CLUNY CROSS

A MAD MEDIEVAL TALE

MARK BLACKHAM

OLIVEWOOD
Publishers

Published by:
Olivewood Publishers
PO Box 381 Union Bay, BC, Canada
V0R 3B0

The characters and events portrayed in this book are fictitious or are used fictitiously. Any similarity to real persons, living or dead, is purely coincidental and not intended by the author.

Blackham, Mark

Cluny Cross: A Mad Medieval Tale/ by Mark Blackham

ISBN: 978-0-9877878-0-4

1. Middle East – European - History – First Crusade -11th century – Fiction.

Revised edition (February 2012)

Printed and bound in the United States of America

MAPS

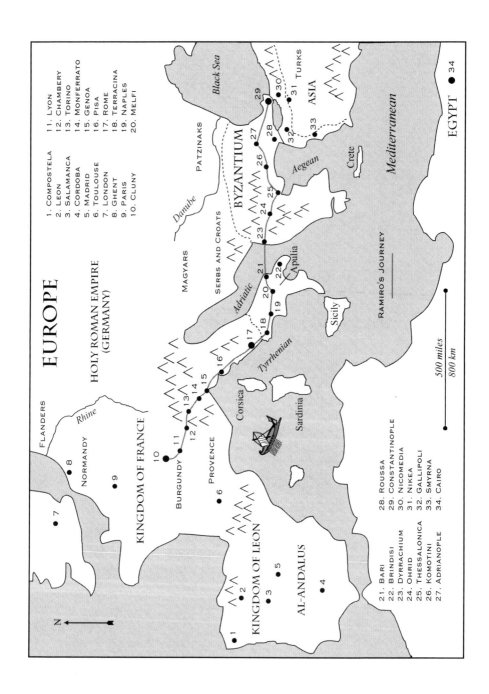

EUROPE

HOLY ROMAN EMPIRE
(GERMANY)

1. COMPOSTELA	11. LYON
2. LEON	12. CHAMBERY
3. SALAMANCA	13. TORINO
4. CORDOBA	14. MONFERRATO
5. MADRID	15. GENOA
6. TOULOUSE	16. PISA
7. LONDON	17. ROME
8. GHENT	18. TERRACINA
9. PARIS	19. NAPLES
10. CLUNY	20. MELFI

21. BARI	28. ROUSSA
22. BRINDISI	29. CONSTANTINOPLE
23. DYRRACHIUM	30. NICOMEDIA
24. OHRID	31. NIKEA
25. THESSALONICA	32. GALLIPOLI
26. KOMOTINI	33. SMYRNA
27. ADRIANOPLE	34. CAIRO

FLANDERS

Rhine

NORMANDY

KINGDOM OF FRANCE

BURGUNDY

PROVENCE

KINGDOM OF LEON

AL-ANDALUS

Corsica

Sardinia

Tyrrhenian

Sicily

Adriatic

Apulia

MAGYARS

SERBS AND CROATS

Danube

PATZINAKS

BYZANTIUM

Black Sea

Aegean

Crete

Mediterranean

ASIA

TURKS

EGYPT

RAMIRO'S JOURNEY

500 miles

800 km

N

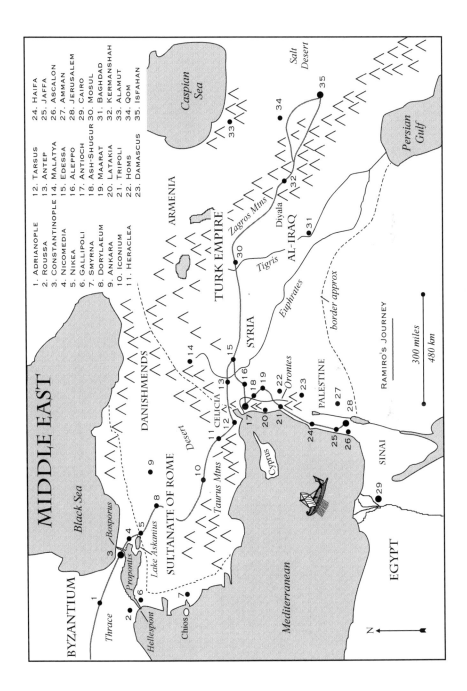

MIDDLE EAST

BYZANTIUM

SULTANATE OF ROME

DANISHMENDS

TURK EMPIRE

ARMENIA

SYRIA

PALESTINE

AL-IRAQ

EGYPT

SINAI

Black Sea

Caspian Sea

Persian Gulf

Salt Desert

Mediterranean

Bosporus

Propontis

Hellespont

Thrace

Lake Askanius

Chios

Cyprus

Orontes

Euphrates

Tigris

Zagros Mtns

Diyala

Taurus Mtns

Desert

border approx

1. ADRIANOPLE
2. ROUSSA
3. CONSTANTINOPLE
4. NICOMEDIA
5. NIKEA
6. GALLIPOLI
7. SMYRNA
8. DORYLAEUM
9. ANKARA
10. ICONIUM
11. HERACLEA
12. TARSUS
13. ANTEP
14. MALATYA
15. EDESSA
16. ALEPPO
17. ANTIOCH
18. ASH-SHUGUR
19. MAARAT
20. LATAKIA
21. TRIPOLI
22. HOMS
23. DAMASCUS
24. HAIFA
25. JAFFA
26. ASCALON
27. AMMAN
28. JERUSALEM
29. CAIRO
30. MOSUL
31. BAGHDAD
32. KERMANSHAH
33. ALAMUT
34. QOM
35. ISFAHAN

CELICIA

RAMIRO'S JOURNEY

300 miles

480 km

N

PROLOGUE

In the seventh century, on the west coast of the Arabian Desert, a man by the name of Muhammad Ibn Abdullah inspired a religious transformation not seen since the days of Christ. Known to his followers as *The Prophet*, his teachings ignited flames of holy fervor throughout Arabia and incited an unprecedented sense of Arab brotherhood and unity. His zealous devotees, convinced they were the chosen of God, stormed out of Mecca to conquer the world in the name of Al-Lah, *The* God.

By the year 1000, Muslim empires had reached their zenith, controlling the whole of the Middle East, North Africa and Spain. Their ships ruled the Mediterranean, seizing Sicily, Corsica, Sardinia and southern Italy. And, much to the horror of all Christians, they managed to breach the mouth of the Tiber to plunder Rome.

But while the Arabs were busy building their empire, Europe too underwent sweeping change. Charlemagne, King of the Franks, created a new European empire, a Christian empire, which he strengthened and solidified by reforming language, religion, money and government. Over time, the new Europeans forgot their humble past and came to believe they lived in a resurrected Holy Roman Empire. The Pope of Rome was their Supreme Bishop, and they were the chosen of God.

Meanwhile, in the East, the remains of the Roman Empire teetered on the brink of extinction, losing Egypt, Syria, and Asia Minor to Muslim armies. This once indomitable empire, commonly known as Byzantium, was reduced to a stub of its former self, barely hanging on to a shred of the Balkans, Greece and Thrace. The people of Byzantium followed Roman bureaucracy and law, but in language and culture they were Greek. They believed the Church of Constantinople was the true center of Christianity and their Patriarch was the True Protector of the Faith, and they were the chosen of God.

The two churches, West and East, one Latin, the other Greek, vied for full control of the Mother Church and squabbled endlessly over points of rank and liturgy - even as Muslim hordes beat on their doorsteps. But as the eleventh century came to a close, both churches began to realize that the preservation of Christendom, the Domain of Christ, required a new solidarity and a new direction. And so, with a desperate sense of urgency and fear, they began to turn their concerted efforts against an intelligent and terrifying opponent – *Dar Al-Islam* – the Domain of Islam.

Part One

EUROPE

~~~~~~

ABBEY OF CLUNY

JUNE 1089

Ramiro fumbled with the envelope. It was dry and brittle and water stains nearly obliterated the writing. The wax seal was already broken... but that came as no surprise because the Abbot scrutinized all mail. The courier said it came all the way from Jerusalem.

"Jerusalem!" he muttered, still standing by the door. "Who in God's name do I know in Jerusalem?" He groped inside with thick fingers, pulling the folded page out slowly. It was made of fine paper, a paper rarely seen among the rough parchments of Burgundy. It was old and yellowed and crackled like a small fire when he opened it. He straightened the folds as carefully as he could, expecting to see Latin or Greek, but it was neither. For a moment, he stared at the odd words, written poorly in a faltering hand. So familiar... "Why... it's Castilian!" he said aloud. He struggled for a bit before the tongue of his youth came to his head.

> *To my beloved son, Ramiro, son of Sancho of León, blessings and God's love be upon you. From your mother, Isabella Agueda, daughter of Eustace of León.*

My mother? He felt his heart pound. He teetered where he stood, putting a hand to the door to steady himself. What cruel farce is this? He staggered back to his cluttered desk by the window, gripping the back of his chair to ease himself down slowly. "Impossible!" he shouted to the stone walls.

The brass bells of the Abbey sounded the call to Lauds, but their rich peal did not reach his ears. He pulled back the long sleeves of his black robe to hold the letter up to the waxing light of dawn, straining at the letters.

> *I write to you from the Church of the Holy Sepulcher in Jerusalem. To my great happiness, I learned of your whereabouts through a conversation with a fellow monk, Russell of Maines, who said he met you some years ago while visiting the Abbey of Cluny.*

Russell! I remember him... but this cannot be! He looked at the envelope again, turning it in his hand. It was old, but it looked authentic, as did the remains of the seal. He looked again at the letter heading, written in Latin and Greek. And my name – my full name - my father's name. Who would know these things? But it cannot be her...

Below his window, fellow monks shuffled along trimmed pathways, on their way to sing Psalms in praise of Our Lord, but he took no notice. He read on.

> *With deep sadness, I must tell you that your brothers have all died in war, and your poor sister passed away in childbirth. After you disappeared, we feared you were dead too and we lost all hope. In our grief, your father and I embarked on a pilgrimage to the Holy Land, where we hoped to receive God's forgiveness and the remission of our sins. But, alas, it is to my great sorrow to tell you that your poor father died of a fever in Tripoli. Only by the Grace of God did I manage to arrive in Jerusalem without him. And by His Will, the Church has taken me in as a bride of Christ.*
>
> *I am pleased, my dear son, that you too have dedicated your life to God. The Abbey of Cluny is held in high regard, even in these distant lands. But now I enter the twilight of my life and you must come to me before I take the hand of Jesus. How I long to look once more upon your gentle face. I entreaty you, my dear son. Come, and I will bestow upon you a holy relic, one I have had in my possession for many years. Come to Jerusalem so that I may place this cherished piece in your hands and gaze upon your dear face one last time.*
>
> *In the year of Our Lord, 1088.*

Tears dripped from his round cheeks and his chest ached with a gnawing pain that was all too familiar. I thought they were slaughtered by the Moors! I saw the ruins of our home! ... the charred remains... the devastation. They said there were no survivors! He had wept then, and he wept again – for his father, a kind and intelligent man, and for his brothers who were so full of life and fought so bravely. And my dear sister, oh dear God, she was always so happy. But even as he wept, a glimmer of joy began to dance amid his gloomy thoughts. He wiped away his tears with a sleeve and smiled a little. My dear mother lives and she is safe in Jerusalem.

THE ABBOT

"Jerusalem? You want to go to Jerusalem?" Abbot Hugh stared at him strangely. "That is very curious indeed."

Ramiro tipped his head, showing a glint in his dark-brown eyes. "Why is that, Reverend Father?" he asked in a rich baritone.

"How did you find out?" asked Hugh in an aging voice. "What do you know?"

"About what, my Lord?"

"About Jerusalem."

"Well... apart from Biblical passages and rumor, I know little indeed, dear Abbot."

The Abbot's long robe hung loosely to the floor. Unlike the black habits of the monks, his was the color of burgundy and had a peaked hood that wrapped tightly around his pale, clean-shaven face. With narrowed eyes, he scanned the stout, swarthy monk who stood in front of him. *Perhaps he knows nothing*, he thought, *but can I rely on him?*

Hugh had accepted Ramiro to the abbey only because he came from a distinguished family of León, and because he wanted to please Alfonso, the King of León, who petitioned on his behalf. Ramiro was just twenty at the time and now, ten years later, he had become an influential figure at the monastery. Hugh had reluctantly appointed him to the position of dean only because he proved so popular among the monks. *But he's too odd. And too damned dark for my liking - black hair, black eyebrows - even his eyes are as black as ink. His skin... it's as tawny as that stinking German ale.*

Whereas Ramiro was a foreigner, Hugh was born to a noble family in the Kingdom of Burgundy. In his early life, he showed such religious zeal and piety that his father gave him to the priesthood and, by the age of fourteen, he became a novice at Cluny. He was so inspired and devoted to the work of God that he quickly rose in the ranks and, by the young age of twenty-five, was unanimously elected Abbot. Now sixty-five, Hugh had become one of the most powerful figures in Western Christendom, a shrewd advisor to popes and kings.

Despite his power, Hugh had trouble meeting Ramiro's intent gaze. The monk's deep, dark stare rattled him, like the baleful, penetrating glare of a... well, of a demon. Alarmed by his thoughts, he dropped his eyes to his desk. "Uh, tell me, Brother Ramiro, why do you have a sudden urge to make a pilgrimage to the Holy Land?"

Ramiro told him about the letter from his mother.

"Oh, yes. I remember that letter. None of the priors could read it."

"It is written in Castilian, Father, the tongue of León."

"No matter, Brother Ramiro. I understand your concerns about your mother," he paused and put his hands together as two fists. "But when you made your vows to the Church, you willingly forsook your earthly family. You should be more concerned with the divine family of God."

"Of course, Reverend Father," he said with a twinge of regret. It had been easy to give up those things he never had... but now it was different, his mother lived. "May I suggest, Abbot, that the holy relic would be a wonderful addition to our collection." He opened his big hands in a conciliatory gesture. "We could place it beside the vial of Christ's blood."

"Yes, yes, perhaps, Brother," said Hugh, somewhat ruffled by the suggestion. "And what exactly is the nature of this relic?"

"Alas, my mother did not say, but whatever it is, it must have originated in the Holy Land itself."

Hugh tapped his fingers on his desk, daring to glance up from time to time. If the relic was real, it might indeed be a powerful one. "But you are one of my deans. And one of our best *medicina*. Who would replace you?"

"Brother Anselm is quite capable, Abbot."

Hugh nodded slowly, his face deadpan. "Perhaps, but nonetheless, I cannot afford to send another monk to Jerusalem."

"Another? What do you mean?"

Hugh scowled. "Must I remind you, Brother, to speak only when asked?"

Ramiro bowed his head. "Forgive me, Reverend Father, for I have sinned."

"If you must know, I am sending Brother Bernold on a special assignment."

"Forgive me again, Father, but Brother Bernold? Why would he want to go to Jerusalem? You know he's more than sixty."

"And so am I, Brother Ramiro."

"Oh, excuse me please, Abbot, I meant no offense."

"Never mind. Bernold is in fine health, and he will be safely accompanied by men-at-arms." He rubbed his smooth chin, pausing in thought. "So you know nothing of this?"

"Of what, Reverend Father?"

Hugh leaned forward over his desk and studied Ramiro for a time before he finally spoke. "When your letter arrived in our last mail, we also received a letter from Pope Urban, may God protect him, and I was asked to choose one of my monks as an emissary to Jerusalem. His Holiness feels that, on certain matters, he can trust only his brethren here at Cluny."

"It came in the same mailing?" Ramiro blurted with a little too much enthusiasm. "Then perhaps it is God's will that I go to Jerusalem."

Hugh glared at him with gray eyes. "Hold your tongue, Brother! And do not presume to lecture me on God's will!"

Ramiro bowed once more. "Forgive me, Father, for my errant ways."

The Abbot waved a hand of finality. "I've already arranged to send Brother Bernold. He knew our blessed Pope when he was the grand prior here. Besides, he's the best qualified."

"But... but Brother Bernold is in poor health, my Abbot. I know, I've treated him many times. His heart is bad. And... and he cannot even speak Greek. And he... he has no experience with the Muslims as I do."

Hugh leaned back in his velvet chair, brushing the desktop with the wide sleeves of his robe. The lips of his clean-shaven face curled on one corner. "What arrogance and pride, Brother Ramiro. Must I remind you of your vow of humility? Must I whip you for your self-obsession?"

Ramiro bowed his head again. "Lord, I am a sinner not worthy to lift my eyes to heaven."

"Not all of us view your experiences as advantageous, Brother," he said, tapping his fingers in a drum roll. "In fact, they can lead us to view you and your actions with some ambiguity. Frankly, I doubt your full commitment to our Holy Cause. Your opinions are much too heretical for my liking, and you spend too much time in the library instead of attending to your duties in the infirmary. The librarian tells me you prefer manuscripts in the heathen tongue."

"That's Arabic, Reverend Father," he said quietly. "But I am only translating the works you suggested – those dealing with science, medicine and healing, nothing more."

Hugh lowered his wrinkled forehead and raised his eyes skeptically. "And I admire your perseverance in this regard, Brother, but you must not ignore your other duties to the Holy Church."

"Yes, Abbot," Ramiro persisted. "And consider, my Lord, how my talents may assist the Church. I speak several languages and know some customs of the land."

Hugh slapped the desk, making a loud whack. "I am well aware of your many talents, Brother Ramiro!" he said with annoyance. "And you would do well to remember that it is only by the Grace of God they come to you. He who glories, let him glory in the Lord!"

"Yes, of course, Reverend Father."

"These are difficult times," said Hugh with a scowl. "And I must be cautious. I worry more about your inclinations." He stood up from his chair. "Besides, you well know the monastery itself is considered *to be* Jerusalem, do you not?"

"Yes, of course, Father."

"Then you must understand that, in the eyes of God, there is no need for your pilgrimage to the Holy City and that fact alone should be enough for you." He shook his head. "I deny your request."

MEDICINA

In a fit of frustration, Ramiro threw the book he was reading onto his desk, which was stacked with Arabic manuscripts obtained from the Moors in Spain. Many of them were translations of Greek, Persian, and Hindi, extremely rare in the West. He was always astounded by the science of these people and greatly moved by their literature, arts, and sublime architecture. But the complicated mathematics of Al-Khwarizmi was beyond him, he simply could not fathom *al-jabra*. Books on medicines and herbs were more to his liking, especially those by Ibn-Sina, an Iranian physician, and those by Ibn-Ishaq, the Christian scholar from Iraq.

But even these subjects no longer caught his interest, he could not concentrate. He closed his eyes and bowed his head, chewing absently on a hairy knuckle as he prayed. Dear Jesus, help me get to Jerusalem, help me to see my dear mother. I beseech you, my Lord, I will offer many prayers of thanksgiving at the Holy Sepulcher... if only, by your Grace, you grant me this prayer. His eyes glistened.

There was a knock at the door.

"Enter!" he said, just loud enough.

A disheveled monk opened the door, his face pale, his eye sockets darkened. He held a hand to his rounded stomach. "Brother Ramiro," he said. "May God's grace be with you. I could not find you in the infirmary."

"What is it, Brother Andrew? You look unwell."

"It's my guts, Brother. I feel nauseous whenever I eat. And I have no strength."

Ramiro stood up. He noticed a small leather sac hanging from Andrew's neck. "What have you got in that?"

"It's angelica, Brother."

Ramiro nodded, he knew it was used to ward off evil spirits. "Do you have diarrhea?"

"No, Brother."

"Are you passing blood?"

"No," he said, slowly shaking his long head. "In fact, I can hardly pass a thing."

"Hold still," said Ramiro as he put a hand to his stomach. "Do you feel any sharp pain?"

"Not really, Brother. I just feel like I'm going to vomit."

Ramiro took his arm and felt his pulse, it was strong. He looked into his eyes and studied their color – they seemed sharp and clear. "Very well, Brother Andrew, follow me to the herb house, I believe you have a bout of worms. We'll see what a few feedings of buckbean will do." He recalled an Arab phrase. "For every illness, Brother, God has given a cure."

STRANGERS

It seemed that everybody came to watch Brother Bernold leave for Jerusalem. They gathered in the courtyard near the gate and prayed for his safe journey.

> *The Lord will keep you from all evil*
> *He will keep your life.*
> *The Lord will keep your going out*
> *and your coming in*
> *from this time on and forever more.*

They were captivated, not just because the Abbot allowed him to ride a horse, which meant it must be a very important journey indeed, but also because of those who waited for him. Just outside the monastery walls, a small army of unfamiliar knights milled about, making a tremendous racket. The monks could hear their strange guttural voices, the constant clack of armor, and the neighs and nickers of many horses.

"Who are they?" Ramiro asked Brother Andrew.

"I don't know," he replied. "It seems no one knows."

"How's your stomach today, Brother? Are you feeling better?"

"Yes, thank you, Brother Ramiro, much better."

"Praise God," Ramiro said before he left suddenly and headed to the library. He scrambled up three floors with an agility that belied his stocky physique and rushed to a nearby window. There they were, a small but noisy horde, hundreds of armed men and over a thousand horses along with many servants, even women and children. He caught a few words on the breeze, it sounded like a German tongue. Their banner was unfamiliar but their dress told all - the heavy armor, the flat-topped helmets, the war hammers, the flared axes, the heavy broadswords, the furs, the stink. They must be Normans, maybe worse. He shuddered as he watched Brother Bernold join them with his novice in tow, and the long procession began to head south, taking the road to Lyon.

"Back to your work!" the Prior shouted from the forecourt. "This is no business of yours! Back to your work!"

Ramiro ran back down the stairs, returning to his work in the herb garden.

A CANTICLE

The stained glass windows seemed to come alive in the first light of day. Biblical scenes, full of brilliant colors, cast a warm kaleidoscope across a long series of white stone columns towering to an ornate roof far overhead. The monks filed in through the main doorway, gathering on the cool, wooden benches of the nave and choir. After they took their seats, the presiding monk raised his voice from the apse.

> *O God come to my assistance,*
> *O Lord make haste to help me...*

He made the sign of the cross on his forehead and all monks chanted in unison.

> *In the name of the Father,*
> *and of the Son,*
> *and of the Holy Spirit.*
> *Amen.*

Ramiro made the motions and mouthed the words but his thoughts drifted to other things. He looked up to the glistening windows, resting his eyes on a simple scene of color, one depicting the glorious city of Jerusalem bathed in a golden light. Here, in a lull of prayer, he fixed his gaze, staring until his focus blurred, the vibrant colors blending as one.

After a long pause, the presiding monk looked down on the large hymn-book spread open on the lectern before him. Its thick vellum pages, bound between leather-covered boards, were inscribed in a lyrical calligraphy with bright illustrations of angels and biblical themes in the margins. "*The Gloria,*" he said loudly, and all monks stood to sing.

> *Glory be to God on high*
> *And on earth peace, goodwill towards men,*
> *We praise you, we bless you,*
> *We worship you, we glorify you...*

A deep chorus reverberated through the enormous church, the sound echoing from its granite walls like the harmony of a second choir. Ramiro moved his lips but his mind still wandered, preoccupied with rending thoughts. He had given his life to God and the monastery, now he wanted to leave. He had an overwhelming, defiant urge to head for Jerusalem, with or without the Abbot's consent. But his heart pounded. What of my vows of obedience? Dear God, will I be excommunicated? Could I ever return? He closed his eyes and prayed for an answer.

The Gloria ended and they all began to chant a Psalm. Ramiro had no need to look at his prayer book, he knew the words by heart. He began to relax and was feeling somewhat soothed by the time they rose again to sing the Canticle of Zechariah.

Blessed be the Lord, the God of Israel
He has come to his people and set them free...

Israel..., he dreamed wistfully. O Jerusalem!

• • • • •

The days passed and Ramiro spent his time making herb potions, tending to the sick, translating texts for the library, or making copies of the Bible. He was on his knees pulling weeds in the herb garden when a panting novice ran up to him. The skinny lad stood twitching in a turbulent mix of agitation and excitement, but he said nothing.

"What is it boy?" Ramiro asked, not looking up. "Can't you see I'm busy here?"

"He's dead, Father," the novice blurted.

Ramiro looked up. "Who's dead?"

"Brother Bernold, Father," he choked, sweeping a tear from his cheek with his fingers.

Ramiro stared up at the boy, unsure if he had heard correctly. "You say he's dead?"

"Yes, Father Ramiro. Died on the road to Chambéry. In the mountains of Savoy. They say he just collapsed - dead on the ground."

Ramiro paled. "Father of mercies! Dear, oh dear." Still on his knees, he put his hands flat to the ground to steady himself. Fear and guilt gripped his thoughts as he recalled, with growing remorse and horror, his earlier prayers. *I prayed to get to Jerusalem, my Lord – but not this way, not by the death of Brother Bernold. Forgive me, Father. Forgive me if I have sinned in my deepest petitions.*

A CROSS

Abbot Hugh was shocked at the news of Brother Bernold's death and began to wonder, with mounting trepidation, if Brother Ramiro was right – perhaps it is God's will that he go to Jerusalem. After all, his letter did arrive the same day as the Pope's - perhaps this is a part of Our Lord's Divine Plan. Could it be so? These anxious thoughts compelled him but he had to fight hard to swallow his aversion to this nettlesome monk. "Well, Brother Ramiro," he said begrudgingly, "you did try to warn me about Brother Bernold's health. I must admit, I never believed it was that serious. A sad business indeed." He glanced down for a moment, trying to appear distressed, but he soon raised his head, changing his tone abruptly. "And now I am faced with the regrettable and difficult task of choosing another to take his place." He paused, watching Ramiro. "Prior Michael has shown an interest. He speaks Greek, you know."

"Yes, Abbot," said Ramiro, standing three paces away with his hands joined at the waist. "But his grammar is poor, and he has been confined within the walls of the monastery since the age of six."

Hugh scowled at the brawny monk, it was all he could do not to belt him across the head as he would a disobedient novice. He well knew Ramiro was the best qualified but he deeply resented his cocky self-assurance and his light-handed disregard for authority and, because Hugh was a man of letters himself, he deeply resented his gifted erudition. With considerable effort, he quelled his rising ire and spoke again. "And now, with some reluctance, I am also forced to consider your request to go to Jerusalem. But tell me, do you know anything at all of current affairs in Italy or among the Greeks?"

"Well, Reverend Father, I know the rightful pope, His Eminence Pope Urban, is kept out of Rome by King Henry's army. And... and that the King has appointed his own pope, a man called Giberto."

Hugh slapped his hand on the desk. "The damned antipope!" He spat the words.

Ramiro's cheeks reddened, he had never heard the Abbot speak so vehemently. He said nothing.

Hugh went on. "And now, Pope Urban must hide like a thief among the Normans of Italy. He cannot even set foot in Rome!" He fell silent for a moment, then rose from his chair. "But His Holiness, may God protect him, he's the only one who can continue our reforms." His voice grew louder. "Only he can unite the Church." His fingers clenched in a fist. "We must unite! Or the heathen will destroy us!"

Ramiro nodded cautiously. "Yes, yes, Abbot, I agree wholeheartedly."

"Are you aware, Brother Ramiro, that the very existence of Christendom is at stake?"

Ramiro's round eyes widened. "Well, I... I know of the battles with the Muslims, Reverend Father. I was once a soldier, as you know. But does it indeed threaten all Christendom?"

"Indeed it does!" he cried, raising his thin gray eyebrows. "Even now, the infidels beat on the shores of southern France. They have seized the Middle Sea and the islands within it!" He banged a fist on his desk. "Have you forgotten already that one of our very own abbots was abducted by these vile creatures?"

"I remember, my Lord, it was Abbot Maiolus, about a hundred years ago."

"Yes, Maiolus. You see!" He pointed a finger at Ramiro, as if proving a point. "These pagans are a perennial threat. Meanwhile, we squabble amongst ourselves like children!"

Ramiro fidgeted, not sure how to respond.

Hugh glanced briefly into his eyes. "To start, we must drive that devil, Giberto, from Rome... him and his German thugs. Once this is done, we can control the West countries." He paused for a moment before shaking his head sadly. "But, alas... the Church does not yet have the power to oust them – even with the help of those conniving, bloodthirsty Normans. We need the armies of the Greek King and the support of the Greek Church. We must find a way to convince their chief bishops... you know the ones I mean."

"They are called patriarchs, Abbot."

"Yes, patriarchs, of course. We need to settle our differences and to unite under a single banner of Christ. We need someone to confer with them and attempt to reach some compromise on our disagreements."

"It is God's will, my Lord."

"If we can unite our forces, then we will seize the Holy Land and secure it for the True Faith."

Ramiro raised his thick brow. "That will be a formidable task, Reverend Father."

Hugh sat down again. "There are many dangers on the road to Jerusalem. I need a man who is not afraid to face them – a man who does not fear for his life. Can I rely on you, Brother Ramiro, to complete this assignment?"

Ramiro could barely mask his glee. "Oh yes, very much so!" But then he hesitated, tipping his head a little. "And uh,... and what would this assignment be, Reverend Father?"

"You will act as my legate, my personal representative. You will meet with these bishops... I mean patriarchs, and attempt to resolve our differences. I want you to write down all you see on your journey. I need to know what people think, the social order, the roads, the lay of the land... military capabilities and such."

"Military capabilities?"

"As a precaution, of course. For the safety of Christian pilgrims."

"Oh, of course, Abbot. Uh, do you mean among the Greeks?"

"The Greeks, yes... and among the vile heathen who corrupt the blessed Holy Land." He leaned forward. "You must send me a full report every three or four months. You can take ample stationary supplies from the scriptorium."

"Thank you, Reverend Father."

"It is an important journey," said Hugh. "You may take two of our horses and you will need a donkey for your gear. First, you will travel to Terracina, south of Rome. Here, you will hold council with His Holiness. I expect he will give you official permission to travel to Jerusalem. And he should give you some letters - for the King and for these patriarchs."

"It is an honor to obey, Father," he said, thrilled at the thought of an audience with the Pope himself. "May God bless His Holiness. But uh... which king?"

"The Greek King, of course. In Constantinople... what's his name?"

Ramiro thought for a moment. "Alexios, I believe."

Hugh glanced at him in astonishment. "Yes, Alexios... of course. He pleads for Pope Urban's help to defeat the pagans, to drive the devils from the Holy Land! Already this God-forsaken race has destroyed the Holy Sepulcher!"

"Uh, if you would excuse me, Abbot," Ramiro said softly. "But that was some time ago. The Sepulcher has since been rebuilt by the Greek King."

Hugh glared at him. "The heathen are still a threat, Brother Ramiro. Do you not agree?"

"Yes, of course, Reverend Father." He bowed a little.

"And now for your second objective," said Hugh, leaning back in his chair. He pulled open a drawer and took out a small package wrapped in oiled linen. He placed it on the desk, undid the string, and opened the wrap slowly. That was when Ramiro first saw it.

It was a simple cross made of polished olivewood - quite plain except for a small bloodstone embedded at its center and a thin chain of brass looping through a hole drilled into its top.

Hugh pushed it towards him. "This is what I gave to Brother Bernold. By the grace of God we recovered it. After you complete your business in Constantinople, you must deliver this cross to Jerusalem, where you will present it to the Patriarch along with the Pope's letter. The Patriarch's name is... uh..." He picked up a letter from his desktop and looked at it briefly. "His name is Symeon. He will then give you further instructions."

Ramiro stepped forward. "A cross, Reverend Father? But what is there about this cross that could be so important?"

"Yours is not to question, Brother, but to obey."

Ramiro reached out and picked it up gently, as if it were made of fragile terracotta. He turned it in his hand, studying it closely. It was not large, neither was it small, and it fit nicely across the palm of his thick hand. "It is an artful work, Abbot, although perhaps a little ostentatious for a Benedictine."

"Do not worry about that," Hugh croaked, waving his hands impatiently. "Keep it close to you at all times. And keep it intact. Take off your other cross right now and put this one about your neck."

Ramiro exchanged the crosses, then he glanced down at his new cross to inspect it again. Perhaps it contains a message, he thought. He looked for a plug but saw no seams of any kind.

Hugh leaned forward again. "It is vital that you present this cross to Patriarch Symeon."

"May I ask why, Reverend Father?"

"I will tell you bluntly, Brother Ramiro... it is time to defeat these heathen who threaten the Word of Christ. We can no longer tolerate this wickedness. It is time to put Jerusalem into its rightful hands – the hands of Christians. Only Christians can restore the Mother Church to Jerusalem. Only then can the City of God rule all Christendom!"

Ramiro shook his head. "I'm not sure I understand."

"We need to persuade the Patriarch to join us – to unite the churches. We need to form an alliance," he said in a haughty tone. "To do this we need lines of communication, Brother. As my legate, you will report on all you see and hear."

"And delivering this cross will assist the alliance?" he asked skeptically.

"Yes, for reasons you will understand when you reach Jerusalem. In the name of God, do you vow to do so?"

Ramiro balked. "My Lord, I... I will obey you in all things and I will vow in the name of God that I will do *all in my power* to deliver it to Symeon."

Hugh nodded. "Very well. And there is no need to mention the cross to anyone. Is that understood?"

"Yes, Father."

"And you will report to me on all you see and hear."

"Yes, of course," Ramiro said warily. The responsibility of this assignment already began to weigh on his thoughts. "And where shall I stay in Jerusalem?"

"Why, at the monastery, of course," said Hugh. "The Monastery of... of Saint Mary, I think it's called. Managed by the Benedictine Order. The abbot there is uh.... uh... what's his name?"

"I have no idea, Abbot."

Hugh picked up another letter. "And you will take this letter to His Holiness. You must deliver it yourself."

Ramiro nodded, receiving it carefully, as if it were a holy relic, and worried about how he would carry it. Then he reflected on his journey. "Tell me please,

Abbot. Once I deliver the Pope's letter to the Greek King, how will I get to Jerusalem?"

Hugh drew his thin lips into a tight smile. "Nothing is wanting to those who fear God, Brother Ramiro. Do not fret about these things and trust our good Lord to guide you."

"Yes, Abbot."

Hugh tapped his fingers. "But I expect the Greek King will put you on a ship sailing to Palestine. Once you have completed your assignment, you will return to Cluny by the same means."

"Thank you, Father."

Hugh reached for a purse sitting on his desk and put it forward. "There should be enough here to fund your journey. If you need more, ask the Patriarch to assist you when you reach Jerusalem."

Ramiro picked it up. It had been a long time since he had used money.

"You must hurry, Brother Ramiro. Count Robert's men will not wait. They have already left Lyon and head east again for Chambéry in the mountain passes."

"Count Robert?"

"Yes, Robert of Flanders."

"Is he the one who leads these knights? "

"No, not personally. He dispatched these men to serve the Greek King. A promise he made when he last took a pilgrimage to the Holy Land."

Ah! Ramiro thought, then they're Flemings - just as odious as those wretched Normans.

Hugh scribbled out a short note and handed it to him. "This is your letter of commendation for Count Robert's captain. His name escapes me. I do not anticipate trouble, and you should be able to return to us within two years. You will not travel alone. I have assigned two assistants to accompany you - Aldebert the novice and Pepin the groom."

"Aldebert?" Ramiro asked in dismay. "Please forgive me, Reverend Father, but the man is a complete imbecile. Surely, anyone else would be up to the task. And Pepin... well he is a mere boy."

The Abbot shook his head with a disheartened look, like that of a disappointed parent. "They will submit to your orders, Brother," he said with frustration. "That is enough. And I command you to review Benedict's *Rules* before you go. In particular, I want you to give special attention to his advice on humility and obedience."

Ramiro bowed. "I will obey, Most Reverend Father."

"Now go," he said with a flip of his hand. "You must leave tomorrow and ride fast to Chambéry."

CHAMBÉRY

Ramiro felt a rush of exhilaration. For so many years, he had worked, prayed and worshiped within the confines of the Abbey, giving his life to the service of God. Now he was, once again, free to roam the compelling, carnal world of men, free to make his own determinations, and free to act. Thoughts of daring adventure raced through his mind and aroused in him a long subdued wanderlust. Jerusalem! I head for Jerusalem and the Tomb of Christ! I will see my beloved mother once again! He felt so vibrant, so alive.

His old gray mare trotted merrily along the road to Lyon, following the wide waters of the Rhone. A warm summer breeze whistled past his ears, carrying with it a thick scent of rosemary from sprawling fields of deep purple. Behind him, a lanky Brother Aldebert fought awkwardly with his flustered horse as he rushed to keep up, his pale, pockmarked face grimacing in frustration. Young Pepin, a thin, scruffy boy of twelve with long, blonde hair and brown eyes, sat behind him in the saddle, hanging on frantically as the befuddled mare lurched in all directions. A laden donkey trailed behind reluctantly, secured by a long leash to Aldebert's horse.

Aldebert rode nervously, gripping his reins with white knuckles, pulling hard one way, then the other. Unwittingly, he pulled back and dug in his heels. His mare whinnied and tossed its head, confused by mixed signals. It wandered from side to side as he overcorrected, first to the left, then to the right, all the while clashing with other travelers on the road.

Ramiro slowed his horse, waiting for them to catch up. "Brother Aldebert! Must you torture that poor beast? You cannot pull back on the reins and expect it to move forward. Have you never learned to ride?"

"Sorry, Father Ramiro," he said as he loosed the reins and dug in his heels. The mare lurched forward at the signal, almost tossing Pepin from the saddle.

"Whoa! Whoa!" Ramiro yelled as he bolted past. "Now what are you doing? Rein back!"

"Sorry!" Aldebert yelled as he jerked on the reins. His horse whinnied again, shaking its head madly, as if to rid itself of a giant pest.

"Really, Brother Aldebert! Perhaps Pepin should take the reins. He could do no worse."

Aldebert frowned, creasing his spotted white face. He looked askance, giving a sneer to the younger Pepin. "No, no, Father. I'll be fine. It's just that my backside is sore."

"That's because you have yet to learn how to post to the trot, Brother Aldebert. You must move with your mount." He sighed heavily. The man is a complete idiot! May God help me!

Aldebert looked at him sheepishly with round, pale-blue eyes that seemed too big for his long, drawn face. His nose was almost as long, ending above thin, red lips that he constantly licked. His large cow-ears hung like wilted flowers, jutting out below his blonde tonsure, the ring of hair left on a monk's shaved head.

Ramiro spurred his mount. "Come on! We must hurry!"

They pushed through the bustling streets of Lyon, an old Roman settlement rivaling Paris in its metropolitan grandeur, and crossed over the Rhone. From the road, they could see the walls of the Basilica of Saint-Martin d'Ainay, another Benedictine abbey, and Ramiro was sorely tempted to visit but he hurried on. He took the road east, heading to Chambéry, a quaint town nestled in a wide valley among the foothills of the Western Alps. Finally, three days after leaving the abbey, they came across Count Robert's men just east of the Isère River. The slow-moving line of knights, squires and servants stretched far ahead.

"There they are!" Ramiro shouted. "Come on!" He spurred his horse forward to join them and soon met up with stragglers crossing the bridge. He pushed on to the front, trotting beside the long line.

Aldebert and Pepin rushed to follow, but Aldebert was not used to such delicate maneuvers in a crowd and barged into pedestrians and nearby riders.

"Stupid monk!" someone cried out in a language he did not understand. "Watch where you're going!"

"Please excuse me," Aldebert muttered as he struggled with his horse. But a moment later, he rammed into a group of surly, weatherworn knights.

"What the hell?" one shouted. "Get out of the way, monk!"

"Have you got horse shit for brains?" cursed another. "Move your foking horse!"

Ramiro heard the commotion. He knew some of the tongue, enough to know it was not good. But he ignored them. May God have mercy on us. And the stink! I wonder how long we'll have to tolerate these vulgar brutes. He reached the front of the line and shouted to one of the knights. "Who leads you?" he yelled in northern French.

The knight looked annoyed. "Who are you? What do you want?" he replied with a Flemish accent.

"I am Ramiro of Cluny. I want to know who commands these men."

"Humph! Of Cluny you say? So you're from the Abbey?"

"Is that not obvious, soldier?"

The young knight nodded sheepishly and pointed. "That's the Captain over there. Drugo the Red we call him. The tall one with red hair and shield."

Ramiro left without a word and rode toward the man. But as he neared, two of Drugo's lieutenants, who were riding on either side of the captain, left their positions to stop him. "What do you want, monk?"

"You will address me as Dom Ramiro, soldier. I hail from Cluny and have come to speak with your captain. You will let me pass."

One of them smiled, the one called Otto. "I suppose you've come to replace the old monk who died past Lyon. Maybe you'll last a little longer." The other knight chuckled.

Ramiro glared at the two young men, who soon stopped smiling, avoiding his eyes. "Let me pass," he said with cold authority, and they parted timidly.

Drugo's red hair poked out beneath a domed helmet and hung below his shoulders. A bushy beard covered his freckled face. He dressed in expensive mail armor from head to toe and, when he moved, the chain links tinkled like a spring of water. Ramiro thought him no more than twenty-five. But he was older than most of his men - some as young as sixteen.

Drugo watched the monk approach and rolled his eyes. "Another one?" he posed sarcastically.

"Good day to you too, Sir Drugo. May God in Heaven deliver you from evil." He moved alongside. "I am Ramiro of Cluny and you have been selected by the Church to escort me to the Greek Kingdom." He stuck out his arm, offering him the Abbot's letter of commendation.

Drugo yanked it from his hand and, without pausing to look at it, shoved it into his belt, crushing it in the process. "Let me make this clear, Ramiro of Cluny. I don't want any damn monks on this journey. I'll take you with me only because my Lord Robert ordered me to do so. So keep in mind that you will do as I say, and you will go where I tell you to go. Do you understand?"

Ramiro's eyes flashed as he stared at the impudent man. "No, I am afraid I do not understand, Sir Drugo," he replied with equal strength. "I am a man of God and I follow God's will. I will do as He commands me and I will go where He commands me. Do *you* understand?"

Drugo scowled, his face reddened and, by force of habit, his hand moved to the hilt of his sword. "Take care with your words, monk, lest no one raise a sword to protect you."

"God will protect me, by his Grace. And you will address me as Dom Ramiro."

Drugo clenched his teeth, returning a silent, hostile glare.

Ramiro held out his hand. "Please return my letter if you cannot be bothered to read it."

Drugo pulled it out of his belt and flung it at him.

Like a toad to a fly, Ramiro snatched it out of mid-air. "And I'm sure your heart will rejoice, Sir Drugo, when I tell you that I will be conducting prayer services twice a day, at sunrise and at sunset. That would be Prime and Vespers, in case you have forgotten. It is an undemanding schedule of prayer... but I am impressed with the urgency of this mission and, thus, will forego the other five hours of prayer."

Drugo did not reply, but when Ramiro turned to ride away, he could hear his vile curses.

MONFERRATO

Ramiro nestled into the dry grass to begin his morning meditation. He turned his eyes to the west, looking back towards Torino and the snow-capped Alps they had left some days before. Wood warblers whistled in the still of dawn as he sat alone on the rise above the camp, which was set up near the round, green hills of Monferrato. He pushed back the hood of his black robe, letting the soft glow of dawn warm his face, and took hold of his new cross, raising it to the thin clouds overhead to begin his morning invocation in silence.

Glory be to God who has shown us the light!
Lead me from darkness to light...

Then he prayed aloud, "And give me strength, Father in Heaven, that I may complete the mission before me." But his prayers soon wandered into loving thoughts of his mother, Isabella, always dear to his heart. And, for a while, he dreamed wistfully of Jerusalem and the Holy Sepulcher. But a creeping feeling of uneasiness slowly dispelled these grand dreams.

He tried to focus and began to mutter the Pater Noster in a dull monotone while gazing across the fertile Po Valley, which rolled east all the way to Venice on the Adriatic Sea. A blanket of orange haze began to dissipate in the brightening shimmer of a summer sun and he squinted in the growing light. "Kak-kak!" a jackdaw sounded and his concentration faltered.

The spectacular panorama did little to dispel his anxieties. It is a long way to Jerusalem and many, like his father before him, had died on the journey. "Deliver us from evil, if it is Your will, my Lord." His gaze drifted to the Flemish campsite below, to the hodgepodge of oiled canvas tents and makeshift shelters. A thin grove of chestnut and oak cast long shadows among them.

The morning sun rose to full light, urging pink and purple wildflowers to open in greeting. Tents rippled and flapped, and cold ash puffed between the stones of dead campfires where jackdaws tussled over scraps dropped the night before. Servants began to rise, rekindling their fires with dry twigs collected from the grassy forest floor. Before long, he caught the aroma of baking bread and roasting boar, a scent broken only by the briny smell of skins and furs stretched out to dry in frames of wood.

Clanging pots and angry bellows soon disturbed the quiet of dawn. He tried to ignore the rising din below him, but before the sun rose a full hand above the horizon, a deafening scream for mercy brought the noisy, bustling camp to a silent standstill.

• • • • •

A terrified tradesman wrestled in the grip of two soldiers, his voice shaking the cool morning air. "I stole nothing, I swear! Nothing! Let me go!"

Otto pulled out his knife, putting the tip to the man's neck. "Settle down, scum! Or I'll slit your throat from ear to ear!" He called out, "Captain! We've caught a thief!"

Drugo the Red pulled his tent flap aside and looked out. A servant girl with long, raven-black hair peeked out behind him. He squinted. "What is it, man? I have yet to eat breakfast." He stepped out and stood tall against the three men in front of him, his open robe revealing tight muscles on a barreled chest bristling with red hairs. Long locks of straight, red hair draped across his shoulders.

"We've caught a thief, m'lord," said his lieutenant, Fulk. "Caught him with the silver locket lost by Otto's wife last week."

The tradesman's eyes widened in fear. "I took nothing, m'lord, I swear in the name of God!" The man was terrified. He had heard the fearsome stories about Drugo, about how the knight was once accused of theft by a lowly peasant and how, right there in front of everybody in Count Robert's court, he had drawn his sword and lopped off the man's head with a single blow. The Count, enraged by his audacity, ordered him to do penitence and seek remission for his sins. He sent him off to serve the Greek King, to whom he had promised fighting men and horses, and ordered him to atone for his evil ways by visiting holy places along the way. Drugo did as he was commanded, but showed little remorse.

He looked to his henchman. "This is a serious accusation, Fulk. Are you sure?"

"We are, m'lord. The locket was sighted in a bag among his possessions."

The tradesman squirmed. "I swear, Sir Drugo, I have no idea how it got there! You must believe me! I'm not a thief!"

"Then how do you explain its presence among your personal things?"

"M'lord, I cannot explain it, but I have never been near Otto's tent. I swear it!"

"So... I ask you once again... how did the locket come to be in your bag?" He glared at the man.

The tradesman squirmed under his hostile, blue stare. "I don't know, m'lord."

"Who accompanies you, tradesman?"

"Well... my wife and daughter, m'lord – and fellow tradesmen."

"Perhaps your wife or your daughter took it?"

"Oh, no, no, m'lord." He struggled. "They are good, honest people!"

"Well then, it must have been one of your fellow tradesmen."

"Oh no, Sir. I... I can't imagine they would do such a thing."

A crease of irritation crossed Drugo's sunburned face. "Then perhaps the fairies put it there in the middle of the night?" His men chuckled. "You must think us fools, man," he sneered. "We have no place for thieves in our midst. You know the law, ... thieves will hang!"

"Please, m'lord! In the name of God's mercy, please!"

Drugo paused and looked at the tradesman with feigned forbearance. "Thieves must be punished... I will not tolerate criminals among us. But I'm in no mood for a hanging first thing in the morning. You will see that I am not a cruel master, tradesman... I will let you live... with the lesser sentence." He turned to his men. "Cut off his hand. That is the law."

"Mercy, m'lord, I have done nothing wrong!"

"Take him away." Drugo shouted. He spun to his tent and the girl within, opening the flap viciously. "Get my breakfast, woman!"

They dragged the pleading carpenter to an opening in the camp, tied his right arm to a large block of wood, and stuffed his wailing mouth with a linen scarf. Knights, servants and slaves rushed in to watch, jostling and pushing for a better view. A line of soldiers held them at bay. The camp fell silent except for the shrieking wails of the tradesman's wife and daughter.

A tall, broad-shouldered Northman stepped up to the block with a wide battle-axe in his hand. He hoisted the blade high above his head, focusing on the tradesman's wrist, poised to strike...

"Stop! Stop at once, in the Holy Name of God!" A booming voice rattled the air. The axe-man held his weapon, staggered slightly, and turned his gaze to the intruder. People jostled for a view and a hundred voices spoke at once.

Ramiro burst through the crowd like a wild bull, knocking people off their feet as he charged forward. His black ring of hair tussled in the morning breeze and his black robe flapped behind him. He strode forward in wide, strong steps, infused with the brazen courage of an ancient prophet, pushing right up to the axe-man and staring defiantly into his big, square face. The towering executioner strained to keep the heavy blade above him. Ramiro stood firm, his dark eyes flashed and his beardless face puckered. "In the name of Christ, I demand to know the sin of this man!"

The executioner shouted down at him. "He's a stinking thief, monk! We caught him with a stolen locket. The Captain sentenced him!" His dark locks swung off his shoulders as he yelled. He steadied himself as his axe grew heavy.

Ramiro glared at him. "You will let me speak with this man... and with the Captain!" The axe-man hesitated, stepped back, and lowered his blade to the ground. An audible sigh of disappointment rippled through the crowd.

"The evidence is clear, monk. The man is guilty," cried Otto, the blonde-haired lieutenant who owned the locket. "Do not meddle in our affairs."

Ramiro turned sharply to face him. "God meddles in your affairs, Otto of Bremen. Are you so sure this man is guilty? Exactly what evidence do you have? Will you stand in the presence of God on Judgment Day and proclaim his guilt with certainty?" He took three long strides, right up to Otto's thin, pallid face. "I must speak with your Captain... at once!"

Otto averted the monk's powerful black stare. His pale green eyes darted about fretfully as he looked for support from his men, but they were too afraid to interfere. Finally, he summoned courage, folding his arms and sticking his chin forward. "He's a rotten thief, monk! Are you here to protect sinners and shit like this? We should hang the bastard!" The crowd roared their approval.

Ramiro spun on the crowd, facing soldiers and servants alike. "Who among you will throw the first stone?" he shouted. "Who is without sin? Are you?..." He pointed. "Are you?... are you?" He swung an accusing finger at the crowd, pointing to individuals in turn, who now backed away in a panic, each in mortal fear of having their sins made public.

He turned again to Otto. "I am here to enforce God's law and to save souls, soldier. You would do well to heed my request. Perhaps the Church should learn of your arrogance and disrespect!" He folded his arms across his broad chest and stood firm, glaring at Otto. The crowd remained quiet, some slipped away.

Otto could feel his testicles recede in fear. He knew Ramiro was Benedictine, as was the Pope himself. Beads of perspiration flushed to his brow. He turned away suddenly, muttering a curse. "Have your way monk... I will summon the Captain. But he won't be pleased."

Before Ramiro could console the terrified tradesman, Drugo exploded onto the scene, still half-dressed in pants and a loose shirt but now wielding a bare sword. Red with rage, with his big nose wrinkled in a hard sneer, he leapt forward like a wildcat to its prey and jabbed the point of his blade to Ramiro's neck. A cry of shock came from the crowd.

Ramiro stood motionless.

Drugo's deep voice blasted across the campground. "What is it, monk, that you must interrupt my breakfast? I have heard the evidence and sentenced this man! That is enough!" The blade trembled in his outstretched arm, scraping the skin of Ramiro's throat.

Ramiro showed no expression. Blood trickled down his neck. His wide eyes glinted for an instant, then darkened. He stared past the dull gray blade, straight into the eyes of the Captain, breaking the silence in a calm voice. "I am a man of God, Captain. Do you intend to kill me?"

Drugo shifted from one foot to the other, then back again. He said nothing.

"Would you kill a man of the Holy Church because you have missed breakfast?" A few people chuckled.

Drugo turned his head sharply in one direction and then the other, glowering at the masses, who again fell silent. He withdrew his sword a hand's length to dally it in Ramiro's face. He spat as he spoke. "Perhaps I would, monk!"

Ramiro countered his fiery response with a slow blink. "Have you forgotten the Peace of God, Captain?" he asked, referring to the papal decree that protects commoners and clergy from the exploits of nobles and knights. "If you commit this nefarious deed, Drugo of Flanders, there can be little doubt you will lose all honor among men. You will be excommunicated from the Church of Christ and your Christian soul will sink to the dark depths of Hell."

Drugo hesitated and a disquieted look replaced his scowl.

There was a tense pause and it seemed that the only sound was Drugo's heavy breathing. "And in those dark pits," Ramiro continued, "you will forever be consumed by the fire of brimstone, your flesh devoured by the beasts of iniquity... day after eternal day. Forever, you will remain a wretched, tormented slave of Satan." He moved his left hand slowly, taking hold of his cross and pushing it forward as far as the chain would allow. The bloodstone sparkled. "Neither crusade nor pilgrimage will absolve your sin. Is this your destiny?"

Drugo's sword wavered as he stared at the cross. A breath of terror swept across his face before he lowered his blade, holding it stiffly at his side. "This is my command, monk!" he shouted as loud as he could. "I am the law! You will not question it!"

"I follow God's law, Captain, not that of man," said Ramiro firmly before changing his tone. "Let me speak with the accused. I know him. He is Louis the Carpenter... a good man. Can we judge him so quickly? Give me some time to know the true events."

Drugo fumed at the challenge, taking a long stride to the left, and then another to the right. His men shuffled out of the way, the crowd moved too. He struggled with his anger, turning again to glare at Ramiro. "Know you, monk, that I will cut off this man's head if it pleases me!" He glowered at the crowd again, daring anyone to defy him. But the people quickly turned away, dropping their eyes to stare at the dust on their worn boots. More began to shuffle away.

Drugo seethed. Why did I ever vow to protect this foking monk? I could slit his fat throat. He straightened his tunic, composed himself, and spoke again. "I can show mercy, monk. I will grant your request. You have till noon before I hear you again."

"Only till noon?"

Drugo ignored him and turned to his men. "Leave the thief here. I'm going to finish my meal. Don't call me again!" He turned away in anger, swaggering back to his tent. The crowd parted in a hurry, giving him wide berth.

• • • • •

Louis' wife was a plump woman who, despite the increasing heat, wrapped herself in a woolen shawl and headscarf. She rushed to her husband, pulling the rag from his mouth before embracing him. "Thank you, Dom Ramiro, thank you for sparing my husband!"

Louis, a short man with shaggy brown hair, a flat face and a big nose, looked up with an expression of blank shock as his large wife fell on him. "Thank you... thank you, Dom Ramiro. This is my wife, Mathilda." A young woman dashed from the crowd and ran to his side. He motioned to her with his head. "And my daughter... Adele."

Politely, Ramiro looked up at the girl and nodded. He was about to turn back to Louis when he looked at her again, suddenly captivated by her enchanting hazel eyes and mesmerized by her small mouth and shapely lips. The smooth skin of her delicate face had the sheen and vitality of youth.

In a sudden rush of shame, he turned away, hesitating awkwardly for a moment before nodding to her again. Quickly, he knelt to comfort Mathilda, taking her hand. "We have not saved him yet, Mathilda. But, God willing, we will solve this matter."

"My husband is an honest man, Dom. He would never steal a thing!" She pressed Louis' head to her large bosom as she knelt.

Louis pulled back in embarrassment. "Mathilda, please, let Dom Ramiro speak."

Ramiro lowered his voice. "Louis, you must tell me everything if I am to help you. Did you take the locket?"

"No, Dom, I swear, I don't know how it came to be in my bag. I swear it in God's name."

Ramiro looked pensive as he scratched at the night's stubble on his chin and stared absently at Louis. "Is there anyone who would want to do you harm?"

Louis lowered his head in thought, he seemed to forget he was still tied to the block. "What do you mean?" he asked, lifting his head again. "You think someone put it in my bag?"

Ramiro's thick lips smiled with compassion, widening his round face. "If you did not steal it, Louis, then that is the only other explanation."

"Why would anyone do that?"

"Perhaps to see you hang... or lose your hand," Ramiro said with a grave expression. "But for what purpose? That is the question." He frowned in thought. "Have you argued with anyone?"

Louis pondered a while. "Nothing more than the occasional quarrel, Dom."

"What about the other carpenters?"

"We get along fine. Perhaps the odd disagreement." He dropped his gaze again to his tethered wrist. "I don't understand, I believe I get along with most everyone."

"Give me the names of your fellow workers and I will enquire."

"Well... there's Pierre, Ramón, Charles, and Raul. They're all good men."

Ramiro put the names to memory. "Who told Otto the locket was in your bag?"

"I don't know, Dom," he choked.

Ramiro stood up. "I must leave you now, but I promise to return soon." He rushed off in the direction of Otto's tent, leaving Louis to Mathilda's bosom.

• • • • •

Otto sat near a small campfire, his long blonde hair draping across his small, shaven face as he sharpened and polished his broadsword. Ramiro confronted him without any pleasantries. "Who told you the locket could be found in Louis' bag?"

The lieutenant stood and slung his sword into its sheath. "My wife's slave girl accused the man."

"And why was that?"

He lifted his long chin. "She said she saw him lurking about my tent the night before."

"You would convict a man on the testimony of a slave?"

Otto shrugged. "So? He's just a tradesman."

"He's a Christian!" Ramiro flushed. "And a valued asset to this company!" He looked towards Otto's tent. "Where is this slave, that I may speak with her?"

"That's her right over there. We call her Sara." He pointed to a girl with long, strawberry-blonde hair who sat on the grass under the shade of a beech tree. She was mending a garment.

Without further ado, Ramiro approached the girl. She lifted her head to toss her hair over one shoulder and noticed him coming. Abruptly, she dropped her eyes.

Ramiro noticed her aversion. "Good morning, Sara."

She looked up again and fidgeted with her needle and thread. She spoke with a heavy, Slavic accent. "Oh, greeting Father. What... what I do for you?"

"You can tell me why you accused Louis of stealing the locket."

She blushed. "I saw him near mistress tent night before."

"Surely, there are many about your tent at all times of the day. Why did Louis attract your attention?"

"He look inside," she blurted. "Inside tent." She dropped her thread in the grass and groped for it in a distressed manner. "I... I must finish chores, Dom. Excuse." She got up suddenly and rushed away, clutching her sewing in both hands.

Ramiro followed after her but could not keep up. "I will know the truth, Sara!" he yelled after her. But she vanished like a ferret into the throng of animals, people and tents.

• • • • •

He stomped back to his own tent, calling out for Pepin, who was waiting for his master to return from his morning meditation.

The boy rushed over. "Yes, Father."

Ramiro took him by the arm and held his elbow in the firm grip of his right hand. He guided him out of earshot. "Pepin, do you know the servants of Otto, the Captain's lieutenant?"

"Well, I... I know them a little, Father. We talk around the campfires." He squirmed, his young face grimacing from the pain of Ramiro's vice-like grip.

Ramiro leaned to his ear. "Discover what you can of Sara, his wife's handmaiden. Does she have any connection to any of the carpenters?" He looked into his eyes. The boy stiffened, returning a vacant stare. Ramiro waited, raising an eyebrow. "Have you gone daft, lad? Did you hear? A man's life is at stake!"

Pepin lowered his eyes. "But Father... everyone knows," he said apologetically.

Ramiro tipped his head, scowling. "And what do you mean by that, boy!" he asked in a harsh whisper. The boy's face reddened. Ramiro tightened his grip. "Well...? Out with it!"

Pepin winced again. "She's Raul's mistress, Father," he cried, tears streaming down his smooth cheeks. "Please, Father, my arm!"

Ramiro stood still, momentarily shocked. Slowly, he gained expression and released his grip. "Forgive me, son," he said, putting a hand to his stubbled chin. "His mistress? Are you sure? The one they call Sara?"

Pepin wiped his face, then rubbed his arm vigorously. "Yeh, the blonde girl, the one Otto bought from a Venetian trader. But Otto doesn't know."

"Is that so?" Ramiro smirked. "And where is Raul's tent?"

"Over to the east, by the carpenter's wagon under a large oak. Do you see it?" He pointed across a hundred tents to the distant tree.

Ramiro peered through the pluming camp smoke. "I see the oak," he said and dismissed the boy. "Not a word to anyone, or I will cleanse your soul with my whip! Now go about your chores." Pepin rubbed his arm again before scampering off to feed the horses.

Ramiro rushed back to poor Louis, who was still tied to the chopping block. "Tell me more of Raul. Who is he and what does he do?"

Louis looked up at Ramiro. "He's one of the guild, Dom. A carpenter, as I said."

"Have you argued?"

Mathilda intervened. "Not really, although he did ask for Adele's hand in marriage, but she refused."

"Why is that?"

"My daughter is a strong-headed woman," said Louis. "She spurned him despite my approval. Look at her, she will be an old maid if she does not marry soon."

Adele rose up from her father's side and flushed. She was eighteen. "I cannot marry him, Dom Ramiro," she said pleadingly. "He's a cruel and deceitful man - I despise him!" She spoke with disarming poise.

Ramiro locked his eyes to her pretty face. She was a striking woman, beautiful round eyes, a delicate nose, her features perfectly proportioned, a voluptuous Keltic goddess. Long auburn hair, half covered with a red shawl, dangled in soft curls about her delicate shoulders. She stood with a look of defiance, resting her hands on curved hips. Her shapely bosom, emphasized by a tunic of tight-knit wool and by the sash tied about her thin waist, rose and fell with every breath. Ramiro continued to stare, fascinated by the flutter of her long eyelashes.

"Dom Ramiro?" she asked when he did not reply.

Ramiro's cheeks reddened in another rush of shame. He lowered his eyes. "Uh... tell me... tell me Adele," he asked, lifting his eyes again. "What did Raul do when you refused him?"

"He was very angry, Dom Ramiro," she said with a serious look. "He rushed out and kicked some poor dogs standing in his way. He never said a word to me after that." She lowered her eyes briefly. "Forgive me for disobeying my father, but I cannot marry a man I detest!" She spat on the ground.

With effort, Ramiro pulled his gaze from her and turned again to Louis. "What would Raul gain with you out of the way?"

"I can guess," said Mathilda. "Myself and Adele would be alone in this strange land with no man to speak for us. She would have to marry then, or we risk being indentured to another master."

"Then he'd inherit all I have," Louis blurted. "Including my position in the guild!" His face soured. "That bastard!" He glanced at Ramiro. "Forgive me, Dom."

"It is only a possibility, Louis. That is all." He avoided looking at Adele. "Time is short, I must investigate." He rose from his knees with a muffled groan and strode off.

Louis looked about helplessly. A soldier stood watch nearby.

• • • • •

Pepin served bread and cheese to Ramiro, whose thoughts ran as he ate. *If I accuse Raul and Sara, they will both die. By the mercy of God, I cannot send them to their deaths - but I must save Louis from this deceit!*

An idea gripped him and he realized what he must do. He put his food down and set off to find Raul in the thick crowd, following Pepin's directions. After a few inquiries, he found the man tending horses at the edge of camp. "Good day. Are you Raul the Carpenter?"

Raul, a short man with shoulder-length brown hair, turned to Ramiro. "Yes, Dom, I am Raul. What brings you to my tent?" he asked as he tethered his horse.

Ramiro wasted little time. "Surely, you must be aware that Louis, one of your guild, has been accused of theft and is about to lose his hand?"

Raul shrugged. "What can I do, Dom? He has been charged by the Captain."

Ramiro scowled and stepped up to face him nose to nose. "Yes, but you know the charges are false, do you not?"

Raul backed away, speaking nervously. "It's a terrible tragedy, Dom. I... I would never suspect Louis of theft. But they found the locket in his possession. What can I do?"

Ramiro continued to move closer to him and he backed away again. "I think you can do something, Raul. Is it not true that the Russian slave, Sara, is your mistress?"

Raul stood still, he looked down, his crafty eyes shooting from side to side. "That is not your affair, monk."

"Only the Lord Jesus Christ determines my affairs, carpenter," he said as he studied the fear in Raul's eyes. "And did you not instruct Sara to accuse Louis of theft so that you could eventually take Adele's hand in marriage and inherit his wealth and position?"

Raul paled, his eyes blinked nervously.

Ramiro persisted. "I know your plot, Raul. You have committed a deadly sin. Only God can forgive you!"

Raul betrayed himself with a guilty look and a quavering voice. "I... I know nothing of this... this affair."

"You have sold your soul to Satan!" Ramiro blurted in disgust. "And now you face the fires of purgatory for accusing another unjustly. You would send another to his death simply to satisfy your own greed and lust?"

Raul tried to speak but could form no words.

Ramiro gripped the cross about his neck and held it up to Raul's face. "May God have mercy on your pitiful soul," he said, as if he were a divine judge passing final sentence. "Now you will face many accusations... that of a thief, and now perjury and deception. You will surely hang."

In a moment of dread, Raul realized his ruse had failed. He dropped to his knees, tears of fear and repentance streaming his cheeks. "Forgive me, Dom. Forgive me! What am I to do?"

"You can submit yourself to Saxon law, Raul... or take what you can carry and return to France as quickly as possible. There is nothing I can do for you." He turned away.

"But Dom, by myself? I will die on the road!"

Ramiro glanced back. "No, Raul, not by yourself, you must take Sara with you. The soldiers will drown her if you do not." He pitied the man. "Your choice is to lose your life here, or face the road. Decide!"

Sara soon heard of Ramiro's threat and before a half-hour had passed, they took Raul's only horse, a few supplies, and rode west at full gallop.

• • • • •

"Brother Aldebert! Wake up!" Ramiro yelled. "How can you possibly sleep through all this commotion and noise? Come, man, it is time to recite morning prayers and get a meal. Must I remind you that slothfulness is a sin?"

Aldebert, jarred from his dreams of Burgundy, bolted upright and slid off of his horse-hair mattress. His bloodshot gaze met Ramiro's scowl of concern. He still wore his black habit, as Benedictines do when they sleep. It was spotted with food and grease stains and hung heavily from his shoulders. His wooden cross dangled from a chain about his neck. For a long moment, he stared at Ramiro with squinting eyes, as if not sure where he was.

Aldebert was still uncomfortable speaking openly to a fellow monk, especially to a dean, a superior. Monks were discouraged from idle talk in the monastery but as they travelled further and further from the Abbey of Cluny, the rule became more and more untenable.

"Father Ramiro,..." he said in a strained voice. "...good morning – and praise the Lord!" He rubbed the sleep from his eyes with dirt stained hands, and again looked up at Ramiro from darkened sockets. "What commotion...?"

Ramiro stood at the entrance with his hands on his hips, his eyes glittering with annoyance. "In all my thirty years, I have never encountered a man who can sleep through such noise."

"Tell me, Father... what happened?"

Ramiro related the morning events. "I'm giving Raul and Sara time to flee before I approach Drugo again. We almost lost a good man, ... and a good carpenter, to the deception of that villain – wretched man!" He shook his head and whispered. "These Normans are a treacherous lot, Brother Aldebert."

Aldebert whispered back. "I thought they were Flemings."

"I suppose most are Flemings, but the rest are Normans. What's the difference, Brother? They are all bastard sons of those barbarous Northmen. Their tongues differ somewhat but they are all the same - greed infects their bones and the sight of blood amuses them." He plopped down on his mattress with a huff of breath. "You should have seen them, Brother Aldebert, hooting for the blood of Louis the Carpenter... with little more than the accusation of a slave." He got up again and began to roll up his mattress. "Come now, we'll take our mattresses outside to air in the sunlight. It is beginning to stink in here!" He could hardly tolerate the reek of the man. "We'll get a servant to wash our robes."

"But we just had our laundry done," Aldebert said.

"Just? That was over two weeks ago, Brother. Quickly now, we must prepare for morning prayers, the faithful rely on us to guide them to our Heavenly Father, to the praise of God."

In a large space, they set up a small altar, placing on it an icon of Christ on the Cross and another of Mother Mary. Almost the whole camp came to worship, while Ramiro and Aldebert led them in prayer, knowing that few, if any, could read the scriptures.

"*Lord open my lips,*" Aldebert chanted.

Ramiro responded, cueing the crowd to repeat his words.

> *And my mouth shall proclaim your praise.*
> *Glory be to the Father*
> *and to the Son*
> *and to the Holy Spirit...*

Drugo prayed, too. He prayed for Divine Providence to favor him with many rewards and riches. After all, I am a soldier of the True Faith, sent to destroy the infidels who threaten the Holy Church and the Holy Land. Guide my sword, oh Lord, that it may pierce the black hearts of your enemies. Surely then, my sins will be forgiven...

● ● ● ● ●

As noon approached, Ramiro sauntered up to Drugo and related his story. "Raul the carpenter and Otto's slave girl have fled in fear, Captain, thus confirming their guilt."

Drugo spun to Otto. "See if this is the case. Be sure to check the whole camp and return to me as quick as you can."

"Yes, m'lord."

Otto left with two other men before Ramiro spoke again. "It is also well to consider the merits of the tradesman, Captain. He is a master carpenter, and few mechanics can repair a wagon wheel as Louis can. You should also know he has considerable experience with catapults and other war machines. But he will be of little use to you with only one hand."

Drugo sat on a stool under the awning outside his large tent, his long legs sprawled out in front of him. He grunted as his black-haired servant girl combed his red locks and trimmed his beard. Cursed monk! But he's probably right, the carpenter could be useful when the time comes.

Otto returned within the hour. "Captain! Raul and my servant girl have fled."

"Well go after them! They cannot be far. Bring me their heads!"

"Yes, m'lord."

"And release that wretched carpenter! I have had enough of this business! Tomorrow, we break camp and ride to Genoa. Leave me now!"

Without another word, Ramiro spun on his heels and hurried back to the chopping block, arriving just as the guard untied Louis' arm. Mathilda gushed in tears and flung herself on Ramiro in a forceful embrace. He stood firm, patting her back awkwardly.

Adele strolled forward as Mathilda loosened her grip. She reached out to take Ramiro's hand. "Thank you, Dom, we are forever in your debt."

Her gentle touch sent a pleasant shock through his arm, and her adoring look sent waves of warm passion pulsing through his chest. For a long moment, it took his breath away. He felt his ears grow hot and gently pulled his hand from hers. "It is, uh... it is my pleasure to serve God and His righteousness. I... I must go now to attend to my duties." He turned away quickly, stumbled on a stone, chuckled nervously, and muttered goodbyes.

Adele stood watching him. A warm gust blew the shawl from her head, tossing her long hair about her shoulders. She traced Ramiro's departure with a keen look and some amusement before shaking her head in a slow reprimand. He's a monk, you fool. Go about your business.

By nightfall, Raul and Sara could not be found, and Otto had given up the chase.

• • • • •

Ramiro tossed and turned in the hot silence of night. Try as he may, he could not sweep the carpenter's daughter from his mind. He thought dutifully of his vows and chided himself for his lack of continence, struggling again and again to redirect his unruly thoughts to prayer.

> Lord in your kindness, we ask you to lighten the
> darkness of this night and grant that your ser-
> vants may sleep in peace...

But it was in vain. She appeared again, like a bewitching angel who had found some secret entrance into the back of his mind. Please forgive me, Father, for my licentious thoughts. Purge my soul of all wantonness that I may devote my mind only to Your Cause. For a while, he managed to distract his thoughts by concentrating on his mission and the upcoming ride to Genoa. It is in the hands of God, he conceded as a fitful sleep finally overcame him.

GENOA & PISA

The merchant galleys at harbor in Genoa were larger than any vessel Ramiro had seen before. Racks of oars perforated long, swooping hulls sitting high above the water. Both lateen and square sails of light-gray canvas draped from their huge yardarms. On the docks, longshoremen unloaded cargo by hand or with rough-hewn cranes, stacking wooden boxes, barrels and canvas bags filled with goods of all kinds. Exports of grain from the Po Valley and precious ores from the Alps lay beside imports of silk, spices, and sugar from the East. All of it moved around the shoreline, slowly making its way to rows of neat, square merchant houses.

Genoa was a vibrant and wealthy city-state excelling in trade, shipbuilding and banking, with branches throughout the Aegean and as far afield as Byzantium. Its navigational instruments and cartographic skills, many of them borrowed from the Greeks and Arabs, were among the best in the western world. But as the power of Genoa increased, so did that of its arch-rival, the city-state of Pisa.

Like Genoa, Pisa exploited the seas and benefited from the plunder of Arab settlements. The two republics grabbed all they could and fought each other over cities and regions fallen to their prey. But by the time their hostilities ceased, Pisa ruled supreme in the Tyrrhenian Sea and Pope Urban the Second awarded control of Corsica and Sardinia to the growing republic. He decreed that Pisan rules of navigation would establish the 'laws and customs of the sea.'

JUST WAR

But there was little time for the wonders of Genoa or Pisa and they kept moving south, following the worn flagstones of the Aurelia Way. With a heavy sigh, Ramiro pulled back the hood of his black robe, exposing his circle of matted hair to the warm sun creeping out of a thin cloud above the rolling, grassy hills of Tuscany. He felt exhausted and longed for the quiet comfort of his private room at the Abbey. Rarely did he have a decent night's sleep in his flimsy tent, which was incapable of shielding his ears from the constant clacking and banging of the servants, or the bellicose bragging of drunken knights.

He thought again of his mother's letter, still not sure what it meant. Was she really dying or just heartbroken? Soon, God willing, I will reach her in the Holy Land and walk the cobbled paths of blessed Jerusalem, the Holiest of Holy cities. His heart raced at the thought of entering the Church of the Holy Sepulcher, where he would finally place his lips to the Tomb of Christ. This would be his supreme act of penance and thanksgiving, and he had no doubt it would bring him God's love and favor, as it did for all who took this sacred journey.

His quiet reflections vanished when two knights barged through the line, bumping and pushing at everything in their way. Women and children lurched to the side, shrieking in surprise. Aldebert's horse stumbled to the edge of the road and Ramiro fought to steady his own mount.

"Mother of God!" He tugged at his reins. "Pull left, Brother Aldebert! Before you throw me into the brambles!"

Aldebert pulled the other way, barging into a nearby wagon.

"Good Lord!" Ramiro chided in exasperation. "When will you learn to ride?" He steadied his mare. "And how long must I forebear these arrogant marauders? I tell you Brother, their impertinence would test the patience of our beloved Saint Paul, may God bless his name!" He reined his horse back to the road, attempting to regain his composure.

Aldebert still struggled with his confused mare. "Were you not once a soldier yourself, Father Ramiro?"

"True enough, Brother Aldebert, but that was long ago. For the past ten years, my life at the abbey has been a simple one, and I suppose I have grown unaccustomed to the brutish ways of a warrior. But it seems to me these men are particularly crude and uncivilized," he snorted. "Never before have I been treated with such contempt!"

Aldebert was not aware the knights were 'crude and uncivilized,' but nodded anyway. "I heard you once fought in Spain, Father Ramiro. Is this true?"

Ramiro hesitated, such idle chatter was unbecoming to a monk, but the boring, monotonous ride compelled him. "Yes, yes, although that now seems like another lifetime," he said, giving in to his propensity to tell a tale. "I was the seventh of eight sons, Brother, so I had little hope of inheritance and sought my fortunes elsewhere. I come from a proud and noble family in the city of León, in the Kingdom of León, ruled by the great king, Alfonso. We served our king well."

"You fought the Moors?"

"That's right. But I was wounded outside Salamanca and captured." He grew quiet for a time. The horses clopped on, people chatted, pots and tools rattled and clanked. "I spent two years as a hostage in Cordoba before I was released."

Aldebert shuffled in his saddle. "Did you return to fighting?"

"Oh, no, no. I could no longer bear the guilt of war. So I retired from Alfonso's service and went on a pilgrimage to Santiago de Compostela, to pray for my sins and to seek forgiveness."

Aldebert gushed. "Did you visit the tomb of Saint James the Moor Killer?"

Ramiro winced. "Yes, some call him that, while others would say Saint James the Great. I worshipped at his tomb day and night, praying for God's grace. I was troubled, Brother. I have killed, though the Commandments say 'you shall not murder.' I have taken booty from the enemy, though we are told 'you shall not steal.' And I have struck in anger, though the Lord Christ teaches us to turn the other cheek. How can I live the life of a soldier, I thought, and still follow the path of Our Savior?"

"But surely, what choice did you have, Father? It is a Just War sanctified by the Mother Church. How could God not favor your actions, even if it means killing another?"

Ramiro shook his head slowly. "I could never completely reconcile the two notions, Brother."

Aldebert pulled an apple from his saddle bag and began to devour it feverishly. He ate quickly and loudly and spoke through a sloshing mouthful. "Truly, God has touched you with His Grace, Father Ramiro."

Ramiro could not drag his gaze from Aldebert. The red sores on his skin were as red as his nose. And when he talked, he spat the white flesh of the apple from blackened teeth and red lips. At the same time, he swallowed whole chunks, as if he had gone without food for weeks on end. The poor boy could use a bit of God's grace himself, he thought. So ugly, so uncultured... and deprived of all common sense.

NORTHMEN

Normans loved to fight. After all, they were the sons and daughters of the fearsome Vikings who pillaged Europe as far afield as Russia and Byzantium. But it was not so much the bloodlust of battle that drove them as it was the rich booty of war.

The Lombards were the first to hire Norman mercenaries in Italy. But in less than thirty years, these clever freebooters began to conquer southern Italy for themselves, taking Arab strongholds to the south, defeating Lombard princes, and driving the Byzantines from the port of Bari in 1071. They were first led by the resolute William Iron Arm and, later, by an ambitious adventurer, Robert Guiscard, once a roving highwayman.

After securing southern Italy, the Normans began to invade Sicily to the south and infringed on Papal lands to the north. The Pope fought back and skirmishes broke out between Guiscard's knights and the Papal Guard.

Not long afterwards, in 1084, King Henry of Germany also invaded the Papal lands and seized Rome from Pope Gregory. The King was annoyed because the Pope had challenged his authority and so he decided to install his own pope, a man by the name of Giberto of Ravenna, named Clement the Third.

Now King Henry became the real enemy of the Pope, forcing Gregory to swallow his pride and to seek shelter among his former foes, the belligerent Normans. And after Gregory died, Pope Urban had to do the same.

And so it was for the next five years, the possession of Rome and the Holy See oscillated between the Germans, who backed Pope Clement, and the Normans, who now fought on behalf of Pope Urban.

• • • • •

Drugo's company neared Rome when the scouts came charging back. "The Germans come! Hundreds of men!"

Drugo peered forward. He saw the heavy knights thundering towards them. "To the field!" he yelled. "Move to the field! Take high ground! Everyone! Form a circle!" Men and women hollered and shrieked, children screamed.

Knights and squires were the first to get to the mound, taking their horses and wagons with them, leaving everyone else to fend for themselves. Aldebert rode off in terror, toppling people to the ground as he went. Women and children ran to catch up, tripping and scrambling into the field, abandoning carts and dropping their bags. Pepin rushed away, leaving the laden donkey standing alone. His blonde hair twisted over his shoulders as he looked back. "Hurry Father! Hurry!"

Ramiro watched in disgust. He looked around at the few stragglers running to catch up. That's when he spotted Louis. His wagon was stuck in a hollow and his Belgian workhorse struggled to get it free. Mathilda and Adele scampered around it, picking up tools and supplies thrown to the ground.

"Leave it Louis!" he cried as he rode up. "Leave it! Go with the others!"

Louis ran to him. "Dom Ramiro. My horse, my tools – I cannot leave them."

"For the love of God, Louis. What good are tools without hands to use them?" He glanced over to Adele, who stopped what she was doing and looked up. Their eyes met and, despite the urgency, he felt swept away. "Adele," he said, strangling his words. "You... you should go now. Please go."

She looked down, hesitant. But when she looked up again, she had fire in her eyes. "Everything we have is here, Dom Ramiro. Would you have us leave it to these damn Germans?"

Louis approached her, taking the tools from her hands. "Go my dear," he said kindly. "Do as Dom Ramiro asks."

"Come on everyone!" Ramiro shouted and they ran across the field toward the circle of knights. They were still sixty paces from the others when the Germans were on them. Three of them raced forward, lances out.

Ramiro stopped. "Keep going! Go!" he shouted to Louis before he spun to face the knights. "Stop!" he shouted, holding up his cross. "Stop in the name of God!"

To his surprise, the knights did stop, turning their mounts around and moving back before holding position about fifty paces away. Well, well..., Ramiro thought with an air of righteousness. But when he turned around to join the others, he saw Drugo's archers stationed behind him.

A wall of shields faced out from the large circle where Drugo's men huddled, long lances jutting out between them - horses, gold, women and children put to the center. The infantry took positions to the outside, wet with sweat and breathing hard under a hot, Tuscany sun.

"God be praised!" Aldebert shouted as Ramiro joined them. "Help us tend the horses, Father Ramiro."

"Horses do not concern me, Brother Aldebert. What of the safety of these poor people you so quickly abandoned on the road. Would you save yourself first? Is this the way of a Benedictine monk?"

Aldebert bowed his head sheepishly. "Sorry, Father, I was only following the Captain's orders."

"You follow my orders, Brother Aldebert. Is that clear?"

"Yes, of course. Forgive me, Father, for I have sinned."

Ramiro turned to Pepin, slapping him on the back of the head. "And you, my boy, you made no attempt to lead the donkey. Do you wish to be known as a coward?"

Pepin flushed bright red and lowered his head. "No, Father Ramiro."

Ramiro left them without another word, pushing his way past hundreds of mounted knights who watched and waited for any signal, their steeds stomping and snorting. He reached the front of the line, standing behind the shielded infantry, who couched lances on their shoulders to spear the enemy's horses. He looked over their shields to study the gathering army.

The Germans stopped at arrow distance and fanned out to face them, their archers ran to the front, kneeling on the dry ground.

Drugo ordered his own archers to the front, relieved to see the enemy had no more men than he did. He opened up the back of the circle to face them in a wide arc and his knights jostled to form a long line, matching the German formation. He did not want a battle, the Germans were strong fighters and there was no prospect of gold here.

A German knight wearing a peaked iron helmet with a wide nasal strip rode out to parley. He was a weathered, husky man with long, brown hair and a thick goatee. High over his head, flapped the banner of the Holy Roman Empire, a black eagle on a gold flag.

Drugo reached out to one of his men, grabbing the banner of the Count of Flanders, a black lion on a gold flag. He rode out slowly from the wall of shields. Ramiro followed him, pushing past the soldiers on the outer ring just as the German knight and Drugo stopped to face each other at shouting distance.

"Who leads you?" the man shouted in colloquial Latin.

Drugo's Latin was rusty, and what little he did know was in the vernacular of Flanders. "I leading men," he replied haltingly. "I Drugo of Flanders. Travel to Gr... Greek land."

"Who are you and what is your business here?" The German spoke quickly.

Drugo strained at his words. "Rome," he replied uncertainly.

"What do you mean, Rome?" The German asked, shaking his head. An army of idiots! He tried again. "Who... are... you?" he enunciated slowly, as if speaking to a child.

"We Fl...," Drugo started but he could not remember the word.

Ramiro sprang to his side. "Perhaps I can help, Sir Drugo," he said fluently.

Drugo stared at him. Then he looked behind to see if any others had followed him out. But no, just this pestering monk. "If I need your help, monk, I'll ask for it," he said in northern French.

"Well," said Ramiro, "unless your German is better than your Latin, Sir Drugo, I'd say we are in trouble."

"Well, monk?" the German shouted impatiently. "Perhaps you can say from whence you come and the nature of your business here."

Ramiro faced the knight with a broad smile. "Of course, sir. I am Ramiro of..." He hesitated to mention Cluny. "... of León, sir. I would be glad to speak on behalf of our noble Captain Drugo." He waved an arm in gesture before speaking again. "And to whom do I have the honor of speaking?"

The man held his chin high. "I am Frederick, Captain of the Papal Guard and Defender of the Holy See." He looked down at Ramiro. "And you are Benedictine," he scoffed. "Just like the false pope himself, the one you call Urban."

Ramiro shivered a little but kept smiling. "We are on our way to the Greek kingdom, Captain Frederick. And we hope to visit Rome on our way."

Frederick's horse raised its head and snorted. "You are Normans?"

"A few, yes. But most are Flemish."

"What is your business in Rome?"

"We simply wish to visit the holy shrines and Saint Peter's Church."

Frederick lifted his chin, shaking his head slowly, his iron helmet glinting in the sun. "No soldiers are permitted in the holy city, especially Normans. The Emperor of the Holy Roman Empire forbids it."

"But Captain, we are pilgrims as well as soldiers. We promise to be brief before continuing to Terracina."

"No, I cannot allow it. You are not welcome in the Holy See."

"As I said, Captain, you will have no trouble with us."

"I cannot let you go that way. I will direct you east, around Rome and across the Apennines."

"What did he say?" asked Drugo, who struggled to keep up.

"He wants us to take another route."

"We could do that," he said, eager to avoid any losses.

"But the Holy Father is in Terracina," said Ramiro. "I have been ordered there."

Drugo sighed heavily. "You can always travel back to Terracina after we get to the Norman duchy."

Ramiro ignored him and turned back to Frederick. "No," he said.

"What do you mean?" Frederick asked, astounded.

Ramiro folded his arms. "We will forego Rome but we must get to Terracina."

Frederick sputtered in disbelief. "You dare to defy me? I will not allow it!" he bellowed.

"You will let us pass," said Ramiro, mustering courage. "Or must we do battle to resolve our differences?"

The big German leaned forward, looking him straight in the eye. "You want a battle, monk? We do not fear your riffraff! I need only draw my sword to begin a fight! And your head will be my first trophy!" He put his hand to his sword hilt.

Drugo watched in alarm. "What's going on?"

Ramiro ignored him. "Riffraff... indeed, Captain Frederick. They may look a little haggard from our long journey but mistake not these men. They are warriors born and bred. They consider it an honor to die with boots on."

Frederick drew his sword. Drugo quickly matched his movements, raising his blade. A great commotion stirred on both sides, knights fixed their lances for charge and the archers readied their bowstrings.

"What did you say to him?" Drugo shouted.

"I told him that we are going to Terracina whether he likes it or not. I told him we would stand and fight."

"You said what? You bloody idiot! We did not come all this way to fight Germans!"

Ramiro waved him down. "Quiet, Sir Drugo or he will think you weak. Hold your head high and be not afraid. God is with you. Look angry, look stern."

Drugo, unsure, sat upright, looking straight at the German. Damned monk! Horses tossed their heads, stomping and snorting. Behind them, the men waited anxiously for any signal. An eerie quiet settled on the field, broken only by the odd neigh of a horse or a cough from the men.

Frederick frantically weighed his chances, glancing over Drugo's well-armed men. He studied the look in Drugo's eyes before his gaze fell to Ramiro, feeling unnerved by the monk's bold, unflinching stare. "You may go to Terracina," he said, breaking the silence. "But we must escort you."

● ● ● ● ●

Many cried when they crossed the Tiber. Rome is the second most sacred destination for Christian pilgrims, but it was a destination denied for Drugo of Flanders and his band of knights. The Germans pressed them ahead, coaxing them forcefully along the ancient Appian Way. But when the Pontine Marshes came into view, the Papal Guard suddenly turned back to Rome.

The road through the lonely marsh was rough and upturned. In many places, paving stones were washed away or sank into the muck of the mud-flats. Stagnant pools lined the weather-worn flagstones and the whole place stank.

"God curse those Germans!" Aldebert ranted as he swatted at mosquitoes. "And curse their devil pope!" He pulled his hood tight around his face.

"Now, now, Brother Aldebert," said Ramiro as he too pulled his hood over his head. "I doubt our loving and merciful God would curse any poor soul." He brushed a swarm of mosquitoes from his face. "We must pray for their errant ways."

Pepin shook his head, tossing his long hair to brush the insects from his face. He covered himself with a cloak and swatted at his arms as he led the donkey. "What's that stink?" he asked.

Ramiro looked back at him. "It's the marsh, boy. The still waters are the home of many foul things."

A long, pleading cry grew from the thicket. Then another, and another, all followed by sharp screeches. People stumbled to a stop, men drew their swords and children ran to their mothers.

"Ghosts of the marsh!" someone shouted. "Souls of the dead!"

"Wood devils! Dear Jesus!" Aldebert cried out, frantically making the sign of the cross.

Ramiro rolled his eyes. "For the love of God, Brother Aldebert. It's a bird!"

Despite the poor condition of the road, they made good time through the foul marshes, eventually arriving at the dry fields of Terracina.

TERRACINA

Ramiro and Aldebert waited anxiously in the wide plaza of the Cathedral of Saints Peter and Cesareo, the very place where the Cardinals of Rome had elected Pope Urban the Second. With their backs to the cathedral steps, they looked out to the deep blue waters of the Tyrrhenian Sea where the craggy promontory of Monte Circeo rose high above the flat, sandy beaches of the littoral.

Drugo waited too, but he ignored the monks, still livid with Ramiro for challenging his authority and putting his men in danger. He paced nervously, eyeing his Italian guards with suspicion, feeling vulnerable without his small army, which was intercepted on the outskirts of Terracina by the Prince of Capua and ordered to remain out of the city.

Aldebert fiddled with his wooden cross, making the sign on his forehead every few minutes. Sweat dripped from his high brow and he wiped it away with a sleeve. He looked behind him, up the stone steps of the cathedral to the pillared entrance. "Will he see us? Why doesn't he come?"

"Patience, Brother Aldebert," said Ramiro. "All things in God's time."

"There he is!" Drugo yelled, pointing to the cathedral entrance. He rushed up the steps in long strides.

"That's a bishop," corrected Ramiro as he hurried behind.

"Aha!" cried the bishop when he saw them approach. "Greetings and God bless. I am the Bishop of Apulia. And clearly, you two are from Cluny. And you, sir," he said to Drugo, "you must be the captain from the Far West. Welcome to Terracina."

"Yes, Your Excellency," Ramiro piped up, glad to be recognized. "We are here to arrange a meeting with His Holiness."

"Yes, yes, the Holy Father has been expecting you. Unfortunately, he cannot see you at this time and offers his sincere apologies."

"But Your Excellency, we have come a long way and Abbot Hugh of Cluny said I must see His Holiness on important business."

The bishop smiled compassionately. "As you will, as you will. But not here. He will meet you at the synod in Melfi in two weeks' time."

MELFI

AUGUST 1089

The Castle of Melfi stood high on the hill above, glowing the color of pure gold as the sun set below the mountains. It was a massive fortress with sheer granite walls, guarded on all sides by rectangular towers. This was the hub of Norman power in the Duchy of Apulia, ruled by Borsa and his half-brother Bohemond, the sons of the Norman warlord, Robert Guiscard.

Bohemond was first-born, a giant of a man and a better warrior. But he was common-born of a Norman mother. Borsa, however, was high-born with Lombard blood and, through the intrigues of his own wily mother and the intervention of Pope Urban, it was he who finally won the duchy.

In the grassy fields below the Castle of Melfi, the Flemings hastened to erect their tents, kindling their fires before the ghosts of the night crawled out from their lairs in the dark woods nearby.

The townspeople, alarmed by the new-comers and wizened in the ways of war, drew in their livestock and huddled inside their small brick homes. They feared these strangers, even though some of them spoke the familiar tongue of their grandparents.

Pepin struggled with the tent. "Do you really think the blessed Pope himself is in the castle, Father Ramiro?" he said, pulling a corner taut.

"I should think so, boy. By the Grace of God, we will all meet on the morrow, either there or in the Bishopric Palace." He readied a peg. "Now don't pull it till I get the peg in." He hit the peg once with the flat of his axe and it sank easily into the chalky soil. He looked over to Aldebert, who sat staring, doing nothing. "Brother Aldebert!" he shouted. "Get over here and give us a hand!"

• • • • •

A hundred voices echoed inside the cavernous hall of the Bishopric Palace. Seventy bishops crowded a huge oak table and they all seemed to be talking at once. To either side, sat dignitaries of the secular world, the warlords of Italy. Dominant among them was Duke Borsa, a quiet man with black hair hanging off his head like the shag of a dog.

At a distance, sat Bohemond, his face shaved smooth, his yellow hair cropped short, Roman-style. The fair countenance of his large, square head was set cold and hard, like the chiseled granite of the castle. He sat well away from Borsa, not because he feared him but because he was sorely tempted to break his neck. The two brothers had just fought for the rule of Apulia and, only recently, was Bohemond dispossessed.

Drugo and Otto shuffled beside Ramiro, uneasy about giving up their weapons at the door. Drugo held his helmet under one arm and fiddled endlessly with his empty sword sheath. Otto looked more pale than usual and his thin, wiry hands twitched at his side. They were both tired of the boring, endless talk of things they did not entirely understand and about which they could care less.

Despite the noisy and lengthy proceedings, Ramiro was ecstatic. What a blessed day! The Holy Father himself! The Pope was much bigger than he imagined. A long, red cape of damask silk draped from his broad shoulders, hanging all the way down to his red leather shoes, and a white stole, decorated with gold crosses, wrapped his neck. His curly, gray hair sprung out from a red skull cap, a full beard jutted from his chin, and a heavy brow gave his deep-set eyes a dogged look.

Urban banged his staff on the granite floor. "Come to order!" he shouted in a croaking voice. In an instant, the hall fell silent. All eyes turned to the head of the table. "How do you say?" he asked the bishops.

The Bishop of Apulia rose to his feet. "We have reached agreement, Your Holiness, and concur that the clergy should not marry, neither shall they abide concubines."

"Very well," said Urban. "I shall decree it so." A hubbub of chatter rose in the hall. He banged his staff again. "And what of simony? What have you decided?"

The bishop spoke again. "We agree also, Your Holiness, that no payment shall be received or paid for the appointment of any ecclesiastical office."

"As you say, this also shall be decreed," he replied. "And now, as the last matter before us, you have been asked to consider lifting the ban of excommunication against Alexios, the Emperor of Byzantium. What have you decided?"

"It remains a difficult matter for us, Your Holiness," said the bishop. "The Greek patriarchs still refuse to accept the Church of Rome as the mother church of Christ. Nor do they agree to the *filioque* clause, among other things." He referred to the Latin belief that the Holy Spirit emanates from both the Father *and* the Son, rather than just the Father, as the Greeks believed. "But we have hope," the bishop continued, "that we will reach a compromise."

The other bishops nodded in unison and the room filled with a clamor of agreement. "Therefore," said the bishop, "we agree to lift the ban of excommunication against the King of the Greeks."

Ramiro watched the Pope's big moustache rise slightly and he thought he saw a smile. "Praise be to God and His mercy," Urban said loudly. "Today's outcomes will help us unite the churches, to free the clergy of vice, and to bring us all closer to God."

He waved to a servant, who came rushing up with a golden box. Urban took hold of it with both hands and placed it on a small pulpit about ten paces from the table. Then he turned his eyes to the crowd. "And now I say to the lords of Italy, it is time to renew the Truce of God. Come to me and swear on the skull of Saint Peter that you will uphold the peace and remain loyal to the True Faith."

The richly-attired men rose from their seats, some with reluctance, and approached Pope Urban one at a time. The first of these was Duke Borsa, who put his hand to the relic and swore his allegiance before kneeling to kiss the Pope's gold ring. His brother, Bohemond, did the same, but only because he felt trapped by circumstance, and others followed suit. After they all made their vows, the bishop from Terracina approached Urban and whispered in his ear.

Urban scanned the crowd before speaking. "Drugo of Flanders! Come forward!"

Drugo, aghast at the sound of his name, nervously made his way through the throng. He did as he saw the others do, placing a hand to the skull of Saint Peter and swearing his allegiance to the Church of Rome.

"Rise to your feet, soldier of God."

Drugo stood awkwardly and the Pope continued. "See you all! Here is a brave man who goes to fight for the True Faith! He hails from distant Flanders, serving the Count of Flanders. And he marches to the Greek Kingdom to scourge that land of the godless pagans and, for this, his sins will be forgiven and he will walk among the angels, as it will be for all who seek to free the blessed Holy Land from the blight of the heathen." He took a moment to scrutinize the lords of Italy, making it clear the words were meant for them. Then he waved a hand in the direction of a man wearing Roman armor. The Byzantine stood and approached.

"Drugo of Flanders," said Urban. "I introduce you to Commander Manuel, ambassador to the Greek Emperor."

Manuel appeared regal in his manner and dress. A soft light winked from the plate armor on his broad chest, half-covered by a long red cloak. He was about thirty, a handsome man of average height who kept his chestnut-brown hair and short beard impeccably groomed. His eyes were aqua blue and seemed to shimmer under his dark brow. He nodded silently to Drugo.

"Commander Manuel will escort you to Constantinople," said Urban. "You are fortunate to have such a distinguished companion and I suggest you take advantage of his position. You both receive my blessing, may God go with you." He dismissed them before ending the long synod with lengthy prayers.

The big Bohemond towered above the others as he milled about the hall, deep in thought. The Greek king wants fighting men, he thought. By God, there must be a way I can seize opportunity here. But the bastard won't even speak to me. He referred to Manuel. And he knew why he was being ignored. After all, only seven years ago, he had invaded Albania in the Greek kingdom with his father, Robert Guiscard.

Ramiro bowed his head in prayer and fingered his cross anxiously. What about me? What of the letters? And when a final chant of 'amen' brought the prayers to a close and his name was not mentioned, he worked his way through the dispersing crowd, hurrying to make his way toward the Pope. But Papal bodyguards stepped forward to stop him.

"What do you want?" asked the chamberlain, stepping from behind.

"Please, Your Grace, I am Ramiro of Cluny. I must speak with the Holy Father. I have urgent business. I have been sent by Abbot Hugh."

"Hugh of Cluny?"

"Yes, indeed. On a critical matter."

"Well then," he said with a grin. "I believe I can arrange a brief meeting on the morrow. For the moment, His Holiness is tired and needs his rest."

"Yes, of course, Your Eminence. Thank you."

• • • • •

Urban, once again in a red cape and red shoes, slouched on his gilded, portable throne as the thick fragrance of incense hung in the air of an elegant room in the Bishopric Palace. Attendees lined either side of the walkway, falling quiet when Ramiro approached to kiss the papal ring.

"Ramiro of Cluny," he said in a deep, tired voice. "I have been expecting you. I believe you have a letter for me."

"Yes, Holy Father, from Abbot Hugh of Cluny." He reached into his habit and drew out the creased envelope. "And I await your instructions, Your Holiness."

The room fell quiet, hot and humid, the air stifling. Urban opened the letter and read. After a while, he put it aside and signaled for Ramiro to rise from his knees. He looked at him squarely, his long nose looming over his thick beard. "And how fare my brethren at Cluny?"

"By God's Grace, all is well, Holy Father. And the monastery is nearly finished."

"That is good. So you are the one who travels to the Greek King?"

"Yes, Holy Father."

"My chamberlain tells me you ride with Count Robert's men."

"That is true, Your Holiness."

"That is good," he said, raising a hand to another page, who rushed up with three letters, each sealed with the papal insignia. "And you will ride with the Byzantine ambassador. You will be well protected." He nodded to the page, who then turned to Ramiro and offered him the letters. "You are to deliver these letters personally. One you will see, I have addressed to the King. It introduces you as my legate and should serve you well. Another is addressed to the Patriarch of Constantinople, and the last to the Patriarch of Jerusalem. Do you swear on the blood of Christ to deliver them on behalf of the Mother Church?"

"Uh, yes, Holy Father, I do," he said with a growing sense of unease. He put his hand to his olivewood cross and rubbed the bloodstone. "And I have the cross."

"The cross?"

"Yes, Holy Father, for the Patriarch of Jerusalem."

Urban nodded as if he understood. "It is good to bear gifts. You leave soon, I hear. May God speed your journey."

BARI

"So what was he like, Father Ramiro," asked Aldebert as the mountains of Melfi gave way to the Murge Plateau with its broad, dry plains and low-lying hills. In the distance, the Adriatic Sea glimmered under a blue sky.

"Who?"

"The Holy Father! What a blessing!"

Ramiro smiled, leaning forward to pat the neck of his mare. "He seemed a just and holy man," he said. But his smile faded when he recalled mentioning his cross. The Pope showed little interest in it. Did he know? The Abbot cautioned me to mention it to no one. Did he mean the Holy Father, too? And what of his talk of war? Popes had waged war in the past, it was true, but Urban... well... after all, he is Benedictine.

His thoughts dissipated when they reached the port of Bari. It was a hive of activity and, despite the heat, people, carts, horses and donkeys plied along the paved streets in easy gaits. Brick buildings, all topped in red tile roofs and built wall-to-wall, lined the way to the docks. By the time Drugo's men got to the departure berth, they found themselves in a noisy mass of people - strange people who, by their dress, were not townsfolk. Many were dark-skinned, some Arabs and Jews, while many others were slaves bound with thick ropes.

Ramiro gazed over the blue-gray waves while they waited for official permission to enter the port. He felt a peculiar excitement, laced with apprehension. Across this sea was an entirely new land, the home of Greeks, Turks and Arabs.

• • • • •

Ramiro leaned on the starboard rail as the hull of the galley chopped against the short rolling waves of the Adriatic. He felt a wave of nausea and wished he had postponed his lunch of calzone. He stuck his head into the wind, feeling it rush past his ears, and when a cool ocean mist brushed his face, he began to feel a little better. Seagulls screeched above in a clear, blue sky and the sound of the oarsman's drum beat below the deck. The oars, as long as twenty feet, swung in tight circles, up and down to the rhythm of the drum. He could feel them strain against the wind.

Knights and servants crammed onto the galley decks with their horses and farm animals, gathering in small groups to chat amongst themselves. And when the ship hit a swell and the bow lifted up, horses staggered and people stumbled. More rushed to the rails to join Ramiro.

"How are you feeling, Monk Ramiro?" someone asked, using the Greek form of address.

Ramiro turned to see the Byzantine ambassador, Manuel, who stood steady on deck, despite the sway of the ship. "A little better, thank you, it's been many years since I rode the waves."

Manuel still wore his fancy helmet and full plated armor as if expecting a battle at any moment. He moved across from Ramiro, leaning on the rail, his long red cape slapping about him in the wind, his blue eyes sparkling with energy. "I'm sure you will soon regain your sea legs." He pointed eastward. "Look! You can just see the cliffs of Dyrrachium."

"Is that in Byzantium?"

"Yes, although we've had some trouble holding it."

"What do you mean?"

"Have you heard of Robert Guiscard?"

"I have heard mention. He was the father of Duke Borsa, was he not?"

"And the father of Bohemond. He was a very cunning Norman who thought he could conquer Byzantium."

"What did he do?"

"He and Bohemond assembled an army of many thousands and launched an attack by taking the same journey we take today. We fought some terrible battles with that cursed man and lost many good men. 'The Weasel' we called him, damn him to Hades – but I have to admit, he was a good commander."

"What happened?"

"Our King instigated a revolt in Italy and Guiscard had to run home to subdue it. Then we drove the rest out."

"And that was the end of it?" asked Ramiro.

"Oh, no. Guiscard refused to give up, even though he was an old man by then. He gathered another huge army for yet another invasion. We were greatly outnumbered. But much to King Alexios' joy, he died of a fever before it was launched."

"Your king sounds like quite a man," said Ramiro, feeling better with his mind off the waves.

"He has saved the empire many times, Monk Ramiro," he said with a touch of gratitude in his voice. "And you will meet him soon. Your Abbot must consider this an important assignment."

"He does," Ramiro nodded. "It is his hope to unite all Christians under one church."

"A noble task, Monk Ramiro, but is not the Latin Church itself divided?"

Ramiro thought of the anti-pope, Giberto, and nodded his head. "Alas, that is also true, Manuel. We can only pray that King Henry realizes his folly."

ROME

Deep within the walls of Rome, Giberto's secretary rushed up the stone steps of the Lateran Palace. Huffing and puffing, he came to an arched doorway, clutching two letters, and banged nervously with the brass knocker. A voice cried from inside and he entered cautiously.

Giberto reclined on his sofa, his wild, black-gray eyebrows crossed in aggravation. "What is it? I asked not to be disturbed."

The secretary bowed low, still breathing heavily from the long climb. "Your Holiness, please... please forgive me but I have just received important letters."

"Letters?" He stood abruptly. "From whom?"

"The Po...," he almost said 'Pope.' "... I mean Odo... Odo of Lagery." He glanced at the seal on the other letter. "And another is from one of our emissaries."

Giberto snatched them from his hand. "That will be all."

"Yes, Your Holiness." He bowed and backed out the door, shutting it quietly.

Giberto, a thin older man with a thin angry face, was once the Archbishop of Ravenna, but he stood opposed to the reforms of Pope Gregory and was excommunicated. Shunned by the clergy of Rome, he turned to the German emperor, Henry.

He strolled back to his desk, looking closely at the addresses on the envelopes. He picked one out, the one from Odo, and sat down heavily. He broke the wax seal recklessly and tugged out the parchment.

> To Giberto, Archbishop of Ravenna, from Pope Urban the Second, his bishops and cardinals, greetings in the name of Our Lord Jesus Christ.
>
> Know you, Giberto of Ravenna, that on March 12th in the year of our Lord 1088, I, Odo of Lagery, by the grace of God, was appointed the Bishop of Rome by the College of Cardinals. I am, therefore, the legitimate heir of Saint Paul and overseer of the Mother Church, in the name of Our Lord Jesus Christ.
>
> It saddens my heart to know that, in spite of these proceedings, you continue to defy the Holy See by calling yourself Pope Clement. Know you that your appointment by Emperor Henry of Germany is not sanctioned by the Church and is, therefore, illegitimate. I beseech you to forsake your false claims and return Rome and the Lateran Palace to its rightful occupants. Be warned that until such pretense is revoked, you will remain excommunicated from the Church of Christ. We pray for you, may God have mercy on your soul.
>
> August 26, in the year of our Lord 1089.

Giberto flushed. "Damn you all!" he said aloud. "You will never hold the Lateran! It's the King's God-given right to appoint the pope and his bishops. You will *never* control Rome!" He rose to his feet fuming, pacing the tiled floors. "And *I* will excommunicate *you*, Odo of Lagery!" he yelled to no one, dashing back to his desk. He sat down hard, his pale face flushing red as he snatched up his quill. In angry strokes, he scratched a note to his secretary. Then he paused in thought and glanced at the other letter. It was from William, his spy among Pope Urban's men. He ripped it open.

> To Pope Clement the Third, by God's grace Lord of the Holy See, from William, your humble servant.
>
> In as much as the protection of the Holy Church depends upon your care, Your Holiness, I must inform you of events that transpire in Melfi. Recently, Odo of Lagery, who now claims to be Pope Urban, was visited by a large company of Northmen, about five hundred in all with some infantry as well as wives, children and servants. These men are knights of Robert, the

Count of Flanders, and are on their way to the Kingdom of the Greeks, where they have been hired as mercenaries.

What may be of concern to your Grace is that two monks from the Abbey of Cluny accompanied these Northmen. One goes by the name of Ramiro, who holds the position of dean, the other is a novice. I know only that the one called Ramiro held council with Odo at the synod in Melfi but, despite my best efforts, I have been unable to discern the reason for the visit. It is said they plan to sail from Bari with Greek ambassadors.

Forever at your service.

August 15, in the year of our Lord 1089.

The last line caught Giberto by surprise. August fifteenth? Why has it arrived so late? He strode to his door and pulled on the bell-rope. Moments later, his secretary huffed into the room.

"Tell me, why did this letter from William take so long to reach me?"

The secretary bowed. "What I have been told, Your Holiness," he heaved, "… is that the Normans shot him off his horse as he rode out of Melfi."

Giberto scowled in anger, they had discovered his spy.

"The messenger's family found the letter weeks later when they went through his bags, Your Holiness. It was sewn into the lining. They sent it right away."

"Cursed Normans!" Giberto fumed. "Damn them to hell! They are the only reason Odo survives!" He left the room suddenly, striding in a silent rage. He flew down the steps and stormed through the enormous hall of the Lateran Palace, ignoring the Holy Steps and the statues of Saint Peter and Saint Paul. He rushed past the motionless German guards who stood erect, dwarfed by towering, marble pillars. His white cloak billowed behind him as he held his white cap firmly to his graying head, stopping only when he came to a large, oak door where two more guards stood on either side. Before entering, he spun to one. "Bring Captain Frederick to me! Immediately!"

"Yes, Your Holiness," the guard bowed low before marching off.

• • • • •

Frederick, the same man who had stopped Drugo's men outside Rome, swept into Giberto's office before the sun rose a quarter hand. He wore mail armor and a sheathed broadsword hung from his left side. He tucked his iron helmet under one arm and bowed before Giberto. "Your Holiness, may the saints preserve you, my Lord." His graveled voice broke the cold silence of the stark room. He straightened, holding out his chin so that his thick goatee stuck forward, then he swept a lock of curly, brown hair from his eyes and waited.

Giberto sat twitching behind an expansive, polished desk strewn with papers. Behind him, a fresco of a tortured Christ adorned the stone wall. He leaned forward over the desk and glared maliciously, his clean-shaven face scowling in fury. "Tell me, Frederick, are you not the captain of my guard?" The vessels in his neck throbbed as he spoke.

A look of concern crossed Frederick's face. "Well, yes, my Lord, you know I am." He shuffled his feet uneasily, rustling his chain-link armor.

Giberto's eyes bulged. "And is it not your responsibility to keep me informed of *all* events?"

"Yes, Holy Father."

"But I am not informed!" he screamed. "I hear my news from petty peasants in the streets! From fish mongers! From idiot plebeians!" He rose from his chair with a start and stomped back and forth in the hollow room. "The Benedictine monks of Cluny plot against us! And you know nothing?"

"Forgive me, Your Holiness."

"Was it not you who stopped a group of Normans just north of Rome?"

"But they said they were Flemings, Holy Father."

Giberto rolled his eyes. "Do not be so naïve, Captain! What's the difference?"

Frederick bowed his head.

"And you failed to mention one was Benedictine."

"Well... I did not think that..."

"You did not think!"

Frederick kept his eyes lowered.

"Do you know how these men got to Melfi?" he asked impatiently.

"We escorted them south, Your Holiness, as far as the Pontine Marshes."

"Are you telling me you provided safe conduct to our enemies and their spies?"

"Well, you must understand, Holy Father, it was a formidable force of Northmen. At first, they were very persistent on entering Rome, but we reached a compromise."

"A compromise?" Giberto yelled. "You cannot compromise with a Norman! I should send you back to King Henry in disgrace. Perhaps you would care to explain your incompetence to him!"

Frederick bowed low. "Please forgive me, Your Holiness, I was only trying to protect the Holy See."

"You fail at your duties, Captain!" He put his hands on his thin hips. "If I am to remain Pope, I must control Rome. I cannot crush these insidious plots if I know nothing of them!"

"What have you heard, Holy Father?"

Giberto gestured madly to the papers laid out on his desk. "Those traitorous..." he sputtered at the thought, "... those cursed, conniving cardinals and this... this Odo work against us. A wretched Benedictine no less! Pope Urban indeed! He schemes against our King and plots to take the Lateran Palace for himself." He threw his hands in the air. "And now I fear he gains support from the Greek Kingdom. He has already sent emissaries there."

Frederick shrugged. "You should not be concerned, Holy Father, our forces will keep Odo out of the Lateran."

Giberto looked cynical. "Well I *am* concerned, Captain Frederick. Odo meets secretly with the lords of Italy and France in order to turn them against us. And now the Greeks!"

"But what do the Greeks want with Rome, Your Holiness?"

Giberto fumed. "This Greek King... what's his name? He's not a fool, he manipulates events to suit his own evil plans and to strengthen his empire, may God curse him! He dreams of regaining the Holy Land from the infidels and he needs all the men he can get to drive them out." He glared at Frederick. "And where do you think these mercenaries will come from?" He paused briefly before answering himself. "From the Normans! Do you not understand Frederick? The Greek King must recognize Urban as the rightful pope in order to get help from the Normans."

"We will stop them, Your Holiness."

A sickly smile crossed Giberto's face. "I hope so, Captain, for your sake. I have the name of one of these monks - Ramiro he's called. Apparently he's a Cluny dean. He's the important one. Travels with a novice."

"What are your instructions, my Lord?"

"I want you to send three of your best men to discover all they can about this meeting in Melfi. And I want these monks arrested before they reach the King."

"But they have a week's head start, Holiness."

"That is your problem, Captain. Just find them. They've probably left port by now."

"But Your Holiness, how will we get our men past the Normans at Bari?"

Urban shook his head in mock rebuke. "Think Captain! Have you no good men familiar with their barbarian tongue?"

"Yes, of course, Holy Father," he said, although he was not sure. "And what shall we do with these monks?"

Giberto put the letter down and rested his palms on the table before looking straight into Frederick's cold eyes. "In the name of God, you must finish them."

Frederick nodded. "As you wish, Your Holiness."

Giberto dismissed him bravely with a wave of his hand. But after the door shut, his angry face dissolved in turmoil and he sank into his armchair, dropping his head into his hands. "May God forgive me."

Part Two

BYZANTIUM

Dyrrachium

September 1089

Excited cries came from the galley deck. Ramiro wrapped his arms around the foremast and held on with all his might. He was trying to keep his place as people pushed and shoved for a better view of the cape and the castle fortress of Dyrrachium, the western bastion of the East Roman Empire.

The whole shoreline was a solid wall of crag, a long escarpment that jutted above the sea so suddenly there was hardly a strip of beach along its length. It served as a natural defense for the fortress, which sat imposingly on the southern point where the hills diminished, giving way to the wide, flat valley laying to the east.

Except for the gentle splash of oars, the galley moved with hardly a sound as it drifted to harbor, passing the huge gray fortress that sprung up from the rock of the shore as if built by Hephaestus, the god of stone. It stood square, its walls rising the height of six men and stretching over a hundred paces on a side. They were so thick, said Manuel proudly, that four horsemen could ride abreast on its battlement. And on each corner, a massive square tower rose from the bare rock and spired above the castellations, each ending in a conical roof of red tile.

The harbor was strangely quiet for a usual day of trade. The governor, John Doukas, ordered all ships out of port and closed the markets. The streets were nearly deserted and townsfolk peeked out nervously from their small windows.

John stared out from the watchtower. He bit his lip as he watched the four Venetian galleys curl their sails and row to port. *Am I ready for them? Over five hundred God-damned Kelts!* He brushed a lock of curly, black hair from his tanned forehead and rubbed at the black stubble on his chin. He shuddered at memories... memories of vicious battles against Guiscard and Bohemond. His eyes moved to his fleet of war-galleys and biremes, which flanked the

Venetians around the point. Then he glanced down to the waterfront where a large contingent of his infantry waited near the docks.

"Do you see Commander Manuel?" he asked.

"He has just left the ship, my Lord," said his lieutenant.

"Bring him to me right away."

"Yes, my Lord."

• • • • •

Ramiro took five awkward steps off the ramp. "Good God! Three days at sea and I must learn to walk again!"

Pepin laughed aloud as he tugged at the donkey.

"Move on, Pepin!" Aldebert shouted from behind. "You're always in the way!" He yanked at the reins of the horses - but he pulled too hard and the frenzied mares rushed forward suddenly, sending him tumbling down the ramp.

Pepin laughed again and pushed ahead to join up with Ramiro. "Look at all the soldiers," he said, pointing to hundreds of men lining the rise above the docks, all armed with sword, shield and bow. "Yes," said Ramiro. "We have quite a reception."

"Are we being honored, Father?"

Ramiro chuckled, remembering Manuel's stories about the Normans. "I doubt that honor plays much of a role in this grim theatre, Pepin."

"What do you mean?"

"Those men, my boy, stand guard not because they come to honor us, but because they fear us."

• • • • •

"Governor John is honored you are among us," said the Byzantine lieutenant to Drugo. "And he welcomes you to Dyrrachium. He is happy to provide you with food and drink, and anything else you may need. However, he regrets to inform you there is little accommodation within the walls and offers his sincere apologies. But we have provided a suitable campground for you and..."

"How long are we expected to wait here?" Drugo interrupted.

"I do not know, my Lord."

"Is your Duke ever going to meet with me?"

"Yes, my Lord, if I may be permitted to continue."

Drugo nodded. "Get on with it man."

"The governor invites you to sup at his table tomorrow afternoon. An escort will arrive at the ninth hour."

• • • • •

Many people came to Ramiro about many different things. Some came to ask for his blessings, others to confess their sins even though he told them repeatedly he was not a priest. And many others, hearing of his healing skills, came to him for medical attention. But he had never been as busy as he was on this particular morning, his tent crowded by sick Flemings of all ranks. Most had fits of vomiting and diarrhea and many had spent hours burning incense in their tents, kneeling and praying, and appealing to the saints for divine intervention. But none of it seemed to work so they came to Ramiro in hopeful assemblies, asking for his blessings and a sprinkle of holy water to cure their ills.

Ramiro did what he could, telling most to eat whole grains and to drink lots of water before he sent them away. He had set up his tent close to Louis the Carpenter and often glanced over to watch Adele as she went about her work. Carts of food and drink arrived from the fortress and when she returned with an armload, he rushed to lend a hand.

"Thank you, Dom Ramiro. You are most kind." She smiled at him, a broad beautiful smile.

He fumbled with the bags and dropped one to the ground. "Oh dear," he said. "I guess I'm not much help really."

She stooped to pick it up. "I believe you are the most helpful of men," she said, rising up slowly and placing the bag back into his arms. "I will be forever in your debt."

He felt a stirring and his skin tingled. He nodded quickly with a tense smile before turning away like a bashful child.

• • • • •

Ramiro stared up at the eastern wall of the fortress, a solid wall of stone running from the sea to the hills, blocking any further landward approach. The base of the wall flared out to form a rampart, used to impede the approach of war machines, and a wide, dry moat ran the entire length. The only entrance was through a massive wooden gate reinforced with an iron shield and the only access to the gate was across a simple wooden bridge, as narrow as a Roman cart. The gate door opened, letting Ramiro, Drugo and his two lieutenants into the fortress grounds.

Bottles of wine, roasted pork and fowl, vegetables of all kinds, pastries and other sweets, as well as many strange dishes, spread out across a long table positioned at the center of a wide dining hall. Six men occupied one end of it, John sat at the head and closest to him were Drugo and the Byzantine commander, Manuel. Servants stood only a few paces away, waiting for a signal. Near the doors, stood a small squad of soldiers. And wandering about the room, sniffing at every corner, were two large Dalmatian hounds, their hard nails clacking back and forth across the gray concrete floors.

John Doukas had been questioning Drugo for some time. "It sounds like you have had an interesting journey, Sir Drugo. I'm sure you will be well accommodated on the way to Constantinople. I have arranged for a platoon of my men to accompany your Kelts on behalf of the Emperor."

Drugo bristled. "What do you mean - Kelts? We're Flemings."

"Of course," said John. "No offense meant. We refer to all your countrymen as Kelts."

"And we need no protection," said Drugo with belligerence. "Our company is strong enough to look after itself."

John smirked. "Perhaps your small army is considered large in the Land of the Kelts, but here, and further south, it is not unusual to encounter hostile armies of many thousands. My men can help you should that happen, even though they are few."

Drugo looked up from his plate. "I'm sure we can deal with the situation, if it arises."

John leaned forward, black curls fell across his clean-shaven cheeks. "Let me tell you something, Sir Drugo. Only two years ago, the Emperor battled an army of ten thousand Patzinaks in a region southeast of here. Have you ever seen an army that size? I doubt your troops would be much competition for them. We've lost a lot of good men to those pagan bastards!"

Drugo stiffened but tried to remain calm. "So who are these...Pasaks?"

"Patzinaks is what we call them. They're an abomination... a filthy pack of Turkoman barbarians who steal everything they can!" He tore a chunk of bread from a loaf.

Drugo shuffled in his seat. "Well, whatever they are, we'll make our own way."

John didn't really care if these stinking Kelts were fed to the wolves, but he had his orders. "I'm afraid you have no choice, Captain. You will almost certainly be mistaken as hostile if not accompanied by a Byzantine guard." He eyed Drugo carefully as he swallowed a draft of wine from his pewter mug. He had no liking of Normans. And the reek! Like a herd of goats!

Drugo seethed at the rebuff, his face set hard. "As you wish," he muttered through a mouthful of pork fat.

John wiped a dribble from his smooth chin before he clapped his hands together with a loud whack. Drugo jumped in his seat, dropping his meat to the floor. In an instant, the two hounds scrambled for it, snarling and nipping in vicious competition. Ramiro and the others lifted their feet out of the way, teetering in their chairs. John and Manuel laughed aloud.

John grinned at Ramiro. "Do not fear, my man, they rarely eat monks." He laughed again. "Sorry if I alarmed you. I was merely summoning the servant. What is your name, monk?"

"I am Ramiro of Cluny, sir."

"I hear some of your countrymen have fallen ill."

"I'm sure it's just the travel, sir. The people are weary."

"Well, you and your company are welcome to stay until you recuperate. I have a physician who can tend to your sick."

"Thank you, Governor John. And if possible, perhaps you could help us find some more opium for my medicine bag, and some spelt or wheat for the sick."

"Of course." He raised his hand to his scribe, who came running over. "Deliver whatever you can to Monk Ramiro."

Drugo leaned back in his chair, his long red hair falling behind him. "My astrologer says the illness is because Saturn is ascending in Aries," he stated confidently. "That would explain it - it will pass."

John looked at him incredulously. "I believe I would put more faith in my physician, Sir Drugo," he said, trying not to smile.

Drugo's face reddened, he felt a boiling urge to kill this Greek... or Roman... or whatever cursed race he was. "I appreciate your offer," he said in a bellicose voice, "but our women folk know the ways of medicine." He turned to look at Ramiro. "All approved by the Church, of course."

"Well, of course," said John. "The decision is yours, but the physician is a good man, he seems to work wonders."

"Is he a magician?" Drugo asked facetiously.

"No, actually he's a Hebrew from Thessalonica. He's very good."

Drugo stood up suddenly, knocking over his chair. "A Hebrew!" he sneered. "They're nothing but a pack of crooked traders and stinking money-lenders! What do they know of medicine?"

John pushed his chair back in an instant, reaching for his sword hilt. His guards moved in. "I advise you to sit down, Sir Drugo! Before you are cut down!"

A servant rushed over to right his chair. Drugo sat down hard, glaring at John.

John pulled his chair forward and calmed himself. "I am not aware of events in the West, Captain. But in our lands, Hebrews are also physicians, philosophers, and men of learning. You would be wise to enlist their services.

They give us no trouble and we let them be." He forgot to mention that, centuries before, the Romans had expelled all Jews from Jerusalem. Only after the Muslim conquest were they allowed to return.

"I'll have no polluted Hebrews among my men." Drugo fumed. "Any good Christian knows they're the scourge of Christ and unclean. They destroyed the Holy Sepulcher! Now they conspire against the people of Christ!" Otto and Fulk nodded in agreement.

Drugo spun on Ramiro. "You should know, monk. Wasn't it one of your own monks at Cluny who claimed this was so?"

Ramiro shuffled uneasily, he had heard the same. "Yes... but I..."

"So?" Drugo shouted at him. "Was it not the case? Can you not support what I say?"

"Well," Ramiro muttered, "not all of us agreed, we..."

"It was not the Hebrews," John interrupted vociferously. "You speak of the mad Caliph of Egypt, a man called Al-Hakim. And it happened about eighty years ago, but he had no help from Hebrews. On the contrary, my dear sir, the Caliph persecuted both Christian and Hebrew, demolished both church and synagogue. Everyone knew he was crazy, but what could they do?"

"You can't trust them!" Drugo belted. "We purged our cities of Hebrews when we learned of their complicity."

"You may think as you like, sir," said John as he slammed his food down and wiped his hands briskly with a napkin. "The physician's services will be your own loss." He cursed to himself - bloody ignorant Kelts, or whatever detestable race they are!

ITALY

Three assassins galloped out of Rome on the best of King Henry's stallions. Sent out by the anti-pope, Giberto, they rode hard for Bari, rising high in the stirrups to rush east on the Appian Way, their long cloaks flapping madly in the wind. They travelled light, with mail vests and little gear, daggers and swords their only weapons.

In the lead, rode a thin, wiry man with shoulder-length black hair, a big moustache and a shaved chin who went by the name of Wiker. Some say he was from Koln but he didn't speak much and never talked about himself. His neighbors liked him and said he always paid his bills on time, but those who knew him well, knew him as Wiker the Blade, a relentless assassin who considered it a matter of professional pride to fulfill every assignment.

DYRRACHIUM

Drugo the Red was glad to leave Dyrrachium. He rode quietly, still brooding over his confrontation with Governor John and deeply resenting Ramiro for not standing behind him when he cursed the Hebrews. Foking monk! Nothing but God-damn trouble!

Knights and servants followed him briskly. Those who had fallen ill soon recovered and, as their health returned, so did a new-found sense of adventure. They spoke excitedly of the wonders and riches to come.

The escort out of Dyrrachium proved to be a rough band of Bulgar and Romani mercenaries led by a Byzantine sergeant who answered to Commander Manuel. They kept to the fore, flanking the head of Drugo's troops while sporting the banner of the East Roman Empire, a black double-headed eagle on a gold flag.

"I don't like this!" Drugo complained to Otto as he eyed the escorts suspiciously. "We have come to serve the King of the Greeks and we are treated like his enemies!" His face reddened as he spoke. "Look at these miserable dogs! We could kill the damned heretics with a slash of our swords!"

Otto flung his blonde hair across one shoulder and leaned over in the saddle, shifting his shield as he did. "No doubt, m'lord. I don't like the look of the bastards either, they're a strange lot. But there's little we can do about it. Besides, they're well equipped and may prove useful. Look... not only do they carry sword and lance, but the bow too."

Drugo looked around again. "All that gear is too much for a horseman. You only need a sword and a lance. How can anyone shoot an arrow from horseback and hope to hit anything?"

• • • • •

Wiker and his two accomplices disembarked in Dyrrachium and wasted little time getting on the Egnatia Way. They continued to race east, heading through the Dinaric Alps to Thessalonica.

THESSALONICA

The Axios River rushed down from the Alps before it leveled off on a wide, marshy plain. At its mouth was Thessalonica, a large port on the Gulf of Therma and home to merchant galleys and a Byzantine war fleet. Manuel led them past the city, sending a small party to the markets for supplies before heading east again. A dreary, overcast sky hung overhead and it rained the whole way. Ramiro and Aldebert covered themselves with oiled cloaks while Pepin held a sodden blanket over his head.

Ramiro often roamed through the long line of travelers with Aldebert at his heels. He offered greetings and support to the sick and weary, helping out whenever he could and, as the day wore to a close, he would wander back to join Louis at his wagon. He rode up front, squeezing beside Louis while Mathilda and Adele sat in the back.

Snow-capped mountain peaks loomed to the north and east, soaring almost two miles into the sky. The road ran right up to their steep foothills before it snaked along the base of the southern range. Ramiro pointed to the lofty peaks where white, wispy clouds curled up from the green forests below. "Look over there... at the mountains. The people here say those are the Rhodope, home of the Greek hero, Orpheus. They say, if you listen, the wind will carry the melodies of his lyre." He smiled.

"Louis has a lyre!" said the plump Mathilda. "And Adele plays it just beautiful. She sings too, Dom Ramiro. Like a songbird she does."

"Mother!" Adele snapped.

"Ah well," said Ramiro. "Then Adele truly is a follower of Orpheus, he is known as the 'father of songs.'"

"My, my, Dom Ramiro," said Mathilda. "Where do you learn such strange things? Does this Or... Orphy still live there?"

"No, Mathilda," he laughed, "no he does not. It's an ancient legend of the Greeks. They have many legends."

Louis rubbed at the bristle below his big nose, wrapped in his own thoughts. He held the reins loosely, allowing his heavy Belgian workhorse to plod along at its own pace, its wide hooves thumping in the dry dirt. And when a wagon wheel squealed in complaint, he raised an eyebrow. "Those wheels need grease again."

"What do you use, Louis?"

"Hog fat. But it's important to mix the right amount of lime with the fat. If you have too much, the grease becomes thin and won't last long."

"Would you like a drink, Dom?" asked Mathilda. "I have some nice spring water from Thessa... Thessa... whatever it is."

"Thessalonica," said Ramiro. "And, yes, Mathilda, a cool drink would be most welcome."

She filled a cup. "Well, Dom, I'll let you worry about the names, it's too much for me. Doesn't anybody here speak Flemish or French?"

Ramiro laughed. "It's unlikely that you'll hear anybody but ourselves speak those tongues in this land. Best to learn Greek."

Adele peeked out from the wagon cover. "Dom Ramiro," she said softly, "I made some barley bread this morning. And there's a little cheese. Would you like some?" She leaned forward, offering it to him in a wooden bowl.

Ramiro grinned at the mention of food and turned on the bench to face her. She looked as becoming as ever. "Yes...yes Adele, thank you." He groped at the bowl, holding it awkwardly, daring to look into her eyes.

Adele smiled. She had no idea why she was so fond of Dom Ramiro. But she could feel his warm, easy strength and his endless vitality. He seemed a little odd and was not particularly handsome, but there was something else about him... perhaps his kindness... his courage or... She caught herself locked to his gaze and, in a timid blush, quickly lowered her eyes.

KOMOTINI

Komotini was a fortress town constructed to protect the Egnatia Way, but it had fallen into disrepair and a Byzantine garrison was no longer stationed there. The people of the village had learned to fend for themselves, so when they saw Drugo's army approaching, flying the familiar gold standard of the Roman Empire, twenty armed riders came out to greet them.

"Greetings, we come in peace," Manuel assured them. "Do not be alarmed." He could see a scurry of frantic activity over the low village walls.

"Welcome... welcome to Komotini," stammered a fat man in a squeaky, nervous voice. "I'm the village headman." He approached uneasily on his small horse. "If you come in peace, why are you so heavily armed?" His small eyes darted about.

"The road is not safe, as you must know," said Manuel, scrutinizing the small party of men. "We are on our way to Constantinople to serve Emperor Alexios in his fight against the infidels. May God protect him."

The headman's stubbled face broke into a smile and he chuckled. "Well then, you could start right here, the Turkoman raid us from the north."

"They have come this far?" Manuel asked, trying not to sound surprised. He looked up to the hills as if expecting to see a horde of savages at the crest.

"We haven't seen them yet," said the man. "But people coming from the north and east say they have. No one is safe anymore. Where are the Emperor's men to protect us?"

"We are doing what we can," said Manuel in a tone of sufferance. "Perhaps your men here would like to join us in the fight?"

"Uhh...," he mumbled, "well, they're not really fighting men. We are only poor farmers, my Lord." He nodded in deference. "But an enemy of the Turks is a friend of ours." He leaned to the side to look at Ramiro. The curious shaved heads of the Benedictine monks were an unwelcome sight in these parts. He had dealt with Westerners before and did not trust them and, being a Greek Christian, he did not trust the Pope's men either. He was anxious to see them on their way. "May God speed you my good men," he said with a thin smile. "And when are you sending us another garrison?"

"That's not possible yet," said Manuel. "We need all the fighting men we can muster if we're ever going to push the savages out of Thrace."

● ● ● ● ●

When they broke camp next morning, dark clouds billowed in the south and a damp southerly wind beat at their tents. "We ride too slowly," Ramiro complained as he packed his gear. "We could reach Constantinople in half the time if we were all mounted. And look at all these women and children. God bless them, but they can be nothing but trouble. Why do the knights insist on bringing them to war?" He tied a belt around his waist and tucked a small dagger into it.

Aldebert watched him. "Why do you carry that knife, Father Ramiro? Are we not men of peace?"

Ramiro smiled, exposing yellowed teeth through his thick lips. His dark eyes twinkled. "A knife is useful for many things, Brother Aldebert. And, while I am a man of peace, many others are not. We are entering a strange land with many enemies and I'm afraid our black robes give us little safety."

"God will protect you, Father. You must have faith."

Ramiro glared at him. "Mind your tongue, Brother Aldebert! And do not presume to lecture me on faith!"

Aldebert flushed red and fell silent.

For many hours, they rode without a word between them, following the road through dark green forests that seemed strangely quiet. Even the birds fell silent and the only sounds were the clop of hooves and the unceasing cacophony of rattling armor and clanging pots. A cool breeze licked their faces as the clouds above grew thicker.

"We must be careful along this stretch, Sir Drugo," said Manuel. "We have little control here or to the north, where the Turkoman roam." He scoured the land. "We must be wary of ambush from forests and high ground."

Drugo picked at his red beard, his eyes darting across the rounded hills. "You mentioned Patzinaks and Turkoman, are they the same?"

"Yes, that's right," said Manuel. "The Patzinaks are one tribe of Turkoman, but there are many others."

"So when you speak of Turks, do you mean Turkoman?"

"No, not really. When we speak of Turks, we speak of the men of the Seljuk Empire, the ones who took Persia, they are Muslim."

"What do you mean?"

"The Turkoman are not Muslim," he said. "They are nothing more than vile pagans who worship stones and drink the blood of their enemies."

Drugo had spent most of his life fighting Normans and Flemings as they vied for control of the rich vales of Flanders. He was one of the Count's most valiant men, but here in this alien land he felt a chill. Perhaps it was the strange landscape, the strange people, or the strange smells. These Patzinaks sounded unnatural. "Where are my damned scouts?" he bellowed.

• • • • •

A scout pointed to one of the young women working in a roadside field. "Look at that! She's a pretty one," he said to the small group of men.

"Ha, ha, ha!" a knight roared. "You have good eyes, like a scout should!" He laughed again as they rode at a trot towards the women. "We should grab the heathen bitch for our own." He leered. "It's been a long time since I had me a woman. Too long."

The first scout hesitated. "Careful. Captain Drugo told us he'd hang any man who raped..."

The other sneered. "Aye, but Drugo already has his French wench to satisfy him." The other men laughed. "Besides," he said, "there's no law against buying one of the bitches." He rode up to the women and dismounted.

The farmers stopped their work, watching them cautiously.

The knight strode up to the pretty girl and pointed. "How much for this one?" He held out some coins. The girl backed away.

The farmers could not understand his strange tongue but when they saw his money, they soon got the gist of his words. A scowling young man stepped forward aggressively, holding his pitchfork like a lance. Other farmers rushed to his side.

The knights laughed aloud, drawing their swords. "So you want to fight, do you?" They laughed again.

The farmers backed off and the girls ran away.

"Let's have some fun!" one yelled as he jumped in the saddle to give chase, but a sudden pounding of hooves distracted him.

A messenger barged into their midst. "Scouts!" he yelled. "You better get back. Drugo wants you. He's as mad as a caged bear."

• • • • •

"Where've you bastards been?" Drugo bellowed. "Why are you not scouring the land ahead? I'll have your balls cut off and fed to the foking pigs if you leave your stations again!" The scouts paled, lowering their heads in fear. "Spy the land ahead and check those hills to the north." He pointed ahead. "Go! And report all you see as quick as you can." The two men, lightly armed with dagger and sword, rode off at full gallop before Drugo could utter another word.

Another unusual silence fell upon the long procession of knights. The further from France they rode, the more unnatural the countryside became; the land, the trees, the animals, the mountains – even the air was different, the people, the dress, the languages – all so unfamiliar. Nervous knights toyed with their weapons, archers inspected their quills.

The southern wind, once a gentle breeze, now gusted through the treetops, whipping back and forth, twirls of dust dancing along the road. People hung tight to their shawls and capes while others ran after bags caught by the wind, yelling as they tumbled away. The twirls soon grew to thick billows, pushing north in long, rolling waves. Overhead, the clouds darkened and broiled. Hours passed. The scouts did not return.

Ramiro covered his mouth with the hood of his robe and shielded his eyes to peer ahead. The dust was too thick to see clearly but he noticed a commotion at the front of the line, where Drugo and the Byzantines were in the lead. There was much shouting.

Drugo held up his arm suddenly. "What's this?" he shouted in alarm. "By God's grace and mercy!" He backed away, quickly making the sign of the cross, which was something he rarely did. Curious knights rushed to look for themselves. They too, staggered back and crossed themselves.

Ramiro got off his horse and rushed over. He pushed his way past the knights and, as the haze cleared, he saw the grisly sight. There, on the side of the road, impaled on two rough poles, were the gaping heads of the scouts, still dripping fresh blood.

Before they could regain their senses, a rising chorus of long, piercing shrieks chilled the air. In a single motion, all heads turned to the shrill cries coming from the hilltop. They saw them, about one hundred paces up, the dark silhouettes of armed horsemen.

Drugo felt his heart beat cold. He shouted above the commotion, "Are those your Patzinaks, Commander?"

Manuel looked up, shielding his eyes. "Sounds like them but it's difficult to see. I doubt they will charge, but we should get out of arrow range."

"We are out of range, they're a hundred paces away."

"That's not enough!" Manuel shouted. "A hundred paces is not enough for a Turkoman arrow!"

Drugo looked up the hill. He knew what he had to do. "Formations! Now!" he bellowed. "Keep it tight! Shields up!"

The knights jostled into position and spun to meet the enemy, hearts pounding at the thrill of battle. But before they could form a line to protect themselves, a deadly hail of Turkoman arrows rained down from the dark sky. Servants, women, and infantry writhed to the ground, screaming in pain and horror. All around them, arrows thudded into the dry earth, others glanced from armor or lodged in wooden shields. Horses fell wounded, squealing and braying, tossing their riders to the ground. Squires rushed in with new mounts.

Chaos followed and Drugo feared they would be slaughtered like pigs in a pen. He held his shield high to protect his face. "Commander! Take the rest of the company to the south, out of range!"

Manuel motioned to him excitedly and shouted, he was trying to warn him about something but the howl of the wind and Drugo's own bellows drowned him out.

"For the love of God, my men, take courage!" Drugo yelled, trotting behind the lines. "Fear not! Get ready for charge! Lances at the ready!" He waved his arm in a wide arc. "Archers to position! Shoot at will!" The archers loosed their arrows, shooting five or six a minute. "God is at your right hand, my men! We will purge the earth of these pagan bastards! Chaaarge!" The knights pushed up the dry, rocky slope, the banner of the Count of Flanders whipping in the wind. They hooted in bloodlust and spurred their war-horses closer and closer to the heathen. The wind followed them up, matching their rage as it blasted from behind.

The Turkoman held position, continuing to shoot. But as the galloping knights loomed closer and closer, they wavered. Their strategy relied on arrows to create havoc and cause the enemy to break rank. Then they would charge in to finish them off with lance and sword. For days, they had watched the long party lumber eastward across the plain. What booty they would take! Horses and gold - and women!

But the blast of wind coming up the hill now carried with it the heavy dust stirred up as the knights charged. It blinded the Turkoman and they faltered with their arrows. They had underestimated the resolve of these strange horsemen, better armed than most on this lonely road, and the sight of five hundred of them charging directly up the hill, lances out, was enough to unnerve even the most courageous among them. Their shields of thick rawhide offered little defense against the heavy steel of broadswords. In an instant, they spun around and fled along a winding path leading north into the mountains. They rode fast, unencumbered by infantry or servants. Even as they rode, they continued to shoot arrows to the rear.

The Flemings charged onto the level crest of the hill, only to find the enemy had fled. Feeling vindicated, they galloped after them in mad pursuit, howling insults as they went, keen for the blood of revenge. But they had little hope of catching them. Their European mounts were slow and clumsy compared to the sleek ponies of the Eurasian steppes, and the weight of their armor slowed them even more. After a fruitless chase, the Patzinaks were nowhere to be seen.

Drugo called a halt to the charge and ordered his men to regroup, it was time to return to the company. But as he turned his steed near the crest of the hill, something caught his eye. He looked to the west, peering down the smooth slopes to the dark plain beyond. Then he saw them. "What's this?" he shouted to Otto. "Look!" He pointed. "There they are! On the plain below!"

"They're heading back to the main road!" Otto shouted. "They're going back to the camp!"

Drugo suddenly realized the ruse. He panicked, thinking of his gold and horses. "Back to the company!" he screamed. "Ride like the devil! The sons of bitches are heading back to camp!" They galloped off in a frenzied fury, the line of charge no longer an ordered affair, every man riding as fast as he could, leaving the slow and the wounded behind.

• • • • •

In the initial attack, Ramiro's fighting instincts returned. He jumped off his horse, using it as a shield to escape the rain of arrows. The horse screamed when an arrow pierced its hind quarter, kicking its legs high in the air in a vain attempt to dislodge it. Ramiro fought hard to hold it steady, Pepin rushed over to help. Together, they tied the frantic animal to a nearby tree. It screamed again as he pulled the arrow from its flesh.

Ramiro shoved a wad of cloth into Pepin's hands. "Come! Take this! Dress the wound. I'll tend to others!" In a flash of dread, he thought about his mission. Frantically, he groped under his robe. Ah! There it is. A look of relief washed over his face. The pouch holding the Pope's letters remained intact. Then, as if to verify its existence, he clutched at the cross hanging from his neck.

The wind died down and the wounded came into view, sprawled along the road or laying in nearby meadows, writhing and wailing in agony. Ramiro's head spun and his heart pounded in his throat. He sought desperately to regain his senses. "Where's my help when I need it?" he said to no one. "Where's Aldebert?" He ran closer to the woods. "Aldebert! Aldebert! Where are you, man? Come to help the wounded!" People began to creep out of their hiding, but no Aldebert.

He ran down the dusty road, looking about frantically, checking the wounded and dead sprawled in the dirt or along the pavement. Then he saw him. He knew it was him from his black robe, now covered in a thick layer of yellow dust. Aldebert lay on his side, his arms and legs splayed out in a peculiar manner. "By all saints! Aldebert! Are you hurt?" He rushed over to crouch beside him.

Aldebert lay face down in the dirt. Ramiro rolled him onto his back and gasped. "Dear Lord!" His assistant's face was cut and bruised, his mouth full of dirt. An arrow pierced his left shoulder just above the heart. Only a splinter protruded from his skin, the shaft had snapped off in his fall.

"Oh no! Dear God, no!" Ramiro gasped as he cleaned out Aldebert's mouth with his fingers and bent down to listen for breath. "Oh dear Lord. Thank you, Mother Mary, he lives!" He knelt in the dust and wept quietly as he wiped Aldebert's face, then he propped his head on a flat stone and made sure he could breathe easily.

He ran back to his horse and rummaged through the saddlebags, grabbing his medicine bag. When he got back to Aldebert, he knelt again to pull the blood-stained robe off his shoulder. He wiped the wound and, with a pair of iron pliers, grabbed hold of the broken arrow shaft and, in a practiced maneuver, swayed it back and forth to dislodge it from the bone. It came free and, to his relief, the steel point came out too. Blood spurted from the wound and he let it bleed for a moment before covering it with a wad of cotton, holding it in place by wrapping a strip of linen under Aldebert's arm.

An anguished scream jarred him from his work and he looked around. A wounded woman writhed in the dirt far to his left, a Patzinak arrow protruding from her side. With a moan of worry, he rushed over to her. She was crying and screaming, clutching at the arrow. "Help me monk... help me!"

He inspected the wound but said nothing. He had seen this kind of injury many times before and knew the inevitable outcome. "Quiet, woman. I will do what I can." He could see by her expensive dress that she was no servant girl, but the wife of a knight. She was small and slight, her black hair, usually covered with a shawl as required by custom, was clumped and soiled. He attempted to stop the flow of blood as it drained into the dust. "What's your name, and who do you accompany?"

"I... I'm Hellad, wife... wife of Arles," she sobbed and convulsed. Ramiro looked around for help. To his great relief, he saw Mathilda coming out from her hiding in the woods. Adele trailed behind her. "Mathilda!" he shouted, "come to help!"

The two women rushed to his side. "Dom Ramiro, what can we do?"

"One of you hold her still while I remove the arrow!" Mathilda hesitated at the sight of blood and staggered a little. "Quickly now!"

Adele hastened to take her mother's place, dropping to her knees beside the wounded woman. "Keep her arms down!" he said as she positioned herself at the woman's head. Ramiro glanced up at her as he worked. "How's Louis?"

Adele flipped her hair from her face with a toss of her head. "By God's mercy, Dom Ramiro, he is well."

"God be praised," he muttered as he placed a hand around the bloody wound and in a slow, steady movement, pulled the arrow from its lodging. Hellad screamed in agony. More blood spurted from the wound, drenching her green linen dress in swathes of red. He halted the flow with a cloth and looked again at Adele, whose face had gone pale. "Quickly, wrap your scarf around the wound. We must stop the blood." Despite the severity of Hellad's wound, he was careful to keep her clothing in place. It was not acceptable for him to view her naked skin. "Get some help to move her to the woods. Tend to her there."

She nodded and looked up to Mathilda for help.

Ramiro looked to God. "Please Father, take this poor woman's soul into your bosom." He made the sign of the cross and prayed. "May the Father of mercies, the God of all consolation, be with you."

He had studied medicines and surgical practices and was familiar with the medical yore of France. He even studied the works of Abu Al-Qasim, a resident of Cordoba considered the greatest surgeon of his time. But despite all his knowledge, it grieved him deeply to know there was nothing he could do for Hellad. The wound was fatal.

• • • • •

Manuel wasted little time taking control with his band of men from Dyrrachium. He trotted his white steed through the disarray, holding his broadsword high and barking orders into the chaotic crowd. "Move the bodies south of the road and take the wounded to rest near the wood!" Those left behind were glad he had the courage to lead and they followed his directions willingly, even though he was not one of their kind.

The wind died down, leaving small eddies of dust swirling about. The knights had been gone too long. Manuel was familiar with the tactics of these Turkoman and regretted not taking the time to discuss them with Drugo. He feared the pagans would return. "All who are armed and can fight, join me now!" The men took up their arms and huddled around his horse. "Get everyone back into those woods," he shouted. "The wounded too! All of you with arrows will ring the outside. Use the trees for cover. Those with lance and sword, stand ready for combat."

Men and women rushed to do his bidding but many failed to hear his warning. A number of servants and infantry were still far down the road collecting supplies and valuables dropped during the initial commotion.

The Turkoman appeared suddenly, thundering around the western foothills like a black scourge. They came fast, startling the stragglers, who dropped their bags and ran as fast as they could. The Turkoman came faster still, hooting and yelling, their long, black cloaks whipping behind. One by one, they ran the Flemings down with their lances and their long, curved swords. One of the pagans leaned off his saddle and scooped up a young girl as she ran screaming, but the rest of them hardly slowed for the slaughter, they had their eyes on the wagons, the pack horses, and the women.

Wails of fear and loud, desperate prayers howled from the woods. Anxious archers faced west, their strings half-drawn. Manuel watched the Patzinaks charge, gauging their distance. "Hold your arrows!"

The heathen approached fast. Still at full gallop, they steered their nimble steeds with their knees and, in a single motion, sheathed their bloodied swords and pulled out their bows, their greedy eyes fixed on chosen targets. At forty paces, they shot their first volley and a barrage of arrows pierced the woods. More screams.

"Loose your arrows!" shouted Manuel. The archers shot their own volley. At forty paces, even the Flemish arrow was deadly. The front row of galloping Turkoman staggered, horses and riders toppled in the dust. Those charging behind leapt over the bodies, or faltered and crashed into rocks and dirt, but the rest galloped past to the right, where the archer's aim was hindered. They shot as they rode and more shrieks pierced the air.

Manuel barked orders and the archers hustled frantically to new positions. The raiders now approached the grove from the east but, just as they began their second charge, Drugo and his furious knights came charging down the low slopes. The Patzinaks saw they were out of time and grabbed what they could before turning to flee.

Drugo led the charge, attacking them head on. While his steed was not swift, it was heavy and strong, trained to kick and bite the enemy. Fully armed and weighted with armor, he fell on the Turkoman with the ferocity of a Russian bear. The rest rushed in with their lances, stabbing at faces, legs and chests. With their lances spent, they brought out broadswords, axes and maces, hacking at arms, legs, and heads with the crazed bloodlust of battle. The Patzinaks, unprepared for this killing frenzy, tried again to flee, but Drugo's right flank closed in for the kill. Over forty escaped the pincer but the rest, outnumbered and outmaneuvered, were slaughtered to a man by the hooting knights, who hacked at flesh and bone, laughing with the relish of victory.

• • • • •

The deadly commotion died down and all seemed quiet and eerie in the aftermath. Ramiro ran from the woods to survey the battleground. The earth was slippery with blood and the air thick with its smell. Gored bodies, strewn across the ground, mingled with hacked arms and legs. Saddles, swords, shields and lances lay scattered between the corpses of men and horses. Five knights lay dead, thirty-one wounded. Infantry and servants fared worse, Ramiro counted over forty dead and a hundred wounded - men, women and children.

Squires and archers ran in to finish off the wounded Turkoman. They wanted some booty of their own. But the knights drove them off with threats, rushing madly between the corpses, hoarding it all for themselves. They soon came to blows.

"I killed him!" shouted one. "His sword is mine! And so is his horse!" Two men stood defiantly, nose to nose.

"I killed him!" The other shouted. "Look – that's my lance!"

Drugo stepped in, yelling above the fray. "Quiet, you stupid bastards! Listen to me!" The squabbling subsided. "A man is entitled to anything he captures, regardless of rank! That is the law. If you have disagreements, then I will decide." The men grumbled and cursed, flashing greedy eyes at their luckier counterparts. They lay claim to weapons, horses, armor, and money. Only the shields were tossed aside, for who would display the crest of an enemy?

Archers pulled arrows from bodies or ran about between the road and the hills collecting those that had missed their mark. Squires cut the throats of wounded horses and left them where they fell. Servants and infantry threw the dead Turkoman to the side of the road, where they rotted for three days before being burned by local peasants. Meanwhile, they buried their own dead with ceremony on the crest of the hill.

"Captain!" said Ramiro, tired and filthy. "I must speak with you."

Drugo, who was trotting around in an attempt to keep order among his troops, turned to him with a scowl. "Yeh, monk, what is it?"

"Who is Arles? His wife is wounded."

"Many are wounded, monk." he said accusingly, as if Ramiro were to blame. "But if you mean Arles of Ghent, he's over there, the tall knight with dark hair, the one holding a black stallion." He pointed briefly and turned away.

Ramiro looked in the direction of Drugo's finger and saw the man, who was waving his arms wildly while cursing a fellow knight. He recognized him, it was the tall executioner who held the axe over Louis the Carpenter some weeks before.

"Are you Arles, husband of Hellad?" he asked, stepping up to the two quarreling men.

Arles looked down on him, frowning at the interruption. "Yeh, what of it? What do you want?

"I regret to tell you, sir, that your wife is badly wounded."

"What?"

"An arrow struck her side, sir. I'm very sorry but there is little I can do. May she rest in God's mercy."

"What do you mean, monk? She will recover, will she not?"

"It has pierced her bowels. I regret to say it is unlikely she will live the day."

"You lie! Stinking monk! Where is she! Tell me before I hack off your fat head and feed it to the crows!"

Ramiro stood his ground, although he knew rogue knights thought little of killing monks and robbing churches, as they had done so often in the past. "She is over by the grove with her servants."

Arles ran off without another word, ignoring the booty. He found Hellad in the throes of death, poisoned from her ruptured bowels, her face ashen white and dripping in large beads of sweat. "Hellad! What's happened?" He fell to his knees beside her. "Don't die, my love! Promise me you won't die!"

Years before, Arles had taken Hellad from her home in Wales when he fought with the Normans to seize that land. She had little choice and was betrothed to him as a payment of mercy, an effort by her family to avoid destruction. Nonetheless, she knew no other way and had become fond of the man, despite his blundering cruelty.

She could barely talk. "I... I can... cannot hold much longer, Arles. The monk tried to help, but the wound is too deep. He... Oh God..." she flinched. "... he has prayed for me." Another spasm of pain gripped her and she wailed in torment.

In a fit of rage, Arles stood up and spun on his servants. "What are you doing you useless pigs? Have you dressed her wounds? Can you do nothing but stand there like idiots?"

A young girl braved a reply. "We have done all we can, m'lord. There is nothing more we can do for her now."

Arles swung his arm out in a fit of frustration, striking the girl on the side of the head and sending her flying into a thicket, where she lay unconscious.

"You stupid bastards!" he shouted through tears. "Go away! Go away! Before I slit your throats!" The rest ran for safety, leaving the poor girl in the bushes. He knelt again beside Hellad, the iron rings of his mail leggings digging into the flesh of his knees, but he felt no pain. In his awkward way, he attempted to comfort her but grief overcame him and tears streamed through the grime on his cheeks. He threw off his helmet and sword to embrace her. And there, in a grove of hornbeam, he held her in his arms and swayed on his knees, still clinging to her long after she died.

• • • • •

The dark clouds finally burst in a torrent of heavy beads. Men and women, too exhausted and too shocked to resist, simply succumbed to the downpour, letting it wash away the dust and grime from their sunburned faces. The dry earth at their feet soon became a thick mud, caking in heavy layers to the thin soles of their boots.

Aldebert lay on his back in the grass with the other wounded, rain pelting at his upturned face. Slowly, he began to regain consciousness, weeping silently from the gnawing pain in his shoulder. The rain stopped as suddenly as it began and he opened his eyes. Clouds dissipated and a few rays of afternoon sun swept across the people of Flanders.

Ramiro tended to the wounded all afternoon and returned to Aldebert's side before dusk. "Brother Aldebert, I see you remain alive and well." He pretended not to notice his tears. "Come now, I must finish tending your wound." He knelt beside him and began to pull back his wet, blood-stained robe to expose the dressing he had applied earlier.

Aldebert quailed. "Aaagh! O, my God... O my God. Blessed Mary have mercy on a pitiful sinner!" His lips curled in anguish and he heaved from the stabbing pain. "Father Ramiro, is this where I am to die... in this... in this God-forsaken land? Among these godless heathen? Aaagh! Careful, careful!"

Ramiro pulled the dressing from the open wound as gently as he could, but he still tore at the fresh scab cemented to the cotton wad. "God willing, Aldebert, you will live another day. You have no choice but to brave the pain as best you can." He took out a bloodied, curved needle from his kit, one he had already used many times that day, and squinted as he threaded it with linen string. Then he wiped dry blood from the wound and prepared to sew the skin. "Pepin!" he shouted. "Pepin, come to help!"

Pepin left the horses and rushed to Ramiro's side, gawking in macabre fascination at Aldebert's open wound. The threat of death and the fray of war had brought him to new heights of awareness and his heart pounded.

"Come on, lad! Take that cotton and dab at the blood so I can see what I'm doing."

Aldebert began to pull away at the sight of the needle but Ramiro put a heavy palm to his chest to flatten him back down. Aldebert gave up, eyeing the needle with terror and wailing like a child when it pierced his skin. He spun his head away. "Our Father who is in Heaven, holy is Your name! Your kingdom come, Your will be done…" he recited the prayer feverishly.

"Come, come, Brother Aldebert, hold still." Ramiro's eyes strained to guide the needle. "You will never survive in this land if you cannot take a little pain. You wanted adventure, and now you have it. You wanted to come as my aide, well aid me now by lying still. I cannot do this work if you squirm like an eel." He lifted his head and nodded to his left. "Look at those soldiers over there, they sew their own wounds!"

"Father Ramiro! I never thought I would have to be sewn back together! They told us the road to Jerusalem was safe! Now look at my sorry state! Blessed Mary!"

"Hold still! My eyes are tired. I will give you something for the pain." He finished tying the wound while Pepin sopped up the blood. From his bag, he pulled out a pouch of crude pills. "Here, take one of these, it will ease your pain."

"What is it?"

"Opium and mandrake. It will dull the pain and help you sleep. Trust me, young man, the soldiers use it to relieve the pain of their wounds… and the ancient Greeks say it's good for diarrhea, too," he smiled.

"But mandrake, Father? Witches use it to summon dark spirits!"

"Why should witches alarm a man of God?" he said, holding out the pill. "If it gives you any peace of mind, my friend, it was uprooted at midnight with appropriate prayer and ritual. Take it… or live with the pain, the choice is yours."

Reluctantly, Aldebert swallowed, washing it down with a long draught from Ramiro's water-skin. He continued to pray but, before the hour was up, he fell sound asleep with a rare look of contentment.

The Flemings staggered three miles further to remove themselves from the shadow of the hills and to find shelter. They carried their wounded on wagons to a camp near a creek at a small abandoned village, where the inhabitants, hearing that alien warriors approached, fled to the hills in abject terror. Drugo found this amusing and his men went about pillaging what they could from buildings and farms. Manuel and Ramiro tried desperately to discourage them, but to little avail.

$$\bullet \quad \bullet \quad \bullet \quad \bullet \quad \bullet$$

Aldebert awoke to a flash of pain and sat up suddenly. Ramiro was gone and his bed was already packed. "Father – where are you?" Pain seared through his shoulder when he yelled. "Father Ramiro!... the pain... it's insufferable!" He felt alone and attempted to rise but fell back in a grimace. "O Blessed Virgin! Don't let me die in this heathen land!"

Within the hour, Ramiro flung open the skirt of the tent. "How do you fare this bright morning, Brother Aldebert?"

"I cannot move, Father Ramiro. The pain... it's so painful."

Ramiro smiled. "The pain is painful, you say. Well, well. I'll give you a little more opium."

This time, Aldebert took the medicine gladly and before long he was smiling quietly. He managed to raise himself up with Ramiro's help. "I will ride today, Father. I feel just fine."

"You will not. Too much motion will break your wound. I talked to Captain Drugo and we decided to stay here for a few days before we head for Adrianople."

ADRIANOPLE

From the crest of a small hill, the city of Adrianople sprawled out on the plains of Thrace below. Ramiro looked down, thinking of another good meal and a mug of Dalmatian wine. After weeks of grueling travel, it sounded as heavenly as meeting Saint Peter at the pearly gates. Maybe he would get a chance to sleep in a real bed! But when he turned to say something to Aldebert, his enthusiasm vanished. His assistant rode bent and sagging in the saddle, his pale face whiter than ever. Ramiro had done all he could to tend his wound but it continued to fester. "How do you feel?" he asked him. "Brother Aldebert! Are you alright?"

Aldebert lifted his head lazily. "What?"

"We will rest soon. Not much further now."

TATICIUS

The small room in the citadel of Adrianople was stark and simple, furnished only with several rough-hewn chairs and a plain wooden table, marred with cuts and scratches. The men sat awkwardly as General Taticius entered the room and sat across from them. Ramiro looked twice. Drugo and his men stared too, not sure what they were seeing. Taticius was a short man with cropped, dark hair and olive skin, but these common characteristics are not what caught their attention. There was something else about him that was extremely peculiar - the man had a metal nose. It was strapped to his face with a fine cord that crossed his cheekbones and wrapped above his ears. And while everyone stared at this gray oddity, he stared back with fearless, resolute eyes. The spectacle unnerved them all, even more so when he spoke because his castrato voice belied his aggressive look and athletic build.

Taticius was a half-breed, his father an Arab and his mother a Greek slave. Taken as a young slave himself by the Byzantines, he soon found himself employed in the Royal household. His intelligence and level-headed courage quickly earned him a name on the battlefield and, by the time he was twenty, he had become a lieutenant. But he fell in battle with the Turks, who cut off his nose and sent it to Byzantium along with a ransom note.

He sat with his elbows resting on the table top, his fingers laced together in front of his iron nose. "I have heard of your troubles with the Turkoman, Sir Drugo."

"I lost five good men," Drugo said accusingly. "We had no idea the road was unsafe."

"My apologies," said Taticius, opening his hands in a conciliatory gesture. "But this is a recent development. The Patzinaks have gained courage since defeating us in battle. Now they believe they can seize Constantinople too. The Emperor is doing all he can to crush them once and for all."

"I'll fight the bastards, General, but right now we need more supplies and medicines. Many of my men still suffer from their wounds."

Taticius nodded. "I will get you whatever you need, and I can send surgeons to your camp if you wish."

Drugo said nothing for a while, remembering his bitter argument with John Doukas over the Hebrew physician. He refused to allow impure heretics and heathen among his men, it would curse them all. "Thanks for the offer, General, but we just need supplies."

For many hours, Drugo, Manuel and Taticius huddled in discussion while Ramiro listened and translated. They talked about the food, the weather and the land, and they talked about the Turks and Patzinaks, about battles and strategies.

"You will be interested to know," said Taticius, "that I have quite a large detachment of Normans under my command. Some of them are here right now. After we settle in, I will introduce you."

After much wine, Drugo and his exhausted men stumbled to their tents while Ramiro dawdled behind. "General Taticius, may I speak with you?"

"Yes, Monk Ramiro, of course, what is it?"

"Is it possible, sir," he asked quietly, "for one of your physicians to attend to my fellow monk? He was badly wounded in the attack and does not heal. He needs help, but I cannot afford to displease Captain Drugo, who is quite particular about who tends to his men, if you understand my meaning."

"Yes, of course, I will make the arrangements. Bring him here this evening. If it offends your Captain, tell him you go to the Church of Sophia to pray for his healing."

"Thank you, sir. I will do as you say." And he rushed away with hope in his heart.

A PHYSICIAN

When he got to his tent, Aldebert was nearly unconscious and the air reeked of infection. "Come Brother Aldebert, we must leave now. I have found some help for you. Come, get up, you will die if you lay here any longer."

Aldebert nodded in a stupor. "I cannot die here Father," he mumbled "… please Ramiro, … take me home… I just want to go home."

Ramiro took hold of his good arm, ignoring his pleas. "Come now, ease your weight on my shoulders and try to walk as best you can. We are going to pray." Aldebert made an effort to raise himself but fell back. Ramiro stooped to catch him, pulling him upright. They left in an awkward amble, heading for the city gates.

Taticius rose from his chair when they came in. "Welcome, Ramiro of Cluny, this is Fawwaz Al-Baghdadi, my physician." He motioned to the man, who sat in the spacious guest room, adorned with colorful rugs and blue ceramic tiles. Fawwaz, dressed in a long white tunic and a white linen cap, was a tall man with a round face, aquiline nose, and a full black beard.

Ramiro was a little surprised to see an Arab physician in the employ of a Byzantine, although he was starting to get accustomed to it. He nodded slowly. "Greetings, Sayyid Fawwaz. It was kind of you to come."

Fawwaz returned the greeting and motioned to his right. "Bring your fellow monk over to the couch so I may tend to him." He studied the two monks quietly and voiced several pleasantries before beginning his inspection. With Ramiro's help, he removed Aldebert's robe and carefully pulled back the old dressing. The stench of the wound struck his nostrils and his head reeled back in repulsion. Taking a deep breath, he leaned forward to examine it closely.

"Take the man's garments," he said to servants nearby. "Wash them in hot water! And bring me a basin of hot water with salt and vinegar, and another kettle just boiled... and strips of clean cotton cloth, just washed and dried. Go, go!" After they scurried off, he picked up his medicine bag and opened it on a nearby table, where he laid out several instruments on a clean cotton cloth. "Who fixed his wound?"

"I did," said Ramiro. "I have done this many times before and I know a little of medicine, but it refuses to heal. I even poured some wine on it."

"Your stitching is good, Ramiro of Cluny, but you have failed to clean the wound."

"But I let it bleed."

"Sometimes that is not enough. A man knows not to offer food with his left hand because it is unclean, so too, you should guard the wound against the foul matter the eyes cannot see. Come, you may assist me. Cover him with that blanket. What have you given him?"

"Just some opium for the pain, but I also have a sleeping potion."

"Good, give him some of that. Then we will wait a while."

After what seemed like an endless wait, Fawwaz sat down again on his small stool beside the couch and began his operation. With a small, razor-sharp knife, he cut away Ramiro's stitches and the wound immediately spurted pus and blood. He dabbed at the secretion with a small cloth and turned his head impatiently. "Where are those servants?"

Taticius, who was watching the affair with some fascination, rose from his chair and strode to the hallway. He barked down the hall to his chamberlain. "Get those servants in here... quickly!"

Fawwaz opened the wound as wide as possible, washing it in strong vinegar before examining it again. "As long as the infection is not in his blood, he may live," he said as he washed his knife and began to cut away dead flesh. When finished, he sewed the skin and dressed the wound with a poultice of linseed, mustard, and borax. "Wash the wound with vinegar and place a similar dressing on it every day. I will give you the ingredients."

Ramiro gleamed. "I cannot thank you enough, Doctor Fawwaz. You are a true Samaritan."

"Well, actually, I'm Sunni. But I understand what you say. Give thanks to Allah."

"Yes, yes, of course. Praise God Almighty." He turned to Taticius. "May I stay with Aldebert tonight, General?"

"Yes, of course. I will have the servants arrange a bed for you."

• • • • •

Aldebert sat in a daze, staring at the plate in front of him, a breakfast of fruit, bread and eggs.

Ramiro watched him anxiously. "Eat, Brother Aldebert!" But Aldebert just continued to stare, glassy-eyed. Ramiro slapped a hand on the table and Aldebert jumped. "If you will not eat, you will not heal! You will do as I say and finish your meal!"

Aldebert looked up, seemingly unaffected by Ramiro's ire. His left arm hung in a new sling. "I feel better, Father, thanks to our good Lord, but my shoulder still hurts terrible." He shuddered and pulled his robe tight around him before rubbing his eyes with hard knuckles.

"Give it time, give it time, Brother. But God cannot help you if you do not eat!"

"It was good of those people to wash my robe," said Aldebert quietly. And my wound looks better. Who was the physician?" His hand shook as he reached for bread.

Ramiro looked into his bloodshot eyes and hesitated, he was not about to tell him the physician was a Muslim and that he had been given a bath. "He was a very good man, Brother Aldebert. Now please... finish your breakfast."

They left Taticius' house before midday, making their way to the church. "We must go to church, Brother, to pray and to thank God for healing your wound."

"But I have not healed yet."

"Nonetheless, we will thank God anyway." He had told Drugo he was taking Aldebert into the city to pray at the church, and he could not lie.

"Do you have any more opium, Father? I think my pain is getting worse."

"You have had enough. I will administer more when I see fit. Let us pray."

BATH HOUSE

Smoke rose in wispy trails from Drugo's camp, lacing between hundreds of canvas tents sprawled out in messy rows outside the south wall of Adrianople. Except for the constant shouting and clang of steel, the air was still, allowing the smoke to rise in thin columns before it flattened into a thin, gray cloud high above. Weary servants rushed about to serve the whims of their masters while knights and squires fought mock battles, trained their horses and, as the day wore on, gambled and drank. Many arrived late to Vespers in a heady state of mind.

A huge crowd milled about Ramiro as he recited the last prayer.

> *May the peace of God, which passes all under-*
> *standing,*
> *Be with us throughout this day*
> *And with all those we love.*
> *Amen*

After the crowd dispersed, Manuel arrived at Drugo's tent. "The bath houses are ready, Sir Drugo."

"Bath houses? What are you talking about?"

"For your presentation to the Emperor. We will arrive in Constantinople within the week and the baths in Adrianople are the only ones until we reach the capital."

Drugo laughed aloud. "You expect us all to bathe?"

"Yes, Sir Drugo. You cannot arrive in the city like this."

"Like what?"

"Well... you... your men are filthy, sir. They stink. We must make them presentable. The servants too, if you like."

"You jest, man," he said before quaffing the last of his beer.

"I jest not, sir," said Manuel, becoming annoyed. "It is an order."

"An order?"

"Yes, Sir Drugo. You should remember that you and your men are now in the employ of the Roman Emperor and you will do as he bids."

Drugo reddened. "I have yet to make my oath to him."

Manuel could barely mask his contempt and his blue eyes flashed beneath his smooth, tanned brow. "If you are unwilling to follow simple instructions," he said with disdain, "you should turn back now."

• • • • •

"It is immoral!" Aldebert sputtered. "It is a sin in the eyes of God, Father. How can you condone such activity, let alone participate?"

"Why is it immoral, Brother Aldebert?" he asked, remembering the pleasures he had enjoyed while a prisoner of the Moors. "Where does it say in the Holy Scriptures that we shall not bathe?"

"Well... uh, well... what about Saint Benedict himself, Father? He says only the sick should bathe!" He had a smug look, feeling righteous in his quote.

Ramiro's tan cheeks widened in a broad smile. "If that is the case, it seems all the more reason for you to join in, Brother. And if you read his *Rules* carefully, he did not say we should *never* bathe, but to do it sparingly. "

"But Father, our physicians say bathing removes protective films from the skin, letting in vile humors. They say it causes sickness ... even death!"

"Well, perhaps our physicians are wrong, Brother Aldebert. The Byzantines and the Muslims all bathe regularly and they seem healthy enough to me."

"How can you say such things, Father Ramiro? The Byzantine faith is blasphemous and the Muslims are heathen!"

"You may deny their faith if you wish, Brother, but how can you deny their knowledge? Can you not admit they may know more of such things?"

"But even if you allow men in the baths," Aldebert fumed, "how can you justify exposing the women too? The thought is too much, Father Ramiro, for women to bathe openly in a public place!"

"The women bathe alone, Brother. Only women exposed to women. Even the slaves who tend them are women. How can a woman's body offend another woman?"

"Well, I think it is wicked, Father - wicked! I will say no more."

Ramiro rolled his eyes in exasperation. "Think what you like but you *will* bathe, even if I have to scrub you myself. I command it and the Emperor commands it."

Tears welled in Aldebert's eyes. He got up and stormed out the tent.

A NORMAN

"Sir Drugo," said Taticius, "I would like you to meet Captain Humberto, a Kelt who has served me well. I trust you may have some interests in common." He forced a tight smile before leaving them alone in a large hall with marble columns, a hall that served as a tavern for his men. A small fire blazed in one corner and long tables to the side held roasted pork, venison, and kegs of ale.

Drugo surveyed the bulky, weather-worn man who approached him, a soldier dressed like the fighting men of Italy. He tried out his feeble Greek, "Greeting Humberto."

Humberto strode up to him smiling, his green eyes glittering through a mass of reddish blonde hair and beard. "And greetings to you Drugo of Flanders." He said in Norman French.

"You're a Norman?"

An uproarious laugh came from Humberto and his men. "Well, we've never been to Normandy, but we are of the Norman line." He filled Drugo's cup from a flask of ale he carried. "Come, we will sit at table, talk, and enjoy the best food the General has to offer."

Drugo had some trouble understanding him. Like the Normans of Melfi, Humberto's French was anachronistic, he used words and expressions that had long fallen out of use in the old country. "From where do you come?"

"We hail from Apulia. Come... we will sit here." They swung their legs over benches and sat down to meat, bread and beer.

"Apulia?"

Humberto nodded.

"We just came that way," said Drugo.

"Then you have heard of Robert Guiscard?" He lifted his red-blonde eyebrows.

"Well... I have heard a little."

"He was not a very popular man in this region!" Humberto laughed and wiped his lips on his sleeve. "He was a cunning bastard... and ruthless. He got rich by marrying the daughter of a local prince. But that wasn't enough for him. He wanted power... so he murdered the prince!" They laughed. "Then the Pope made him a Duke!" They roared again.

Humberto took a long draught of ale and wiped his lips again. "After that, he tried to seize the Byzantine crown for himself. And almost did! So, as you can imagine, Normans are not always received kindly here."

Drugo nodded in understanding and wiped his hands on his greasy pants. "So tell me, Humberto. What brings you to the service of the Greeks?"

Humberto smiled wide, lifting his flat nose. "Gold...," he laughed, "just gold."

"And to what house do you claim allegiance?"

"Well, I'm actually a nephew of Guiscard."

Drugo squinted at him and smirked. "You jest!"

Humberto laughed. "I'm quite serious. Alas, I am not a very popular relative, other members of our house saw to that." He poured more ale. "They cut off my inheritance and I was forced to seek my fortunes elsewhere. So here I am. King Alexios pays well."

"Why would the king hire you if you're a Norman *and* a nephew of Guiscard?"

"They are happy to employ me as long as I swear allegiance to the Emperor." He smiled. "Besides, they need us to fight those devil Turks," he said, tearing at a loaf of bread. "And what brings you to this far away land?"

Drugo drained his cup. "I owe fealty to my Lord, the Count of Flanders," he said, not mentioning he was forced to come. "The one called Robert of Flanders. He made a pilgrimage to Jerusalem a few years ago and met with the Greek King. The King asked him for a few hundred fighting men and some horses, so here we are. We were promised land and gold for our troubles."

Humberto chuckled. "Gold you will get, but the King wants all the land. I once made the mistake of turning against him. He took away my fief and everything I had and sent me away. I was lucky not to have my eyes burned out."

Drugo frowned. "And he took you back?"

"Yeh, after I renewed my oath of fealty to him. He'll hire just about any fighting man you can imagine," Humberto chuckled. He tilted his head towards Taticius, who stood at a distance conferring with some men. "You see our commander over there? We call him Iron Nose. He used to be a slave, captured as a boy by Alexios' father. They made him a eunuch."

"A eunuch? Why?"

"Because he was trained to be an officer of the king's household. Slaves are more trustworthy when their balls have been cut off," he chortled. "He's done well. Now he's a general... and a damned good one. The King likes to put him in charge of us Kelts."

"Why's that?"

"I'm not sure. Maybe because he understands men from the west. His Latin is pretty good too."

Drugo shook his head in disbelief. "From a slave to a general. I've never heard anything like it. And a eunuch!"

Humberto laughed again. "Let me tell you something, Sir Drugo, it would serve you well to learn the lay of the land and the customs of these Turks. They fight their battles differently and are not easily defeated, but I can tell you some things I have learned over the years."

"I've already learned a few lessons, Captain Humberto, but you must tell me all you know."

THE BLADE

Wiker the Blade had seen the Patzinak corpses left on the side of the road past Komotini and wondered if the barbarians had saved him the trouble of killing these monks.

He arrived at the walls of Adrianople at first light, riding right up to the Fleming camp to confront a squire tending horses. "Where is your captain?" he asked softly.

The squire eyed the strangers warily, noticing their accents. They were covered in road dust, but their dress was Italian. "He stays with General Taticius, near the citadel."

"What's his name?"

"Captain Drugo, Drugo of Flanders."

"And what of the monks who accompany him?"

"The monks? Oh... yeh, I think they're staying inside too. Why do you ask?"

Wiker ignored him. He twirled his big black mustache in thought before spurring his mount to the city gates.

"Have you seen a company of Flemings pass through?" he asked the weary gatekeeper.

The gatekeeper looked puzzled, he shook his head and replied in Greek.

Wiker enunciated slowly. "Flemings... Frenchmen. Where?"

The man shook his head again before summoning another man, the scribe who kept accounts. "Can you understand what these barbarians want?"

The scribe turned to Wiker and spoke in hesitating Latin. "What you want?"

Wiker replied impatiently. "We seek the Frenchmen."

The scribe frowned. "Frenchmen? You mean Kelt like you?"

"Yes, Kelts. They were accompanied by two monks."

A look of recognition passed over the scribe's face. "Oh, yes, those Kelt. They come yesterday. Must be important. They dine with General."

Wiker swung a leg over his horse and dismounted. He shook the dust from his cloak. "So where are these men now?"

The scribe looked annoyed. "Who you and what your business here?"

Wiker continued to dust himself. "We are soldiers of fortune. We come to serve the Empire. Where is your general now?"

"General Taticius stay in quarters outside citadel." He pointed to the citadel, which towered above the other buildings. "Take this street. Turn north at market."

"And where is the leader of the Kelts? The one they call Drugo of Flanders."

The scribe checked his documents. "They in same place."

Wiker started to pass through the gate but two sentries moved in front of him. "I not finished, sir," said the scribe as he raised his pen. "What your names?"

Wiker hesitated. He thought of using aliases but realized the confusion this could create among his own men. Besides, no one knew them here. "I am Wiker," he said, before offering the names of his accomplices.

"And where you from?"

"We hail from Italy."

The scribe's face soured. He didn't like Kelts from Italy. "You may enter. Leave weapon and horse at stable." He pointed to the stables.

"Our weapons? Is the city that safe?"

"Those the rule. Weapon and horse stay here."

Wiker stepped back to talk to his men. "Turn in your weapons to the gate keeper." Then, he lowered his voice. "But keep your daggers in your boots."

• • • • •

Drugo's head throbbed from the ale, his throat was as dry as dust, his stomach rumbled and groaned. He had already made two rushed visits to the public toilets and feared a third when he arrived at the door of the General's war-room.

Taticius was quick to notice his bloodshot eyes. "I trust you enjoyed yourself last night, Captain?"

"Yes, General."

He motioned to a chair. "Please, sit."

Drugo slumped into a chair, his head spinning.

Taticius, impeccably dressed, wore a lamellar corselet over a long brown tunic and covered his shoulders with a freshly ironed blue cape. His short, dark hair was clean-cut, his face smooth-shaved. "Can I get you something to eat or drink?" His plated armor creaked as he sat down.

Drugo nodded, trying not to stare at his metal nose. "Water please."

He barked an order to one of the guards before turning back to Drugo. "Soon, you will reach Constantinople. There, the Emperor will decide your course of action. I presume he will dispatch you to Nicomedia, where I am often stationed. If I am correct, you will be joining forces with Captain Humberto and the other Kelts." He paused. "Do you have any questions?"

Drugo looked blankly at him. "No... no," he mumbled.

Taticius straightened in his chair. "How is your Greek coming along?"

"I try learn," he said in Greek as he rubbed his forehead.

"I will assign a tutor to you. All commanders must learn Greek."

Drugo shrugged.

Taticius ruffled at his apparent detachment. "I order it, Captain. Your life and the lives of your men depend on it."

A soldier returned with a large jug of water and two cups. He banged them down on the table and left the room. Taticius motioned. "Please, Captain... drink."

Drugo filled a cup and drank it all. He filled it again.

Taticius observed the unkempt barbarian with some revulsion, the reek of his breath, the yellow and black teeth, and the stink of liquor exuding from his skin. May God help us, he thought before he spoke again. "Have you tried the baths, Captain?"

Drugo nodded.

"Ah, very good. I advise you to use them often."

Drugo stared at him.

"Furthermore," said the General, "it appears you could use a toothbrush. It can help rid your teeth of those worms. I will arrange for you to see our dentist."

Drugo closed his lips unwittingly and ran his tongue over his teeth. His ears reddened. God damned foreigners! Treat us like children!

Taticius did not wait for a reply. "I have hired three more mercenaries. They came to see me yesterday. From Italy, they say. Not the most trustworthy credentials. I have put them under your command until they reach the city. The Emperor will decide their fate."

Drugo drank another cup of water and wiped his face on a sleeve. "As you wish."

• • • • •

Taticius hired Wiker and his two henchmen and they joined Drugo's long procession as it left Adrianople. "There they are." Wiker twirled his mustache as he nodded towards the monks at the front of the line. "We will introduce ourselves tonight. And remember... do nothing without my instruction." A soldier riding ahead turned in his saddle when he heard German. Wiker greeted him in Latin. The soldier nodded and turned forward again. Wiker looked askance at his men and they rode in silence.

TZURULOS

The sun was low in the sky when they arrived at the fortress of Tzurulos, where they prepared to camp for the night. It rested high on a hill and had a good view of the plains of Thrace. But there was little room within the walls, so they rode around the foot of the hill seeking a place to raise their tents. Soldiers dismounted and the quest for tent space began.

Ramiro pointed to a spot. "We camp here. Quickly Pepin! Lay out the tent before one of these louts takes our place."

"Yes, Father." He rushed to unpack the donkey.

Ramiro glanced at Aldebert, who sat idle on his mare. "Come Aldebert! Off that horse and lend a hand. It will be dusk soon. Find us something to eat."

Aldebert dismounted with some difficulty, moaning from the pain in his shoulder as he began to rummage through the saddlebags. Pepin, who was driving tent nails into the hard ground, scowled as he watched him make a mess of his packs. He rushed over. "Brother Aldebert, not to worry, I have some bread and cheese that I got yesterday. And there's still some dried fruit... I'll get it."

Aldebert left the bags and stood looking helpless.

Ramiro began to spread out the tent. "Brother Aldebert... do something besides standing there like an idiot!"

"What can I do?"

Ramiro stood. "We've been on the road for weeks doing the same thing almost every day. And still, you don't know what to do. Think man! Take our flasks and fill them at the river."

"But I have only one good arm and the river is over a hundred paces away."

"That's not far for a young man like you. If you prefer, you can tether the horses and feed them."

"But that's Pepin's job. I'm not a groom."

Ramiro scowled. "Your job is to serve God, Brother. And since we are on a mission of God, then your job is to accomplish that mission. That means doing anything you can to help. Surely, you can feed a horse."

• • • • •

Wiker the Blade wandered through the crowd. He nodded toward the foot of the hill. "Over there," he said to his two henchmen. "Look for a space as close as possible. But not too close."

They spread out to search the ground. Before long, one of them began to wave above the crowd and the other two converged on the spot. The monk's tent was about twenty paces away.

Rolf scoured the ground. "I can see why nobody has jumped on this spot. Look at the rocks!"

Wiker looked around. "Do not concern yourself with the rocks, Rolf. It is doubtful you'll have any sleep tonight." He kicked at the sharp stones. "Level it out as much as you can and set up the tents. Try to look like the rest of them."

After they put up Wiker's large tent and fed the horses, they huddled inside to talk. "I will approach their tent and introduce myself," said Wiker. "That will give me a chance to study their campsite and to know something of their habits. The rest of you find some food and prepare for a fast ride. We meet back here at sunset."

• • • • •

Ramiro sat on a smooth stone beside his tent. He was busy cleaning the dust from a figurine of Mother Mary when Wiker arrived. He looked up when the stranger loomed. "Greetings, my son. What can I do for you?"

Wiker looked down on the stout monk and the bag of religious paraphernalia in front of him. "Tell me, Father, do you hold Vespers tonight?"

Ramiro smiled broadly. "Yes, yes, we do... every night, God willing. I hope you will join us." He motioned to the icon. "As you can see, I am preparing the Mother herself." He looked around. "Have a seat if you like." He pointed. "There's a suitable stone. What is your name, sir? You are new to us, are you not?"

Wiker studied the ground. "I am Wiker and, yes, I joined up yesterday."

"Are you my neighbor here?"

"I'm camped over there." He pointed.

Ramiro smiled. "On that rocky ground?"

"Yes, well, there were few places left."

"Where are you from?" Ramiro asked as he studied the wiry man.

Wiker pulled up his pant legs and squatted on the stone. "From Venice," he said with an empty, cold look.

"A cavalryman from Venice? We don't see too many in our travels."

Wiker forced a smile. "And I see few monks from Cluny in mine."

Ramiro's eyes narrowed for a moment. He switched to the Latin dialect of the north. "It is a beautiful island, is it not?"

Wiker stiffened a little before speaking in the same tongue. "What island?"

"Why, Venice, of course."

He laughed artificially. "Oh, yes, yes, very beautiful," he said before making an attempt to change direction. "Are you traveling to Constantinople?"

"Yes, we are."

"What does a Benedictine monk do in that city? I hear they have closed the Latin churches."

Ramiro shrugged. "Perhaps we can open them again, by the Grace of God."

Wiker hesitated. "Yes, yes, hopefully."

Ramiro put his cloth away and closed the bag. "Have you heard the news from Rome?"

Wiker shook his head. "And what news is that?"

"Odo of Lagery was appointed Pope by the cardinals. He was ordained Urban the Second, and is now the legitimate heir of Saint Paul."

Wiker feigned a smile. "Yes... yes, I have heard - that was last year... but what of Pope Clement? Was he not appointed by the Holy Roman Emperor, His Highness Henry?"

"Ah, but as you must know, good sir, there is much disagreement about who has the right to install popes and bishops. One side believes only servants of the True Church have that right, while the other claims that kings and queens have the right to choose."

Wiker shuffled uneasily, staring at him. "I can guess your position, Dom Ramiro."

"Yes, I agree with Pope Gregory's reforms, may God rest his soul."

"But what of the divine right of kings?" Wiker asked with a hint of annoyance. "Are they not also ordained by God?"

Ramiro looked hard at the man. "No, I don't believe they are. They simply want to control the Church by controlling its people. Kings pay their bishops too well. They twist and pervert the truth to suit their own selfish designs."

Wiker stood up suddenly, flushing red. He hesitated and fought for composure. "Forgive me, but my travels have made me a little agitated. I... I will leave you now and take some rest."

Ramiro glared at him. "It would appear some rest is in order, soldier. Farewell, Wiker of Venice. May God's peace be upon you."

Wiker climbed the hill in long strides. You fool! He cursed himself for losing his temper. The rebel monk is sharp - but he's still nothing but a minion of the false pope and speaks blasphemy. He must be stopped! Halfway up the hill he paused, ostensibly to peruse the countryside. But he was more interested in the position of Ramiro's tent, which was set up adjacent to the hill. The place was crowded and he knew their escape relied on getting to the main road as fast as possible, so he took note of the best route and returned to his tent to wait for his comrades.

By dusk, his men had returned. "We wait until everyone is asleep," said Wiker. "Remember Rolf, to stab in the neck first so they make no sound." His beady eyes moved to the other man. "You take the horses. Tether them near the road. They must be fully saddled and ready to go." He leaned forward and spoke quietly. "This is my plan..."

● ● ● ● ●

Campfires roared under a clear, starlit sky and a festive mood hung in the air. Constantinople was only a few days away and the barbarians were behind them. At least, that was what they hoped. And this was the day to celebrate Michaelmas, the day to rejoice in the Archangel Michael, the patron saint of horsemen. It was he who defeated Lucifer in a battle for the heavens and it was he who came to earth to protect us from the coming days of darkness.

Drugo, like many knights, revered Saint Michael, the heavenly warrior who defeated the Evil One and who now stands against the Antichrist. He hovered on Ramiro's words, reciting after him the Prayer of Saint Michael.

> St. Michael the Archangel, defend us in battle; be
> our safeguard against the wickedness and snares
> of the Devil...

The prayers ended and the dancing began. Servants and soldiers alike brought out their flutes, horns, bells, and drums. And Louis had his lyre. A group of knights and a few women danced a clumsy jig in the trembling firelight. A servant girl with long, black hair spun around them, keeping out the forces of darkness by spinning circles with her outstretched arms. Soldiers leered at the pretty lass, emboldened by wine and beer brought down from the village. One knight, a slim man with black hair hanging below his ears, staggered to the center and moved lecherously towards the girl. But he only teased before he turned on his heels and, almost falling down, he began to bellow.

We in our wandering,
Blithesome and squandering,
Tara, tantara, teino!

Eat to satiety,
Drink to propriety;
Tara, tantara, teino!

He managed to sing through several verses before he collapsed to the ground. The audience laughed and clapped. The music started up again and more came in to dance.

Aldebert sneered, "Father Ramiro! We should be reciting Psalms and hymns of the mass! Not these vulgar pagan songs."

Ramiro laughed. "Enjoy the music, Brother Aldebert. God knows it is a rare event since we left the abbey. And remember, Saint Gregory said dance was fine if done in honor of God."

"Well," he sputtered, "this is hardly in honor of God."

"Why do you say? They celebrate Saint Michael do they not? And levity is a healthy balm to the miseries they have endured. Let them enjoy."

The night wore on, the music waned, and many stumbled to their tents. When all was quiet, Adele came into the circle carrying her father's lyre. Ramiro rushed out carrying a wooden box and glowed like a candle when she smiled and thanked him. She sat down, tucking her legs under her, strumming the chords gently to test the tune of the strings. She slung her long hair over one shoulder with a toss of her head and slowly, she struck up a melody, playing an old Keltic tune. She lifted her eyes to the stars and, much to Ramiro's surprise, began to sing in a lively soubrette.

Alas, my love, you do me wrong,
To cast me off discourteously.
For I have loved you well and long,
Delighting in your company.

She tilted her head to the lyre, her voice clear and angelic, singing with such feeling that she swayed the whole crowd, who hung on her every word and every chorus.

Ramiro was captivated. Her words sang to his own heart, to his own secret longings. It was a yearning he could not understand, yet it welled up in his chest in a flood of sorrow. And when she finished the last chorus, he pulled a kerchief from his pocket and wiped his eyes. Many others did the same, wrenched as they were by her lyrics of unrequited love.

Adele seemed oblivious to the delight of the crowd because, no sooner did she put down her lyre, when she got up right away and began to hand out bread to the soldiers.

Ramiro's eyes followed her every move as she mingled cheerfully with the crowd. She was so beautiful, so graceful. And with wry amusement, he noticed she was a feisty lass who had little trouble holding back the greedy ones. When she came to Wiker and his two friends, he took a moment to watch them, but the men noticed his look and averted their eyes. And every so often, one of them would look askance at him. That is when he stopped thinking of Adele.

● ● ● ● ●

The festivities tapered into silence and night darkened to its deepest pitch. A half-moon rose in the east, shining dimly through a thin blanket of white cloud. Wiker could hear a distant cough and the low rattle of snoring. He stepped out of his tent and Rolf followed him. They tread carefully in the cold light, making their way towards the monk's tent. A flap rustled. They stopped and stooped to the ground. A man wearing only trousers stumbled out of a nearby tent. Wiker waited, dagger in hand. He watched the man grope to the foot of the hill, almost feeling his way before stubbing his foot on a rock and cursing under his breath. Moments later, they heard him pissing in the dirt. Wiker motioned to Rolf to keep still and they waited until the man returned to his tent. We have been out too long, he worried, standing up cautiously to look around. He thought he heard the clink of armor. He stiffened and motioned to Rolf again, waving him down. After a long silence, he signaled with his hand and they continued to skulk forward.

They both clenched their long daggers in a tight fist, ready for the kill. Still crouching, they took their positions in front of the tent, preparing to lunge. In an instant, Wiker threw the flap back and they burst in. Wiker dove to the right, Rolf to the left, stabbing and stabbing.

● ● ● ● ●

Adele jumped from her bed. She heard people yelling and the clash of steel. "What's going on, Papa?" she called out from the tent.

Louis stood outside brandishing an oak club. "I don't know, girl. There's a big ruckus over by the knight's quarter. I'll go take a look."

"I'm coming too!" she yelled, heaving a cloak over her shoulders.

"No you're not!" said Mathilda. "You're hardly decent!"

"Mama! Please! I'll stay with Papa. I promise."

"Stupid girl! Well at least show some manners and cover your hair."

"Yes, Mama." She grabbed a scarf and fitted it in haste.

"What's happened?" Louis asked a man coming from the direction of the uproar.

"The two monks have been attacked," the man said as he walked by. "Stabbed by German assassins."

Adele shrieked. The flap whipped open and she rushed out, bumping into Louis. She stopped for a moment, staring at him with wide, terrified eyes. Suddenly, she spun around without a word and ran straight for the knight's quarter. Mathilda came bumbling out behind her. "Wait for your father!"

"Adele!" Louis shouted. "Stop girl! Wait for me!"

• • • • •

Wiker was only ten paces out of Ramiro's tent when he ran straight into Arles of Ghent, who picked him up as easily as a sack of grain and threw him down hard onto the rough ground. He put his foot on the German's neck, holding his axe above his head, ready to strike. Meanwhile, Rolf stood motionless with the tip of Drugo's broadsword at his neck.

"Where's your other man?" Drugo shouted. They said nothing. Drugo pressed the tip of his sword into Rolf's neck and blood poured from its touch. "Where is he?"

Rolf panicked and clutched at his neck. "He's down the road with the horses!"

Drugo lowered his blade and turned to Otto. "Take your men. Bring him alive if you can." They rushed off, swords drawn.

• • • • •

Twenty paces away, Aldebert clutched his head in his hands. "How did you know, Father Ramiro? How did you know they were sent to kill you?"

Ramiro watched with arms folded and a palm to his chin. "Well, there were several clues."

"Like what?"

He pointed to the German tent. "Why would anyone camp on that rocky ground, Brother Aldebert? You remember, we looked at it earlier. That seemed odd to me."

Aldebert lifted his brow, eyes bulging. "That's it? The rocky ground?"

"No, no. There's more. When we talked, he knew I came from Cluny. Now, how would he know that after being with us for just a day? He also said he was from Venice but clearly he was not fluent in the local tongue. Nor did he seem to know much of the city. Besides, how many armored mercenaries come from Venice? Venetians are merchant men or pirates. And look at his dress, hear his accent. He's a German. And so are his two friends. Now why is a German in Italy I ask you?... Only to protect Henry's pope," he answered himself. "And then, when I challenged the king's right to choose bishops, well that was the final clue, that's when he became angry and stormed off."

Aldebert shook his head. "But Father, why would they want to murder you?"

"Murder *us*, Brother Aldebert. They were going to kill you too."

Aldebert fidgeted wildly. "Blessed Saints! Wood devils and savage heathen! Now this! May the Lord protect us! What are we..."

"Dom Ramiro!" cried a girl's voice.

Ramiro spun around. It was Adele. She stood in bare feet with her father's cloak wrapped tight around her. She was crying. "What's wrong!" he asked in alarm.

But she could not speak and covered her face with her hands to mask her tears.

"Are you alright?"

She nodded with her hands still at her face.

"Is it your father? Your mother?"

She shook her head erratically and, as suddenly as she had arrived, she spun away and ran off without a word.

Ramiro leaned towards Aldebert. "Women are indeed the strangest creatures, Brother Aldebert. I doubt any man could live long enough to understand them."

"Really?"

"Oh yes, Brother, and this is why God, by his mercy, has given us love."

● ● ● ● ●

Drugo shouted to Otto. "Did you get the man with the horses?"

"He drew his sword, m'lord. We cut him down," he said, still wielding his bloodied sword. "And we've taken their horses."

They stripped Wiker and Rolf of their armor and tied them to a tree. Otto and Fulk held the points of their spears to their necks. The crowd milled closer, eager to see in the torchlight.

Drugo bellowed at them. "Back to your tents! There's no business for you here. All is well. Back to your tents." The people shuffled away reluctantly and he turned to stare down on Wiker. "Who sent you?" he asked, jabbing his sword at him. Wiker said nothing. Drugo gave a nod to Otto, who jabbed his spear into his leg. Wiker clenched his teeth but made no sound.

Drugo turned to Rolf. "Who sent you?"

Rolf shuffled his legs uneasily. Blood still ran from the cut at his throat "I don't know. I only do as my Lord asks."

Fulk jabbed his spear into Rolf's side. Rolf shrieked and Drugo asked again. "What's your mission?" Rolf moaned but said nothing more.

Drugo lost patience. "Kill him," he said and, without hesitation, Fulk heaved his spear through Rolf's throat. Blood spurted from the man's neck with the last beats of his heart. Unaffected, Drugo turned again to Wiker and glared at him. He held his sword to the man's neck. "I will kill you next. Who sent you?"

"We are servants of Pope Clement," he said in a defiant voice.

Drugo sneered. "So, you are bootlickers of the antipope. What business does that papal snake have with these monks?"

"I don't know." Wiker eyed Drugo's sword. "I swear on Christ's name. I don't know."

Again, Drugo pushed his sword into his neck. Wiker's eyes widened in fear and he tried to move back but Drugo pushed further.

"The monks betray the Holy Roman Emperor!" Wiker shouted suddenly.

Drugo kept his sword at his neck. "Filthy pig! Your master usurps the Holy Church. Pope Urban is its rightful heir."

Wiker spat into the dirt.

Drugo spat too, raising his sword to take his head. "Heretic! I'll send you to hell!" But he hesitated in half swing as his senses returned. *I will discover nothing more if he is dead.* He lowered his sword and turned away to let his anger cool. "Leave him here till morning light. We will decide his fate at that time."

He returned to his tent wondering why these cursed monks were so important that Giberto would send assassins after them. How could they possibly threaten the German king? Why do they travel to the Greek Kingdom? It was pointless to ask that damn monk, he had asked him many times already but he would say nothing of any substance. Still, he had sworn to get them safely to the Greek King, and that is *all* he would do.

• • • • •

Fulk rushed to Drugo's tent just before dawn. "Captain, Captain! He has escaped!"

Drugo stumbled out of his tent and hurried to the tree where Wiker was bound. The ropes were cut.

Drugo reddened. "Who was watching him?"

One soldier offered a meek reply. "Sorry, m'lord. I fell asleep."

Drugo lunged at the man, striking him hard across the head with the flat of his sword. The soldier collapsed to the ground. "Find him!" he yelled to the others.

Otto dared to speak. "He has taken a horse, Sir Drugo."

"Then mount up and go after him!"

"Captain!" shouted Manuel the Byzantine, who rushed to the commotion. "We cannot delay any longer. Emperor Alexios awaits you. Besides, it is much too dangerous to turn back... or to wait here. A scout says the barbarians repelled the Roman army. So the Turkoman still roam the area and approach this village again. Wiker can do no harm now. It is unlikely he will reach Rome alive."

Drugo bristled. He stomped away, waving an arm in a wide circle. "Then we are done with this business. Prepare for travel in the morning."

Aldebert fretted. "He has escaped! What shall we do? Holy Mother of God, what shall we do?"

"Calm yourself, Brother Aldebert," said Ramiro. "We will do nothing but trust in our good Lord and our own good judgment."

CONSTANTINOPLE

OCTOBER 1089

The Egnatia Way skirted the rocky northern shore of the Propontis, winding its way along the coast, where it headed straight for the Golden Gate of Constantinople. A cool easterly wind blasted against the cavalcade of knights and servants and beat at the dark blue waters of the sea, churning up white crests on rolling waves before they crashed on the rocky shore. Sunburned fishermen pulled in their nets from clinker-built dinghies while gulls squawked overhead, waiting for them to clean their catch.

Ramiro reveled in the thick, briny air and a thrill of excitement overcame his worries about Wiker, although Aldebert still looked over his shoulder in furtive glances. The outline of the massive city walls emerged over the horizon and Ramiro began to imagine a Byzantine banquet served with vats of Dalmatian wine, or maybe a new vintage for him to try. And, although he would never admit it to Aldebert, he happily anticipated another hot bath.

"Do you see the city in the distance?" asked Manuel.

"Yes, Commander, it looks magnificent. It's enormous."

"It is larger than Rome, Monk Ramiro, and the center of our world," he lifted his chin with pride. "It is the Queen of Cities. We trade with merchants from as far away as the Land of the Rus, the kingdoms of the Indus Valley, and further still, the Land of the Sung."

Ramiro and Aldebert stared blankly. They had never heard of such places.

"Our city," said Manuel, unabashed, "has been a bastion of the Christian faith since Emperor Constantine made it the capital seven hundred years ago. And it is the seat of the Great Bishop, Patriarch Nikolas."

Aldebert bristled at Manuel's pride and the mere mention of the Patriarch. He pulled his horse closer to him and strained forward. "But surely, Commander, the ultimate authority of the Christian Church *must* lay with Saint Paul and the Popes who inherit his seat at the Lateran. After all, was it not Saint Paul who first brought Christianity to Rome, and from there, by God's will, the Word came to Constantinople?"

Manuel pulled a water-skin from his bag and took a long draught. He could sense Aldebert's indignation. "I agree, Monk Aldebert, that Saint Paul introduced Christianity to Rome, but remember that he also converted the Greeks of Antioch, who were the first to widely embrace the teachings of Christ. Did you not know Christianity was well established here long before it reached Rome?" He tried to be polite but was mildly annoyed. What arrogance! And now they want to rule the Church too!

Aldebert fumed at an imagined challenge, his heart pounded and blood rushed to his head in hot waves, clouding his mind in fury. His pocked face reddened. Unable to restrain himself, he gushed in anger. "Paul was the creator of the Christian Church! A position inherited directly from Christ himself! The only true allegiance must be to Saint Paul and his successors!"

Both Manuel and Ramiro were taken aback by his ill-disposed outburst. But before they could respond, he continued to rant. The veins in his neck and temple bulged. "The only true spiritual lineage of Christ is through the Pope...."

"That's enough, Brother Aldebert!" Ramiro snapped.

Aldebert stopped. In a rush of shame, he lowered his head. "I beg your leave," he muttered.

For the most part, Ramiro's views were similar, but a sliver of doubt pierced his thoughts. Manuel's grasp of Roman, Greek, and Christian history was much more comprehensive than his own. Could there be more to this? Surely, God ordained the Pope. Could the Patriarch also be ordained? Why would God create two earthly rulers for His Church?

Manuel could barely conceal his contempt for Aldebert. The people of Constantinople had heard of the Abbey of Cluny and its strong allegiance to the Pope. The infamous Pope Gregory was also a man of Cluny and he had betrayed them to that Norman bastard, Guiscard. Without another word, he swung his horse out of line and trotted away.

"I told you, Father Ramiro," said Aldebert. "I told you we would have nothing but trouble with these Eastern heretics! Why did you not defend me? You know we are God's chosen people, the Pope said as much. It is we who carry the true message of Christ our Lord. Why do they not see that?" He flung his arms about as he talked and winced from the pain in his shoulder.

Ramiro observed Aldebert's hard red sneer. "Are you going out of your mind, Brother Aldebert?" he said in a piqued voice. "If our mission is to be a success, then we must remain tactful and patient. We cannot afford to fail." He took a drink of water to clear his dry throat. "If you are going to engage yourself in hot-headed arguments all the way to Jerusalem, I will leave you in Constantinople and you can return to Cluny in your own time. Regardless of what you believe, I will not allow you to jeopardize this assignment. Do you understand?"

Aldebert fell silent, paling with anxiety. "Forgive me, Father Ramiro, for I have sinned." Then he looked askance at Ramiro and fidgeted with his reins. "But how can we tolerate such vile thoughts?"

"Tolerate them you will, Brother Aldebert. And you will learn to control that bitter tongue of yours. It affords us nothing."

• • • • •

"Who are these men?" Drugo asked, noticing a platoon of troops riding out from the city gates. The men had darker skin and high cheekbones, many had thin beards, and they all had braided black hair.

"They are Turks, going to fight the Turkomans we just left." Manuel raised his voice over the increasing din of the road, now swarming with people and animals. Shoppers headed to market while merchants carried their wares on donkeys or carts. Cattle, sheep, pigs, and even crates of strange clucking birds filled the air with their scents and sounds.

"So how do we know which Turk is an enemy and which is not?"

"Just as you would anywhere else, Sir Drugo, ... by their banners. These Turks fly the Byzantine flag."

Drugo shook his head. "It's all very confusing."

"Not really," said Manuel. "Some fight against us, and some for us. Turks fight Turks, just as I'm sure Normans fight Normans under different banners. They are fierce fighters. Many have bought their freedom and now seek their fortunes in the booty of war... just as you do, my friend." He smiled. "The men you see here are called mamluks."

"What? Mam...loo?"

"Mamluk. It means 'slave warrior.' These are the men you must learn to fight. Most of them are Turkoman taken from Iran and Khorasan when young, and trained for a life of war. By the time they become men, they know of little else and have no loyalty to other Turks. Besides, they are well rewarded for their efforts and are often envied by those who seek their fortunes elsewhere."

"But why use slaves in the first place?" Drugo asked. "Are there no fighting men among the Turks or Arabs?"

"Of course there are. The Arabs started using slaves as fighters because their religion forbids Muslims to kill Muslims. So when the Arab kings fight each other, they use the mamluks, who are pagans taken from the far north."

Drugo found it bewildering, the concept was new to him. True, they had mercenaries in Europe, but nearly all knights were the sons of the wealthy, they were men of rank and means. Few others could afford fine horses and weapons. Lesser men could become knights after gaining wealth, some through pillage, but they were seldom accepted as equals.

The enormous walls of Constantinople towered over them, distracting his thoughts. These walls were a far cry from any he had seen in Italy, and there was nothing at all like them in France or Flanders where palisades were still made of wood. He knew of few places built of stone, although he had heard of the Tower of London, built by the Norman conqueror, William the Bastard. But never in his life had he seen walls like this.

The Greeks first settled Constantinople six hundred years before the birth of Christ. They called it Byzantion. Its location was vital, guarding all sea traffic to and from the Black Sea and all land traffic from Asia Minor to Europe. The Romans realized its strategic value and seized it four hundred years later, calling it Byzantium. The Roman emperor, Constantine, made it his official capital in 330 and renamed the city after himself. And after the Roman Empire split into East and West, it remained the capital of the East Roman Empire for more than one thousand years.

The city sprawled out on a peninsula, shielded to the northeast by the Bosporus and the Golden Horn, and to the south, by the Propontis. Its walls stretched over twelve Roman miles, lining the shores and slicing across the north-west approach. The first line of defense to the landward side was a wide moat. Next, were three walls, a lower, middle, and inner, all spaced about fifty paces apart. If attackers managed to get past the moat and the first wall, they had to cross the space between to scale the second, which stood the height of five men. They would then have to contend with raining arrows and burning tar thrown down from the battlement and towers. If they managed to scale the second wall, they would be forced to climb the inner wall, the height of seven men, and face similar obstacles. Built into these walls were ninety-six rectangular towers. Drugo could not see them all, but he could spot them as far as the eye could see. And he could think of no army able to penetrate these defenses.

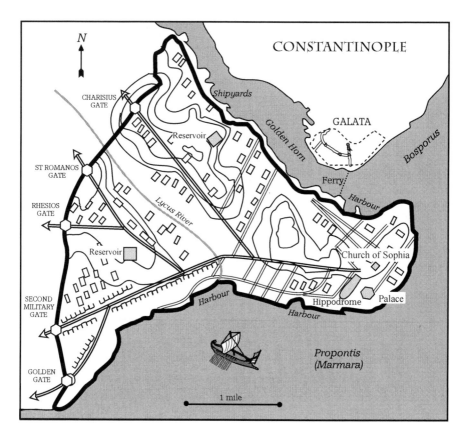

They no sooner reached the Golden Gate when a team of Byzantine slaves rushed out with wagons of food, clothing, and jugs of wine and water. They even brought fodder for the horses. With practiced efficiency, they cleared ground and set up latrines.

"We have permission to enter the city," said Manuel, who returned with blonde-haired Byzantine guards carrying huge battle-axes. "But only ten knights and the monks are allowed in today."

• • • • •

Ramiro smiled when he heard the news. He grabbed Aldebert by the arm and pulled him over to the horses in order to prepare.

"Another bath? Father Ramiro. It goes against all common sense!"

"You will do as I tell you to do, Brother Aldebert. I remind you of your position here. We are about to meet the Emperor of the Greek Empire, and we must do as he wishes." Already, his assistant was filthy and smelled like a wet dog.

"It is against God's wishes!" Aldebert protested.

"What do you know of God's wishes, Brother Aldebert? Did he personally commute this revelation to you?" He paused and bit his lip to control his words. "If you will not cooperate, you will stay in camp with the servants and horses!"

Aldebert scowled and his big ears drooped.

"Pepin! Prepare our horses... quickly now! Quickly!" The boy was stuffing his mouth with fruit taken from the Emperor's wagon. "Did you think you would starve here, boy? Quickly now, give these horses some water. The Emperor awaits us. You will remain here with the donkey and our baggage. Guard them carefully. Do you understand?"

"Yes, Father, don't worry. I'll sleep on top of everything."

"Just take care, boy. I'm not sure when we will return but we'll try to keep in touch." He reached for the Pope's letters under his robe and relaxed when he felt the soft crush of vellum.

• • • • •

A narrow bridge crossed the moat, bringing them to a plaza guarded on both sides by huge rectangular towers that funneled to the entrance of the Golden Gate, a large archway with a massive iron-clad door as thick as a man's forearm. Inside, the gate opened onto an expansive courtyard where stunning statues of elephants towered over them.

They passed through the Castle of Seven Towers to follow a paved avenue lined with a colonnade of tall stone pillars. To the north, the waters of a huge reservoir glimmered in the sun. The long avenue stretched more than four miles across the city, lined on either side with luxurious mansions, and ended at the tip of the peninsula in the vicinity of the Imperial Palace, the Hippodrome, the Churches of Sofia and Irene, and the ancient Acropolis of the Greeks. Here, Manuel led them through the doorway of a sprawling three-story building that overlooked the Hippodrome and the sea. A wide flight of marble stairs took them to the third floor, where lavish rooms awaited their arrival.

From the windows, Aldebert peered down on the huge Hippodrome. He gestured to Manuel and pointed out the window. "Why is it so big?"

"Like the one in Rome, it's where we hold sporting events, chariot races and special ceremonies."

Aldebert pointed into the center of the arena. "Look! What's that?" he said, referring to a huge pile of ashes near the center. Looks like there was a fire."

Manuel nodded solemnly. "An intentional fire, Monk Aldebert. I hear the Emperor sentenced a heretic to the flames."

Aldebert stared at him. "You mean someone was burned alive?"

"Yes... that is the sentence for heretics."

They all rushed to the window for a look, staring at the cold ashes of the pyre. Visions of hot flames licking at their feet soon haunted their thoughts.

"I will leave you now," said Manuel. "My mission is accomplished and I return to my family for a few days of rest. You will now be under the tutelage of the chamberlain."

He was no sooner out the door when Aldebert blurted. "Father Ramiro! They will burn us alive! God help us!"

"Contain yourself, Aldebert. I'm sure the Emperor will spare you as long as you keep your mouth shut."

Drugo and Otto grinned. It was one of the few times Ramiro had seen them smile. "They will burn you monks first," said Drugo with a nervous chuckle. "At least we are of some use to them."

"How can you laugh at the sight of this?" Aldebert cried. "Mother of Mary, I feel sick! We are in the hands of heretics who would burn *us* for being heretics!"

"Keep your head," said Ramiro. "There is little we can do now but attempt to please the Emperor. We are at his mercy." But despite his outward calm, he felt a seed of fear.

• • • • •

"I am chamberlain to Emperor Alexios. Most men know me as Little John and you may address me as such."

Little John was anything but little, he was a huge man of fighting proportions. Clearly, he was a warrior-monk because he dressed in a simple black robe, yet a long sword hung from a shoulder strap and its hilt looked well-worn. He had a full head of black hair, a beard, and a face laced with battle scars.

Drugo and his men, dwarfed by Little John's presence, remained silent, uneasy without their weapons.

"I have arranged for breakfast in your rooms. Give your garments to the servants for cleaning. Please take advantage of our baths to refresh yourselves. Before dusk, you will meet with the Emperor at the Palace. And, as you are all strangers to our Empire, let me give you instructions on Palace protocol."

• • • • •

Aldebert stood timidly at the edge of the large bath, his face red with shame. In fear of Ramiro's wrath he said nothing and dropped his tunic to the floor. He stood silently for a moment, feeling conspicuously naked in his breeches.

Ramiro wasted no time climbing into the warm pool and looked back to see Aldebert's thin, white frame standing in solitude. The arrow wound on his shoulder had healed nicely but left a large, rippled scar. He gestured to him. "Come on in man, the water is warm."

Aldebert reluctantly sat down on the rim of the pool and stuck his legs in the water.

"Come, come, Brother. Get in." He scooped a handful of water and threw it at him.

Aldebert jolted. "Father Ramiro, please!"

"It's not going to kill you. Now get in!"

Frowning, Aldebert lowered himself slowly into the pool, squatting carefully on a low bench under the water.

Ramiro threw him a bar of soap. "Now, rub that all over you. And you see this? Scrub yourself with it." He tossed over a strange object.

Aldebert cautiously picked up the floating sponge. He had never seen anything like it. It squashed in his fingers. "What is it?"

"Never mind, just scrub."

• • • • •

The sheer size of the city, its grandeur, and its ostentatious wealth, overwhelmed and daunted the Flemings as they made their way to see the King. The Imperial Palace dominated their view, rising up in elegance and opulence, a gigantic marble and stone structure spread out over acres of carefully manicured gardens. The royal courtyard, a beautifully paved area interspersed with colorful flowers, exotic trees, and bubbling fountains, was unlike anything they had seen before.

Guards led them through to an antechamber, where they were told to wait until the Emperor summoned them. Red sofas lined the walls of the ornate room where bowls of strange fruit and vases of flowers adorned marble tables. The men sat awkwardly, unused to such conspicuous luxury. Drugo wandered around aimlessly, pretending to inspect some corner of the room. He appeared to be looking for an escape route and reached constantly for the hilt of his missing broadsword.

"Emperor Alexios will receive you now," said Little John formally. "Follow me."

A wide hallway bustled with servants rushing to and fro with platters of food and drink, clean linen, flowers, and all manner of things. And when Ramiro arrived at a massive door straddled by more guards, he could feel his heart beat furiously. Behind this door was the heart of the Roman Empire, the throne room of Alexios Komnenos, Imperial Emperor of the East.

THE KOMNENOS THRONE

The hall fell quiet when they filed in. The only sound came from bright birds fluttering high above in the dome of the ceiling. But they were no sooner through the door when Drugo stopped suddenly and stepped back. The other men stumbled into him. Aldebert jumped behind Ramiro. "By God's mercy!"

A huge beast roared and clawed the air in their direction, held back by a towering man with sapphire skin and rippling muscles who pulled hard on its chain. Courtiers titillated with amusement.

Little John smiled. "Have you never seen a lion? Come, my brave men. Follow me."

The men kept turning their heads back for another look at the lion and its black attendant. They trailed Little John in an awkward amble along the wide, red carpet where whispering courtiers lined either side.

The path led to an elaborate dais rising about two feet above the floor. On this dais, was the imperial throne, and on the gilded throne, was Emperor Alexios Komnenos. Behind him to his right, sat a man of about the same age and height and, to his left, an older woman of graceful poise.

Little John approached and knelt. "Your Majesty, may our Lord bless your reign. I present to you the Kelts sent by the Count of Flanders, as well as two monks, emissaries of the Latin Church." He moved to the side.

"Welcome to the Roman Empire," Alexios said in a soft tenor. "I trust you have been treated kindly?"

For a moment, the men were a little dumbfounded. The Emperor spoke in fluent Latin. He was about thirty-five and of medium height. Curly, dark-red hair outlined his ruddy face and hung to his broad shoulders while a full, trimmed beard tapered to a point from his chin. A lamellar corselet covered his chest and a long, purple cape draped to the floor. Peeking out of his cloak, were red leggings and scuffed riding boots. Indeed, the only sign of royalty about him was his purple cape and a simple diadem.

Drugo managed a reply. "Greetings, Your Highness. Yes, we have been well cared for."

Alexios smiled thinly. "You must forgive my dress," he said, as if guessing their thoughts. "I have just returned from another campaign against the Turkoman and have had little time to refresh myself." His green eyes sparkled in a menacing way, a look emphasized by his elegant and expressive eyebrows. "I hear you had your own troubles with these barbarians."

"Yes, Your Highness," Drugo answered stiffly.

Alexios twirled the end of his trimmed moustache and said nothing. He waited and watched. The throne room fell silent and Drugo became noticeably agitated.

"And how fares your lord, the Count of Flanders?"

Drugo shuffled uneasily. "He fares well, Your Highness, and is glad to be of help to your Christian nation."

Alexios sat motionless, leaning on one arm of the throne. "And we are pleased that the Count has fulfilled his oath and has seen the wisdom of protecting the True Faith. We send our thanks to God on High that you have arrived safely. You will be well rewarded. I trust you are the commander of these troops?"

"Yes, Your Highness, I am Drugo of Flanders," he said as prospects of gold and glory danced through his mind.

"Welcome Drugo of Flanders." The Emperor waved his arm to the man sitting on his right. "This is my brother and trusted advisor, Isaak Komnenos." Isaak had similar red hair and beard, but was thin and pale. He acknowledged the Flemings with a wan smile and a nod.

Alexios then gestured to his left. "And this is my mother, Anna Dalassene, also one of my most trusted advisors." Anna, a dignified woman in her fifties, nodded towards them with an expressionless face. A small gold diadem adorned her ashen-blonde hair and a light application of eye shadow and lip paint highlighted her fine facial features. Despite her age, her graceful beauty equaled that of many a younger woman.

All of them bowed in turn when the royal members were introduced. "We are honored, Your Highness," said Drugo. "And I am pleased to announce that the Count of Flanders presents you with a gift of one hundred and fifty of our finest horses."

A loud murmur came from the courtiers. Alexios raised his long eyebrows. "That is extremely generous of the Count. I will send him a letter of appreciation. Your lord is one of the few men in the West who is aware of the present danger to Christendom and we are grateful that you have come to assist us in our divine cause."

Drugo bowed again, smirking in the attention of the Royal Court.

"And I am informed these two monks are representatives of your church," said the King as he peered beyond Drugo. "Step forward saintly people, that we may know you."

At the Emperor's call, Ramiro and Aldebert, who stood directly behind Drugo, momentarily hesitated. Ramiro had been studying the Emperor, who seemed an eloquent man, although he spoke with a slight lisp, especially when he sounded an 'r.' He summoned his courage and stepped forward. Aldebert, petrified, staggered behind. "Greetings, your Serene Majesty, it is indeed an honor to be before you. I am Father Ramiro, Dean of the Abbey of Cluny." He motioned to Aldebert. "This is my aide, Brother Aldebert."

"Welcome, Father Ramiro of Cluny and Brother Aldebert. I am also honored that you have come so far in the interests of your faith." He examined the two monks for a long while. A green parrot squawked overhead before swooping over the silent courtiers. "I hear you have encountered some enemies on your journey. May I presume that some of your countrymen are not pleased with your mission here?"

Ramiro looked up. He was about to say they were Germans, not countrymen, but he was sadly aware that few in the Royal Court perceived any difference. "Yes, Your Majesty, it appears to be so."

"So tell me, Monk Ramiro, what brings you to our Empire?"

Ramiro did not expect such direct questioning in the presence of the court. He had hoped for a private audience with the King. "Well, Your Majesty, the venerable Pope Urban has charged me with the task of working towards the reunification of our churches. He is eager to have our differences reconciled."

Alexios raised an eyebrow. "Is this your sole objective?"

"Uh... yes, Your Majesty. I am here as liaison to His Holiness, Pope Urban the Second."

Alexios kept his keen gaze on Ramiro. He had a playful twinkle in his eyes. "I believe you have something for me, Monk Ramiro."

Ramiro was taken off-guard. How could he know?

Alexios smiled. "Do you have a letter for me?"

"Yes, Your Highness," he said, groping into his robe and drawing out a leather pouch. He selected one of the three letters which, like the others, bore the papal seal.

Alexios motioned. "Come forward, good monk."

Ramiro approached, placing the creased letter on a silver plate held out by a waiting page. "My letter of commendation, Your Highness."

The page offered the letter to Alexios, who passed it to his brother, Isaak, who held it unopened. "We will review this letter and speak to you afterwards."

"Yes, Your Highness," Ramiro said, proud to offer credentials from the Pope himself.

Alexios leaned forward in his throne. "And you have another letter, I believe?"

"Well, uh, yes, Your Majesty," he flustered. "But I was instructed to deliver it personally to Patriarch Nikolas."

Alexios smiled genuinely. "Well here he is." He waved his arm towards Nikolas who stood a few paces from the throne. A few chuckles came from the courtiers. Nikolas, a tall thin man, wore a draping white gown decorated in red crosses. A conical hat with a red cross on the front towered above his square face, which was almost hidden by his dangling, curly black hair and a bushy beard. "I introduce you to Patriarch Nikolas," said Alexios. "He is eager to discuss with you all things ecumenical." Nikolas bowed to the men and they bowed in return.

Ramiro smiled. "And I also look forward to these discussions, Your Highness."

"You may give him the letter now," Alexios persisted.

This was not what Ramiro had expected. He had hoped for a face-to-face talk with the Patriarch before handing him the letter. "Yes... yes, Your Majesty."

Alexios waved a finger and another royal page rushed up to Ramiro, who handed over the letter reluctantly. The king sat leaning on one arm, staring at Ramiro for a long time.

Ramiro stood silently. He bowed and began to back away.

Alexios raised his long eyebrows. "Monk Ramiro, you have a third letter, I believe."

Ramiro stammered. "But... but Your Highness, it...it is bound for Jerusalem."

"For the Patriarch of Jerusalem?"

"Well... yes," said Ramiro, flabbergasted. "It is for Patriarch Symeon, Your Majesty. But... I... I made a solemn vow to His Holiness, Pope Urban, that I would deliver it personally."

Alexios looked amused. "And how do you intend to do that, pray tell? A gauntlet of murderous Turks lines the road to Jerusalem. Just how long do you think two Latin monks would fare on that road?"

Ramiro flushed, seeing the direction of his thoughts. "Your Imperial Highness!" he said desperately. "How can I forsake my explicit duty to the Church? I have given my oath."

"And what was the nature of that oath?" asked Alexios with a stern face.

"As I said, Your Highness, it is to deliver this letter, as quickly as I can, to Patriarch Symeon of Jerusalem."

"Well then, would not your duties be fulfilled if you gave the letter to Patriarch Nikolas, who is of the same Church? Surely, you cannot believe that it would go undelivered?"

"Of... of course not, Your Highness. It was not my intention to suggest..."
"I give you my promise that it will reach Patriarch Symeon. And rest assured, he will receive it long before you could possibly arrive. Do you accept my pledge?"

The blood drained from Ramiro's face. "Yes, of course, Your Majesty."

"Then I will accept your letter on behalf of Patriarch Symeon."

Ramiro's hands shook as he reached again into his purse and pulled out the third letter. In a quavering, uneasy motion, he handed the letter over to the page. His heart beat heavily at the thought of betraying his abbot and the Pope and, much worse, at the terrifying thought of excommunication. After all, he had sworn on the blood of Christ.

"We have much to discuss, Monk Ramiro. I will summon you to council at a later date."

"Yes, Your Majesty." He bowed again and stepped back.

The King returned his penetrating gaze to Drugo and, again, he paused for a while. "Drugo of Flanders. It is your custom, is it not, to swear fealty to your lord?"

Drugo brushed a lock of hair from his eyes. "Yes, Your Majesty."

Alexios stared hard at the man. "Then you have no objection swearing your allegiance to me?"

Drugo hesitated. It meant he would serve no other master and that all lands and booty he seized would become the property of his lord. But he, too, felt trapped by circumstance. "I will swear my allegiance, my Lord, second only to my master, the Count of Flanders."

"The Count is a long distance from here, Drugo of Flanders. Did he not send you to serve the Roman Empire?"

"Well, yes, Your Highness."

Alexios said nothing, he just looked down on Drugo and raised his eyebrows.

Drugo felt cold under his glare. "Of... of course, Your Highness, I will swear my allegiance to you."

"Then be so kind as to offer me a formal pledge."

Drugo flushed. "Now, Your Highness?"

Alexios nodded and smiled. "Yes, Sir Drugo, so that your oath is acknowledged in the eyes of God and witnessed by the whole court."

Drugo summoned his courage and spoke in a loud voice. "I swear, by the Passion of Christ Our Savior, by His Invincible Cross, and by the Holy Gospels that I, Drugo of Flanders, will serve the Emperor as his vassal, and will arm myself against his enemies."

Alexios studied him, pausing momentarily. "And you swear to guard the Holy Sepulcher?"

"With my life, Your Highness." He bowed deeply.

Alexios clasped his hands in his lap and spoke with gravity. "I accept you as my vassal, Drugo of Flanders. My scribes will draw up a contract to this effect and I trust you and all of your men will put your names upon it."

"Yes, Your Highness, I will speak to my men."

"Good. Then this matter is finished. I will assign you and your men to the stronghold of Nicomedia, east of the Propontis. The Turks there are giving us much trouble and we need strong fighting men like yourselves to whip them back. You will rest here for a time as we fear no attacks in the winter months. But by early spring, you will be stationed to your posts." He scrutinized each of Drugo's men as he spoke. They shuffled uneasily, averting their eyes. "I believe you have met Captain Humberto?"

Drugo raised his eyebrows. "Well... uh, yes, Your Highness, in Adrianople."

"Good. When you get to Nicomedia, you will join forces with him and follow the orders of General Taticius."

Drugo bowed. "Yes, Your Majesty."

Alexios stood up. "Thank you gentlemen, you are dismissed."

THE POPE'S LETTERS

Rainwater beat on the mullioned glass windows of the Palace meeting room. Inside, Alexios and his advisors reposed in elegant armchairs, huddling around a single table. The servants laid out Cretan wine, fruit and honeycakes before slipping out the door.

Only after they left, did Anna speak. "Alexi, do not keep us in suspense, my dear. What did the Pope say in his letter to Nikolas?"

Alexios glanced at Nikolas before turning back to Anna, grinning from ear to ear. He paused momentarily as the others leaned on his words. "Well, mother, I am glad to report that Pope Urban has lifted his ban of excommunication against me." He handed her the letter.

Her eyes narrowed a little as she read, a wry smile crossing her thin, red lips. She said nothing.

"I don't see why it would make any difference to you, Alexi," Isaak blurted. "You are not of the Latin Church."

Anna put down her fork. "Because, my son, it now means the way is paved for communion between our two churches. With official communion, we are now in a much better position to negotiate terms of reconciliation. And hopefully, we'll be able to get some military assistance."

"So, what do you think of this letter to Nikolas?" asked Alexios.

She held the letter in her hands, reading it again as she brushed a lock of blonde hair behind her small ears. "For the most part, it looks as though the Pope is being quite conciliatory. There is much hope in this letter. However, there is no mention of providing troops."

"I also found the letter encouraging," said Nikolas through his bushy, black beard. "As I see it, Urban has only two main requests. First, that we reopen all Latin churches in the Empire and, second, that we return the Pope's name to the sacred rosters."

Alexios grinned. "By the Lord Jesus Christ! That is simple enough."

Anna glared at him. "Please son, do not use the Lord's name in vain. You must remain pious in order to receive God's favor."

"Yes, mother, sorry. But this is wonderful news! Reply at once that we agree with his requests."

Nikolas shook his head. "It is not that simple, Your Highness. We closed the Latin churches thirty years ago for a number of reasons. We cannot make any ecclesiastic changes without a synod – the council of bishops must decide. Besides, the Latins continue with their abominable rituals – like using unleavened bread in Communion. This is not acceptable. And they insist on believing that the Holy Spirit emanates from the Son as well as the Father. This is an absurd notion of the divine Trinity."

"Surely, these are not insurmountable problems, Nikolas. The Empire is at stake. Call a meeting of the bishops, we have no time to loose!"

Anna contemplated her somewhat impetuous son. "Use tact and diplomacy, Alexi. We also need to convince the patriarchs in Jerusalem and Antioch."

"Yes, yes, and then we should draft a reply to the Pope," said Alexios, putting a hand to his forehead. "What about the letter to Symeon, Nikolas? What does it say?"

"I haven't opened it."

"Well, do so now. Our forgers will reseal it."

Nikolas broke the papal seal and opened the letter. He read it and passed it on to Alexios. "You can see that Pope Urban reiterates the need to unite the Churches, which is encouraging. But there is something here not in our letter. Here, he argues for the primacy of the Pope, which means, of course, that Urban himself would head this new church. This is nothing new," he scoffed. "But we can never agree to his demand... I will also send a letter to Symeon."

Alexios glanced at him. "Do not jeopardize this delicate balance, Nikolas. Tell the Patriarch anything that pleases him. And tell the other patriarchs only what they need to know. We must manipulate the situation to our advantage, for the sake of the Empire!"

Isaak turned in his chair, his pale cheeks flushed. "Why bother with all this. Why not recruit more men from the Bulgars or the Vlachs?"

Alexios stood to pace the room. "We send our recruiters everywhere looking for mercenaries, brother, but there are few left. We need the Latins and their bloodthirsty men, whether we like it or not. The Patzinaks attack from the north, the Turks from the east, Bulgars and Serbs from the west. We have lost Asia, Syria, and Palestine ... even Antioch!" He paused, sincerely regretting the recent loss of such an important stronghold. "Our only relief is that, by the grace of God, that bastard Guiscard is dead, or we would have those black-hearted Normans on our doorstep as well!"

"This is my point, Alexi," said Isaak. "How can we trust these Latins? Lest we forget, it was not that long ago that they tried to defeat the Empire. And they even had the blessing of Pope Gregory! And did not Gregory vow he would raise an army of the faithful and lead them personally to Jerusalem to recover the Holy Sepulcher? What if Pope Urban thinks the same? Do we really want him roaming our Empire with a vast Norman army?"

Alexios shuddered at the thought. He strode to the table and put both hands down. His broad shoulders squared over them all. "Of course not, but it is unlikely this will happen."

"It seems sadly ironic," said Isaak, "that the Normans, who were so recently our mortal enemy, are now our potential allies."

Alexios smirked. "I suppose, but not all of them are Normans and we must do whatever possible to save the Empire. We fight God's war to preserve Christianity."

Anna leaned back in her chair, fingering prayer beads in her hand, moving them one by one. "So how will Urban raise an army to assist us if he cannot even hold the Lateran?"

Alexios dropped his head. "I don't know, mother, but what other hope have we? We need to find a solution that brings the Latins to our aide with the least cost. Somehow, Urban must put fire in the bellies of these Kelts. We need to give him a cause... a cause that appeals to these barbarians." He paused with a mischievous grin. "And I believe I know what it is."

"Alexi, darling, please dispense with the melodrama," she said, tapping her stylus on the table. "What's your idea?"

He became more animated. "The answer is the Holy Sepulcher. On many occasions, I have heard how much these Kelts revere the Tomb of Christ. They come from the ends of the earth to worship it. John Doukas of Dyrrachium met with these men and he confirmed how they remember the misdeeds of Al-Hakim, the Egyptian king, and that he destroyed the Sepulcher. They are indignant about this. There is a pent-up fury here. We can take advantage of it. Did you observe that Kelt in court today - that Drugo? When I asked him if he would defend the Holy Sepulcher, he said 'to the death' without any hesitation. I sincerely doubt he would jeopardize his life for anything else... except perhaps a purse of gold."

Isaak looked up knowingly. "Gold is all these Kelts want. They would kill their own fathers to get it."

"I agree, we cannot trust them any more than we can trust a Turk. We just have to remain one step ahead of them." He turned back to Anna. "But let me continue with my idea, mother. We will draft a letter to Urban telling him the Holy Sepulcher has fallen again to the hands of heathen Turks, who desecrate the place with their pagan filth."

"But Alexi, that's a lie!"

"Is it? The Turks govern Jerusalem and control all within it."

"But they leave the Christians alone. They are neither threatened nor harmed."

"I know, I know, but the Latins know nothing of this. Let's take advantage of it." He took a sip of wine. "And it will be no lie to tell Pope Urban that the Romans, good Christians, now suffer in Asia. The Turks steal everything they own, ravage their crops, desecrate their churches, rape the women..."

"Yes, yes, that's enough, my son," said Anna with disgust. "We will consider sending another letter to Urban. Perhaps that monk could deliver it... what's his name?"

"Ramiro," said Nikolas. "It sounds like a Latin name, like the kind used in Andalusia." He glanced at her. "But I thought it puzzling that the Pope would give his letters to that monk. Why not give them to Commander Manuel or one of our other ambassadors when they were in Melfi?"

"Remember," said Anna as she wiped her hands on a napkin, "that the Pope was once the grand prior at the abbey of Cluny. He trusts few people but his own monks, which means it is likely he sent them as spies."

"I agree," said Alexios. "We cannot afford to expose our weaknesses to these Kelts. We must take care to control what they see and hear."

REPORT: ITALY AND BEYOND

The library writing desk was stuffed with the finest papers, made from cotton they say. And there was ample ink of the best quality and many fine quills. Ramiro dipped his pen and began his first report to Abbot Hugh.

To my Lord, Reverend Father Hugh, Abbot of Cluny, from his
humble and faithful servant, Ramiro in Constantinople, Empire
of the Greeks, greetings full of peace and gladness in the Lord.

By the Grace of Almighty God, we have reached the Greek city
of Constantinople, although we encountered many difficulties
and hardships along the way. I will attempt to recount to you,
faithfully and truthfully, the nature of these events...

He went on to tell the Abbot how the Genoese and Pisans had made tremendous strides in the Tyrrhenian Sea with their improved war galleys and seafaring skills, and how they had beat back the Arabs and took control of profitable merchant routes. He mentioned the German troops and how they had, by force of arms, stopped them from entering Rome, even to worship at the holy sites. And he told Hugh about the Normans and how they had taken Bari from the Greeks and southern Italy from the Arabs, and that they continued to fight against the pagans in Sicily. He wrote, with mixed feelings, that the Normans were Pope Urban's only allies against the German king. Then he mentioned the synod in Melfi and the ecumenical council's canons on simony and chastity. Here, he paused in his writing when a troubling image of Adele hovered in his mind. With effort, he dispelled it and went on to tell Hugh about the attack of the Patzinaks and how several men had died in fighting and that Brother Aldebert had been wounded. And he gave his first impressions of Byzantium, its amazing city, its king, its lords, its people, its sizable warships and its standing army of well-armed men of all races.

But he failed to mention the Pope's letters.

• • • • •

In another corner of the city, a thin wiry man with a big mustache sat in a small, cold room he rented near the Church of Sophia. Wiker the Blade stared absently at his long, gleaming dagger as he honed its razor edge carefully with a fine Belgian whetstone. Satisfied with the edge, he took up a cloth of sheepskin and began to polish it slowly, all the while thinking about two Benedictine monks and a mission unfulfilled.

• • • • •

Ramiro paced back and forth like a caged animal. "This is intolerable! Intolerable, I say! We have been here three weeks...three weeks, Brother Aldebert! And still I have heard nothing from the Emperor! When will I meet with the Patriarch? What am I to do? Symeon's letter was my only excuse to get to Jerusalem, and now that is gone." He said nothing of the Cluny cross.

Aldebert perched himself on a soft couch, spooning a breakfast of yogurt, rice, and olives. "Let's go to Jerusalem ourselves. We'll get Pepin to bring our horses to the city gate. I'm sure he'll be glad to get out of the King's stables."

They were alone in their apartment overlooking the Hippodrome. On Alexios' instructions, Drugo and his men moved across the waters of the Golden Horn to the suburbs of Galata, far from the city walls. But Ramiro had no idea what happened to Louis or Adele. They were camped outside the walls for a time but now the camp was gone. Were they also moved to Galata?

"Aldebert!" said Ramiro with frustration. "You heard the Emperor, it's unlikely we'd make it alive on the road south. And how could Pepin bring us horses unnoticed?"

"Then let's go by sea. I hear they have boats sailing to Palestine."

"Yes, but it is very expensive. We have only a few coins between us. And how will we make any money here?" He sat down with a thump and let out a heavy sigh. "We are so close to Jerusalem and the Holy Sepulcher. It would be a travesty to fail now. And how will I ever be able to face Abbot Hugh if the Pope's letter is not delivered as the King promised?" He thought again of his mother. What if she really was dying? I may never see her again. He fingered his cross, rubbing the bloodstone. And I've got to get this cross to the Patriarch! God give me strength!

Aldebert gazed over the whitecaps of the Propontis. His acne had almost disappeared and color returned to his cheeks. "We could take another walk around the city. Or go to visit Pepin again."

"I'm tired of sightseeing. Besides, everywhere we go that wretched guard follows us."

"Oh, that reminds me," Aldebert said with eyes bulging. "The guard said someone was asking about you."

"Who?"

"He said the man didn't give his name. He just asked if you lived here."

"That's odd. What did he look like?"

"Black hair and mustache was all he could recall."

"Well that could be anybody. Did he say anything else?"

"No, except that his Greek was poor."

"A foreigner then. Very odd."

ALEXIOS

"What's this?" Alexios asked.

Little John looked at the front of the envelope. "I got it from the post office, Your Highness. You said to intercept all mail from those Latin monks. One of them mailed this yesterday."

"Did you read it?"

"Yes, my Lord."

"And what does it say?"

"Nothing of any surprise or import. The monk tells his abbot about the Normans and reports on their skirmish with the Patzinaks?"

"Does he say anything about Byzantium?"

"Nothing of strategic value, my Lord. In fact, he complements you and the empire."

"Very well, let it pass."

• • • • •

A hazy sun cast its low rays through the windows of the Palace morning-room where Alexios sat at breakfast with his young wife, Irene.

"Tell me, Alexi, how went the call to synod?" she asked in a melodious voice, her light blue eyes sparkling. "Did the bishops agree to your ideas?" She wrapped her hands around a cup of lemon tea.

Alexios glanced up at her across the long table. Her blonde curls whitened in the sunlight and her rose-colored lips complemented the taint of her cheeks. He had married her when she was only fifteen and was infatuated with her beauty. But it was a marriage hotly contested by his mother, Anna, who hated her family, the House of Doukas. And it was one of the few times Alexios dared to defy his overbearing mother, even when she cried and groaned, because he realized he needed the Doukas family to hold power - and because he was madly in love. Now, Irene was twenty-three and she looked more alluring than ever. "There is progress, my love," he said. "But the bishops can be difficult at times." He motioned to the servants and they left the room. "They just need to recognize the Pope."

"How did they respond?" she asked, gazing out to sea.

Alexios stabbed at his breakfast. "They argue over clauses, unleavened bread and points of ritual. They say too much time has passed since the rift between our churches began. But by God's mercy, we eventually managed to reach a compromise. Urban must send his profession of faith to Constantinople - and he must accept the holy canons adopted at the sixth ecumenical council."

She adjusted the shoulder of her blue silk dress. "So what was their response to the Pope's claim that only *he* can head the church?"

"I honestly doubt that will ever come to pass. Nonetheless, we can avoid that topic as long as necessary and let Urban believe what he likes. The most important thing is to get some Norman or French troops to help us against the Turks."

Irene picked up the servant bell and rang it for a short moment. "Alexi, you spend much time on the affairs of the Empire, but do not forget your children. They have not seen you for days."

"Yes, my love. I will see them after breakfast."

• • • • •

Ramiro bathed anxiously and put on his freshly-washed habit. King Alexios had finally summoned him. Aldebert helped him to shave his head and face, and to trim his thin circle of hair. An escort arrived at noon, leading him through a maze of Palace hallways to a single door at ground level where one guard stood by. He knocked.

"Enter!"

The escort opened the door and Ramiro entered alone. "Good day, Your Majesty, may you receive God's grace."

"Come, Monk Ramiro, come in and sit," said Alexios as he sat alone in a decorative armchair. His bright white tunic, embroidered in gold and belted at the hip with a golden tie, contrasted starkly with his blood-red leggings and sandals. The room was full of books and letters, and maps were strewn about. Through an archway, the room opened to a wide, flowered garden, where golden orioles whistled from the branches of cherry trees.

Ramiro walked slowly through the room, attempting to read some of the book titles before he sat.

"You are a man of letters," said Alexios. "I can see your interest."

"I am, Your Majesty. Many things interest me." He sat stiffly.

"I hear you speak Arabic?"

"Uh yes, Your Highness," he said, wondering how he knew.

"Perhaps you would like to see our library collection?"

"I would like that very much, Sire. And I thought I might take the time to learn Turkish as well."

"Turkish? Well, I suppose that could prove very useful indeed. If you like, I can arrange for you to receive a Greek-Turkish dictionary."

Ramiro smiled. "Thank you, Your Highness."

"So be it. Please, have some wine." He filled a fine glass goblet.

Ramiro picked it up cheerfully and took a sip right away.

"You have been treated well?" Alexios asked as he settled back.

"Oh, yes, indeed, Your Highness. Very well, thank you."

Alexios clasped his hands in his lap. "So Monk Ramiro, what brings you to our Empire?"

"As I mentioned in court, Your Majesty, Pope Urban has entrusted me to confer with the patriarchs so that we may resolve our differences, hopefully to bring about the unification of the Christian church." He sat on the edge of his seat. "Consider, Your Majesty, the implications for the whole Christian community. Think of the strength of One Church, One Faith under One God."

Alexios scratched at his beard. "But who shall rule this church? Is that not an issue of concern to both parties?"

"Well, yes, I pray that we can reach some agreement on that point."

"Perhaps this discussion is best left to the Patriarch," said Alexios with some impatience. "Now tell me, how does Pope Urban react to my requests for fighting men? Does he realize the gravity of the situation?"

Ramiro nodded. "I believe so, Sire. He attempts to sway the lords of the West but they see little profit in this enterprise. He understands that a greater purpose must be devised in order to provoke them to action."

"There is much profit to be had," said Alexios. "Tell the Pope we have an opportunity to retake Jerusalem and the Holy Land and, in the name of Christendom, we have an opportunity to reclaim the Holy Sepulcher from the Muslim infidels. The soldiers will profit in the booty of war. Think of the riches in Antioch, Aleppo and Damascus."

"I will write to him of these things, Your Highness. And how large an army will you need for this venture?"

"Many thousands are needed. We are terribly outnumbered. I beseech the Pope to send as many warriors as he can."

"I will mention this too." Ramiro paused before beginning his plea. "Your Majesty, I still hope to travel to Jerusalem. It is my desire to visit its holy shrines and especially to pray at the Holy Sepulcher." He was careful not to mention the Cluny cross, which seemed to be the only thing Alexios knew nothing about.

Alexios rubbed his chin in thought. He did not want the Pope's men meddling in Jerusalem where it was difficult for him to oversee their actions. "This is a bad time to travel that road, Monk Ramiro. Only when we reconquer Nikea and Antioch will there be much hope of safe travel to the south. The sooner we receive assistance, the sooner you may undertake your journey."

"But Abbot Hugh said you would arrange for a ship to take me to Jaffa."

"Did he? Perhaps he forgot that it is a long and dangerous journey by sea. We are plagued by Turk pirates on the Aegean and by the Egyptians further south." He leaned on one arm. "Nonetheless, I will do my best to secure safe passage for you. In the meantime, we need you as a chaplain to the Latin soldiers in Nicomedia. There are many more Latins there. I trust you met Humberto?"

Ramiro nodded, but he did not like the sound of this. "But, Sire, I must get to Jerusalem."

"Ah, yes, of course." Alexios tried to look concerned. "There will be plenty of time for that. But if you wish to aide Christendom and help pilgrims to Jerusalem, there is no better way than to support the soldiers."

Ramiro's dark brow converged in a heavy frown. "Is there no one else to fulfill this duty?"

Alexios smiled congenially. "There are few Latin monks or priests in the Empire. And your countrymen respond poorly to our Greek clergymen."

"But what could I possibly do there?"

"As all men of the cloth do for their soldiers, lead them to prayer, oversee their rites, urge them into battle in the name of God, rally them to fight for the True Faith, to destroy these vile heathen who attack the Churches of our Lord and threaten the Holy Sepulcher itself." He fingered his trimmed, red beard. "And if Pope Urban urges the faithful to wage war against the Turks, you will be doing a service to your men and to your Faith."

Ramiro slumped in his chair. What does he mean... my men? Not those cursed Flemings! He tried to remain calm. "And for how long will my services be required, Your Highness?" he asked, fighting to control his mounting frustration.

"I am not sure, perhaps six months or so. Think it over. If this is not agreeable to you, I can arrange for your safe travel back to France."

His veiled threat did not evade Ramiro. "I will give it some thought, Your Highness. I foresee no problem serving with Drugo's men for a period of time, but you realize that I cannot accept any permanent commission without the approval of the Abbot of Cluny."

"I will write to Pope Urban and relate to him the importance of your position here. Surely, he will relay the message to your Abbot?"

Ramiro felt a wave of despondency. "Yes, I'm sure he would, Your Majesty. And if the Abbot does agree, I hope that you will, after a term of service, facilitate my journey to Jerusalem."

"I will," said Alexios, but his tone carried little conviction.

"Thank you. And one more matter, Your Highness. When am I scheduled to meet with the Patriarch?"

Alexios smiled. "I will make arrangements." He paused, changing the subject. "How are your funds?"

"Well, Sire, ... I did bring a purse but it is not much. We were somewhat dependent on Sir Drugo. But now that he has moved to Galata..."

Alexios rose from the sofa and strode to a large desk in one corner of the room. He dipped a quill and scribbled a note. "Take this to my treasurer, he will provide you with the monies you need."

Ramiro got up and moved to accept it. "This is very kind of you, Your Majesty. May God bless your reign."

"And should you accept my offer to go to Nicomedia," said Alexios. "I will provide you and your assistant with a monthly stipend." He handed him the note and gestured again to the chair. "Now, Monk Ramiro, please have a seat and tell me about your journey... and of events in Rome. How does Pope Urban fare against the forces of the German king?"

Ramiro related much of what he knew as Alexios prodded him on with endless questions about the affairs of Europe. After hours of discussion, he rose abruptly to signal the meeting was over. "I'm pleased we had this meeting and I look forward to your response."

Ramiro stood and nodded. "May God be with you," he said as he left the room.

Alexios was satisfied. That should keep the damned monk occupied for a time. But we shall see, I may find a good use for him yet. He opened the door and spoke to the guard. "Send instructions to Commander Manuel. The Latin monks are not to leave the city without my consent. Continue to intercept all messages."

● ● ● ● ●

Aldebert paled when Ramiro told him of his meeting with the King. "And where on God's earth is Nicomedia?"

"It's beyond the Propontis, near the battle line of the Turks."

"Blessed Mother Mary, Father Ramiro! We did not come to fight Turks. We are here on the Pope's business!"

"I know that, Brother Aldebert, but I am no longer sure what the Pope's business is. It's beginning to look like the Venerable One himself condones a war against these Turks. Now I recall how he encouraged and blessed Drugo's soldiers just before we left the outskirts of Rome. It did seem a little zealous. I wonder what he said in his letters..."

Aldebert slumped in a chair and began to rub at the scar on his shoulder. "I have no desire to be a target for another arrow. We should just return to France. We delivered the letters. Our mission is complete."

"No it is not, Aldebert."

Aldebert looked up at him with pleading eyes. "Perhaps you could make a pilgrimage to Jerusalem another time?"

"Brother Aldebert, I'm thirty. There is no other time. Besides, there is more to this journey than my desire to kiss the blessed Tomb of our Lord."

"What do you mean?"

Ramiro hesitated and bit his lip. He may have said too much and warned himself not to mention the cross or the nature of his mission, so he said the next thing in mind. "If you must know... my mother is in Jerusalem." This was the first time he had mentioned this to anyone but the Abbot.

"Your mother?"

"Yes, I received a letter from her when at the Abbey. I thought she was dead."

"By the cross! Then you really must get to Jerusalem!"

"Yes, and she promised me a holy relic. I hope to secure it for the Abbey so that we may use it to venerate Our Lord and the Martyrs of the Faith." He crossed himself and prayed inwardly for God to forgive his mangling of the truth.

Aldebert jumped from his chair. "A holy relic! Perhaps a piece of the True Cross! A Holy Nail... or the bones of a saint! Some have found vials of the blood of John the Baptist!"

"Yes, yes, Brother, I have heard these stories."

"Do you really believe we could return with a holy relic, Father? We would become heroes at the Abbey!"

Ramiro frowned. "Do not let vanity rule your thoughts, Brother Aldebert. It is our duty to the Church."

Aldebert lowered his head. "Yes, Father... may the Saints forgive me." But he soon looked up, his round eyes bulging. "We must get to Jerusalem! We just need some money."

Ramiro dug into his purse. "That reminds me. The King gave me a note for the treasurer."

"Really? For how much?"

"I haven't looked." He pulled it out and unfolded it. "It's quite straightforward, the King has given us... let's see..." He squinted to read Alexios' scrawl, moving the paper back and forth. "No, wait, that cannot be."

"What is it?"

"Aldebert, brace yourself. The King has given us ten gold bezants and fifty electra, whatever they are."

Aldebert jumped about like a giddy child. "That's a fortune, Father Ramiro! That's enough to get us to Jerusalem and back!"

Ramiro sat down with a gloomy look. "But how can I betray the King with his own money? And how far would we get with that guard watching us all the time? Even at the city gates they check the names of all who come and go."

Aldebert slumped back into a chair. "We are prisoners of this King."

"Not entirely. He would let us return to France, but as long as we stay here, we are at his whim and mercy."

"Do you intend to stay, then?"

"What choice do I have? I must get to Jerusalem. I will tell the King that we agree to go to Nicomedia."

"May God help us," Aldebert sighed.

A knock came from the door. They looked at each other. "Go see who it is, Brother."

Aldebert returned shortly, holding a book. "The guard brought this for you."

Ramiro looked at the title. "It's the Turkish dictionary!"

Aldebert raised an eyebrow. "Turkish? I don't see how that's going to help."

Ramiro got up suddenly. "Come along, Brother. Now that we have a bit of money, let's do some shopping."

A JUG OF WINE

The markets of Constantinople were the finest Ramiro had ever seen. The busy shops housed themselves neatly in long brick buildings lining both sides of clean, cobblestone streets. Each shop had its own archway and a locking iron gate, the typical Roman style. Ramiro and Aldebert huddled in one of them, looking over a selection of wines stored in large jugs.

"This is our very best," said the ruddy-faced wine-maker pointing to one. "And the most popular."

"Is it spiced?" Ramiro asked.

"Yes, yes. With fresh anise," said the man.

Ramiro curled his lip and shook his head. "I'm not fond of it," he said, thinking of its overwhelming licorice flavor.

The vintner picked up another bottle. "I've got posca if you prefer," he said, mentioning a sour wine spiced with coriander.

"No thank you," said Ramiro. "It's too hard on my stomach."

"Aah," said the man. "Then you are a connoisseur. I think you will like this." He went behind the shelf and pointed to another jug. "We import it from Mesopotamia. It's made from the finest black dates. "It's expensive but you must try it," he said, blowing off the dust before pouring a little into a cup.

Ramiro took a sip and rolled it on his tongue. "That is surprisingly good," he said after he swallowed. "I'll take a jug."

"This is heavy," said Aldebert as he left the shop carrying the thick, ceramic jug. "What now?"

"Now we find the bookstores, Brother. I'm eager to see what they have."

As they left the shop, two men watched. One was the Byzantine guard who always followed at a distance, and the other was Wiker the Blade, who glared out from a spice shop across the street. He noticed the guard and felt for the hilt of his dagger.

"We should go home," said Aldebert, who was tired of carrying the wine and looking at books. "It's getting dark and the markets are closing anyway."

"Look at this, Brother Aldebert," said Ramiro eagerly. "It's a book written by Saint Euthymius. *Barlaam and Josaphat* it's called."

The book seller overheard. "A very interesting book," said the man, walking over.

"What's it about?"

"It's a story about a man from the Indus. One called Siddhartha the Buddha."

"Interesting," said Ramiro, turning it in his hand. "I'll take it."

They stepped into the dim street as the book seller closed shop behind them and rushed off in the other direction.

"Where's the guard?" Aldebert asked.

"Perhaps he got tired of watching us shop," said Ramiro as he stuffed the book into a canvas bag hanging about his neck. "But he's never left us before."

Aldebert bit his thin red lips and looked around nervously. The street was quiet and deserted. "Let's go home, Father. I can't carry this jug much longer."

Wiker the Blade watched from the dark corner of a narrow alleyway as he wiped fresh blood from his dagger. The dead guard lay at his feet, a gaping slash across his throat. Wiker pulled his head back and waited for the right moment. He listened as Ramiro and Aldebert approached and stooped low when they passed by. They were only a few paces past him when he started out to strike from behind. But he tripped over the legs of the sprawling guard and, as he reached out to steady himself, his dagger clanked against the wall.

"What's that?" Aldebert asked as he jerked his head around.

Ramiro glanced behind. A dark figure stirred. He yanked at Aldebert's sleeve. "Come quickly, Brother," he said in a harsh whisper. "Quickly!"

But before they could take another step, Wiker sprang out from the alleyway as fast as an Armenian viper. Ramiro heard him and spun around. Wiker backed away for an instant, but then he lunged again, plunging the dagger into Ramiro's guts. Ramiro staggered back, the knife jutting from his stomach. Aldebert yelled in shock and backed away. Ramiro toppled to the cobblestones, writhing and grasping at the dagger.

Wiker lost his grip on the hilt as Ramiro fell. He reached under his cape and pulled out another dagger before jumping over Ramiro to slash his throat. But before he could make the deadly cut, Aldebert regained his senses and came running towards him, raising the wine jug high over his head and, with all his might, he smashed it down on Wiker's skull. The jug shattered as it met its mark and Wiker collapsed in a deluge of dark Mesopotamian wine.

GALATA

Alexios paced back and forth behind the long table before he suddenly stepped up to his map and tapped his finger on Nikea, a fortress on the eastern shores of the Propontis, just south of the Byzantine stronghold of Nicomedia. "And to the east, we have more trouble with Abul Kasim," he said loudly to the assembly of generals. Holding his finger on the map, he turned and looked around the room. "...the Sultan of Rome," he added sarcastically. They all laughed.

He continued in a more somber tone. "You all know Abul Kasim controls Nikea since the death of Sulayman and now extends his grip over our eastern provinces. Now, we hear, he schemes to take Nicomedia, the very gateway to Constantinople."

Isaak moved forward in his chair. "Then we should send those new Kelts to reinforce General Taticius' position there."

"I agree," said Alexios. "The Normans are tough fighters and they may as well stay with their own kind. But we must control them!" He looked straight at Taticius. "I want you to put spies among them. Your informants will report directly to you ... and you to me."

"Yes, Your Highness."

He looked down at his papers. "Very well, we will move the Kelts from Galata to Nicomedia immediately."

"I thought you were going to leave them at Galata until the spring," said Anna.

"I was, but apparently they create havoc there. I'm told they drink and fight almost every day. They've been in several drunken brawls with the Russians, the Italians, and even amongst themselves! Their rooms are pig-sties. Our slaves are mistreated, some even raped. They fear to clean their rooms."

Anna sneered in disgust. "They're all the same. Uncouth savages! They seem content only when inebriated into a stupor. Thank God we put them in Galata with the other pagans."

"They are hardly pagans, mother," Isaak piped in. "They are Christian."

Anna's jaw tensed, she made no reply.

"You're right, brother," Isaak continued. "We may as well move them to Nicomedia right away. At least they could vent themselves against our enemies and do some good."

"That's what I thought. They should be able to keep that little bastard, Abul Kasim, at bay."

Anna looked worried. "Are you sure you can trust so many Kelts in one place?"

Alexios shook his head. "No, I'm not. But General Taticius has much experience with these western barbarians. We must trust his abilities." He rapped a knuckle on the table. "We just need them to hold the walls of Nicomedia. And when the opportunity presents itself, we will send them on raiding parties to harass Abul Kasim's forces whenever they stray. They must learn how the Turks fight to be of any use."

"It's difficult to get Kelts to fight that way," said Taticius. They just want to charge in and start hacking." The men chuckled.

"They're a hot-headed race, General, but you must train them. Our success depends on it." A shock of red hair dangled over his face. He smiled. "We'll use that Latin monk to control them, the one called Ramiro."

"Did you hear what happened to him?" Commander Manuel asked.

Alexios shook his head. "No. What?"

"He was stabbed in the markets yesterday, apparently by the same man that attacked him in Tzurulos."

"Is that so?" Alexios asked as he pondered the monk's usefulness. "Is he alive then?"

"Fortunately, yes. The doctor said the killer's blade was slowed by a book he carried in his bag, so only a short length of blade managed to pierce his stomach. By the grace of God, it missed his liver."

"What about the assassin?"

Manuel smiled. "The other monk hit him over the head with a wine jug. It split his skull open like a melon."

"Are there any more after him?"

"We don't believe so, Sire."

"So how long will it be before Monk Ramiro can travel?"

"The doctor said he'll be fine in a couple of weeks."

"Good," said Alexios. "So we can still send him off with the Kelts. Hopefully, he will tell them the safety of the Holy Sepulcher depends on their success, or he can tell them they will not receive any gold unless they follow our directions. Either way should work." The men roared.

Anna smiled. "So the Latin monks have agreed to serve with the Kelts in Nicomedia?"

Alexios smiled back. "With some convincing, mother. It will keep them busy until I find a better use for them. But Monk Ramiro wasn't very happy about it."

"Why not?"

"He said he was very anxious to make a pilgrimage to Jerusalem."

"Good, keep him anxious," said Anna. "He may claim to be a man of God, but remember he is allied to Rome - not Byzantium. And the very fact that assassins are after him means he must be important."

"If he is a spy, I want to keep him away from the Holy Land," said Alexios. "We should make an effort to control all information going west so I will keep him at a safe distance in Nicomedia. Then he can report as he pleases and it will make little strategic difference. Once I'm sure about his loyalties, I may find a use for him."

"How?"

"I'll think of something. He seems to have a gift for languages. I gave him a Turkish dictionary."

"If he could speak Turkish, he could be some help to us," said Anna. "Give him one of our best tutors to take with him to Nicomedia. Someone to keep an eye on him."

"Yes, yes! And I know just the man," said Alexios. He moved over to his secretary, speaking softly. He returned again to the map on the wall. "Now, my generals, let's finish our plans."

REPORT: TROUBLED EMPIRE

Ramiro scratched his head, trying to think of what to say next to Abbot Hugh. He put a hand to the bandage over his stomach as he thought about Wiker's attack. He had no desire to tell Hugh about the latest attempt on his life, nor how Brother Aldebert had killed the man with a wine jug. Poor Aldebert was beside himself for days.

But as far as the rest of it goes, he had been unable to discover much of Byzantine internal affairs. He knew what everyone knew, that pagan enemies surrounded the empire on all sides and that it fought desperately to survive each onslaught. He wrote of the encroaching Turkomans from north Bulgaria who raided and pillaged, leaving death and destruction in their wake, and he wrote of the Turks on the eastern frontier and how they had laid waste to Greek farms and continued to assault Greek cities. He mentioned how the Byzantines fought back with mercenary armies gathered from every corner of the empire, even from the ranks of their enemies. And he emphasized King Alexios' desperate request for thousands more to fight the hordes.

He also told the Abbot how the Orthodox Church continued to defy the views of Rome on a number of issues. But alas, he was at a loss to suggest a compromise. And the Patriarch had made it clear he was unwilling to cede ecclesiastical power to the Pope. On this, he cited the decisions of the Council of Chalcedon and suggested, in his humble opinion, that perhaps both the Patriarch and the Pope could share power, just as the council had decided many years before.

TATRAN

Aldebert ran about the room in a frenzy. "God help us, Father Ramiro! Why are they rushing us off to the end of the world like this? I thought we were here for the winter. Now we're being ordered to Niko... Niko whatever."

"That's Nicomedia, Brother. It's the Emperor's last stronghold in the east. It can't be that bad," he said, secretly hoping to see Adele again. "I hear it has a magnificent palace and was once the capital of the Empire. Come now! We must go. The escorts are waiting and Pepin has our mounts ready."

There was a knock at the door.

"See who it is, Brother."

Aldebert scurried to the door. He opened it a bit and peeked out. A short man with a dark, leathery face stared back at him. He was broad-shouldered with long, braided hair and a thin moustache.

"Who are you?"

"Greetings. I am Tatran. The Emperor sent me." His long braids swung about his shoulders as he talked and his wide moustache bobbed below high cheekbones. He wore Roman armor and carried a sword.

Aldebert sputtered at the sight of the man. "You... you teacher?" he replied in stammered Greek.

The man smiled and his narrow, brown eyes gleamed. "Yes, I am Tatran. Are you Master Ramiro?"

"No, no." He pointed. "He inside. Wait here."

Tatran nodded. "Yes, yes."

Aldebert shut the door with a bang and sprinted back to Ramiro. He spoke in a breathless, hushed voice. "Father! Father! The tutor is here!"

"Ah! That's good... so why in the name of God are you so flustered?"

"Father, he's a Turk!" Aldebert brushed a finger across his cheek. "He's got those strange eyes! And he's got a sword!" He motioned to an imaginary sword at his side.

"Calm down, Brother. He's my tutor. He's come to teach me Turkish. Why is it such a surprise that he's a Turk?"

"But he's got a sword, Father! And he carries a dirk in his belt!"

"So? Any man in his right mind would carry weapons to Nicomedia. He's loyal to the Emperor, Aldebert. We have nothing to fear. Now let's go."

"He's a heathen! He could be another assassin! May God help us!" He made the sign of the cross before fumbling with the ties on his bag.

• • • • •

Clean, gardened streets stretched for miles along the shores of the Golden Horn. Here were the luxurious mansions of privileged foreign merchants, the Genoese, Pisans and Venetians, those who had assisted the Empire at one point or another. Now the Emperor rewarded them with the best markets of Asia. Their warehouses were close at hand, clustered along the waterfront near the bustling shipyards. Other less privileged merchants lived in Galata, just across the water, where Drugo and his men waited.

Tatran led them down to the ferry port. The dock swarmed with longshoremen, carpenters, traders, and travelers from afar. Carts and wagons of goods from all over the known world came and went. A large crane lifted logs from the hold of a Russian vessel, loading them onto long wagons pulled by teams of oxen. Other vessels carried crates of spices from distant Indus or copper from the mountains of Armenia.

Tatran raised his arm. "The ferry comes. Prepare to load!"

• • • • •

Loud cheers greeted them when they reached Galata. The knights were rested. Their wounds had healed and they were once again greedy for battle and booty.

Ramiro looked around the courtyard, his thoughts elsewhere. "Where are the women and tradesmen, Sir Drugo?"

"Only a few were allowed to go to Nicomedia," Drugo replied with a hint of regret. "We have our squires, archers, and a few manservants. The others must stay in Galata. But the Emperor gave them all work."

Ramiro frowned, still looking over the crowd. "And what of Louis the Carpenter? Where is he?"

"Why are you concerned with carpenters?"

"Do you know where they are, Sir Drugo?" he asked with irritation.

"If you must know, the Emperor ordered them all to the shipyards. He's building a new fleet of war galleys."

Drugo appeared to have forgotten about Louis and the stolen locket. But Ramiro said no more of it. "And where are these shipyards?"

Drugo swung his arm north, his chain link armor rustled. "Along the coast of the Golden Horn, further north. But you can't get in. They won't let anyone in or out. The tradesmen and their families must stay in the compound until the ships are finished." He mounted in an agile move. "We must leave." He spun his horse to shout at his men. "Move out, everyone, move out!"

Ramiro tried to hide his disappointment at the turn of events. He spun to Aldebert and Pepin, shouting above the crowd. "Quick, mount up before we're all trampled!"

In an eager leap, Pepin swung into the saddle of his new horse. And it came with a new saddle! He grinned from ear to ear.

Aldebert fumed. "Pepin! This horse does not excuse you from your duties. And put those weapons away!"

Pepin's smile faded as he covered his short sword and knife with his cloak.

"Father Ramiro, how can we permit him to carry these weapons? We are men of God!"

"Brother Aldebert, be practical. These are gifts from the Emperor himself. It would be rude for the boy to refuse them. Besides, it can do no harm for him to learn their use. We are entering a dangerous land."

Aldebert spread his arms wide and raised his voice. "*Yea, though I walk through the valley of death, I will fear no evil, for You are with me, Your rod and Your staff they comfort me.*"

"I know the Psalms, Brother Aldebert," Ramiro said with a scornful glance. He swung his leg over his gray mare. "Nonetheless, I commend you on your faith. May God be with you." He felt for the knife beneath his robe. "We pray the next Turk arrow won't land between your eyes."

Pepin giggled.

Aldebert glared at the boy before swinging back to Ramiro. "You mock me, Father!"

"Forgive me Brother Aldebert... but you would do well to keep your wits about you." He spurred his horse forward to hide his broadening smile and they all clambered to board the ship waiting to take them across the Bosporus to Chalcedon. Beyond this point, lay a vast and mysterious land that the Romans call Asia.

Part Three

ASIA MINOR

~~~~~~~~~~~~~~~~~~~~~~~~

1090

East of Constantinople, thrived a vibrant world the people of Europe knew little about. Although they were aware of the Holy Land and believed it was the 'land of milk and honey' as they were told in the Bible, only a few returning pilgrims had any idea of what it was really like. And even these few knew almost nothing of the triangle of power and intrigue that encompassed the region.

In the northwest corner sat the Byzantine Empire, a tired relic of the East Roman Empire, now revitalized under the rule of the clever and ambitious Alexios. To the northeast, was the young Turk Empire, built on the civilization of ancient Persia and now ruled by the Seljuk Turk, Malik Shah. And to the south, was timeless Egypt, forever a potent force in the affairs of the Mediterranean. It was ruled in name only by the Caliph, but real power rested in the hands of the vizier, Al-Afdal, commander of the armies.

The Byzantines were Orthodox Christian, the Turks were Sunni Muslim, and the Egyptians were Shia Muslim. Although they traded extensively, they harped on their differences more than their similarities. And, ironically, the pathological hatred between the Sunni and the Shia was cause enough for the Egyptians to form a loose alliance with the Byzantine Christians. Each saw the other as an evil heretic or a misled pagan, creating a milieu of animosity, fear and distrust. They settled disputes with pacts or intrigues or, when diplomacy failed, by war. And the harsh, arid landscape of the Middle East was their battleground.

TURKS

The old Roman road ran east, following the rocky northern shore of the Propontis, where it wound through thick forests of fir, pine and beech. Above the trees, gray clouds rolled in from the Black Sea, billowing in thick waves across a brooding sky. Lightning laced through them and the resounding thunder sent a shudder through Ramiro's chest. He tried to look up but spun his face away when a hail of sleet pelted him. He pulled his hood about his ears and tucked his heavy cloak under his legs.

Tatran the Tutor seemed unperturbed by the cold forces of nature. He rode with his shoulders squared and his chin up, combing the sleet from his long moustache with the fingers of one hand. A heavy cloak swathed his shoulders, covering a coat of armor, a long wool tunic, thick leggings and fur-lined boots.

Ramiro pushed into the wind and pulled his horse alongside. "Where are you from, Tatran?"

Tatran rode at a near trot and Ramiro had to spur his horse on. "I was raised in the mountains of Bulgaria," he said loudly. "I was a slave once - but now I'm a freeman." His eyes gleamed. "Tatran the Scyth at your service, your Excellency."

"Are you Christian?"

"Yes, yes, of course," he chuckled nervously. "King Alexios insisted."

"So you really believe Jesus is Our Savior?" Ramiro asked with a hint of skepticism.

Tatran squinted as he forced a smile. "Of course... he... uh... he was a great prophet," he said before praying inwardly, 'may Allah forgive me.'

Ramiro nodded. "And what brought you to the service of the Emperor?"

"I am a mercenary, Your Excellency... and the Emperor pays well."

Ramiro held up his hand. "Please, Tatran, do not address me for a station I do not occupy. You are my teacher. Just call me Ramiro."

"Very well, Master Ramiro." He maneuvered a muddy turn in the road. "And if I am to teach you, let's begin now. From now on, we speak only Turkish."

Ramiro shivered from the wet cold but managed a smile. "I, too, am eager to learn your language, Tatran, but first you must tell me about your people... who are the Turks?"

Tatran beamed as he related his story about how Chinese armies cruelly harassed his people and forced them to flee their ancient homeland near the Altai Mountains far to the north. That was many years ago and they wandered in search of a new home, but the aggressive Chinese pushed them further south and they finally settled into an uneasy existence in Khorasan, north of Iran. He told Ramiro how, over the following years, they were raided and enslaved by the Arabs and Iranians, but how one family of Turks, the Seljuks, managed to free themselves by fighting back. "Then, one fateful day, by the will of God," he said proudly, "the grandsons of Seljuk defeated the King of Iran in a glorious battle. You have heard of the Battle of Dandanqan?"

Ramiro shook his head.

"No? It was a famous battle... only fifty years ago."

"Forgive me Tatran, I know little about this part of God's world."

"Well it was an important day for the Turks," he said, brushing sleet from his brow. "Now the esteemed Seljuks rule a great empire. They are the masters of Iran, Khorasan and Al-Iraq... and now they hold Roman lands." There was a touch of pride and arrogance in his voice, even though he was employed by the Romans. He raised his voice. "And now it is all ruled by Malik Shah, the Great King, the Sultan of the World."

"And he is a Seljuk?"

"Yes, yes, Master. The Great Sultan is the son of Arslan the Magnificent." His long, black braids bounced across his shoulders. "He is the one who defeated the Romans only a generation ago. The Seljuks have taken all of Asia from the Romans. King Alexios is not pleased about this."

"I'm sure he's not," Ramiro agreed. "What of this 'Sultan of Rome'? Is this the same man?"

"Aah! No, no. You speak of Abul Kasim. He claims the title because he now rules over Roman land... although not easily. But he should not call himself 'sultan'. This makes Malik Shah very angry. He's just an emir."

"An emir? Like a prince?"

"Not really... a military commander."

Ramiro nodded. "And have you met this Sultan of Rome?"

"Yes, I've met him," he said with a sneer. "He is nothing. He is a little man who thinks he is a giant among men. He is a sly fox who rules only because his master, a true Seljuk, died in battle. But I tell you the fox plays with the wolf. He plots to take Nicomedia from the Romans. He is the man King Alexios wants us to destroy."

NICOMEDIA

FEBRUARY 1090

The tail of the storm abated and the skies cleared just before sunset. Now they could see for miles along the flat road running east to Nicomedia. In the distance, the long walls of the city rose up over a low hill, where it guarded the main roads leading west to Constantinople, east to Ankara in the heart of Asia Minor, and south to Nikea and Antioch. As they neared the gates, a watchman signaled their approach with trumpet blasts and the thick, iron-clad doors opened to receive Drugo's small army.

General Taticius was there to greet them. Although he rarely smiled, perhaps because doing so dislodged his iron nose, the arrival of more fighting men brought a happy gleam to his eyes. "Welcome, Sir Drugo!" he shouted over the clamor of men. "Welcome again to the service of the Emperor. I hope your quarters will be adequate. Tomorrow, we will discuss strategies."

Drugo nodded. "Yes, General."

"Ah, Captain, you understand," said Taticius. "Can I presume your Greek is improving?"

"I learning," he smirked. "Women help me."

A loud hoot came from above. Humberto was on the battlement. His big belly shook when he shouted down. "Hail, Sir Drugo!" A cheer went up and they jabbed their fists in the air.

Ramiro could not share in their joviality. His quick smile of greeting faded into a look of profound disenchantment. This place was nothing like Constantinople. His heart sank at the sight of the decayed and austere surroundings. Moss and grass grew between stones and bricks, paint and plaster peeled from the walls, no color, no design. Crumbling buildings lined the streets, doors hung askew from their hinges and smashed roof tiles littered the pathways. The filthy streets, the litter, and the stink of raw sewage in the air made him nauseous. He shivered and folded his arms for warmth. Blessed Virgin, what have I come to?

• • • • •

From his room in the dilapidated Palace of Diocletian, Ramiro enjoyed a commanding view of the Gulf of Astacus and the Propontis beyond. The mountains of Bulgaria glowed in the distance. "If nothing else, Brother Aldebert, we do have a beautiful vista. Although I cannot say much for the city below us."

Aldebert looked up from his meal, juice ran down his chin as he talked with a mouthful. "They say this was once a home of..." he paused to chew, "... a home of Emperors. There's a theatre and a large market. And many old temples... though to pagan gods."

"So they say," said Ramiro. "But these buildings are nearly falling down. And the people who live here appear no better than beggars. Look at their filthy tunics and worn boots! There is no color... no joy among them."

Aldebert wiped his face with his sleeve. "They should embrace the True Faith, Father. That would cheer them."

Ramiro looked at him in dismay. "I believe there is more to it than that, Brother Aldebert. These people are on the front lines against the Turkoman. Their fields are raided and their orchards plundered."

Aldebert didn't seem to hear. "What are we to do here, Father Ramiro?"

"Honestly, I have no idea. The King wants us to lend spiritual and moral support to the troops, the 'Latin' troops as he called them. I am no more than a chaplain. Drugo could easily do without us. And we did not receive much of a welcome from the citizens. They seem to despise our presence."

"Have we not come to help them? Why are they so cold?"

"Perhaps they tire of the constant warfare. Turks on one side, Greeks on the other. Perhaps they just hate Kelts. I don't know."

Aldebert got up and moved to the window. "How long must we stay here? When will we ever get to Jerusalem?"

Ramiro let out a long sigh. He moved his hand to his cross, thinking of his mother and his mission. "I don't know, Brother. The King has sent us here and we are at his mercy... for the moment."

RAIDERS

"Good morning, Captains," said Taticius as he rubbed his hands. "I call you together so we can discuss the tactics to use against Abul Kasim." He unfolded a map and placed it before them. "Our primary mission is to stop him from advancing any further in the east while the Emperor attempts to out-maneuver the Patzinaks in the west. Abul Kasim imagines himself as the new Emperor of Rome and we must foil his wretched plans as best we can."

Drugo looked down on the map. His long, red hair draped across his face as he moved his finger along the coast of the Propontis. "What's the distance from Nicomedia to Nikea?"

"About thirty miles," said Taticius. "Nikea lies at the eastern end of Lake Askanius." He pointed to the map. "We must pass through the mountains to reach it." He moved his finger along the south coast of the Propontis. "From Nikea, Abul Kasim plans to conquer this region. He has taken the town of Kios on the shore of the Propontis. You see? It is just west of the lake."

"I see it," said Drugo, staring in fascination, amazed at the quality and detail of Byzantine maps.

"For his plan to work," said Taticius, "he must take Nicomedia. Our job is to stop him."

Drugo tapped his fingers impatiently. "When do we attack the heathen bastard?"

"We will let him come to us. We have too few men for a frontal assault on Nikea. When we travel beyond the city walls, it will be only to harass his forces whenever they stray. Our tactic must be to attack and retreat, attack and retreat." He brushed a hand across his short black hair and adjusted his nose strap. "Abul Kasim will wait for spring. He cannot do much in the rain and mud. In the meantime, we'll scout the coast from here to Kios and take care of any resistance we find."

Drugo put a hand to the hilt of his sword.

Taticius glanced at him. "Has it been a long winter, Sir Drugo?"

"Too long, General," he grinned.

• • • • •

A large fire blazed in a corner of the expansive hall, its loud crackle competing with the boisterous laughter and rowdy voices of the knights.

Arles the Executioner swaggered as he recounted their recent raid on Turk settlements. "You should have seen that little shit try to run," he said. "Ha, ha. I took his head off with one cut - but he still ran another ten paces!" The men laughed aloud and slapped each other's backs.

Taticius entered the hall. "My men, you fought bravely against the Turks today. But do not let these minor victories swell your heads. I have told you all before, you must strike and retreat, strike and retreat. This is the only tactic that will endure. The pagans are experts in ambush."

There were mumbles and curses. "Must we fight like cowards?" asked the big Arles. "Where's the honor in that?"

"There is no honor in defeat, Arles of Ghent. I'm telling you, unless you understand the tactics of the Turks, you will not win the day."

They continued to curse as they turned back to warm themselves by the fire.

"And where are the prisoners I need?" Taticius asked a little louder. "I need captives for interrogation. It is not to our advantage to kill everyone!"

APRIL 1090
Ramiro pretended to read one of his books on Turkish grammar. He stomped his feet on the cold stone floor. "Where's Pepin?"

Aldebert shook his head. "I think he's at the stables."

"Well, when he returns, send him right back out for more charcoal. It's freezing in here. The forty days of Lent have long passed and still this winter is upon us. Will it never end?" He slammed the book shut and put it down. "May God give me strength, Brother Aldebert. I will go mad here - completely mad! Three months!... and still we have nothing to do and nowhere to go. It's a prison!"

Aldebert crouched in a corner of the room. He was mumbling a Psalm as he looked up. "But Father Ramiro, are we not doing God's work here? Our men fight to destroy the heathen Turks and free good Christians from their evil grasp." He quoted a line from his book. "*He subdues peoples under us and nations under our feet.*"

"You quote out of context, Brother," Ramiro said with chagrin. "You must be careful not to twist God's word to suit your own designs." He let out a heavy sigh. "Anyway it could take years to defeat the Turks... if ever. I don't have the time to wait. I must get to Jerusalem."

"How?"

"I wish I knew Brother Aldebert. We're prisoners in a strange land. We know almost nothing of its customs, nor can we speak Turkish."

Aldebert got to his feet and stepped over to the window. "At least you're learning it from Tatran, although it's too much for me, I'm still struggling with Greek."

"Well," Ramiro muttered as he snatched up his book again. "I suppose we may as well prepare ourselves in the meantime."

"Surely you please God by holding mass for the soldiers, Father?"

"Perhaps, but I am completely ostracized by the Greek clergy. They will have nothing to do with me after our uh... our debates over doctrine. All I tried to do was express my views on the nature of the Trinity. They became quite upset. Now I fear to enter their churches, such is the degree of their hostility. And there are no Latin churches."

Aldebert sneered. "They're ignorant fools!" He stared out the window. "Maybe we should try to leave, Father. There must be a way to get to Jerusalem."

Ramiro shook his head with concern. "Brother Aldebert, even the soldiers dare not take the road south. How long would we last? I have told you of Taticius' briefings. He said Abul Kasim controls Nikea and beyond. And bands of roving Turkoman dominate the roads further south, down the Aegean coast."

"But Father, some of the Greek priests say that pilgrims take those routes every year. And many arrive safely."

"Perhaps... perhaps it is not as dangerous as we are led to believe. But in all truth, our black robes would attract unnecessary attention."

● ● ● ● ●

A cold rain pelted the walls of Nicomedia and General Taticius shivered. His thick tunic, wool cloak, and wool leggings failed to keep him warm. He rubbed his legs, thinking briefly about donning the fur-lined trousers worn by these Kelts. He had to admit they seemed more practical, especially in this weather. Servants stoked the coals and brought food and wine before he dismissed them with a wave of his hand.

Ramiro settled into a low chair. Torches burned from two corners, casting flickering shadows across the plastered walls. The men seemed ill at ease in the dim light.

Taticius leaned back. "You have done well over the last few months. Now our forces have some mobility on the coast." He put his hands together, fingers meshed. "But it seems Abul Kasim is determined to stop us. We must prepare for the worst."

"What do you mean?" asked Drugo.

"He prepares for a spring advance from Nikea. His forces are much larger now. The Turks who raid the countryside flock to him on promises of gold and booty. Somehow, he has managed to convince them Nicomedia will fall and that Constantinople will follow. We must prepare for an assault."

RAIN & FIRE

Overcast skies and a thick fog hid the Pontic Mountains from view. Ramiro had never seen so much rain. It rained all night and all day for weeks on end. Rivers of rain surged through the streets of Nicomedia. Moss and mold gained new life, crawling along cracks of stone in wriggling streaks of green and black. The sprawling lowlands flooded, wagons bogged down in mud and people sloughed through mire. But the Byzantines pressed on. Anyone who could walk was sent out to collect stones of all sizes and wood of any kind. Tradesman and soldier alike worked in the armories or reinforced sections of wall. Women and children made leather coats and water-skins and collected wood and feathers to make arrow shafts.

Ramiro and Aldebert, soaking wet, returned to their room as night fell. "Quickly Pepin, stoke those braziers!" said Ramiro. "We must warm ourselves or risk falling ill." He shuddered as he removed his thick cloak, heavy with rain. "Brother Aldebert, tie some ropes to hang these up."

There was a knock at the door and Ramiro answered it. A small man with a flat, round face and a big nose stood in the doorway, his leather cloak dripping rainwater into small pools at his feet.

"Greetings, Dom Ramiro," said the man.

Ramiro gawked.

"Who is it, Father?"

"Brother Aldebert, it is our old friend, Louis the Carpenter!"

Louis' big cheeks cracked into a broad smile. "Dom Ramiro... God bless you! It's good to see you're fit and well."

"And you look good too, Louis, by God's Grace. Come in, come in. You must dry yourself, poor man."

Aldebert rushed over and they clasped hands. "What brings you to Nicomedia?"

"Let the man sit first, Brother!" Ramiro said before he clapped his hands in glee. "Pepin! Bring us some warm wine." He motioned to a stool. "Please, Louis, sit."

Louis pulled off his cloak before he sat down. "I'm here, Brother, because the Emperor ordered me here, along with other tradesmen."

"And what of your wife, Mathilda?" Ramiro asked. "And, uh... your daughter, Adele?"

Louis took a cup of wine from Pepin. "They are well, Dom Ramiro, but were told to stay in Galata. They will join me here at later date."

"Oh... oh, that is good news indeed!" he blurted with a little too much enthusiasm. His ears grew hot.

Aldebert shuffled into the silence. "What will you do here, Louis?"

"They want me to make catapults. General Taticius says he wants ten of them."

Aldebert scratched his long nose. "Catapults? What for?"

"For war, Brother Aldebert," said Ramiro. He turned to Louis. "What else is said, my friend?"

"They don't tell us much, Dom Ramiro. But we've been building ships, one after the other, in the yards along the Golden Horn. And all kinds of siege engines... "

"What's a siege engine?" young Pepin asked as he poured more wine.

Louis opened his hands as he spoke. "Catapults are one type, Pepin, my boy. Some of them big enough to throw a horse. And then there are battering rams to smash through the gates, and big drills and towers."

"Drills?"

"Yes, boy, big bow-drills. Miners get up to the base of the wall and drill through the mortar to loosen the stones, then they dig down 'neath the wall and build fires to make it collapse." He looked around the room, squirming in his chair and lowering his voice. "Dom Ramiro, the Byzantines have a terrible weapon."

"What kind of weapon?"

"It's a special fire, a liquid fire of sorts."

"What do you mean?"

"Uh, well... I don't know much about it. I saw it once. It's a thick, black gooey stuff – smells like rotten eggs but shimmers like it's got silver in it. Burns anywhere, they say. Sometimes they shoot it out of brass tubes, or they put it in small pots, and then sling'em with catapults or crossbows."

"So?" Ramiro asked. "Why not use flaming arrows instead - or burning tar?"

"Yes, that's what I thought at first, Dom, but this is quite a different fire. The flame cannot be put out. It will even burn under water!"

"Under water?" Ramiro shook his head. "How in the name of Heaven is that possible?" He finished his wine and motioned Pepin to fill their cups again.

"I don't know. They mix together certain ingredients. It's all secret. Some say the Arabs and Turks have copied it, but the Greeks say it's not the same stuff."

Aldebert sat back, his heart pounding. "It sounds like the Devil's work to me, Father."

"So when can we expect an assault?" Ramiro asked in a somber tone.

Louis shook his head. "I've no idea, Dom. They tell me little. As soon as it dries out, I'd think."

•　•　•　•　•

The rains stopped by the end of April and the roads hardened by May. The weeks passed, but Abul Kasim had not come. Sentries strolled the battlements of Nicomedia with an eye to the south. Most of them appeared distracted by the monotony of their task but, on this day, one was more vigilant. He peered in the direction of Nikea, shading his eyes from the bright sky, straining into the distance. There, just out of the foothills, a thin ribbon of dust wandered across the flatlands. He pointed. "To the south! Rider approaching!"

Taticius and Drugo rushed to the battlement.

"It's a messenger!" the sentry shouted.

"What banner does he carry?" asked Drugo.

"I can't see it yet!"

A crowd of men joined them. They all strained to the hills. A young man shouted. "Yes! It's yellow! It's our banner!"

"He rides at full gallop!" cried the sentry. The dust cleared for a moment and he shouted again. "Look! He's being chased!"

They could see them now. There, about two hundred paces behind the messenger, and in hot pursuit, rode a band of mamluks.

Taticius recognized them. "Those are Abul's men! Ready the gates! Put twenty men out right away!"

Before the messenger had galloped another mile, the south gate opened for Arles and nineteen others and they charged out to challenge the band of Turks. When Abul Kasim's men spotted the heavily-armed infidels bearing down on them, they hesitated and reined to a stop. One barked an order and they pulled their steeds around to flee back to Nikea.

The messenger sped past Arles and charged through the city gates. "They're coming!" he shouted. "They're coming!"

• • • • •

A whole day passed before they spotted Abul Kasim's army. The Turks came through the foothills by the thousands, gathering on the plains below. Farmers had long since fled and whole villages lay abandoned for the safety of the walls of Nicomedia.

Taticius watched from a window of the citadel. "Look! They bring a tower and catapults!" He said to Humberto and Drugo.

"I see that, General," said Humberto, "we are prepared."

Taticius paced. "Do not allow any miners near the walls. Put people on the battlements to drop stones, get the women if needs be."

"Yes, General."

Taticius watched helplessly as the Turks assembled their tower far out of arrow range. The warriors spread out around the base of the hill, concentrating their forces on roadways and gates. "Captains, we are now under siege," he said, strolling the battlements with Drugo and Humberto. "And we can expect no help from Constantinople. The King is leading an army to Roussa to stop the Patzinaks. We are alone."

• • • • •

Ramiro watched as the Turks assembled their war machines with amazing speed and alacrity. "It won't be long now, Brother Aldebert. They will advance."

Aldebert rubbed his hands in a fit of frenzy. "Blessed Virgin, what are we to do?"

"We will do what we must to survive. If needs be, we will throw stones on their heads."

"But we are men of peace, Father," said Aldebert, who was still praying for God's forgiveness after killing Wiker. "What of the Rules of Benedict?"

"Brother Aldebert, the rules concern only the manner of everyday life and prayer. They say nothing specific about self-defense. If we let these Turks within the walls then you may as well throw yourself from the battlements... because that is exactly what they will do with you."

Aldebert raised his nose in a huff. "Then I will pray for peace and place my life in the hands of Divine Providence."

Ramiro glared at him. "And you will throw stones if you must!"

ABUL KASIM

Abul Kasim was not an imposing figure, nor did he have the countenance of a king. Instead, he appeared an average man of plain features with brown eyes, dark hair and a thin beard. Were it not for his gold-laced turban and the small rubies sewn into his vest, he might have looked like an ordinary man of time and place. But Abul Kasim was the governor of Nikea and now, since the death of his lord Sulayman, he was the Sultan of Rome.

His black stallion pranced through the long lines of men and sunlight glistened from the polished chain-link armor exposed below his rich vest. He made sure all was going to plan and, as he looked again to the walls of Nicomedia, he dreamed of riches and power. I will conquer Nicomedia... then I will seize Constantinople. I will be the new Emperor of Rome... and my enemies will fall on their knees to worship me!

Beside him rode his brother Bolkas, the eldest son of his father's second wife. "You see, brother," he said to him. "We have encountered no opposition. The Roman Empire is weak. The King is preoccupied with the Turkoman near Gallipoli. This is our best chance to take Nicomedia. Do you still disagree, brother?"

Bolkas bit his lip. He was a slim man with a long face and sullen eyes. "By the will of Allah, I agree it is wise to enlarge our territory, my Lord, but why dedicate so much time and effort to the Romans? Did not our lord Sulayman reach an accord with King Alexios?"

Abul Kasim raised his voice in anger. "I am the Sultan now, my brother - not Sulayman!"

"But please consider, Efendi. Perhaps we should take control of the south and east. Already, some upstart pirate has seized Smyrna. Some Turkoman by the name of Chaka. How can we allow this? It seems to me that his forces along the Aegean are more of a threat than those of the Roman King!"

"All in good time, my brother. Think of the riches in Constantinople. Even a portion of that wealth will allow us great power!"

Bolkas rode a little closer, a long, yellow cloak draped from his shoulders. "I agree, but we should be careful not to offend Malik Shah, may Allah preserve him. He is not pleased that you call yourself Sultan. You would be wise to pledge allegiance to him. Then we could rule in peace."

"What does the Shah know about these lands?" Abul sputtered. "All he wants is Syria and Palestine. All he wants is to destroy the Shia heretics of Egypt!" He slapped his small hand against the saddle. "I want Byzantium!" His stallion whinnied and stomped.

"And the Turkoman want Byzantium!" said Bolkas with agitation. "And now the pirate Chaka wants Byzantium!"

Abul sneered. "What do I care about Chaka and the rest? Let them all weaken themselves in battle with the Roman King. The barbarians will take their loot and leave, as they always do. Then we will take care of this Chaka."

Abruptly, he changed the subject. "What of these new mercenaries of the Romans? I hear that the eunuch, Taticius, leads these pale-faced men."

"That is true, Efendi. They call themselves Franj."

Abul shook his head. "I have heard of these Franj. Alexios is a fool. How can he trust these filthy pigs?"

"They are vulgar fools, my Lord, may Allah curse them all, but I hear they can be dangerous in close battle. And they become even more dangerous when their many gods are aroused."

"No matter," said Abul. "Let them pray to their heathen mother-goddess. Tomorrow we start the catapults. "

BATTLE FOR NICOMEDIA

The sun was not yet over the horizon when the first boulder smashed into the walls of Nicomedia. Screams of panic filled the air and children wailed amid the clash of steel. Ramiro felt the building shudder. He jumped from his bed. "It begins! Aldebert! Pepin! Let's go!"

Taticius watched Abul Kasim aim his big catapult for the south gate. He shouted to his captains. "Humberto! Set our catapults against theirs. We have the advantage of height."

"With pleasure, General."

"And keep the archers ready. Allow no one to advance."

Louis ran about the battlement checking the condition of his catapults. His were lightweight, stood the height of a man, and could be operated by one or two men. The lower end of the throwing arm pivoted on an axle wound tight with rope. The upper arm held a sling pouch loaded with a single stone about as big as two hands could hold. One man could crank down the arm by winding the rope around a spindle. Once released, the rope spring snapped the arm upright, slinging the stone into a long, upward arc.

"Release!" barked Humberto.

A sharp whacking noise accompanied each launch as the arm of the catapult reached its stop. A rain of stones came crashing down on the Turks, pummeling men to the ground while others ran for cover. Hastily, Abul's men erected short, wooden walls for defense and continued their own volleys.

A boulder slammed into the battlements, smashing through the castellations and sweeping two archers to their deaths before it crashed into the courtyard, crushing people below and spinning to a stop against a stone building. Before long, another boulder came soaring towards them, scoring a direct hit on the south gate, breaking the beam. A door burst open, twisted and gnarled. The battlement shook and Humberto fell to his knees.

A loud cheer came from the Turks. They shook their lances above their heads all the while shouting taunts.

Abul Kasim laughed. "We will soon have Nicomedia!" he gloated. "Charge the south gate and prepare the tower! Get the men ready!"

• • • • •

Humberto yelled. "They're moving the tower!"

Taticius was overseeing the gate repair. He looked up at Humberto. "Get the archers into position! Keep the catapults on them!" He turned back to the men at the gate. They managed to close the broken door and replaced the locking beam but the gate was cracked and weak. "Quick, my men! Put a pry beam up against it! Secure it with braces! Let's go! The heathen are upon us!" He turned to one of his men. "Get the fire ready!" he shouted.

The tower advanced slowly. Stones from Louis' catapults continued to smash it while the archers of Nicomedia took careful aim. The Turks shot back, aiming for the archers on the battlements in order to keep their heads down while they continued to advance the tower closer and closer to the damaged gate.

Taticius placed more men at the gate towers. From here, they continued their barrage of arrows and stones. The Turks responded with their own salvos. The Byzantines were outnumbered.

Ramiro and Aldebert grabbed stones from the stockpile and ran with them to the base of the walls. From there, Pepin carried them up to the battlements. Arrows thudded into the ground around them and ricocheted from stone walls.

The tower came closer and closer and soon began to loom above the wall. "Where are the fire grenades?" Taticius yelled.

"They are coming, my Lord. They were not prepared."

"God damn them! If they don't arrive soon, our heads will be impaled along these walls!" The tower crashed against the wall above the gate and its door slammed down on the battlements. "Humberto! Drugo! Get your men ready!"

A mob of Turks raged out, screaming war cries but many fell dead or wounded in a hail of arrows. More and more clambered out behind them. And they kept coming. The archers could barely keep up and the Turks began to push them back along the walls. Soon they fought their way into the main compound.

The Kelts charged at them, first with lances, then sword and dagger. But the Turks were good fighters and well-armored. More and more kept rushing in from the tower door.

Two soldiers ran up to Taticius carrying modified crossbows in one hand and a burning wick in the other. From their belts, hung a bag of fire grenades. Taticius rushed them to positions along the wall. "Move! Move! Shoot as soon as you can!"

The men ran to the corner turrets to attack the sides of the wooden tower. "Cover those men!" shouted Taticius. But as one grenadier neared position, an arrow struck him in the throat and he plummeted from the wall, taking the crossbow with him.

The dead soldier thumped to the ground right in front of Pepin, who stopped and stared at the sprawled, limp body. Smoke from the dead man's wick trailed into the air beside him. The crossbow lay at his feet. Pepin dropped the stones he carried and picked it up. All but one of the grenades was broken, their gooey contents oozing along the ground.

Men on the battlements shouted to him in panic. "Bring it up, boy! Get the wick! Bring it up the ladder! Grab the grenades!"

Pepin snatched up the crossbow, the wick, and the last grenade. Then he scurried up the ladder as quick as a squirrel.

Ramiro shouted after him. "No Pepin! Give it to a soldier! Come back!" He ran back and forth along the wall, keeping his eye on the boy.

Pepin did not hear. The fighting raged around him as he reached the battlement. "How does it work?" he yelled at the men around him, but they did not hear him over the din of steel.

Humberto watched the boy anxiously and shouted as loud as he could. "Load the crossbow, boy! Put the grenade on it. Light the fuse and pull the trigger!"

Pepin stopped. He studied the crossbow frantically. He had seen one used before and sat down to place his feet on the inside of the bow, pulling the string back as hard as he could with both hands. But he could not pull hard enough. A mamluk ran up behind him, howling as he raised his sword to strike.

Humberto shouted a warning, fighting his way toward Pepin, rushing up behind the attacking mamluk. The Turk spun around to face him. But Humberto did not stop for swordplay. Instead, the heavy man put his shield up and barged right into the Turk, sending him spiraling off the battlement. He hurried to Pepin and, with little effort, loaded the crossbow. He placed the grenade into the crux and put the wick to the oiled cover, blowing gently. It erupted in flame.

Something caught Pepin's eye. "Watch out!" he screamed.

Humberto turned to see more Turks running towards them. He handed the crossbow to Pepin. "Move towards the tower" he yelled. "I'll hold them off!"

Pepin held the bow awkwardly and hesitated.

Humberto gave him a push. "Now! Now! If that tar catches, we're all dead!" And he spun around to fight.

Pepin looked down on the tower. An arrow whistled past his ear. He pointed the crossbow and found its trigger.

Humberto shouted again, all the while clashing his sword against the enemy. "Quick boy! Let it go before it blows your face off!"

Pepin steadied his wavering sight and, with a shaking hand, he squeezed the trigger. The crossbow recoiled sharply, slamming into his shoulder and throwing him off balance. With a loud scream, he toppled off the walkway and dropped flat onto the roof of a side building. Unconscious, he began to roll off.

Ramiro watched in horror. He rushed to the building, arriving just in time to catch the boy before he hit the ground and they both collapsed to the pavement.

Pepin scored a direct hit on the tower. The grenade exploded in its center and burned with a strange and ravenous fire. It burned bright, like the white light of the sun, clinging to all it hit, sizzling and crackling. Thick clouds of choking, white smoke engulfed all nearby. Then another blast of fire hit the tower from the rear. The Turks inside died a fiery, white death, their short-lived shrieks piercing through the clatter of battle. Burning men screamed out before collapsing into flaming balls of flesh. The rest fell back in a mad panic, stumbling and trampling the soldiers behind them.

Taticius saw the advantage. "Quick! Get the tower away from the wall before it burns through the gate!"

● ● ● ● ●

Abul Kasim watched from his camp. He saw the flames shooting skyward from the tower and cursed as his men retreated in terror. It was already dusk. The battle was lost. "May Allah damn them!" he screamed in a pitched voice.

Bolkas watched the long flames soar into the air. The Kelts had pushed the remains of the tower down the road, where it burned rapaciously. "And what do you propose to do now, my brother?" he asked calmly.

Abul cast him a furious look. "We will build another tower and pound them again with the catapults! We will kill them all!"

Abul Kasim continued his siege for another month. He tried many times to construct new war machines but the Byzantines managed to thwart his every effort. There was little wood available because Taticius had the foresight to collect it all for miles around.

And Abul was pressed for time and money. The weather warmed and it was the season to plant crops. The Turks would not work for free and expected their salaries to be paid on time. Many simply rode away to seek better prospects elsewhere. And he had trouble from another quarter. The rebel Danishmends to the east were attacking his cities. In a fit of desperation, he finally abandoned his siege and returned to Nikea.

REPORT: NICOMEDIA

Ramiro scribbled another report to the Abbot. He described in detail the attack of Abul Kasim and even provided some drawings of the war machines used on both sides. He mentioned the ferocity of the Turks and their skill at battle, especially with the bow. But he also gave credit to the Flemish knights, telling him how they had routed Abul Kasim's forces along the coast of the Propontis and drove them from the walls of Nicomedia. He wrote about the Greek tactics and their defenses, including the strange Greek fire. He told him of young Pepin's heroism in battle and of their ultimate victory. But he also mentioned the sorry state of affairs at the frontier of the shrinking empire. The Greeks once prospered across all Asia, all the way to Armenia, wherever that is. But now they lived in fear of their lives and no harvest was safe. The Turks blocked the roads south to Jerusalem and demanded protection money from merchants and pilgrims. The route was perilous and almost impassable.

He sealed the envelope and rushed it to the courier's office.

AUGUST 1090

A hot wind blasted through an open window of the Palace, blowing Drugo's map off the table. He cursed as he chased after it, grabbing it off the floor and slapping it back on the table. Otto and Fulk smiled but dared not laugh. "Look at this," he said, placing candlesticks on the corners. "Do you see?" He tucked his long hair behind one ear.

"See what?" Otto asked, rising from his seat.

Drugo held a caliper in one hand, spreading it between Rome and Nikea. He lifted a point off Rome and swung the caliper end towards Jerusalem. "The Holy Land is eight hundred miles from here. That's almost the same as the distance from here to Rome."

Otto leaned over his shoulder. "That's a great distance, Sir Drugo. And nothing but heathen Turks and Arabs along the way."

Fulk was not interested. "When does this damned fast end? I could eat a whole pig."

"The Dormition Fast lasts till mid-August," said Drugo. "You'll just have to put up with it."

"How long can a man go without meat, Captain? Not even milk or cheese. And no wine! Christ! It doesn't seem right."

"Don't worry. They plan a feast tonight."

"What in hell is this one?"

Drugo smiled as much as he ever did. "They call it the Great Feast of Transfiguration."

"Can we finally eat what we want?"

"No meat, just fish. But at least we can drink wine, by the mercy of Christ."

• • • • •

Ramiro licked his lips. The long tables were stacked with wine and food; bluefish with leeks, mackerel in onion, grilled tuna, anchovy, mussels, shrimp and lobster. It was time for the feast to begin and they all rose to their feet to sing praises to the Lord.

> *You were transfigured upon the mount, O Christ*
> *our God, and Your disciples, insofar as they could*
> *bear, beheld Your glory...*

And when the long prayers ended, they all delved in.

"You eat too much!" Aldebert snapped at Pepin, who was busy sampling almost every dish.

"Leave him be, Brother Aldebert," scolded Ramiro. "Can you not see he is growing into a man?" Indeed, Pepin had grown considerably since leaving Cluny. He seemed a foot taller and a stone heavier. His voice had deepened a little and fine, blonde hairs grew on his chin. And now, since he had shot the fire grenade against the Turks, he enjoyed some fame among the men. They even talked of his improving speed and skill with the sword.

"It's been a long time since I've had food this good," said Louis. "Although the fare in Byzantium was pretty good too." He wiped his face with his sleeve before reaching for more shrimp.

"So tell me, Louis," Ramiro asked with as much indifference as he could muster, "when do you expect your wife to join you?"

"I was hoping she'd come soon, Dom, but she sent a letter. She's got a fever and wants to wait till next spring. Suits me fine. At least I know Nicomedia will be safe when they get here."

"I will pray for her health, Louis. And uh... your daughter, Adele? Will she come soon or... or has she found a husband?"

Louis shook his head in frustration. "No, she's not married yet. Too stubborn and fussy, I say. Stupid girl. She'll be an old maid soon."

A little elation fluttered deep within Ramiro's chest, but he pretended not to notice. "Yes, Louis, she should marry soon. She's a beautiful girl." He paused a while. "Did you say she's coming too?"

"Yes. It will be good to see them again. I hope they have a safe journey."

For a moment, Ramiro felt enraptured, thinking of her smiling face. Then, in an instant, he blushed with contrition. "I pray so too, Louis. By Our Father's grace, they will arrive safely."

CONSTANTINOPLE

DECEMBER 1090

Winter closed in on Constantinople. A freezing wind swept down from the Black Sea and lashed against the city's stone walls. For the first time in living memory, the waters of the Golden Horn and the Bosporus were thick with ice. Snow fell for weeks on end, covering the trembling city in a thick, white blanket.

Icy blasts pelted those brave enough to venture out to market, where shivering vendors waited painfully, hoping to earn a few copper coins. Commoners wrapped themselves in heavy woolen capes and rushed home to huddle through the night in one small room of their brick houses where mattresses, cushions and blankets lined the floors and walls. Charcoal braziers of ground stone or rough iron were the only source of heat.

But in the Emperor's palace, and in the ornate mansions of the wealthy, sweating slaves in busy basements stoked ovens with wood and coal to heat thick marble floors. And hundreds of obedient servants rushed about to meet the capricious demands of their masters.

• • • • •

A huge map of the Empire, past and present, draped from the plastered wall of the war room. Sconce oil lamps flickered lightly in cool drafts while servants scurried about with trays of bread, cheese and warm mead, leaving as quickly as they came. Alexios sat at the head of a square table, greeting his advisors and generals as they sat. Satisfied all were present, his warm smile changed quickly to a look of consternation. He tapped a wand on the table top and furrowed his brick-red brow before standing abruptly. "This is a dangerous time, gentlemen. I need your undivided attention." The generals fell silent. "As you know, we have had success keeping Abul Kasim from the walls of Nicomedia and we continue to harass his forces whenever possible. He is subdued for the time being and licks his wounds in Nikea."

He turned and pointed to the map, swinging his wand along the Aegean coast of the Asian provinces, to the region south of Constantinople. Then he pointed to the end of a deep harbor, just east of the island of Chios. "But we have more trouble elsewhere. A Turk pirate by the name of Chaka has taken Smyrna and our governor has fled. Now he controls the coastal road and builds ships to take the islands of Chios and Lesbos."

He swung his purple cape out of the way as he stepped to the other side of the map. His red slippers flashed below him and the gold trim on his belt twinkled in the orange light. He moved his pointer southwest to the Hellespont, a narrow strait that was the only access to the Propontis from the south, controlling all maritime traffic between the Mediterranean and the Black Sea. "And, to make matters worse," he said, "the Patzinaks have taken Roussa. They plan to strangle us at Gallipoli."

"What of the Patzinaks to the north?" asked John Doukas. "Are they not a greater threat?"

"They are a terrible threat, Governor. But we are short of men and are forced to make a decision on how to divide our armies." He swung his right arm back to the map. "Like John said, more Patzinaks, and now Kumans march again from the north. As most of you know, they have crossed the Danube and we've been unable to resist their advances. They are on their way to join their comrades already in Roussa." He paused, staring at the map. "We have lost too many good men to these barbarian hordes."

"There's more to it," said Isaak. "It's a three-pronged attack. This is a plot!"

Murmurs of laughter rumbled through the room.

Alexios frowned. "I believe Isaak is right. The Patzinaks in Roussa will attack from the west, Chaka from the south, and Abul Kasim from the east. Our spies say many messengers run between all three. Chaka is plotting with Abul Kasim as well as the Patzinak chiefs. They know we spread our forces too thin. Their plan is to lead a three point, concerted assault on the Empire." He put his hands on the table. A serious look crossed his face. "We need a solution... and we need it now!"

"How long will it take the barbarians in the north to reach Roussa?" Isaak asked.

"Fortunately," said John, "it's a cold winter. Snow and ice traps them in the mountains of Bulgaria. They won't be able to move till late spring. And if we can find a small army to trouble their journey, we could possibly delay them until the spring of next year."

"That's a good plan," said Isaak. "But what of the pirate, Chaka? We cannot allow him to place an armada at the Hellespont... nor to land thousands of barbarians on our shores."

Alexios nodded. "I would say Chaka and the Patzinaks at Roussa are the greatest threat right now. As soon as the ice melts, we will put the full of our forces against them. We need to attack them both at the same time."

"I think we can do it," said John.

"Yes, but we will need every sword we can find," said Alexios. "We must recall the Kelts from Nicomedia. We will use them against the Turkoman."

"But we cannot forget about Abul Kasim," said Isaak. "If he takes Nicomedia, we'll be cut off from the land route."

"That's the chance we will have to take. If we are to survive as a Christian nation, we will need everyone to fight the Patzinaks."

NICOMEDIA

FEBRUARY 1091

A scream echoed from the dungeons of the old Palace. Taticius had caught a spy. Ramiro winced, bowing his head so it almost touched the desk. "Blessed Saint Benedict, guide me to the path of solitude with God and bring peace to my heart." He looked up from the desk and raised his eyes past the rows of books to the ornate dome above the library. "It befuddles the mind, Brother Aldebert, that men could be so cruel and evil. It defies everything Christ teaches! It even defies all that Muhammad teaches!"

"Muhammad? How can you speak his name, Father Ramiro?"

"He is who he is, Brother Aldebert. One should know the ways of the Muslims and how they think. You would do well to study the Quran."

"I can't believe my ears, Father! It's the work of the Devil!"

"Really, Brother? How can you believe such nonsense? Do you see now why you are still a novice and why we restrict the books you may read?" He looked directly into Aldebert's astonished eyes. "Do not mistake me, there are many points on which I cannot agree and the Holy Testaments remain my guiding truth. But truth comes to us in many ways, Brother. From the word of a stranger, from a sentence in a manuscript, or from your own mind when it grasps new meaning. If you could read Arabic, you may see the Quran as I do, full of many ideas shared by Christian and Hebrew alike."

Aldebert flushed white, his thoughts stark and panicked. Is Father Ramiro possessed by demons? And now he speaks well of Hebrews? His heart pounded, fear clouded his mind and twisted his tongue, his breathing labored.

Another scream echoed through the cavernous halls. Ramiro stood abruptly. "How can any man of God condone such cruelty?"

Aldebert could not speak. His fear of losing Ramiro to the fires of Purgatory overwhelmed any reasonable thought, and the screams of torture only worsened his condition. His eyes rolled in his head and he slumped off his chair, collapsing onto the cold tiles.

Ramiro put his hands on his hips, looking down on the unconscious man. "You really are an idiot, Brother Aldebert!"

• • • • •

Taticius waved a letter in an upraised hand as he spoke to his captains and lieutenants. "The Empire is in serious trouble, my men. Another horde of Patzinaks march south past Adrianople and threaten Thrace and the capital itself. They gather again near Roussa. Our spies report over forty thousand."

The men gasped.

"Forty thousand!" Humberto bellowed. "How can we possibly gather enough men to fight them?"

"That's the problem, Captain," said Taticius as he rattled the letter at him. "That is why the Emperor himself has personally requested your services in Gallipoli. He needs as many good warriors as he can get." He lifted his arm and scratched the back of his head. "But that is not all. They say a pirate gives us trouble. He has built a whole fleet of warships and has taken Chios."

"What of Abul Kasim?" asked Drugo.

"Abul Kasim will have to wait," said Taticius, falling into his chair. "At this time, the King wants you to ride down the coast to join him against the enemy."

Drugo and Humberto glanced at each other. They were tired of endless raids – but forty thousand heathen!

Ramiro felt a glint of hope. Maybe now I can get away - leave for Jerusalem.

"Alas," said Taticius, "we must abandon Nicomedia for a time. We will leave a small garrison to guard the gates but, for the most part, the people will have to fend for themselves until we can return."

Ramiro's hopeful thoughts vanished in worry. What of Adele?

• • • • •

"You're leaving?" asked Louis, who was obviously not pleased.

"I've been ordered to join the men going to Gallipoli," Ramiro replied gently. "I have little choice at this point."

"But I haven't received instructions. What am I to do? I'm still waiting for Mathilda and Adele to arrive." His big eyes turned down.

Ramiro deeply regretted missing Adele again, although he would never admit it, even to himself. He put his hands on Louis' shoulders. "Don't stay here, Louis. It's no longer safe. As soon as your wife and daughter arrive, you must turn them around immediately and head right back to Constantinople. Promise me this."

"Of course, Dom Ramiro. I've no desire to stay here myself."

● ● ● ● ●

Aldebert looked despondent. He had just heard the news. "So now we go into battle again, Father Ramiro? Am I to take up the sword too?"

"No, no, of course not. Nonetheless, we still have to accompany these Norman brutes. May God give me strength! Why does the Emperor send me galloping around the countryside like this? I have more important duties to attend to." He lowered his voice. "Brother, this may be our only chance to get to Jerusalem. Perhaps..." He looked about nervously. "Perhaps we could sail there."

Aldebert glanced at the door. "A dangerous journey, I'm sure," he said softly. "And we would defy the Emperor's orders."

Ramiro answered in a harsh whisper. "I have the Abbot's orders, Brother. Whose shall I follow?"

"The Abbot of course, Father Ramiro, but the King has given us a large purse for our services. Would we use his money to flee to Jerusalem?"

"It is a moral dilemma, I must admit. But our loyalty to the Holy Church must precede all other loyalties."

Aldebert looked wary. "What do you plan to do?"

Ramiro shook his head. "I'm not sure... but I must find a way. As I said, if the road is impassable, we should try sailing to Jaffa." He paused as another thought came to him. "And think of this, Brother, our robes would attract little attention on a sailing ship. And by the time we get to Jaffa... well, there must be many monks in the Holy Land."

"Where do you think we could commission a ship, Father?"

"I don't know. But I do know we ride down the coast soon. Hopefully, an opportunity will present itself." He stood and paced the room as his thoughts raced. How much longer must I defer my arrival in Jerusalem? I must find a way to deliver this cross to Patriarch Symeon. He made a fist and slapped it against a palm. And the Abbot is waiting for my report. What will he think? He stopped pacing and looked out the window. Will I ever see my mother again? God bless her soul. And what of the Holy Sepulcher? He slumped into a chair, dropping his head into his hands.

REPORT: MORE PAGANS

The library in Nicomedia was always quiet. Times were tough on the frontier and most of the upper classes had fled for the safety of Constantinople. Those who remained had little time for books or letters. Ramiro could imagine the place was once a grand institution of exquisite design, teeming with books and librarians. But, like most buildings in this sad place, it had fallen into disrepair. Many shelves were empty, their contents removed to safer locations. There was no heat except for a single brazier, over which huddled a lonely attendant, a middle-aged man who knew little of the collection and seemed to care less.

The place was freezing. Ramiro rubbed his legs and pulled his thick wool cloak tighter around his shoulders. Despite the cold, his eyes began to droop and he put his head down, resting it on an outspread arm. His report to the Abbot was already late but, until now, there was little to say that had not already been said.

He mentioned that he was still posted to the eastern frontier and that his movements remained restricted to the mercies of King Alexios but, because of serious trouble from the pagans, they would be moving on soon. Perhaps now, by the will of God, the way would be open for Jerusalem. He wrote again of the countless hordes of savages that, even now, invaded the Greek Kingdom, raiding and pillaging, threatening the very existence of this good Christian nation.

GALLIPOLI

Taticius' army of Kelts left Nicomedia on a cold April morning. Their combined forces proved over twenty-five hundred men, all on horseback. They rode hard down the coast, making short work of any resistance. But it did not take long for Abul Kasim's spies to discover their departure.

The sun sat low in the western sky when the small army arrived at the northern entrance to the Hellespont, where Byzantine ships were going to take them across the strait to Gallipoli and then Roussa, but they had not yet arrived.

Pepin and Aldebert set up their tent without a word, both exhausted from the ride. But Ramiro could not rest. "I'm going to take a stroll down to the water," he said to Aldebert.

"At this time, Father? It's almost dark."

Ramiro spoke softly. "We are out of time, Brother. This may be our only chance to escape the Emperor's bonds. Did you see the skiffs on shore? I will have a talk with the fishermen. Perhaps we can start our journey right away. By morning, it may be too late."

Aldebert chewed on a filthy nail. "I wish we had more time... I'll come with you."

"No. You must stay to answer any questions and to divert suspicion."

"Then take Pepin, he's armed."

"No, I will go alone." He left before Aldebert could protest any further, sauntering down to the waterfront in the twilight and turning south to greet the fishermen coming home from a day at sea. He mingled among them, most of them Greek, asking questions about their trade. Many just stared at him but Ramiro gave no thought to his strange appearance. He asked if any boats would be sailing for Palestine.

The fishermen laughed aloud. "None of our boats could make that journey," said one. "It is many leagues to Palestine. And the waters are dangerous."

Ramiro felt desperate. "I can pay you well... in gold coin."

The men stopped laughing. "How much?"

"Five bezants."

They whistled in disbelief. One of them shrugged his shoulders. "All the gold in the world will not get my small craft to Palestine."

Another man stepped forward. "I will take you," he said in accented Greek.

The fishermen laughed again. "Not in that little skiff of yours."

The man rebuked them angrily. "I know this! But I can arrange passage on a larger ship stationed south at Lesbos." He faced Ramiro. "I will take you there."

"How far south?"

"Not far. About seventy miles. If you like, come to my house in the village and we will make arrangements."

Ramiro hesitated. He wondered when Alexios' ships would arrive and how much time he had. "I need to leave very soon."

"Yes, yes, we can leave at first light."

"Very well, let's discuss your terms."

The other fishermen looked puzzled, shaking their heads as they went back to work.

Ramiro followed the man to the village. It was getting darker and the way was not easy. He could see a few dim lights in the mud-brick houses up ahead. He looked behind him in an attempt to situate himself. All seemed very quiet.

He followed the fisherman to the gray, mud walls circling the village and passed through a narrow gateway. Here, the man stopped and grinned. "Wait here. I must tell my wife to prepare for a guest." He strode to the door of a nearby house and entered.

Ramiro stood alone. He could hear people talking excitedly. It sounded like Turkish.

After a time, the door opened and the fisherman waved him in.

Ramiro walked up briskly and entered. But he was only two steps inside when he hesitated. The room was empty. "What's this? What... ?" But he never had a chance to finish his question. In a flash, another man jumped out from behind the door and clubbed him across the head. Ramiro collapsed to the floor.

"What have you done? You idiot! You've killed him." The fisherman looked down on the sprawling monk and the blood oozing from his head.

The young man stooped, the club still in his hand. He rolled the monk on his back and listened for breath. "He lives." He inspected the wound. "His skin is cut, that is all."

The fisherman peered anxiously out the small window. "Search him."

The young man patted the black robe until he found a pocket inside. "Here it is." He pulled out a purse and opened it hastily. "Look! It's full of bezants."

The older man smiled. "Anything else?"

"Just a roll of paper. Looks like a letter."

"What does it say?"

The man shrugged. "I don't know. It's in some strange script." He tossed it on the floor. "Oh now, look at this." He pulled out a short dagger.

The fisherman inspected the weapon. "Just a cheap knife... poor steel. What's that about his neck?"

The young man tugged at the chain and pulled out the cross. "It's his cross. Look! It has a gem!"

"Give it to me... and the purse. Tie him up and gag him. Move quickly! The Roman army is on our doorstep."

The young man pulled some rope from his bag. He turned the monk over and tied his hands before wrapping a cotton gag around his head. He tried to lift him up. "Ugh! He's as heavy as a mule. Help me carry him to the horse."

The older man smiled again. "What fortune! We'll get a good price for this one. Let's take the road to Nikea. Hurry!"

• • • • •

Aldebert was worried sick. The night was as black as tar and Ramiro had not returned. He waited for another hour, pacing outside the tent, chewing his lips, wringing his hands. *Would he leave without me?* He fretted for hours before, in a final fit of anxiety, he dashed to Taticius' tent. "General! I must speak with you!"

A soldier stopped him. "The general has retired."

"It's important!" he shouted, looking around the guard. "General! It's Aldebert! Father Ramiro is missing!"

Taticius poked his head out, still fitting his iron nose. He looked annoyed. "What is it, monk?"

"Father Ramiro went for a walk along the shore and he hasn't returned."

"How long has he been gone?"

"Since before sunset. What could have happened to him?"

Taticius turned to his guard. "Send out five men with torches. Ask questions in the village."

"Yes, m'lord."

They searched in futility. Several fishermen remembered seeing him and said he went off with a Turk fisherman. They thought that was odd because, as far as they knew, no Turks lived in the village.

Taticius formed a larger search party in the morning and they scoured the area. Nobody had seen him since he left the fishermen on the shore so Taticius ordered a full search of all houses. The Kelts barged through the village, breaking down doors when not opened at their first shouts, oblivious to the fact that no one understood their tongue. They searched every room among screaming women and children who huddled together for safety. And they stole what they could.

Arles banged on a door. It was unlocked and flew open. The house was empty except for some debris and paper strewn across the floor. He looked down, noticing a pool of blood near the threshold. Stooping, he put a finger to it. It was still soft. "Captain! Captain! Over here!"

At the sight of fresh blood, Drugo dispatched ten men down every road and pathway. They stopped everyone they encountered, but Ramiro was not to be found.

Taticius became noticeably agitated. "Captain Drugo, we cannot send any men out now. Look! The Emperor's ships have arrived. We must leave immediately."

Aldebert was beside himself. "We cannot leave now! We must find Father Ramiro!"

"We have searched everywhere, Monk Aldebert. There is nothing more we can do. The very existence of the Empire is at stake! Thousands of barbarians are on our doorstep - and many thousands more are coming. We cannot delay."

Aldebert folded his arms in protest. "Then I will stay until he returns."

"You will not! Look at you! A black robe and a shaved head in this land? You will not last the night."

Aldebert began to argue with him but Taticius interrupted. "And tell me, why did Monk Ramiro leave the camp in the first place?"

"I... I don't know," Aldebert lied.

"It was a foolish thing to do. Now he will have to make his own way back. Get your gear and come with us!"

In a dour state of melancholy, Aldebert plodded back to his tent. Tears welled in his eyes as he began to pack. He set about collecting their things in an attempt to dispel his grief with practical chores. But as he bent to pick up Ramiro's book of Psalms, thick tears gushed down his cheeks, his shoulders heaved and he collapsed to his knees with a wail of despair.

NIKEA

Abul Kasim tapped his calipers against an open palm as he leaned over to study a large map laid out on a wide oak table. He glanced over to Bolkas who sat reading recent reports coming in from scouts and spies. "Well, brother, what is news?"

Bolkas' sullen eyes looked down at the letters before him. "My brother, our scouts say the Romans have abandoned Nicomedia. They hasten to Gallipoli to stop the advance of the Turkoman, the ones they call Patzinaks. And Chaka has taken the islands of Lesbos and Chios where he has built another fleet of ships. He prepares to sail against Constantinople."

Abul Kasim tapped his finger against a spot on the map. "Good, good... all is going to plan, dear Bolkas. Now that the Romans no longer harry us along the coast, we will start building our own ships on the Propontis." He pointed to a spot on the coast, just west of Lake Askanius. "And we will send another force to Nicomedia. Let's take control of it while the opportunity presents itself."

"But we have a pact with Chaka. We are supposed to go after the Romans and stop them at the Hellespont."

"Forget Chaka. He has enough men to fend for himself. We must take Nicomedia."

"Brother, please, I urge you to reconsider. I have reports from our spies. Malik Shah is sending more troops to Edessa. He is angry because you do not pledge allegiance to him and now he plots to send an army against us. We cannot risk losing Nikea. By the will of Allah, we must make peace with the Shah."

Abul's face reddened. He threw his calipers against the wall. "To hell with the Shah! We are strong! Did we not drive those rebel Danishmends back to Malatya? Now we control all the land to Kayseri! The Shah will have to cross mountains and desert to reach us. Our ramparts are high and thick, our reserves are good. We have nothing to fear!"

JUNE 1091

The months passed and Abul Kasim continued his machinations to defeat Constantinople. Bolkas reproached him again, fearing the wrath of the Romans. But Abul dismissed him in another fit of rage.

Bolkas seethed as he stomped to his quarters. My brother has gone mad! The idiot will destroy us all with his ridiculous schemes. He spoke harshly to the guards at his doorway and chastised his second wife as she rushed to take his cloak. He slipped off his shoes and washed his hands in a brass basin. His wife, a slender woman with full lips and almond eyes, offered him a towel. He grabbed one end of it and spoke with venom. "Where is that useless son of yours?"

She frowned and flipped the rest of the towel at him. "*Our* son, my esteemed husband, makes good use of his time learning the arts of war."

"I will be in the men's room," he snapped. "Bring me some hot lemon tea... and something to eat."

She turned in a swish of green silk and left without a word.

He called after her. "And tell your thick-headed son to meet me there!"

• • • • •

Hasan took off his sword and shoes before he stepped in. "Peace be upon you, father."

Bolkas looked up from his papers. "Sit down."

Hasan sat across from him on one of the large cushions spread along the floor. He was an attractive young man with a thin moustache, a smooth face, and full lips like his mother.

Bolkas sat back to sip tea from a small porcelain cup. "Now, tell me, what have you learned today?"

Hasan was the eldest son of Bolkas' second wife and, at nineteen, he was a good spy. "Yes, esteemed father," he said dryly. "Caravan drivers from Samarkand report the Silk Road is open again. It seems the Sung still rule China. Many exotic goods and silks have arrived with the last caravan from Xian. We can buy these through the governor of Samarkand."

"So?" scoffed Bolkas. "The governor is greedy. We can buy silks from Constantinople."

"Yes, father, but they are inferior. And the recent wars among the Romans have disrupted production. Prices are very high."

Bolkas rubbed his beard. "Very well, I will consider it." He wrote briefly on a memo pad before looking again at Hasan. "So, come on boy! What else did you hear?"

"As you probably know, esteemed father, Nicomedia has fallen into our hands without much of a fight. The governor had few troops left. We took booty and slaves... and killed the rest."

"I know this," Bolkas said impatiently. "Tell me something new."

Hasan rubbed his cheek. "Well... we have hired many good tradesmen to build our ships on the Propontis."

Bolkas shook his head. "Why does your uncle persist with this fleet? With this... this mad craving for Constantinople? The Romans are strong again. Against all odds, King Alexios has defeated the Turkoman near Gallipoli. And once again, he has destroyed Chaka's fleet. Now Abul Kasim stands alone. We are wasting valuable resources."

"I agree, my father, the King even now plots against us. He has built many new ships and plans an assault by land and sea."

Bolkas put his cup down. "So now we have the Romans attacking from the west and soon the Sultan's army will assail us from the east. We cannot hold both sides!" He paused. "What have you heard from Edessa?"

"There is little new, my Lord. No army marches against us at this time. The Shah has vowed to defeat the Danishmends at Malatya before besieging the walls of Nikea."

Bolkas stewed. My brother is a moron and will be the demise of Nikea. Our heads will be impaled on the Shah's spikes and set in the market for all to see. I must convince the Great Sultan that I am loyal - that I want no part of my brother's reckless schemes.

Hasan cleared his throat.

Bolkas turned to him. "Drink your tea. Your mother makes it with rose hip. It's good for you."

"Yes, father."

"Anything else, boy?"

"Yes, I hear the Hashashin are causing more trouble for the Sultan."

"Shia Fanatics!" said Bolkas, although a chill ran through him when he heard the name. "Murderers!"

"Some say they are crazed drug addicts."

Bolkas sneered. "Damned heretics! May Allah curse them." But he was truly worried, the Hashashin were relentless assassins. Malik Shah is our only hope of peace, he thought. Our only hope of a strong Turk empire.

Hasan shifted on his cushion.

"Is that all, my son?"

"One small thing, esteemed father. Apparently, there is a Christian monk in our slave-quarters. His captors request payment or release for ransom. They claim he is not a Roman monk but instead hails from the Far West, a strange land with strange customs."

Bolkas was about to take a sip of tea but put his cup down suddenly. "He must be one of those barbarians the Romans hired... the ones who call themselves Franj."

"Possibly, father. His captors wish to sell the monk. They believe the Emperor will pay a royal ransom for him." Hasan paused for a reply but none came. "What do you wish us to do with him, my Lord?"

Bolkas stared blankly before he narrowed his eyes. "Buy him. Offer them the regular price. Then bring him to me."

"Now, my Lord?"

"Yes, now. Is that a problem?"

"I have seen the monk, Efendi. He is badly beaten and he stinks!" Hasan's face screwed as he recalled the reek of the slave-quarters.

"Then deliver him to my chamberlain with instructions that he is to be bathed and fed, his wounds dressed. I will see him tomorrow. Bring an interpreter. Go."

Hasan stood and bowed. "Yes, father. May Allah keep you."

Bolkas sat quietly, mulling over the latest events. *I must find a way...*

SLAVE QUARTERS

"Get up! Get up you filthy pigs or I'll cut off your balls and feed'em to the dogs!" The slave master carried a heavy bull whip in one hand, cracking it against the iron bars. Spittle sprayed into his black beard as he shouted. Long black hair, tied at the back, fell below his thick leather helmet and a black cape draped his shoulders. He was a man of girth.

Ramiro clutched the wall and pulled himself erect. Like the nine other slaves in his cell, he moved to the back, avoiding the shit pail in the corner. The slaver opened a grate and other slaves working outside pushed in wooden buckets of barley gruel and water. As soon as the grate slammed shut, the captives moved forward to scoop food into their clay cups. This was the only meal they would get that day.

If Aldebert were present, he would not have recognized his master. His robe was in filthy tatters. He had grown a full head of black hair and a small beard, both matted and greasy. His former bulk dissipated, his face thinned, and visible sores laced across his head, hands and feet. But there was still one thing Aldebert may have recognized, and that was the persistent twinkle in his dark eyes.

Ramiro filled his cup with gruel and sat on the straw beside a young man just thrown among them that morning. "Peace be upon you. I am Ramiro of Cluny," he said in much improved Turkish, albeit with a western accent.

The youth swept his long, black locks from his face but continued to stare forward. He had not eaten any gruel yet... but this was only his first day. He replied politely. "And to you peace."

"I can see you are despondent, my friend. Tell me your story."

The man scowled. "I am not in the habit of discussing my life with strangers, especially foreigners."

Ramiro grinned weakly. "Perhaps not now, but the time will come. We can help each other. I can see by your hands that you are neither a servant nor a tradesman. And you still wear a fine tunic, even sandals."

"I'm a scribe," he said flatly.

"A scribe and a Turk," said Ramiro looking into the young man's clear brown eyes. "How did you come to arrive in a place like this?"

"I... I was..." he bowed his head and fell silent.

Ramiro tried another approach. "May I have the honor of your name, Efendi?"

The young man held his head high. He was no more than seventeen and a whisper of a beard hung from his chin. "I am Ozan, son of Kubad, of the family Seljuk." An awkward silence ensued. Rats squealed along the rafters.

"You have an honorable name, Efendi," said one of the captives, a muscular young man with brown hair.

"Yes," said another. "How is it that a son of the great Seljuks becomes a slave?"

"Because it is the wish of Abul Kasim," he replied forlornly. "I was accused of the most licentious crimes, but I have done nothing wrong. May Allah be my judge."

The captives nodded. They understood.

Ramiro did not. "Please explain."

"He is of the Seljuk family," interjected the brown-haired man.

Ramiro shook his head.

"Do you not see, old man?" asked Ozan. "I am a nephew of Sulayman, the man who used to rule Nikea. Abul Kasim does not want any of Sulayman's relatives in the palace lest we seek to overthrow him and take the Roman lands for ourselves. So he drives us from power and position. We are exiled and enslaved."

"I pray to Allah that Kilich will return to rule," said the brown-haired man. Others nodded in agreement.

"Who is Kilich?" asked Ramiro.

"The eldest son of Sulayman, the rightful heir to Nikea. The Sultan keeps him in Isfahan."

"Where's that?"

The men looked at him with amazement, wondering if his mind was addled.

"Clearly, you are a foreigner," said Ozan. "Isfahan is a marvelous and wonderful city to the east, through the high mountains of Iran. It is the capital city of the great Seljuk Empire and the home to the Great Sultan, Malik Shah."

"Aah," replied Ramiro, nodding in understanding. The prison cell fell quiet again. His mind wandered. He thought of Drugo and his Flemings. "Tell me, Ozan, have you heard any news of the Roman king and his battles with the Patzinaks?"

"Patzinaks?" Ozan looked around at the other men. They shook their heads. "Do you mean the Turkoman?"

"Yes, yes the Turkoman."

"I have heard the Roman king was victorious," said Ozan indifferently.

"Really? But I thought he was greatly outnumbered." He tried to hide his pleasure.

"Yes, he was. But the Roman king is sly. Thousands of these Patzinaks came to do battle with the Romans and then many thousands of Kumans joined them. But the king, a truly deceitful man, managed to turn one tribe against the other. He convinced the Kumans to come over to his side and together they slaughtered these Patzinaks. Then the king turned against the Kuman, the very ones who had helped him, and drove them north, out of the land around Constantinople."

"And what of your lord, Abul Kasim? Has he given up his fight against the Roman king?"

"No," he said, looking around carefully. "May Allah curse him," he whispered. "He took Nicomedia and now builds warships on the Propontis."

Ramiro put a hand to his chin, his eyes downcast. Nicomedia has fallen? What of Louis and his wife? What of Adele? Oh, dear Jesus, I hope they managed to get back to Constantinople.

A shout rang out through the prison cells. "Up, you sons of whores!" yelled the slave master. The captives backed against the wall. The slaver's whip cracked against the bars. "Which one of you is the Roman monk? Answer me!"

Ramiro stepped forward. "I am the monk."

The gate clanged open. "Come with me!" He grabbed him by the arm.

BOLKAS

Ramiro shuffled into the room, the ropes about his ankles impeding his steps. He wore a clean, brown tunic and his hair and beard looked freshly trimmed. But the red sores on his face were a testament to his treatment. Hasan held him by the arm.

Bolkas rose from the cushions, putting a hand to his heart. "Peace be upon you, holy man. Please, come and sit." He offered him a thick cushion and motioned to his guard. "Remove these ropes!"

Ramiro sat down with a thump and stuck his legs out for the guard. "And peace unto you, Lord Bolkas."

Bolkas was stunned. "You speak Turkish?" He turned to Hasan. "He speaks Turkish, you moron! Why do I need an interpreter?"

"Forgive me, Lord. I did not know." He bowed his head.

Bolkas turned back to Ramiro. "Do you understand everything I say or did you just memorize a few pleasantries?"

Ramiro returned a thin smile. "I have memorized quite a number of pleasantries, Efendi."

Bolkas looked at him for a long time, and then he waved his hand. "The rest of you... Out! I will speak with him alone."

"But, Master, are you sure...?"

"Out! Out!" he shouted and they scurried out the door. The room fell quiet. Ramiro rubbed his ankles.

Bolkas offered him sage tea from the low round table in front of them. "You have an accent but your grammar is fairly good. Have some tea."

"Thank you, Efendi." Ramiro was careful to accept it with his right hand. He fingered the blue and red floral designs on the small porcelain cup before taking a sip, then another. It tasted strange, but it was sweet and appealing. Better than the slop I've endured for weeks, he thought.

Bolkas offered him *khabis*, a sweet made with dates and cream, and *qubayta*, a pastry stuffed with sugar, almonds and pistachios. Ramiro stuffed his mouth. It was all he could do to restrain himself.

"What is your name, holy man?"

"I am Ramiro of Cluny," he mumbled through a mouthful of cake.

"And where is Cluny?"

"Far to the west, in a land called Burgundy."

Bolkas raised his eyebrows. "Burgundy? Never heard of it. You must be a long way from home. But you look a bit like an Arab. What brought you to our country?"

Ramiro took another sip of tea. Many insolent replies came to mind but he thought it best to hold his tongue. "My master sent me to the Roman king to discuss religious matters. I am here because I was captured at the Hellespont."

"So you have met with King Alexios?"

"Yes."

"Do you think he will pay for your release?"

"I don't know, but I certainly hope so."

"What do you know of the King's plans? Will he attack Nikea?"

Ramiro hesitated. "I only concern myself with religious matters, my Lord."

Bolkas forced a smile. "You were caught with his troops - surely you know something about his plans?"

"I know the troops were on their way to Gallipoli. That is all I know."

"How many men do you have? Who leads them?"

"I have no men, my Lord, but General Taticius leads about two thousand."

"And what of these Franj? Who leads them?"

"They follow Taticius."

Bolkas squinted. "Are you attempting to frustrate me, priest? Perhaps, you would prefer I return you to the dungeon for interrogation."

Ramiro clenched his jaw, looking squarely into Bolkas' face. "What do you want with me, Efendi? I can tell you nothing you don't already know. Do you really think I am privy to the King's council?"

Bolkas leaned back on the cushions. The man had spunk. He let out a derisive snort, then chuckled. "I suppose not." He folded his arms and put a hand to his chin. A pensive look crossed his face and slight crease came to his brow. How can I make use of this barbarian? Perhaps I should just sell him back to the Roman king. Suddenly, he had an idea. "Tell me, priest, what languages do you speak apart from Turkish?"

Ramiro rubbed at the sores on his wrists. "I speak Arabic, Greek, Latin, French, Castilian, some German... some Flemish."

"Allah's blessing! Remarkable! But I have never heard of the latter tongues. Are they languages of the west?"

"Yes."

"Can you also write these languages?"

"I am still attempting to master Turkish and Flemish."

A sly grin spread across Bolkas' narrow face. "Thank you, Ramiro. You will leave now. I will give you a room for the remainder of your stay."

"Thank you, Efendi. May I return to Constantinople?"

"We shall see."

"And please, Efendi, what of my possessions?"

"Your what?"

"My money and my cross, Efendi. Especially the cross, it means much to me."

"Does it? Then I will see what I can do."

• • • • •

Hasan removed his boots and entered Bolkas' study room. He felt uneasy. "Peace be upon you, esteemed Father. I am at your service." He bowed.

Bolkas did not look up. He was rummaging through a stack of papers on his desk. "Do you remember getting a letter from the Shah's vizier?"

"You mean Nizam Al-Mulk?"

"Of course I mean Nizam! Who else would it be, you idiot!"

"We have several letters from Nizam, noble father."

"Well, where in Allah's name are they?"

"If you please, Efendi, they are filed over here." He walked over to an ornate cabinet embedded with mother-of-pearl designs and opened a drawer. "Here they are."

Bolkas rushed over, snatching the folder from his hand. He flipped through the pages anxiously. "This is it!"

"This is what, my Lord?"

"It is a letter sent by Nizam's office to all the far western cities of the Empire. He requests translators and scribes for the Royal Library in Isfahan. Apparently, they have collected many western texts but have few who can translate them. This is just what I need, Hasan! Just what I need!"

"For what, Master?"

Bolkas hesitated and looked at Hasan with some reservation. "My son, I will put forth to you some of my ideas. These are never to be repeated to anyone. Do you understand? No one!"

"Yes, of course, Father."

Bolkas went to the door and opened it slowly. He looked out briefly then shut it quietly before strolling to the window. "If one word of this gets out, our heads will roll and our families put to death."

A look of disquiet lined Hasan's face.

Bolkas continued in hushed tones. "I believe your uncle has gone mad. The Romans have defeated the Turkoman in the west and Chaka to the south, yet he still plots against their Empire. Now he has taken Nicomedia and builds ships on the Propontis. He has learned nothing. Soon, the Roman king will send an army against us."

"And so will Malik Shah," piped Hasan.

"Do not interrupt me."

"Forgive me, esteemed Father."

"We must appease the Shah. And do it before Abul Kasim destroys us all. We must find a way to return Kilich, Son of Sulayman, to the walls of Nikea."

"Kilich? He's just a boy," said Hasan before he leaned over to whisper. "Why not betray your brother and rule yourself?"

"It is not a position I aspire to, my son. Emirs have much wealth but rarely die in bed. I am content with my holdings in Cappadocia. Besides, the people will not follow me willingly. They yearn for the return of the Son of Sulayman. He is the only one who will unite us with strength."

"Excuse me, father. But why would Malik Shah allow Kilich to return? Was not his father a traitor to the Empire?"

Bolkas sneered. "And Abul Kasim is also a traitor. Malik Shah is very angry and plans to send an army against us. But if he conquers this land, he will have trouble governing it at such a distance. We must convince him that Kilich is the best choice, and we must offer our professions of loyalty."

"So what is your plan, my Lord?"

"I will send a secret envoy to the Shah telling him of all that passes. We will plead for the return of Kilich. And we will send him a gift."

"A gift? Of what?"

"A gift of a scribe, Hasan. We will send him the Christian priest."

"You do not wish to ransom him?"

"That would gain us nothing but a bit of gold. It is more important to curry the Shah's favor and save our heads."

"As you wish, father. And who would you like to send on this mission?"

"You will go. Prepare for a journey to Isfahan."

"Me? To Isfahan? My Lord - please! That's a one month ride! Even more!"

"All the more reason for you to hurry, my son. The weather is good. You will take five men with you – all family."

"But we will be gone for at least two months, my Lord. What will you tell Abul Kasim?"

"The Hajj is next month. I will tell him you went on the pilgrimage to Mecca."

Hasan clenched his jaw in rage. His high cheeks reddened and he bowed quickly to hide his animosity. "As you command, my Father."

"I will give you a letter for the Shah to authenticate your mission and to explain events." He sat down at his desk and, in a neat hand, finished the letter and sealed it. "Oh, that reminds me," he said, handing the letter to Hasan. "The priest wants his money and his cross."

"His cross?"

"Yes, the cross that hung about his neck. You know how much these Christians like their talismans."

"But any cross will do, father. Why does he bother with this one?"

"Get it anyway. I need to appease this man for a while."

• • • • •

"Isfahan?" Ramiro was stunned.

"Yes, Isfahan," Hasan replied dryly.

"But I hear it is a great distance to the east, Efendi. Many months of travel."

"So it is, slave. But that is of no concern to you."

"May God have mercy on me! I beseech you, my Lord, please send me back to Constantinople. I promise you the Roman King will pay a generous ransom!"

"I cannot. My father ordered you to Isfahan. That is the end of it!" He fumed. Damned Christian barbarian! I must leave my fief and family to embark on this dangerous and ludicrous journey - all for a cursed Christian. Damn my father to hell!

"But why?" Ramiro asked. "What am I to do in Isfahan?"

"You will translate books for Nizam."

"Who?"

"Nizam Al-Mulk is the Sultan's vizier. Apart from the Great Sultan himself, he is the most powerful man in the Empire. It is an honor."

"An honor I can do without!"

"Do not presume upon my patience, slave. I would gladly slit your pagan throat and throw you to the dogs."

Ramiro's mind raced as he studied Hasan. He thought him a handsome man with a delicate nose and a strong chin, covered as it was by a thin black beard. Braided, black hair hung to his shoulders and a long yellow cloak covered his new corselet of mail armor. But Ramiro could sense his seething hostility and felt he needed a friend at a time like this. "May I at least make one request, lord Hasan?"

"What is it?"

"There is another slave who can also read and write. I believe he would also be an asset to Malik Shah."

Hasan raised one eyebrow. "A scribe? What's his name?"

"He is Ozan, son of Kuban. I met him in the slave-quarter."

"Ozan son of Kuban? Why in the name of Allah is a Seljuk in the dungeon?"

"Your master, Abul Kasim, condemned him. He was accused of consorting with his wives."

Hasan turned away, folding his arms. My father is right, he thought, my uncle has gone mad. If the Sultan hears that one of his kin suffers at the hands of Abul Kasim, he will have an even greater pretense to send his armies against us. But if I free him and take him with me, it may help my negotiations. He turned back. "I will see what I can do."

"Thank you, Efendi. And ah... just one other matter...did you find my things? I don't care about the money but I would like my cross."

"Your money? I know nothing of your money."

Ramiro sighed. "And what of the cross?"

Hasan dug into his pocket. "You mean this wretched thing?"

Ramiro looked down on the remains of his cross. It was in two pieces. The slavers had torn off the arm and pried the beautiful bloodstone from its setting, leaving splinters and a rough gouge. His heart leapt to his throat. The message! Was it removed? Was there a message? Slowly, he picked the two pieces from Hasan's hand, looking at them closely. But he could see no cavities. What will I say to the Patriarch when he sees this? Tears of frustration and grief welled in his eyes as he tried to refit the arm. He shook his head in disbelief. "It's mutilated!"

Hasan hissed. "Ignorant Christian! It's an icon... superstitious and idolatrous! Sinful in the eyes of Allah."

"I am not ashamed to be a Christian, my Lord," Ramiro said with strong conviction. "My cross reminds me of my duty to God," he pointed to a small tubular amulet hanging from Hasan's neck. "Just as that amulet you wear reminds you of Allah. Can you deny me that?"

Hasan touched his amulet briefly. "What do you know of my amulet?"

"I know it contains chosen verses from the Quran. And that you believe it will protect you from the Evil Eye and other unseen perils."

Hasan smirked. "Impudent slave... you had better watch your tongue or it will be cut out."

TO CILICIA

Hasan and his five men raced out of the southern gate of Nikea in the cold light of a full moon. With Ramiro and Ozan in tow, they pushed east, making their way up the steep mountains bordering Lake Askanius, and they kept riding until they were well out of sight of the city walls. Up and up they went, following tight winding trails until, by evening, they came to the dry, grassy Plains of Dorylaeum set amid the rolling hills of the vast Anatolian Plateau.

Ramiro marveled at the horse he rode, a sleek and spirited gelding, faster than any he had ridden before. Lean, quick and strong, the beast could keep a steady canter for miles at a stretch. When prodded, it would run at terrifying speeds, even along thin mountain passes. And now on the open plain, it charged fast and smooth. His ears whistled in a hot wind.

He tried not to think of the rattling chain that bound his wrists and locked him to the saddle. And he tried not to think of Jerusalem and his mission. But he began to wonder if he would ever again return to the Abbey of Cluny, or if he would ever again see Aldebert, or Pepin or Louis or... Adele. Dear God, somehow I must escape!

He felt for the cross around his neck. He had taken the time to repair it by binding the arm with string, which he wrapped in a tight crisscross pattern. Hasan, of all people, told him to wear it conspicuously because, despite his scorn for it, he knew all Christians must wear one in Muslim lands.

Ozan rode alongside, but he was not encumbered by chains. He was Seljuk, so Hasan freed him as soon as they were out of the gates.

They camped near the ruins of a Roman trading post just as the sun settled below distant mountains. And here they washed in preparation for *salat*, the time of ritual prayer. Before sunset, Hasan said '*Allahu Akbar*' aloud and they all knelt on the hard ground, prostrating themselves before God, facing the Kaaba Mosque in Mecca, far to the south.

Ramiro knelt too, praying in his own way.

> *Support me, O Lord, according to your word and*
> *I shall live*
> *Let me not be disappointed in my hope*
> *Glory be to the Father and to the Son and to the*
> *Holy Spirit...*

• • • • •

At morning light, Hasan gave strict orders to fill every water skin and canteen for the ride to Iconium. They would stop at every watering hole to allow the horses a long drink. The dreaded sun was on the rise and soon it would torment them with its blistering heat.

Before long, the air was as hot as the blast of a kiln and the whole ground shimmered with heat-waves along the shadowless road snaking southeast, where it skirted the arid northern foothills of the Taurus Mountains. They entered a wasteland. Whole villages lay abandoned, wells blocked up, cisterns ruined, fields uncultivated, roads and bridges in a state of decay. This was the work of the Turkoman, who raided, pillaged and scorched the earth, forcing Greek Christians to flee in their wake.

Ramiro covered his head with a small turban and, despite the heat, he draped a thin, wool cloak over it to hide the sun. Every beat of his heart pounded in his head. He swooned and panted for breath.

Water ran short and the horses stumbled, forcing them to dismount. Trudging on foot, nearly fainting from exhaustion and thirst, they finally found relief at a small town nestled in the mountains, one of the few places spared by the Turks. Here they refreshed themselves, bought supplies and took rest at an inn before preparing for the last leg to Iconium.

Three days later, when they reached the green valley of Meram, Iconium seemed like a veritable oasis. Rivers drained from the nearby mountains, flowing across the valley to irrigate hundreds of fields, orchards and vineyards before petering out in the lifeless desert.

"You see, slave?" asked Hasan waving his arm in a broad arc. "You see all this land to the north?"

Ramiro looked north across an immense barren land where lakes dried to a white salt and lifeless volcanic peaks pierced the rocky soil. To the east, the Taurus range rose suddenly from the plateau, towering almost two miles above them. "I see it," he said.

"That is Cappadocia - that is my land," Hasan said with pride. "My father seized it from the Romans. One day, by the will of Allah, we will rule the whole Roman Empire and the Romans will be our slaves, just as you are."

• • • • •

The ride to Iconium had been torturous, but the ride to Heraclea at the base of the Taurus proved to be the most pressing journey of all. Hasan heard of its dangers and bought a mule to carry extra water. They trudged on across the searing, waterless and lifeless land and, weak with fatigue, eventually arrived at the green foothills, entering the cool reprieve of mountain forests, thick with fir and black pine.

But the beauty of the mountains had its own lurking perils. The wooded pass, known as the Cilician Gate, was a dangerous route ideal for ambush from cliffs overhead. Armenian Christians stalked these mountains after fleeing the advancing Turks. Many of them still professed loyalty to the Byzantine emperor and, as a matter of course, they did not receive Turks kindly. The men of Nikea soon discovered this. They no sooner entered the pass when an armed band of Armenians rode out from a military checkpoint to challenge them.

"Halt," cried the lead man who, like the others, dressed in billowing tunics and pants, striped in vibrant colors. "You enter the land of Oshin, son of

Hatoum." It was clear these men were Turks. "You must pay the toll or turn back," he said without pleasantries.

"We will pay your toll," said Hasan calmly, "and leave you in peace." But when they demanded one dinar, he was incensed. "That is outrageous!"

"That is the fee for Turks," said the man with undisguised hostility. "Give us no trouble or we will hang your heads from the trees as a warning to others."

The Armenians were not the only predators along this route. The place teemed with bears, wolves, jackals and wildcats, all surviving on plentiful herds of deer and mountain goat. And when Hasan and his men made camp, it seemed they were hunted too.

· · · · ·

"Cursed Armenians!" Hasan seethed as he warmed his hands over the fire. "One day, by the will of Allah, we will destroy them all!"

They wrapped their cloaks tight to keep warm in the cool mountain air. Ozan and Ramiro sat together. Ozan felt he owed a debt of honor to Ramiro for saving him from Abul Kasim's dungeon, and perhaps a tortured death. They had talked often on this journey and came to like each other, though Ozan was careful to appear indifferent.

"Who are these Armenians?" Ramiro asked Hasan. Ozan tugged nervously at his sleeve, urging him to keep quiet.

Hasan glared at him. "How many times must I tell you, slave? You will not speak without permission!"

"Perhaps we should cut off a finger to remind him," said Sebuk, a brother of Hasan.

Ramiro could abide Hasan, who was a devout man of some moral character, but he detested Sebuk, a cold, heartless creature with a hateful, sneering face that seemed to delight in cruelty. "If you cut off my fingers, Efendi, what good will I be to the Sultan?"

Sebuk rose up in fury and belted him across the face. "Know your place, slave! Or I will gouge out your eyes and throw you to the jackals!"

Ramiro staggered from the blow and put a hand to his cheek. "Then kill me now!" he shouted, red-faced, "so that I no longer have to endure your vile presence!"

Sebuk flushed and drew his sword. "Stinking kafir!" He raised it to strike. "Son of pig shit!"

"Stop!" Hasan shouted. "That is enough!"

Sebuk sheathed his sword slowly before he sat down again, glaring at Ramiro with thin, dark eyes.

• • • • •

On a hot August day, they began a steep descent from the mountains, passing through pistachio forests and ripe olive groves before coming to the wide, fertile Plain of Cilicia hemmed between the mountains and the sea. Ramiro looked down on the green plain far below. It seemed as flat as the vast ocean beyond and spread eastward like a green blanket for as far as the eye could see, right up to the mountains of Hatay on the Syrian coast. When Hasan told them they were going to Cilicia, he thought little of it, although the name sounded remotely familiar. It was only when he heard they were heading to the city of Tarsus at the foot of the mountain did the truth come to mind. Tarsus! – home of the blessed Saint Paul! What fortune! Perhaps God does not curse me, after all.

EDESSA

Hasan pressed them on for Edessa, leaving the lush plain of Cilicia by way of the Syrian Gate to the east. They travelled past ancient Antep, crossing smooth rolling mountains where only a few trees of hardy black pine managed to survive alongside cultivated groves of pistachio. Off the mountain and down they rode until the path flattened onto the rolling Plain of Haran where a ferry waited to take them across the gray waters of the mythical Euphrates. From here, it was only a day's ride to Edessa, a city once conquered by a Macedonian, a man known in these parts as Alexander the Infamous.

Edessa, the birthplace of King Nimrod who built the Tower of Babylon, lies near the center of the Haran plain. Here, it is ringed on three sides by low limestone hills that rise up to a plateau and mountains beyond. Its high walls, built by the Romans centuries before, loomed above the flatlands. So protected, it controlled the road running south into a vast alluvial lowland, a place the Greeks call Mesopotamia, 'The Land between the Rivers.' But the Arabs call it Al-Jazeera, 'The Island,' and among the Persians it is Al-Iraq, 'The Lowlands.'

Edessa, rich in commerce and a powerful regional center, was a sophisticated city with churches, schools, mosques and monasteries. It was the first city to embrace Christianity under Armenian rule. Once ruled by Arabs long before the coming of Muhammad, it passed between Armenians, Romans, and Persians before falling to the newly invigorated Muslim Arabs in 638. It was now ruled by the Turks under the Sultan, Malik Shah, who seized it only four years prior.

Outside the city gates, and crushed along its walls, hundreds of busy caravans gathered to exchange cargo. Men rushed about in a flurry of activity, shouting and cursing, loading hundreds of camels, horses, mules and donkeys, ready to begin travel to all cardinal points.

• • • • •

Ramiro wallowed in thick, billowing clouds of steam. He was naked except for his breeches and the mended cross about his neck. Sweat drenched his face and body, emphasizing the strong tone of his muscles. His face and neck, burned by the summer sun, stood out against his pale skin. "How I love these Roman baths! Can there be a more refreshing feeling, Ozan?"

Ozan lay on his stomach while a servant scrubbed his back with a soapy sponge. "We call them Turkish baths, Ramiro. But I agree, I cannot think of any alternative at the moment. Albeit, if I have to ride another day, I fear there will be little left of my ass."

Ramiro laughed lightly. "Tell me, Ozan, if I am a slave, why am I allowed such treatment."

"Because you are a valuable slave, Ramiro. Hasan wants you in good condition before we reach the Sultan. Besides, we Turks are not barbarians. Slaves are given opportunities and can advance in rank." A servant poured cold water over him. Ozan shivered as the soap washed away, exposing his sleek copper skin.

Ramiro waited for the servant to leave. "Ozan, tell me, how far is Jerusalem?"

Ozan laughed mockingly. "For a man who can speak many languages and who claims to have read so much, you seem very stupid about many great places and people."

Ramiro blushed. "And what do you know of *my* land and people?"

"I know you come from a distant wilderness inhabited by crude barbarians. And I have met many of your kind from the west. I admit, most are not like you, they are ignorant and vulgar and have not learned to wash."

"I could agree." Ramiro chuckled. "But what do you know of our famous people and places?"

"Why is that important? Is your civilization as great as that of the Romans? Are your backward villages as significant as the magnificent cities and wonders of the great Seljuk Empire?"

"Do you know what our cities are like?"

"Well, you must know. So tell me, are they as wonderful?"

Ramiro sighed in resignation. "No, they are not... so how far is Jerusalem?"

"It's about one hundred and fifty farsakhs." Ozan moved his fingers in thought. "Over six hundred of your Roman miles. That's at least ten day's ride from here."

"Only ten days!" Ramiro said a bit too loud. He waited for the servant to leave before he spoke again. "Ozan," he said softly, "I have told you that I must get to Jerusalem. Do you think there is any way to escape?"

Ozan's eyes went wide with shock. He put a hand to Ramiro's lips and waved a finger of silence before getting up to inspect every corner of the steam room. Satisfied, he sat closer. "A very stupid idea, Ramiro. It is my job to watch you. Do you want me to lose my head too? Look at the robes you must wear, the cloth of a slave. And by your accent alone, people know you are not one of us. And where are your papers?"

"My papers?"

"Yes, man. People are known by the papers they carry, even slaves have them when they travel. Only the rebel Turkoman roam with impunity."

"I have no papers."

"That's my point. Any free man could seize you as a runaway slave. You have no family here, no tribe, there is no one to speak for you, no one to wield a sword for you. Say no more of this or we will be whipped and chained in our rooms."

"Can you show me one of these papers?"

"Sure, when we get back to our room."

Ramiro fingered his damaged cross. He had sanded the edges but it still bore the rough gouge suffered when the bloodstone was pried out. Its original chain was gone, now replaced with a leather strap.

Ozan pointed at it. "Do you worship it?"

Ramiro looked at him then glanced down to his cross. "No, I do not worship it. It only reminds me to worship God."

"Muslims have no idols. There is only one God... and He is so great, He cannot be portrayed with idols or pictures."

"I understand your words, Ozan. And, yes, many Christians revere sacred objects and let their minds fall from God's way. But to me, this cross is a symbol of many things. For instance, when they nailed Jesus to the cross, he did not cry out in anger or pain. Instead, he asked God to forgive the man who drove the stakes through his hands. That, I believe, is the response of a powerful and holy man."

Ozan scoffed. "He sounds like a weakling! And if he was so powerful, why did he allow the Romans to execute him in the first place?"

"Well, Ozan, I think I can explain..."

Heavy boots clapped on the tiles. It was Hasan. "Your bath is finished. Tomorrow we leave for Mosul."

• • • • •

Ramiro slipped from his bed in the dark of night. Fully dressed, he picked up a small bundle of things he had collected secretly. The room was quiet except for the sound of Ozan snoring. He peered out the window. The moonlit street one story below was empty. He crept to the door in bare feet, holding his shoes and the bundle in one hand, and opened it a crack. By the dim light of an oil lamp, he could see one of the men slouched in his chair, breathing heavily. He watched him for several minutes until he was certain he was sleeping. Then he opened the door a little more. The hinges creaked and the guard stirred. He held his breath. All was still. He stepped out slowly and, without a sound, tread lightly down the steps. The inn was quiet and dark. He tried to see the front door but could not. Carefully, with an arm outstretched, he felt his way along the furniture, the faint moonlight in one window was his only reference. Just two more steps. But his foot hit the leg of a table with a thump. He froze in silence. All was quiet and he continued to grope in the direction of the door. He touched the wall and ran his hand across it until he felt the latch. It was barred on the inside. He tried to move the iron shaft but it was stiff. He wiggled it in slight movements and it began to squeal from the effort. He stopped again and worked up some spittle, applying it as lubrication. He pulled again and it moved silently.

Outside, he put on his boots and a long cloak taken from his bag and walked briskly down the cobblestone street, heading for the city gate. It was almost dawn. The gate was closed and barred, illuminated on either side by flaming torches. Two sentries stood talking.

They noticed him approach. "Where are you going at this hour?"

"Peace be upon you," said Ramiro. "I leave to join a caravan."

The sentry noticed his accent. "What caravan?"

"There is one leaving for Jerusalem at first light."

"Show me your papers."

Ramiro reached into his bundle and brought out a fresh sheet of paper. He gave it to the sentry and waited in trepidation. He had gone to the library yesterday after seeing Ozan's identification. He hoped his forgery would pass the guard's scrutiny in this dim light.

The guard looked at the paper. "Khoril Far? An Armenian. What was your business in Edessa?"

"Only to rest before I resume my journey."

The sentry returned his paper. "Very well, on your way." He opened a small door set in the larger gate and let him through.

Ramiro headed straight for the caravans parked outside the city walls. "May God forgive my deceit," he muttered. The sky lightened and he could see the caravan drivers preparing their mules and camels. He approached one. "Peace be upon you."

"And to you, peace," the driver replied.

"Do you travel to Jerusalem?"

The driver stood in a long green tunic, wearing a small turban of the same color. "No, we head north for Kayseri."

"Is anyone here going to Jerusalem?"

"Not that I know of. You could see Mahmoud over there." He pointed to another caravan. "He heads for Aleppo."

"Thank you." Ramiro said, and made his way over.

"Aleppo? I will take you there, stranger," replied the burly Iranian. "For one dinar."

Ramiro rummaged through his bag and pulled out several coins, showing them to the driver. He had no idea what they were worth.

The Iranian looked at the coins in his outstretched hand. "For this, I will take you one farsakh," he scoffed.

"Perhaps I could be of use?"

"Have you driven camels before?"

"No, but I speak many languages."

The Iranian laughed and held up his whip. "The camels speak only one language."

A shout came from the gate and the large doors began to creak open. Ramiro left the driver suddenly, rushing across a harvested field to a nearby village. He was halfway there when Hasan and three others rode out. There was nowhere to hide. He ran into the village where he managed to slip behind a tall, conical silo.

Hasan shouted to the caravan drivers. "Runaway slave! Runaway slave!" The Iranian driver pointed down the road to the village and Hasan rode off in pursuit.

Ramiro saw him coming and cowered in the crevice of a wall. But a farmer waved his arms to catch Hasan's attention, pointing to his hiding spot. Ramiro took off again, running through the narrow streets looking for shelter. The peasants dodged him in fear, running to their small houses and slamming shut their doors.

Hasan charged into the village. He spotted Ramiro dashing down a dirt lane and went after him.

Ramiro ran as fast as he could, gasping for breath. He sprinted out of the village, but there was nowhere to hide. He looked back to see Hasan bearing down on him, he stumbled, tripped and crashed head first onto the rocky ground.

MOSUL

A fresh welt burned on Ramiro's left cheek. He was cut, sore and bruised from his fall, and from the beating he received afterwards. They put a rope around his neck and tied it to his saddle before cinching it again to Hasan's horse.

Ramiro hung his head, fighting against his deepening depression. Every day, Jerusalem becomes further and further away. And what can I do? Now we travel east again. Always east. Always away from glorious Jerusalem. How many years will it take? Does my mother still live? Will I ever reach the Tomb of Our Lord? He raised his face to the sun and prayed. Father in Heaven, deliver me from the clutches of Greeks and Turks. Guide my path to your Holy City. He looked up to the steep mountains on his right, and to the snowy peaks beyond. I wonder how Brother Aldebert is doing, poor lad. At least Pepin has some sense. Then he turned to look left, to the expansive lowland that ran flat, straight to the horizon. And I hope Adele is safe.

They could already see Mosul, miles in the distance. The city seemed to stand above the flat plain, its eerie mirage rippling in the hot air. All around them, vast fields of ripened cotton rose and fell in an undulating sea of white bolls. The road was thick with caravans carrying all kinds of strange goods, some from as far away as China.

But Hasan had little time for Mosul and headed to one of the many ferries crossing the Tigris. From there, they followed the foothills south to Kirkuk where they skirted the Diyala Plain before heading east, up into the thick Zagros Mountains of eastern Iran.

Part Four

IRAN

~~~~~~~~~~~~~~~~~~~~~~~~~~~

ARYANS

Iran is a vast, rugged country with steep mountains, salt deserts, and rich river valleys. Few travelers can follow its meandering paths through thin forests of scrub oak and pistachio without sensing the great antiquity of the land, a place called Parsa by the Achaemenids, Persis by the Greeks, and Persia by the Latins. But for thousands of years, the people of this turbulent land have called themselves Aryans, and Iran is the Land of the Aryans.

It was here, in the time of the Biblical Abraham, that Zoroaster taught his people to worship the One God, Ahuramazda. It was here, in this harsh land, where the Medes built the first Iranian Empire over two thousand seven hundred years ago. And centuries later, under the rule of the Achaemenids, it became the largest and most powerful empire in the known world, stretching from the Mediterranean Sea to the mountains of China. These were the Persians, the chronic archenemies of the Greeks and Romans.

But over time, this great empire weakened, as all do, and eventually it succumbed to the armies of Alexander the Macedonian in 330 BC. It was resurrected for a time by Sassanids and Parthians, only to fall again to Muslim Arabs in the seventh century, and then to invading Turks four hundred years later.

While King Alexios fought desperately to save the crumbling Byzantine Empire, the Turk Empire flowered under the powerful rule of Jalal Ad-Dawlah Malik Shah, the Great King, the Sultan of Iran. From his throne in the luxurious capital of Isfahan in central Iran, he controlled a new empire that spread from the Aral Sea in the north to the Persian Gulf in the south, from Syria in the west to the foothills of the Himalayas in the east.

THE ZAGROS

Campfire flames billowed and flickered in a gusting mountain wind, causing wispy silhouettes to dance like demons of the night across the canvas tents. Ramiro pulled at the rough hemp rope tied about his neck, trying to ease his pain. His raw skin bled from the chafe and every move of his head brought sharp grinds of agony. He glared across the fire at Hasan, who huddled in talk with his brother, Sebuk.

Ozan watched him. He leaned over, speaking in hushed tones. "You see, now you suffer for your foolishness. Hasan is very angry with you. And with me."

Ramiro scoffed. "I don't give a damn what Hasan thinks."

Ozan turned away quickly, fearing Hasan might overhear.

But Ramiro cared no longer, he was desperate, furious, and ready to die. He stood up suddenly. "Ya, Hasan!" he yelled. A lull fell around the fire. Ozan pulled away, astonished that Ramiro would be so stupid.

Hasan rose up and reached for his sword. "You dare to interrupt me, slave?"

Ramiro pulled at the gritty rope about his neck. "Take this off!"

Sebuk snarled and bolted forward before Hasan had the chance. Seething, he drew his sword and rushed around the fire. He swung his blade in a feint, stopping it just a finger away from Ramiro's neck. "Perhaps I should remove your ugly head, stinking kafir!" he shouted. "Then the rope will come off easily." The men smiled.

"And just how will you explain my headless body to your father?" Ramiro asked derisively.

Sebuk stuck his gnarled face right into Ramiro's, shouting with a vengeance. "That is the fate of slaves who try to escape!"

"Better that fate," Ramiro shouted back, "than to be dragged around this God-forsaken land like a wild animal on a leash!"

Sebuk glared at him, his sword trembling in his hand. "Filthy heathen! Kafir dog! How dare you speak to me like this!" He grabbed Ramiro by the hair and pulled his head back, putting the blade across his throat.

"And what of Nizam?" Ramiro strained. "What will you tell him?"

Sebuk hesitated. He looked askance at Hasan before returning his glare to Ramiro. "What do you know of Nizam?"

"I know you should fear him."

Hasan stepped forward. "Hold your sword, brother. We must consider the consequences... and the importance of our journey."

Sebuk made no reply. He released Ramiro's hair and shoved him to the ground. Ramiro got up defiantly and Sebuk slapped him across the head. Ramiro winced from the blow but soon steadied himself, running his fingers through his hair and straightening his tunic. "Is this how you want me to appear to Nizam? Will he see the bruises and cuts? Is this how your scribes are treated?"

Hasan brandished his sword and raised his voice. "We treated you well! But you tried to run!"

"You rescued me from one prison," Ramiro shouted back, "and threw me into another! What did you expect?" He made an effort to calm himself. "I beseech you, Efendi. Remove the rope about my neck and you have my solemn word I will not attempt another escape."

Hasan stood glaring at him. "Swear it in the name of Allah!"

Ramiro looked around the campfire. All eyes were on him. He took time to look each man straight in the eyes before turning slowly to face Hasan. "I swear it in the name of Allah, the merciful and compassionate." The camp fell silent. It was more than expected from a Christian. Ramiro continued. "We are all slaves of Allah and, as you have all read in the Holy Quran... Allah is not unjust to His slaves. And does He not exhort us to treat our slaves with kindness?"

The men were pleasantly surprised, never before had they heard the Quran cited by a kafir. Some began to squirm at the thought of Sebuk's injustice. Others looked down.

But Hasan's deadpan face showed neither regret nor admiration. He simply nodded. "Very well. Cut his ropes!" Then he waved his sword at Ramiro in challenge. "But I swear to you, monk, I will skin you alive if you run again!"

ISFAHAN

SEPTEMBER 1091

The cold, damp air of the high plateau began to warm as the men of Nikea descended to the valley floor below. The clouds cleared and their wet gear steamed under a dazzling sunlight. The further down they went, the hotter it became.

There, far below, was the huge oasis of Isfahan, a green jewel bounded by steep, snow covered mountains on the west and the great Salt Desert on the east. Meandering through the lush oasis was the olive-green Zayandeh River, draining from a watershed high in the Zagros.

"You see! Isn't it beautiful!" shouted Ozan as if he owned the city. "This is the magnificent home of the Great Shah, the most powerful man in the world – King of the East and the West!" He nudged his horse forward. "And they say... if you have seen Isfahan, you have seen half the world!"

But Ramiro said nothing, brooding over his sorry state.

"Look Ramiro!" said Ozan. "This will be much better than Nikea!"

"Perhaps for you, young man," he said, "but I do not belong here. My home is far to the west."

"You must forget this, old friend," he said, leaning over in his saddle. "You must do the best with what Allah gives you. How many of your brethren have seen glorious Isfahan?"

Ramiro said nothing.

Forty days after leaving Nikea, Hasan and his men arrived on the outskirts of Isfahan, where an old scribe in a guard house compared their names to a long list of wanted men. He held the list close to his face, squinting as he read. Then he looked up and studied Hasan carefully. "You say you come from Nikea? That is a long way. What is your business in Isfahan?"

Perspiration dripped from Hasan's smooth brow as he breathed the thick, hot air of the valley. "We have come to see the Vizier."

The scribe smiled through a thin, gray beard. "To see the Vizier, eh? Are you a prince, Efendi?"

"I am Hasan, son of Bolkas, son of Mahmud of the Oghuz clan. Cousins of the Seljuk."

The scribe nodded. "There are many Seljuks in Iran, may Allah bless their name. What is your business here?"

"My father received a letter from the office of Nizam in which he requested scribes for the new library. We have brought a scribe for this service."

"I know of this request," said the scribe. "Does your man have knowledge of the barbarian tongues?"

"Yes, Efendi."

The scribe wrote a brief note and handed it to Hasan. "Take this to the Vizier's secretary, a man by the name of Qubad."

Extravagant mansions of wealthy landowners lined the road to Isfahan. Sunlight glistened from their blue tile facades as tall, leafy trees of elm, willow and mulberry swayed in a hot breeze. Only the blue domes of mosques and the peaks of minarets spiraled above the canopy of lush, green foliage.

Hasan found a respectable inn near the thick walls of the Shah's compound, the one called the Square of the Shah, and settled in before they all headed straight for the baths where they wallowed for hours in cool pools of clear water.

● ● ● ● ●

Ramiro rose in the hazy, amber light of dawn. All was quiet except for the soft song of warblers. He stepped out onto the small patio and looked across gardened boulevards stretching out in all directions. He glanced down, two stories below, where three merchants sat near the compound wall, washing their hands and feet in preparation for the call to prayer. Their words echoed softly from the stone walls.

bismi-llahi ar-rahmani ar-rahimi

He knew what it meant. 'In the name of God, most gracious, most merciful.' The words rang true to his heart. Soon, he heard the vibrant call to prayer sounding from the minarets. The merchants below knelt on their prayer mats to face Mecca, prostrating themselves to God.

> *God is the greatest*
> *I bear witness that there is no lord but God*
> *Make haste toward prayer*
> *Make haste toward success*
> *God is the greatest*
> *There is no lord but God*
> *Muhammad is the Messenger of God*

Truly, God is the greatest, Ramiro thought in a reflection of worship. He raised his head to the sky for a moment then lowered his gaze to the Square below, impressed by its magnificent beauty, the bubbling fountains, the manicured gardens, and the marbled pathways winding through beds of bright flowers. At the north end, the elaborate Friday Mosque rose majestically beside gushing fountains. To the south, stood the Mosque of Ali and, to the east, the Sultan's magnificent palace towered above it all.

Despite the disarming beauty of Isfahan, Ramiro could not dispel his overwhelming sense of gloom. He fell to his knees as a wave of melancholy swept over him. With tears welling in his eyes, he began to recite the twenty-third Psalm.

Ozan watched from his bed, listening to the strange words.

> *The Lord is my Shepherd; I shall not want.*
> *Yea, though I walk through the valley of the*
> *shadow of death, I will fear no evil, for You are*
> *with me...*

"Ya! Ramiro!" Ozan shouted as soon as he ended his prayers. "What are you doing on your knees? Have you become a good Muslim?" He laughed.

Ramiro, jarred by the shout, wiped his face with his sleeve and rose to face the young man. "God is the greatest," he said quietly.

Ozan smiled. "Of that there is no doubt, old friend. But come, we must eat."

A SECRETARY

Ramiro squirmed on the cushion, still having trouble crossing his legs on the floor for any period of time. He put his hands behind his waist and arched his back. Ozan shuffled uncomfortably beside him while Hasan leaned forward, resting his elbows on his knees. They had been waiting six hours for an audience with Nizam's secretary, a man by the name of Qubad.

The call to sunset prayers reverberated along the walls. Hasan and Ozan rose from their cushions and knelt on the central rug to pray, glad for a change of position. Ramiro knelt too and prayed in his own way. Two grim-looking askari, the elite guard, watched them in silence.

No sooner had the prayers ended when an aide opened the door. "Come!" he said gruffly.

The secretary's office was an expansive room decorated lavishly in fine furniture and vessels of bronze and silver. The best Khorasan carpets adorned the floors and cushions of Samarkand silk spread out in patches of vibrant color against the mosaic walls.

They were not invited to sit. The two askari shut the door and stood behind them without a sound. On a small dais, the secretary sat in a chair of polished wood, writing busily. He did not look up for some time. When he did, Ramiro saw he was not a Turk but an Iranian bureaucrat. He was neither young nor old, had a fine moustache, a keen look and square features. His tunic was of the finest cotton embroidered with silk and gold thread. Over it, he wore a purple vest hemmed in precious gems.

Qubad appeared comfortable with power. He looked them over casually, as if judging cattle for slaughter. They lowered their eyes. "And who are you?" he asked Hasan.

Hasan lifted his eyes. "Me, Efendi?"

"Yes, you!"

"Forgive me, my Lord, may Allah bless your name. I am Hasan of Cappadocia, son of Bolkas, son of Mahmud of the Oghuz clan."

"And this is the letter you brought?" he said, holding up Bolkas' letter of introduction.

"Yes, my Lord."

"You are from Nikea in the Roman lands?"

"Yes, my Lord."

"You may be of the Oghuz clan," said Qubad disparagingly, "but you cannot dare to ally yourself with the great family of Seljuk!" He raised his voice. "We have heard of your treason. Do you know what we do with traitors?"

Hasan shifted uneasily, he knew all too well. Cold perspiration dripped from his underarms. "Please, Efendi I can..."

"You conquer the Land of Rome in the name of the Great Shah and then you decide to keep it for yourselves! How do you reply?"

"My esteemed lord," said Hasan, trying to choose his words carefully, "we are embarrassed by the follies of our lord Sulayman and wish to pledge allegiance only to the Great Shah, may Allah bless his name."

Qubad leaned forward, as if to emphasize his words. "If you wish to pledge allegiance, then why does your emir call himself sultan? First, Sulayman dared to reject our ambassadors and now your cursed uncle, Abul Kasim, does the same. How do you reply?"

Hasan fidgeted. "My Lord, my father and I do not approve of Abul Kasim's actions. He is a fool and would destroy us all with his thoughtless schemes. The people of Nikea and those living in the Land of Rome want only peace. The Romans seek to destroy us and the Turkoman roam the countryside killing and pillaging. Our people would welcome the safety and stability of the Empire."

Qubad waved his hand. "We are well aware of your difficulties, but they appear to be of your own making." He shook the letter. "And now you expect us to release Sulayman's son?"

"My esteemed Lord, the people humbly request that the Son of Sulayman be permitted to rule Nikea in the name of the Great Shah, may Allah keep him."

"The one named Kilich?"

"Yes, Efendi."

"He's just a boy," Qubad scoffed. "Besides, how can we trust the son if we could not trust the father?" He shook his head. "I think the Sultan, may Allah keep him, would rather give the rule of Nikea to an experienced man of his own choosing. Even now, the Shah leads an army to conquer the rebels in the west, and General Buzan of Edessa heads to Nikea with orders from the Shah to depose this Abul Kasim."

Hasan's eyes darted to Qubad. The Great Sultan himself! My father was right!

Qubad noticed his look of surprise. "Is this not what you wanted, Hasan son of Bolkas?"

He forced a weak smile. "Yes, yes, of course, my Lord."

"We will soon sweep away this mess," said Qubad. "Your uncle is weak. And this Roman king... this Alexios, now he sends an army of those western barbarians against him. Fearsome fighters, we hear... like wild animals. And smell like them too. They come from the hills of Andalusia."

Ramiro piped in. "Actually, Efendi, most come from further north."

With a ring of steel, Qubad's askari whipped out their swords, lunging at Ramiro, ready to run him through. They watched Qubad for a signal.

"Enough!" Qubad shouted, holding up his hand. "He is a stupid foreigner. We must excuse his bad manners... for now." The guards sheathed their swords slowly and returned to position. "If you wish to keep your head, foreigner, you will hold your tongue." He faced Hasan. "Is this your scribe?"

"Yes, my Lord."

"And how do you name yourself, scribe?"

"I am Ramiro of Cluny, my esteemed Lord."

Qubad smiled. He studied Ramiro for some time. "Your Turkish is very good for a foreigner," he said with amusement, as if a monkey had learned to talk. "You are a Christian?"

"Yes, Lord."

"Can you read and write Turkish?"

"Yes, Efendi."

"Do you know anything of mathematics or philosophy?"

"Yes, my Lord, I have read some manuscripts on these topics."

"Then perhaps you would like to meet one of our honored academics?" Qubad smiled condescendingly. "Surely, you have heard of Omar Khayyam?"

Ramiro looked puzzled. "Excuse me, Lord, I know not of this man."

Qubad raised his eyebrows in a feigned look of surprise. "You have never heard of Omar Khayyam, the greatest mathematician of our age?" His voice had a measure of contempt. "Theories of cubic equations? Euclidean geometry? No? Well, well... perhaps we cannot expect western barbarians to possess the intellect required to understand such complicated topics."

Ramiro bowed but did not reply.

Qubad nodded to Ozan. "And who is this?"

"Ozan of Nikea, my Lord," said Hasan. "Another scribe we have brought to the service of the Sultan, may Allah bless him."

"And as a price for these scribes, you expect us to release Sulayman's sons?" asked Qubad, curling his lips on one corner.

Hasan bowed. "As my Lord pleases."

"We will consider your request. You may leave."

THE LIBRARY

The months passed in monotonous procession. Ramiro thought again of escape, he always thought of escape. But what's the point? It was not as though they penned him up in a dingy dungeon, albeit his small room in the basement of the library was windowless, dark and depressing. But, strangely enough, he was free to go almost anywhere in the city, as long as he showed up for work on time. At first, this new-found freedom seemed to present a good opportunity for escape. But on deeper reflection, the task seemed almost impossible. To get through the city gates, he needed official papers. And once outside, he needed money. Besides, he had a foreign accent and wore the dress of a slave, a simple brown tunic with no markings and belted at the waist with a black sash. Even if he did get out, where would he go? Who could he trust? He recalled the peasants of Edessa who were so keen to turn him over to Hasan when he last tried to escape.

It's been almost three years since my mother wrote to me. Does she still live? And what of the Patriarch of Jerusalem? How can I approach the man and say that I have allowed the cross to be desecrated, that I have failed in my mission? What will the Abbot think? What perils have I brought to the True Faith? More doubts and regrets swirled through his mind as he leaned over his desk to study the volume handed to him by the library administrator. He brushed the dust from its leather binding and opened it to the title page. It was a copy of Aristotle's *Politica*.

"May the saints preserve me," he muttered in French.

"No talking!" scowled the administrator, a lean man with a sour look who sat behind an ornate desk at the head of the room, glaring in his direction.

Ramiro nodded. "Forgive me, Efendi."

"Do you know what you should be doing?"

"Yes, Efendi. I must submit a synopsis of the text to you."

"Then get on with it!"

"Yes, Efendi." He turned to the first page and began to read, taking notes as he went. He was astounded by Aristotle's frank discussions on the character of royalty and aristocracy, and of his theories on constitutional government. Ramiro had always accepted his kings and lords blindly, almost religiously, as if they were part of the natural order of things. But Aristotle challenged the whole concept. He found himself captivated and the hours passed unnoticed as he read through the day.

"Give me what you have," ordered the administrator when afternoon prayers ended.

Ramiro stood up and shuffled his notes together in an orderly fashion before handing them over.

The administrator stood by his desk as he read. "Your Turkish needs work. Obviously, you have not mastered all verb conjugations." He read for a long time before he threw the notes back to Ramiro. "That is enough. Give me the book."

"But I have not finished, Efendi."

"And you will not finish. This book is inappropriate."

"Inappropriate? Why?"

"The Great Shah, may Allah bless his name, does not want his loyal subjects to learn dangerous political ideas. What is this nonsense about democracy? The people rule together? It can only lead to anarchy and chaos. Everyone for themselves... how can it work? Do you have this kind of government in your own country?"

"Well... no."

"And men creating laws! Even a foreigner should know by now that God has written all laws. These are put down in the *Sharia*. This is what you should read." He shook his head in disgust. "Give me the book, it is finished. I will get another."

NIKEA

JUNE 1092

Far to the west in distant Nikea, Abul Kasim wrung his hands and chewed on a lip. A bead of sweat dripped from his brow as he looked out nervously from a citadel port, watching General Buzan's army amass in the distance. Bolkas stood behind him and a messenger waited by his side.

"General Buzan has requested your surrender, my Lord," said Bolkas in deference. "What is your reply?"

Abul Kasim considered the size of Buzan's army, it was huge. But can it breach the walls of Nikea? What will happen if I surrender? What a fool I have been! Bolkas tried to warn me. And this army may be just the first. He turned and waved the messenger away. "Return to General Buzan and tell him I wish to negotiate."

They waited many long, tortuous hours. But Buzan did not bother to reply. Instead, his whole army rode off in the direction of Ankara. Abul Kasim watched in trepidation and confusion, although he was somewhat relieved.

"You see?" he said in a shaking voice as the army faded into the distance. "General Buzan is no threat to us."

Bolkas could not hide his contempt. "More are coming, my brother. Of that you can be sure. Another army fights the Danishmends in the east, and it is led by Malik Shah."

"By the Sultan himself?" Abul was shocked. "Here?"

"He is camped near Malatya. Soon he will come this way. He is determined to take firm hold of the Roman lands."

Abul Kasim felt the blood run from his head. He stumbled to some cushions and sat down. "I... I offered to negotiate. Why did he not accept?"

"The answer is obvious!" Bolkas sneered in fury, becoming emboldened by Abul Kasim's despair. "They want us dead!"

Abul Kasim fidgeted. "I have done what I can, Bolkas."

"You have done nothing but endanger us all!" Bolkas shouted. "The Sultan will slaughter us - our sons, wives, brothers, our cousins! And what have you done? You waste your time fighting the Romans! You let the Roman king deceive you. You thought you were smarter than him – but instead he has led you astray with vain promises of gold! Now we are weak on the western frontier while the Sultan's armies march on us from the east. If you do not make peace with him soon, we will all lose our heads!"

• • • • •

Abul Kasim tossed and turned, he could not sleep. Fear rattled his thoughts. Bolkas was right, I must appease the Sultan. He rose early and went straight for the treasury. Before noon, he had fifteen donkeys loaded with gold. He was sure he could appease the Shah by pledging his allegiance and offering tribute.

Bolkas watched in disgust. What an idiot! Now he depletes our treasury and the Sultan will probably take our heads anyway.

Abul Kasim set off to see the Sultan with a train of servants and a squadron of his men. They travelled for five days when, just outside of Ankara, a surly band of askari thundered down on them.

"I am Abul Kasim of Nikea!" he shouted at them. "I have come to speak with General Buzan."

The askari said nothing. They charged with their lances right up to Abul's men and ran them through with hardly a fight.

Abul Kasim cringed in terror atop his mount, thinking he was next. "I come in peace!" he yelled.

The askari dismounted quietly and dragged him from his horse.

"What are you doing?" he wailed. "I come with gold for Buzan!"

They forced him to the ground. "General Buzan thanks you for the gold, traitor!" one said smirking, and before he could utter another word, the askari slipped a garrote around his neck and pulled hard. Abul Kasim's eyes bulged in terror as he writhed and struggled in vain. And there he died a silent death. The askari hacked off his head as a trophy for Buzan, leaving his bloodied corpse to the hungry vultures circling the dry steppe of the Anatolian Plain.

CONSTANTINOPLE

"Ramiro's alive?" Aldebert cried, jumping out of his chair and knocking it over. "He's a slave?"

"He was captured by the Turks," said Manuel, the Byzantine commander. "The Emperor's spies say he was kept prisoner at Nikea."

"Then we must pay the ransom!"

Manuel shook his well-groomed head. "I am afraid it is more difficult than that, Monk Aldebert. It seems that the Shah's men murdered Abul Kasim and now his brother, Bolkas, rules Nikea. I made further enquiries but got little cooperation. Apparently, Ramiro is no longer there. Rumor has it they sent him to Isfahan."

"Isfahan? Where on God's earth is that?"

"Far to the east. It's the capital city of the Turks."

"But how can we be sure he's there?"

"It would be very difficult," Manuel admitted. "We have no spies there."

"Why not just ask them? Ask the Shah."

"We could try but it may lead to nothing. How do we know the Shah is even aware of him? We would have to include something in the letter that would not only pique his interest in Ramiro but also prove to us that he's there."

Aldebert fell into a sullen mood. He righted his chair and slumped back into it. "Dear Jesus! What can we do?"

Manuel put a hand to his shoulder. "I am sorry Monk Aldebert. I wish we could think of something but you must realize the Emperor is very preoccupied with serious matters."

Aldebert had a rare flash of insight. He sprung to his feet again, his eyes lighting up. "I know what to do!"

ISFAHAN

JULY 1092

Hasan knew nothing of events transpiring in Nikea and still hoped for the release of Kilich, Son of Sulayman. But Qubad did not summon him, so he reluctantly stayed on in Isfahan for the winter. He planned to return to Nikea in the spring, when the mountains were free of ice and snow. But winter passed and his repeated requests for an audience with the secretary were summarily dismissed, as were his petitions to visit young Kilich. So he waited through the summer, hoping for the best, but he gradually became more and more anxious as the months wore on. And then, much to his relief, he was once again called to Qubad's office.

He stood alone, daring not to speak.

"Hasan of Cappadocia," said Qubad with feigned interest. "You have come to make a request?"

"Yes, Efendi, for the release of Kilich."

The rubies on Qubad's turban sparkled when he laughed. "I deny your request. But perhaps you would like to join him?"

Hasan frowned a little. "I do not understand, my Lord."

"We have news that should be of great interest to you," he said, giving him a sinister look. He rose from his chair and motioned to the guards, who strode up to take Hasan by the arms.

"What is going on, Efendi?" Hasan panicked as the guards gripped tight. His shiny black hair tousled over his eyes.

Qubad smiled. "The good news, Hasan, son of Bolkas, is that Abul Kasim is dead."

"Abul Kasim, my Lord?"

"Yes. It seems he disappointed the Sultan and General Buzan had him strangled. Now your father has taken control of Nikea." He paused. "Do you know what that means?"

Hasan understood. "That means my father Bolkas now rules the Roman lands."

"Yes," Qubad laughed again. "And so now *you* have become a hostage of Malik Shah, may Allah keep him. We must have some influence over your father, and unless he does as he is told, we will deliver your head to him. Let's see how well he negotiates under the circumstances." He glowered. "Take him away!"

• • • • •

A knock came to the door. "Who is it?" asked Ramiro.

"It's me! It's Ozan. Let me in!"

It was not unusual for Ozan to visit, but he sounded distressed, which made the back of Ramiro's neck tingle as he rushed to the door. "By all saints!" he said, swinging the door open. "Come in, come in. What is it?"

"It's Hasan, Ramiro! They've put him in the dungeon! His brother, Sebuk too!"

"But why?"

"Because they are sons of Bolkas."

Ramiro shook his head. "You will have to tell me more than that, my boy."

"The Sultan has taken Nikea. Abul Kasim is dead. They strangled him."

Ramiro let out a low whistle.

"Yes, and now Bolkas rules – and he has pledged allegiance to the Sultan."

"Then why do they keep his sons?"

"To keep him an honest man, of course."

"Of course. Come in, sit and we will have some tea. I want to hear everything. But first, what about you? What will you do?"

"I could have returned to Nikea but I want to wait until it's safe. Besides, I have a good position here."

"And what about the other men who rode with us?"

"They were released and head back to tell Bolkas the fate of his sons."

Ramiro thought again of Adele. "Any more news of Nicomedia? Does Bolkas rule it too?"

"I don't know. No one here is interested in Nicomedia."

POETRY

Young girls twirled, dancing in unison to the winding melody of flutes, drums, tambourines and four-stringed ouds. Their fine raiments of colorful silk billowed around them as they spun, all the while singing old Persian songs in a loud soprano.

Thousands of people crammed the market square to watch them. But they really came for the poetry competition. Near the stage, sat the judges and distinguished guests, while members of the royal house looked down from the balcony of an adjacent mosque. Commoners pushed and shoved for a better view. The music stopped and the dancing girls rushed back to their quarters.

Poets from all walks of life came to the stage, one by one, to recite their stories of heroism, of honor, and of unrequited love. Some were soldiers, others philosophers or mathematicians or physicians. After each finished their delivery, the crowd would voice their approval accordingly.

"Look!" Ozan cried. "Look – it's Omar Khayyam!" They had come early and struggled to hold their place beside the wall while others forced their way past. He pointed to the stage.

Omar Khayyam stood in a long, flowing tunic that looked expensive. He wore a white turban, had a long face and a full, gray beard.

"The mathematician?" asked Ramiro, holding out his elbows.

"He is many things. He is a great man."

Ramiro looked up to the balcony of the mosque. "Which one is the Sultan?"

"He's not there. They say he's still on campaign."

"Still in Asia as Qubad said?"

"So it seems. Shush! It begins."

Ramiro wondered if the Sultan would attack Byzantium next. What would King Alexios do? Are my friends safe? I pray so. May the grace and peace of Christ be with them.

Ozan chuckled at the poet's words and Ramiro tumbled out of his daydream. The quatrain of Omar reached his ears.

> *Did God set grapes a-growing, do you think,*
> *And at the same time make it a sin to drink?*
> *Give thanks to Him who foreordained it thus--*
> *Surely He loves to hear the glasses clink!*

The crowd laughed. Ramiro chuckled. It brought to mind a bottle of fine red wine. He poked Ozan's arm. "I thought Hasan said Muslims don't drink? And yet I see taverns everywhere and now your famous poet attributes wine to the works of God."

"Hasan is a very devout man," said Ozan. "Perhaps he is too serious," he said with a crease of his smooth brow. "But of course," he was quick to add, "no one would dare go to prayers while drunk. This is forbidden."

"I should hope so, Ozan. And what of Hasan and his brother? Have you heard anything more?"

"I hear they locked them up with Kilich."

"In the dungeon?"

Ozan smiled and his thin beard seemed to crawl up his face. "No, it seems their rooms are much better than that. The Sultan keeps them in a compound for special guests."

"Where is this compound?"

"I don't know," he said, eyeing Ramiro suspiciously. "Why do you ask?"

SEPTEMBER 1092

Once again, Hasan stood in Qubad's office, escorted in by a single guard. He looked healthy and stood in a clean tunic and cloak, his long hair freshly braided and his beard clipped short.

"And so we meet again, Hasan, son of Bolkas." Qubad sounded oddly courteous.

Hasan bowed. "Peace be upon you, Efendi."

"I trust you have enjoyed your stay in Isfahan?" he said, his eyes twinkling with malice.

"Yes, Efendi."

"And you have had much time to chat with young Kilich, I presume?"

"Yes, Efendi."

"That is good," he said as he picked up a letter from his desk. He held it up between two long fingers, showing his manicured nails and gold rings. "Now we shall turn to other matters. I have this letter – a very strange letter, indeed. It vexes me." He motioned to a guard. "I want you to have a look at it." The guard handed it over to Hasan. "And I want you to tell me what it says."

Hasan stared at the strange words. "I do not know, Efendi. The letters are Roman but I have never seen these words before."

Qubad twirled an end of his moustache. "What about that barbarian scribe of yours? Perhaps it is one of his tongues?"

"Yes... yes, perhaps, my Lord."

"Then I will summon him." Qubad leaned back, resting an elbow on his chair. He gestured, opening his hands. "So? Do you have any further issues of concern that you wish to address?"

Hasan felt disarmed by Qubad's apparent kindness. "Forgive me, Efendi, may Allah bless your name, I have only one."

"And what may that be, son of Bolkas?"

"Will we be released soon, Efendi?"

Qubad laughed, like the chortle of a hyena. Then his face hardened. "Take him away!"

● ● ● ● ●

Ramiro's hair was disheveled, his face stubbled. Two askari had barged into his room, pulling him from bed in the middle of the night. He hardly had time to get dressed before they rushed him to Qubad's office.

Qubad looked tired too, and covered his night dress with a decorated cape. He held a letter in one hand. "Welcome, Scribe."

"Peace be upon you, Efendi," Ramiro muttered.

"I want you to look at this letter," he said impatiently. Once again, a guard passed it over.

Ramiro opened the page, not knowing what to expect. But a look of astonishment soon rushed across his face. "By the love of Mary!" he exclaimed in French.

"Aha! You can read it," said Qubad eagerly. "You must tell me exactly what it says - exactly, do you understand?"

"Uh, yes... yes, my Lord," he said with distraction. The letter was written in Provençal but King Alexios had signed it in Greek. He recognized Brother Aldebert's handwriting and was greatly relieved to know he had survived the Patzinaks. He could not help but smile after he read it through.

Qubad frowned. "You smile? What can be so funny? Is this a joke of some sort?"

"Forgive me, my esteemed Efendi. No, it is no joke. This letter was sent by the Roman Emperor, Alexios Komnenos, and is addressed to the Great Sultan, may Allah keep him."

Qubad rose from his chair. "From the Emperor? Why does he use this strange tongue? Read it to me!"

Ramiro shook his head. "I will not, my Lord."

Qubad glared in amazement. "You will not? Is that what you said?" The guards drew their swords.

Ramiro looked calmly at Qubad. "This letter is for Malik Shah... and his eyes only."

Qubad's eyes went wide with fury... and fear. His ruthless uncle, the Vizier Nizam, had given him the letter with the critical task of interpreting it. "I will have you skinned alive! Read it to me!" he yelled again.

"But my Lord, it is for the Sultan."

Qubad clenched his jaw, rippling the muscles in his square cheeks. He spun around and took a moment to compose himself, his face scowling with a look of contempt. "The Sultan," he said in a controlled tone, "is still on campaign in the Roman Lands. He has yet to return."

Ramiro shrugged. "Then I will wait, Efendi."

"You will tell me now!" Qubad screamed with a reddened face. Spittle flew from his lips.

"Forgive me, my Lord. I must not."

"Ah, but you must, infidel. And you will." He drew his jeweled dagger and leaned into Ramiro's face while the guards still brandished their swords. "Or I will begin by carving out your eyes! And, if that fails to induce you - I will slice off your manhood! Do you understand? All of it... so you will forever squat like a woman to piss!"

Ramiro stared into Qubad's frothing face. "When I meet the Great Shah, I will be sure to inform him of your hospitality."

Qubad paled, eyeing Ramiro for some time, the dirk trembling in his hands. He turned away for a moment and then suddenly spun on his heels, slapping Ramiro hard across the face. "Take him to the dungeon!"

THE ISMAILI

Black rats squeaked and rustled on the rafters overhead. Ramiro sat idly on a few strands of straw, trying to avoid the filth around him while resting his back against the cool stone wall. Five other men sat cross-legged around him, staring intently but saying nothing. He closed his eyes and reached to his neck to grasp his mended cross, but it was not there. Qubad took all he had, which was not much. He prayed silently.

After some time, a gaunt young man with a full, black beard spoke to him. "Who are you? Why are you here?"

Ramiro was in no mood to explain himself.

The gaunt man raised his voice. "You're a spy for Nizam!"

"Do you really believe I'm a Turk spy?" Ramiro said with irritation.

"You're a foreigner!" The man blurted. "I can tell from your speech. Why are you here?"

"Because I am a slave who refuses to cooperate."

The thin man laughed, a cackling laugh. "If that were true, you'd be dead."

Ramiro smiled. "I suppose. Perhaps Allah has intervened."

The prisoner put his hands together. "Praise be to Allah."

"And why are you here?" Ramiro asked him.

"Because I am Shia," he smirked.

"Because you are Shia? Is that all?"

"No, it's because I am both Shia and Ismaili."

"Ismaili?... the Hashashin?"

The man scoffed. "Do you even know what that means, foreigner?"

"I was told you are hash eaters and that you kill people when crazed by the drug."

All of the men laughed aloud. One started to cough and hack.

"That's what they want you to believe." The gaunt man chuckled. "It's all propaganda... filthy lies spread by the accursed Seljuks! Those Turk bastards."

Another man waved his hand down, warning him to lower his voice.

"What do I care?" said the man. "Tomorrow I die."

"Tomorrow?"

"Yes, I am to be executed."

"For what?"

"For complaining," he said despondently. "I complain about the mistreatment of Iranians... about the land the Turks have stolen from us. They take everything and give us misery and poverty in return. Ignorant barbarians!" He lowered his voice. "This is why I joined the Ismailis. Don't you see? Iranians have followed the wrong path, only the Shia know the Truth, only the Ismailis have the courage to fight back against these evil Sunni, may Allah curse them!"

"But I was told that *you* are the fanatics."

"Of course you were. These Turks believe they rule by the will of Allah. The Sultan and Nizam seek to destroy all Shia. Our people hide in the hills to escape their persecutions. But now we have a savior."

Ramiro saw the other men look askance at the iron door. Dread filled their eyes. "Who is this savior?" he asked softly.

The man leaned forward. "Why, Hassan i-Sabbah, of course," he whispered. "Leader of the Ismaili. He will free us from Turk shackles. He is not afraid to kill those who kill us. Even now he gains power. Then the Iranians will rule Iran once again... and it will be Shia."

THE VIZIER

The only sound in the lush courtyard of Nizam's mansion was the nasal trill of a trumpeter finch as it flitted in the orange trees. Nizam reclined lazily under a huge umbrella while a slave cooled him with a wide fan of peacock feathers. Qubad sat nearby and five more servants stood at a distance.

Nizam was an Iranian, a strong-looking man even in his seventies, with a big head, a prominent nose, and a heavy brow. His gray beard bobbed up and down as he chewed on ripe, purple grapes, and large emeralds glistened from his red silk turban whenever he spat the seeds onto a napkin spread out over his tunic of fine red brocade. He held the letter from King Alexios and stared at the strange, undecipherable words. "So you say the infidel will not translate this for us?"

Qubad fidgeted in his chair. "He refuses, my Lord, despite our best attempts to persuade him."

A look of concern crossed Nizam's face. "I hope you have not harmed him."

"Not where visible, my Lord."

Nizam's long nostrils flared and his bushy brows furrowed. "He had better be in the best of health by tomorrow, nephew. Or you will find yourself stationed on the Russian frontier. Is that clear?"

"I will obey your command, Oh Lord," he said, lowering his eyes.

"You will offer this barbarian the hospitality of the Sultan, as Allah demands it. Have you forgotten the ways of a good Muslim?"

"No, my Lord. I will obey."

"Bring him to me tomorrow. I want to know what this letter contains. There is little sense presenting it to the Sultan if it is merely trivial." He forced a thin smile. "Don't you agree?"

"Yes, Master, of course."

"And give me this Christian cross he wants so badly."

"Yes, Master." Qubad took it from his pocket and a servant delivered it to Nizam.

Nizam waved a delicate hand. "Leave me now."

"May Allah exalt you, my uncle."

• • • • •

Nizam was visibly frustrated. "All we want to know is the gist of this letter, man. Will you not at least tell us that?" He held Ramiro's roughly mended cross in his left hand, twirling it between his fingers.

Ramiro stood neatly groomed in a clean white tunic. He was glad to be out of the dark, stinking dungeon. But his legs still burned and bled from the whips of Qubad's jailers. "Please forgive me, my Lord, but I must obey Emperor Alexios. This letter may be delivered only to your king, Malik Shah, may Allah keep him."

Nizam fumed. "How dare you! I am the Sultan's vizier! What impertinence!" Impulsively, he started from his chair but he caught himself and settled back down. The guards leaned forward, fingering their sword hilts. He raised a hand to stop them.

"Forgive me, exalted Lord." Ramiro bowed. "I have no intent to belittle your station. You must understand... I am a man of honor, great Vizier, and cannot, therefore, oblige your request."

Nizam tapped the cross on a low table. His voice was cold. "Do you realize your life is in my hands?"

Ramiro bowed slightly. "Yes, esteemed Vizier."

Nizam observed Ramiro's calm face. He could detect no fear in his eyes. None at all. How unusual. What should he do? He did not like it when only the Sultan was privy to news. How could he prepare? Knowledge was the base of his power. Yet killing or torturing this cursed infidel would accomplish nothing. He stewed for a moment before he relented. "Very well. I will arrange an audience with the Sultan, who is now returning from his campaign in the west. My chamberlain will advise you on court protocol."

"Thank you, great Vizier. And, if it pleases my Lord, may I have my cross?"

Nizam glanced down at the wooden cross, its center wrapped tight with string. "I understand these crosses carry much weight for Christians. This one looks badly damaged. Why is it so important to you?"

"I have owned it for some time, my Lord."

"Then it has sentimental value?"

"Yes, my Lord."

"Muslims do not worship idols of wood or gold. They worship only God."

"As do I, my Lord. My cross is only a symbol that inspires me to do the will of God."

Nizam, despite his power and wealth, was a devout and deeply religious man. He examined Ramiro with interest. "Do you consider yourself a servant of Allah?"

"I serve God whenever I can, Efendi."

"Forgive me, Ramiro of Cluny, but your religion seems quite grotesque to me. Is it not true that you have rituals in which you feign to drink the blood of your prophet, Jesus, and to eat his flesh?"

"Yes, Efendi, but the ritual is only symbolic. By doing so, we imbibe the spirit of Jesus and of his wholehearted commitment to do the will of God."

"But do you not also pray to the bones and blood of your holy men? It sounds barbaric."

"Yes, my Lord, many believe the saints offer divine intervention."

Nizam shook his head. "Christians have many strange beliefs. Why do you worship this Jesus? Muslims worship only God."

"As do Christians, Efendi. But some Christians revere Jesus just as some Muslims revere Muhammad. At times, my Lord, it seems the messenger is mistaken for the One who sent him."

Nizam smiled. "You speak well, Scribe. I can see you are a true servant of Allah."

"You are most kind. Uh... my cross, great Vizier?"

Nizam paused and looked at the cross again. "I will return this to you when I am satisfied. In the meantime, you will obtain another cross and wear it about your neck."

Ramiro bowed. "Yes, my Lord."

Nizam waved his hand. "You may leave."

THE SULTAN

Shortly after Malik Shah returned from his summer campaign in Asia, two askari came for Ramiro. They rushed him from his room and, without a word, pointed and prodded him along gardened pathways leading to the Royal Palace.

The ostentatious grandeur of the Palace stunned Ramiro. A vast, glimmering pool reflected a clear blue sky amid bright crimson flowers of weeping ironwood along its edge. The entire building, archways and pillars, were all fashioned from an exquisite cream marble quarried from the steep, barren mountains of Fars province. A series of arched windows and doorways crossed its front, each wrapped in a flowery façade of purple and gold tiles.

Inside, the splendor continued with high vaulted ceilings, marble colonnades, piers and arches, all laid out in rhythmic, radiating patterns. Over all this, a dazzling display of light beamed through stained glass windows, splashing about the halls in blue, gold and teal like a shower of water-colors.

Ramiro's awe shattered under the heavy hands of four guards, who searched him brusquely from head to toe, looking for hidden weapons or poisons. Satisfied, they led him into the enormous meeting hall.

The Great Sultan of Khorasan sat on a small throne, crossing his legs on a footstool. A loose, purple tunic with a red sash, draped from his square shoulders. He was about thirty-five, a handsome man of fine features. Large, almond-shaped eyes swept up to the corners of his wide face, accentuated by thin black eyebrows that almost converged above his small nose. A thin moustache curved down into a barbered black beard running along his jaw line. His crown, a domed hat with a gold rim and a brush of peacock feathers, towered from his head.

Nizam stood beside Ramiro below the stepped dais. They stooped slightly, careful to keep their heads lower than the Sultan's. On one level below him, sat his eldest son, Berkyaruk, a glowering young man with long, black hair, a thin moustache and heartless eyes.

The Sultan demanded privacy, dismissing all but his son and four heavily armed askari. Two young pages remained, but their discretion could be assured, their tongues had been removed.

A weak smile crossed the Sultan's face. He spoke softly. "I hear you must be either a fool or a man of strong conviction to defy the orders of my vizier. Tell us your name."

Ramiro bowed. "O Great Shah, I am Ramiro of Cluny. May God keep you."

"So, you are a man of God, I hear. A Christian. Is this true?"

"Yes, my Shah."

"Tell me, how did you come to Isfahan?"

"It is a long story, Your Highness."

"I have the time," said the Sultan smiling, as if amused by a child. "Please continue."

Ramiro spent almost an hour summarizing his journey, careful not to say too much and careful not to speak ill of Turks.

"So you have spent time at the court of the Roman King?"

"Yes, my Shah."

The Sultan folded his arms and put one hand to his chin. "We must talk more of this at another time." He paused, noticing a bruise on Ramiro's cheek. "How have you been treated?"

Ramiro hesitated. "I... I am thankful for your hospitality, my Shah, may God keep you."

The Sultan glanced suspiciously at Nizam, who bowed his head in deference.

"And now, Ramiro of Cluny, would you be so kind as to read this letter for me?" A page offered it to Ramiro.

Ramiro picked it up and read it through in his mind. Only the squawk of a caged parrot interrupted the ensuing silence. An Iranian scribe dipped his quill, preparing to take down the words. Ramiro cleared his throat and began to read aloud. He read slowly, translating into Turkish.

> *From Emperor Alexios Komnenos of the Roman Empire, greetings.*
>
> *To my Servant, Ramiro of Cluny, may God protect you. You must deliver this message to no one but the Great Sultan, Malik Shah* _____
>
> *To Jalal Al-Dawlah Malik Shah, the Great Sultan of Persia, Lord of the Turks.*

*Be it known that I have received your letter in which you make
a generous offer to return the cities of Nikea and Antioch to my
possession in exchange for my daughter's hand in marriage to
your eldest son, Berkyaruk. I am presently considering your
generous proposal.*

*I have written this letter in the tongue of the French because
it has come to my attention that you are in possession of one
scribe and holy man by the name of Ramiro of Cluny. If you
choose to reply to this letter, then I will know that he lives and
remains safe in your care.*

*I can verify that Ramiro of Cluny is a man of peace who
walks the path of God. He has come to you only because he was
captured in Gallipoli while serving as a spiritual leader to my
men.*

*As a sign of good intention, I ask you, in the name of God, to
release the holy man so that he may return to his rightful home
in the west. Upon his release, if it is your wish that peace be
negotiated, I will dispatch an envoy to seek terms.*

Alexios Komnenos

August 10, in the year of our Lord 1092.

Ramiro finished and stood quietly. The throne room remained silent except
for the scratching of the scribe. Malik Shah had concentrated on every word
and continued to stare at him, not with distraction but with amused interest.
Berkyaruk watched him too, but with an expression of malice and disdain.

"This letter," said the Sultan, "speaks very highly of you, Ramiro of Cluny.
But how do we know you have interpreted it correctly?"

Ramiro bowed. "On that issue, Great Lord, I can offer no proof. I could
merely suggest you send the letter to Antioch for verification. I hear some
western foreigners live there."

"He is a spy!" Berkyaruk blurted. "A spy for the Romans!"

Malik Shah quieted his son with a piercing glance. Berkyaruk lowered his
head. The Shah swung his eyes back to Ramiro. "If this letter is as you say,
then there are two things of which we can be sure." He held up two fingers and
touched one with his other hand. "One is that the Roman king has his spies
everywhere." He paused while continuing to stare at Ramiro. Then he touched
his other finger. "And two, is that you must be a valuable man, Ramiro of
Cluny." He smiled sparingly. "You have both a king and Allah appealing for
your release."

Ramiro avoided eye contact by looking at the Sultan's feet. He said nothing.

The Sultan continued. "I am not familiar with your Christian calendar, can you convert the date of this letter to the Hijra calendar?"

"Please forgive me, Great King, but I do not know how."

The Sultan murmured some words to a page who rushed out of the room. While he was gone, Ramiro suffered under the hostile glare of Berkyaruk, who seemed ready to run him through at the slightest provocation. After a very long and uncomfortable wait, the page returned with a sheet of paper which he presented to the Sultan.

"Ah! The fourth day of Rajab. That's six weeks ago." He continued to stare at the note. Then he looked down on Ramiro. "You may leave now."

Ramiro hesitated, he wanted his cross.

"You heard the Sultan!" Berkyaruk said loudly. The young man glowered with a look of utter hatred, causing Ramiro to shiver as he backed away.

● ● ● ● ●

Malik Shah sat elevated at the head of a long, low table, his legs folded under him. "We had a successful campaign in Asia," he said to his generals. "And we have eliminated that troublemaker, Abul Kasim. But we must be careful to keep King Alexios at bay. If we can bring his daughter as wife to my son, we may gain some hold over his decisions. But the only correspondence I have received from the King is a strange letter written in a barbarian tongue. In it, he requests that we return a holy man, one called Ramiro, who is now in our possession." He looked around the table. "What is your advice, General Buzan?"

Buzan was a slender man, his smooth facial features interrupted by a gnarled arrow scar on one cheek. "Return him, my King," he said. "It is a token offering, a small price to pay. And we gain the advantage of time."

"But what if he is a spy?" Berkyaruk challenged loudly. He was only seventeen but already thickset, wide shouldered, and a head taller than most. If he lived, he could be the next Sultan.

"Has he been here long enough to learn anything of import?" Buzan asked.

"If he has travelled this far," said Berkyaruk with unbridled defensiveness, "he would know many things of interest to our enemies. Take no chances. Execute him!"

"Patience, my son," said the Shah. "Life is never that simple. This man could prove useful to us." He took several sips of mint tea before he spoke again. "Recently, I received an envoy from Nikea with a request to return the Son of Sulayman to rule." He looked around the room for a reaction. "Do you think this wise, Nizam?"

Nizam sat to his right, folding his hands in his lap. "There is little doubt the people in Asia would follow Kilich, my Shah. And there is little to be gained by keeping him here now. But will he remain loyal to the Empire?"

Malik Shah nodded. "That is the question. I will consider it. We have time." He paused and sighed heavily before speaking again. "Now what of these Shia heretics? They grow stronger in our midst. We must destroy them! Especially these Hashashin! May Allah curse their sons! They are evil men... agents of the Fatimids who spread their filthy propaganda everywhere."

"Forgive me, my Lord," said Buzan. "But we need more men. We already have one army besieging Kohistan, another still fights the Danishmend in the Roman lands, and our men in Syria are far away and have their own troubles."

"My Shah," said Nizam. "May I suggest we use the Caliph's army in Baghdad. We know the Caliph is becoming an embarrassment with his political meddling. We should exile him to Basra, put one of our generals in his place, and use his army to attack the Hashashin stronghold." Several generals and advisors nodded in agreement.

The Sultan rubbed his chin and smirked. "Yes, this is a good idea, my Vizier. I believe the Caliph has become an irritant to the Empire." He paused for a moment. "You will go to Baghdad to make the necessary arrangements."

"Me?" Nizam said, astonished. "To Baghdad, my Shah?"

Malik Shah nodded. "Yes. You are the only one with the necessary credentials. He is the Caliph, after all."

OCTOBER 1092

"Ramiro! Ramiro!" Ozan yelled as the door flew open with a bang.

Ramiro jolted up in bed and instinctively felt for his knife, but it was not there. "By the love of Mary, Ozan! Are you trying to stop my heart? What's the matter now?"

Ozan ran up to Ramiro's bed and fell to his knees. "You will not believe this! The whole palace... no, the whole city... no, even the whole country wails in grief!"

"You had better tell me soon, boy, or I will wring your neck! Out with it!"

"Nizam is dead, Ramiro! Murdered by the Hashashin on the road to Baghdad!"

Ramiro jumped out of bed. "The Vizier?"

"Yes, yes!"

"When?"

"Two days ago!" He flung his arms out. "What will happen now, Ramiro?"

Ramiro went to the window. He looked out onto the teeming streets where everyone seemed to be talking in high voices. "How did it happen?"

"Two wicked men..." Ozan choked. "May Allah damn them to hell! Just two men, Ramiro... when there were hundreds of the Shah's askari all about! They came to Nizam's litter in the guise of presenting gifts - then they stabbed him with poisoned knives! The askari hacked them to pieces... but it was too late for Nizam!"

Ramiro stayed by the window. He shook his head in disbelief and reached for his wooden cross, but it was not there. In its stead was a gray iron cross, the only one he had managed to find. "This is a sad day for the Turks," he said sincerely. "Nizam was a great man who did much for the empire." He thought about the Vizier's influential manuscript, the *Book of Government*, which he came across in the library. And he thought about his great accomplishments - the distinguished schools of academia and the many hospitals with the best physicians in the world. He bowed his head in sorrow. "What now, Ozan? Who will take his place? Hopefully not Secretary Qubad." He turned from the window. "And how will I ever get my cross back?"

"But you have another cross," said Ozan, pointing a finger.

"I want my own cross," said Ramiro.

"The one you wear is beautiful. Why do you want that broken old thing?"

"I must have it, Ozan. I will say no more."

RESURRECTION

Ramiro tidied himself frantically. Two weeks after Nizam's murder at the hands of the Hashashin, he was summoned again to the Royal Court. Already, he was sweating, and he just had a bath. Noon prayers ended and it was time for his audience. Have I got everything? What do I need? Nothing. I need nothing.

The Sultan sat as before, flanked by his personal bodyguards and two pages while a squad of soldiers stood near the palace door. His eyes looked dark and tired, his complexion pallid, and when he spoke, it was with a hint of melancholy. Ramiro offered lengthy greetings but the Sultan wasted little time with social pleasantries.

"My son, Berkyaruk, would have you executed," he said in a straightforward manner. "But I have decided to release you to King Alexios instead. Times have changed and I must find a way to appease the king and secure my western frontier while I attend to more serious matters at home." He waved an arm out slowly, as if to encompass his kingdom. "And it is time for the Feast of Eid, a day to forgive and forget our differences, a day to make amends."

Ramiro could barely contain his glee. He had to lower his head and bite his lip to suppress a smile. But he said nothing.

The Sultan looked at him kindly. "You have served me well. My librarian tells me you have done the work of three scholars," he paused for a while and seemed to drift off in thought. And then, as if realizing where he was, he spoke again. "I will arrange an escort to take you to Nikea. From there, you may continue to Constantinople. I want you to deliver a letter to the Roman King."

"As you command, Great Shah," said Ramiro with elation.

"For your troubles," said the Sultan, "you will be richly rewarded." He nodded to a page standing nearby. The boy held a silver platter covered with a napkin of red silk. He walked over to Ramiro, holding the platter before him. With finesse, the boy pinched one corner of the napkin between finger and thumb and folded it back.

Ramiro gasped. He stared at the object on the plate. It was a cross. A golden cross on a golden chain. He reached out slowly and picked it up carefully, as if it were a strange creature from another world. "It is beautiful, O Shah."

The Sultan nodded and smiled. "Look closely," he said.

The cross was not solid gold. Instead, it was an exquisite outline of gold and silver, a frame of sorts. And encased within that frame was a simple wooden cross.

Slowly, it dawned on him. My... my cross? Yes, yes, it is my cross! By all saints! It had been resurrected in new form. Each arm splayed out slightly, like the tail of a fish, embellished with fine, floral designs. And in the center, the frame artfully covered the gouge where the bloodstone had been, while still leaving a slot of exposed wood on the post and arms. The old frayed wood was polished smooth and seemed to glisten along with the gold. He had never seen anything like it. "Thank you, Great Shah, may Allah keep you." He held the cross to his chest. Tears welled in his eyes and he choked back a sob.

"I tried to find the bloodstone you spoke of," said the Sultan in a calm voice, "but, alas, to no avail. Nevertheless, it may be of some comfort to you to know it was made by a Christian, an Armenian jeweler. He is very good. You see - the gold and silver alloy gives it strength."

Ramiro nodded. "It is beautiful, my Shah, thank you."

The Sultan signaled to a page. "And for your journey home, I present you with another gift." The page came forward with a bulging bag of coins, offering it to Ramiro. It was heavy.

"Thank you, Great Shah, you are very, very generous. May Allah and the Prophet be praised!"

The Sultan waved his hand to another page. He too, stepped forward with a silver platter, on it was a piece of paper. "This document grants you full privileges in any part of my empire. You should find it useful." He straightened his back. "You will be provided with two horses and all supplies. Is there anything else you require for your journey, Ramiro of Cluny?"

"May Allah bless your sons, my Shah." Ramiro paused. "I have only one enquiry, Great Lord... what of my associates, will they also be released?"

The Sultan appeared puzzled. "Who is this?"

"Hasan of Cappadocia and his brother. They brought me here from Nikea and were detained by the Vizier, may Allah's mercy rest upon his soul. Will these men accompany my return?"

"You mean the ones who are kin to Abul Kasim?"

"Yes, my Shah."

The Sultan nodded with distraction. "I will consider the matter."

"And if it pleases the Shah, will Kilich also be permitted to return home to Nikea?"

"The Son of Sulayman?"

"Yes, my Shah."

"I will consider that matter also," he said with a hint of annoyance. "We are finished."

SON OF SULAYMAN

Kilich wiled away his time in the Shah's detention compound along with several other political prisoners who were lucky enough to have some future value. It was a golden cage, quite unlike the prisons visited by Ramiro. Its occupants enjoyed baths, servants, and lavish meals while they studied Islam, the arts, science and literature. And shopping excursions were allowed under escort. It was here that young Kilich had spent most of his life, and it was here where Hasan and Sebuk were detained.

Kilich sat under the shade of apricot trees. The courtyard was quiet except for the din of the market in the distance and the chirps of reedlings. Pleasing aromas of barbecued lamb and garlic hung in the air. Servants brought out bowls of oranges, dates and almonds.

Hasan and Sebuk joined the young man and they were deeply embroiled in a discussion of political affairs, discussing all that had come to pass in Nikea, the execution of Abul Kasim, the new-found strength of the Roman King and, of course, what would happen in the Seljuk Empire now that Vizier Nizam was dead.

Kilich fingered dates from one of the bowls. His braided, black hair hung over one shoulder. A simple white tunic, belted with a blue sash was all he wore. Hasan thought he looked healthy and fit, his skin glowed with the flush of youth. At fourteen, he already stood the height of a man.

The boy stared into the distance, his big brown eyes unfocused, his neat black eyebrows furrowed in thought. "Tell me Hasan, do you think the Sultan will release me now that Nizam is dead?"

"Soon we hope. The servants say Ramiro met with the Shah to plead our case. Perhaps he will release you too." Kilich's maturity impressed Hasan, despite the fact that the young man had yet to grow a beard. In all things, he acted with composure and carried himself confidently. He was well read, gifted in the arts of war, and thoroughly indoctrinated in Sunni Islam. "One thing is sure," said Hasan, "the people of Nikea would welcome you gladly."

Kilich smiled. "I would like to meet this Ramiro, he sounds like an able man."

"He is very talented, but difficult to subdue," said Hasan, remembering Ramiro's flight in Edessa and his fearless confrontation with him around the campfire in the Zagros Mountains.

"Do you remember much of Nikea?" asked Sebuk.

Kilich shook his head. "Not really. I have only the memories of a child. But I have learned all I can of the Roman sultanate and of my father's life, may Allah have mercy on his soul. And I know it is my rightful inheritance, by the will of Allah."

"Praise be to Allah," the others chanted.

FEAST OF EID

Ramiro felt privileged - for an emancipated slave. Since his meeting with the Sultan, he was moved from his small, spider-infested room to a compound right next to the library. His new rooms were spacious and furnished, and a small balcony overlooked a common courtyard, beautifully adorned with a circular fountain at its center. Wrapping around the fountain like a waiting audience, was a larger circle of gleaming marble benches interspersed with green lemon trees.

The courtyard was unusually busy today. It was the end of the month of Ramadan and great preparations were being made for the Feast of Eid, which marked the end to fasting. He looked down on the tables of delicious delicacies and smacked his lips. But, alas, he was Christian and could not attend.

"Look at this, Ramiro!" said Ozan as he shuffled through the rooms. "You live like a king now!"

Ramiro pulled his eyes away from the tables of food and turned to Ozan with a sad smile. "For a while, my friend. It will be better for a while." Inwardly, he was thrilled to be leaving but many disparate thoughts tugged at his heart. What should I do? Should I head straight for Jerusalem? But I promised the Shah I would deliver his letter to King Alexios, a letter I already have in my possession. And I accepted gifts on this very premise. But do I have the time? So much time wasted! I must get to Jerusalem!

"Ramiro!" said Ozan with a flicker of a frown. "Did you hear?"

Ramiro shook his head to dispel his thoughts. "I am sorry, Ozan. What did you say?"

"I asked - when are you leaving?" Ozan had matured somewhat since they left Nikea. His beard had filled a little, as had his shoulders which he now swathed in a copper-brown cloak. He wrapped his long hair in a small turban, wore sandals on his feet, and looked like a true scholar.

"In the spring, I would think," said Ramiro after a lengthy pause. "I cannot imagine traveling through those steep mountains in the winter."

Ozan nodded as if he should have known. No route west could avoid the mountain snows until late spring. "Take me with you," he said suddenly. "You have to go past Nikea anyway."

Ramiro moved from the balcony and gestured for Ozan to sit. "Can you get away?" he asked, moving two large pillows for a seat.

"I see no problem. I am free and I am Seljuk."

"What of Nikea? Will you be welcome there?"

"Abul Kasim was my only enemy, Ramiro."

"I suppose," he muttered as his thoughts drifted again. Could I send Ozan to Alexios on my behalf? That would leave me free to pursue Jerusalem. He had said nothing to Ozan about the Sultan's letter, deciding to keep it to himself, unless the moment demanded otherwise.

"Ramiro?"

"Uh... yes, Ozan."

"Will you take me along? It would be my honor to escort you."

"Yes. Yes, I think that would be wise."

BLACK NOVEMBER

Five months seemed like a long time to Ramiro, a long time before winter ended. To ease his boredom and anxieties, he went on a shopping spree, buying new clothes - a cotton cloak for summer, a fur-lined leather cloak for winter, a money-belt, boots and bags, even a new turban. No longer would he have the dress of a slave. He was a freeman now and had official papers stamped with the seal of the Shah himself.

But he found it difficult to pass the time. He tired of his studies, although he still went to the library to help out, but more to keep himself busy. He found little to do around the house because maids and servants attended to his chores. So this particular morning, he occupied his time stuffing his leather money-belt with the Sultan's gold coins. He felt little apprehension about traveling with so much gold. After all, he would ride with a band of the Sultan's mamluks. He decided to keep two coins for spending money, putting these in his purse, which dangled from his outer belt by a bronze chain.

As yet, nothing had been said to him about the release of Hasan and Sebuk. Nonetheless, he was feeling lively, if not giddy. Perhaps he would get to Jerusalem after all. He tingled with new-found excitement. "Thank you, glorious Father in Heaven!" he said aloud. "Blessed is your Son. I will say a hundred Hail Marys!"

When he finished stuffing the money-belt, he leaned over and picked up his reworked cross. Reflections of morning light flickered and danced along its gold and silver framework. He was pleased to get it back, although he could never tell the Sultan that it appeared far too ostentatious for a Benedictine monk. And any highwayman would slit his throat for it. Indeed, the pious would be so tempted. So he wrapped it in a soft cloth and put it into his vest pocket, leaving his iron cross about his neck.

When all was done, he sat on his bed to reminisce. He thought kindly of Brother Aldebert and Pepin and prayed they fared well. He wondered about Drugo and his Flemings and whether they still lived. Images of Adele came to mind. Did she ever arrive in Nicomedia? And if she did, did she escape before Abul Kasim seized the place? *Mother Mary, saint of all women, I pray you watch over her.*

The rising timbre of a woman wailing in the distance distracted him from his thoughts. It was the wail and ululation of death. The sound grew in intensity, louder and louder, until the whole palace choked with screams and cries. "What in the name of God?" He went to the balcony and looked out from his room. In the twilight of dawn he saw a great commotion in the streets. People scurried back and forth like a mass of rats. *Something is very wrong,* he thought. He ran to the door and opened it. The hall was empty. He rushed into the main library but not a soul was there, the whole place was deserted. He turned and left, hurrying outside and onto the busy street. All eyes wept and all hearts sorrowed.

"What's happened?" he asked a man in the street, but the man brushed him away with a stark look of grief, big tears coursing his cheeks. Then he spotted the librarian dashing back into the building and went after him. "Efendi, Efendi, please tell me what has happened!"

The librarian was crying too, his eyes red, his cheeks wet with tears. "Today, Ramiro, we have been cursed by Allah! It is a terrible day! A terrible day indeed. What will happen now? What will happen to the Empire?"

Ramiro shuddered. He gripped the librarian by the shoulders. "Efendi, what has happened?"

The librarian began to sob and he had to squat on the steps. He was barely intelligible. "The Great Shah is dead!"

"Malik Shah is dead?" Ramiro parroted in astonishment.

The librarian nodded his head.

"How? How could this happen?"

The librarian shrugged. "Some say he was poisoned. They blame the Hashashin!"

Ramiro's heart began to pound. May God protect us. Now what? Who will be the next Sultan? Berkyaruk came to mind and he shivered when he recalled his encounter with the malevolent young man, the one that would have him executed. Anything can happen. Now everything is different. Now Berkyaruk takes the throne. Will the Sultan's escort still come for me in the spring? Will Berkyaruk let me go... or will he slice off my head? He soon realized what he had to do. Once again, he took the sobbing librarian by the shoulders. "Where's the Shah's detention compound? Where is it?"

The librarian pointed south-east. "On the Street of Flowers."

Ramiro rushed back to his room and grabbed his bag. Ozan! Where's Ozan? He ran through the building, heading towards his room. "Ozan!" he yelled. "Ozan!" When he got to his door, he flung it open. Ozan was sitting on the floor, swaying back and forth. He was crying.

Ramiro rushed over to him. "Ozan! Come man! We must go!"

"Haven't you heard, Ramiro?" he sobbed, wiping his cheeks with his fingers. "The Great Shah – he's been murdered!"

"I have heard, Ozan. And now is a dangerous time. Come. Get your things. We are leaving Isfahan."

"Now? What about..."

"Get your things, Ozan! Trust me! We have to go!"

With all their baggage, they hurried down the crowded cobble streets to the Sultan's jail. When they arrived, there was only one nervous guard at the main gate.

"What do you want?" threatened the young man as he put his hand to his sword.

"I... I want you to release some prisoners," Ramiro panted.

"On whose authority? Where are your papers?"

Ramiro hesitated. Then he remembered the Sultan's document. He pulled it from his belt and handed it to the guard.

The guard recognized the insignia and handed it back to Ramiro. "And where is your release form?"

Ramiro stared intently at the guard, his black eyes flared. "The Sultan is dead! The Vizier is dead! The Empire is in chaos! The men I want can do no harm now."

The guard looked around. His eyes darted from the street to Ramiro and then to the gate. He was clearly flustered. "How much?"

"How much?" Ramiro repeated. "Oh! How much. Yes, yes, of course. He dug into his pouch for a gold dinar and handed it to the guard. It was a small fortune.

The guard stared at the coin for ages, glancing suspiciously at Ramiro before shifting his eyes back to the coin. He put it to his teeth. It was real. He smiled. "Who do you want released?"

Ramiro told him.

"Kilich too?"

"Yes."

The guard opened the door. "Hurry! Go into the courtyard and summon them. You must return by this door. I will not wait long."

Ramiro rushed through and hurried down an arched walkway before entering the courtyard. "Hasan! Sebuk! Where are you?"

The men dashed out of their rooms and ran to him. The other prisoners joined them. "What are you doing here? What's going on? What's all the noise about?" shouted Hasan.

"The Sultan is dead. Poisoned in the night."

The men fell mute, returning blank stares. "Malik Shah?"

"Yes, yes, there's no time to explain. I just bribed the jailer and we must go - now! Come! Forget your things! Come!" He headed for the exit. The men hastened behind. They rushed through the gate. The other prisoners did the same. The guard was gone.

"First we need weapons," said Hasan when they reached the streets. "Then we need horses."

"I have two horses!" Ramiro shouted as he remembered the Sultan's gifts.

"You have horses? But you are a slave," said Sebuk with a look of disgust.

"Not any more, Sebuk. But I will explain it all later. We must go."

"Two horses are not enough!" said young Kilich. "We'll need two more!"

"And we need arms – at least a sword."

"I know a place," said Ramiro, remembering his walks around the shops. But when they arrived, the shop was closed. Sebuk banged on the thick, wooden door. "Open up! Open up! Or we will smash the door in!"

A worried old man opened the door a little. Sebuk pushed it hard and it flung open, sending the poor man sprawling to the floor. They all moved into the shop.

"We mean you no harm, old man," said Ramiro. "But we need weapons. Your best swords, knives and shields. And we need bows."

"I have no bows, Efendi. I'm a blacksmith."

"Then show us what you have." Ramiro dug into his money belt and paid the man handsomely.

Weapons in hand, they rushed to a stable and offered the groom twice the price for good horses and saddles. But he refused. "These are not my horses!" he shouted. "You can't take them!"

Sebuk drew his newly-acquired knife, slashing the man across the face. The shocked groom screeched in pain, slapping a hand to his bloodied cheek. "But we will take them anyway," he sneered. Hasan and Kilich drew their swords and the groom backed away. They took saddles and mounted.

Before they rode off, Ramiro threw two dinar to the terrified groom. "Forgive me, Father," he muttered under his breath.

They were no sooner out on the streets when Ramiro shouted. "We will need food and warm clothes to get through the Zagros!" The men agreed and they went in search of provisions.

Before the sun rose another hand, Ramiro retrieved his two horses from the Sultan's stable and met the five men at the city gates. The guards stopped them. "Show your papers!"

Hasan and Sebuk kept a hand on their sword hilts. Ramiro sensed trouble and took the lead. He handed them his pass. The guards were impressed. "My friends have no papers, Efendi, but we will gladly pay the fine." He threw them a dinar each. The guards hesitated momentarily, exchanging glances before rushing them through the gates.

Hordes of terrified citizens and slaves fled Isfahan and the road choked with horses and carts. People prayed aloud, wailed in grief, or cursed the Hashashin. The men barged their way through the chaotic throng until they reached the open road. Here they pushed hard, riding west to cross the Zagros in the dead of winter.

AL-IRAQ

Ramiro was chilled to the bone. He wrapped his wet cloak tight about his chest and adjusted his turban to keep the freezing rain and sleet off his neck. They plodded mile after mile through thick mud and wet snow, looking hard for something to feed the horses in the cold, barren mountains of Iran.

Just south of Qom, they turned west for Daskerah to camp in the warmer valley. Ramiro helped to put up a canvas tarp, their only shelter from the sleet and snow. He shook his head sadly as they huddled around a small fire. "Who would murder the Sultan? Who could commit such an odious deed? Was it really these Hashashin?"

Ozan rubbed his hands close to the flames. "They murdered the Vizier didn't they? – why not the Sultan?"

"Some in the markets said the family of Nizam plotted his death," Kilich said with a serious look on his boyish face. "They blame the Sultan for his death. They say he was the one who ordered him to Baghdad."

Ramiro did not look convinced. "Why would the Sultan plot to kill his own Vizier?"

"Maybe because he was a very powerful man and an Iranian. The Sultan may have worried about this," he nodded his head as he spoke.

"But it could also have been his half-brother Tutush," said Hasan. "There were rumors that he met with the Hashashin to plot an assassination."

Ramiro frowned. "Why would he do that?"

"Tutush was angry when the Sultan sent his army to Syria and took control of the Roman lands that he wanted for himself. To this day, Tutush covets those cities for his own and now he will want to be the next Sultan."

"So what do you think will happen?" Ramiro asked.

"There will be war," said Sebuk, who stood near the fire drying his cape. His tone towards Ramiro had changed considerably. "Tutush will claim the Empire, as is his right. But it is also the right of the Shah's son, Berkyaruk." He slung his cape across his shoulders and squatted near the fire. "Oh yes, there will be war. But the timing is good for you, Lord Kilich. You may claim Nikea with little opposition."

Kilich nodded. "I believe you are right, Sebuk. But what will happen to the Seljuk Empire?"

• • • • •

They rode west, trotting through the deep, cold valleys of the Zagros, galloping past the wonders of Bisitun and finally charging down the western slope, down to the Diyala River and onto the vast, warm plain of Al-Iraq. It was here, and only here, that Ramiro began to feel renewed hope. And as they headed northwest to Kirkuk and Mosul, a twinkle returned to his eyes. "If it is your will Father," he said softly. "I pray she still lives."

"What will you do, Ramiro, after you return to Constantinople?" Ozan asked.

"I'm not sure." He felt for the Shah's letter, which he kept folded in his money belt. Should he fulfill his obligation to deliver it? Or did it really matter now that the Sultan was dead? "Perhaps I should return to Constantinople," he said, thinking of Aldebert, "and then I will continue to Jerusalem." Yet doubt plagued him. What if Alexios holds me prisoner or appoints me to some other God-forsaken heathen land?

• • • • •

Ramiro had his first spasm of pain just past the ruins of Uwaynat outside Mosul. He slouched in the saddle and his horse slowed to a halt. Ozan noticed and yelled to the others. Ramiro tried to dismount. Grimacing in pain, he swayed in the saddle and started to topple.

Ozan jumped from his mount and rushed to his side, catching him just before he slid to the ground. "Ramiro! What's wrong?" he asked, kneeling down beside him.

Ramiro lay flat on his back at the side of the road and tried not to scream from the gripping pain in his guts.

"Are you alright?" Hasan asked as he rode up and dismounted.

Ramiro waved a hand. "Yes, yes. I just need a little rest." He slapped a hand on Ozan's shoulders. "Help me to the bushes before I vacate into my breeches."

• • • • •

Ramiro thought he was feeling better after a night's sleep but the pain soon returned. It started in his stomach with flutters of nausea before grinding straight into his bowels. Then came the diarrhea and the vomiting. It seemed they had to stop every farsakh so he could relieve himself.

"Bad water," said Sebuk. "I've seen it before." He took Ramiro's water skin and threw it away. "You can no longer use it."

Ramiro sat on the ground, hunched over from the sharp, searing cramps, oblivious to his surroundings.

"We must get to Edessa," said Hasan. "To the hospital." He went over to Ramiro and put his hand on his shoulder. "Can you make it to Edessa, Ramiro?"

Ramiro nodded and started to get up but he faltered. Hasan took him by the arm. But Ramiro was no sooner erect when he fainted, crumbling to the ground.

Hasan turned him over onto his back. "We'll have to get a horse and cart. He cannot ride like this."

"We have no money for a horse and cart," said Sebuk.

"No, but he does, and the money will be used to save his life."

"Take something for us," Sebuk urged. "We'll need it for the journey."

Hasan hesitated. "We can leave a note. And if he returns to Nikea, we will compensate him."

Sebuk nodded impatiently. "Yes, yes, brother, do it."

Hasan dug into Ramiro's money-belt. He took out two gold dinar. "This is more than enough."

"Take more," said Sebuk as he crouched down beside him.

Hasan scowled at him. "Have we become common thieves, my brother? Have you no honor? This man saved your life."

● ● ● ● ●

The cart rattled and bounced along the rough road, jarring Ramiro to consciousness. With effort, he lifted his head from a soft bundle and saw Ozan driving. He reached for the cross tucked in his vest, and felt relieved when he felt its familiar form. Then he thought of a prayer and tried to speak but no words would come. His mouth was as dry as summer dust and his tongue swollen. The thick, fur blanket that covered him seemed to offer no respite from the cold and he shivered violently.

Ozan turned around to see he was awake. "How do you feel, old friend? You look terrible."

Ramiro looked at him but could not respond, although he managed to raise a trembling hand in greeting.

"We will be in Edessa soon, my friend." Ozan tried to sound cheerful but spun his head away to hide his fear and sorrow. He rapped the horse's rump with his wand. "Yella! Yella!" he shouted.

Ramiro closed his eyes and fell into a thick fog of fleeting images and distant dreams.

EDESSA

"Will he live?" Hasan asked.

The physician folded his hands across his bright white tunic. He had a broad face and a long, flat nose that seemed to run up through his forehead where it disappeared into his dazzling white skull cap. Shocks of black hair dangled to his ears and, when he spoke, his long black beard barely moved. "Probably not. The man is in shock and severely dehydrated. His pulse is slow and weak and his eyes rheumy. We have put him in quarantine and have begun treatment. We should know in four to five days. But only Allah knows if he will live or die, by His mercy."

Hasan's brow furrowed. "Does he talk?"

"Once in a while. He keeps muttering about something. Does the name 'Adele' mean anything to you?"

Hasan shook his head.

"And several times he mentioned the Shah, at least I think he did, and something about a letter. I thought he was delirious at first, until I found a letter in his money-belt."

"A letter?" asked Hasan suspiciously.

"Yes. It bears the seal of Malik Shah and is addressed to the Roman King, Alexios. Do you think it important now that the Sultan is dead?"

Hasan shrugged a little. "Perhaps not. Whatever arrangement they had is bound to be moot."

"Are you willing to deliver this letter?"

"Me? To Constantinople?"

"You can send it on from Nikea, can you not?"

"I suppose. Very well, give it to me." He reached out.

The physician had a cautious look. "Will you swear to deliver this letter?"

"I will do it," said Hasan with a hint of impatience.

"You swear in the name of Allah?"

"In the name of Allah, I swear, by the will of Allah."

The physician reached into his tunic. "Here it is."

Hasan looked at it briefly before putting it in a pouch about his waist. "Is his money safe?"

"Of course it is. The guards allow no one in."

Hasan nodded skeptically. "Is there anything we can do for Ramiro?"

"I think not at this time. I will prescribe lots of water, a dose of lobelia, raw lemons and simple soups. And, of course, he is in much need of rest. Then we wait. Allah will decide."

• • • • •

Sebuk paced the room. "We cannot wait, my brother. We must return Kilich to Nikea as soon as possible. Already, General Buzan plans to take Malatya - and the Danishmends attack Kayseri from the north. If Buzan discovers the Son of Sulayman in his midst, he will have him in chains – or even executed."

"You are right, Sebuk," said Hasan. "Even if Ramiro does recover, he will be in no condition to travel for some time."

"I should stay to look after him," said Ozan.

"No," said Kilich. "You are my cousin. I will need you by my side."

Ozan wavered for a moment, he felt deeply obliged to stay with Ramiro - and yet returning to Nikea with Kilich was a great honor and privilege. He would share in his power and wealth. He had to go back. "But we must do *something* for him, Efendi, by the mercy of Allah." Tears welled in his eyes.

"Perhaps we could use some of Ramiro's money to buy a slave," suggested Sebuk. "Then he would have someone to look after him... if he lives."

"That's a good idea, Sebuk. We will talk to the physician about this." He rubbed his chin in worry. "We cannot wait for him to recover. We will see the physician now and ride for Nikea at first light."

CONSTANTINOPLE

DECEMBER 1092

Emperor Alexios was stunned. "Unbelievable! Are you completely sure?"

"Yes, my Lord," replied the envoy, still covered in a film of road dust. "There is no doubt, Malik Shah is dead. The Turk Empire is in chaos. His son, Berkyaruk, claims the throne, as does his brother, Prince Tutush." He reached into a small leather bag. "I return your letter, my Lord."

Alexios took the letter, one which he had given to the envoy to deliver personally to the Sultan. It had followed the letter he sent in French to appease Monk Aldebert. But now this. He slouched low in his gilded chair and his thoughts raced. Now there is no need for us to make a pact with the Sultan. And my daughter will be pleased to know she is no longer required to marry the Sultan's son. He smiled. The Sultan is dead. Praise be to God! Now we have an opportunity to regain an Empire. He composed himself and turned again to the envoy.

"Who is responsible?"

"There are many rumors, my King. Some say the Ismailis..."

"You mean the Hashashin?"

"Yes, my Lord. And others say his brother, Tutush, plotted his death, or that Nizam's family sought revenge."

Alexios stood up and wandered in thought. His red cape hung to the floor, where it swished around his red boots. "What else? You said you had three messages."

The envoy looked into the king's weatherworn and scarred face. "I have news of Nikea, my King. Our spies report that the Son of Sulayman has returned."

"Kilich? But he's just a boy! Who will be his military advisor?"

"He's fourteen, my Lord. And I hear that Al-Khanes will be his atabek. They say the people cheered him home, and Bolkas, the brother of Abul Kasim, handed over the city without argument. Now Sulayman's family has gained control again."

Alexios cursed under his breath. I should have seized the place when I had the chance. He put his hand to his chin. "How did he get to Nikea so quickly?"

"I heard he escaped the day after the Sultan's murder, O King. They say his jailer was bribed."

Alexios grew impatient. "And the last news?"

The envoy shuffled, his chain link armor clinked. "I have a letter from the Sultan."

"From Malik Shah?"

"Yes, my King." He handed it over.

"How did you get it?"

On my return, sire, I stopped at Nikea. This was just after Kilich returned. One of Bolkas' sons, a man called Hasan, he recognized my dress and approached me. He almost begged me to take it and gave me two dinar."

Alexios' face brightened. "So this letter must be a response to the one we sent on behalf of that Latin monk. Do you remember? We heard rumor he was captured by Turks and, only God knows how, he ended up in the Sultan's court. I agreed to test the rumor by sending a letter in his own tongue. I was just amusing the monk, I thought."

The envoy looked puzzled.

"Perhaps you know nothing of it. It was a favor I did to appease his ranting associate." He brushed a lock of red hair from his eyes. "Any word of him?"

"Who, my Lord?"

"Of the Latin monk. The Kelt with a ring of dark hair." He twirled one finger over his head.

The envoy shook his head. "I heard nothing of a monk, my Lord."

Alexios continued. "This man who gave you the letter, did he mention any names?"

"Oh, yes, yes. He said he got it from a man called Ramirah..."

"Ramiro," said Alexios. "What did he say?"

"He said they left the man for dead, my King. That he probably died of dysentery in Edessa."

Alexios shook his head. "Most unfortunate," he muttered. "Most unfortunate, indeed." He opened the letter. It was written in Turkish. He handed it back to the envoy. "What does it say?"

The man read slowly. "He says he received your letter written in a... strange tongue on behalf of the holy man. He is... glad that you are considering the... betrothal of your daughter to his son, Berkyaruk. And he says he will let the monk return as a sign of good faith."

"So the monk really was alive in Isfahan. How in hell's blazes did he get there? And how did he get out? And how did he end up in Edessa?"

"I have no idea, my Lord."

• • • • •

Aldebert collapsed in tears. "Ramiro's dead?" he choked. "No! No! I will not believe it! May God have mercy!"

Commander Manuel tried to comfort him. "Well... we are not entirely sure, but it seems likely."

Aldebert lifted his head out of his hands, his long face wet with tears. "You're not sure? You mean he may still live?"

"We have no firm word, as yet."

"When did he fall ill?"

"I don't know. He was last seen near death in the hospital at Edessa."

Aldebert stood suddenly, brushing tears from his face. "Then I will go to Edessa. I will find him. Alive or not!"

Manuel shook his head. "It is a dangerous journey. And worse if you travel as a monk. The Turk Empire is in chaos, warlords and Turkoman plunder with impunity. No city is safe."

"To hell with the God-damned Turks!"

"Please, Monk Aldebert, you can barely wield a sword."

Aldebert stuck out his chin. "I will take Pepin," he said defiantly. "He has learned to use a sword."

"Please," Manuel sighed in desperation. "We have many experienced men at our disposal. Let me send a messenger to Edessa to find the truth."

"Who will go?"

"I will ask for Tatran. He knows Ramiro and he can speak the languages. He will take a homing pigeon."

"A what?"

"A homing pigeon – we breed them in our lofts. No matter where you take them, they will always return to the loft. It is a part of our spy network."

"But Edessa is hundreds of miles away!"

"No matter. The pigeon will return... unless it is shot down."

"And what can the pigeon tell us if it does return?"

"We will tie a marking to its leg. If it is white, Ramiro lives. But if black..."

Aldebert waved his hand - he didn't want to hear. "How soon will Tatran leave?"

"With the Emperor's permission, I will send him off tomorrow."

SPRING 1093

Alexios paced in fury. "Chaka has betrayed us again! Any treaty with that man is worthless!"

"And for the third time he builds more ships to attack our ports," said John Doukas.

"We must destroy him once and for all!" Isaak ranted. "We should send an army to Smyrna and capture the coast."

"We can send only one division, brother," Alexios moaned. "Even though we have managed to defeat the Patzinaks, we are still threatened by a Kuman horde approaching from the north and will need most of our men to drive them back. We *must* think of another way to dissuade Chaka."

John stood up, leaning with his fingers on the table. "And already Chaka has betrothed his daughter to Kilich of Nikea. We can only assume he has made a pact with him to surround our eastern shores."

Alexios raised his hands in the air as he paced the room. "How can Kilich trust that treacherous fox? Damn him to Hades!"

Anna glared up at him, creasing her small, pale forehead. "Please, Alexi, do not curse. How can our Lord God stay with you when you entertain such vile thoughts?"

"Sorry, mother," he said ruefully. "But this man drives me to rage."

Anna tapped her finger on her note paper. "Remember," she said, "there is no use wasting the lives of our good men when other means present themselves. We should send young Kilich a letter. Something that would lead him to distrust Chaka... we need to turn these infidels against each other, like dogs over meat. That would save us much trouble. We might even be able to persuade Kilich to ally with us."

"But now Chaka is his father-in-law."

"My dear Alexi, you should know by now that any notion of kinship will dissolve like salt in water when it comes to money and power."

"Yes... yes," he mumbled. He thought for a moment and then smiled. "Let's tell Kilich that Chaka plans to conquer his sultanate, and not Byzantium, which is probably true anyway."

Isaak grinned. "It's worth a try."

"I will gladly compose the letter," said Anna with a sly grin.

NIKEA

Kilich dressed in the fine raiments of a sultan. Now fifteen, he was a little taller and, having a fine growth of stubble, looked more of a man. He read the letter from Alexios to his advisors. "Do you believe this letter, cousin?"

"I do, my Sultan," said Ozan. "Chaka cannot possibly win the Roman throne. And why else would he assemble an army and build a fleet in Smyrna? If we allow him to come up the coast with his ships, he could attack us from land and sea."

Kilich paused for a moment, looking at his men. "But can we trust King Alexios?" He caught the eye of his atabek, a rough-looking and battle-hardened mamluk who had advised his father about military matters. "What do you think, Al-Khanes?"

"I don't trust Chaka any more than the Roman king," Al-Khanes said in a deep, nasal voice. He was a big man with long braided hair, a scarred face, and a gnarled nose, smashed by a war hammer years before. "May Allah curse them both. But the king's words ring true, my Prince. If we allow Chaka to strengthen, he will be a threat. We must do all we can to bring the Aegean coast under our control. For now, I say we ally with the Romans to defeat him."

Kilich nodded. "Then so be it!" he shouted with the eager naiveté of youth. "We will join the Romans on this venture. Assemble an army."

SMYRNA

Chaka looked over the walls of Smyrna. His weathered face creased with concern when he heard that a Byzantine army rode down the coast. But he was truly alarmed when he learned that his new son-in-law, Kilich, had joined them. So when both armies reached Smyrna and camped outside his walls, he sent a messenger to Kilich's camp, seeking terms.

The messenger returned with good news and, much to Chaka's surprise, he was warmly received in Kilich's large tent, where he was subsequently plied with food and fine wine. Guards stood outside while six mamluks guarded the young Prince as he sat, as did Ozan and Al-Khanes. They exchanged pleasantries and began to feast.

Chaka put on his finest robe for the occasion. He cut his hair short, Roman style. His face was rough, scarred by war and adversity. As was the custom, he talked at length about the weather, about the crops, and about their sons before approaching the matter at hand. Finally, he could wait no longer.

"I am your father-in-law, Prince Kilich. Why do you side with these Romans?" he complained through thick lips. "You cannot trust them. You know they will betray you. And if you drive me out, the sons of bitches will attack you next. Join me and we will rule the Roman lands together." He downed his mug of wine.

Kilich eyed the man with disgust. He's as vulgar as a barbarian. He stinks and eats like a pig. He leaned forward and reached for the wine jug. "And how do you foresee this arrangement?" he asked with barely disguised hostility. "If I join you to defeat the Romans, how will the spoils be divided?" He filled Chaka's mug.

Chaka took another long draught. "Well... you can take all land west of Nikea, as far as the Propontis. I will hold Byzantium and the Roman lands west of the sea, and keep the Aegean coast."

Al-Khanes leaned over, his long braids swept the table and his dark eyes glared over his gnarled nose. "It sounds like you will get the lion's share, Lord Chaka."

Kilich scowled. "My atabek speaks well. How do you reply? What of our position?" He dreaded the thought of being surrounded by Chaka's forces. "If you lay claim to the Roman lands, I want Smyrna and the coast."

Chaka looked at him with glassy eyes, the wine was taking its toll. "I have paid the price for Smyrna," he scoffed, "while you have done little. Why should I cede it to you?"

"Because you offer me nothing I do not already have," said Kilich. "You must pay the price if you want my help."

Chaka banged his mug onto the low table. "You're nothing but a young upstart. Do not think you can defeat me!" He took another drink, then raised his voice. "My armies could easily overrun both Nikea and the Roman lands!" he smirked.

Kilich stared at him with wide eyes. "The Roman king spoke the truth!" he shouted, jumping to his feet. "You plot against us!" He drew his sword in an impetuous flash of rage. "Conniving old bastard! May Allah curse you!" And, catching them all by complete surprise, he thrust his blade right through Chaka's ribs before the shocked man could utter a single word.

The tent fell dead quiet. Chaka stared up at Kilich, his eyes bulging in total shock. He tried to speak but the only sound was the gurgle of his own blood. His eyes flickered and he collapsed headfirst into a bowl of cold hummus.

Part Five

SYRIA

LAND OF DREAMS

Syria was not always dry and barren. An Egyptian account from the Middle Kingdom describes the land as '...afflicted with water, difficult from many trees, the ways thereof painful because of the mountains.' Another says it is '...overgrown with cypresses and oaks and cedars which reach the heavens,' where 'lions are more numerous than leopards or hyenas.'

It was here in this lush, salubrious land where one of the world's most ancient civilizations evolved, a great Semitic empire, the motherland of Arab and Jew alike. But over the millennia, the climate dried out and the bright flower of the empire withered and died. Rather than a center of domination, Syria soon became dominated, remaining strategic only because it was a vital crossroads for the armies and caravans of Egypt, Greece, Rome and Persia. Even so, much of its ancient culture persisted, and its arts, literature and science flourished in the midst of conflict and turmoil. And to this day, Syria is the land of a thousand nights, it is the land of a thousand dreams.

EDESSA

Ramiro stared at the two angels. They appeared to shiver in a bright, blue light, and yet he could see them so plainly.

"What do you seek, Ramiro?" one asked.

"I seek Jerusalem, O Holy One," he said without moving his lips.

"Why Jerusalem?" asked the other.

"Why... why because it is the Holy City of God, the most sacred place on earth. And the place of our Savior's crucifixion and death. I wish to pray at His tomb." He had no sooner spoken when a vivid image appeared before him - a huge, gray stone cube oozing blood from its top, a thick blood that drenched its sides in scarlet swaths. "Blessed Mary!" Ramiro jolted. "Is this the Holy Sepulcher? What does this mean?" Then, just as suddenly, the vision disappeared.

"And you have a cross?" the angels asked, unfazed.

"Uh, yes, yes, I do, for the Patriarch. I promised to deliver it to the Patriarch."

"Is it important?"

"Oh yes, it is very important, for the sake of Christendom," he said sincerely, but he thought he could hear the angels laugh, if indeed angels laugh.

"And you seek a woman, one close to your heart," one asked.

"Yes, Spirit, my mother."

"And you think of another."

"Uh... yes, yes," he felt himself blush. "I... I pray for her safety." The angels did not respond, but again he felt they were amused.

"Do you believe you will reach God in Jerusalem?" both angels chorused.

"I believe the power of God is greater in Jerusalem," said Ramiro with candor.

"Do you?" they asked wistfully. "But do not your scriptures tell you the Domain of God is within? Have you not learned that God lives in your heart and mind? And there, he waits patiently to guide you... if you would only listen and obey."

"Yes, I do believe that, Blessed Spirits. But is not the Holy Sepulcher a sacred place? The center of the earth?"

"There is no sacred place," they said lovingly. "Only a life in the service of God is sacred."

"I lead a pious life," Ramiro said defensively. "What more can I do?"

"You lead a troubled life, Ramiro of Cluny, your heart is rent with doubt - your mind clouded by tradition - your actions impeded by ritual. How is it possible to serve God in such confusion?"

"But I... I believe I have devoted my life to God."

"So you say."

Ramiro felt a rush of remorse. "Please, Holy Ones, what must I do?"

"Listen to the Spirit," they chanted, "... and obey." Together, they took his hands and led him toward the light. It was cool, white and bright.

"What's this?"

"Heaven's Gate," said one. "Prepare to enter the Domain of God... fear not."

• • • • •

The young man stood in the doorway. He wrung his hands in a fuss, bit his lip and bounced on his knees. He could hardly contain his excitement as he waited for the physician to acknowledge him.

"What is it, Jameel?" the physician finally asked with some annoyance.

"Sayyid! I saw him move!" The young man's brown hair fell into his eyes.

"You saw Ramiro move?"

"Yes, Sayyid, I saw his eyelids flutter and his body twitch."

The physician rose from his cushion. "Well then, he is either dying or recovering." He rushed to the room and bent over Ramiro's limp figure. He smelled his breath and listened to its labor. He took his thin arm and felt his pulse. "I see no movement but I detect a slight quickening of his pulse. Otherwise, he appears much the same." He made an entry in his notebook and prepared to leave. "Stay with him, boy. Keep that brazier burning and keep him warm. If he awakes, by the will of Allah, you must give him hot soup. If he doesn't eat soon, he will surely die." He left the room and the young man sat down to wait.

ALEPPO

KHUDA THE MAMLUK

The sun was high overhead by the time Khuda the Mamluk approached the southern gate of Aleppo, one of the longest inhabited cities in the world. The high mound of the Citadel dominated the view, a natural formation of limestone rock that rose one hundred and sixty feet above the city center. Its sheer rock sides served as steep ramparts and the imposing walls and towers of the Citadel itself, which sat on the flat summit of the mound, could house a garrison of thousands.

Aleppo was a trading mecca. Merchandise from as far away as India and China made its way to the Persian Gulf and then up the Euphrates to the markets of southwest Asia, including luxuries such as musk, aloes, camphor, cinnamon - and Samarkand slaves.

"Toros! Son of camel shit!" Khuda yelled to one of his men. "Put that whip aside or I'll hack off your feet and leave the vultures to pick your miserable bones!" He shouted with his chin up to carry his threat to the back of the caravan train, a procession of six pack camels, seven armed horsemen, fifteen Turkoman horses, and a string of Samarkand slaves. The slaves, twelve barefoot children roped together at the waist, were dragged along by the strong pull of a sand-colored dromedary.

Khuda, a brawny Turk with a battle-scarred face, scratched his scruffy, black beard in vexation. They had travelled the road from Baghdad, following the Euphrates to Raqqa. From there, they crossed the Syrian Desert, a flat wasteland of rock and gravel, and skirted past the oasis at Al-Jabbal before taking the long, hot road to Aleppo. His slaves suffered on this last leg and he knew it would concern his employer, Harun the Slaver. He scowled and adjusted his turban. Long braids of black hair swung across his broad shoulders.

The gatekeepers of Aleppo recognized him and let his party through. Khuda returned their greetings, dodging people and animals while the loud, brazen cries of hawkers reverberated from the stone walls and gray pigeons fluttered overhead, cooing from nests set along thick wooden beams.

He dismounted with effort, shifting the scabbard of his sword as he swung a leg over his mount. Long days in the saddle had made him stiff and he grunted as he hit the ground. He walked unsteadily to the tax collector, an Arab employee of the Turk Emir, and greeted the man politely.

The tax collector combed his fingers through his black beard, impeccably groomed, and darted a glance in Khuda's direction before scratching at his short hair, which peeped out under a white cotton cap. In front of him, lay a stack of paper held in place with flat stones. He spread one out on the table and dipped his quill in a pot of Indian ink. "How many slaves do you bring? And what do you carry on the camels?" He sat stiffly, swatting slowly at the flies on the scroll in front of him.

This idiot has no manners, Khuda thought before he reached into his belt and pulled out a piece of paper. He threw it on the table. "Here's my list."

The collector looked askance in disgust, then he turned to the list and read aloud. "Fifteen horses, twelve child slaves, one talent of silk, two talents of silver dishes, a talent of pepper and one of cinnamon, and four talents of sugar." He transcribed the tally at his desk, making the entries on a long scroll before ordering one of his assistants to check the cargo. The man rushed out while Khuda waited in the heat.

When the servant finally returned to confirm the accounting, the taxman finished his calculations. "You owe the Emir, may Allah keep him, a tax of twenty-two dirham."

"Twenty-two dirham?" Khuda growled, perhaps a bit too loudly. He gritted his teeth and reminded himself to keep calm. "That is more than I have ever paid for similar merchandise. Are you sure?"

The collector looked directly at him for the first time. "That is the fee, trader. Would you like me to advise the Emir of your discontent?"

Khuda paused. "No, no. That will not be necessary. I will pay your fee," he fumed, knowing the amount was exorbitant.

Harun the Slaver arrived at the gate just as the collector handed Khuda his receipt. He rode up on a heavy Barqah mare, a working breed from North Africa known for its big head and thick legs. It was not a beautiful horse but it was the only one capable of supporting the man's weight. Harun was eager to inspect his new merchandise. "Ya, Khuda!" he shouted in an excited, gasping voice.

Khuda looked up from the table. "Peace be upon you, Harun. May you receive Allah's blessing."

Harun, a huge fat man, dismounted with considerable difficulty. He grasped the horn of his saddle, twisting the harness and causing his poor horse to neigh in pain. A muscular slave dashed to his aid, but he could barely cope. "Get away you stupid oaf," Harun shouted at him, raising a kerchief to dab at the sweat pouring from his chubby face. He waddled over to inspect the young slaves, who were filthy and teetering under the blazing rays of the noonday sun. "Khuda!" he yelled. "Are you trying to put me out of business? These waifs are barely alive! Get them to the house before they all die on me!" His shrill voice managed to rise above the deafening din of hawkers and hucksters who lined the narrow, teeming streets.

Khuda clenched his teeth. You fat pig! What do you know of the trouble and misery we endure just to fatten your purse and belly? He turned a piercing glance to Toros, an Armenian slave with light brown hair and green eyes who also worked for Harun.

Toros immediately sensed trouble and rushed to get the slaves in line, eight girls and four boys, before pulling them along the dry and dusty street, some sobbing from exhaustion, others silently morose. "Let's go! Let's go!" he yelled, cracking his whip. He turned on a crying slave boy, a frail lad of nine with thick, black hair, belting him across the head with the palm of his hand and knocking him to the ground. The boy screamed as he fell. Toros glared at the cowering lad. "Shut up! You miserable little dog! Who will buy you in such a sorry state! We'll sell you to the whorehouse! - Quiet! Get up and clean your ugly face!"

Toros' shouts did not escape the attention of Ibrahim, a clergyman who stood at the door of the bakery across the street. He counted out a few copper coins for his hot flat bread before storming over to Toros.

"You, ... slave-driver!" he shouted in a deep, throaty voice that belied his tall, slender frame. So powerful was its resonance that the people around the bakery fell silent or began to talk in hushed whispers. Many in the gathering crowd recognized his dress, a white turban and a long black tunic with sleeves that covered his hands. Ibrahim was a *mufti*, a legal scholar and a Sunni Muslim known and respected for his knowledge of the laws and traditions contained in the Sharia and the Hadiths. Those who knew him told others and the word spread quickly throughout the crowd of shoppers and merchants.

Toros recognized Ibrahim's dress and tried to move away as fast as he could. Meanwhile, Harun turned awkwardly on his small feet to see why such a hush had descended on the boisterous street. That's when he saw the mufti striding toward one of his drivers.

"You!" Ibrahim shouted at Toros in indignation. "In the name of Allah, must you beat these slaves for no reason? Is your heart so devoid of compassion that you would treat these poor wretches with such malice?" His stern face scowled at the young man.

"No Mufti," Toros replied respectfully, he briefly met Ibrahim's fiery stare before lowering his eyes.

Harun waddled back with servants in tow. Sweat ran freely down his pale, round face. "O Noble One," he interjected before Toros could say another word. "Praise Allah for your presence among us!" he gasped. "I am Harun. How can I assist you today, O Great Mufti?" He took another deep breath. "Has my unworthy boy dared to offend you? If so, forgive him, he's a stupid Armenian and knows no better." Spittle flew from his bulging lips, drooling into his graying beard.

Ibrahim's stern face curled in a sneer of disgust. "You offend God, Harun, son of slavers, with your vile language and cruelty!" he said, laying Toros' sins on his head. The crowd closed around them. "Do you not obey the Sharia, the Holy Law of Islam?"

"By all means, Great One," Harun flushed, he could feel his heart pound. "We are simply on our way to the market to sell these Turkomans, Holy One. We meant no harm or offense, they are merely infidels," his voice labored.

Ibrahim persisted in the same strong voice. "And how does the Sharia instruct us in these matters, Slaver?"

"Well..." Harun struggled for words, not really sure what to say. "It is the right way, Sayyid, the law...the way a good Muslim lives," he stammered. He could not draw his mind from the cool comfort of his mansion. He grasped for ways to escape the mufti, but his brain fogged in the stifling heat. The crowd smirked at his difficulty.

Ibrahim raised his voice for the edification of all. "The Sharia is our guiding principle," he instructed with righteous indignation, "it specifies the laws and moral principles by which every good Muslim should abide. It instructs us in the duties each Muslim owes to God and his fellow man." He paused to give his words effect. "Remember, in the words of the Prophet, you should give slaves the same food you eat, the same clothes you wear, you must burden them lightly, and torment them not." After another pause, he added his own comment. "Even if they appear inferior."

"Yes, Mufti," agreed Harun quickly as his small eyes shifted down the street toward the gathering crowd and the slave market. "Your wisdom precedes you - and your knowledge of Islam is unmatched. May Allah and the Prophet be praised! I go now to obtain good homes and admirable occupations for these poor waifs. May Allah preserve them, by the will of Allah." And he began to turn away while signaling to the others. The young slaves stared wide-eyed at the tall mufti, who showed such courage in the face of the cruel slavers.

Khuda watched. His scruffy beard could hardly hide the derisive grin on his lips or the glint of amusement in his narrow eyes.

Toros gave gentle tugs on their ropes and they all began to slip away to the waiting market.

Ibrahim could see them inching away... without his leave. "Go, then, and do not forget your prayers!" he cried in an effort to save face. He hesitated to press the issue, he had done all he could. He knew he could not prevent the mistreatment of slaves despite the laws and admonitions of Islam. And it was foolish to think slaves would eat and dress as their masters. Indeed, slaves were marked by their dress and grooming. Further protest was unwise. There were many wealthy people in the dispersing crowd, Christians, Muslims, Jews, and Zoroastrians alike, who relied on slave labor to work their homes and businesses. And the ruling Turks needed slaves to fight their battles. They came from near and far; the infidel Turkoman of the north, the Armenians of the Caucasus, the Slavs of the Dnieper, and the Greeks of Byzantium. And here they all mingled on the streets of Aleppo.

Thick odors of human sweat, animals and dung hung in the air as an endless stream of people, horses, donkeys, camels, and carts carved their way through the narrow streets. But at times, more pleasing aromas of grilled lamb and roasting camel would drift across their path.

Hundreds of shops crowded the streets near the mosques. Further out, lay warehouses, factories and guild schools. Slaves darted about cleaning the pavement and picking up garbage, supervised by freemen from the Office of Municipal Works. Soldiers strolled back and forth. Itinerant traders and craftsmen set up stalls and tents in the central plaza. Artisans and merchants sold ornate glass, books, dyed cloth from Damascus, copper utensils, iron tools and weapons, saddles, shoes, herbs and medicines, pottery, and beautiful silks from Samarkand.

Harun's long procession finally came to a stop at the wall of his luxurious mansion, a two-storied stone building cornering the market at Slave Alley. "Open the gate!" he cried out.

His head eunuch and chamberlain, a small balding man who appeared highly agitated, stood by the entrance. "Ya, Harun, my Lord!" he shouted at the door. "Surely it is Allah's blessing that you have returned to us safely. May Allah preserve you, Master."

"I have no time for your babble," said Harun. "I've been away only a few hours. Get these slaves inside. They need food and drink... And bathe them!" He wheezed from the long walk. "Check the goods in store and tend to the horses. I will take my meal as soon as I wash and dress. Go! Go! Go!"

"Yes, Master, at once!"

"Come Khuda," Harun muttered, "You must brief me on recent events. We will bathe and dine."

A big woman with a wide, heavy face met them inside. "All is prepared for you, my husband," cried Huda, who was nearly as fat as Harun. She raised her voice. "Your bath awaits you at your leisure." Harun did not reply and she huffed off with her nose in the air.

The main door opened into a wide foyer where wool carpets, woven in colorful animal themes, spread across floors of blue ceramic tile. They passed into a small courtyard adorned with pear and orange trees wrapping a marble fountain. The place was quiet except for the tinkle of water. Even the birds fell silent in the heat.

Khuda was eager to wash away the dust and grime accumulated on his long journey from Baghdad and he headed straight into the bath.

"So tell me Khuda, what news have you heard?" Harun asked before emptying a large glass of orange juice. A slave gave him another.

Khuda shook his head, tightening his lips. "Trouble is brewing, Master. Everywhere, local emirs fight amongst themselves, trying to grab more land and cities. Raiders and thieves haunt the roads. It's too dangerous to return to Baghdad. Berkyaruk still fights for the Sultan's throne. His uncle, Tutush will challenge him. I have heard he leads an army to Isfahan."

"Apparently not," said Harun. "I heard he abandoned the campaign and returned to Damascus."

"Why? What happened?" Khuda asked, drying his long hair with a towel.

"Not enough men. The emirs of Aleppo and Edessa failed to follow him into battle as they had promised. Now he schemes to destroy them in revenge."

Khuda nodded in understanding. "And what of Antioch? Do you think Tutush will besiege it too?"

Harun shook his head. "It's unlikely that even Tutush could breach the walls of Antioch."

"I suppose that's true. And what of the west? What of the Roman lands?"

Harun smiled, lifting his huge cheeks. "Oh yes, there is trouble there too. But it bodes well for me. I just bought some young Roman women captured up north near Nikea. Some with colored hair. I'll get a good price for them."

They fell silent and gazed into the garden. The whitewashed walls of the courtyard glowed in the waning rays of the desert sun and the air began to cool. Sparrows revived and fluttered between branches.

• • • • •

While Harun and Khuda sat down to a meal of roast lamb, onions, beans and olives, the slaves in the cells below ate bowls of cold, barley gruel. The large basement of Harun's expansive mansion served as a slave-quarter, divided into dim cells separated by stone walls. The boy slaves were thrown into one and the girls in another. Four other cells held more. One held only black slaves, another held Turkoman women, while another contained eight white women, the Roman slaves.

Toros the Armenian and Dmitri the Slav sat on goat-hair cushions to enjoy a meal of dates, goat cheese and flat bread spread on a low wooden table. They ate greedily.

Dmitri, a blonde boy of twelve, was captured in the upper reaches of the Dnieper by the Rus, descendants of Viking raiders and the fathers of Russia, and shipped down the Volga to a port on the north Caspian Sea. From there, he was sent to the slave markets of Bukhara to be castrated. His white-blonde hair, blue eyes and tanned skin made him a rare sight. His owner, Harun, thought he was pretty and bought him in the markets of Baghdad.

"Did you see Harun's face when the mufti scolded him," Dmitri smirked.

"I thought his beady eyes would burst out of his fat head!" Toros sputtered through a piece of flatbread and they both laughed aloud. "Careful - be quiet, we don't want that bitch, Huda, to hear us."

"Toros, let's go to the market today. I want to buy a knife from the old armorer." He stuffed a date in his mouth.

Toros put his food down and yawned. "I'm too tired to go anywhere. Besides, you stink of camel shit."

Dmitri groaned. "You talk like an old man."

Above them, an iron door squealed on its hinges and slammed shut. "Huda comes!" Toros whispered. They cleaned up their meal in a hurry and sat waiting.

Huda huffed down the long, stone stairway. Two slave girls accompanied her, one carrying stacks of rough linen robes and the other stooping from the weight of two pails of steaming water. "Toros! You Armenian bastard! Come and help us before I sell you for dog meat!" she shrilled as she labored her way down the steps. Her faded, yellow tunic brushed the floor.

Toros rushed to the base of the staircase. Dmitri followed. "Yes, Mistress. Your wish is my command."

She thumped to the floor, panting as if she had run a marathon, and looked up into Toros' watchful green eyes. "It's a wonder you didn't kill them all, you stupid infidels. Look at their condition! I should have you both whipped!" Her heavy jowls fluttered and her thick lips sputtered.

Toros looked down into her pale face, distracted by the thin, black hairs growing out of her chin. Her big head and bulging body bobbed as she heaved her words. You ugly old hag! But he lowered his eyes lest they betray his thoughts. "Welcome, Sayyidah, your kindness and mercy precede you."

Huda clicked her tongue in disapproval before turning on the slave girls carrying the pails. "Prepare our new arrivals for a washing. The physician is coming to tend their wounds." Then she plodded over to the cell holding the Roman women. "And make sure one of you takes care of these girls. Make sure they're well fed and clean. And I want their hair brushed." She looked carefully at the women. Some were sobbing and others stared vacantly. Only one of them showed any spirit, the one with red hair, the one who spoke a strange barbarian tongue. She was a beautiful woman, but too old for the best price. "Well, well my pretty ones," Huda screeched at them. "Soon you will have the pleasure of a prince's harem." But the women did not understand her words. The red-head snarled at her, screaming something no one understood.

Huda stepped back in alarm, then laughed nervously. "Well, come on Toros!" she shouted. "Unlock the doors so my girls can get to work. We have one month to transform these heathen bitches into precious dolls. Then we take them to market."

EDESSA

JUNE 1093

Ramiro had another dream. He soared like a bird over the rolling hills and lush valleys of Burgundy. There, far below, was Cluny and the monastery and the vast farmlands that spread out around it. A small hamlet caught his eye and down he came, slowly, slowly, until he found himself alight in a garden of bright flowers surrounding a small, thatch-roofed house. Adele was there, she held a babe in her arms. The child looked at him and smiled.

He opened his eyes with a start, he had no idea where he was. He stared at the ceiling. It was white. He looked down to the walls. They were white. The door was white. Is this heaven?

With effort, he tried to get up but could not. He managed to rock to his side and propped himself on an elbow but he had no strength and flopped back. He tried again and, this time, managed to balance. He looked around, soon realizing he was in a small room, all plastered white. A window opened behind him and he could hear the twitter of birds.

He lay back down for some time, trying to collect his thoughts. Suddenly, the door swung open and he jolted. He turned his head and stared at the young man in the doorway. The boy grinned from ear to ear. Ramiro tried to speak but only a dry squawk emerged and he fell to coughing. The boy reached for a jug of water on a nearby table and rushed to the bed, helping him to drink.

"Are you a... an angel?" Ramiro croaked in southern French.

Jameel shook his head and replied in Arabic. "What are you trying to say, Master?"

Ramiro stared blankly for some time.

"Master, can you hear me?"

Ramiro heard the words, like someone calling from far above, and he began to pull himself into the present, inch by inch, as if clawing out of a deep well. Slowly, he began to recall the tongue of the land and repeated the phrase in rasping Arabic.

The boy looked astonished, then smiled broadly. "No, Master, I am Jameel. I am the one your right hand owns."

"What?"

"Your friends bought me for you, Master."

"My friends? What do you mean?" his voice a harsh whisper.

Jameel stood by the bed looking demur. "I am your slave, Master."

"My slave?"

"Yes, Master. Your friends bought me to care for you."

Ramiro stared at the boy as a flood of memories returned, washing away his lingering dreams. "Where are my friends?"

"They left almost one month ago. They left for Nikea."

Ramiro rolled to his side. I'm still alive, he thought, and a wide smile cracked across his pallid, round face.

"Please, Master," said Jameel in a pleading tone. "You must eat."

Ramiro tried again to pry himself up. "Come on, then," he said softly. "Make yourself useful, my boy. Help me sit up."

Jameel put one arm under Ramiro's knees and another to his back. He lifted him to a sitting position. The boy was about fourteen and, except for a few minor blemishes, he was strikingly attractive. He had dark brown hair,

blue eyes and a small nose. So young and beautiful, Ramiro thought, just as
the slavers like them. He raised a weak hand to scratch an itch on his chin and
was startled by a mangled mass of bushy, black beard - and his hair, it hung to
his shoulders. "Blessed saints!" he grated. "I need a barber."

Jameel laughed. "Now you look like a holy man, Master. I was told you are
a holy man."

"Where am I?" Ramiro asked.

"Why, you are in hospital, Sayyid."

"What hospital?"

"The hospital in Edessa, Master." Jameel began to wonder if his new master
was addled.

Ramiro's eyes widened in a sudden thought. "Where's my cross?"

"Your cross? Oh, yes, the Christian cross. Do not worry, Master, it is in
the cabinet with all your possessions. Now I will get some soup for you." He
turned and ran out the door.

• • • • •

"This is not a good time to ride, Master," Jameel protested. "It's too cold
and wet. And you are still weak." He followed Ramiro along the winding path
of the hospital garden. Dark, rolling clouds threatened in the distance and the
air cooled, giving strength to his words.

Grudgingly, Ramiro knew the boy was right. He had lost weight and strength
and was still in no shape to travel. "But that's not what I asked you, I want to
know the best route to Jerusalem," he said with a touch of exasperation.

"Yes, Sayyid, forgive me." Jameel was right on his heels, like a friendly
shadow. "First you must go to Aleppo, then head south on the long road to
Homs and Damascus. I'm not sure how to get to Jerusalem from there. I think
you will have to travel down the Jordan River."

Ramiro studied the slight young man, beautiful but poorly educated... and
he was not a warrior. "How do you know these things?" he asked skeptically.

Jameel smiled. "Everyone knows this, Master."

"Is this the only route?" he asked as he ran his fingers through his neatly
barbered beard. His hair had been cut just below the ears, the current fashion.

"Oh, no. You can travel the coast from Aleppo to Latakia, from there to
Tripoli, Beirut and Tyre. After that, I'm not sure."

It started to rain and they took cover in a small shrine at the riverside. Here
they sat and watched as it poured down in heavy beads. "So which route is
the best?"

"It all depends, Master. The road to Homs and Damascus is flat but it's hot,
although you can follow the river to Homs."

"What river?"

"Why... the great Orontes, Master." Jameel said proudly, happy to demonstrate his knowledge.

"And the coast road?"

"Many more Christians live along the coast road, Master. But there are still problems."

"Such as?" Ramiro asked, rolling his hands to urge him on.

"Well, there are many hills to climb and ... and further south, the Egyptians wait to enslave us."

"Why would they enslave us?"

"Because we are not Shia, Efendi."

"Are these the Ismailis... the Hashashin?"

"No, no, Master." Jameel laughed. "Not all Shia are Ismailis. The Egyptians are Fatimid Shia."

"And which are you Jameel, Shia or Sunni?"

"Oh, no, neither Sayyid, they tell me I was born a Christian."

Ramiro looked surprised. "Really? But you're an Arab."

"There are many Christian Arabs, Master."

"So are you a member of the Greek church?"

"No, no, Sayyid. My last master said I was a stinking Maronite. But I am not sure what a Maronite is... and I have never been in a church."

Ramiro brought out his golden cross. "You have seen this?"

"Yes, Master, it is very beautiful."

"Where is your cross?"

"I was not allowed to have one," Jameel said sadly.

"I thought all Christians had to wear one?"

"Slaves are slaves, Master. There are no Muslim slaves."

"Well, now you will have one. We will go to the markets."

"You are good to me, Master," he beamed. "I will serve you well."

"You do not need to serve me, Jameel, I set you free."

"Free, Master?" Jameel had a sudden look of fear. "But what will I do, Master? I have no money, no family... no position."

"I will give you some money."

"Please, Master, let me come with you. I have nothing here."

He stared at the young man and wondered if it was wise to bring him along. He pursed his lips in hesitation, then he smiled a little. "Oh, very well, you will come." He stood up. "In the meantime, we will continue with your reading lessons. And then we will prepare for Aleppo. I want you to find us two horses."

"Horses, Master?"

"Yes, horses. We will ride soon."

"But Master, Christians are not allowed to have horses."

"What do you mean? I rode a horse all the way to Isfahan!"

"Yes, Master. Please excuse me, but you said you travelled as a slave of the Muslims. South of here, you may not own a horse or a weapon. It is the law."

"Can we ride a mule?"

"Yes, or a donkey. But you must remember to dismount when passing important Muslims."

REPORT: EDESSA

Ramiro focused his mind to finish a long overdue account to Abbot Hugh. He first told him of his capture by the Turks, his escape, his illness and subsequent brush with death. Then he went on to describe the Turk Empire and its vast extent, its power and civilization, its hospitals and universities, its literature, mathematics, architecture and art. And with genuine sadness, he wrote of the assassination of the Great Sultan and his Vizier and how their deaths had caused the empire to spiral into a state of chaos. He told Hugh about the lay of the land, its deserts and mountains, and he told him about the cities of Isfahan, Mosul, Edessa, Antioch and the blessed Tarsus, home of Saint Paul.

But he said nothing of the cross. He had promised Hugh he would deliver it intact. How could he tell him it had been broken and its bloodstone torn out? And how could he tell him it had been remodeled in gold by heretics?

He put his pen down and rubbed his stubbled face. *I have said enough. Now I must send a letter to Aldebert - he must be back in Constantinople by now.*

A SCYTH

Weeks later, a Byzantine messenger arrived at the Edessa hospital. "May Allah keep you. I am Tatran the Scyth," he said to the physician. "I'm looking for a man by the name of Ramiro of Cluny."

"He was here for some time," the physician replied. "But he left for Aleppo over a week ago."

Tatran smiled. *Ramiro was alive.* "Did he say any more about his destination?"

A look of concern crossed the physician's face. *Whoever this man is, he thought, he is clearly a Turk.* "And what is your business, Sayyid?"

"I have been sent by the Roman Emperor to find this man, Ramiro." He dug into his vest. "Here are my papers."

"The Emperor?" the physician asked skeptically as he perused the document, written in Greek. It looked authentic. He raised his eyes. "Ramiro gave me an envelope," he said, looking Tatran square in the face. "He addressed it to a man by the name of Aldebert of Cluny, now residing in Constantinople. Do you know this man?"

"Well, yes, I know him well."

The physician turned to a cabinet next to his desk and retrieved a large envelope made of thick, Baghdadi paper. He put it on the table. "Ramiro asked me to send this on with the next courier going to Constantinople. Perhaps you could deliver it? Otherwise, considering the turmoil these days, it may be some time before I can send it off."

"Of course, Sayyid, I would be glad to."

He handed it over. "Ramiro told us he was going to Aleppo, but he often talked of Jerusalem. His friends from Isfahan have returned to Nikea. That is all I know."

"His friends from Isfahan?" asked Tatran. "What friends are these?"

"Four men from Nikea who were imprisoned, like himself, by the Sultan in Isfahan, may Allah's mercy rest upon his soul. One of them was the Son of Sulayman."

"You mean the boy called Kilich?"

"That's right... that was his name."

Tatran returned to his room. What was Ramiro doing with the Son of Sulayman? How did he get to Isfahan? He could make no sense of it and paced the floor. Finally, he sat down and scribbled tiny words on a small piece of parchment. He waited patiently for the ink to dry before he rolled it tight. Then he reached for a small birdcage sitting on the floor, removed the cover, opened the cage door, and took hold of the cramped pigeon inside. It flapped weakly as he tied the note to its leg with a white band. He carried it to the windowsill where it fluttered for a long while before spreading its wings and venturing off. At first, it flew unsteadily, and then, with renewed confidence, it soared high into a clear blue sky, flapping northwest for Byzantium.

ALEPPO

The muezzins of Aleppo sounded the call to evening prayer just as Ramiro and Jameel came to the north gate. Ramiro had come to enjoy the mesmerizing resonance of the *adhan*, its chant instilled in him a sense of mystery and awe. They dismounted when others did and knelt to pray at the side of the road. They prayed to the same God and faced the same direction as the Muslims, but in their hearts they turned to Jerusalem.

Prayers ended and the crowd milled through the gate. "Halt!" The gatekeeper cried when they tried to pass through. "Where are your papers?"

Ramiro groped into his bag. "I have them here," he said, bringing out the certificate given to him by the Sultan.

The Gatekeeper read the document, then he looked at Ramiro with some suspicion. "You are Christians?"

"Yes, Sayyid."

"Where are your crosses?"

Jameel reached inside his tunic and brought out his new cross. Ramiro showed him the iron cross he purchased in Isfahan while keeping his golden cross tucked safely inside his vest. He offered apologies.

"Christians must always show their crosses so we know who you are," he scolded. "And you must wear a yellow sash too. Get them at the market."

Ramiro bowed slightly. "Yes, Sayyid," he said, turning away.

The Gatekeeper held up a hand. "Wait! I need to see your tax receipt!"

"Tax receipt?"

"The poll tax. Don't play dumb with me."

Jameel shook Ramiro's arm. "All Christians must pay tribute to the Emir, Master. Once a year."

Ramiro forced a smile. "Of course, Sayyid. Please excuse me, I am an ignorant traveler."

The man pointed. "Give your names and your money to the scribe. He will issue your certificates."

• • • • •

Ramiro stormed out of the building in long, heavy strides, heading for the Christian quarter in the northwest corner. "A dinar each! That's outrageous!"

"All who are not Muslim must pay, Master," Jameel puffed as he struggled to keep up.

Ramiro prayed silently, trying to calm himself. '*O God, come to my assistance...*'

They looked for accommodations along the dim and narrow cobbled streets, hemmed on either side by the tall, stone walls of adjacent buildings. The walls were plain with no windows at ground level and there was nothing to see but stone and brick and flat iron doors, the odd starkness broken only by flashes of color from bright buds of jasmine and rose blooming in window-pots one story up. A thick fragrance of orange blossom wafted in from nearby orchards, dominating the spring air.

A small brass plate inscribed in Arabic and Greek was all that identified the Christian hostel. The innkeeper was a talkative man and Ramiro had little trouble extracting information from him.

"Oh, no." The innkeeper waved a finger and shook his head. "Do not travel to Jerusalem by way of Damascus. It is too dangerous. Tutush, brother of the Great Sultan, is taking revenge on all those disloyal to him. Even now, I hear, he prepares an army to ride north against us here at Aleppo."

"Why?" Ramiro asked.

The man looked at him and raised his brow, which seemed to lower his long ears. "Haven't you heard? Tutush went to Iran to claim the Sultan's throne but returned in disgrace. The Emir of this city and Buzan of Edessa did not follow him as planned. Instead, they showed their loyalty to Berkyaruk instead."

Ramiro felt a chill, the last thing he wanted was more trouble. He had to move south, and fast. "I should pay more attention to politics, my friend. So, what route do you suggest?"

"Go south to Maarat before Tutush rides to war. It's the fastest road. Then continue south to Homs. From there, you head west through the Homs Gap to avoid Damascus. That will bring you to the coast road where you head down to Jaffa."

"And from Jaffa, one travels east for Jerusalem." Ramiro interjected, pleased that he knew a little geography.

"That's right. It's a short journey from there." He offered more tea.

Ramiro held out his cup. "I hear the Egyptians might be a problem."

The innkeeper shook his head. "Not yet. They haven't had much say on the coast for some time, except further south. But not long ago, they ruled the whole seaboard right up to Antioch. They even seized Aleppo for a while." He leaned forward, resting his elbows on the desk. "I think Jaffa may still be ruled by the Egyptians - but not to worry, the Romans still do a lot of business there."

"So you would feel safe on that route?"

"Only God knows what will happen," he shrugged. "Nowhere is safe since the Sultan died. Now everyone fights for themselves, taking what spoils they can."

"And what of Jerusalem? Is it safe?"

"Oh, yeh, usually, anyway. The governors change from time to time. Now Tutush rules it, but he stays at his palace in Damascus and he's left some cousins to govern... can't remember their names. Idiots, really." He shook his head again. "But I'll bet those Egyptians are just waiting for a chance to seize it."

• • • • •

Ramiro strapped on his money belt. The hospital in Edessa had kept all his possessions safe and he was startled when they refused to take any money for his treatment. But in true thankfulness, he insisted on making a generous donation.

He donned an expensive new tunic with embroidered arm bands, leggings and a wool coat, and then wrapped a yellow sash about his waist. He fitted a blue turban and trimmed his black beard. Then he hung the iron cross from his neck with a leather lace. He looked in the mirror, turning from side to side, and chuckled. "Come, Jameel," he said cheerfully. "Let's return to the market for supplies. Then we'll take the road to Maarat. I talked to the innkeeper yesterday and he said this is a good time to travel that route." He unconsciously put a hand to his money belt. He still had about half the gold given to him by the Sultan, Malik Shah. It seemed so long ago now.

"Yes, Sayyid, I'm ready," said Jameel, standing behind Ramiro. He was pleased with his new clothes and could hardly drag himself away from the mirror. No longer did he dress in the rough cloth of a slave.

The markets were busy, they were always busy. And Ramiro was always amazed at the quality and variety of merchandise sold in the hundreds of small booths set up in the plaza next to the mosque. But even more remarkable goods were sold in the brick and stone stores of the *souk*. Here were the finest cloths, silks and satins, wools and cottons, fine leatherworks, bronze and silver dishes, ornate candlesticks, and spices from the Far East.

And then there were the goldsmiths and jewelers who catered to the wealthy with sweetened fruit drinks while their hired guards patrolled the clean cobblestone streets. Each shop had its specialty. There was gold and silver of every design and stones of jade, lapis lazuli, and opal. And, for the right price or the right people, emeralds, rubies, sapphires and pearls would be brought out from their strong-boxes.

But such treasures did not occupy Ramiro's thoughts. He could only think of getting enough supplies for his journey south to Jerusalem. Finally, he would be able to complete his mission and see his mother. He said a prayer of thanks.

"That will be five fals, Sayyid," said the storekeeper.

"What? Oh, yes, of course," he said, handing the bag of dried fruit to Jameel and pointing to another stall. "Here, take this money and buy some nuts and cheese for our journey. I need to find some medicines. I'll meet you later at the inn." Jameel ran off, happy to have an important errand.

"Where can I find an apothecary?" he asked the store-keeper as he paid him.

The man pointed past throngs of shoppers and noisy hawkers. "Go to the end of the street, near the women's corridor."

Ramiro wandered for some time but could see nothing that looked like an apothecary. The narrow street wound endlessly through the city but no one he asked seemed to know the way. I must have passed it, he thought. He came to an intersection and stopped. He wasn't sure where he was. The crowds of shoppers had trickled to just a few. He looked around for shops or signs but there were none to be seen. Then he noticed two men watching him from a doorway, so he strode over. "Peace be upon you, Efendi. Tell me please, where is the women's corridor?"

Toros the Armenian returned a sly smile. "This is it," he said, waving a hand to the door. He looked at Ramiro's fine clothes. "Come inside."

Ramiro stepped into the hallway of a poorly lit stone building teeming with activity and echoing with loud voices. He followed it to a vast room with a pillared open space. Men and women dressed in plain brown tunics sat in groups on the floor while guards with whips strolled between them. He lifted his eyes to one corner of the room. On a raised platform, two men held a naked woman by the arms as she squirmed under the prodding fingers of another man, who was richly attired and jeweled. The man stuck one finger in her mouth to check her teeth, and then he felt her breasts and inspected her thighs.

Ramiro went pale and turned away. Oh, blessed Saints, what have I come to? This is a slave market!

Khuda the Mamluk looked at him suspiciously. "Over there," he growled and pointed to an area where several well-dressed men sat on plush cushions. "Please, sit."

Feeling trapped, Ramiro walked over to join the merchants, some of whom nodded in greeting. One of them was a huge fat man supported by several large cushions and two muscular slaves.

He moved sheepishly to an outer seat and sat down. Red with shame, he turned his eyes from the naked woman and looked over the sad lot of dejected slaves waiting to be sold. They were mainly children or young men and women. Most were white, a few black. Shameful! Father in Heaven, deliver me from this vile place of misery! He bit his lip to stem tears of pity.

He remained quiet as the bartering continued, considering how he could excuse himself and leave politely. But it would be bad manners to leave right away so he endured the auction of three slaves before he looked around to see his way out. He was about to get up when something in the crowd of captives caught his eye. In one group, he spotted several women with pale skin, most had light hair, some blonde, another red, an uncommon sight in these parts. He looked at the red-head and watched her for a moment or two, curious to see if she was Greek or Latin. The woman turned her head towards him, as if she sensed his presence. She looked straight into his eyes.

Ramiro gawked. The blood drained from his head in a cold chill. No! It can't be! He blinked several times before wiping his eyes and looking again. His heart began to pound. Oh dear God! It *is* her! How can this be? May God have mercy! He became oblivious to his surroundings. All he could do was gape at the woman sitting on the floor. It's Adele!

He bolted up from his cushion. "Adele, it's me!" he yelled in French. The slave market fell silent, all eyes went to Ramiro.

The woman jolted at the sound of her name, a name she had not heard for some time. She stared at the man shouting at her but did not recognize him. He had a full head of hair and a beard and dressed as a man of leisure.

"Adele! It is Dom Ramiro!"

She knew the voice. She stared into his eyes, those dark, twinkling eyes. A flood of recognition and shock came to her face. "Dom Ramiro!" she wailed. "In the name of God! Help me!"

Khuda moved up behind her and lashed out with his whip. "Shut up, bitch!"

Adele flinched, then she turned in anger and grabbed at the whip. Khuda took hold of her hand and twisted it. She cried in pain and he slapped the back of her head. Then he turned to Ramiro with a snarl. "And you, foreigner! You have no business talking to the slaves!"

"I will buy her!" Ramiro shouted impetuously. "I will pay twice her value!"

Khuda hung his whip near Adele's face. "The bitch is sold already. You are too late."

Ramiro turned to the buyers. "Who bought her? I will double the sum!"

The men shook their heads in disgust. What terrible manners. Cursed foreigners!

Harun the Slaver was outraged. He even forced himself to rise, balancing his fat, bulbous body with the help of two slaves. His jowls flapped as he ranted. "May Allah curse you. How dare you! I will have you whipped and thrown into the streets! This woman goes to Antioch - to the House of the Emir, may Allah keep him." His voice grew hoarse. "Your money means nothing to him! Desist!" He fell to coughing.

"Please, Sayyid," Ramiro pleaded. "I will come to any agreement."

Harun waved a pudgy hand in repulsion. "Throw him out!"

Toros marched towards him, resting his hand on the hilt of his dagger. Khuda came too and they both grabbed Ramiro by the arms. They hustled him to the doorway. The buyers laughed as he struggled in vain. Adele slapped her hands to her mouth to stifle a scream.

"No, no, please! We must talk!" Ramiro shouted. More laughter.

The two men opened the door and together they heaved him into the street. Ramiro spun and stumbled onto the dark cobblestones, falling to his hands. Khuda yelled from the doorway. "Don't show your face again, kafir... or we'll gut you like a dog!"

• • • • •

Ramiro barged into his room. He was disheveled in every way and his new tunic soiled. Jameel dropped an apple he was eating and backed away.

"Come Jameel! We leave now! We're going to Antioch."

"Antioch, Master? What of Jerusalem? What has happened?"

"Jerusalem will have to wait. I have important business to attend to. I'll explain it all later." He studied the skinny, defenseless Jameel and compared him to the gnarled slave-driver, Khuda. Secretly, he wished he had a more aggressive companion. "Move now! Pack our bags!"

• • • • •

Harun the Slaver fidgeted on his cushions while slaves served cakes and wine in his mansion. He was flabbergasted. "What? What do you mean you will not renew your contract? Have you been offered a better price? We could renegotiate. I have been good to you all these years. Does that mean nothing to you?"

"Forgive me, Master," said Khuda, "but I tire of slave trading and seek my fortunes elsewhere." He spoke with no hint of regret.

"But what will you do?"

"I leave to join the emir, Yaghi Siyan in Antioch. He is hiring and pays well."

"You will take up the sword again?" Harun stuffed his wide mouth with baklava and washed the pastry down with a gulp of red wine.

"I always have my sword, Efendi. I am mamluk," he bristled, straightening his shoulders. His short beard had been clipped, his hair washed and braided into four tails, two down the front and two at the back. His helmet sat beside him. "The Emir hired me as one of his personal askari. I might even get a diwan."

"A diwan? For how much?"

"One percent of taxes."

"Who offered you this?" Harun asked as he picked at his teeth with a little finger.

"Yaghi Siyan's buyer. At the market."

"He's just a buyer," Harun scoffed. "You cannot take his word."

Khuda stiffened. "He's an emissary as well. He's come to talk to the Emir of Aleppo about uniting against Tutush."

"Against Tutush?" Harun shook his head slowly. "That sounds like more trouble than four wives."

"My business is trouble, Efendi." Khuda paused to sip his wine. "The emissary has hired me to escort his new slaves to Antioch."

"Including that red-haired woman?" Harun chuckled.

Khuda smiled. "Yeh. Who was that madman at the market today?"

"An accursed Christian, I hear. He sure wanted that woman."

"Terrible manners," growled Khuda as he reached for a cake. "And do you remember the mufti? The one who stopped to berate us in the market?"

Harun nodded. "Yes, the one called Ibrahim. Damned clerics. Ranting and raving. Why do they make our lives so difficult? And what about him?"

"The emissary wants me to escort him to Antioch as well," said Khuda. "He says the mufti fears to travel the road unguarded. The Shia have gained confidence since the death of the Sultan."

Harun snorted. "Well, good riddance. That will be another thorn out of our side."

There was a long moment of silence before Khuda spoke again.

"And I have another matter to discuss, Sayyid."

"What is it?"

"Toros asked me to approach you. He has served you well and can now pay for his freedom." He paused, watching Harun.

Harun bristled, his beady eyes narrowed and he flushed red. "What! What? No! This is too much, Khuda. You are leaving, and now Toros – one of my best drivers! I will not allow it!"

Khuda tried to remain calm. "You have many drivers... besides, it is the custom, noble Harun."

"I curse the custom! Nobody enforces it. Toros stays!"

Khuda lifted his head and tossed a braid over his shoulder. "I am willing to add to Toros' purse. I will pay you more than his value."

Harun shook his head, his jowls flapped. "No, no, I cannot."

Khuda's face hardened and his voice became cold. "I could take the matter to the judge... or to the Emir himself."

Harun glared at him. "Are you threatening me?"

Khuda stared hard into Harun's little eyes. "Maybe the Emir would like to hear about your trading activities outside the city walls?"

Harun turned his head from Khuda's malicious glare, his testicles shrinking in fear. If the Emir discovered his tax evasion, he would be skinned alive and his bloodied corpse hung in the square for all to see. His fat nose wrinkled in a sneer of disgust. "May Allah damn you! Go! Leave me!"

• • • • •

"We'll camp here." Ramiro gestured to the campsite near a spring of cool water.

Jameel pulled the mule to a stop. "But Master, we are only a few hours from Antioch."

"Nonetheless, we will camp here so I can watch the road."

"You look for your lady friend?"

"Yes, Jameel. By the grace of God, they will have to go by eventually. I know we left before they did."

"But what will you do, Master? How will you recognize her? She is sure to be covered and veiled. And even if you do, you cannot seize her. They will kill you. And once she's in the emir's harem, how will you get her out? It is heavily guarded."

"I don't know yet," Ramiro sighed. "I don't know. I will just have to put my faith in God."

"Praise God," Jameel said softly.

• • • • •

"Here they come!" Ramiro shouted.

Jameel left his stone seat and rubbed his buttocks. "Praise to the Lord, Master, finally! It's been two days." He shivered as he looked down the road. "How do you know it's her?"

Ramiro nodded towards the small party. "The two men in front, they're the ones who threw me out of the slave market." He took cover behind a hawthorn. "You stay there."

Khuda and Toros, along with the mufti, Ibrahim, and three of the emir's men, escorted a procession of horses on which the slaves rode. Ramiro watched them go by. He could see the women were covered as Jameel had said and he was disappointed, he hoped they would stop at the spring, as many did on this route, although he had no idea what he would do if they did. He stood up. "Let's go. We'll stay a hundred paces behind."

CONSTANTINOPLE

"He lives!" shouted Aldebert. "He lives! Oh, Blessed Mary, Mother of God. He lives!" Tears rolled down his cheeks as he fought to catch his breath.

Commander Manuel put a hand on his shoulder to comfort him. "We will find him. Tatran sent a brief note along with the pigeon. It says Ramiro went to Aleppo and he has gone to follow."

"Aleppo?" asked Aldebert through another sob. "Why?"

"We are not sure," said Manuel, running his fingers through his neatly-trimmed beard. "Apparently he heads for Jerusalem."

"I will go to Jerusalem too!" Aldebert cried as he jumped to his feet.

"Now wait before you do anything rash," Manuel said patiently. "He also mentioned that Ramiro had sent on an envelope."

"An envelope?"

"Yes, he entrusted it with one of our caravans heading this way. It should arrive in a week or so."

AUGUST 1093

Aldebert stared at the large envelope for some time. It vibrated in his trembling hands. Ramiro had written the address in three tongues, Latin, Greek, and Arabic to 'Aldebert of Cluny at the Court of Constantinople.' He bit his lip to summon his frail courage and, with sudden daring, as if he were about to hurl himself off a cliff, he tore it open. It ripped in half and two sealed letters fell to the floor. "Mother Mary!" he squawked. He fell to his knees to pick them up. Only one was for him. The other, much thicker, was addressed to Abbot Hugh of Cluny.

His hands continued to shake as he held Ramiro's letter in front of him. He wanted to open it – but was afraid to. He stared out the window of his small room and could hear the bells of the Church of Sophia in the distance. Can I finally leave? In a fit of anxiety, he fell into a chair and tried to break the wax seal carefully but tore the paper. "Dear, oh dear," he muttered. Still shaking, he opened it and read.

> From Ramiro, Dean of Cluny, to Aldebert of Cluny, greetings in the name of Our Lord Jesus Christ.
>
> My dear Brother Aldebert, I pray you have not worried much for my well-being. I have survived these last years as a captive of the Turks and managed to secure my freedom only when the Great Sultan died. At the moment, I reside in Edessa, where I had fallen ill some months ago. By God's grace, I was renewed of spirit and spared to live again in the world of men.

Do not seek me out, my friend. It is much too dangerous to travel these roads. I head again for Jerusalem and when I arrive, God willing, you can join me there. At that time, you must arrange passage on a Genoese or Byzantine vessel and sail to Jaffa on the coast of Palestine. From thence, travel east to Jerusalem and seek out the Christian area.

But if you do not hear from me within the year, you must return to Rome to give a full account of all you have seen and heard to His Holiness, Pope Urban the Second, may God bless his name. Then it is your duty to return to the Abbey to explain events to our Reverend Father, and I leave you the vital task of forwarding to him the enclosed letter. This must be done with immediate haste.

I pray for your safety.

June 12, in the year of Our Lord 1093

Aldebert jumped around the room like a schoolboy, laughing and crying at the same time. "I'm going to Jerusalem!"

ANTIOCH

The road to Antioch ran straight out of the western gate of Aleppo. It skirted the basalt foothills just north of the Syrian Desert and pushed through the mountain pass called Bab Al-Hawa before opening onto the wide Plain of Antioch. To the right, was Lake Antioch, a body of water twenty miles wide, glittering like topaz between the mountain ranges. Straight ahead, the Nur Mountains towered more than a mile above the plain. The road went straight towards the mountains before turning south into a wide gap that ran all the way to the port of Saint Simeon on the Mediterranean Sea. At the mouth of this gap, the city of Antioch nestled between Mount Silpios and the River Orontes.

The enormous walls and towers of Antioch seemed to reach to the sky as Ramiro made his way through the Gate of Saint Paul. Only the walls of Constantinople could begin to rival their height and extent. Massive square towers studded the fortification every hundred paces as it climbed steeply up the ridge of Mount Silpios, which rose sixteen hundred feet above the plain. It followed the ridge for almost two miles before dropping back down to cross the valley floor at the Gate of Saint George where it continued to the wide Orontes, along which hundreds of dhows plied their trade. From here, the wall turned north to skirt the river past Bridge Gate and Dog Gate

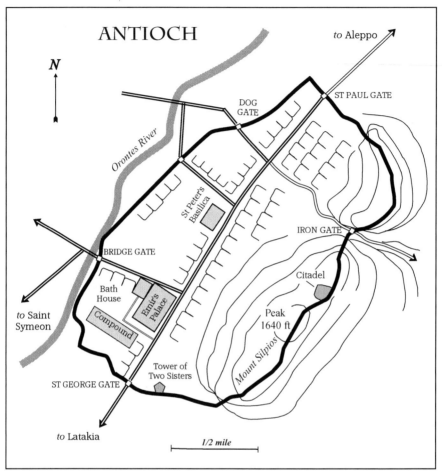

before swinging east to complete the circle back at the Gate of Saint Paul, a circumference of over seven miles.

With its back against the mountain, Antioch spread out onto the flats of the river bend, where it dominated all traffic from the Mediterranean to inner Syria. Although long past its moment of Roman glory, it remained a wonder of the world and was the cosmopolitan home to hundreds of thousands. Most of them were Greek Christian, even when the Turks ruled.

The emir of Antioch was Yaghi Siyan, a Turk appointed by the late Malik Shah. He was a wily, seasoned warrior and, by his firm hand, the city enjoyed a period of prosperity and peace.

A HAREM

Ramiro looked ahead anxiously. New minarets spiked above the buildings in all directions. To his left, Mount Silpios jutted to the sky and he could see the

Citadel and the long wall at its peak. On the streets, busy shoppers in colorful dress haggled with merchants in their storefronts, and hawkers outside peddled their wares in Greek, Arabic and Aramaic. The slave procession was just ahead. He looked behind to make sure Jameel had not lost his way in the chaotic crowd. "Stay with me!" he shouted to him. A cart blocked his way and he pushed past with apologies.

The main street ran straight through the city for over two miles before reaching the opposite wall at the Gate of Saint George. From here, the road continued south along the coast to the city of Latakia.

Almost a mile down the main street, stood the majestic Cathedral of Saint Peter, the official residence of the Patriarch of Antioch and one of the few Christian churches not converted to a mosque by the conquering Turks. He longed to enter its doors but pressed ahead, following Khuda and the slaves.

Traffic slowed and stopped. Hundreds of noisy people jammed the streets and hundreds more crammed into the main square.

"What's going on?" Ramiro asked a merchant.

"It's an execution," said the man. "Enemies of the Emir are about to lose their heads." He whipped a finger across his throat.

Ramiro ignored the execution and pushed his way through the masses, inch by inch, keeping a close watch on Khuda's procession. Another mile south, the opulent Palace of the Emir came into view. Just past the palace, he saw Khuda turn right, heading towards the river. He rushed to keep up, coming to the corner just in time to see Khuda turn again, wrapping around the palace grounds on a narrow street. There, the procession stopped.

Ramiro dismounted and took note of his surroundings. Jameel joined him. "Keep quiet," he whispered. The street was not busy. One side opened onto a treed parkway and a bathhouse. On the other side, stood the palace. He walked his mule down the street, pretending to be a sightseer and watched the slaves dismount. He ambled past the door just as it slammed shut.

Most buildings had no windows at street level, but this particular building had no windows at all. He strolled across the street to the park and Jameel followed. There they sat watching as innocently as they could. "Get out some food, Jameel, and we will have a picnic."

They watched for hours but saw no more signs of activity. Ramiro noticed a patron leaving the bathhouse behind them, the man wore a cross. "Peace be upon you," he said to him. The man returned the greeting.

"Can you tell me, Sayyid, what is this building here?"

"That one?" he pointed. "That's a wing of the Emir's residence... I think it's his harem." He nodded discreetly towards the Palace. "You can hear the women in the courtyard."

"Thank you, and where can a Christian rent a room?"

The man pointed north. "In the area around the cathedral."

• • • • •

With careful discretion, Ramiro asked many questions about the Emir and his palace. But exhausted from his daily excursions, he returned to the inn to rest. "It's hopeless, Jameel. It's as though she's disappeared from the face of the earth."

"It's a harem, Master. It's got more guards than the treasury. You will probably never see her again."

"I cannot accept that, my friend. I must find a way."

JOHN THE OXITE

Soft rays of red, blue and yellow streamed in through the stained glass windows of the Cathedral of Saint Peter, spreading kindly across the stone pillars towering overhead and bathing the smooth, tile floors where Ramiro knelt in prayer. He faced the altar, nested between two massive pillars, and looked up to a life-sized image of a crucified Christ towering behind it. He waited an hour before he heard someone approach behind him. He got up and turned to see the Patriarch.

A black cylindrical hat rose high on the Patriarch's head and his simple black robe draped loosely to the floor. In one hand, he held a long, black staff capped in gold, and a yellow-gold pendant hung from a thin chain about his neck. John the Oxite spoke quietly through a long, blonde-gray beard. "Forgive me for interrupting your prayers, my son, but my time is short. Do you seek an audience with me?"

Ramiro held his turban with both hands, and bowed to the man. "Yes, Your Eminence, may all the saints keep you. I am Ramiro of Cluny."

"Cluny? That name sounds familiar."

"I hail from the Monastery of Cluny and, despite my dress and appearance, Your Eminence, which... which I can explain, I am a disciple of Saint Benedict."

The Patriarch raised his chin. "Do you mean to tell me you are a Cluny monk?"

"Yes, Your Grace."

"Well, well." John took some time to look him over, he appeared skeptical. "I would agree, your dress is certainly not that of a monk. Where is your robe?"

Ramiro smiled apologetically. "I would gladly tell you my story, but it would take many hours to relate."

"Your new Pope is a man of Cluny. Is that not correct?"

"Ah, yes, Your Eminence."

"And tell me, what is the Pope's name?" John tested.

"Why... it is Pope Urban the Second, Your Eminence, born Odo of Lagery and formerly the Bishop of Ostia."

John nodded gently and the top of his tall hat swayed. "So what is it you want from me, Ramiro of Cluny?"

"Well, Your Eminence, to be honest, I... I hope to save a woman from a life of slavery."

"To save a woman? A very odd request, indeed. Perhaps you should take the time to tell me your story. Come to my chambers."

● ● ● ● ●

John shifted uneasily in his chair. "That is quite a tale, Monk Ramiro." He opened his hands in a despairing gesture. "But you must understand, there is little I can do for you. Our church remains unmolested by the authorities only because so many Christians live and trade here. But make no mistake, the Emir sees us as allies of Byzantium and thus as potential enemies. If I begin to meddle in his affairs, it could cause much trouble for all of us. I hope you understand." He rose from his chair. "But please come to worship with us any time you like."

Ramiro stood up at the same time, still clutching his turban. "Surely, there must be something I can do?" he said with mounting frustration.

"You can ask the Emir for an audience," said John. "Though it may take some time. Christians are not often heard at court. It may be best to approach a mufti on the matter."

"A mufti?"

"Yes, a lawyer. Some of them can be very effective. Once they hear your case, they may present the matter to a qadi, the judges who enforce the Sharia. The Emir has the ultimate say, of course, but his actions are constrained somewhat by the religious courts."

Ramiro nodded politely. "Thank you, Your Eminence. So where can I find a good mufti?"

THE MUFTI

Ibrahim, the stern-looking mufti with big, fiery eyes and a wide mouth, squatted behind a low table on a slightly raised platform. His big ears stuck out below his white turban and a gray-black beard almost covered his face. Behind him, sat a scribe holding a writing board across his knees, and a servant rushed in with a tray of lemonade before moving quietly to the side.

"You say you wish to free a female slave owned by the Emir, Yaghi Siyan?" Ibrahim asked in his throaty voice, somewhat taken aback by the odd request.

"Yes, Mufti," Ramiro replied, shifting on his cushion.

Ibrahim worked his fingers through his long beard. "The Emir is a powerful man, this could be very difficult."

Ramiro leaned forward, putting his hands to his knees. "I am willing to pay all I have."

Ibrahim looked at him warily and cocked an eye. "Is this woman a kin of yours?"

"No, Mufti, but she is the daughter of a dear friend," he said with some reservation.

Ibrahim tipped his head, wondering if he should probe further into this delicate matter. "Money cannot be the sole issue when it comes to dealing with a wealthy and eminent man like the Emir," he said, staring at the table top, "even when the most tactful negotiations are employed." He looked up. "You say the woman is a Christian?"

"Yes. Is that a problem?"

"Not really. More lemonade?" He paused to refill Ramiro's cup before he spoke again. "Islam discourages the enslavement of the People of the Book - the Christians and Hebrews. This may work in our favor but the tenet is largely ignored. Tell me, how was she captured?"

"As far as I know, she was taken when Abul Kasim seized Nicomedia."

"And I presume this was a holy war?"

Ramiro shook his head. "I don't know. Why?"

"If it was not a holy war, then her capture is illegal."

"How can you tell if it was a holy war?"

"If it was a war against unbelievers, it was a holy war. Who held Nicomedia?"

"The Romans."

"Then holy war could be justified."

Ramiro leaned forward to press a point. "But the Roman king had a pact with the Sultan, and Nicomedia was to remain unharmed and intact."

"Really? Are you sure? Can you verify this?"

Ramiro looked down and shook his head. "I am not sure. And it would be nearly impossible to get any verification from Isfahan at this time because of the wars."

The mufti looked at him with deep, sympathetic eyes. "Then what can I do?"

"Well," Ramiro said, with a hint of desperation, "you say that, as a Christian, she may be freed?"

"Ideally this is the case... but it is not always practiced. It is considered an act of great benevolence to free a slave, but most masters demand a good reason. Although..." he paused, "freeing a slave is also seen as a way to expiate sins."

This caught Ramiro's attention, the forgiveness of sins is a Christian specialty. "What sins in particular?"

"Usually murder, or perjury before the courts."

Ramiro sighed heavily. The chances of a Christian bringing serious charges against the Emir were slim at best. "Can we simply ask for her release with an offer of compensation?"

"We can try, but it will take time."

"How long?"

"Maybe a year."

OCTOBER 1093

Ramiro sat in his room reading a copy of the Quran. The lyrical beauty of Arabic always moved him in strange ways - but this copy was written in a fanciful script and he struggled with the elaborate letters. Once in a while, he scribbled a note on some thick, hemp paper, which he sorted into piles related to different topics. He pondered on a phrase about slavery and was so absorbed with its meaning that he failed to hear a light tap at his door. The tapping got louder, finally breaking into his thoughts. Book in hand, he wandered to the door and opened it a little. A short man with long, braided hair and a drooping, black moustache stood outside.

"Excuse me, Sayyid," said the man in Turkish. "I am looking for Ramiro of Cluny."

Ramiro beamed. "I am that man, Tatran!" He swung the door open and rushed to clasp his hand.

Tatran backed off suddenly, putting a hand to his sword.

Ramiro stopped. "It's me! It's Ramiro!"

Tatran stared at him. "Master Ramiro? Is it really you?"

"Yes, yes," Ramiro laughed. "Come in, my Tutor. Please, come in."

Tatran entered cautiously, never taking his eyes off Ramiro. "You look so different, like a Christian merchant, Master. I can hardly believe my eyes. And your Turkish is very good."

Ramiro laughed again. "You look well too, Tatran. Please sit. How did you find me?"

"I met your innkeeper in Aleppo," he said, still standing. "He seemed to know all about you."

"Oh, him. Yes, a talkative fellow. Would you like some wine?"

"Please, Master."

Are you still a warrior for King Alexios?" he asked as he filled a cup.

"Not really. I'm rarely on the front lines any more. I spend most of my time in negotiations and running errands for the King." He looked down and nodded towards Ramiro's hand. "And you are reading the Quran? May Allah be praised!"

Ramiro smiled. "I thought you were a Christian?"

Tatran blushed. "Christian... Muslim. Both are good, are they not?"

"Yes, both are good," he chuckled. "And I thought it best to review the book."

"Ah, yes, of course. You look fit, Ramiro, although a little thin. We all feared you dead. The Emperor sent me to find you at Aldebert's request."

"Brother Aldebert? Is he well?"

"Oh yes," he nodded. "But he worries very much. He waits like a nervous schoolboy for you to summon him to Jerusalem."

Ramiro smiled kindly. "And what of my servant, Pepin. Is he still with Aldebert in Constantinople?"

"He is still there, but not with Aldebert. They had many disagreements."

"I can imagine."

"Yes. Now he is a horseman for the King."

Ramiro lifted an eye. "Is he now? Perhaps he has found his calling." Again, he motioned to a cushion. "Please sit down, Tatran. You must be exhausted from your journey. I am eager to hear all that has come to pass." He brought out another bottle of spiced wine and they sat down for a long talk. Tatran briefed him on recent affairs while Ramiro told him of his adventures in the east and of his sickness in Edessa. "So, did you get my letter?"

Tatran nodded with a serious look. "Yes, Master, and I sent it forward with reliable men."

"So why do you seek me out, Tatran?"

"Why... to see that you are well, Master Ramiro. To see if you need help. Nothing more." He took a sip of wine. "I came here thinking you travelled to Antioch to board a vessel, or perhaps took the road south to Jerusalem."

"No, there is more to it, my friend," he said with a shake of his head. "Although my heart is still set on Jerusalem." He leaned back on the cushions and folded his legs. "Do you remember Louis the Carpenter?"

Tatran shrugged. "I don't think so."

"He was the man who built the catapults at Nikea."

Tatran nodded. "Yes... yes, now I do. He was very good for a Kelt. It was very sad."

Ramiro scowled. "What was sad?"

"Well, Master, you remember when we all abandoned Nicomedia to fight the Patzinaks with General Taticius and your French barbarians?"

"Yes, of course."

"Well, Abul Kasim knew we had left and, later on that year, he came back with another army. But we had too few men to fight him off, everyone was killed."

"That is old news, Tatran," Ramiro said impatiently. "But are you sure everyone was killed? You never saw this man again?"

"No Ramiro, not even in Byzantium."

Ramiro was stunned and took a moment to gather his thoughts. "May God have mercy on his poor soul."

"Yes," said Tatran as he shook his head sadly. "They killed all the men and the old women. The rest they took for slaves."

Ramiro stood up and walked to the window. He bowed his head as he thought of Louis and Mathilda. I pray, Lord, they did not suffer. He lifted his head again. "So that explains how Adele ended up in Aleppo."

"What? Who is Adele?"

"She's the daughter of Louis the Carpenter." Ramiro told him what happened in Aleppo, and how he had followed the slaves to Antioch.

Tatran leaned over and put a hand to his shoulder. "You can do nothing now, Master Ramiro. Leave her. I will ride with you to Jerusalem."

"No, no, Tatran, I must rescue the girl. I cannot bear the thought of her suffering as a slave. And it's the least I can do for Louis."

Tatran shook his head. "But what can you do? It is an impossible situation."

"I must free her. Dear God, somehow I must free her. Will you help me?"

Tatran sighed heavily. "So where is she now?"

• • • • •

Ramiro pointed to the western wall of Yaghi Siyan's palace. He pulled his cloak tight to his chest and fought off a shiver. A haze of cold light was the only sign of dawn and a soft drizzle fell as the call to prayers reverberated through the moist air. "That is where she went in," he explained to Tatran. "Somehow we must get her out."

The sheer wall of the building sided most of the narrow street, which ended abruptly at the iron gates to the Emir's Palace, an entrance for servants and goods. Behind the gate, sat two guards.

"So where's the courtyard?" Tatran asked, his narrow eyes darting about.

"Why is that important?"

"The courtyard. The women must have an outside area."

"Well, I don't know," said Ramiro. "And how can we tell?" He looked up. The walls were the height of two men.

"I will climb that tree, Master," Jameel piped in, pointing to a tall bay tree. "Then I can see over the walls."

Ramiro looked up at the billowing green tree, which stood majestically across the street near the entrance to the park. Then his eyes wandered cautiously, first to the baths on one side of the street, then to the guards. "Very well, Jameel. Climb quickly when I give you a signal." He led them over and they waited until the guards looked preoccupied and all was clear. "Now! Go, go! Keep out of sight. You must tell us all you see. Come down as soon as I whistle."

"Yes, Master," he said before he scrambled up a branch.

Ramiro and Tatran sat on a bench under the tree and tried to look like tourists seeking shelter. Within a few minutes, Jameel had reached the upper branches. He stayed there for a long time. The sky cleared.

Finally, they heard women's voices and laughter coming over the walls. The two guards came out of the gate to march around the palace periphery. Sometime later, they passed by again. One of them stared over at Ramiro and Tatran.

"We cannot stay much longer," said Ramiro as he turned his head away.

"I agree," said Tatran nervously. "We will be skinned alive if caught."

The guards talked for a moment, then strolled away to continue their rounds. Ramiro looked up and whistled softly.

Jameel rustled through the leaves and jumped to the ground. Ramiro stood up. "Come! We must leave."

● ● ● ● ●

"So, tell us everything you saw, young man." Ramiro ordered after they returned to their rooms. He lit two candles and placed them on the table. "Ah! Better still..." He grabbed a pad of paper and a pen, which he dipped in ink before handing it to the boy.

"But Master! I don't know how to write very well."

"I want you to draw, Jameel. Draw everything you saw."

Jameel held the pen awkwardly. "Well... um...let's see..." he mumbled.

Ramiro fluttered his hands. "Get on with it, boy! Draw the road to start."

Jameel drew two straight lines across the page. Then, wall by wall, in a jittery hand, he drew the western outline of the Emir's Palace.

Tatran could make no sense of it. "Tell us what you are drawing, Jameel."

"Yes, yes," he said in an eager voice. "This is the door where the slaves were taken in. Here is the building. Now, right beside it... to the right..." he pointed, "is part of the grand entrance to the palace. It is very nice, there are many beautiful fountains and wild animals, Master. Just running around."

"Very good, Jameel," Ramiro said impatiently. "But what about the women's courtyard? Could you see it?"

"Oh yes, it is here... on the other side of the building. Did you hear the women laughing?"

Tatran nodded. "That was just after sunrise prayers. It's likely they will come out again after sunset prayers."

"I think you're right, Tatran. The first time Jameel and I were there, it was dusk and we heard them. Do you think we can assume the courtyard is used every day in the same fashion?"

"Probably, except perhaps on Friday, the holy day. These things are generally routine."

"The court is very big, Master Ramiro," said Jameel. "Its wall goes to the end of the street... where you see the gates."

"Can we get to the end of the wall without going through the gates?" asked Tatran.

"I think so..."

"What did you see inside the walls?"

"Over here," said Jameel, pointing, "beside the far wall... I guess that's the north wall, there's a line of trees. They're as tall as the wall." He moved his pen to the right. "In the center is a fountain and a small pool, and there are four kiosks around the pool where the women drink and eat."

Tatran scratched his head. "Where are the guards?"

"They are at this end, beside the door of the building. And eunuchs serve the women."

"Did you see any women with colored hair?"

"Their hair is mostly covered, Master, but I think I glimpsed one or two."

Tatran tapped on the drawing. "The far wall is best - we have the cover of the trees."

Ramiro threw his hands up. "Then what? How do we know Adele will be there?"

"If she belongs to Yaghi Siyan, it is very likely she will be there," said Tatran.

"Somehow... we must tell her of our plan," Ramiro said, staring down at Jameel. "Tell me, boy, how old are these eunuchs?"

"They are about my age, Master."

Ramiro smiled. Tatran looked at him, then he smiled too.

Jameel watched them both and his eyes went wide. "Me? You want me to be a eunuch? No, no. That is very dangerous, Master Ramiro, yes, very dangerous. If they catch me they will burn out my eyes with hot irons! Then they will skin me alive! Chop me into pieces!" He went to his knees. "Please, Master, no!"

"Get up foolish boy! I will give you a gold dinar."

"A gold dinar?" His pretty face broadened into a wide smile and he got to his feet.

"Now tell us, what did the eunuchs wear? You must remember exactly."

"Yes, I remember."

Tatran swung a braid of hair over his shoulder, his battle-scarred face moved like wrinkled leather when he talked. "We could give her a letter."

"A good idea, Tatran, but it's unlikely she can read, although, she may speak some Turkish or Arabic by now. And Jameel cannot speak French, of course."

"We could draw pictures," said Jameel.

Ramiro sat down and huddled up to the table. "That's a good idea, Jameel, we will do just that. And Tatran, you must get another fast horse. This is what we will do..."

HARAM

Ramiro waited for the guards to begin their morning rounds before approaching the Palace gate warily. Tatran and Jameel followed, and when they reached the corner of the wall, they darted into the tall myrtle bushes growing along its edge. Without a word, Tatran stooped and Jameel climbed onto his back. Jameel, now dressed like a royal eunuch in billowing striped pants with matching tunic and turban, put his feet on Tatran's shoulders. He bent down to grab a rope from Ramiro before straining upwards to grasp the top of the wall. He could not quite reach so Tatran took hold of his feet and raised him up with his arms. Meanwhile, Ramiro tied one end to a stiff branch of a bush, disguising it as best he could. Then he moved out to watch the gate and the street, looking around the wall to see if the guards returned. He looked back just as Jameel scurried over the top. They waited. It seemed an endless wait before Jameel gave the rope a tug, letting them know he was down. Ramiro peeked around the wall again. All looked clear and he re-entered the quiet street with Tatran. They were just around the corner when they heard a voice.

"Stop! Stop and identify yourselves!"

They turned to face the guards coming across the street.

"Where are you going at this hour?" one of them asked.

"Peace be upon you," said Ramiro. "We enjoy a morning walk before prayers, Sayyid. Nothing more."

"Let me see some identification," he said in a gruff voice.

Tatran reached into his tunic and brought out a worn document. He handed it to the guard, who squinted in the low light as he read.

"You work for the Romans?"

"Yes, Efendi, I come to trade."

The guard looked at him suspiciously, then he turned to Ramiro, noticing his cross. "And yours?"

Ramiro handed him the document given to him by the late Sultan. Then he gave the guard his poll tax receipt.

The guard studied the documents. A surprised look crossed his face. He gave Ramiro a sheepish glance and handed the papers back. "My apologies, Efendi, but it is my job to check everyone around these gates."

Ramiro smiled. "You do your job well, guard, now go about your business."

Tatran looked at Ramiro in amazement after the guards continued their rounds. "What is that document you have? It must be of great authority."

"It was a gift from Malik Shah."

"The Sultan himself?" Tatran stared at him, tripping over his own feet.

• • • • •

Jameel hid behind a cluster of rose bushes at the far end of the courtyard. He could feel his heart pounding against his ribs and began to regret he had agreed to Ramiro's scheme. The court was empty, the air cool. The chant of morning prayers began and he looked to the sky, praying in Aramaic. Please, God, help me now. I will go to church every day.

The sun rose a hand above the horizon. That's when he heard the noises, the women were coming into the courtyard and the eunuchs followed. He sat and watched. Cold perspiration dripped from his skin. The women strolled about the fountain in their shawls, glad to be out for a walk in the fresh, morning air. Several eunuchs spread out bowls of fruit, hummus and hot flat bread in the kiosks. Jameel recalled Ramiro's description of the girl - long auburn hair, hazel eyes, slim, fine features. He studied the women closely, looking at their hair.

"What are you doing there? You stupid boy." A young woman approached from his side.

"I am so sorry, Sayyidah," said Jameel. "I am looking for a brooch lost by another." He stood quickly and pretended to search behind the roses.

"Whose brooch?" the woman asked.

"Uh... uh... I think her name is Adele, Sayyidah. I am new here."

"You do look unfamiliar," she said, staring at him with a puzzled look.

Jameel avoided her eyes. "Adele, Sayyidah, the lady with red hair and light-brown eyes."

"Oh, Adelah." She nodded. "The rebellious one."

"Yes, Adelah, where is she now?"

The young lady pointed. "She's sitting in that kiosk, the brooding one. Never says much. Speaks a strange tongue."

"Oh yes, I see her now. Thank you, Sayyidah." He brushed off his pants and tried to appear relaxed as he strolled towards the kiosk. He was almost by her side when a concubine sitting near the fountain raised her voice to him. "Boy! Bring me some bread."

"Yes, Sayyidah," he said, stepping into the kiosk where Adele sat alone. She stared blankly into the distance and did not seem to notice him. He leaned towards her as he took one of the plates of bread. "Ramiro," was all he said.

Adele turned and looked at him in surprise. "What?" she said in Arabic.

Jameel held a finger to his lips before he rushed off with the bread. He returned a moment later. "Ramiro," he nodded, saying the name again. Carefully, he reached into his tunic and took out a small sheet of folded paper. He discreetly placed it on the table and put the plate over it. Adele looked around nervously. One of the guards seemed to be staring in their direction, so she waited. Eventually he turned his back. She tilted the plate and snatched the paper, stuffing it into her bosom.

With a nod of his head, Jameel made a slight gesture to the north wall before walking in that direction with a plate of fruit. A while later, Adele followed, pretending to stroll. She wandered to the wall where Jameel offered the fruit to nearby ladies. He caught her eye and motioned with his head to a spot on the wall. She walked under the trees but saw nothing. She glanced back at Jameel. He looked up with his eyes. She looked up too. Then she saw the rope and quickly diverted her eyes in fear. Jameel ignored her and went about serving the ladies.

Their time ended and the Harem Master called out in a high voice. The ladies of the court rose slowly, keeping their poise while they strolled in procession to the main door. The eunuchs followed but Jameel held back, slipping into the bushes as the crowd dispersed. When the courtyard emptied, he went over to the rope and pulled himself up and over the wall. He lowered himself to the ground with a thump, tore off the eunuch's clothing, and slipped on a plain tunic left in the bushes.

Adele rushed to her room. She was alone. Nervously, she pulled out the paper before her roommates returned. What will I do? "Oh, dear God. I can't read." Her hands shook as she opened the small page. She stared at it for a short while, flipped it upside down and stared again. Then, with another quarter turn, she understood. There was the wall. And Ramiro, dressed as a monk, stood on the far side. She smiled a little when she thought of him. God bless the man! And on the far right of the paper, was a familiar depiction of the sun. Sunset! Tonight! She slapped a hand to her mouth. Mother Mary, give me courage, I beseech you. She heard women laughing and stuffed the note between her breasts.

• • • • •

"You're sure it was her?" Ramiro asked.

"Yes, Master. It was her."

"And you gave her the note?"

"Yes, yes, as I said."

"I just hope she understands it," he said, biting his lip.

• • • • •

The call to sunset prayers sounded from the minarets and Ramiro knelt to the ground. He said a prayer for Adele and then for Jameel and Tatran. The guards prayed too. He watched them. Soon they would change shifts.

Prayers ended and he waited under the bay tree that Jameel had climbed the other day. Tatran sat some paces behind and Jameel stayed with the horses at the end of the street.

The time had come. The guards walked away and their replacements had not yet arrived. Ramiro strode briskly to the wall and fell in behind the trees, waiting. He heard the women in the courtyard and waited until it was almost dark. Everything fell quiet. Despite the cool night, he dripped in sweat. There was a tug at the rope. The bush rustled and he rushed to hold it still, taking the weight in his hands. He could hear her grunting softly and the rope heaved against his arms. She appeared atop the wall and he motioned to her frantically.

A yell came out from the courtyard. "Stop! Stop in the name of the Emir!"

Adele looked behind her, then she looked down in terror. It was a long drop.

"Jump!" Ramiro hissed in French. "For the love of God, woman. Jump!"

"Stop at once!" came another shout.

Ramiro heard the guard's footfalls running across the courtyard to the wall. And from the gate, the new guard cried out. "Who goes there?"

Adele looked behind her again before looking back at Ramiro. In a panic, she opened her arms and leapt from the wall. He caught her fall and they both collapsed flat to the ground. Her long hair fell over his face and he caught the scent of rose. He rolled her off and got to his feet. "Are you alright?" he whispered.

"Yes, Father. What do we do now?" she whispered back.

"Come! We must go!" He took her hand and they ran to the street.

Tatran waited nervously by the bay tree. He ran towards them just as two guards came out of the gate. "Take her!" Ramiro shouted. "Take her to Jaffa!"

"I will fight!" Tatran bellowed.

"No! Take her now!"

Tatran hesitated, then he grabbed Adele by the hand and they ran towards Jameel and the waiting horses. Ramiro turned on the two guards, who now drew their swords and shouted to their comrades. He pulled out a knife and threatened them both. They stopped and began to parry. Tatran reached the horses and Ramiro could hear them gallop away.

Ramiro swung his knife back and forth and tried to fall back towards his mount but the guards noticed and blocked his path. Six more guards ran out from the gate and surrounded him. He held up his knife in surrender before dropping it to the ground. Four guards seized him, beating him down and tying his hands. The other guards ran to the end of the street, but the culprits had disappeared. "Get the horses! Search the streets! Check the gates!"

THE RECKONING

Ramiro had committed a grave offense. The harem was sacrosanct, a forbidden place. Apart from the master of the house, the only men allowed into these inviolable quarters were eunuchs, who were there only to protect and serve. For all others who dared to enter, the penalty was death.

Ramiro clawed at the wall of the cell as he tried to get up. It was pitch black, small and stark. The only light came through the cracks of a poorly fitted door. He sat back down on the cold, stone floor and rubbed his shoulder, bruised from the fall he suffered when the soldiers hurled him inside. He heard a commotion and, soon, two of the Emir's askari opened the creaking door and entered. He looked up. One carried a torch, the other held a whip.

The one with the whip spoke with a snarl. "Before you die, kafir, you will tell us all you know."

Ramiro recognized him, it was the slaver from Aleppo. The one who threw him out the door and onto the street. He said nothing.

Khuda the Mamluk put his whip aside and drew his knife. He grabbed Ramiro by the hair and held the point to his face. He was about to spit more curses at him when a look of amazement crossed his face. "It's you! The infidel from Aleppo!" he said, smiling in derision. "The man who wanted the red-haired slave girl." His smile contorted to a sneer. "Where is she, you stinking kafir? Where has she gone?"

Ramiro did not respond and Khuda pressed the point of his knife under an eye. "First I will gut you," he smiled with pleasure. The light of the torch flickered across his scarred face. "Then I will peel off your skin, one strip at a time. Do you hear me! You mound of dog shit! Speak now and enjoy a quick death!"

"I... I wish to see the Emir," Ramiro strained to talk.

Khuda looked at his companion. He smiled and the two askaris roared in cruel amusement. Then the one with the torch made a fist and struck Ramiro across the head, sending him reeling to the floor. "You arrogant pig!" Spittle flew from his lips. "The Emir does not waste his time with thieving infidels." He drew his sword and poked it into Ramiro's side. "Where is she? Who are your friends? Speak!"

Ramiro got to his knees and put a hand to the side of his head. Blood ran between his fingers. He fumbled into a pocket and brought out the Sultan's document, holding it up for Khuda with a shaking hand. But as he did, the golden cross fell out his vest pocket. He picked it up in a snap and shoved it back into his vest. But the guards noticed.

Khuda grabbed the paper. He held it to the light of the torch. There was a long moment of silence. "Where did you get this?"

"From the hands of the Great Sultan," Ramiro grunted. "From Malik Shah, may Allah's mercy rest upon his soul."

"Search him," Khuda said to the other askari, who pulled Ramiro to his feet and took all he had, drawing out the golden cross with a low whistle.

"Give it to me," Khuda ordered. The guard handed it over, looking at him suspiciously.

"And look at this," said the guard as he stared in amazement at the gold coins in Ramiro's money belt.

"Those are mine," said Ramiro, rubbing the side of his head. "You have no right to take them! I will report your bad manners."

Khuda wavered, looking again at the paper and then back to Ramiro. He had an angry look, like that of a man deprived of certain pleasures. He had hoped to hack off this man's head, but the papers in his hand appeared important and he was loathe to commit some grave offense that may cost him his own head. He motioned to the other askari and they both left the cell with Ramiro's money and his cross. Outside, Khuda shouted an order. "Move him to the prisoner's quarter. We will let the Qadi decide his fate."

• • • • •

No one entered or left Antioch without being checked at the gates. And now, with all the trouble after the death of the Shah, security had been tightened even more. The guards at the Gate of Saint George were busy inspecting papers as Tatran and Adele waited in a long line-up of people, donkeys and handcarts. A merchant at the front of the line fumbled for his papers and tax receipts. Tatran tried to remain calm. He already had his papers in his hand and glanced ahead to Jameel. The boy has his papers too, he thought. But what do I do about the girl?

Adele sat behind him on the horse. She covered herself head to toe in a long, black hijab that Jameel had bought for her in a rush. A black veil covered her face, hiding her pale fear. Where's Dom Ramiro? she thought anxiously, looking behind, but the veil obscured her vision. Dear God. Where is he?

Jameel glanced back to Tatran while he toyed with the certificate that Ramiro paid for in Aleppo. He tried to assure himself that all was going well, but he feared for Ramiro. He brought out his tax receipt and put a hand to his cross.

Tatran watched as Jameel showed his papers. Everything seemed fine. There! There he goes through the gate. The boy is safe.

"Papers! Receipts!" a guard shouted.

Tatran handed him his papers.

"And her?" the guard pointed to Adele.

"She is my wife, Efendi," he replied in a calm voice.

"Then show me your marriage certificate," said the guard.

Tatran opened his hands in apology. "I cannot find it, Efendi. I will replace it as soon as I return to Aleppo."

The guard eyed him suspiciously. "What was your business in Antioch? You carry nothing."

"I... I am looking for work, Efendi."

But Tatran had hesitated too long. The guard waved and five more guards joined him. "Your wife must remove her veil for identification. We have orders from the Emir. She must dismount."

"How dare you!" Tatran shouted, but he was not very convincing and the guard remained unmoved.

"Remove your veil!" ordered the guard.

Tatran studied his surroundings carefully before shrugging his shoulders a little and, with a toss of his head, he ordered Adele to get down.

Adele's heart beat in her throat and she felt feint. In shaking movements, she worked her way off the saddle.

No sooner was she on the ground and out of the way, when Tatran jabbed his heels into his stallion's ribs and pulled on the reins at the same time. The horse reared up and flailed its hooves at the guards - a trick he learned from the Normans. The guards scattered and he barged through the crowd filling the gate. People screamed and carts flew to the side.

"Stop him!" the guards yelled. "Stop him!"

The soldiers near the gate began to close in. Tatran charged right for them, swinging his sword. With a signal from his knees, the stallion lurched into the air and vaulted over them. He landed in a crowd, scattering people in all directions, and galloped south as fast as his steed would go.

"After him!" a guard yelled. Ten askari rushed to mount up and thundered out of the gate. More people scattered to the sides. The horsemen rode hard and fast but Tatran was already out of sight.

Adele kicked and beat at the guards and tried to flee, but she did not get far. They grabbed her by the arms as she kicked some more. "Let me go!" she screamed. "Filthy pigs! Bastards! God curse you!" The men laughed at her futile struggle and her strange tongue. They tied her up and dragged her back to Yaghi Siyan's harem.

Jameel, who had been waiting down the road, jumped up when he saw Tatran coming fast. The girl was gone. He sensed trouble, and when Tatran swung his arm in a frantic motion for him to stay behind, he moved into the crowd of traffic to escape the eyes of the askari. Tatran raced away. Moments later, the askari flew past in determined pursuit.

Jameel waited anxiously near the road for two days, sleeping at a campsite. But Ramiro never came. I will wait for them in Latakia, he thought tearfully. They will have to pass through sooner or later. But doubt gnawed at him. Will I ever see him again?

SPRING 1094

A messenger stood waiting as Yaghi Siyan stared out the eastern window, watching gray and white clouds billow over the dry hills leading to the plains of Aleppo. His council of advisors sat behind him in the expansive war room, which had a commanding view from the Citadel, high on Mount Silpios. The wrinkles in Yaghi's huge face seemed deeper than usual and his white hair and beard made him appear old by warrior standards, but his age did not hinder his ambition. He turned to the messenger. "You are sure about this?"

"Yes, Beyfendi."

"Does Prince Tutush plan to besiege Antioch as well?" He stroked his long, beard as he spoke.

"We... we are not sure, Beyfendi, but we think not. He has his eye on the Sultan's throne. He wants to lead an army back to Iran and has no time to waste besieging Antioch."

"Then why did he attack Aleppo and Edessa?" he asked, although he already knew the answer.

"Because the Emirs betrayed him, my Lord. They did not follow him into battle when he marched to Isfahan last year."

"And they were both executed?"

"Yes, Master, as I reported." The messenger fidgeted. "And now that Tutush has conquered, he claims the loyalty of their men. He will increase the size of his army and march again to Iran, where Berkyaruk stands ready to defend the throne."

Yaghi waved his hand. "Go." He turned to his advisors after the messenger backed to the doorway and left. "May Allah curse him! How long will it be before Tutush takes our heads, too?"

"Some say he made a pact with the Hashashin to kill the Great Shah," said one of Yaghi's sons. "May Allah bring death to their families!" The councilors shuddered at the mention of the Hashashin.

Yaghi Siyan fell quiet for some time. The whole room fell quiet. "All we can do is wait," he said. "We will prepare our defenses and wait. We will see how Tutush fares against Berkyaruk." He looked to his secretary. "What else do you have?" The secretary bowed and handed him a letter. Yaghi pretended to read but his sight failed him. He handed it back. "Read it to me."

The secretary cleared his throat. "It is a letter from the Qadi, my Lord. In this particular case, he has failed to reach a verdict and refers the matter to your judgment, for your personal pleasure."

"What matter is this?"

"It is to do with the trouble we had in the harem, with the one that your right hand owns."

"The red-haired one?"

"Yes, Beyfendi. One of the men was caught and remains in prison."

"That was many months ago. He should have been executed by now."

"Yes, my Lord," the short, chubby secretary began to tremble, his voice squawked. "But the man possesses authentic papers delivered and sealed by Allah's Chosen, the Great Sultan, may Allah's mercy rest with him. The Qadi cannot determine if the late Shah's document is still valid, Beyfendi. At least, not until a new Sultan is determined."

Yaghi frowned a little. "What document?"

"The Christian was a scribe of the Sultan, Beyfendi. The document gives him all the rights of a freeman and says specifically that he is not to be harmed in any way."

"A Christian scribe? Favored in the courts of Isfahan?"

"Yes, my Lord."

Yaghi returned the Qadi's letter to the secretary. "This may prove amusing. Bring him before us. And bring the Qadi too. The council will decide his fate."

• • • • •

"Please, sit," said Yaghi from the head of the table.

Khuda gripped Ramiro by the arm. He shoved him to his knees before the council. Ramiro looked pale and thin, his black hair and beard disheveled, his movements stiff, his fine clothes in tatters.

Yaghi waved a hand and Khuda stepped back to the wall. A servant offered Ramiro a cup of apple cider, lightly fermented, and he took it with both hands. There was a scent of lemon. He drained the cup and the servant refilled it.

"What... is... your... name?" Yaghi asked slowly.

Ramiro cleared his throat. "I am Ramiro of Cluny, my Lord," he replied fluently.

Yaghi had seen Ramiro's iron cross and was surprised when he spoke in Turkish. "And you have been charged with abducting one of my girls, have you not?"

"Yes, Beyfendi."

Yaghi Siyan spoke to his secretary. "Who arrested this man?"

"Why... why the askari Khuda did, my Lord," replied the secretary, pointing to the soldier, who now stood to the side.

Yaghi Siyan stared at Ramiro's document before looking again at Khuda's report. Long creases rippled his large face when he scowled. He looked directly at Khuda. "Is this your report?"

"Yes, Beyfendi," he replied in his graveled voice.

Yaghi looked again at the Shah's document. He held it at arm's length. "It states that he was an accomplished scribe in Isfahan and has been discharged with honor, given all the rights of a full citizen of the Empire."

Khuda kept his dark eyes lowered. "Yes, Beyfendi."

"And this is the man who abducted one of my girls?"

"Yes, my Lord. He arranged her escape from the courtyard." His eyes narrowed.

"Tell the council what you know of this man," interjected the Qadi, who had previously heard Khuda's tale.

Khuda related the story of his encounter with Ramiro in the Aleppo slave market. He told them about the infidel's outrageous behavior.

"Is he related to this woman?" Yaghi enquired.

"I do not know, Beyfendi, but he was desperate to buy the girl."

Yaghi adjusted his jeweled vest and flipped his fingers at a servant, who ran up with more cider. His thick lips curled under his broad, white moustache as he glared at Ramiro. "Are you related to this woman?"

"No, Beyfendi."

Yaghi raised his voice. "Yet you dare to invade my harem! I should have you skinned and hung in the market!" He leaned over and rapped a knuckle on the table for emphasis. "What do you say in your defense?"

Ramiro cleared his throat. "May Allah look kindly on your mercy, Great Emir," he said meekly before telling them briefly of his journey across the Balkans and how Adele had accompanied them to Constantinople as the daughter of a tradesman and a friend. He recounted that Abul Kasim had seized Nicomedia when the Romans left it undefended in order to go fight the Patzinak barbarians. And that Abul had enslaved the women and children of Nicomedia. "I felt a moral obligation to free her, Beyfendi, despite the danger."

Yaghi scoffed. "You are a brave man, Scribe. But you are also a fool. You accomplished nothing."

Ramiro looked at him with a rush of foreboding.

Yaghi Siyan smiled as if reading his thoughts. "I still have my girl. She was captured at the gates."

Ramiro lowered his head as the truth set in. He had failed. A crushing wave of anguish gripped him and he could think of no reply.

"Is this all you have to say?" Yaghi taunted.

Ramiro had a sudden thought and forced himself to remember what he had read in the Quran as well as the conversations he had with the mufti, Ibrahim. He raised his head slowly. "If I may speak boldly, Beyfendi, I feel her capture and enslavement may be contested on two points."

"Go on," said Yaghi, somewhat amused.

Ramiro held out his hands in a gesture of appeasement. "Council members, I cannot profess to know the law as you do. I am a Christian, as is the woman now in our Lord's possession. But does not the Sunni faith discourage the enslavement of the People of the Book? Does not the Prophet, may Allah exalt him, show mercy for these people?" He paused for effect.

The council was astonished and marveled at the barbarian's Turkish. But the Qadi, a corpulent man who covered his drooping shoulders and big belly with the most expensive silks, was not impressed. He shouted in anger. "Only if the infidels accept the domination of Islam! Christians are filthy and corrupt!"

Yaghi waved him down. "And what is your second point?"

Ramiro glanced up at the long-bearded Qadi as he took more cider. "My second point, Beyfendi, is that the woman's capture cannot be justified by holy war. Abul Kasim's capture of Nicomedia was against the wishes of the Great Sultan, who was negotiating a pact with King Alexios at the time. Abul's foray was not a holy war and cannot, therefore, be used to legitimize the woman's enslavement."

The councilors chatted amongst themselves, some of them arguing loudly. Yaghi Siyan quieted them while smiling condescendingly at Ramiro. "You are indeed a man of letters, Ramiro of Cluny, and you defend your points with eloquence... for a Christian. I will consider leniency." Most of the councilors nodded in agreement.

But Ramiro was not finished. "If you accept my argument, Great Emir, I wish to negotiate the girl's freedom."

There was a hubbub from the council. Yaghi glared at him, taken aback. What impudence! But then he took a moment to reflect on his personal experiences with the barbarian slave girl. What trouble she is! Wild and untamable! Brings nothing but grief to my household and refuses to submit, despite the lash of my whip. He pulled himself from his thoughts and studied Ramiro with some suspicion. "What makes you think you can buy her? I could save myself this trouble and behead you tomorrow."

"But my Lord," Ramiro pleaded. "Does not the Holy Quran say it is good to free slaves, as the Prophet himself did? That your sins will be forgiven?" He stared straight into Yaghi's eyes.

Yaghi stirred uncomfortably under Ramiro's dark gaze. Many sins filled his mind and he felt embarrassed, as if Ramiro had brought them into the room for all to see. A flicker of fear crossed his face before he composed himself.

Ramiro continued. "And does not Allah urge you to 'Force not your slave-girls to prostitution so that you may seek enjoyment of the life of the world, especially if they would preserve their chastity'?"

The men were aghast. Never before had they heard a dhimmi recite a passage from the Quran, especially in challenge to the Emir himself. They looked at Yaghi to see his reaction.

Yaghi Siyan found himself in an awkward position. At this point, to deny Ramiro's eloquent and just request would look miserly and he sought to gain face. "You cannot afford to buy her," he said.

"But I can, Beyfendi, if you return my money."

"Your money?" He motioned to his secretary. The secretary shuffled his papers and brought one out. It was an accounting of Ramiro's possessions.

"How much?" Yaghi asked in amazement. The secretary showed him the figure and his eyes went wide.

Yaghi turned to his councilors. "It seems the man can indeed afford the girl. What is your opinion, my Councilors?"

"Let it be the will of Allah," said the Qadi, glad to have this case settled. "But an unwed Christian cannot own a female slave unless he marries her." The others nodded their agreement.

Ramiro sputtered. "Marry her? But, Beyfendi ... no, no, I... I cannot!"

"You must," the Qadi huffed. "It is the only honorable thing to do."

"But I am a... "

"Enough!" Yaghi shouted. He was pleased to save face, get rid of the girl, and get his money back. "You will pay the price and marry the girl, or I will have you both executed before the sun sets!"

Ramiro bit his tongue and lowered his head. "As you command, my Emir." He paused for a moment. "And if it pleases my Lord, will you return my cross for the wedding?"

"What cross? You are wearing it."

"No, Beyfendi, the other one, the golden cross. It must be in the report."

The secretary read through the list again. He shook his head. Yaghi Siyan opened his hands apologetically. "There is no golden cross listed here."

Ramiro stared at him for a moment. Then he turned to look at Khuda, but the man did not look back. He pointed to him. "He has it, Beyfendi. He took it from me at the gate."

Khuda turned to glare at him, a piercing glare. His right hand twitched near his empty sword sheath and his lips curled in a snarl. He could barely contain his indignant fury and almost lurched at Ramiro before stopping himself.

Yaghi noticed, as did the others. "Is this true, Askari?" he asked Khuda.

Khuda shook his grizzled head. "No, Master," he said. "He must have dropped it outside the wall when he was about his thieving business."

"Liar!" Ramiro shouted.

The councilors gasped. Khuda lunged at Ramiro but several guards jumped in to hold him back.

"Enough!" Yaghi shouted to Khuda. "Leave! Now!"

Khuda's face turned to stone. "Yes, Beyfendi, may Allah bless your name." He bowed stiffly and turned to leave. As he did so, he hissed at Ramiro. "I will see you die a slow death, kafir!"

Yaghi fumed. "And you!" he said to Ramiro. "You are in no position to call any Muslim a liar. You will show respect for your masters! Or you will not live another day to worship your vile mother goddess!" He turned to his guards. "Get him out of here!"

A RELUCTANT GROOM

Yaghi Siyan wasted little time. He arranged for the Patriarch himself to marry them in the Cathedral of Saint Peter.

In torment, Ramiro grappled with his faith. *Marry her! But I am a disciple of Saint Benedict! I have taken sacred vows... a vow of chastity and obedience.* In distress, he recalled the synod at Melfi, where Pope Urban and the bishops decreed that no clergy were to marry or take concubines. *Blessed saints! But for the love of God, what choice do I have? Is it worth our lives? After all, I can still remain chaste. Yes, yes. And perhaps the Abbot will annul the marriage when he learns it was Orthodox and unconsummated. But what if he cannot? Will my sins ever be forgiven - even if I do reach the Holy Sepulcher?*

• • • • •

Adele wore a full-length, white dress with long, draping sleeves. A white shawl and veil covered her head. Although Ramiro was a reluctant groom, he still wanted to please her, so he had it made especially for her, French style.

John the Oxite faced them both. "You will exchange your rings now."

Ramiro and Adele did so, giving each other a slim gold ring.

"Have you, Ramiro of Cluny, a good, free and unconstrained will and firm intention to take to wife this woman, Adele, daughter of Louis, who you see before you?"

"I have, Reverend Father," said Ramiro, his stomach churning.

"Have you promised yourself to any other bride?"

"I have not promised myself, Reverend Father."

No sooner did the ceremony end when Yaghi's men whisked them back to the Emir's compound, where they were given a spacious apartment and expected to consummate their marriage.

Ramiro was visibly agitated. He wandered to the balcony while speaking to Adele in a loud affected voice, as if she were a complete stranger. "The rooms are pleasant enough," he said much too loudly. "And we have a nice view of the gardens from the balcony... and the baths are just down the hall... and... and we will have a servant assigned... and..."

"And we are alive, Dom Ramiro," she said kindly.

Hesitating, Ramiro turned to face her. She tugged at her shawl and it slid from her head, leaving her long, soft curls draping across her shoulders. She was no longer the young girl he once knew, although her enchanting beauty still unnerved him. And she still retained a glint of determined fire in her eyes. "Please... please, Adele, just call me Ramiro."

Adele walked over to him and took his hands in hers. He stiffened and almost pulled away, but he could not. Just the touch of her electrified his whole being with emotion and desire. She smiled. "I owe you my life, and for that I am truly grateful."

Ramiro caught the scent of bergamot orange. He could feel the warmth of her body, her face was so close. He tried to look into her caring eyes but could not find the courage, so lowered his head as he spoke. "Thank you, Adele. And I am grateful that God brought your affliction to my attention." He raised his head again.

Adele smiled and he could feel his heart leap. She raised her thin, red eyebrows, her hazel eyes sparkled. "Tis surely God's fate," she said, "and we should make the best of it."

"Yes, yes, of course." He stared at her full lips as she spoke. It was all he could do not to embrace her with a passionate kiss. But he lowered his head to hide his shame.

"Am I that ugly that you can't look at me, Ramiro?"

He raised his head, his eyes went wide. "No, no, not at all, Adele. Forgive me, I think you are a... a beautiful woman. But I am unused to a woman's presence, especially one so near."

Adele, still holding his hand, led him to the cushions lining one wall and motioned for him to sit. "Well, you better get used to me, at least for a while," she said as a matter of fact. "And we can't go on not looking at each other when we speak." Her small nose wrinkled with a light-hearted smile.

He dared to glance into her eyes. "Of course." He looked away, then he looked back again. "Just give me some time to get used to it."

She looked at him sympathetically before rising to her feet and swinging out onto the floor, gliding in a slow pirouette, her white dress billowing in front of him. "I'm going to change my clothes," she said, stopping suddenly in her turn. "And you, *my husband*, should call the servant for some food and drink."

"Uh... yes... very well." She looked like an angel.

"And think of a way to get us out of here," she said, walking to the bedchamber.

• • • • •

Yaghi Siyan summoned Ramiro to his chambers. Only his atabek sat with him. "Sit down," he ordered.

Ramiro squatted on a cushion.

"You spent some time in the courts of Isfahan. Is this correct?"

"Yes, Beyfendi."

"Tell me what you know. What of Berkyaruk? Do you think he will take the throne?"

"He is young, strong, and ruthless, my Lord. And many men flock to his call."

"Do you think Tutush will defeat him?"

"I do not know. But the mamluks of Isfahan will not harken to Tutush. He is seen as a rebel and a troublemaker." Ramiro went on to discuss matters of the court, the murder of Nizam by the Ismailis, and then the death of the Shah under mysterious circumstances.

Ramiro's mention of the Hashashin again sent nervous shivers through Yaghi Siyan. He was all too aware that troublesome Ismaili devotees lived just to the south, in the hills of Lebanon. "Now tell us what you know about the Romans.... will they attack Antioch?"

"I have heard little, Beyfendi. I know only that the Roman king looks to hire mercenaries from the west."

Yaghi Siyan asked him many more questions. When he could think of no more, he ended the discussion abruptly.

"My Lord," said Ramiro as he stood up. "I have received my money but not my cross. Will it be returned soon?"

Yaghi waved a hand of dismissal. "You were told it was not on the list. I will hear no more of this. Leave me."

Ramiro bowed and left.

The door closed. Yaghi fumed. "I do not trust him."

"But the Great Shah trusted this man, Beyfendi," said the atabek.

"And the Great Shah is dead! This man knows too much. What if he returns to the Romans?" He stroked his long beard. "We will keep him here for a while. Until things settle down."

"As you command, Beyfendi. And what of the Romans? What will we do?"

"You heard the man. The Roman king plots against us. I know it!" He stood and stared out the window. "We will send more spies to Constantinople. Damned Christians! May Allah curse them all!"

• • • • •

Months passed and Ramiro waited patiently for Yaghi Siyan to release them, but no word came. He asked time and again for an audience, but his pleas were ignored. They were prisoners, that much was clear. But it was not an unpleasant prison, their apartment was luxurious, servants cooked and cleaned for them, and almost anything they desired could be had by sending one to the markets.

Their rooms formed part of a compound situated across from the palace. It housed favored prisoners, servants, staff, and the askari of the emir. It had only one entrance and that was heavily guarded. But they were free to roam the lush courtyard with its gardens and fountains and here they soon discovered many others in the same predicament, people of position who had fallen out of favor with Yaghi Siyan.

At first, Ramiro and Adele settled into an awkward existence. He slept on a mattress on the floor of another room while she took the bedchamber. He managed to acquire some books and stationery and occupied his time reading and writing. Adele went about collecting a new wardrobe and dedicated much of her time to sewing and embellishment. In the evenings, Ramiro would try to teach her to read and write, but she was not an eager student of letters.

Adele was glad to be out of the harem but she was not entirely happy. Ramiro showed little interest in her and kept his conversations formal and aloof. Nonetheless, she could sense his eyes on her on many occasions and wondered about his affections. Sure, he was a monk, but now they were legally married. What now? Years ago, she had grown fond of him and she thought that he felt the same. And why had he gone through so much trouble and danger to rescue her if only to disregard her now in such a cold manner? She was still attracted to him, even more so as she came to know him intimately. He was kind and strong, a resolute spirit who showed no fear of life's travails. How she longed for his love and attention - just one embrace.

Ramiro was obsessed with her. Every time she swished and swayed past him, he could barely refrain from reaching out and pulling her into his arms. Her little movements, her quaint mannerisms, they were a rhapsody to his heart. But he could not reconcile his faith and turned to his books for comfort and distraction. With considerable effort, he dismissed the seductive demons harassing his troubled mind and constantly reminded himself of his sacred vows, taken in the sight of God. He thought of the Abbot and the Pope. They had trusted him. How could he betray them and all that he had vowed? But now he had made another vow, a vow to Adele.

Adele picked with distraction at a salad of banana, mango, and watermelon. She stared over the balcony, across to the verdant gardens of the Palace. "Why is life so full of horror and fear, Ramiro?" she asked without moving her head.

Ramiro looked up from his writings. He knew he could not begin to imagine the treatment she had endured at the hands of her captors. And she showed no inclination to discuss it. So far, all he had learned was that she and her parents had fled Nicomedia only to be caught by a band of highwaymen who put Louis and Mathilda to the sword before carrying her off into slavery.

He tried to think of something heartfelt to say but felt so constrained by the tenets of his faith. "Life is like this because mankind refuses to accept the love of God," he said after some thought.

Adele shook her head sadly. "How can so many men profess to follow God in word but not in deed? How can they be party to such atrocities?"

"Weak minds have not the courage to live in the domain of God," he said softly. "They are afflicted with sin and justify their actions by twisting God's words to suit their own evil plans. These are the worst of men." He put down his pen and rose to stretch his back.

She stared into her fruit bowl. "Do you think Yaghi Siyan will ever let us go?"

"I can only pray," he said. "Somehow, I must get to Jerusalem. But first I need that cross." He looked down to his study desk, askew with books and papers, books to translate, letters to write. But the Emir allowed no letters out and he thought of the futility of it all. The Abbot must think the worst by now. He looked down on his stack of undelivered letters and sighed heavily. He longed for his freedom.

CONSTANTINOPLE

OCTOBER 1094

Aldebert still waited anxiously for Ramiro's letter from Jerusalem. But it never came. In his previous letter, sent over a year ago, Ramiro had instructed him to leave for Rome in a year if he heard no further word from him. Now he began to fear the worst.

Did Ramiro mean to wait a year from July? Or from the date I received the letter, three months later? He convinced himself it must be the latter and used this excuse to wait until October. But now that time had come and he could wait no longer, winter was upon them and this was his last chance to sail to Italy until next spring.

And so, with a heavy heart, he returned to Rome to tell the Pope all that had transpired in the Greek kingdom, just as Ramiro had asked him to do. But after this, he did not return to Cluny as instructed. He knew that, if he did, Abbot Hugh would never allow him to leave the monastery again. So he dallied in Rome for a time, given the task of helping the bishops re-establish themselves in the Lateran, which was, once again, in the hands of Pope Urban. This was how he encountered the Bishop of Apulia, the same bishop he had met years ago at Terracina and Melfi.

"You cannot stay here indefinitely, Brother Aldebert," said the Bishop. "And you cannot go to Jerusalem. You are Benedictine and you must have the permission of your Abbot."

"Yes, Your Grace," said Aldebert plaintively. "But it is my heart's desire to go. I know Father Ramiro will send another letter."

"You have said this many times. How do you know he is still alive?"

"I feel it in my bones, Your Grace."

"Well, I sincerely doubt that argument will hold sway with Abbot Hugh. And my duties here are fulfilled. I must return to Bari and my diocese."

"Please, Your Grace, help me compose a letter to the Abbot. If I cannot go to Jerusalem, perhaps he will let me stay to serve you in Bari?"

"That is unlikely, Brother Aldebert," he sighed. "But he may be satisfied to let you join the Allsaints Abbey at Valenzano. It is Benedictine and is just a few miles from Bari.

"Thank you, Your Grace," Aldebert beamed. "Thank you."

"And since you seem to know more about affairs in the East than many of us, I will let the Abbot know how indispensable you are to me as an advisor. But if he declines, you must return to Cluny. Is that understood?"

Aldebert bowed his head. "Yes, Your Grace."

ANTIOCH

MARCH, 1095

There was a rap on the door. "Come in!" Ramiro shouted. A servant entered with a covered silver tray. "Your hot meals, Sayyid."

"Thank you, Boris."

Boris, a proud and elegant man, moved across the room like a gentle breeze, placing the tray on a low table surrounded by four cushions. "You will enjoy this, Sayyid. It is a special Magyar recipe, just like I used to have at home."

"What is it?" Ramiro asked as he lifted the lid a little.

"Chicken and rice, very good."

"Boris... how can you claim this dish is Magyar? I've eaten chicken and rice from Constantinople to Isfahan."

Boris lifted his square chin in defiance. "This is a special dish, Master," he said as if he had a personal hand in its creation. "With special Magyar spices."

Ramiro smirked. "My dear man, I have read that both chickens and rice come from Hindustan, not Hungary."

"Humph! You are so smart, Master Ramiro. Sometimes too smart." Boris motioned to a cushion and turned to Adele. "Please Sayyidah, sit and try it."

He lifted the lid. "It is the spices that are so special," He looked askance at Ramiro in mild defiance.

Adele smiled. "Thank you, Boris. It does smell good."

Ramiro ignored the meal. "Sit down, Boris," he commanded. "Tell me again all that you have seen and heard."

Boris put the lid aside and sat down uneasily. "I really should not be speaking with you about such things, Master."

"All I want is news, Boris," Ramiro smiled congenially. "Nothing more." He sat across from him.

"Your supper will go cold, Sayyid," he said, squirming on the cushion.

Ramiro stared straight into his eyes. "It is weeks since we have had a good chat, Boris. Tell me, has Prince Tutush won the throne?"

Boris glanced into Ramiro's dark, twinkling eyes and shivered a little. "Oh no, Master Ramiro, Tutush was killed by his nephew, Berkyaruk, who is now the new Sultan."

Ramiro whistled. "Tutush is dead? By all the saints! What now? Has any peace returned to Syria?"

Boris shook his head. "Oh no, Sayyid. It is worse. Now Berkyaruk is too busy fighting his brother to worry about us. There is no peace. They all fight. Now Tutush's sons squabble over Syria. The one called Ridwan fights with his brother Dukak and now he challenges Yaghi Siyan."

Ramiro shook his head slowly. "Cannot Ridwan and Dukak rule together?"

"That is not the custom, Sayyid. Two swords will not fit into one sheath."

"My Lord! What a mess!"

Boris nodded in agreement. "And Yaghi Siyan, may God keep him, has formed an alliance with Dukak." He nodded again. "But Kerboga sides with Ridwan."

"Wait a minute, Boris. Who is Kerboga?"

"Kerboga rules Mosul."

Ramiro thought for a moment. "It is all very confusing," he said quietly. "So... if I have understood you correctly... does this mean that Antioch and Damascus are allied against Aleppo and Mosul?"

"It seems that way for now, Sayyid... are you going to eat?"

"What of the coast? Is the route to Jerusalem safe?"

"No, no. The Egyptians have taken many cities on the water – they claim the entire coast south of Dog River. There is no peace." Boris looked around the room and whispered. "I have heard they were here."

"Who?"

"The Egyptians, the Fatimids. They came to speak with our Emir."

"Why?"

"He needs their help to defeat Ridwan. People are very nervous. Pilgrims fear to travel."

Ramiro stood up slowly and wandered to the balcony. "This chaos bodes ill for Syria. Everyone is weak. And the more they fight, the weaker they get. Soon, no house or road will be safe."

Boris nodded. "Yes, Sayyid. Even now, many people flee their farms for the safety of city walls."

"Ramiro," said Adele as she dabbled with her food. "Come and eat. Leave poor Boris alone."

"Just a moment," he said before turning back to Boris. "And what of the west? Have you heard anything about the Romans?"

"I know they have taken ports along the Aegean coast since the death of the pirate Chaka. And they still hold Cyprus. So this too, has Yaghi worried. He fears a naval strike. He knows the Byzantines have built many ships, and the Genoese side with them."

Ramiro furrowed his brow. "What of Nikea?"

Boris pushed up his lips and shook his head. "I haven't heard much. Except that the Son of Sulayman still holds it."

"Thank you, Boris. Keep your eyes and ears open." He handed him a silver coin.

THE LAW

Mufti Ibrahim was unaccustomed to house visits, especially to the home of a Christian. But he found himself unable to turn down Ramiro's request since he had already been paid well for his advice and, furthermore, he knew Ramiro could not come to him.

"I have presented your case to the Qadi," he said. "But you have made my pleas for clemency less forceful by interfering with another man's woman and violating sacred customs."

"I understand, Mufti," said Ramiro. "But now I have done all that is asked by the Emir. I have wed the woman and paid the fines. Am I not redeemed? On what charges can he still hold me prisoner?"

Ibrahim smiled politely as he brushed a crumb of almond cake from his white tunic. "The Emir needs no pretense to hold you, he can do as he pleases. The best we can hope to accomplish is to convince him you are no longer a threat."

"What threat can I possibly be to the Emir? I have no power, no position – the Christians here are Orthodox and will not follow my lead."

"The Emir, may Allah keep him, must see some advantage to your detention, although I admit it is unclear to me."

"Is there nothing contained in Sharia or the Hadiths that could aid my case? Can I not ransom myself?"

Ibrahim shook his head. "Only if your master agrees."

"What of the expatiation of sins? Surely the Emir has transgressed the laws of Islam at one point or another. Is there no way we could use this to our advantage?"

"I have tried to position your case in this way," said Ibrahim, "but you must realize it puts me in a very delicate and possibly dangerous position. My pleas were dismissed. Nonetheless, I am impressed by your knowledge of the Quran. And this brings to mind something that may help your case considerably."

"Really?" asked Ramiro as he offered more tea. "And what is that?"

Ibrahim offered up his cup. "You must become a Muslim," he said as a matter of fact.

Ramiro looked up suddenly, missing the cup and pouring hot tea on the table. "A... a Muslim?"

"There is no other way, Ramiro. Yaghi Siyan would be very pleased, and the Qadi too. It is the best way to ensure your release."

Ramiro shook his head as he lowered the teapot. "I value your advice, Mufti, but this is asking too much. I have taken solemn vows. I have dedicated my life to the teachings of Jesus."

Ibrahim opened his hands in appeal. "Understand that Muslims do not revile Jesus. We believe he was a great prophet. You are asked only to uphold the seven pillars of Islam. One of which is to assert that Muhammad was also God's prophet – his last prophet."

"With all due respect, Mufti, it does not appear that simple to me. There are many divisions in Islam, are there not? How am I to know what to believe?"

"And there are many divisions among Christians. Does that dissuade you? Besides, there is only one True Faith in Islam – and that is Sunni."

"So you say, but I'm sure the Shia would not agree."

Ibrahim's cup shook in his hand and the muscles of his jaw drew taut. "Heretics!" he hissed. "Blasphemers!"

Ramiro held up a hand in defense. "Of course, Mufti, of course. I was only pointing to the differences."

"Yaghi Siyan is Sunni," Ibrahim explained, as if talking to a child. "The Turks are Sunni. Only becoming a Sunni will guarantee your release." He rose from his cushion. "That is my proposal. I will leave you now."

Ramiro followed him to the door. "I will consider your proposal, Mufti. In the meantime, can I count on your continued support?"

"I will see what I can do," he said tersely.

CONSTANTINOPLE

Alexios leaned in his saddle and swung hard. There was a resounding whack and the leather ball streaked between the goal posts. The crowd cheered and his team mates raised their polo mallets in victory. He pulled hard on the reins and his Palomino stallion whinnied, skidding to a halt on the dry grass before rearing its front legs high in the air. "A good game, Taticius!" he shouted. "Your team played well."

Taticius held his fidgety mount steady. He bowed his head slightly. "Not as well as yours, my King... congratulations."

Alexios pulled his horse around and looked over to his wife, Irene. She smiled and waved back. A lock of blonde hair fell out of her headscarf. He grinned back, admiring her beauty. When the groom came to take his horse, he dismounted and walked over to her. The crowd began to disperse.

Irene rose from her chair and took his hand. "You were wonderful, darling. I so seldom get to see you ride."

"He rides like a Turk," said Anna, who sat next to her.

Alexios smirked. "The Turks ride well, mother. We would win more battles if our men could do the same." The thought of the Turks brought Alexios' thoughts back to his struggling Empire.

Anna clicked her tongue in disapproval. "We must talk, Alexi."

• • • • •

"I have sent letter after letter to the Pope!" Alexios shouted in his war room. "I have pleaded for help. I told him the heathen Turks hold Jerusalem and have desecrated the Holy Sepulcher. Indeed, that they have desecrated the Holy Land itself!"

"Patience, my son," Anna consoled. "Pope Urban has just regained the Lateran from the Germans. Give him more time. Even now, we hear, he gains support in the north."

"We are out of time, mother. Now is the time to strike. We have destroyed the Patzinaks and the Kumans. Thrace and Bulgaria are again in our hands. And we have rid ourselves of that pirate, Chaka." He smiled. "Murdered by his own son-in-law!" The men laughed.

Alexios continued with convincing force. "And now the Turks are weak. They fight amongst themselves." He swung his arm in a wide arc. "Now that we have regained the Aegean, we can afford to put some pressure on young

Kilich. We must devise a way to occupy Nicomedia and take Nikea." He paused. "And then we will besiege Antioch." His men stirred in their seats.

"Antioch?" said Isaak. "How many Kelts did you ask for?"

"As many as I can get, brother. If we can find more men to fight like those barbarians, we could take Nikea and then head straight for Antioch."

John Doukas spoke up. "But you know the Kelts are trouble, my King. They are difficult to control."

"You're right, John. But they fight like a pack of dogs... and we have few good fighting men left."

Isaak shook his head. "You cannot trust them!" he hissed. "Have you already forgotten that weasel, that... that Norman bastard Guiscard? They'll take your money with one hand and stab you in the back with the other. All the while claiming it is God's will."

Anna raised her small chin, her long, ashen-blonde hair tied at the back. "I agree, Isaak. I believe they are the most deplorable race of men." She pointed at him with her quill. "But what do we do? Are we content to let the heathen Turks hold Nikea, only miles from Constantinople? Every day they harass us."

"But we don't need the Kelts to take Nikea." Isaak protested. "Kilich is not that strong. We should gather up all our fighting men and make an assault."

"Then what, dear brother?" Alexios joined in. "Once the new sultan consolidates his position, he will return in force to retake Asia and all of Syria. We need to establish our positions now - and then begin to reinforce them. But to do that, we need more men. That's why we need the Kelts. That's why we must take this chance, a chance to regain the full extent of the Roman Empire. It is our God-given right!" He slapped the table with the palm of his hand. "We must attack now!"

John raised a calm voice. "So what have you heard? Will these Kelts come?"

Alexios stroked his short, red beard with his manicured fingers. "Pope Urban is holding a council at Piacenza and I have sent representatives to plead again for help. I have made clear the atrocities of the Turks and the defilement of our holy places."

"What's this council all about?" John asked.

"The Pope is consolidating his power. Many important people will be there. Bishops and lords. Even the King of France will grovel on his knees to appeal his excommunication." Alexios placed his hands on the table. "Our representatives have been charged to seek military assistance wherever and whenever they can... and they are in a position to make generous offers."

"Whatever happened to those Latin monks who came years ago with letters from their Pope?" Anna asked. "Surely, they could speak well on our behalf."

"It's too late for that, mother. Only one survived and he returned to Rome last August."

"Which one?" John asked, remembering the two black-robed monks he had first met in Dyrrachium.

"The stupid one... Aldebert I think his name is. Lieutenant Tatran said the intelligent one was lost to the Turks at Antioch."

CLUNY

With the help of the Normans, Pope Urban tightened his grip on Rome. Then, at a feverish pace, he set out to make personal visits to the lords and bishops of Lombardy to the north. If he was going to hold Rome against the Germans and reassert his papacy, he needed their unswerving support.

In March of 1095, he held a council in the small town of Piacenza. Two hundred bishops attended, as well as thousands of church officials and nearly all the lords of Italy. In all, nearly thirty-five thousand men gathered here to discuss religious reform, the antipope, heresy, and the marital problems of the King of France.

Also present was a delegation from King Alexios, which made emotional and elaborate pleas to the lords of Europe for aid in their battle against the accursed barbarians who had seized and desecrated the holy places of Christendom.

Pope Urban kept up his tireless campaign and, in the fall of 1095, he entered Burgundy to pay a visit to his old monastery, the Abbey of Cluny. The Abbey rang with excitement. Monks fell to their knees and praised God for the safe arrival of His Holiness, who now blessed their monastery with his very presence.

● ● ● ● ●

"Do you have any more news from your spies in the East?" asked Pope Urban as he made himself comfortable in Abbot Hugh's private chambers.

"Alas, no, Your Holiness," said Hugh. "Not since the report we received last year from Edessa. We were quite surprised to get it because we heard nothing for a number of years and feared he was either dead or captured. As events turned out, he actually *was* captured by the pagans but, by the grace of God, he managed to escape. Said he was heading for Jerusalem."

"And this came from your monk? The one I met in Melfi?"

"Yes, Holy Father. The one called Ramiro. Apparently, the Persians imprisoned and enslaved him, which accounts for the absence of his reports.

"Yes, I heard of this from your other monk, the one now in Rome."

"Brother Aldebert?"

"Yes, that's him. He seems to know much about these Greeks and their affairs."

"He wrote to me recently," said Hugh, "requesting to be moved to a Benedictine monastery near Bari."

"That would serve us well," said Urban. "Many pilgrims and soldiers come and go from Bari. He can report on all he hears."

Hugh was initially angered when he read Aldebert's request to go to Bari and was about to order him back to the monastery. But now he had a change of heart. "As you wish, Holy Father."

"Do me the favor, Abbot, of recounting these reports. I am afraid my memory does not serve me well in old age."

"Of course, Your Holiness, would you like some refreshments?"

"Just some water, if you will."

Hugh got up and poured him a cup of water from a sideboard. "Well," he said, "it seems the Greeks are having much trouble holding against the Persians and have lost vast tracts of their Christian empire. Good Christians are driven from their homes, tortured or enslaved. Holy places are defiled, churches profaned. Antioch, home of our blessed Saint Paul, is scourged and oppressed."

Urban shook his head in sadness and shame. "We cannot allow this to continue, it threatens the whole of Christendom."

"But there is some news in our favor," Hugh went on. "It seems the King of the Persians was murdered and the country has fallen into civil war. And the princes of Syria fight amongst themselves, few with any real power. So you see, Your Holiness, God has cleared the path for our Holy Crusade."

"Praise God!" said Urban. "Did you know the Greek King sent a delegation to our council in Piacenza?"

"I heard rumor, Holy Father. What did they say?"

"No more than we have come to expect. That Holy Jerusalem itself suffers at the hands of these Godless heathen, violated and polluted by their very presence, that the Tomb of Christ is corrupted and that the alms of pious Christians are pilfered from the Church of God. They persecute the devout, enslaving and massacring them by the thousands, their bodies left to rot in heaps. We can no longer tolerate this villainy and heresy!"

"I agree, Holy Father. We must destroy them."

"For many years," said Urban, "the Greek King has pleaded for the soldiers of Christ to come to his aide. The time has come to harken to his call, in the name of God."

"It has been too long, Holiness. We should have rallied forces years ago. The men of France undermine themselves with their petty quarrels and battles. We need to redirect their energies to a more noble and Godly cause."

Urban nodded. "I have been urging them to Byzantium for some time. Finally, they begin to listen. I have talked to some of the lords and I believe Count Raymond of Toulouse is the best man to lead a Holy Crusade."

"I agree, Raymond is a good choice," said Hugh. "He has the money and is devoted to our cause. And surely, Holy Father, these men will receive God's grace and the remission of their sins for entering on the divine path to the Holy Sepulcher and wresting the Holy Land from such an evil race."

"They will," said Urban. "And now it is time to rally the people to this cause. I plan to hold another council in France for this purpose, for a call to Holy War. Perhaps Cluny would be appropriate."

"Here, Your Holiness? At the monastery?" Abbot Hugh was visibly unnerved.

"You think not, Abbot?"

"Forgive me, Holy Father, but is it a good idea to associate the Benedictine Order with war of any kind?"

"Perhaps not, what do you suggest?"

Hugh thought for a moment. "I suggest Claremont. It is about eighty miles to the southwest and closer to central France. Several important councils have been held there in the past and the new cathedral is splendid. It would serve our purposes well."

"So be it, Abbot Hugh. We go to Claremont."

ANTIOCH

Ibrahim paid another visit to Ramiro. "I'm leaving for Jerusalem," he said bluntly. "There is little more I can do for you here."

"Jerusalem?" Ramiro felt a flood of envy. "Why Jerusalem?"

"I have been asked to take the position of Qadi there. It is a great and rare privilege. I must go."

"But what of my case?"

"Like I said, you should embrace Islam. This is your only hope of release."

"I cannot do this, Mufti, my faith in Christ is too strong."

"But your situation here is unlikely to improve, Ramiro."

"Dear oh dear, may God help us. If only I could go with you."

"I doubt that is possible."

Ramiro had an idea. "But perhaps you could do something for me?"

"And what is that?"

"Deliver a letter to the Patriarch."

Ibrahim shook his head. "The Christian leader? No, no, I do not dare. If anyone should discover this, I would be accused as a spy, as a traitor."

"But I promise, Mufti, there will be nothing of vital military interest in the letter. It is only to explain my absence to the Patriarch. He must wonder what has happened to me. Please, I beg of you."

Ibrahim glanced at Ramiro with a look of exasperation. "Very well, but I reserve the right to review and approve this letter. Do you have it?"

"One moment, Mufti," he said, rushing to his desk. "It will only take one moment to write." He began to write in Latin before he realized that Ibrahim would not be able to read it. So he tore it up and wrote another in Greek. He briefly told the Patriarch all that had expired and beseeched him to forward his message to Abbot Hugh of Cluny. He blew on the ink to speed its drying before handing it to Ibrahim for his approval.

Ibrahim looked it over. "Very well," he said. "God willing, I will deliver it. Although it is against my better judgment."

December 1095

Yaghi Siyan ranted. "That son of a whore! May Allah curse the day he was born!" The messenger pulled back in fear as Yaghi shouted at him. "How far has Ridwan advanced?"

The messenger went pale. "He has taken the eastern townships, Beyfendi. But he is not equipped to lay siege to Antioch."

"How dare he!" Yaghi pulled his knife and held it up to the messenger. "I will slit his throat by my own hand!"

The messenger's eyes flickered briefly, he looked faint.

"And where is his brother, Dukak?" he shouted again. "Do we not have an alliance?"

"Yes, Emir," the messenger gulped, glad to still be of some use. "Dukak rode north from Damascus to help us, but he had to turn back because his brother Ridwan took advantage of his departure and attacked."

Yaghi turned to his commanders. "Enough of this! Enough of Ridwan! Prepare for battle! We will move against him in the spring."

Holy War

Weeks became months and months became years. Still, Yaghi Siyan would not hear their pleas for freedom. Ramiro refused to give up and continued to take notes for his reports to Abbot Hugh, reports that he could never send out. Month on end, he tried to keep up hope, but despair gnawed at him, like a rat through wood.

"Checkmate!" Boris yelled.

"For the love of Mary, Boris! There's no need to shout." Ramiro glared at the chessboard. "I don't understand," he confessed, unable to suppress his anger and frustration.

Adele could not stifle a smile as she added more charcoal to the brazier.

Boris was too eager to help. "You see, my castle attacks your king. But you cannot move because your only escape is here." He pointed to a square. "And my horseman covers this square. Your king is dead," he smirked.

"What of my vizier? Or my qadi? Can they do nothing?"

Boris was still smiling. "Oh yes, some moves ago. But you missed your opportunity."

Ramiro rubbed his hands as cold drafts of winter crossed the room. "Enough, I'm tired."

"Do you want to play backgammon instead, Master Ramiro?"

"No, Boris. I've had enough of games." He leaned away from the table with a feeling of despair. How much longer? How much longer must I waste my time playing games? Has Abbot Hugh forsaken me? God knows my mother must think the worst. If, indeed, she still lives.

There was a knock at the door. "You have a visitor, Ramiro!" a guard shouted from behind the door.

"A visitor?" he shouted back as he got up and moved to the door. "But I have no appointments today."

The guard opened the door a little and motioned behind him with his eyes. "It is a very important visitor."

Ramiro gestured to Boris. "You had better leave."

Boris got up and swept out the door. The guard moved aside for him and John the Oxite stepped in, his black cape flowing behind him.

"Your Eminence! May God bless you. What a pleasure this is."

The Patriarch made an apologetic gesture as Boris slipped out. "Forgive me for appearing without notice. Until now, the Emir has been reluctant to let me see you."

Ramiro bowed. "Please, Your Eminence. Sit down."

Adele rose from her seat when John arrived. "Would you like some juice?" she asked.

John sat down on a sprawl of cushions. His long face appeared ashen and drawn and his gray-blonde beard seemed a little grayer. He waved his hand in refusal. "No, no, dear woman. I won't be long."

Adele retired to her own room, as was the custom when men talked. But she could still hear every word.

John looked tired. His long, black robe rustled as he shuffled on the cushions. He spoke with heavy eyes. "How have you been, Monk Ramiro?"

Ramiro gave a small shrug. "As well as can be expected, given the circumstances."

John smiled tautly. "If you had followed my advice, you would not be here now. Why didn't you use the mufti, as I suggested?

"I was too impatient, Your Eminence. The mufti said it would take over a year for my case to be heard."

John opened his hands. "But now you have been held captive for an even longer time. So what have you gained?"

Ramiro raised his chin stubbornly. "I saved the woman from an unthinkable fate, Your Eminence. That is reward enough."

"You are indeed a strange man, Ramiro of Cluny, perhaps a foolish one. But I admire your principles and your resolve."

"I asked to see you many months ago, Your Eminence," said Ramiro, brushing his long hair from round cheeks. "But I heard nothing. And they will not allow me letters."

"I was never informed," said John sternly. "But there are some events that may interest you. I have news from Rome."

"What have you heard?"

He leaned forward. "The Bishop of Rome has taken the Lateran Palace. The Germans have quit."

"You mean Pope Urban has taken his seat?"

"Yes, last year. Now he asserts his power throughout the West and calls for a Holy Crusade."

"What do you mean?"

"Urban has called for a crusade to liberate the Holy Land from the infidels. He promised the men of France and Germany that God would forgive their sins if they took up the cross to fight a Holy War."

"And... and what was the response?"

"Very good, I hear. Even now, hordes of French and Germans rush to Constantinople. And many lords of the West prepare for a spring advance."

Ramiro rose suddenly from his cushion. He went to the table and poured a glass of wine. He offered one to John, who shook his head. "This is incredible!" he said before draining his cup. "I thought Urban's mission was to unite the churches in peace. Now he goes to war?"

"He still hopes to rule Christendom." John scowled. "Mark my words, this war will be as much against the Greek Church as against the infidels. None of us trust him."

"No, I cannot believe that, Your Eminence. Pope Urban would not wage war on Christians."

"But we are not of his church. You know the deep enmity that exists between us. I pray for the best... but we shall see."

"What does King Alexios think of all this?"

John scoffed. "It was his plan, Monk Ramiro. He has plotted for years to get mercenaries from the West. Now he has succeeded. But I tell you he is asking for trouble."

Ramiro stood up and paced by the window. He thought of the brutal Drugo and his greedy men. "I agree, Your Eminence, they are an unruly lot. But do you really believe French armies can reach Jerusalem?"

"Why not? And if they do, they will surely pass through Antioch."

Despite John's dire predictions, Ramiro felt inwardly elated. "Well, at least it would mean my freedom," he said. "It would put Jerusalem in Christian hands and allow pilgrims a safe passage."

"War is never a safe gambit," said John. "Surely you know that."

REQUITED LOVE

Ramiro and Adele knelt in prayer, as they did every morning and evening. Ramiro laid his iron cross in front of them before praying aloud.

> *O Holy Cross*
> *by which that Cross is brought to mind*
> *on which our Lord Jesus Christ*
> *through his own death*
> *raised us up from that eternal death...*

They prayed for family and friends, for the Pope and the Holy Church, and they prayed for their freedom. When all was said and done, Adele served out two cups of sage tea and went about her sewing at the table. Ramiro sat across from her, picking through a book of poetry that Boris had smuggled in. The author was Abu Nuwas, a man scorned by some for his lewdness, while adored by others for his extensive learning. There were poems about the pleasures of the hunt, about his love of women, and about his love of boys. He read quietly.

> *O moon of the darkened bedroom*
> *I kissed him once, just once*
> *as he slept, half hoping half fearing*
> *he might wake up*

O silk soft moon
his pajamas held such softness
Ah how I'd like a real live kiss
how I'd like to be offered
what's under the covers

In a flush of embarrassment, Ramiro slammed the book shut and put it down. "Blessed saints!"

"What's the matter?" Adele asked.

He shook his head in wonder. "I cannot believe that men write of such things!"

"What's it about?"

He flustered, too abashed to tell her. "It's... it's about love."

Adele looked up from her sewing and smiled in her charming way. "Are you so embarrassed by love, my husband?"

"Well, not really, as long as love remains within the moral bounds of the Church."

"Is our love within these bounds, Ramiro?"

He blushed and turned his eyes away. He could not answer her honestly.

She put down her sewing and leaned across the table, taking his hand and squeezing it gently. She surprised him by her move and he dared to gaze into her round, pleading eyes. "Ramiro," she said, "... we've been living together for almost two years. When will you come to my bed? I am your wife." She paused. "Don't you love me?"

Ramiro reddened. The harried demons of his faith offered him little respite. His face writhed in a torment of confusion and indecision. He thought about the first time he had noticed her on their journey through the Balkans. Her beauty had swayed him then... and it swayed him now. How he longed for her loving touch. "I... I do love you, Adele," he said quietly, with a touch of apology and affection. "But you promised to respect my vows."

Adele smiled and got up. She moved around the table and cuddled on the cushions beside him. "You really do love me?"

Ramiro nodded. "Yes, dear woman, I think I've loved you since I first set eyes on you."

She caressed his arm and whispered into his ear. "And now we have each other, dearest Ramiro." She pulled gently on his arm. "Come with me... come to my bed," she said in a low, seductive voice. "Love me." Her soft lips touched his ear.

Hot blood rushed to his head and his loins stirred with a carnal craving he had not felt since the days of his youth. In an instant, a crushing wave of desire swept away years of denial. Awkwardly, he put his arm over her shoulder, hesitating for a moment before pulling her gently into his chest until they were face to face. At first, their lips met in a timid, soft touch but, in only a few precious moments, they pressed harder and harder in a bold, reckless embrace, releasing long, pent-up cravings in an explosion of passionate love.

JULY 1096

Ramiro was unusually happy as he strode to the courtyard. He enjoyed his walks throughout the whole compound but preferred the courtyard where he was sure to avoid Khuda the Mamluk, who still threatened him on occasion. But he also kept an eye on the Turk whenever he could. And his servant Boris watched him too. He knew where Khuda lived in the compound and made notes about his activities. But today, Khuda was not a concern. Here, around the splashing fountain, he could bask in bright sunshine, talk to fellow prisoners, and hear scraps of news from every corner.

He strolled to his favorite bench under a pear tree. It was already occupied. "Good morning, Rabbi. What a lovely day!"

Rabbi David said nothing, his shoulders were hunched, his face serious, his demeanor morose.

"What is it, Rabbi?" asked Ramiro as he sat beside him. "Do these prison walls weigh heavily on your mind?"

David looked at him with large, sad eyes. "These walls always weigh on me, Ramiro. But today, terrible news has come my way."

Ramiro tipped his head. "And what is that, my friend?"

David reached over and put his hand on Ramiro's arm. "You remember that your Pope called for Holy War against the infidels?"

"Yes, I do," he replied with intrinsic guilt. "But it does not sit well with me. What has happened?"

"Well, it seems it is first a war against the Hebrews." Tears welled in his eyes.

"What do you mean?"

"There have been terrible massacres, my friend. Hundreds of German savages terrorize the Hebrews who live in their towns. They have murdered hundreds, maybe thousands... and they burn and pillage their homes." He put his head in his hands. "What have my people done to deserve this?"

"Are you sure, Rabbi? Where did this happen?"

"Yes, I am sure," he said in a quaking voice. "My son just told me. In Mainz, Worms, and Cologne. Last year. Mobs of Christian fanatics went on a rampage. Now these same mobs travel east to... to Constantinople." He blew his nose in a kerchief.

"But why?"

"Who knows? Because we are both hated and envied. Hated because we are not Christian. Envied because some have money. And our people are always blamed for the death of your messiah. All of this!"

"And their armies march to Constantinople?"

"It's not much of an army, I hear. It is more a band of murderers and thieves who profess to follow God. That God would be so cruel!"

"Who leads them, Rabbi?"

"Hermits and madmen is all I've heard."

Part Six

BARBARIANS

~~~~~~~~~~~~~~~~~~~~~~~~~~~~~~~~~

CONSTANTINOPLE

AUGUST 1096

King Alexios surveyed the grounds with dread. There, far beyond the city walls, gathered thousands upon thousands of zealous Christian peasants and ruffians who had made the long trek from Germany and France, divinely inspired as they were by the fiery oratory of Pope Urban and his call to Holy War. But this was not the mercenary army he had hoped for. Only a few hundred had horses, swords, bows, or armor of any kind. Most carried only knives and sharpened stakes. Among them were thousands of women and children, even the elderly. Many waved palms and wore rough crosses sewn onto their shoulders. Thousands arrived every day and their numbers soon became unwieldy. But there was a ray of hope amid the gloom. He heard that more formidable armies readied themselves for a Holy Crusade and should arrive in a few months.

"May God have mercy on us!" he shouted. "Don't let them inside the city walls. But keep them well-fed. And bring their leaders to me right away!"

The captain bowed and backed away. "Yes, my King."

• • • • •

Peter the Hermit sat with drooping shoulders. Walter the Penniless sat beside him. Both were dressed in soiled wool shirts and pants. Peter was balding while Walter had shoulder-length, greasy hair. They appeared uncomfortable in the splendor of Alexios' palace and shuffled uneasily in their elegant armchairs. Alexios tried for hours to give them advice, but it seemed to fall on deaf ears.

Alexios studied the short man with balding, blonde hair, his skin burnt from the sun and his beard matted with grease. He had heard much about Peter, renowned as a stirring orator who was capable of arousing the masses. But he was a stubborn man, too fanatical for his liking, although not as bad as Walter, who could do nothing but respond with thoughtless, dogmatic tirades. And the stink! Worse than a pig sty! He reached for a scented kerchief and pretended to wipe his nose. "So Peter, I hear you have been here before."

"Yes, Your Highness, I was captured and tortured by these heathen some years ago, may God curse them!" His red face scowled heavily.

"Will you not wait as I ask? I assure you more capable armies are on their way. I hope you will follow my advice and tarry here until they arrive."

Peter opened his hands in a gesture of resignation. "I have led the faithful here, Your Highness, but I cannot control them. They ignore my pleas and continue to plunder the countryside. They are the Chosen of God, chosen for a Holy Crusade to Jerusalem. They are anxious to fight the heathen and will have their way."

Walter broke in, speaking loudly. "We have been sent by the Pope himself to regain the Holy Land! We will not be stopped!" His clotted hair swayed across his face as he ranted.

Alexios stood up impatiently. "Then you leave me little choice. I will move your people across the Bosporus. You may stake yourselves along the Propontis at a fort called Civetot."

• • • • •

Peter and Walter eagerly set up camp at Civetot. It was on the water and could be supplied easily across the Propontis. Shortly after they arrived, thousands of them set out from camp to pillage the countryside, believing they must do God's work, seeing everyone they encountered as godless, evil heathen who must be scourged from the face of the earth. They rampaged, killing Muslim and Christian alike, looting homes, mosques, and even Greek churches. They ridiculed, raped and tortured their captives before burning them alive, screaming on pyres.

NIKEA

Kilich laughed aloud. His commanders laughed too. "So this is the great Franj army," he smirked. "This army of rabble that the Roman King prays will defeat the Turks." He laughed again.

Ozan smiled. "Yes, my Sultan. They occupy Civetot and the Roman king supplies them across the sea. They pillage every village and lay waste. They kill everyone – even the Christians!" The men chuckled.

"How well organized are they?" Kilich asked.

"Not very well, my Lord. There are different tribes with different tongues and they distrust each other. Nonetheless, some armed horsemen are among them. They are crude and violent men, my Lord. They ravage the countryside, destroying all in their path. They like to torture their victims before they kill them. The people say they slaughter infants and roast them on spits!"

Kilich turned away in disgust. "Animals! Barbarians! May Allah damn them to Hellfire!" He looked back. "And now you say they march here, to Nikea?"

"Yes, my Lord."

Kilich turned to his atabek, Al-Khanes. "Kill them all. Send a patrol to confront them."

"Yes, Master. But perhaps we should send a more sizeable army to destroy them."

Kilich smiled. "No. We will show them how mamluks fight."

• • • • •

But Kilich was wrong. His patrol of mamluks was killed to a man, overwhelmed by the sheer numbers of would-be Crusaders.

"Then you were right, Al-Khanes," he admitted, shaking his head. "What should we do now?"

"Watch and wait, my Lord," he crackled. "They advance towards us. We should lure them away, lure them into a trap."

"And what do you propose?"

"Use the fortress at Xerigordon, my Prince."

Young Kilich frowned. "What do you mean?"

"Xerigordon is only a few miles from here. Remove our troops from the fortress and send a spy into the barbarian camp. He will tell them we have fled in fear and that it is free for the taking. Since these barbarians are so stupid and greedy, they will not be able to refuse the offer."

Kilich brightened. "And then we will besiege them!"

OCTOBER 1096

These barbarians are so predictable, Al-Khanes thought as his troops surrounded Xerigordon. And they are so stupid. Could they not see that the well sits outside the city walls? Now they have suffered eight days without water and will not last much longer, not in this heat. My spies say they drink the blood of their mounts, and others drink their own piss. He smiled. May Allah curse them with a slow death!

A messenger ran up to him and bowed. "They wish to surrender, Commander."

Al-Khanes hardened. "Did you tell them they will live only if they renounce their faith and embrace Islam?"

"Yes, Commander."

"Very well. When they open the gates, enslave the converts and slaughter the rest."

• • • • •

Prince Kilich was enthused by his success at Xerigordon. "Filthy kuffar! May Allah curse their ancestors! We will kill them all and rid the earth of this heathen scum! We ride to Civetot!"

"But, Master, they will be prepared. And the Emperor supplies them by sea," Al-Khanes protested.

"Then what do you advise, my atabek?"

Al-Khanes rubbed his bushy beard before scratching at an old scar running down his chin. "Send our spies to Civetot. They will tell the Christians that their comrades have managed to take Nikea and now share in its rich spoils. They will come running - like greedy rats to a carcass. Then we lay an ambush."

"You are a wise atabek, Al-Khanes." Kilich smiled. "We will do as you say. But we must do it quickly before the pagan devils discover the truth."

• • • • •

Walter the Penniless danced with joy when he heard Nikea had fallen to their comrades. "By the grace of God we have conquered!" The whole camp at Civetot screamed with delight. Thousands gushed with tears and fell to their knees to thank God for their divine victory over the wicked heathen. But they soon forgot their prayers of thanksgiving and began to shout with envy. What of the rich booty from Nikea? They wanted their share and began to rush out madly to join the victors.

"What of Peter?" asked Walter. "We should wait for him to return from Constantinople before we head out."

But their greed soon overcame all common sense and they stormed out of the gates, heading for Nikea with Walter in the lead. They had no sooner left the gate when a lone survivor of Xerigordon came stumbling back to camp. He tried to stop them. He warned them that their comrades did not take Nikea, but instead, were cruelly slaughtered or enslaved.

Walter ranted and cursed like a madman when he heard the terrible news. But he was so enraged by the slaughter of fellow Christians that, rather than heeding good advice, he worked the crowd into a frenzy of revenge and they rushed forward in an angry mob. This time, they vowed, they would reach Nikea and they would destroy it.

The Turks lay in ambush at a narrow wooded valley not far from Civetot. As soon as the mass of Christian zealots entered the mouth of the valley, Kilich sent horsemen to face them. But Walter egged them forward, reminding them of their first easy victory over the mamluks. They rushed against the Turks, confident that God would favor them. But these wayward souls soon died screaming in a deadly rain of Turk arrows. Walter the Penniless, riddled by seven, died before he hit the ground. The rest fell back in a stampede of fear, storming out the valley the way they had come. But now, Turk infantry blocked the way. With nowhere to flee, terrified French and German paupers died by the thousands on this bloody battle-ground. Huge mounds of their corpses were left to rot in the burning sun of the valley, where vultures and crows picked the bones clean.

But Kilich did not stop there. He led his men east to overrun Civetot with brutal suppression, killing everyone, sparing only a few pretty boys and girls for the slave markets of Aleppo.

• • • • •

Kilich felt the throb of battle in his veins. "Now we must go to fight the Danishmend to the east! They have grown too bold since the death of the Great Shah. We must ride against them to regain Malatya!"

"But what of the Franj, my Lord?" asked Ozan. "We hear that many more march from the far west."

Kilich burst into a scoffing laugh. "You cannot be serious, Ozan. You saw what they were like. Why should we fear these rag-tag warriors?" He took on a more serious tone. "It's the Danishmend who are the real threat to our domains."

"But my Lord,' said Al-Khanes in his crackling voice. "We have heard these new infidel armies are better equipped and are personally led by their chiefs."

Kilich shook his head. "No. We will not sit here worrying about a thousand more peasants from the West. But you can be sure the Danishmend will continue their raids until they have taken all of our cities. We need those cities! We need the revenues. We must ride to Malatya!"

CONSTANTINOPLE

MAY 1097

Alexios began to worry. The newly-arriving French armies were much larger than he expected, and they continued to come by the thousands. Not just men of war but, once again, thousands of women, children, servants and slaves. They were camped outside the city walls, a mass of filthy zealots who yelled and screamed and sang and danced in the thick, choking smoke of a thousand campfires.

Prominent among these men was Raymond of Toulouse, a dominant lord of Provence and a favorite of the Pope. With him, was Bishop Adhemar, the appointed spiritual leader of the Holy Crusade.

Robert of Flanders also came, the son of the man who sent Drugo the Red to fight for the Greek King. And traveling with him, was the rich and powerful Godfrey of Bouillon.

Raymond and Adhemar were keen to maintain détente with the Byzantine king. In their wisdom, they realized they would have to rely on him for supplies and information. But Godfrey distrusted Alexios and refused to swear allegiance.

Alexios responded by cutting off his food supplies - and that is when the pillaging began. Godfrey's men went on a looting rampage, setting fire to a number of buildings. Alexios sent out the full force of his troops, putting down the rebellion.

But given time, flattery, and some generous gifts, Godfrey eventually yielded to Alexios and swore an oath of fealty to him. So the King moved them all across the Bosporus to Pelekanum, just west of Nicomedia. Then Bohemond arrived.

"Bohemond has come?" asked Isaak.

"Yes, along with his nephew, Tancred. But he has little money and only a small army," Alexios said, as if it were some comfort.

"But we cannot trust him, my King. He is a son of Robert Guiscard. He has only one intention – and that is to take Byzantium for his own!"

"He will take the oath of allegiance. For the moment, he is no threat. But like you say, Isaak, he cannot be trusted."

"It is too much, too fast, my son," said Anna with a sincere look of concern. "We must move them east as quickly as possible, before they do any more damage. We are still recovering from Godfrey's rampage."

Alexios nodded. "I agree, mother. I will send them all to Pelekanum and Nicomedia. Once they have reaffirmed their oaths, we can make better use of their aggression by setting them against the Turks at Nikea."

● ● ● ● ●

Drugo the Red heard the news and was elated, as were his three hundred or so remaining men. "Count Robert comes!" he shouted. "Our lord and master!"

The men cheered with great enthusiasm, drawing their swords and jabbing them into the air.

When the cheers subsided, Otto blurted out. "But we still serve the Greek king! How can we join Robert?"

General Taticius quelled them. "It is true, you still owe allegiance to Alexios. But don't worry. You'll have your chance to fight alongside Robert. We will join them to besiege Nikea."

The men roared their pleasure. "Death to the heathen!" they howled. "God wills it!"

NIKEA

We need more men, Ozan thought with mounting trepidation. These Franj are determined, and they are not like the beggars who came before. Our spies say three thousand of them labor on the road from Nicomedia to Nikea, busy clearing hundreds of trees, pulling the stumps to widen the narrow mountain road for their growing army. And there was no one to stop them. Kilich had left to fight the Danishmend to the east.

Thousands upon thousands of Crusaders camped near Nicomedia, so many that their food and provisions soon ran short. So they split their army in two, both taking different routes, but both heading to one place – Nikea. Days later, both armies converged on the outskirts of Lake Askanius, over thirty thousand men.

Ozan frantically wrote another letter to Kilich. He sent the first letter when he heard the Franj had returned in great numbers and were now camped at Pelekanum. But alas, his master was distracted by the Danishmend's siege of Malatya. His only response was to send a few detachments back to Nikea to appease his wife, who was pregnant and fretting.

Kilich must come, Ozan panicked. And he must come soon! He handed the letter to the messenger. "Ride as fast as you can. The Sultanate is under attack!"

MALATYA

Kilich sat in his war tent reading Ozan's letter. A deep frown crossed his boyish face. He summoned his atabek, Al-Khanes. "What should we do? If we return now, Danishmend will take Malatya. But if we do not, Nikea will fall to the barbarians. Our families are there. Our treasury is there."

Al-Khanes took a moment to think, rubbing his gnarled nose with a finger. "Then you must make peace with Ghazi of the Danishmend," he said.

"Peace?" Kilich shrugged. "How?"

"These Christian barbarians threaten all Muslims, Shia and Sunni alike. It makes no difference to them. They even kill the Christians of Byzantium. No one is safe."

Kilich saw the direction of his advice and felt encouraged. "Do you think we can convince Ghazi to join us in a holy war against these infidels?"

"Yes, my Lord. He hates Christians. I'm sure Hasan of Cappadocia will join us as well."

"Yes, yes." Kilich muttered, thinking of Hasan and his escape from Isfahan with Ramiro and how Hasan had helped him on the long journey back to Nikea. Hasan had proved to be a faithful ally since the death of his father, Bolkas. Now he ruled Cappadocia.

And so it was. Against all odds, Ghazi Danishmend, a fierce man of Islam, was convinced to reach a truce with Kilich and to join him against the heathen Christians. And Hasan came too, inflamed by his own seething hatred of Christians. Their combined armies rushed to Nikea. But by the time they arrived, tens of thousands of Crusaders had already surrounded the city walls, preparing for a long siege.

NIKEA

Nikea's walls and ramparts were two and a half miles in circumference and along these walls were one hundred towers and four gates. The western wall rose out of the waters of Lake Askanius where a water-gate allowed the passage of boats and supplies. The remainder of the wall, standing the height of six men, was surrounded by a moat full with the runoff from nearby streams. Nikea was almost impregnable. But it could never sustain an onslaught of this size and intensity. The Crusaders had enough men to surround the whole city and to attack every gate, except the one on the water.

Kilich looked down on Nikea from a nearby hilltop. The size of the infidel army shocked him, sending a chill of dread pulsing through his veins. The real possibility of losing his family, his gold, and his beloved Nikea struck him as if a cold sword had pierced his heart.

"We are too late, Master," said Al-Khanes with little comfort. "There must be forty thousand. We cannot penetrate their lines. It is better to turn back now and save our men for another day of battle." Ghazi Danishmend and most of the commanders nodded in agreement.

"But there must be a way!" Kilich shouted in despair. "We cannot give up without a fight. Look! They are weak in the south. We will attack there! By the will of Allah!"

Reluctantly, Ghazi and Hasan agreed. They would attack at dawn with the sun at their backs. But Kilich's plan was foiled. The French captured two of his spies among their ranks. So when Kilich charged out, the Crusaders were ready for him. A fierce battle ensued and many died on both sides. But when Bohemond joined the fray, Kilich saw that all was lost and retreated south. Never again would he return to Nikea.

• • • • •

Ozan watched the battle from the city walls. Tears streamed down his cheeks. It was over. They had to surrender. But the Turk garrison refused to give up, despite the overwhelming odds. Even when the Crusaders cut off the heads of their comrades and catapulted them over the city walls, they refused to waiver.

It was only when Commander Manuel and General Taticius arrived from Constantinople that they reconsidered. And when the Crusaders spotted the Byzantine ships on the lake, they rejoiced and gave glory to God. But their cheers did little for the moral of the Turks, who soon let the Romans into the city, where they sued for peace.

At dawn on the following day, the Crusaders were somewhat startled to see Byzantine flags stationed along the walls. They soon realized that Alexios had taken the city by stealth rather than by storm. They were furious when they learned that the King had let the pagan Turks run free because, on their march, they had seen the macabre remains of the French and German peasants killed ten months before. They thought now of these stinking mounds of skulls and bones and the sun-dried flesh of good Christian folk, and were sorely disappointed to be denied their revenge. And they were even more enraged when they thought they were deprived of the booty of war. So when Alexios asked them to repeat their pledges of allegiance, they refused. Only when the King promised them the treasury of Nikea, did they relent.

But Alexios gave them much more than gold. He offered them invaluable advice on the lay of the land and the state of political turmoil among the Turks and Arabs. He rehearsed the enemy's fighting habits, their strengths and weaknesses. He gave them maps and guides, appointing Taticius to serve as an experienced advisor. The King stressed the strategic importance of Antioch and he put fire in their bellies with exaggerated tales about the violations of holy places.

Feeling encouraged and heavy with Nikea's gold, tens of thousands of Crusaders headed south, deep into Turk-held territory. To avoid being unwieldy and inefficient, they again divided the masses into two great armies.

Drugo the Red and his men followed their lord Robert and were glad to be among their own kind again. But Drugo well knew the habits of these Turks. He put his hand to the hilt of his sword. "I don't like this, Humberto. I feel we're being watched."

Humberto laughed. "Of that you can be sure, Sir Drugo."

DORYLAEUM

JULY 1097

"They ride south, Prince Kilich," said the scout. "There are many, many thousands but they have divided into two armies. The smaller one leads the way. They head for Iconium."

"Then they must cross the Plains of Dorylaeum. The road narrows through the valley beyond the ruins," said Hasan.

"And now we have almost thirty thousand men," said Ghazi. "We are ready."

"Very well," said Kilich. "We attack at Dorylaeum."

• • • • •

The Crusaders travelled for days without incident, although some men spotted Turk scouts on the hilltops. A few hours after dawn, they reached the Plains of Dorylaeum. It was here in this low valley, hemmed in by mountains on every side, where the Turks appeared by the thousands. They massed on the plain in front of them and thousands more appeared on the crests. And when they began to blow their trumpets and howl their piercing war cries, fear rippled through the Crusader ranks. But fear soon turned to terror when a deadly hail of arrows began to riddle the masses, and when the heathen hoard came screaming down the hills in a full assault, terror turned to blind panic. Hundreds dropped all they had and began to flee.

Bohemond and Taticius knew that a frenzied flight was just what the Turks wanted, and that it would mean certain death. With level heads, they took control, barking commands to hold them in formation. Together, they managed to form an enormous, defensive circle, putting women, children, goods and horses to the center while the best armored men stationed themselves to the outside. Fast messengers rode back to warn the other army, led by Godfrey.

Another cloud of arrows rained down on the army of God, then another, and another, killing hundreds with every volley. Horses, mules, and donkeys fell screaming to the ground. Thousands lay dead or dying. Frightened priests slinked through the crowd attempting to boost morale. "Stand fast together, trust in Christ and the Holy Cross. Stand fast. Stand fast. Trust in Christ and the Holy Cross."

Kilich came racing down the plain with all his men, charging into the circle head on. They broke through, piercing with lance, slashing with sword. But the harder they pressed, the harder the knights pushed back, closing the circle once more.

Where are the others? Bohemond agonized. Where is Godfrey? When will he come? They huddled all night, dreading the rain of arrows they knew would come with the dawn.

But Kilich no sooner began his morning assault when a thin trail of dust appeared on the western horizon.

Bohemond shouted with relief. "Here they come!"

Kilich saw them too, shaken by the size of the approaching army. But the worst was yet to come. Just as he sighted Godfrey's army, another appeared behind their lines, trapping them in a pincer. Seeing that all was lost and in fear of his life, he fled with the other emirs, racing into the mountains at full gallop. The other horsemen followed, leaving the infantry abandoned and trapped. The Franj cut them to pieces, chasing and killing for hours. Only a few hundred young captives were spared for the slave markets of Byzantium.

Three thousand Turks died on that day. But the Crusader victory was a Pyrrhic one. Over four thousand of them perished, and thousands of their precious horses and pack animals died in the relentless fusillade of arrows.

• • • • •

Where the Turks failed, Mother Nature had more success. Leaving Dorylaeum in the dead heat of summer, the Crusaders took the road south. It was the same destitute route taken by Ramiro years before when Hasan dragged him as a slave to Isfahan. It skirted the blistering, barren desert and headed for the distant, lush orchards of Iconium. Unfamiliar with the heavy demands of the barren land and the scorched-earth policy of the Turks, they soon ran short of water. Even Taticius was unprepared for the devastation they encountered; villages abandoned, wells poisoned or blocked, fields destroyed, animals slaughtered. Thirst and hunger soon ravaged their ranks and thousands upon thousands suffered a lingering, miserable death along this uninhabited path. Children and the old died first, even Godfrey's young son died from the heat. Many of the remaining horses died and the army of knights quickly became an army of foot-soldiers. The pack animals died too and much was left behind.

They took three long months to cross Asia, a journey usually accomplished in a single month. By the time they reached drinkable water, nearly twenty thousand of their corpses lined the desert route.

Taticius survived this journey, as did Drugo the Red, his lieutenant Otto, and the executioner, Arles of Ghent. But the cheerful Humberto succumbed to the heat, along with Fulk and another twenty-four of Drugo's men, who all died with glazed eyes and gaping mouths.

ANTIOCH

The thousands of Crusader deaths barely made the news, but the defeat of the Son of Sulayman at Nikea, then again at Dorylaeum, sent waves of panic throughout the world of Islam. Already shaken by the death of the illustrious Malik Shah, the latest news was even more distressing. A Christian army had defeated the once-indomitable Seljuk Turks. Muslims everywhere quaked in dread and shame, many abandoning cities and towns in the path of the invaders.

Yaghi Siyan, the emir of Antioch, was half-way to Damascus to help Dukak fight his brother Ridwan when he heard the news. "They took Nikea?"

"Yes, Beyfendi," said the messenger, wringing his hands. "And Kilich, Son of Sulayman, lost a great battle at Dorylaeum. No one can stop them, my Lord. Prince Kilich runs with his tail between his legs. He hides in the hills."

"By the Mercy of Allah! And you say they head for Antioch?"

"Yes, my Lord. With an army of many, many thousands."

Yaghi Siyan felt a cold fear grip his loins. He had been preoccupied with his battles against, Ridwan, son of Tutush, but now the Byzantine threat was too close and too dangerous to ignore. "Damascus will have to wait!" he yelled. He turned his army around and rode in furious haste back to the walls of Antioch.

EGYPT

AL-AFDAL

But not all Muslims wept at the fall of Nikea. The Egyptian vizier, a man by the name of Al-Afdal, laughed aloud when he heard the news. Al-Afdal was born an Armenian Muslim, a fighting mamluk and the son of a mamluk. His father was vizier to the Caliph and, when he died, Al-Afdal inherited his position. No sooner had he taken the post, when the Caliph himself died suddenly under mysterious circumstances and all power fell into his hands. To make sure it stayed that way, Al-Afdal appointed a child as the new Caliph.

By the time he was thirty-five, he ruled a nation of seven million people and, with guile and ruthless perseverance, and he would continue to rule for the next twenty-four years. He was an ardent disciple of Fatimid Shia and a firm believer in the doctrine of the twelve Imams. As such, he hated the Seljuk Turks. He hated them because they were Sunni, he hated them because they defeated the Arabs, and he hated them just because they were Turks. For years, he had fought against them in Syria and Palestine. Some even whispered that, despite his hatred of the Hashashin, he secretly supported their stronghold in central Iran and their bloody efforts there to defeat the Seljuks from within. As far as Al-Afdal was concerned, anyone or any army that stopped the advance of the Turks was an ally of his. So when the Byzantines and the Crusaders left Nikea and headed further into Turk territory, he was jubilant.

"Send an envoy to King Alexios," he said. "Let us see how we can assist this new army of his. And we must negotiate who gets what. I want everything south of Dog River, especially Jerusalem."

ANTIOCH

Antioch was in chaos. Yaghi Siyan, filled with dread, began food rations and daily inspections of all fortifications. He laid plans for a long siege and again sent his eldest son to Damascus, seeking help.

"The Christians have rebelled, my Lord. They besiege our outposts and our garrisons have fled," said his atabek. "May Allah strike them dead!"

"We can't trust these damnable Christians!" Yaghi shouted. His advisors nodded in agreement. He said nothing for a while and stood staring straight ahead, stroking his long, white beard with distraction. "That Greek priest, the one they call Patriarch. He plots against me! I'm sure of it. Bring him in for interrogation."

"What shall we do with the others, my Lord?" asked the atabek. "Most of the city is Christian. The merchants and our taxes will suffer."

Yaghi waved a hand in dismissal. "I'm worried about our heads, not taxes. Devise a plan to get them out of the city. And do it soon."

The atabek nodded. "Your wish is my command, Great Emir."

• • • • •

Boris knocked on the door and opened it just enough to stick his head through. "Psst! Master! Master! I must speak with you." He tried to keep his voice down.

Ramiro woke up with a start. He was taking a midday nap, as many do in the heat. He stumbled to the door. "Boris? What is it? Come in man."

"Sorry to wake you, Master. But I have just heard something you should know right away." He shut the door, strode over to the cushions and sat down.

Ramiro went over to a bronze basin. "Well? What is it?" He dipped his hands in the water to splash his face.

"The Roman army approaches Antioch," Boris huffed. "They have thousands of mercenaries! Barbarians from the west!"

"We have heard, Boris," he said, drying his face with a cotton towel. "Do you think we are in danger?"

"Yes." Boris nodded fretfully. "Yaghi Siyan is furious, he blames all Christians. He says the Patriarch is a traitor! He hung him from the walls of the Cathedral and beat his feet with iron rods! God have mercy!"

Ramiro stopped what he was doing. "By all Saints! John the Oxite?"

"Yes," said Boris, close to tears. "His Eminence himself. God help us! And the Cathedral, Ramiro, they have desecrated the Cathedral of Saint Peter! They smashed everything – and now bring in their horses – to use it as a stable! May God curse them!"

Ramiro took Boris' hands. "Do not curse in the name of God, Boris."

"Sorry, Master."

"That's alright, Boris. Calm down. Clearly, Yaghi Siyan fears the Christians will rebel."

"It's true, Master. Even now, they drive out anyone of prominence."

"Does he plot to kill us?"

"No, no, he is not that stupid. But he plans to cast out the clergy and every Christian man of fighting age."

"What do you mean? When?"

"Well, today he sent a large corps of men, all Muslim, to dig trenches around the walls."

"Yes, I heard," said Ramiro, hanging the towel.

"Well, tomorrow he will send out another corps, but this time it will be all Christian."

Ramiro nodded. "So?"

"But he plans to keep them out, Master."

"Outside the walls?"

"Yes."

Ramiro rubbed his bearded chin in thought. "I see. Will I be one of the chosen?"

"Probably. Yaghi Siyan fears you."

"Really? Why?"

"He thinks you could easily rally the Christians to your cause."

Ramiro shook his head. "I have no cause here, Boris. But now we may have a chance to escape to Jerusalem." He went over to Boris and sat near him. "This means that I have only today to retrieve my cross from Khuda. I know he has it. Do you remember the plan we spoke of."

Boris wrung his thin hands and spoke nervously. "Master, you cannot do this. He will kill you! He is a fearsome man."

Ramiro ignored his plea. "This is Friday, Boris! The perfect day!"

Boris looked confused for a moment. A quick smile came and went from his drawn face. "Because today is the day his concubine shops!"

"And today is the day Khuda will be at the mosque," Ramiro added.

They heard a noise and turned. Adele sauntered into the room wearing a long, yellow tunic, decorated at the hems with delicate mauve flowers. She belted it at the waist to show her figure.

Ramiro turned to her. "Did you hear what Boris said?"

"Most of it," she said as she tied her hair back. "So what's our plan?"

ADELE'S VENTURE

"No, you will not!" Ramiro shouted.

"Yes, I will!" Adele shouted back. "It doesn't make sense for you to go. His cleaning slave is a woman. How will you pass for a woman? Are you going to shave your beard and put on earrings?" Her frown turned to a smile.

"Adele, it is much too dangerous."

She ignored him. "And it'll be easier for me to go unnoticed. You'll never get past the guards."

Ramiro shook his head again. "Then we will forget the cross. It is a trinket and not worth a life."

"It's a gift from the Great Shah," said Adele, thinking of the gold. "It's worth the risk. Do you not trust me?"

"Of course I do."

"Am I not capable?"

"Yes, yes. That's not it."

"Then I'll go. And I better go soon!"

"You are an impossible woman!"

She smiled.

• • • • •

Adele put on a simple, gray tunic with a plain sash and wore reed sandals, the dress of a slave. She carried an empty water pail and a mop, making her way to the askari barracks, which were within the same compound. She passed the guards with ease and came to the door of Khuda's quarters where she took out the key that Boris had made at great expense and fumbled it into the lock. She opened the door, picked up the pail and mop, entered quickly and shut it. Once inside, she began a frenzied search for Ramiro's cross. She rummaged through drawers and wooden trunks, careful not to disturb anything. It was not a big place. It must be here, somewhere.

An hour passed and she could not find it. In tears, she sat down and put her head in her hands. She had looked everywhere. She heard approaching footsteps and tensed, but the sound died away and she relaxed a little. She leaned forward on her elbows, watching a tear splash on the mosaic tile. In a state of distraction, she stuck her finger into it and swirled it, following the design. The tile moved slightly.

The tiles! It's under a tile, you stupid wench! She picked at the one that moved. It lifted easily, but there was only mortar underneath. She crawled about the floor, testing every tile frantically. The first room revealed nothing. The second room, nothing. It was getting late. She went into a small, dark storage room. Here! Here's a loose one. Her heart pounded, she lifted it up, revealing a dark cavity. She reached in. This is it! She grabbed a small canvas bag. It was full of gold and silver coins - and there's the cross!

She heard voices, women's voices. The concubine returned. The tile clacked as she dropped it back into place with trembling hands. She rushed over to the door, tossing the bag of coins into the empty pail before rushing out with mop and pail in hand. The concubine's voice grew louder. Adele groped with the key but her hands shook so badly, she had trouble getting it into the lock. Finally, she jammed it in and spun the tumbler before darting in the other direction, walking as fast as she could.

The concubine did not see her come out the door, but she saw her rushing away. "Where did she come from?" she asked the escort. The escort shook her head. "You! Cleaning-Woman! What are you doing here?"

Adele made no reply. She kept walking, rounded a corner of the building, rushed to the other corner, then headed back the way she came. She could hear the woman yelling after her.

• • • • •

"You got it?" Ramiro was astounded, and greatly relieved. He slumped into a chair. "Praise the Lord, my dear! You are an amazing woman!"

"I thought you said I was impossible," she grinned.

"Then I hope you will forgive me for that. Let's see." He reached for the bag. Immediately, he felt the weight of it. "What's this?" He opened it, reached in and pulled out the golden cross. "Adele," he paused. "Adele, I am very grateful to have my cross back. I cannot thank you enough."

"I can think of a way," she cooed.

"I'm sure you can, my dear." He looked in the bag again and frowned. "But you should have left the money. We are not thieves, I just wanted my cross back."

"Sorry. Everything happened so fast... I wasn't thinking."

"Dear, oh dear," Ramiro lamented. "May God have mercy. Khuda will hunt us to the death for this."

"I'll take it back," she said hastily.

"You will not. It's much too late for that."

"Well... maybe we could leave it here with a note."

Ramiro gave her a despairing look. "And do you really believe he will get it?"

She stomped her foot. "Then to hell with the man! We'll just take it with us."

Ramiro shook his head. "I want nothing to do with it!"

Adele grabbed the bag. "Then I'll take it," she glared. "And I don't want to hear another word about it!"

• • • • •

Ramiro slept uneasily in the August heat. He awoke with a start and checked the door locks. Then he went to the window and looked out onto the courtyard. He checked the window latch.

Adele rose from bed and sauntered up behind him. "Do you think he knows already?"

Ramiro jumped at her voice. "By all Saints!" he caught his breath. "You frightened me out of my wits."

"You're awfully nervous," she said.

"I admit, I am very worried. When Khuda discovers his money is gone, he will come to our door - no matter what the hour. He's a seasoned warrior. Our heads will roll. I just hope we can get out in time."

• • • • •

It was the day for the Christians to dig trenches. "The guard will be here soon. We must hurry!" Ramiro fussed.

Adele glared at him. "I'm going as fast as I can!"

"We can't take all of this, woman!" he gestured in hopelessness. "Do you really need all these clothes?"

"I'll carry them myself!" she snapped. "You've no need to worry yourself to death."

He raised his eyes to heaven and prayed inwardly. Dear Father in Heaven, give me strength...

"Come on, Ramiro!" Her auburn hair dangled in her face. "We don't want to be roaming the roads after dark!"

Ramiro prayed again. And especially, my Lord, with this mule-headed woman. He took a bag from her hand. "You don't need to carry all that."

"When can we leave?" asked Adele.

"I'm not sure. We must wait for the guard."

• • • • •

Khuda turned pale. His cache was gone. "Where is it?" he yelled at his concubine.

"I don't know, Master, I swear in the name of Allah!"

He slapped her face and she staggered back. "Where is it, you whore? I'll slit your throat right here!"

The woman cringed in fear and pain. Tears streamed her face. "Please, Master! I know nothing of it. I didn't even know it was here," she cried. "I swear it, my Lord." Khuda stepped forward to beat her again. She moved away. "It was the slave! The cleaning woman!"

He grabbed her by the arm. "What do you mean?"

She told him she saw the cleaning woman rushing away. "I thought little of it, Master. But that is all I saw, by the mercy of Allah!"

"How would she get in? You left the door unlocked!" He struck her again and she crashed to the floor.

She curled on the tiles, sobbing. "No, no, my Lord. The door was always locked."

"Get up! Bring the slave to me!"

She got to her feet cautiously before scurrying out the door.

• • • • •

The cleaning woman screamed in terror. "It was not me, Efendi! I wasn't here!" Khuda beat her again with a stick. Blood ran from her head. "It was the Christian woman!"

"What woman?" he shouted, striking her again.

"The one... the one with red hair," she sniveled. "She paid me to stay away."

Khuda lowered his stick, staring at her. He knew only one woman with red hair. "So how did she get in?"

The slave lowered her eyes to the floor, too frightened to speak.

"You gave her a key! Didn't you?" He hit her again.

Her eyes widened in fear. "I meant no harm, Master. Forgive me!"

Khuda lunged at her, grabbing her by the throat with his big hands. He squeezed hard. She lashed back with arms and legs - but she struggled in vain and he watched her die.

THE IRON GATE

A guard banged on the door. "You will come with me."

"What is it?" Ramiro shouted from behind the door.

"The Emir has ordered you to the work party."

"Very well," he said as he opened the door. "Give us a few minutes to get ready."

The guard looked in and saw Adele standing ready. "Just the men are ordered out," he said. "No women or children."

"But she must come," Ramiro countered.

The guard was unmoved. "Sorry, I have my orders."

Adele stood behind Ramiro, holding a bag in each hand. He knew her temper and could feel her push forward to confront the guard. He turned, putting a hand out to stop her and placing a finger to his lips. Then he turned to the guard again, scratching at his black beard and pursing his lips in thought. It seemed like a long time before he spoke. "Tell me," he asked the guard, "did not Muslim women draw water for the men working outside yesterday?"

The guard shuffled a little. "Uh, yes, I suppose."

"Well then, that is what this woman will do. A Christian woman to draw water for the Christian men. How can you deny her that?"

The young man hesitated, he appeared uneasy. "I will have to check with the sergeant."

Ramiro put a hand into his pocket and pulled out a silver dirham. He gave it to the guard. "Thank you. Thank you very much. Please keep this for your troubles. We will wait here."

The guard walked away, staring at the coin in his hand. He had no sooner rounded a corner when Ramiro took a bag from Adele. "Let's go. This way. Quickly! We will head for the Gate of Saint George." They rushed downstairs to join the others, where the sheer number of Christians leaving the compound seemed to overwhelm the two guards, who tried to check papers at the exit. Ramiro and Adele pushed themselves into the middle. And no one stopped them.

• • • • •

Christian men clogged the streets, all heading out to dig trenches. Ramiro took Adele's arm with one hand and held his shoulder bag with the other. "We must head south and find an inn before dark."

She leaned into his ear, huffing from the weight of her bags. "We should go north and join the Christian army!"

"No, I will take no part in holy war. I'll take you to the port at Saint Simeon. You can get a ship to Byzantium."

"But I'll be safer with my own kind."

"The French? Do you really think you'll be safer with the French or the Germans?" he asked in a harsh whisper. "These people are not farmers, Adele.

They are soldiers of fortune, filled with bloodlust and greed. Gold and glory is all they seek. You will become their slave!"

"The Turks are no better!" she snapped. "They killed my parents and put me into slavery!"

"Your parents died fighting in a war, Adele. And everyone takes slaves in war. I sincerely doubt French masters would treat you any better than Arabs or Greeks." He continued to take long strides along the cobbled streets. "But you are free to take your own direction. I do not hold you." He took a drink of water from his flask, trying to appear indifferent to her decision.

She rushed alongside him. "And what'll you do, Ramiro?" She jutted her chin. "You would leave me alone?"

"I want you to be safe. I can find an escort for you... a Byzantine escort. But I must go to Jerusalem. Only God can stop me."

She dropped her bags and grabbed him by the arm, pulling him to a stop. "Then I'm going with you." she said with a tone of finality.

He shook his head. "No, you cannot. It will be an arduous and dangerous journey."

"Ramiro, my *husband*, every road is fraught with danger, like you always say."

"Blessed Saints, woman! I'm telling you it's too dangerous!"

Adele shook her head in disapproval. "Now, now, dear Ramiro. God would not be pleased with your hot temper."

He reddened, putting a hand to his iron cross while muttering a prayer. Then he bent down to take one of her bags. "Very well, have your way. But I'll hear no complaints." He looked into the sky. "We better go. It's almost noon. We'll head south for Latakia."

"Look!" She pointed. "There's the gate!"

Ramiro looked over to the Gate of Saint George and the long line of men and women waiting to pass through. Guards stood on either side. He took a minute to scan the crowd, then he stopped suddenly and spun around. "It's Khuda!" he said, turning his head away. He motioned for her to do the same. "He's watching at the gate!" He pulled her in the opposite direction. "We must head north - to the Gate of Saint Paul."

"That's too far," she said, pulling back. "Let's go to Bridge Gate... it's closer and we can still head south to Latakia." She referred to the western gate that bridged the River Orontes.

"Very well," he said impatiently. "Let's go, let's go."

They hurried up the main street heading north but had no sooner reached the intersection of the Bridge Gate Road when Ramiro stopped again. "Look," he said, tilting his head to the intersection. "The man on a horse. That's one of Khuda's men. I recognize him from the slave market in Aleppo – do you remember?"

Adele glanced towards the man. It was him – the man called Toros. "Yeh, yeh. I remember that one!" she said with bitterness. But she had no sooner uttered those words when Toros looked in their direction and caught her eye. She turned away quickly, but her quick turn exposed a lock of auburn hair from beneath her headscarf. "He saw me, Ramiro! He saw me!"

Ramiro glanced over. She was right. Toros was heading towards them. "Quick! Down this alleyway! Come!" They took off, walking as fast as they could without drawing attention, and delved into the alleyway.

Long stone fences, standing the height of a tall man, lined the alley on either side. Small wooden gates interspersed the fence, each one leading to a private residence. They rushed along and Ramiro tried every one. They were locked. He looked behind. No sign of Toros yet. He tried a few more gates. One was loose. The hooves of a horse clattered on the flagstones behind them. He put his shoulder to it and it flew open. "Quick! Inside." They slipped into a small courtyard, shutting the gate behind them. The clatter of hooves grew louder. A rider went by. Then another... and another. He held a finger to his lips.

But just as the clatter of hooves became distant, someone screamed behind them. They turned in fright to see an old woman waving a broom. "Please, Sayyidah, please be quiet." Ramiro tried to speak gently. "We mean you no harm. I swear to Allah." Again, he put a finger to his lips.

The woman started to yell. "Get out! Get out!"

Ramiro was somewhat relieved at her cry. Even though he had spoken in Arabic, the woman yelled back in Greek. He held up his palms in surrender. "Please, mother, we are Christian," he answered in Greek before turning to Adele in French. "Adele, give her some money. Quick now. Before Khuda's men return."

Adele fumbled in her bag and found a silver coin. She offered it with outstretched arm.

The woman looked at her suspiciously. Then she squinted at the coin. "What have you got?" she asked in a shrill voice.

"It's a dirham for you," Ramiro said softly. "And I will give you more if you help us."

Toros had heard the woman's scream and turned his mount around. He rode back standing in his stirrups to look over the fences. His men did the same.

The old woman hesitated just as a young man rushed out of the door behind her, raising a club against them. But the woman held out her arm. "Enough!" she said, stopping him in his tracks. "Take the money." A dirham was more money than her son could earn with three month's hard labor.

The man stepped forward, still holding up the club. He took the coin from Adele's hand and inspected it. He looked back at his mother and nodded.

They all heard the horses returning. "Inside!" the woman said. "Inside!"

• • • • •

"You are safe for now," said the young man as he drew away from the window.

"How can we get out?" Ramiro asked. "They're probably watching every gate."

The man sat down as his mother served mint tea. "Take the Iron Gate," he said. "They expect you will try the southern gates to head into Christian territory. And you can bribe the guards at the Iron Gate."

"You mean the gate by the Citadel?" Adele asked. "The one at the crest of Mount Silpios?"

The young man blushed, not used to being addressed by a strange woman. "That's the one," he said without looking at her. "But you must stay off the main road. Use the alleyways."

"Guide us to the Iron Gate," Ramiro said. "And we will give you another coin."

• • • • •

Ramiro let out a heavy sigh of relief. They had just stepped outside the Iron Gate, starting on the rough, gullied road that headed east for Aleppo or south to the Orontes Valley.

"You gave him too much!" she complained.

"Blessed saints, Adele! I would have given him everything I had to get out of this wretched city. "We're free, Adele. Free! Come! We must head for Latakia but will have to take the long route around the mountains."

"We can still afford to sail," she said, "… perhaps we should both get a ship to Byzantium or Italy."

"I'm not going back to Byzantium until I've delivered the cross!" he said, somewhat vexed.

"Have it your way!" she huffed, turning away and lifting one of her heavy bags with a grunt. "But we'll need a donkey, Ramiro. We'll never get to Jerusalem on foot. And now you'll have to use Khuda's money because you've spent everything else."

• • • • •

"They have escaped, my Lord," said Khuda, red with fury. "I ask permission to pursue them."

When Khuda became Yaghi Siyan's askari, he had given up his independence. The Emir, always worried about the loyalty of his men, kept all weapons and armor in the citadel, giving them out only when needed. Even the horses were confined to the Emir's stables.

Yaghi Siyan looked at him in disbelief. "How can you ask such a thing at a time like this? The barbarians ravage the countryside! The Christians side with them and massacre our garrisons!" His long, white beard wagged as he ranted. "And you come to me about your money – about a slave-girl! What do I care about a slave! I need all the men I can muster. You will stay!"

Khuda grit his teeth and bowed his head. "Yes, Beyfendi. As you command."

Part Seven
TURKISH PLIGHT

JISR ASH-SHUGHUR

SEPTEMBER 1097

Ramiro and Adele hurried east across the rough terrain of Mount Silpios before turning south to follow a wending path through miles of dark-green forests, thick with pine and cypress and teeming with deer, goat, wolves and wildcats. They escaped with few supplies, sleeping under rough lean-tos while keeping a small fire to ward off the beasts of the night. Morning brought them off the mountain, where the path dropped sharply to the wide floor of the fertile Orontes Valley. The path soon widened to a road passing through fields of sugarcane spread out in emerald blankets on either side of the slow river. They eventually arrived at the northern foothills of the Ansariya Mountains and the village of Jisr Ash-Shughur, a farming community nestled into the hills adjacent to the river. The villagers shied away, unused to strangers. There were few places to stay but they managed to rent a small room in a quiet tavern, the only tavern. The village seemed a peaceful place, ruled as it was by a petty Turk governor and a single garrison.

Ramiro was glad to be out of Antioch. For over three years, he had lived there as a prisoner, and for over three years, he was forbidden to send out letters. Now he was free, free to go to Jerusalem and free to complete his mission. If, indeed, there was any mission left to complete. Abbot Hugh must think me dead by now. I must get a report to him and ask what I should do. But what shall I say? There is so much to say. Where do I begin?

He looked north from the small veranda of his room, surveying the road to Antioch as it meandered up the hill and disappeared in sparse forests of Aleppo pine and Valonia oak. He clutched a quill in one hand while trying to think of the right words, but his mind wandered to Ozan and Tatran and he wondered what happened to them. He prayed they had escaped the clutches of Yaghi Siyan. He thought of his mother again and feared he had broken her heart. And he thought of the Patriarch and the message in his cross, if indeed there was any message. Then he thought of Khuda and felt a cold tingle down his spine. Will he come?

He felt for his golden cross, still pinned into his vest pocket. He was so relieved to have it back. Finally, there was some hope. "Please Lord," he prayed aloud. "Guide my feet to Jerusalem."

Adele yelled from inside. "Ramiro! Come! Lunch is ready!"

•　•　•　•　•

The innkeeper gesticulated wildly as he spoke. "The barbarians raid and pillage all the land, even to Aleppo," he said in a loud voice. "They are coming this way."

"Are you sure?" Ramiro asked.

"I'm quite sure, Sayyid. My cousin told me. He has seen them!"

Ramiro said nothing. His mind raced. Trouble was brewing. We must leave for Jerusalem, and we must leave now... before the rains come.

The next day, he loaded a mule and a donkey, bought with Khuda's money. "Where's the tent?" he shouted.

It's still upstairs," said Adele. "You get it."

"And where's my new medicine bag?"

"It's right there," she pointed. "You hung it from the saddle horn."

"Are you ready to go yet?" he fretted. "The sun is already a hand up and it's going to be a hot day."

ANSARIYA MOUNTAINS

Ramiro struggled up the steep road leading west through the Ansariya Mountains and beyond to Latakia on the Mediterranean coast. Adele plodded beside him, straining from the arduous climb in the heat of a hot autumn day. By the time the road flattened out, the sun settled behind high peaks and the air began to cool.

"We better camp here," he said. "It'll be dark soon."

A twig cracked and the bushes rustled, then another crack. Adele looked around cautiously. "What's that?"

Ramiro peered into the dimming light. "I don't know, an animal perhaps."

Another noise and he wished he had a weapon. Adele scoured the ground and grabbed a hefty stick of oak. They stood still and watched.

"There!" she whispered, pointing through a cluster of dry buckthorn.

Then Ramiro saw it move. "It's a dog - I think it's a dog."

"Strange dog," said Adele. "Look, it's got black and white stripes."

He looked again. "It's a hyena. I've seen them before."

"Hyena? What's that?"

"It's like a dog... but more vicious and sly."

"Will it attack?"

"Probably not, but we should be vigilant."

"How can we sleep with that thing lurking about? You should start a fire."

• • • • •

Adele slept nervously, waking at every sound. She thought she heard another noise just as the faint light of dawn glowed against the tent. "Ramiro!" she whispered, jabbing him in the ribs. "Somebody or something's out there. I think I heard a horse... or maybe that hyena."

He lifted his tired head. "By God's mercy, Adele. How will I get any sleep?"

She gave him a push. "Go look!"

He groaned loudly before he threw off the blanket and stumbled out. A thin trail of smoke still rose from the embers of their fire. He looked around. "I see nothing," he said. "You will make an old man of me with all this worry."

But then he heard it too. It was the pounding of hooves - and it was getting closer. "Quick! Get out of the tent!"

She rushed out. "What is it?"

"Someone comes. I'll get the mule. You grab the donkey. Move into the bushes!"

They were barely concealed when three riders came charging down the mountain road. They rode straight for the tent and came to a sudden stop. A cloud of dust followed their path and drifted through the bushes. Adele coughed.

The men jumped from their mounts, drew their swords, and ran after them. One of them stopped at the tent, pulled the flap back and looked inside.

Ramiro saw them coming. He moved into full view and held up his hands. "Peace be upon you, Sadah. We mean no harm."

The men wore black kafiyas over their heads, and black capes covered their long, white tunics. Three had moustaches, one a full beard. With cruel laughs, they surrounded the two. "Give us what you have!" said the bearded man. "Before we slit your throats!"

Ramiro and Adele stood in tunics alone. "We have nothing on us," said Ramiro, hoping they would leave.

"Search the tent!" said the highwayman.

One of them went to the tent and threw everything outside. He searched their clothes and bags. That's when they found the purse of coins in Adele's coat. And soon, he found the cross in Ramiro's vest. He held it up for the bearded one to see. "Look at this, Yaqut!" He whistled and smiled broadly.

Yaqut took it from his accomplice and turned it in his hand. Then he grabbed the purse and shook it. His cruel eyes twinkled and he smiled too.

"Please," said Ramiro. "I must have the cross. Take the money and leave us."

Yaqut walked over to him and, without warning, belted him across the face. Ramiro dropped to his knees.

"I will take both your money and your golden cross, kafir!" Then he leered at Adele and smirked. "And I will take your woman too." He moved over to her, grabbed her arm and put a hand to her breasts. Adele slapped him. He slapped her back and her head spun from the impact.

Ramiro knelt on the ground, holding a hand to his bruised face. But when he saw Yaqut slap Adele, an indignant fury boiled in his chest, exploding into his mind with blind rage. Without thinking, he charged forward like a mad bull, crashing head-on into the tall highwayman, lifting him right off his feet and dashing him to the rocky ground. Ramiro got on top of him with all his weight and began to pound his head with his fists. Yaqut, a big man himself, managed to heave him off and they rolled on the sharp stones, entwined in a brutal duel. The money and the cross flew from Yaqut's hand and spewed onto the gravel. But neither man gave heed as they fought for their lives, even when they rolled over it, back and forth in the melee.

The other two highwaymen watched and laughed. They were confident Yaqut would prevail, and then they would have some good sport. They would torture and kill this troublesome kafir before having the pleasure of his woman.

But while the two men watched the scuffle, Adele moved behind them. She picked up the club of dried oak she found the night before and readied it for the highwayman closest to her. Gripping it with both hands, she swung it as hard as she could - right against the back of the man's head. There was a loud, hollow whack, as if she had hit a tree trunk. The man flew forward without a sound and fell face first into the dirt. He lay motionless. The other highwayman turned, staring at his fallen comrade in disbelief. He spun his eyes to Adele, raised his sword, and went after her.

Ramiro's weight was to his advantage. He pinned Yaqut under him and put a knee on his sword arm. Then again, he pounded his fists into the highwayman's face until the man stopped moving. Adele screamed. He looked up to see her dodging behind thin pines as one of the robbers attempted to slash her. She still held the club. Ramiro drew Yaqut's sword from its sheath and rushed over. He raised it as he ran and, in a breathless rage, swung the gray blade against the robber's right side.

The blow severed the man's arm and it fell twitching to the ground. The man shrieked as blood spurted from the stump of his arm. He looked at Ramiro in astonishment and horror before falling to his knees, clutching uselessly at his bleeding stump. "Please, Sayyid!" he yelled. "Have mercy!"

But Ramiro was no more the pliant monk. In the tempest of battle, his soldier's instincts became acutely alive. His black eyes glowered, his heart pounded, and his chest heaved. The flush of battle was on his cheeks and he wanted to kill. He raised the sword again, ready for the fatal strike.

Another loud whack! The highwayman's head flopped forward and he slumped to the dirt. Adele stood behind him, holding the bloodied club.

"Foking bastard!" she yelled. She hit him again, even as he lay motionless. Then she kicked him, and kicked him again.

"Adele!" Ramiro shouted. "He's down. We're alright. Stop now."

A horse whinnied behind them. Yaqut had recovered from Ramiro's beating and, while they scuffled with the other highwayman, he managed to get back to his horse. Ramiro ran after him but Yaqut kicked in his heels and galloped away, heading down the road the way they had just come, down to Jisr Ash-Shughur.

"The cross!" Ramiro cried out. He rushed over to the spot where they had fought and searched the ground. "It's gone!" he wailed. "And the money too!" He picked up several coins dropped in the scuffle. "Quickly, we must go," he said, putting on his vest and coat.

Adele straightened her hair. "What about these men?"

"They're dead."

"Should we bury them?"

"We have no time. The hyenas will clean them up." He threw Yaqut's sword to the ground but took a dirk from one of the dead highwaymen and strapped it to his belt. He looked about. "Come now! Get the donkey. Before any traveler sees us."

"What about the money?" she asked. "What are we going to do now?"

"Did they get it all?"

"No," she sighed. "I put some of it in the saddle bag, but the bastard got most of it."

"It doesn't matter," Ramiro said dismissively. "We should still have enough to get to Jerusalem."

"So, what do you think?" Adele asked as she looked down the road. "Should we still head for Latakia?"

"We can't go to Latakia now. I must retrieve the cross."

She stared at him anxiously. "No, Ramiro. Let's get out of here while we can."

"No, I cannot," he said with a look of annoyance. "I cannot arrive in Jerusalem without it."

She put a hand to his arm. "I thought you wanted to avoid the trouble in Antioch? We can be in Jerusalem in two weeks."

The muscles of Ramiro's face tightened. "As I said, I cannot arrive without the cross."

"God's blood, man!" she shouted, her face crimson. "What about your mother?"

Ramiro scowled. "Really, Adele, must you curse like a Provençal fishwife?" He took her hand. "Believe me, my dear woman, my heart yearns to see my mother again but I have serious obligations which I cannot ignore. I promised in the name of God I would deliver it."

She pulled her hand away. "Can the cross be that damned important?" she asked in a bitter voice. "Are you going to risk our lives over it?"

"No, I'll risk my own life - not yours."

"And what am I supposed to do? Travel by myself?"

"You can stay in Ash-Shughur until I retrieve it."

"God's blood!" she spat. "I think not!"

JISR ASH-SHUGHUR

Jisr Ash-Shughur was as quiet as ever. Ramiro described the highwayman to all he met. "Have you seen him?" he asked. "His face is badly beaten. He goes by the name of Yaqut." But no one had seen the man.

"You were robbed?" asked the innkeeper. "Where?"

Ramiro told him the story.

"You see? This is the trouble when there is no rule, no order." The innkeeper shook his head. "The Turks can no longer protect us."

"Which way would he go?" Ramiro asked.

"He could go south along the Orontes and travel to Homs. Or maybe he went east to Maarat An-Numan. Or north to Aleppo."

"I doubt he went north. The Christian army comes."

The innkeeper pointed east. "Go to the road leading south and ask returning travelers. Someone must have seen him. Then go to the Maarat road and do the same."

• • • • •

Ramiro asked everyone he met on the road to Homs. No one remembered the man. So they rushed to the road going east to Maarat and asked again.

"You've seen this man?"

"Yes, Sayyid," said the farmer. "He was very rude. Took our water without thanks. His face was swollen - like he was stung by bees. He's heading east for Maarat An-Numan."

"Go east? To where?" Adele asked as they rode away.

"To a place called Maarat. It's on the plateau we saw from the other side. It's not far – but we must hurry before the highwayman heads further east."

"You'll never get to Jerusalem that way," she said in a cold voice.

"Adele, please try to understand it is my duty to retrieve this cross. It is the only reason I vowed to go to Jerusalem."

MAARAT

The vast, rolling steppe of Syria opened up before their eyes when they reached the summit of the plateau, a dry and brittle grassland that stretched as far as the eye could see. The road to Maarat wound its way through these low, rounded hills before it disappeared into a hazy distance.

Miles before the city, the grasslands turned to fields of wheat and barley, where peasants worked the harvest. Grain was the gold of Maarat, and the city lay on a lucrative trade route. Although Ramiro and Adele approached from the west, the main traffic through the city was by way of an ancient road that ran south from Aleppo, extending to Hama, Homs, Damascus and beyond. The Romans paved it all the way to Petra in the Transjordan and then west to Egypt. They called it the Via Nova. But the Arabs still thought of it by its old name, the King's Highway.

"We must find the cross as quickly as possible," Ramiro said as they approached the city gate. "Look at this traffic! Head for the stables first – then we'll go to the markets!"

• • • • •

"So what now?" Adele asked as they walked away from yet another storefront. "We've tried every jeweler and pawnbroker. It's not here."

"It's got to be here," said Ramiro. "I can only pray that God will guide me to it."

She let out a long sigh of exasperation. "Let's get something to eat. The food stalls are over there."

They made their way across the paved market, winding their way past stalls and shoppers. A small group of armed men wandered past, led by a plump man dressed in fine attire. Two thin scribes followed him closely as he went from stall to storefront. Adele eyed them suspiciously, avoiding their path.

"Not to worry," said Ramiro, noticing her aversion. "That's the Muhtasib, the market supervisor. He's just collecting taxes from the merchants."

The boy at the stall rolled hot flatbread around a dollop of couscous and vegetables, giving them to Ramiro in paper napkins. They wandered about for a place to sit before taking a low bench recently abandoned by another couple.

Adele was half-way through her meal when she suddenly spat her food to the ground. "There he is!" She jabbed at Ramiro. "Look! Over there!" she pointed. "It's him!" And so it was. Yaqut the highwayman, his face badly swollen and bruised, was arguing with a merchant. He was no more than twenty paces away.

Ramiro saw he had found another sword. He got up suddenly, leaving his bread on the bench before striding briskly toward the thief, feeling for the dirk he had recently acquired from the dead highwayman. "Yaqut!" he shouted.

Yaqut looked over in alarm. Someone knew his name. He saw Ramiro, then Adele following behind. He reached for his sword.

But Ramiro was on him and grabbed his sword arm. "I want my cross, thief!"

Yaqut broke free, jumped back and drew his sword. The crowd around them gasped and shuffled out of the way. Ramiro pulled out his knife and stood defensively, but he knew it was no match for a sword. The merchants started to yell for help. Yaqut's eyes darted around him. He started to back away. Suddenly, the crowd parted and four soldiers of the Muhtasib barged onto the scene. They drew their swords and challenged them both. Ramiro dropped his dirk and held out open palms. The soldiers turned to Yaqut.

Yaqut panicked. He was a known thief, he would be executed. He jumped at one of the soldiers, slashing his arm. The others backed away in surprise, not expecting real trouble. Yaqut parried at another, stabbing him in the side. When the soldier kept advancing, he slashed at his legs, making him stumble and fall. The other two called for help. Yaqut backed away, turned, and barged through the crowd. People screamed and yelled as they fell out of his way. He disappeared into the throng and the soldiers went after him. More arrived, and they too rushed off in pursuit.

Ramiro put his hands down, he had been forgotten in the melee. The two fallen soldiers lay nearby, groaning and clutching at their wounds. He rushed over to one of them, who held a bloodied hand to his side. "I can help," he said to the soldier. "Let me see the wound." Yaqut's sword had missed vital organs. He would live if they could halt the bleeding. "Quick!" he said to Adele as she followed. "Give me your scarf!" He took it from her and wrapped it tight around the soldier's torso. The crowd offered more strips of cloth which he used to bind the cut to the man's leg and to stifle the bleeding of the other soldier's arm.

"What's your name?" someone asked boldly.

Ramiro looked up. It was the Muhtasib. "I am Ramiro of Cluny, Efendi."

The Muhtasib, a well-fed man with a full beard, folded his arms. A jewel sparkled from his red turban. Two soldiers, holding whips, stood beside him.

"Ramiro of Cluny," said the Muhtasib, "I see you are Christian. Don't you know it is forbidden for you to own a weapon?"

Ramiro stood and bowed slightly. "A thousand apologies, Efendi. But that man is a thief. He robbed us in the mountains and was going to kill us."

The Muhtasib ignored his entreaty. "You must also know it is forbidden for a Christian to attack a Muslim? I don't like this kind of trouble in my market."

"But the man drew his sword against me, Efendi. He is a thief. He took my cross."

"Your cross? You fight over a trifle?"

"It is a golden cross, Efendi, of some value."

"Aah," said the Muhtasib in understanding. "You will come with me," he said brusquely. "I want a full report."

Ramiro opened his hands in plea. "There is little else left to say, Efendi, it is a simple theft."

The Muhtasib seemed not to hear. "You will come with me - or do my men have to drive you with their whips?"

● ● ● ● ●

Ramiro sat alone in the small holding cell. He told them all he would dare to tell. He said he was from Antioch but not that Yaghi Siyan held him as a prisoner. He told them of his cross but not that it may contain something for the Patriarch. After hours of questioning, they left him alone on a stone bench. Only after the muezzin sounded the call to sunset prayers, was he released without a word.

"Did they catch the thief?" asked Adele as she rubbed her arms in the cool evening air. She had been waiting outside for hours.

"They would not say," he said as he removed his cloak and threw it over her shoulders.

"Thank you," she said, pulling it tight. "And what about the cross?"

"They said they would look for it. I gave them a quick sketch."

"What do we do now?"

"We wait. Come, we will get a room for the night."

● ● ● ● ●

The Qadi of Maarat sat on a large, golden cushion raised on a dais. A long, white cloak draped from his shoulders, partially covering his red silk tunic. The hood of his cloak hung over his white turban, which sat atop his chiseled, triangular face. "You say he is a physician?" he asked, stroking his trimmed, gray beard.

"Yes, Qadi," said the Muhtasib, bowing before him. "He attended to the soldiers and dressed their wounds in a most professional manner."

The Qadi looked down his long nose. "We could use more physicians," he said, "...even if he is a Christian."

"Yes, Qadi."

"Did you catch this thief?"

"We did, my Qadi. We cut him down at the north gate. He had a bag of coins and the cross was hidden in his tunic."

"Let me see this cross."

The chubby Muhtasib signaled to a servant who rushed to the Qadi's side with a wrapped object. He unfolded the wrap to reveal Ramiro's cross and offered it with open palm.

The Qadi picked it up and studied it. "A beautiful piece," he said. "But it seems a little beaten up. What happened to it?"

"The dhimmi said it was thrown to the ground during his scuffle with the thief."

"Is it really made of gold?"

"The smith said it was made of gold and silver, Qadi. The Christian is very keen to have it back. "

"I'm sure he is," he said before falling silent for a long moment. "You will bring him to me."

• • • • •

Two grim-looking mamluks stood on either side of the seated Qadi. He pulled at the shoulders of his white cloak before gesturing to another cushion beside the platform. "Sit," he ordered.

Ramiro sat down awkwardly. He said nothing.

"What brings you to Maarat An-Numan?" he asked with hands on folded knees.

"My wife and I are on our way to Jerusalem, Qadi. We were robbed on the road to Latakia."

The Qadi studied Ramiro, sweeping his eyes up and down. "Tell me, Ramiro of Cluny, how did such an expensive piece come into your hands?"

"I am just a courier, my Lord. I am bidden to deliver it to the Patriarch of Jerusalem."

"You are Roman?"

"No, Qadi, I come from a land further west."

The Qadi nodded with disinterest. After a long pause, he spoke again. "You are a physician?"

"Well, Efendi, I know something of medicine and have studied the works of physicians and scholars, but I was never trained at your universities."

"The Muhtasib tells me you dressed the wounds of our men. I am in your debt. Is there anything I can do for you?"

"If it pleases my Lord, I desire only to retrieve what was taken from me so that I may continue my journey."

The Qadi's lips spread aside in a thin, contrived smile. "Then you will be pleased to know that we managed to retrieve your cross."

"Why, that is wonderful news, indeed!"

The Qadi held up a hand to silence him. "But it has come at a cost," he lied. "We had to buy it back from a merchant. It was very expensive."

Ramiro frowned. "How expensive?"

"Three gold dinar."

"But what of our purse? Did you recover it as well?"

"Purse? No, only the cross," he lied again.

Ramiro groaned. It was an impossible sum. It would take months to collect that much. "I do not have the money, Efendi," he admitted.

"I am sure we can come to some arrangement for you to work off the debt," said the Qadi in feigned sympathy.

Ramiro glanced at him suspiciously. "And what do you suggest, my Qadi?"

"I suggest you join the hospital," he said raising his bearded chin, "where you can attend to injury and illness. You will be well remunerated for your troubles."

"But Qadi, that could take some time."

The Qadi tried to look compassionate. "Well, if you can think of any other way to obtain the money, that is up to you. But it is unlikely you will find a position with better pay."

Ramiro bowed in defeat, realizing he must play for time. "Yes, my Qadi. As you wish."

• • • • •

"So how long is this going to take?" Adele asked in mounting frustration.

"I'm not sure," said Ramiro as he squatted on the floor of the empty room. "But at least we know he has the cross. How much money do we have left?"

"Not much. It may add up to a silver dirham or two. How much are they paying you?"

"They didn't say and it didn't seem like the right time to ask."

Adele tossed her head back. "Blood of Christ!" She looked around their newly-rented room and her small nose wrinkled in disgust. "Well, I'm not staying here. The place stinks! And the cockroaches are as big as mice!"

He waved a hand to settle her down. "Rest assured, my dear. There is no need to stay here. The Qadi has given us very nice quarters near the hospital."

Weeks passed in Maarat and, over time, Ramiro became popular at the hospital. His jovial manner, linguistic skills, and his first-rate knowledge of medicine quickly endeared him to the staff. He was in the laboratory making a tonic for dysentery when the news reached the hospital.

"The barbarians march on Antioch!"

REPORT: MAARAT

Ramiro stared into the long, yellow flame of the oil lamp. He wondered if his reports to the Abbot were just a waste of time now that the French had begun their invasion. It had been four years since he posted his last report from Edessa and two years since he gave Ibrahim his letter for the Patriarch. Did he get it? If so, did he notify the Abbot? He put his pen down and stood to stretch. What else could he say to the Abbot? He told him all he knew of Antioch, of its impregnable walls and towers and how it guards all traffic coming from the sea into northern Syria. He mentioned that many Christians lived there and said they were free to worship and engage in commerce.

He stared down at the pale, unfinished page and his sense of duty returned. He sat back down and dipped his quill to remind Hugh that the Great Emir of Syria, brother to the Sultan, had died in battle and that now his sons fought internecine wars, letting the country fall into a state of lawlessness where highwaymen roamed freely. Only the walled cities offered any safety, Jerusalem among them. While admitting much was hearsay, he told him the Egyptians fought for southern Palestine and controlled several port cities, including a place called Ascalon and maybe even the busy port of Jaffa.

But he said nothing of the cross, and he certainly could not tell the Abbot about Adele. He finished the report and put it aside before taking up a fresh sheet of paper. He would send another letter to Aldebert to let him know he was safe and to explain his delay in reaching Jerusalem. Ramiro remembered telling him to return to Rome if he did not hear from him after a year. So he must have returned to the Abbey by now, he thought.

ANTIOCH

"Tarsus has fallen, my Lord. And the whole of Cilicia. The barbarians took it with hardly a fight. The Armenians helped them. May Allah curse them!"

Yaghi Siyan wrung his hands as he paced back and forth in the citadel sitting high above the city of Antioch. These unholy barbarians seemed unstoppable, despite their heavy losses, "Damned Christians! May Allah render them helpless. This is the work of the devil Roman King!" He was about to bark an order to his men when he heard a frenzied shout from the sentinel.

"They're here! They're here!"

He peered over the parapets. There, across the broad Plain of Antioch, miles in the distance, rose a huge, billowing cloud of dust. The barbarians had arrived, a writhing mass of flesh and steel that spread across the land like a darkening cloud of locusts.

A prolonged lull of dread weighed over the city as word of their arrival passed quickly from mouth to ear in hushed whispers. Men and women prayed in silent fear and the markets came to a standstill. An eerie silence gripped the air, broken only by a child wailing in the distance, a lonesome sound quickly silenced. And a single warbler trilled from the parapet as if confused by the sudden stillness.

Yaghi Siyan shivered. Why do I worry? These wretched kuffar will never breach the walls of Antioch! Our water is inside. And we have months of food. Even with all their numbers, they cannot guard every gate. We will outlast these heathen dogs! Curse them to Hellfire!

The Franj kept arriving by the thousands in what seemed like an endless procession. There were tens of thousands. They swarmed across the Orontes at the Iron Bridge and, in a rising din of shouts and clacking steel, took up their positions near the three northern gates. The siege of Antioch had begun.

• • • • •

Khuda the Mamluk stared out from the battlements. Thousands of other mamluk did the same, many of them spewing loud insults and vile curses to the stinking foreigners gathering near the gates. But Khuda said nothing. He thought of his money and the golden cross and brooded bitterly over Ramiro and the red-haired woman. Only wrath and revenge burned through his mind. Dog-rutting Christians! They will die! They will take days to die!

Despite his fury, the scene beyond the walls filled him with a sense of overwhelming hopelessness. The barbarian army is huge, and they are everywhere. If I could just get through the Iron Gate. But I need weapons - and I need a horse. Curse the Emir!

• • • • •

Yaghi Siyan's mamluks attacked the Franj whenever they could, picking off strays, foragers, and squads of soldiers. But in every skirmish, they were turned back. Then Dukak came up from Damascus with a great army, declaring Holy War against the infidels. But, alas, to the bitterness and shame of Yaghi Siyan, the man turned away after his first ill-fated battle against the barbarians.

The Crusaders pillaged the countryside for miles around, which forced Ridwan of Aleppo, Yaghi Siyan's arch-enemy, to mount his own attack. Ridwan had a strategic advantage at first but he underestimated the fanatical resolve and ferocity of these barbarians. He hoped to surround them but, when he tried, he made a tactical blunder and found his own forces cornered instead. The tables turned quickly and, in another fateful battle, Ridwan lost a thousand men to the barbarian broadsword. Yet another campaign ended in disgrace.

• • • • •

"Heathen scum!" Drugo the Red shouted as he brought his sword down hard onto the neck of a Turk prisoner. But it was a poor cut and the head did not sever on the first blow. The Turk fell forward spurting blood, his head lobbed to the side. "Foking pagan!" Drugo bellowed as he hacked again, cutting it free. He grabbed the bloodied skull by the hair and threw it onto a pile.

Otto and Arles helped load the large catapult with the grisly heads of Ridwan's men, aiming it over the castellations of Antioch. Otto pulled the release and the bloody payload shot forward. The men around them laughed and jeered as they watched the mutilated heads fly through the air, some soaring over the walls and crashing into city streets while others missed their mark, splattering against the high stone walls.

Robert of Flanders observed from his mount. His flat-topped helmet almost covered his smooth, sloping brow and its nasal strip reached down to the end of his long, hooked nose. His thin lips smiled and there was a glint of approval in his blue eyes. He was pleased with the efforts of his men, as were Godfrey, Bohemond, and Raymond, who also watched from horseback. They all hoped to drive holy terror into the Turks.

And it worked. The morale within Antioch faltered. Yaghi Siyan had trouble getting any more information about the invading Franj, his spies were terrified. The starving barbarians had captured one of them, torturing and killing the man in gruesome amusement before roasting him on a spit and, to Yaghi's horror, eating his flesh. Now, in heightened desperation, he appealed to the only man with an army large enough to save Antioch from the foreign horde, and this was Kerboga of Mosul, far to the east.

NOVEMBER 1097

The siege of Antioch went on for months. Cold, wet weather weakened the Crusader's resolve and they began to starve and die. And when an earthquake shook the mountains, their faith was severely tested. Some deserted in fear and panic, including Peter the Hermit and many others who thought the situation was hopeless. Others blamed Taticius and his men for their troubles, forcing them out. Those who stayed behind endured weeks more of relentless, freezing rain. Illness and starvation forced thousands to scrounge for food - any food – grass and nettles and even seeds picked from piles of horse shit.

In desperation, Bohemond and Robert led raiding parties south along the King's Highway but often had little to show for their efforts. Over the following weeks, they survived by slaughtering their pack animals and, eventually, they began to butcher their remaining horses. By winter's end, only seven hundred horses remained for twenty thousand knights.

MAARAT

JANUARY 1098

The foreign army dominated the news. But the people of Maarat were not overly concerned about the siege of Antioch. They were primarily Christian and Arab and had no love for Turks. Nonetheless, it was an uneasy time. They heard rumors of barbarism, even of massacred Christians. And when Bohemond and Robert raided the countryside as far south as Albara, some fled further south for the relative safety of Homs and Hama.

But Ramiro stayed. Their rooms near the hospital were not spacious but they were clean and well-furnished. He lay on his back on a slew of cushions spaced out on the floor. A wool blanket covered his legs from the cool air of winter. "How much money have we got?"

"Not enough to get the cross," Adele said sharply. "Not even one dinar. You should talk to the Qadi again."

"I agree. We can't stay here any longer. Only God knows what will happen next. And Khuda will come after us sooner or later. I must get the cross so we can move on to Jerusalem in the spring."

Adele studied her appearance with a small glass mirror. "Even if Khuda gets past the French lines," she said, "he won't travel easily."

"That's true, but he knows the ways of this land much better than they do. He will come. We have to get to Jerusalem! God help me!"

Adele brushed a lock of hair behind a small ear. "How do I look?"

Ramiro glanced up. A cream wool shawl covered her shoulders. She wore green, silk pajamas with long, embroidered sleeves, a prize she secured in Antioch. "You look as beautiful as ever," he said with sincerity.

She smiled. "Would you like some more fattoush?"

He lolled his head back and forth. "No, thank you, I've had enough. And if you keep feeding me like this, I'll soon be as fat as the King of France."

She giggled. "So what do you think?"

"About what?"

"Do you think the French will ever march for Jerusalem?"

"I doubt it. I hear they lost most of their men and horses. Many have deserted and the rest starve. And many more will surely die before they reach the Holy City... if they ever do."

"They've been at Antioch a long time," she said as she brushed her hair slowly. "Why do they spend all this time and effort to capture it if they head for Jerusalem?"

Ramiro picked up his cup from the low table and drained the last bit of wine. Then he cleared his throat. "Without Antioch, their supplies and men would be cut off from Byzantium and the West. They must capture it... or die in the attempt."

"Would you like more wine?"

Ramiro held out a palm. "No thanks, I've had enough."

She didn't seem to hear and filled his cup anyway. "We have all we need to travel."

"All but the cross," Ramiro lamented. "The journey should be safe enough if we can leave soon." He stretched his arms out and yawned. "I'm going to bed," he muttered, but made no effort to get up.

Adele rose to her feet. Her hair hung loosely over her shoulders and her silk pajamas whispered as she moved towards him. She bent over to take his hand and gave it a tug. "And I'm going with you," she with a coquettish grin.

"Are you now?"

She pulled at his hand until he rose to his feet. "Come along, dear husband. You have an important duty to perform."

ANTIOCH

On a cool, sunny morning in February, three Egyptian war-galleys skimmed along the calm waters of the Mediterranean. They headed for the port of Saint Simeon, joined by a flotilla of Byzantine triremes sailing out from a port in Cyprus. King Alexios had arranged for the Crusaders to meet the Egyptian ambassadors sent by Al-Afdal and reminded them that Egypt was his ally against the Turks. On the King's recommendation, the ambassadors met with Raymond of Toulouse the following day. Raymond heard them out and noted their demands before calling a council of commanders.

Raymond stood up as the men filed into his large tent. He stood tall, with gray hair and beard, sporting a muscular build despite being in his sixties. He lost his right eye battling the Moors in Spain and a gray, leather patch covered the empty socket. He was a deeply pious man who rushed to Pope Urban's call, believing he was doing God's work by battling the heathen. Certainly age did not hinder his vigor or ambition for he saw himself as the leader of the Holy Crusade and the future ruler of the Holy Land. But the wages of war were beginning to have their toll and he was often ill.

Bohemond of Taranto waited impatiently. He stood towering above them all. Born of brutish Norman blood, he was a gigantic man who stood a forearm's length above all others. His ruthless, light blue eyes shone under a heavy brow, and his short, yellow hair, cut Roman style, crowned his huge head. His narrow waist and broad shoulders, along with his engaging charm, swayed many a young maiden to his bed. But wise men feared him, for under his smiling, clean-shaven face lurked the ambitious, crafty, and savage persona of his father, Robert Guiscard.

Bohemond had no love for Count Raymond. He knew the man wanted Antioch, but he wanted it too. "So, what did the Egyptians say?" he demanded.

Raymond scowled at him, furrowing his eye-patch. But he ignored him and remained quiet until the hubbub of men subsided. Finally, he spoke. "The Lord of Egypt has made a proposal to us. As we have learned, there is no love between the Egyptians and the Turks, even though they are both Muslim."

"Who cares?" yelled Godfrey, who also resented Raymond's command. "They're both foking pagans!" He stood taller than most, but not as tall as Bohemond. He was a big man with long, blonde hair and beard, a barreled chest and thick arms. By the age of sixteen, he was an accomplished warrior whose weapon of choice was the crossbow. Now he was thirty-eight and a nobleman of Lorraine.

Raymond stared at Godfrey with a look of sufferance. "Thank you, Duke Godfrey, for your keen observations. Now, if you will allow me to continue..."

"Get on with it," said Bohemond.

Raymond raised his voice. "The proposal is this – the Egyptians will assist us in every manner by providing supplies to the ports of Syria and Palestine, giving military assistance whenever possible. In exchange for their cooperation, they request that all former Egyptian territory be returned to them and that all other lands jointly conquered will be divided equally."

"What do they mean by former territory?" asked Robert of Flanders. "Does it include Jerusalem?"

Raymond nodded. "Unfortunately, yes. It includes most of Palestine."

"Never!" Bishop Adhemar snapped. "The savages ask us to forsake Jerusalem! The most blessed Tomb of Christ! What good is Syria to us? The devil can have it for all I care."

Raymond nodded in a gesture of peace. "Of course, I agree, Your Excellency."

"It goes against God's will!" said Adhemar with such conviction that all men felt forced to nod in agreement.

"I already told the ambassadors as much," said Raymond. "But I present this to you so we may formulate an official response."

Bohemond spoke up. "It would not be wise to infuriate these Egyptians right now. We are in no position to acquire more enemies. And seeing what little help we get from the Greeks, we could use an ally."

"But we cannot agree to forgo Jerusalem!" Adhemar shouted vehemently.

"I know that," said Bohemond as he raised his palm. "But we can delay our response as much as possible. Anything to gain cooperation and time."

"What do you suggest?" asked Raymond grudgingly.

Bohemond stepped out, then turned to face the men. His huge build almost hid Raymond from view. "We should keep them here as long as possible. When they return to Egypt, we will send our own ambassadors back with them."

"What good will that do?" asked Robert.

"First," said Bohemond, "it will allow us further delay tactics by letting the Egyptians think we will eventually come to some agreement. And secondly, our men will have a chance to learn all they can about Egypt and Palestine."

"They will be our spies," said Robert.

"Exactly. We can make a pact with these pagans if it means our survival. Then... who knows? By the will of God, times change, do they not?"

● ● ● ● ●

The French ambassadors left for Egypt in March and, not long after their departure, an English fleet put in at Saint Simeon, carrying Italian pilgrims and a store of supplies and material from Constantinople - all destined for the siege of Antioch. With this desperately needed shipment, the Crusaders were able to tighten their blockade, as General Taticius had recommended to them long before.

JUNE 1098

Yaghi Siyan paced in the palace. He rubbed at a sharp pain in his left arm. His stomach churned. "When will Kerboga come from Mosul? He's three weeks late!"

"No one knows, my Lord," said the atabek. "We have trouble getting scouts past the barbarian lines. But we hear that one of them, a man called Baldwin, has seized Edessa from the Armenians. Perhaps he challenged Kerboga's army on the way." He spread his hands apologetically.

"He must come soon. We cannot hold much longer, we need more supplies." He pulled at his white beard. "By the mercy of Allah, when will he come?"

● ● ● ● ●

A dawn trumpet sounded. But it was not the horn of Antioch, it was the trumpet of the Franj. "My Lord, wake up! Wake up!" the chamberlain shouted. "The barbarians have taken the citadel!"

"The citadel?" Yaghi gasped. Eight months of siege and now this. "How?"

"We were betrayed, my Lord, by an accursed Armenian! May Allah strike him dead!"

The citadel was the last stronghold, the last hope. The news was more than Yaghi could bear. He staggered in fear. "Get my horse ready! At once!"

In dreaded haste, Yaghi Siyan abandoned his city, his family, and all his possessions. He fled Antioch with a small group of askaris. Khuda was among them. They charged through the Iron Gate and galloped along the thin mountain road to Aleppo. But Yaghi was no more than a few miles from the city when he succumbed to deep remorse. His flight had been frantic and reckless. In wailing grief, he collapsed from his mount and fell to the ground. The askaris attempted to put him back in the saddle but he would not stay and slumped to the ground again, barely conscious. Fearing pursuit, the askaris left him there to die and raced for the safety of Aleppo.

But after an hour's ride, Khuda left the others and turned south on another path. Now that Yaghi Siyan was deposed, he was free and had a chance to recover his gold. And he knew where that damned Christian was heading.

If Yaghi Siyan had kept his head, he soon would have discovered that the western barbarians did not take the citadel. They captured the Tower of Two Sisters on the southern wall. If he had assembled his troops, he could have driven them off. But now, in the confusion, the Franj managed to unlock a city gate. The doors swung wide and the waiting barbarians stormed in by the thousands, swords drawn, hooting and yelling, rampaging through Antioch like a scourge from Hell, hacking and stabbing, raping, pillaging and burning, killing every man, woman, and child. Muslim, Christian and Jew alike died in a frenzy of slaughter. The apocalyptic infidels, drenched red with blood from head to toe, howled above the terrified screams of their victims - "God wills it! God wills it!"

But Khuda gave little thought to the distant screams from Antioch. He raced south along the King's Highway, heading for Maarat. They have been gone ten months... but I know where they go and I will find them, he vowed. And by the will of Allah, I will kill them both!

MAARAT

Salim could barely speak, his big brown eyes glistened, his lips quivered. "Have... have you heard of Antioch?" he asked in a small voice.

"No," Ramiro replied as he filled in the forms for a new patient. "What is it?" He could see that Salim, another physician at the hospital, was highly agitated.

"It has fallen to the barbarians!" he said, his voice cracking in grief. "They slaughtered everyone! They are worse than animals! May Allah damn them to Hell!" He wiped a tear from his cheek.

Ramiro's quill stopped moving in mid-word and he stared straight ahead. Ink began to smear across the paper in a slow crawl. "Everyone?" he asked quietly, still staring at the wall.

"Yes Ramiro, anyone within the walls. Women and children - everyone."

"Not the Christians?" he asked in disbelief. He recalled how Yaghi Siyan drove out thousands of Christian men from Antioch but kept their women and children as virtual hostages.

"Everyone, my friend," Salim replied dolefully.

"Father of mercies! But why?"

"Allah has cursed them. Only Allah knows why."

"What about Kerboga's men? Did they not come as promised?"

"They came too late."

Ramiro felt a gnawing, bitter ache in his chest. "This is unbelievable. Did no one escape?"

"Only a few, Ramiro, may Allah have mercy."

Ramiro thought of all the people he had come to know in Antioch, he thought of his servant Boris and his family, and he thought of the Rabbi and all the others he had befriended, many of them Arabs and Turks. He bowed his head and wept.

• • • • •

"May God protect us!" Ramiro lamented when he was alone with Adele. "This is their Holy War! Most of Antioch was Christian! I cannot believe the blessed Pope of Rome would sanction such cruelty and bloodshed. He is a man of Cluny!"

Adele took a sip of wine. Although she hated the Turks for taking her as a slave, she had made many friends among the women of Antioch, Christian and Muslim alike. She tried not to think about how they had died.

"Not only are these so-called crusaders barbaric," said Ramiro in a voice of reason, "they're stupid! All those people – they provided food and services, they paid taxes. Where's their revenue now?"

Adele dabbed her lips with a napkin. "It is very sad, although there is one small comfort."

"What's that?"

"Khuda must be dead."

Ramiro looked around as if expecting the enraged Turk to come barging through their door. "I hope so, Adele. Nonetheless, the French will be coming south soon and that will be bad enough. We must get to Jerusalem so I can deliver the cross. I must plead with the Qadi to return it to me."

A SHADOW

It was the twenty-seventh day of Rajab, the time of Laylat Al-Miraj, and the neighborhood was unusually quiet. Muslim parents had shuffled their children off to the mosques to hear the story of Muhammad's climb to heaven. There, they were taught to see the event as a symbol of their own soul's journey in the afterlife and to emphasize the need for prayer and piety.

Ramiro took advantage of the quiet to compose a letter to Abbot Hugh. But he was not sure if he could get it delivered. The last one he sent to Tripoli before the French started raiding the countryside. Now most feared to travel, especially if they were Muslim. There was little to say. How could he explain that he had lost the cross? He wanted the Abbot to know that he planned to leave for Jerusalem as soon as he could, but he could not leave yet.

"What did the Qadi say?" Adele shouted from the kitchen.

Ramiro put his quill down. "I offered him a dinar and a half for it but he was unwilling to let it go. We've got to find a way to get more money."

She came out of the kitchen drying her hands on a towel. "Perhaps I could find a job. You know I'm good with leatherwork."

"No, no. I won't have it, Adele. Besides, your Arabic is terrible. I must give you more lessons." He rose from his low table and settled back in the cushions.

"Wait!" she said to him as he picked up a book. "Before you make yourself comfortable, go to the market before it closes. I need some sage."

"Is it absolutely necessary?"

She stuck out her chin. "Yes it is, old man. Or you can eat your meal without seasoning."

He smiled at her spirit. "Very well," he said, raising himself up slowly. "Besides, I could use a little walk."

"Well, don't be gone too long. And stay away from the tavern," she said with a stern look, "...or it'll all be cold when you get back."

• • • • •

Ramiro stuffed a small bag of sage into his pocket. He paid the merchant and continued his stroll home, passing through the quiet marketplace. He caught a scent of rose and took a deep breath. *How I love this time of year.*

His path led him past the door of the tavern and he could hear the boisterous voices of the patrons inside. He hesitated by the door. It was the best place for any news... and they had a very good wine made from the soft, black dates of southern Iraq. *I wonder if there is any more news of Antioch and the French.* He was about to open the door when he heard a voice behind him.

"Good evening, Ramiro," a man said. "Peace be upon you."

Ramiro turned, feeling a little startled and a little guilty. It was Salim the physician.

"Are you going to the tavern?" he asked with some surprise.

Ramiro reddened a little. "Oh no, of course not. I'm just taking a stroll. And you?"

"I'm going to the market before it closes."

"Well, I'm on my way home. I'll walk with you a while."

They had no sooner turned to leave when an angry roar erupted inside the tavern, followed by a crash against the door. A deep, gravelly voice shouted from within. "Mind your own damned business! You ask too many questions!"

Ramiro felt a chill in his bones. *He knew that voice.*

Another voice squawked from behind the door. "Forgive me, Efendi, I was just trying to make conversation."

"Get out of the way!" the voice shouted again.

Ramiro grabbed Salim by the sleeve and tugged him away. "Let's go," he said. "Quick, follow me."

"What's going on?" he asked, just as the tavern door began to open.

Ramiro kept pulling. "Shut up and follow me." He pulled Salim along at a frenzied pace just as a man came out the door.

"Don't look back, Salim. Just keep walking." Ramiro took him down the street and turned a corner. "Alright, we can stop here for a while."

"What is it Ramiro? What's all the fuss?"

Ramiro put a finger to his lips. Then he peeked around the corner. It *was* him. It was Khuda. "May God protect us!"

• • • • •

"He's still alive? Oh Lord – blessed Mary!" Adele cried. "What are we going to do?"

"Don't worry, he's gone for now. Salim sent his younger brother to watch him. The boy said he mounted up this morning and rode south."

"So? What are we going to do? We can't stay here."

"Khuda has no idea we're here. He's heading south, probably to Jerusalem. Or maybe he's just looking for a new employer in Damascus."

She got up and wrapped her arms around him. "Do you think he's forgotten us?" she asked, resting her head on his shoulder.

"After all this time? I'm sure he has," he said with little conviction. "Not to worry."

ANTIOCH

The corpses of Antioch rose in macabre pyramids outside the city gates. Muslim slaves, beaten and bruised, with their heads bowed in shame and defeat, trudged to and fro, pulling carts stacked with the bodies and limbs of the men, woman, and children massacred within the walls.

The plunder of Antioch was disappointing. The siege had gone on for so long, there was little left to steal, not even much money. Nonetheless, the Crusaders wasted little time grabbing all they could. By the rules of war, they owned all they seized. But Bohemond claimed control of the city and flew his banner from atop the Citadel, high above on the crest of Mount Silpios. Count Raymond was infuriated. He resented Bohemond's claim and wanted the city handed over to King Alexios as they had promised. So he thwarted Bohemond's efforts by holding the Emir's Palace and the Bridge Gate, which controlled the road leading to the port of Saint Simeon, a vital supply route.

After the frenzied bloodlust of battle had subsided, the Christians gathered at the now-vacant Cathedral of Saint Peter and fell to their knees on the blood-stained tiles to give thanks to God for their victory. It was here that a young servant by the name of Peter Bartholomew approached Bishop Adhemar and Count Raymond to tell them of his divine revelation. He claimed that Saint Andrew the Apostle had come to him in a vision and had commanded him to retrieve a Holy Lance buried beneath the floor of the cathedral. He was to give it to Raymond for him to use as a sacred standard in battle.

Adhemar was not impressed. He resented any attempt to usurp his heavenly power. Besides, Peter had no station, he was just a servant. But Raymond, in his arrogance, found Peter's predilection compelling and became greatly excited at the prospect of obtaining one of the most holy relics of Christ.

So they tore up the tiles and began to dig, shoveling furiously for hours until a great pit had formed. But no lance was found. Peter jumped into the hole and began to pray fervently. He prayed that God would return His lance to the Crusaders, bringing strength and victory to His chosen people. Lo and behold, Peter discovered the lance when he noticed its point sticking out of the earth. Men fell to their knees in tears of exaltation while others ran off to spread the good news. Cries of great joy and celebration rocked the city.

JULY 1098

But the euphoria did not last long. One month after the occupation of Antioch, typhus raged through their filthy ranks. Thousands of them, weakened by months of hunger, quickly succumbed to high fevers and failing hearts. The leaders and the wealthy stayed outside the city, leaving their men to fend for themselves. Only Bohemond and Bishop Adhemar remained, the former feared for his precious Antioch and the latter for his people. But Adhemar, weak and pale, died by the end of the month.

The men were shocked at his death. They could not understand why God had taken the Papal Legate from their midst in such a cruel and undignified manner. Was he not divinely protected? What sins had they committed to deserve such a harsh penalty?

• • • • •

Bohemond towered above his nephew, Tancred. He lifted one leg and let out a long fart. "I shit on Raymond of Toulouse," he bellowed. "Antioch is mine! I'm the one who broke the gates. I'm the one who seized the citadel!"

Tancred, a slim man in his early twenties, backed away from uncle Bohemond, whose very presence he found intimidating. "We can't control the city until Raymond gives up the Palace and the Bridge Gate," he advised. "We should force him out."

Bohemond shook his close-cropped head. "No, we must be tactful," he said in a rattling baritone. "Raymond has taken possession of the Holy Lance and uses it to draw men to his cause. If we start fighting amongst ourselves, we accomplish nothing. We must lay plans."

Tancred brushed a lock of long, brown hair from his hard-set eyes. "What can we do? We lost three thousand men to the plague. God punishes us! Even Bishop Adhemar has died. And many more are sick and weak. If God does not protect the bishop, what hope have we?"

Bohemond ignored him. He had no interest in theological debates. He crossed his arms and put a hand to his chin before strolling to a northern portal of the citadel, where he looked north across the sea to the rich plain of Cilicia and, behind it, to the rough peaks of the Taurus Mountains. "We will wait," he said. "Like you say, the plague has killed many of our men - but it shows signs of abating. As for Count Raymond, well... he cannot hold for long. He's a self-possessed, deluded old man with one eye. We will push him out. But first things first, my dear Tancred. We must make sure the Greeks do not get Antioch."

"So you will not hand over the city as we agreed?"

Bohemond flushed red. He slammed a thick hand on the table, and the loud noise echoed from stone walls. "What have they done to capture Antioch?" he bellowed. Tancred flinched. "We starved and froze for months outside the walls and they did nothing! Nothing! Only after we conquered did they send an army. And when they heard Kerboga was coming, they turned back like a pack of dogs! God curse them! They do not deserve Antioch!"

"How will you stop them? What if they amass an army?"

"We will secure Cilicia. It is our northern frontier. If we can do that, the Greeks will have no chance to advance on us."

"But I already control Cilicia."

"You have too few men. I will send more."

Tancred eyed him suspiciously. He feared his uncle and knew he was making a sly attempt to usurp his control of the region. But he was out-ranked. What could he do? And what spoils would be left for him? "What of Jerusalem?" he asked, trying to divert the subject. "And what of the Egyptians? They claim the Holy City too."

Bohemond laughed and his crafty blue eyes gleamed. "I'm not concerned about the Egyptians. We'll let Godfrey and Raymond go to Palestine to fight them. I want Antioch. From here, I will control all Syria."

EGYPT

Although the Egyptian vizier, Al-Afdal, had rejoiced when the Roman army of barbarians first defeated the Turks at Nikea, and then again at Antioch, he was now a troubled man. He had met with the barbarian ambassadors from Antioch, and he had heard their demands. So he went to pray. He faced the *mihrab*, which indicates the direction of Mecca, and prostrated himself in the hall of the exquisite Al-Azhar Mosque of Cairo. He begged Allah to lift the terrible plague that racked the people of Egypt, and now he prayed for the death of these fanatics, these Roman mercenaries from the West.

Events were not unfolding quite as he had hoped. The Franj were obstinate. He felt he made a generous concession on one issue of his proposed alliance;

instead of dividing all conquered lands equally, he told the ambassadors they could have all of Syria and any other lands they conquer, all except for Palestine, which he believed belonged to Egypt. He assured them they would have no trouble visiting the holy sites of Jerusalem.

But they flatly refused him. They wanted Jerusalem and would hear no compromise. This was not the bargain he had made with King Alexios and he could not understand why these men were so inflexible. He had an alliance with the Romans. Is this not what the King wanted? To regain the cities of Anatolia and Syria from the Turks? Why do they insist on marching to Jerusalem? And what will I do if they enter Palestine?

He rose from his prayers and left for his offices in the stronghold of Fustat. A long entourage of servants and soldiers followed after him. Along the way, he summoned his atabek.

"Prepare an army for a spring advance into Palestine. I cannot trust the Romans or these barbarians. We must seize Jerusalem before they do."

"Yes, my Lord."

"And send a delegation to the Roman King," he said angrily. "I want to know why his army refuses to negotiate with us, I want to know his intentions, and I want to know the status of our alliance."

The atabek bowed. "As you command, my Lord."

CONSTANTINOPLE

Emperor Alexios had made a grave mistake - a mistake that may have cost him Antioch. He could barely contain his anger and frustration. "I should never have listened to those wretched Kelts!" he shouted at the roomful of generals, admirals and lieutenants. They squirmed in their seats.

"Who was this?" asked his brother Isaak.

"The deserters. They're the ones who told me all was lost at Antioch. They're the ones who said two Turk armies marched on the city. Armies of thirty thousand! That's the only reason I turned back!" He paced the room, his uncombed red hair dangling over his shoulders. "No doubt, the French at Antioch now think of me as a coward! And worse still – against all odds, those bumbling morons have managed to take the city! Unbelievable!"

John Doukas tried to solace him. "They signed a pact, my king. They must relinquish Antioch to your hands."

"But can we trust them?" he asked in all seriousness. "I offered to send another army - but they refused! They had the gall to refuse me! And now – now I fear they will use my retreat as an excuse to claim Antioch for themselves. They will say I have broken my vow." He took a gulp from a glass of water before looking at the men seated around the table. "Who can we trust?"

"I don't trust any of them," said Anna with the inherent authority of a dowager. "They are the most arrogant and fanatical of men. I have to say, I am quite worried about having thousands of marauding Kelts in our midst. I'm sure you all remember the trouble they can cause. They are foolhardy barbarians, their souls twisted by avarice. I fear for the Empire."

"You are right, mother, of course," Alexios said. "But this is the gambit we took in an effort to regain our empire. We must be careful, I know. We certainly cannot trust Godfrey and especially not Bohemond. Those two will make use of any argument to hold Antioch."

General Taticius rose to his feet. A dull flash came from his iron nose. "Bohemond forced me out," he complained. "And then he told the others I deserted, that I was a coward. He's just a scheming, crooked Norman, like all the rest."

"What should we do now?" Isaak asked.

Alexios threw his arms in the air. "Now – we wait. And we negotiate. A plague has fallen on Antioch. Probably typhus. They say thousands are ill, many have died. Even their so-called spiritual leader has succumbed – what's his name?"

"Bishop Adhemar, my Lord," answered Patriarch Nikolas. "He seemed reasonable enough, although some of his views were too fanatical for me. Saw himself as the new Pope of the East."

"This is an unfortunate development," said Alexios. "Like you say, Your Grace, he was one of the most reasonable of these self-proclaimed crusaders. I had hoped he would sway others to our cause."

Anna held up a finger. "There is another matter that needs our immediate attention."

"And what is that?"

She ruffled through her stack of correspondence. "We just received a letter from the Egyptian Vizier and a messenger stands waiting for our response."

"Go on."

"The Vizier seems upset. He wants to know why the leaders of your army in Antioch have refused to negotiate. He says they refuse to compromise on Jerusalem, which leaves him no alternative but to send an army across the Sinai. He wants you to clarify your intentions. And he wants to know if we still have an alliance."

"Perhaps we should tell him we have no control over these savages," said John.

"No, not yet," said Alexios, rubbing his forehead. "We must delay. We may still need their help. Tell Al-Afdal whatever he wants to hear. We know the Kelts are intent on Jerusalem but whether they will ever make it remains to be seen. Many have died, and now the plague ravages their ranks. Who will be left to march to Jerusalem?"

"Then I will tell him we still have an alliance," said Anna, "and that our intentions are to concentrate our efforts on north Syria. After that, we can only hope the Kelts will abandon Antioch and then we will be in a better position to reclaim it."

Patriarch Nikolas raised his voice. "I would not be so sure of that, my Lady. Now the barbarians say they have found the Holy Lance in Antioch, the very spearhead used to pierce the body of Christ at his crucifixion. It was supposedly buried in the Basilica of Saint Peter. They claim this is a sign from God – that Divine Providence favors them to rule Antioch."

Alexios laughed bitterly and shook his head. "That is a preposterous claim!" he said with derision. "Another lie put forward by one of their sham priests! How can they believe this ridiculous account? Everyone knows that *we* alone possess the Holy Lance. It is stored in our own Church of Sophia." The men nodded in agreement.

Nikolas rose from his chair. "The Latins will do and say anything to further their cause! Barbarian heretics!"

Alexios waved him down and the Patriarch returned to his seat, red-faced.

Tatran the Scyth fiddled nervously with a long braid. He stood up suddenly. "My King, is there any word of Ramiro of Cluny?" he asked with an undercurrent of guilt and remorse. It had been four years since he had made his escape from Antioch, leaving Ramiro and Adele to the whimsical mercy of Yaghi Siyan.

Alexios looked bewildered. "Who?"

"The Latin monk, my Lord," Tatran reminded him, "... the one captured by the Turks some years ago. Was he found at Antioch?" His broad moustache rose and fell as he spoke.

"Oh, yes – him. The one who escaped from the Sultan's prison. An interesting man." He paused with a hand to his chin. "I don't know, Lieutenant. We have little information from inside the walls." He glanced at the others. "Does anyone know the whereabouts of this man?"

The men shook their heads, mumbling nays.

"It is unlikely he lived," said Alexios. "We hear the savages killed everyone..." He shook his head with dread and amazement, "...even the Christians."

MAARAT

The woman shrieked and wailed, running through the entrance of the hospital in Maarat. She rushed through the doorway clutching her two-year old son in her arms and ran right up to the administration desk. "Help me! By the mercy of Allah! Help me!" Her child hacked and struggled to breathe, squirming madly in her arms.

At the sound of her wail, Ramiro and Salim came rushing out of the infirmary. They hastened to the woman and briefly inspected the boy. "Quickly," Ramiro said. "Bring him into room number three." Salim, hurried behind.

Ramiro took the boy from his mother's arms and rested him on a table. His small arms struggled against him as he tried to breathe. Ramiro stuck a tongue depressor into the boy's mouth. "His throat is badly swollen and red," he said to Salim.

"Is it croup?"

"I'm not sure yet. But if it gets worse, he will suffocate."

The boy's mother burst into tears at Ramiro's words and Salim made an awkward attempt to console her.

Ramiro reached for a concoction of hyssop, licorice and opium and tried to force the liquid down the boy's throat, but the child could not swallow. His small chest heaved as he spat out the medicine and strained for air. His face began to pale and blue.

Ramiro lifted him to a sitting position and slapped him on the back, but to no avail. "We must do a tracheotomy!" he almost shouted. "Or the boy will die!"

"A tracheotomy! But I have never seen one done, Doctor Ramiro. Have you ever performed such an operation?"

"No, I confess I have not," he said as he moved the boy in various positions, trying to make it easier for him to breathe. "But unless something is done, the boy will suffocate." The child's mother groaned aloud and covered her face with her hands to hide her tears.

"Go get Al-Zahrawi's manual!" he shouted to Salim. "You know the one, *The Method of Medicine*. I'm sure he describes the procedure."

Salim rushed off while Ramiro tried to clear the boy's airway by depressing the back of his tongue. Long minutes later, Salim rushed back with the book in hand.

Ramiro flipped the pages anxiously. "Here! Look! Here it is. We make the incision at the sternal notch." He looked at the boy, who was now unconscious. "I'll get the scalpel. Find a speculum."

When all was in hand, the boy's mother and Salim held the child on his back. Ramiro bent over him with the scalpel and made a slow puncture of the throat. Blood poured from the cut and the boy's mother staggered a little. "Hold him still!" he barked. He pushed the thin knife deeper and deeper until, suddenly, a spray of blood blew from the cut, splattering into his face. He wiped his eyes with his sleeve and grabbed the speculum, a rounded glass tube used for internal inspection. He pushed it into the incision, curving it down into the boy's windpipe. Air hissed through it when the child gulped for breath. In a moment, his breathing steadied and, slowly, color returned to his cheeks. "He will live," Ramiro smiled.

• • • • •

Dawud the Silk Merchant was no sooner through the door when he fell to his knees, prostrating himself in front of Ramiro. "May Allah bless you!" he wept. "May your sons become princes! May you live for a thousand moons! I am forever in your debt, Sayyid."

"Get up, man!" said Ramiro, somewhat flabbergasted. "It is only by God's Grace that the boy has survived. Give thanks to God and say no more of it."

Adele peeked into the hallway. She quickly fitted a headscarf and moved behind Ramiro.

Dawud was a plump Arab merchant who had become wealthy trading Byzantine silks. He rose to his feet with effort and put his right hand to his heart. "Praise be to Allah," he said with conviction. "Please Sayyid," he continued. "If there is anything in my power I can do for you, only say the words and it will be done."

Ramiro put a hand on the man's shoulder. "I am thankful the boy lived. That is enough."

Adele jabbed a finger into his back. Startled, he turned around.

"The cross!" she whispered. "Get the cross."

"Oh, yes... yes, of course," he whispered back. He turned back to Dawud. "Well, actually there is one thing..."

• • • • •

Ramiro stared at his golden cross. Dawud had paid off the Qadi and it was his again. He rubbed it meticulously with a cotton cloth until it began to shine, although some marring remained. He let out a heavy sigh. "Well, it may be a little damaged," he said to Adele, "but at least we can get on our way to Jerusalem."

Adele was busy sewing coins into the hems of their blankets and clothes. "Thank God," she said without looking up. "When do we leave?"

"Soon," he said. "I just have a few things to finish at the hospital and then..."

Sudden trumpet blasts drowned out Ramiro's sentence. A great commotion followed in the streets below. He moved to the patio to have a look. Adele followed behind. From their rooms on the third floor, they could see down the street that ran straight to the city walls and the main gate.

"What's going on?" she asked.

"That was a warning trumpet," he said. "A call to arms. The garrison is mounted and waiting at the gate. We must be under attack!"

• • • • •

A small Crusader army gathered outside the walls of Maarat, no more than a thousand men in all. Since the fall of Antioch, the French and Normans had renewed their courage and confidence and sought to expand their holdings. Raymond still vied with Bohemond for control of Antioch and his plan was to seize as many fiefs as possible to give his claim more weight, so he sent out a small army to conquer towns and villages to the south. Maarat An-Numan seemed like a profitable target.

• • • • •

Ramiro hurried into the market. "What's going on?" he asked the tinker, who seemed to be the best source of information apart from the tavern.

"The barbarians come!" said the wizened old man with bushy, gray eyebrows. Just as he spoke, a gust of wind blew at his stall, clanging a series of brass pots hanging from a crossbar. The noise seemed like an ominous chime and the old man put out a hand to steady them. Then he spoke to Ramiro again. "They will kill us all! May Allah strike them dead!"

Ramiro felt cold, despite the dry heat. "Do you know what they're doing outside the walls?"

"They prepare for siege, Sayyid."

"So what is the garrison going to do? They are at the gates."

"They will attack. They cannot afford a siege. But if they lose, we will all die by the sword... just like they died at Antioch."

The tinker no sooner spoke when the gates flew open and the full garrison of angry mamluks charged out against the Crusaders, catching them off guard. The intruders were too busy making ladders and a battering ram and were barely fit for battle. With fierce determination, the mamluks drove straight into their camp, hooting and hollering and stabbing with lances. They had heard of the massacre at Antioch and decided they would rather die in battle, meeting the devil face to face, than be slaughtered in their beds.

The knights mounted in a mad frenzy but had little opportunity to organize any defense. A wild and fierce battle ensued. The French were routed, suffering heavy casualties, and the survivors fled back to Antioch.

• • • • •

Ramiro and Adele made hasty preparations to leave. He gathered all supplies while Adele took the time to sew their remaining coins into the hems of their cloaks and blankets.

"Quick! We must go. We'll head back to the River Orontes," he said, mounting the mule. He reached out a hand to Adele, who was fumbling, trying to get her foot into the stirrup. "Come on, Adele! Are you sure you know how to ride?"

She frowned as she dragged herself into the saddle and sat behind him. "Never you mind! I'll be just fine."

"We'll take the road that follows the river south," he said. "Then we'll head for Tripoli. It's not safe to stay on the King's Highway."

"Ya, Ramiro," a voice yelled. It was Dawud the silk merchant. He held the reins of another mule, complete with saddle and bags.

"Peace be upon you, Dawud."

"And you, Ramiro of Cluny," Dawud huffed as he approached. "I hear you leave us for Jerusalem."

"Yes, and we must go soon."

"But you cannot travel on a single mule, Doctor Ramiro. Please take this one as a gift of thanks. I would have given you a horse if it was allowed. And here is a purse to fund your journey."

Ramiro held up a palm of refusal. "You have done enough, Dawud. We will take no more from you." Adele poked him in the back.

"Please, Doctor, I insist. The Prophet tells us 'whoever does you a favor, respond in kind...' The life of my son is a debt I can never repay. Please take my gifts and I will pray for you."

Ramiro nodded. "As you wish, Dawud. We pray God will provide you many sons."

• • • • •

When Khuda the Mamluk left Maarat weeks before, he galloped south for Jerusalem. He rode across the vast grassland spreading from Hama to Homs and kept riding past Damascus and further south to the dry outskirts of Amman. From Amman, he headed west, crossing the cool Salt Mountains before taking the steep descent into the blistering hot Jordan Valley. He traversed the deep valley floor at a steady gait, took a bridge over the River Jordan, and headed up into the dry forests of the Judean Hills where the Holy City of Jerusalem sprawled out over its crown.

TRIPOLI

A stunning ocean panorama opened up to Ramiro and Adele when they rounded the crest of the Ansariya Mountains. Far out to sea, across the shimmering waters of the Mediterranean, the setting sun glowed over the island of Cyprus. Swirls of black and white gulls circled and swooped in the briny air. They had journeyed long and hard, hoping to avoid another encounter with highwaymen. And now they were nearing the safety of the coast, where local emirs seemed unaffected by the trouble further north. They turned south, taking the road that runs along the narrow coastal plain, squeezing between the sea and the foothills.

Orchards of oranges and lemons decorated the low foothills on the approach to Tripoli, which lay on a flat, green promontory jutting into the Mediterranean. Dominating the view of the city was the colossal Citadel sitting adjacent to the Abu Ali River, its massive walls and towers forming a huge octagon, rising five to six stories above the city's paved and gardened streets.

"Did I tell you this is where my father died?" Ramiro asked as he reflected sadly on the kind man.

Adele reached out and took his arm in a gesture of comfort. "No. What on earth was he doing here?"

"He was on his way to Jerusalem with my mother. But he fell ill and passed into God's care."

"Do you know where he's buried?"

"Alas, I do not. And I cannot imagine how I would ever know. At least, not until I talk to my mother. No matter, we have no time for excursions. I want to go to the armorer next."

"You plan to buy weapons?" she asked, somewhat surprised. "They can't sell to you."

"They can be persuaded with silver. I want a knife at least, and since you seem so adept with oak, a mace would be a good weapon for you." His eyes twinkled.

"That's not funny," she snorted.

"I'm quite sincere. It's easy to swing and more effective than a simple club."

"And where do you think I'm going to put it?"

"We'll get a leather belt for you. You can cover it with your cloak."

"Do you still think Khuda will find us?"

"If he is alive, you can be sure he will be thinking of us."

REPORT: TRIPOLI

The docks of Tripoli were quiet. It was a Friday, the Muslim holy day. But some people milled around the few Christian stores still open. The office of the Byzantine shipper was among them, a small place nestled between the barrel-maker's shop and the currency exchange.

"Where are you going?" Adele asked.

"I've got to get this report off to the abbot," said Ramiro. "Here's the place." He opened the door to find the attendant sleeping at his desk.

"Hello!" he said loudly.

The young man jumped awake and staggered to his feet. "Yes, Sayyid," he said in accented Arabic. "Peace be upon you." He brushed his shaggy brown hair back with his hands.

"And you," said Ramiro in Greek. "When does the next ship sail for Bari?"

"It should arrive next week," he said as he straightened his tunic. "It's coming up from Jaffa. Then it sails for Saint Simeon before heading for Bari."

"Good, good," said Ramiro, handing him the envelope. "How much to deliver this?"

The courier took the package and weighed it. "Fifty fals," he said.

Ramiro paid the man. "Is Jaffa safe?"

"Safe enough," the man said. "The Egyptians have a garrison there."

"And what of Jerusalem?"

"The Turks still hold it."

Part Eight
PALESTINE & JUDEA

Dog River

Just north of Beirut is the ancient divide called Dog River. Over the ages, the river carved its way through the limestone mountains, creating a deep ravine with almost sheer walls. It was virtually impassable until the kings of old built roads and bridges across it.

To control Dog River, was to control all north-south traffic along the coast, and much blood was spilled to possess it. Some of the victors included the kings of Egypt, Assyria, Babylon and Rome, who boasted of their achievements and conquests by erecting steles along the road or by having their reliefs carved into the limestone cliffs.

Adele looked up at the weather-worn relief of a man wearing a tall hat and a short skirt. People living nearby said it was old Egyptian, but nobody knew it was the Pharaoh Ramses. She stared up at his strange headgear and a warm wind blew a strand of hair across her tanned face. She tucked it into her headscarf. "Why do men always fight, Ramiro?"

Ramiro shook his head sadly as he stared up. "For many reasons. They fight for glory among peers, they fight for land and riches, they fight for revenge, and they fight for their gods."

"Will it ever stop?" she asked in a despairing voice.

"One day it will," he said. "Lord Jesus promised us that. But I sincerely doubt it will be any time soon."

"So what should we do while we wait?"

"We should take courage, have faith, and live our lives as Christ taught us."

"But what of holy war? Isn't it our duty to protect the True Faith?"

"Holy war? Duty?" he scoffed. "How can holy war be any part of the True Faith? The French say they are Christian, yet the Commandments say 'you shall not murder.' Is that commandment so difficult to understand? If Christians – or Muslims or Hebrews - truly believe the Commandments, how can any war be attributed to God?" He sighed in resignation. "Those who kill in the name of God are ignorant or evil – or both. They do not worship God – they worship selfish pursuits."

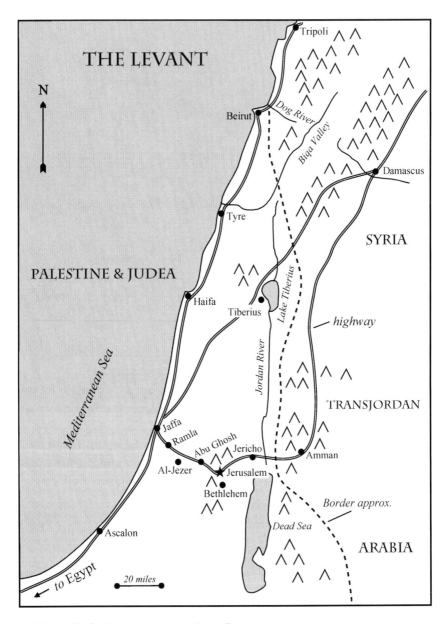

Adele smiled. "So your answer is no."

He nodded with a glint in his eye. "It is."

"So what of the highwaymen we killed?" she asked with growing concern. "Did we commit a sin?"

"I struggle with that," he said, thinking of the moment when he was ready to cut the man down with Yaqut's sword. "But it was hardly murder. I derive some consolation from Saint Augustine, who believed the only justification for killing was self-defense. And make no mistake, those men would have killed us – or worse."

Adele shuddered, recalling her treatment at the hands of slavers.

The steep road dropped to the bottom of the ravine where a stone bridge, built by the Romans centuries before, took them across Dog River. Ramiro scanned the area before he knelt at the riverside to refill their water-skins. He pushed one under water and the air bubbled out. "Let's go for a swim," he said.

"Here? Now?" she asked, looking around.

"Yes, here, now."

"We can't go naked."

"We'll wear what we have on. A good opportunity to do our laundry and have a bath at the same time. Come. We'll move upriver, away from the bridge."

Adele hugged his arm when he stood up. She pulled him close and nibbled at his ear. "It looks like we'll be all alone."

Ramiro smiled. "I presume you are not complaining."

JAFFA

The road south proved safe and prosperous, taking them through the busy ports of Beirut, Tyre and Haifa with little trouble. It was a hot August day when they finally arrived in Jaffa, where they breezed through the gates and pushed their way through the clogged street to make the climb up Jaffa Hill, one of the oldest settlements in the world, where the ruins of nine thousand years of human existence rested far below their feet.

Hundreds of shoppers and merchants of every dress imaginable thronged the streets while Egyptian troops milled about. Screaming peddlers lined the way, laying out their meager goods across worn carpets spread out on the dusty ground.

"Let's stop now!" Adele yelled.

Ramiro was far ahead, striding up the hill like a new man. His bones tingled with expectation. Jerusalem was so near. He turned around and shouted back. "No! I want to go to the top. We'll stop there!" He pulled at the mule's reins. The street wound its way up to the crest of the hill, eventually coming to the crumbling citadel, now occupied by a lone Egyptian garrison.

"Did you notice?" he asked as they sat down on a block of stone.

"Notice what? The magnificent view?" She pushed her hair into her blue headscarf.

"Well, yes that too. But look at all these people, Adele. See there," he pointed. "I think those two are Genoese or Venetians." He nodded to his right. She looked over to see a man dressed in a formed, knee-length tunic. He wore tight, red hose that climbed far above his knees.

"It seems such odd dress now, doesn't it Ramiro?"

"I always thought it was odd," he said, tipping his head again. "And look there. Those are probably Egyptians. And over there," his eyes moved. "The local folk, Philistines and Hebrews."

Adele looked out to sea, taking in the magnificent panorama with a slow turn of her head. "Ramiro," she smiled. "It really is beautiful. We've seen so many wonderful things on this journey." She put up her hand as a swallowtail butterfly flapped past their noses with its bright, yellow wings. She chuckled when it touched her fingers and watched it for a moment before it swooped down the hill.

"Yes, indeed, my dear. Except for a few prisons and beatings, we've done well," he said facetiously. He pointed out to sea. "Look. From here, you can watch every ship for miles around. And look along the coast. Whether south or north, you have a clear view of the roads."

"Ah!" Adele nodded. "Then you are telling me it's a strategic beauty."

Ramiro looked at her, furrowing his brow. "You jest with me."

She chuckled and pointed to the docks below. "Look at all the different ships. And flags of every nation!"

Ramiro pointed again. "There's the Byzantine banner. Now's your chance to go back... back to the safety of France."

She pretended to scowl. "Are you trying to get rid of me again?"

"I'm only thinking of your safety, my love. Soon, the Egyptians will march on Jerusalem. And then maybe the French. No doubt, there will be more trouble."

"I'll be safe with you," she said, taking his arm. "Besides, a child should be with his father." She smiled wide.

At first, her words did not quite register with Ramiro. He stared at her, hoping she was joking again, although it was little to joke about. "What... what do you mean?"

"I am with child, my husband."

"With ch... child?" he stuttered. "You... you mean... that we...?"

Adele nodded, still smiling.

He did his best to return her smile. "Are you serious? You're sure?"

A wisp of disappointment trailed across her face and her smile faded quickly. "I'm quite serious," she said in a maternal voice.

Ramiro said nothing for a long while. One part of his mind was elated with the prospect of fatherhood, while another was greatly disturbed. He had broken his Benedictine vows, and the child would be proof of that. He could never return to the Abbey of Cluny. Will God reject me for my sins, for my weakness? And then he felt a new-found fear. What of Adele and the child?

Adele spoke again, her voice breaking. "I see you are not pleased."

Ramiro turned his head. Tears streamed her pretty cheeks and a drop hung from her small nose. He took her in his arms and she clung to him. "Forgive me, my love. Yes, I am very happy. But you must understand, I am also very worried. More than ever, I want you to return to Constantinople. For your safety and for the child's."

She wept quietly on his shoulder. "I... I can't leave you, Ramiro. Where will I go? I have no one left. I would rather die at your side than roam France without you."

Ramiro's resolve soon vanished in her flood of tears. It was more than his heart could bear, and he knew at that moment that he was deeply in love with Adele, more so than he ever thought possible. And now that she bore his child, he felt an immeasurable bond that surpassed all understanding. He could never leave her. "Then you will stay," he said as he took her hand and pulled her to her feet. He turned to face the east and put his arm out towards the Judean Hills. "And thence lies Jerusalem, my sweet. Soon, we will worship at the Holy Sepulcher and give our thanks to the Lord." He squeezed her hand lightly. "Come. We will find an inn and get some rest."

JERUSALEM

For weeks, Khuda the Mamluk wandered the streets of Jerusalem, visiting the markets, taverns, inns and hostels, and even the churches. "I am looking for a man named Ramiro," he said to the innkeeper. "He is about this tall." He held out a hand. "And he is heavyset. He's got black eyes, like the Devil himself. Speaks with an accent. Travels with a red-haired woman."

The innkeeper looked at Khuda with suspicion. The stranger was clearly a Turk. "There was no one here like that. And what interest do you have in these people?"

"My interests are none of your business." Khuda snarled. "Did you see a red-haired woman?"

"I have seen several red-headed women in my time," he replied sarcastically.

Khuda reached across the desk and grabbed the man by his vest, yanking him forward, right off his feet. "I'll ask once more before I slit your throat!" He whipped his knife from his belt and stuck it to the man's neck.

The innkeeper yelped. "No, Efendi, I swear. I have not seen them!"

Khuda threw the man to the floor and rushed out the door. They must be in Jaffa. But what if the Egyptians come?

RAMLA

The road to Jerusalem was wide and well-travelled. Adele covered her eyes with one hand as the morning sun burst above the dry, Judean Hills. She watched the approaching silhouettes of farmers leading laden donkeys. Most were heading the other way, to Jaffa.

The coastal plain gave way to the irrigated foothills of Filastin, and here they came to Ramla, the capital city of Palestine. It lay at the intersection of the Via Maris and the Jaffa-Jerusalem road and, from this location, it controlled all vital traffic between Egypt and Syria.

A call to prayer greeted them at the gates. "Come," Ramiro urged. "Where there is a mosque, there is a market."

"Let's get a room at the inn first," Adele pleaded. "I'm exhausted."

• • • • •

The old innkeeper turned them away with a shake of his head. "This is a Muslim hostel. This is a Muslim city. You must go to the Christian church outside the city... or to the Christians at Ludd."

"How far is that?" Ramiro asked.

"About an hour's ride north," he wheezed.

Ramiro was about to get more detailed directions when, suddenly, Adele lurched forward, her face red. "Need rest! Need room!" she yelled in strained Arabic. Red hair dangled out of her headscarf.

The innkeeper, shocked at first, made no reply to her. Instead, he turned back to Ramiro. "You see? You Christians cannot control your women," he admonished him in subdued anger. "Any man of honor would beat her. You are not welcome here. Imshee!"

Ramiro scowled at her as they left the inn. "Are you daft?" he snapped. "How can you accomplish anything acting like that?"

"I'm tired!" she spat. "And I can speak my mind if I wish!"

He yanked at the mule's reins. "Words can be foolish or wise," he said in a tempered voice. "A wise man first measures the weight of his words."

She said nothing and walked away, pulling her mule forward.

He followed. "Don't you see, Adele? You must adopt the customs of the land. Do you really expect a whole nation to change just for you?"

She said nothing.

He turned towards the mosque. "Come. We must go to market, we need supplies. Then we'll ride for Ludd."

She followed in simmering silence.

The pale marble walls of the White Mosque glowed with a tint of rose, colored by the setting sun. A square minaret towered above the grounds and its long shadow crept across the courtyard like the hand of a giant sundial.

They found a water-seller near the mosque. The muscular young man drew water from a huge underground cistern, filled by an aqueduct that ran down from springs east of Ramla.

"Your mosque is very beautiful," said Ramiro after salutations.

The young man beamed. "Yes, Sayyid. Some people say the White Mosque is more beautiful and even more graceful than the Umayyad Mosque of Damascus."

Ramiro paid the attendant and asked a few questions before turning to leave.

Adele broke her silence. "Are we going to Ludd now?" She pulled her headscarf tight to conceal her hair.

Ramiro sauntered with the laden mule. "I've reconsidered. I don't like the idea of going to Ludd, it would be like going back. I would rather continue east. The water-man said there's a campsite at a place called Al-Jezer. It's only five miles east."

• • • • •

Khuda eyed the travelers coming and going, always on the lookout for Ramiro and the red-headed woman. He followed the road to Jaffa as it wound down through the Judean hills and kept a steady gait, trying to remain inconspicuous. Before leaving Jerusalem, he changed his dress to that of a merchant, stuffing his long hair under a turban and packing his mail armor and sword among his saddlebags. He was careful to speak only Arabic. But he could not hide his face, he looked like a Turk.

After the death of the Great Sultan, and then of Prince Tutush, Seljuk power in Palestine declined rapidly. East and south of Jerusalem, Turks were not welcome. The Egyptians had taken the advantage, helped by their dubious allies, the Byzantines and Italians. So when the Egyptians advanced into southern Palestine, poorly equipped Turk soldiers abandoned their garrisons in fear and made hasty retreats to Jerusalem or Damascus. There was much to fear, the Turks had no greater enemy than the Fatimid Egyptians.

Khuda stopped in Abu Ghosh, a town between Jerusalem and Jaffa. Once again, he asked at every inn, although he was much more polite here. But no one had seen them. He went to the markets and scrutinized the crowds carefully before riding down every street. They're not here. Maybe Ramla or Jaffa? Can't go to Jaffa, too many cursed Fatimids. And soon, the heretics will march on Jerusalem. May Allah curse them! He rode out of Abu Ghosh, heading for Ramla just as Ramiro and Adele turned off the main road, traveling to Al-Jezer.

AL-JEZER

The village of Al-Jezer sat on the slope of a flat-topped hill. They found the campsite at the summit almost deserted except for one man squatting under a simple lean-to on the other side. Ramiro studied him closely.

Adele pointed to a mass of huge stones jutting from the earth. "Look at these ruins."

Ramiro nodded. "An abandoned city no doubt, robbed of its stone." He spread his arm toward the coast. "But I can see why the place was important. Look at the commanding view of the coastal plain, the valley, and the road to Jerusalem."

Adele seemed unimpressed. She strolled along the grassy platform, glancing cautiously in the direction of the squatter. She stopped and looked down. "Here's a good spot for the tent."

The stranger called over to them. "Peace be upon you!" he said loudly.

"And to you, peace!" Ramiro shouted back. He tied the mules to one of the stones before strolling over to introduce himself.

The man said he was traveling to Jaffa to work for an uncle in the construction business. But he was worried about the Egyptians, who had taken the coast and, as rumor had it, would soon arrive at the gates of Jerusalem.

"Can we still get into the city?" Ramiro asked.

"Maybe. The emir is suspicious of everyone right now and his troops are ready to defend the city. I see you are Christian. You will need papers. Do you have any?"

Ramiro thought of his letter from the late Turk Sultan. It may still prove useful. "Yes, I do," he replied.

After more talk of politics and economic affairs, Ramiro said polite good-byes and returned to Adele. "It seems the Egyptians will soon lay siege to Jerusalem," he said. "This is a dangerous time. We could rush and make an attempt to get in before the army arrives. But if the Turks lose the battle, will we be safe? It may be best to return to Jaffa."

She did not look pleased. "Our child will need a home soon, Ramiro. We can't keep wandering the countryside."

He looked at her with wry amusement. "We will get to Jerusalem. We have plenty of time." He took her hand, raised it to his lips and kissed it. "It's not a long journey from Jaffa to Jerusalem, my love."

"But what about Khuda?"

He shrugged. "Either he's dead or the Blessed Virgin has been watching over us."

She looked around again, as if some danger hid behind the bushes. "Let's set up the tent so I can wash my hair without our neighbor seeing."

• • • • •

Ramiro lay flat on his back. A small fire flickered nearby, heating a pot of water. It was a dark, moonless night and the stars were brilliant. He pointed to the heavens. "The Romans call it the Milky Way. And look there – the constellations of Pegasus, Pisces, and there's Aquarius."

Adele knelt beside him, drying her hair. She smiled. "You could be an astrologer or a soothsayer."

Ramiro smiled back in the dim light of the fire. "And secure a position in the royal courts of France?" They laughed.

"What do the stars tell you, Ramiro?" She yawned. "Is this a good time to go to Jerusalem?"

He looked at her with fondness, brushing a lock of hair from her face with his thick fingers. "For that, my love, we will put our trust in God. I doubt the Lord of the Heavens would doom us to the fate of the stars. If it were not possible to change our lives, why would God send the Prophets and Our Savior to urge us onto a path of righteousness?"

The bushes rustled nearby. Adele tensed. "What's that?"

Ramiro felt for the dagger he bought in Tripoli. The flames flickered in a warm breeze. Was it just the wind? They heard it again. A rustle, a cough. Ramiro threw off the blanket, drew his dagger and crouched low. With a finger to his lips, he motioned to Adele to keep quiet. He stared into the blackness for any sign of life. The mules whinnied and he looked hard in their direction. He thought he saw something move, a low dark figure. He rose up a little and took a cautious step forward, then another.

First he heard thumps on the dry ground, and then a sudden, piercing scream just as the black form rushed straight at him. It smashed into his knees and sent him reeling to the ground. It came at him again, squealing as it charged. "It's a boar!" he shouted. The beast charged again and again, attempting to gore him with its short, sharp tusks.

Thwack! The boar staggered. Thwack! Adele hit it again and, with a terrifying squeal, it fled back into the dark, rustling bushes. She stood alone, the bloodied mace in her hand.

Ramiro sat on the ground, rubbing the cuts on his knees. "You see?" he said. "I knew that mace would be a good weapon for you."

●   ●   ●   ●   ●

A distant rumble brought Ramiro out of a fretful sleep. He rolled off his mattress and crawled outside. In the distance, in the red haze of dawn, a wisp of dust trailed behind a long procession of troops. They were marching to Jerusalem.

Their fellow camper was also awake and watching. He shouted over. "It's the Egyptian army! Look, Al-Afdal leads them. I see his white banner."

Ramiro strained to see the banner, but could not.

Adele peeped out. "They've come already? Now what do we do?"

He still stared out at the marching army. "Now we wait. They will not take Jerusalem in a day. We must return to Jaffa."

"I don't want to go back to Jaffa," she scowled. "Why don't we simply follow the army to Jerusalem? We can always find a place nearby."

He thought for a moment, then shrugged. "I suppose there's no harm in that."

She began to dress. "Then we better get going."

RAMLA

"Oh, yes, I remember those two, alright," said the innkeeper. "Christians with no manners at all. Yes, the raving witch had red hair. I sent them away."

"Which way did they go?" Khuda asked, somewhat excited.

The innkeeper shrugged and opened his hands. "I don't know. I sent them to the Christians at Ludd. But who knows where they went."

"When?"

"Just yesterday." He shrugged again. "Maybe they went to Jaffa, maybe Jerusalem. But it's unlikely they'll get into Jerusalem. The Egyptian army passed by this morning. Surely you saw them?"

Khuda nodded. He had hid in his room until they left. He was beginning to feel uncomfortable. Soon, no place in Palestine would be safe for him. He thanked the mean-spirited innkeeper and returned to his mount. His thoughts turned again to Ramiro and the girl and a menacing grin crossed his dark, weathered face. I know where they are going, he thought. I must return to Jerusalem. By the will of Allah, I will steal my way into the city, even under siege.

• • • • •

By noon, the Egyptian army had disappeared into the hills, following the narrow mountain road that wound its way up to Jerusalem. Ramiro and Adele followed some hours behind. He pointed to a high hilltop as they left the wide expanse of the Ayalon Valley and headed into the steep hills. A few soldiers stood guard on its crest, watching the road. "Egyptians," he said. "Just be calm, Adele. We are ignorant pilgrims and nothing more." He reached into his tunic for a few coins. "We will pay their toll and move on."

But no one rode out to stop them. So they forged ahead and, as the sun set, took a worn path off the main road where they found a place to camp in a sparse grove of oak.

• • • • •

Hours later, Khuda saw the same soldiers. He could see their dark silhouettes standing against the glowing rays of a setting sun. He felt for the dagger about his waist and drew his cloak to hide it. He thought too of his sword, which he had mounted under his saddlebags so that its hilt was barely exposed. He hoped the soldiers would ignore him, but he unwittingly gave himself away. He rode a spirited charger and, by his graceful movements, was clearly accomplished in the saddle. Even from a distance, the soldiers suspected he was mamluk and two rode down the hill to intercept him.

"Identify yourself!" one of them cried as he rode up.

"Salaam alaykum," replied Khuda. "I am Mahmoud of the Shikara family and a merchant of Jerusalem."

"You look like a Turk," one of them challenged. "Where is your merchandise? Where are your donkeys?"

Khuda studied the two soldiers carefully. They were lightly armed. He glanced up the hill for a brief moment. The other soldiers remained on the crest, but they were watching. "I have just returned from business in Jaffa," he said, "and now make my way home to Jerusalem." He forced a thin smile.

"Dismount and show us your papers."

"Of course," Sayyid. They are in my bags." He swung a leg over his horse and hit the ground lightly.

One soldier dismounted and walked over to him. "Let's see what you carry in your bags."

"As you wish," said Khuda, knowing the soldier would soon discover his arms and the mail coat. Without any warning, he grabbed the hidden hilt of his sword and drew it out. There was a dull flash of steel and a shout. "Curse your mothers! Shia bastards!"

Before the stunned soldier could respond, Khuda plunged the blade through his neck and, just as fast, he withdrew the bloodied sword before the man collapsed to the ground. By this time, the other soldier had regained his senses and drew his own blade to fight. Meanwhile, the horsemen on the crest saw the commotion, shouting loudly as they charged down the path towards them.

Khuda jumped to the left side of the mounted soldier, who tried to turn his horse to regain advantage with his sword arm. Khuda was faster. He swung his sword in a backswing, striking the soldier's left leg, cutting it off below the knee and slicing into the ribs of his horse. The horse screamed and bolted. The man howled and tumbled from his saddle in shock. Khuda jumped onto his steed and took off at full gallop. Arrows flew past his ears as four Egyptian horsemen thundered onto the road in dogged pursuit.

• • • • •

Ramiro stared up at the stars as Adele slept beside him. It was another black, moonless night and the stars glimmered like jewels. He was searching the southern sky for the constellation of Libra when he heard the snap of a dry twig. He immediately thought of the boar and felt the pain of his fresh wounds. He thought, too, of brigands and Egyptian soldiers. As a measure of caution, he had forgone a campfire, insisting they set up their tent at a spot nestled against the hills.

Another snap, closer now. He reached under his mattress for his dagger. He listened, the crunch of dry grass, the snort of a horse. Soldiers? Travelers? He rose slowly, crouching on the ground and peering into the blackness. He saw nothing. More noise... then nothing. A long moment passed. He heard a snore, a human snore, and relaxed a little. Another traveler.

• • • • •

Before the break of dawn, Ramiro was fully dressed. He sat facing the direction of the night noise and held his dagger beside him. The morning light waxed slowly between the oaks. There he is! One man, one horse.

The man stirred, as though he could sense someone's gaze. In an instant, he jumped to his feet, rolled up his mattress and packed his bags. That's when Ramiro noticed his long braids. He's a Turk! He's armed!

The man was busy stuffing his braids under his turban when he noticed Ramiro staring at him from a distance. For one brief moment, their eyes met.

Ramiro could feel the blood drain from his face. It's Khuda!

For a moment, Khuda feared Ramiro was an Egyptian soldier, but when he saw his dress, he relaxed. Still... there was something about the man that made him hesitate. He looked back again but Ramiro had turned his face and seemed to be laying back down. He scanned the area around him for other signs of life. There were none.

Ramiro rolled to one side. He poked Adele gently. Her eyelids flickered and she woke with a start. He was about to whisper a warning to her when she blurted out. "What is it? You want some breakfast?" He could not put his hand over her mouth fast enough.

Khuda was already mounted and about to ride away when he heard the woman's voice. It was not Arabic, nor was it Turkish. It was the tongue of those western barbarians. And those eyes! How could I mistake those eyes! The eyes of the Devil. It's the barbarian priest and that red-headed whore! Those thieving kuffar! A wicked grin crossed his face. He jumped off his horse and drew his sword. By the will of Allah, I will have my revenge.

Ramiro watched him dismount and pull his sword. "It's Khuda!" he gushed. "He knows! He's coming this way!"

Adele tore his hand from her mouth and reached for her mace. "That bastard won't kill me without a fight!"

He gave her a despairing look. She had spirit - but both of them together were no match for Khuda, a battle-hardened mamluk. Now here he was, striding through the trees towards them, sword in hand. They would surely die. He looked around frantically. The spot he had chosen, which he assumed was safe, now proved otherwise. The hill hemmed them in and they had no way of escape. "Quick! Pull down the tent!"

"What?" she screamed. "The tent? Are you mad? He's coming!"

"Do it now!" he yelled in a chilling voice, yanking out the pegs. "Now grab a corner! We'll use it as a net!" Khuda was only a few strides away. "If he goes my way – try to wrap around him! I'll do the same. Keep your mace ready and hit him whenever you can!" He put his dagger in his belt, held the tent corner with one hand, and scooped up a handful of dirt with the other.

"I have come to send you to Hell, Christian!" Khuda yelled as he raised his sword to strike.

Ramiro surprised him by stepping forward, throwing the dirt straight into his eyes. Khuda's sword faltered in mid-swing and he staggered, groping at his eyes. Ramiro and Adele fell on him with the tent. But Khuda was too strong and agile and, even with their combined weight, they had trouble bringing him down. Adele hammered on him with her mace but he fought back like a wild bear. Ramiro was about to drive in his dagger when Khuda's sword burst through the canvas and sliced across his right arm. Ramiro clutched at the wound, dropping his knife. Khuda felt the weight shift and threw them both off. He flung out his left arm, belting Adele across the head. She tumbled to the ground. Ramiro rushed to pick up the dagger with his left hand. Blood poured down his arm. Khuda rubbed his eyes, still red and watering. Ramiro moved to strike but Khuda heard the noise and jumped at him, swinging his sword wildly. Ramiro held up his dagger, but Khuda's swing sent it flying out of his hand. Before he could respond, Khuda gained some sight and jumped at him. Too close for a sword thrust, he punched out with the hilt, striking Ramiro in the throat.

Ramiro collapsed onto the rough ground, choking and gasping. Khuda put a foot on his wounded arm and pressed the point of his sword into his neck. "Where's my money? Christian pig!" He pushed down with the point. "Tell me now and you will have a quick death," he smiled.

Ramiro grunted in pain, he could hardly speak. "It's... it's on the mule," he croaked. "In the blankets."

Khuda's face gnarled in another cold smile. He bent down to search Ramiro and found the package in his vest. He cut the string and opened it. The gold and silver cross flashed in a ray of morning sun. "Ha, ha. You see, kafir? What good has this talisman brought you?" His smile turned to a sneer and his sword twitched in anticipation of a kill. "You will have no need of it now, barbarian! May Allah damn your soul!"

Adele opened her eyes and looked around carefully. She was behind Khuda. She rose slowly, reaching for her mace lying on the ground a short distance away. With a firm grip on it, she rushed at Khuda's back. But Khuda noticed a flicker in Ramiro's eye and spun around as fast as a panther. He swung his sword arm out to strike her but Adele had already landed her mace square between his shoulder blades. He crumbled for a moment, but regained his stance before she could hit him again. He turned and belted her across the head. She fell again, blood pouring from her nose.

"You bitch!" he shouted, raising his sword to run her through. Ramiro got up and grabbed at his legs with his good arm. Khuda stumbled. Adele rose to her hands and knees and swung the mace as hard as she could. Khuda howled as it crashed into his kneecap. He fell to the ground and groped for his sword. Adele swung at him again. But he saw the blow coming, dodged and punched her right between the eyes. She toppled down, unconscious.

That's when Ramiro heard the soldiers, only paces away. Khuda heard them too. He cursed aloud and hobbled back to his horse as fast as he could. He mounted with difficulty and grabbed the reins of the mules. Ramiro tried to stop him but was held back by the swing of his blade.

"I'll kill you later, kafir!" he snapped as he rode away into the hills with the mules in tow.

No sooner had he disappeared, when two Egyptian horsemen rode into the campsite. Ramiro clutched at his bleeding arm while pointing the way. They rode off in pursuit.

• • • • •

Ramiro winced as the needle pierced his skin. "Hold still!" Adele shouted as she pushed it through. "You are fortunate, it's a clean cut."

He dabbed at the sweat on his brow. "I would hardly call that 'fortunate,' my dear," he moaned. "In two days, I've been gored by a wild boar and pierced by a mamluk sword. The only good fortunate is that my medicine bag was left behind." He turned his head to inspect her work. "Keep it clean," he ordered, remembering the advice of Fawwaz, the doctor from Adrianople who had saved Brother Aldebert's life.

Adele frowned at him. Her face was badly bruised and cut from Khuda's blows. She strained to see through blackened and swollen eyes. "Never you mind!" she snapped. "It's clean!" She put a hand to his chin and turned his head away. "I know what to do!"

"Khuda took everything," he lamented. "I thought, at last, I could fulfill my pledge and deliver the cross to Jerusalem." He dabbed at his brow again. The shade of a pistachio tree failed to shield them from the torrid heat of day. "I must get it back. I made a promise to the Abbot."

Adele glared at him. "You don't mean you're going after Khuda?"

"I must."

Adele drove the needle in hard. "Bloody fool!"

"Aaagh! Careful! Are you going to stab me to death with that thing?"

"Forget the cross, Ramiro. We're lucky to be alive!"

"I cannot forget it. I made a promise. I swore an oath. Khuda's probably gone to Jerusalem anyway. It would be the best place to sell it."

Adele sighed in frustration. "Well, at least you will soon get to see your mother." She wiped the wound clean and wrapped it tightly in the cleanest cloth she could find.

He nodded. It had been a while since he thought of her, even though they approached Jerusalem by the day. "And, by the Grace of God, the Patriarch too."

"And, praise Mary," said Adele. "... we still have the tent and some gear. And we have some money." She reached for the hem of Ramiro's cloak and shook it. "Remember the coins I sewed into our clothes." She began to roll up the tent. "But we can't stay here long. We'll have to walk to the next town." She winced from a sharp spasm and put a hand to her stomach.

He noticed her waver. She looked terrible. "What's wrong?"

She tried to steady herself. "Nothing... nothing's wrong. Help me to bundle these... these..." Her eyes rolled in her head, her knees gave way, and she crumbled to the ground.

JERUSALEM

Khuda was lucky. He found a grotto carved into the hills and darted in with his horse and the mules. The Egyptians spotted him in their search and rushed in, swords drawn. But it was a trap. And they were no match for the seasoned mamluk, even with a wounded knee.

And when he eventually arrived at Jerusalem, watching from a distance, he could see the Egyptian forces besieging the Jaffa Gate and the Damascus Gate. But there were not enough of them to cover all the gates. So, in the cover of night, he took a long route around the city and approached the unguarded Lion's Gate near the Temple Mount, where the Turk guards gladly let him in.

THE JEWELER

Madteos the Jeweler studied the cross carefully, holding a magnifying glass in one hand and scratching the golden metal with a thin, sharp needle. His liver-spotted brow furrowed beneath a frayed, yellow cap. "What do you want for it?"

Khuda looked down on the jeweler's wide desk, covered with Christian crosses and figurines. "What's it worth, old man?" he growled.

Madteos shrugged his thin shoulders. "I'll give you one dinar," he muttered through a wide moustache.

Khuda leaned forward and grabbed it from his hand. "You insult me! I'll take it to another jeweler – one who knows the true value of gold art."

Madteos shrugged again. He could see Khuda was a Turk. "I might pay a little more. How did you obtain this cross?" he asked warily. "I don't want any trouble. Are you Christian?"

Khuda flushed red. He barged past the desk to grab Madteos by his vest, lifting the thin, old man off his feet and slamming him against a wall. Pendants and idols fell to the floor. "What do you think? Stupid kafir! May Allah curse you! How dare you speak to me like this! I'll knock every tooth from your withered head and gouge out your eyes!"

"Forgive me, Efendi!" Madteos squawked. "Forgive my bad manners! Of... of course it's worth more." He forced a smile. "I will give you two dinar - yes, two dinar."

Khuda released him slowly. "Give it to me now! I cannot abide the filth of this place."

He took the money and limped back to his horse. He mounted with difficulty and rode out from the Christian market as fast as he could. No good Muslim would be seen in these heathen surroundings. He felt unclean and headed for the baths.

• • • • •

I have done well, Khuda thought as the hot steam enveloped him. I got a good price for the mules and found some coins sewn into the blankets, though it's not much compared to what I had. Damn them! Then he smiled a little with a pleasing sense of revenge. At least I got two dinar for that satanic cross. But his pleasure vanished in a flash when a jarring pain shot through his wounded knee. He leaned forward and rubbed at the tight bandages. May Allah curse that demon woman! I should have killed her right away. The priest too!

He moved to a low massage table and lay on his back, letting the masseuse rub rose oil into his scarred skin and squeeze the tension from his roped muscles. His head tilted to the side and his long braids almost reached the floor. He spoke in a low voice. "What have you heard about these Egyptians? Will the heretics take the city?"

The masseuse hesitated. "Uh, maybe, Efendi. We all worry." He could see Khuda's many scars and guessed he was mamluk. "Will you join the Turks to defend the city?"

Khuda grunted. "Perhaps I will. Nothing would give me more pleasure than to drive my sword through a stinking Fatimid."

ABU GHOSH

Ramiro couldn't stop crying. He wiped his cheeks with a kerchief already damp with tears. He paid no attention to the burning pain in his arm, now bandaged with a poultice. His precious cross was gone - but that didn't seem to matter either. Jerusalem, the holiest of cities, where his mother waited, was just a walk away – but he gave no thought to it. "Adele," he choked in a whisper. "Adele."

When Adele collapsed, he panicked. He held her in his arms and stroked the dirt from her swollen face. He saw the blood, there was so much blood, and he felt her pulse weaken. He remembered ripping open the hem of his robe for the coins and running out to the Jerusalem road for help. He rushed to a farmer pulling a handcart full of vegetables and thrust a silver dirham into the surprised man's hands. In a frenzy, he dumped the vegetables on the side of the road and rushed back to Adele. Her head lolled in his arms when he lifted her into the cart and, despite the wounds to his arms and legs, he pushed that cart at a near run – all the way to the hospital in Abu Ghosh.

He took her hand as she lay unconscious on the bed, her body as limp as bread dough. Khuda's blows had taken their toll, she looked like a corpse, the dark bruises around her eyes and cheeks stood in stark contrast to her cold, pallid skin.

The physician, a young man with jet-black hair, put his hand on Ramiro's shoulder. "Praise Allah she lives. She has lost a lot of blood from her miscarriage. When she awakes, by the will of Allah, you must feed her as much barley and chicken soup as she can swallow."

Ramiro raised his head and put his hand to the physician's. "Thank you, Doctor," he strained through tears. "May Allah keep your children."

AUGUST 1098

The news rushed through the markets of Abu Ghosh. Everyone seemed to be talking at once. "Jerusalem falls! The Turks have fled to Damascus!"

Adele sat by the window of their small room, staring vacantly at nothing in particular. The bruises and the swelling were almost gone but her pallid complexion made her look weak and tired. She appeared unmoved by the news.

Ramiro lifted his head from his work. He was making a detailed ink drawing of the cross, which he planned to use in his search. He rose from a cushion. "Did you hear that? I'm going out to learn what I can. Can I get you something?"

She turned her head and shook it lethargically.

Ramiro walked over to her, kneeling down to take her hand. "Adele, my love, you cannot go on like this. It wasn't your fault."

She pulled her hand away and wiped her eyes. "God punishes me for my sins. He has taken my child from me."

"God does not punish, Adele. God is merciful and loving." He took her hand again and squeezed a little. "The trials and tribulations we suffer are accidents of time - or simply the outcome of our actions. Khuda is the man to blame for our loss – not God."

"Why didn't God save our child, Ramiro? Why? What have I done to bring this curse? What have *you* done?"

"We have done nothing, Adele, listen to me. The God I know does not curse people with afflictions."

She put her arms around his neck and rested her head on his shoulder. After a moment of silence, she lifted her eyes, putting the palm of her hand to his cheek. "Will we have another child, Ramiro?"

He kissed her forehead. "In God's time, my love. All in God's time"

ITALY

The Allsaints Abbey near Bari used to be a quiet place, but since the Holy War began two years ago, Aldebert rarely had a moment of peace. Would-be crusaders came to the abbey by the hundreds, usually to ask for something to eat or a place to sleep out of the weather. He spent much time with these people and helped many to continue on with their journey.

Two years ago, much to his surprise, Abbot Hugh had conceded to his request to remain in Italy, but only if he stayed at the Benedictine abbey. He was required to send the Abbot monthly reports on all that was going on. And Abbot Martinus of the Allsaints Abbey had instructions to let him roam the port where, ostensibly, he was to tend to pilgrims. During his escapades, he met several illustrious crusaders on their way to Dyrrachium and Constantinople.

And as the years wore on, he heard of the Crusader's travails on their long march to Antioch, the place where Saint Stephen was martyred, and he rejoiced when he was told that, after a long siege, they had finally conquered, cleaning the city of pagan filth, as was God's will. The news of victory gave others courage and they came from all corners of Europe to join up. Some were true warriors but most were common folk with no horses and few weapons of note. They were ill-equipped and poorly prepared, and often the first to die.

Aldebert was older now, almost thirty, and his thin frame had filled somewhat. His face was heavier and his acne gone, leaving a pale, pocked skin on his cheeks. He had waited, hoping beyond hope for Ramiro to summon him to Jerusalem. But the promised letter never came and he could not bear to think of what dreadful fate may have overtaken his fellow monk. Even now, years later, he had to fight back tears at the very mention of his name. So when a letter from Ramiro finally did arrive, he was beside himself.

He started to cry the moment he took it in his hands. It was the letter mailed from Maarat the year before. Ramiro had sent it to Cluny and the Abbot had been kind enough to forward it through. He tried to read it through his tears but could not and had to settle himself down, dabbing his eyes with a damp kerchief before the words became clear.

> *From Ramiro of Cluny to Aldebert of Cluny, dearest greeting in the Name of Our Lord and Savior.*
>
> *I pray my letter finds you safe and well at the Abbey. Although I have much to tell, I will remain brief. With God's help, we will meet again in more auspicious times.*

I regret to inform you that I have yet to arrive in Jerusalem. Not long after I left Edessa, I was captured again by the Turks and spent the last four years as a prisoner in Antioch. By the Grace of Almighty God, I managed to escape to a lonely city in the heart of Syria. Lord willing, I will resume my journey to Jerusalem in the spring. But I must tell you, no place is safe to travel since the death of the Turk Sultan. I will write again when God, by His will, finally places my feet on the Holy Soil of Jerusalem.

Maarat An-Numan, October 12, in the year of Our Lord 1097

"Praise the Lord!" he blubbered. "Thank you, Jesus!" He continued to wipe the streaming tears from his pale cheeks. Then he had a sudden thought. "In the spring? But spring has passed. He must be there by now!" He imagined Ramiro in Jerusalem, threatened on all sides by evil, bloodthirsty, Godless pagans, and he jumped to his feet. "I'll join the Holy Crusade!"

JERUSALEM

SEPTEMBER 1098

Ramiro tugged at the donkey he purchased in Abu Ghosh, leading it along the winding road through groves of oak and orchards of olive and pistachio. Adele walked alongside, gripping the donkey's harness with one hand. Color returned to her cheeks and vigor to her stride. But she still had a distant, distracted look.

Ramiro had his head down as he walked. He was deep in thought. *Jerusalem is so near. After all these years, does my mother still live? And what do I say to Patriarch Symeon? What of the secret message sent by Abbot Hugh? Or was it a message? Now the cross is gone, stolen again by that heathen Turk. How will I find it?* A yell came from up ahead. A long caravan of camels approached. The lead driver shouted to clear the way. Ramiro pulled the donkey further to the side. The caravan passed and his thoughts returned again to his dilemma. *Perhaps it is too late anyway. How long has it been? Eight... no nine, it's been over nine years since Abbot Hugh gave me the cross. Can its message still remain vital? The Abbot said the fate of Christendom hung on this message. How could that be? Perhaps its meaning is intrinsic. Perhaps the cross itself is the message.* He lifted his head from his thoughts as they rounded a sharp corner of the road. And then he saw it... there it was.

There, across the Valley of Hinnon, the high walls of Jerusalem jutted from a rough limestone plateau as if they were a natural and timeless extension of the rock itself. They towered into a dark blue sky like the majestic walls of a mythical castle. High above, a thin cover of cloud, lit up by the morning sun as it crept over the Mount of Olives, glowed over the city like a golden halo.

He staggered at the sight. The blood rushed from his head and he went feint, his legs weakened and he fell to his knees in the middle of the road. The years of delay, the perilous roads travelled, the long imprisonments, the disappointments, and the years of suffering – it all caught up to him in an overwhelming agony of spirit, twisting his swarthy face in anguish and ecstasy. His shoulders heaved and he began to sob openly, putting his hands to his knees to steady himself. "Oh Jerusalem," he choked aloud as a rush of tears streamed his cheeks. "Praise be to the Heavenly Father and the Son of God." He stared out at the Biblical city of the Hebrews, of the prophets, and of Jesus. It was all true. He wiped his face with his sleeve, unable to stop the rush of hot tears.

"Ramiro!" Adele cried as she abandoned the donkey and rushed to kneel at his side. "Ramiro! Are you alright?" She rested a hand on his shoulder.

Her touch brought him to his senses. He turned to look at her and soon realized he was kneeling in the middle of the road. Some travelers stopped and stared at him, others cursed his obstruction. He wiped his face again. "Yes, yes, of course. I'm fine." He stood unsteadily before moving to the side of the road. "Come, let's get out of the way. I need to rest a while."

• • • • •

The walls of Jerusalem stand the height of ten men and are five paces thick. They wrap around a crest of limestone rock for two and a half miles, interspersed with six main gates and two fortresses. Below the walls, the deep valleys of Qidron, Josaphat and Hinnon serve as a natural defense to the south, wrapping part way around the city like wide, craggy moats gouged from the gray-white rock by the hand of God. Only to the north, does flatter ground allow an easier approach, but here a second outer wall and a series of dry moats defend the main wall.

The Canaanites settled here four thousand years ago near a site that would later become known as the Temple Mount. They called it Jebus, after the name of their tribe. Nearby, was the spot where the High Priest Melchizedek later made a covenant with Abraham of Chaldea. It was called Salem. And the sweep of Jebus-Salem came to form the heart of an emerging Jewish nation.

In year 70, Jewish zealots rose up in rebellion against their Roman masters. But they were soon crushed by the ruthless Roman military machine and paid a terrible price. Thousands were crucified on Golgotha, the Hill of Skulls. And, like the Persians centuries before, the Romans flattened the city walls and demolished the Temple, forever banning all Jews from the city.

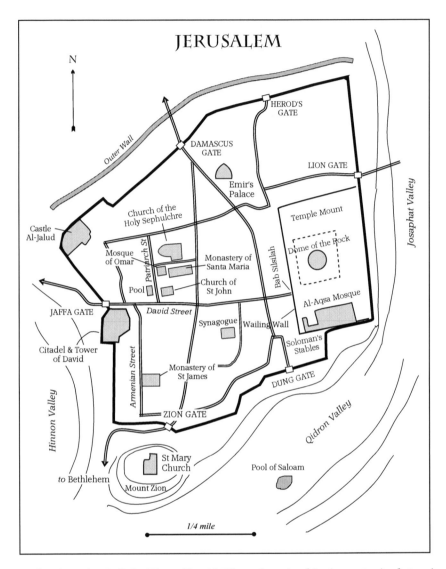

Only when the Caliph, Umar Ibn Al-Khattab, seized it six centuries later, in 638, were the Jews finally allowed to return to their ancestral home.

For Muslims, Jerusalem is where God led the Prophet Muhammad to a meeting with Moses and Jesus before the archangel Gabriel carried him off to Paradise, making it their third holiest city after Mecca and Medina. Not long after the conquest, the new Caliph cleared the Temple Mount of rubble and refuse accumulated over centuries of Roman neglect and here he built a splendid shrine, the Dome of the Rock, which he fancifully envisioned as a place of worship for all faiths.

And for Christians, Jerusalem is where Jesus proclaimed his divinity in the Second Temple, where he taught that God is better envisioned as a Divine Parent motivated by love, and where the same Son of Man was cruelly executed at the instigation of vengeful Sadducees and Pharisees.

Christians of the time believed that Jerusalem was the place where heaven meets earth in a divine union of God and man, and the very point of that heavenly juncture was the Holy Sepulcher, the Tomb of Christ.

• • • • •

When Ramiro and Adele approached the Jaffa Gate, the white banner of the Egyptian Fatimids flapped high above the Tower of David. The conquering vizier, Al-Afdal, allowed the ruling Turks to flee to Damascus, a popular gesture. But he was not so kind to their askaris and others who defended the city, and he put many to the sword. Then without ceremony, he installed his own governor, a brawny, ambitious man by the name of Iftikhar, and manned the barracks with Egyptian troops. Satisfied with his victory, Al-Afdal returned to his pressing affairs in Cairo. He felt confident he had put an end to the Franj invasion of Palestine.

The bureaucrats of Jerusalem wasted little time bowing in submission to their new overlords and life in the city resumed its busy pace. No one really seemed to care whether the Turks or the Egyptians ruled, as long as commerce was good. But Governor Iftikhar remained wary and his guards at the gates checked everyone. The long line-up inched slowly through the dim, narrow entrance of the gate.

"And where are you from?" a guard asked as he perused their papers routinely.

"From Maarat An-Numan, Sayyid," Ramiro offered quickly.

"And what is your business in Jerusalem?"

"We are Christian pilgrims, Sayyid. We have come to worship at the Holy Sepulcher."

"Hmmph," he huffed. He glanced at Adele's pale face and looked them over suspiciously. "Are you one of those western barbarians? The devils who, even now, have taken Antioch?"

"Oh no, Sayyid." Ramiro gushed in fluent Arabic. "We have nothing to do with those barbarians. We have come only to worship."

"How long will you stay?"

Ramiro hesitated. "Uh, by your permission, Sayyid, until the Nativity Feast."

"What? This means nothing to me. How long is that?" he asked impatiently.

"Well," Ramiro thought for a moment, converting the date of Christmas. "That would be until the end of the month of Muharram, Sayyid."

The guard handed the papers back to him. "That's a long time. You must register. Give your names to the clerk." He pointed inside the gate before turning to the next in line.

• • • • •

"Ha, ha!" Ramiro laughed. "We've done it! We have reached Jerusalem, my darling!" He gave Adele a warm embrace. The donkey tugged at the reins and brayed in the commotion.

"Ramiro!" She pushed him away. "Mind your manners. People are all around us." But she smiled too, the first smile he had seen in a long time. She tossed her head with a glitter in her eyes "Where do we go from here? Where's the Holy Sepulcher?"

"I have no idea," he said, shaking his head. "But we will soon know." He took long strides down David Street to ask the nearest vendor, a man selling hummus and flatbread.

"We continue down this street," he said, returning with a snack. "And then turn left on Patriarch Street. It leads north to the church. Come! I must know if my mother lives. And I must meet with the Patriarch as soon as possible."

"What of Khuda? What if he's in the city?"

He scanned the crowd. "I haven't seen a Turk yet. I'm sure they've all left." He looked over his shoulder one more time.

HOLY SEPULCHER

In 325, the first Christian Emperor, Constantine, prodded on by his devout mother, Helena, demolished the Temple of Aphrodite, the Greek goddess of erotic love, to erect a church in Jerusalem. Helena supervised all construction and, in the course of excavations, claimed to have found the remains of the True Cross and the Tomb of Christ. And so she named it the Church of the Holy Sepulcher and it soon became the most holy site in all Christendom.

Under Muslim rule, the church survived until the mad Caliph of Egypt, Al-Hakim, razed it to the ground in 1009. The news of its destruction spread like an angry fire throughout the whole of Europe. But in their shock and ignorance, Christians blamed Jews for the desecration.

In 1048, the emperor of Byzantium rebuilt the church, but it was only a partial reconstruction. So when Ramiro and Adele arrived, the rebuilt church was only fifty years old.

• • • • •

The market on Patriarch Street bustled with business, crowded with bags and barrels of goods from every corner of the known world. Ramiro pushed through a mass of people until he suddenly turned right and headed down Saint Helena Street, a path so narrow only pedestrians and donkeys could pass through. Adele rushed to keep up. The path turned left, then right, before descending a flight of stone steps, coming eventually to a dilapidated courtyard, the entrance to the Church of the Holy Sepulcher.

"This is it," said Ramiro.

"This?" Adele asked with some amazement. "But it's half a ruin!"

"So it seems," he muttered. He had finally reached the site of the Holy Sepulcher, a mysterious place that had eluded him for so many years. But he was disappointed, it was far from the magnificent structure he had imagined from his readings. Nothing remained of the ancient basilica or the atrium, and the once-covered courtyard now stood open to the sky. Here and there, the fractured base of the old walls jutted from the rough ground and, in some places, the shattered remains of a once-beautiful mosaic floor peeked through the dirt.

They made their way through the dim entrance, which led straight to the wide, circular floor of the rotunda. White, stone pillars, joined by arches, stood right in front of them, forming a circle at the center. An ornate, domed ceiling rose high above this ringed, open space. Small windows, way up, let in a pale-yellow daylight that reflected down the plastered walls before resting on a small, stone shrine at the very center of the rotunda. This was the aedicule, and within it, was the Tomb of Christ.

Ramiro knelt beside the shrine and reached out to touch its stone. He prayed quietly with his eyes shut. For years, he had pined for this moment. For years, he had suffered to reach this holy place. It was here, at the very Tomb of Christ, where he had no doubt the Holy Spirit would wash away all his sins and he would be renewed, he would be sanctified. It was here, where he expected some divine revelation and a feeling of spiritual bliss. But he felt nothing. Instead, he fretted in anxious thoughts.

Meanwhile, Adele fondled her prayer beads and prayed passionately to Mother Mary. Tears of bitter grief stained her cheeks, grief at the haunting images of her parents slain by the Turks, grief at being cruelly enslaved, and the unbearable grief of losing her first child. She prayed for mercy and she prayed for the remission of her sins. She lifted her eyes to the soft light overhead and, in a moment of divine worship, she felt a flood of ecstasy. The exhilaration lifted her soul to new heights and she felt released, finally released from the cold bitterness that caged her mind. She cried some more and praised the Mother of God for leading her to the most holy place on earth. Her senses returned only when impatient new arrivals nudged her away.

They moved away from the aedicule to stand between the pillars. "When will you know of your mother?" she asked, wiping her face.

"I have asked. We must wait here for the nun."

Time moved slowly. Clergy and pilgrims came and went and the prayers of the faithful echoed from the unadorned walls. Pilgrims arrived in all kinds of dress, coming from near and far, despite the constant danger.

Adele poked him and pointed. "I think that's her."

A slight woman approached, wearing a long, white habit and a white headscarf. "Are you Ramiro of Cluny?" she asked.

"Yes, Sister. Do you have any news of my mother, Isabella Agueda?"

The nun answered brusquely. "I'm sorry to say, Sister Isabella passed away four years ago."

Ramiro took a moment to absorb her words. And what he heard was not entirely unexpected. He had feared this outcome many times but came to believe he had hardened his mind to it, telling himself that he had done all he could to get here on time and that death was, after all, just a part of life. But when the plain truth sank to his heart, he felt a heave of remorse and grief. He clenched his jaw, struggling to restrain his emotions. "By... by God's mercy!" he choked. "May she rest in peace."

Adele took his arm, holding it firm.

"Who is your mother's father?" the nun tested, oblivious to his pain.

Ramiro blinked through tears. "Why, it is Eustace of León."

She handed him an envelope. "You answered correctly. Sister Isabella asked me to give you this. By the grace of God, she rests in the bosom of Christ."

"Thank you, Sister, thank you," he said in a strained voice and reached for the letter. The nun turned around to walk away.

"Wait, please, Sister," he called after her. "Would you be so kind as to direct me to the Patriarch?"

She turned. "You wish to see Patriarch Symeon?"

"Yes, if you please."

She shook her head. "He was exiled almost a year ago. They accused him of collaborating with the Greeks and the western barbarians and he fled to the island of Cyprus."

"Cyprus? All the way to Cyprus?"

"Yes," she said. "If you must see His Eminence, you will have to return to Jaffa to board a vessel."

"Then tell me, who is in authority here?"

"Bishop Aliphas is our guide for the moment. Unless they throw him out too."

ISABELLA'S LETTER

Merchants, shoppers, priests and monks crisscrossed the small courtyard outside the Church of the Holy Sepulcher. A few steps away, food stalls sold kebab, olives, and rafis. Ramiro bought some olives and they sat on a low, stone bench by the wall. His mind wandered in all directions and he could not help but think, with some remorse, that he would have seen his mother if he had not gone after Adele in Antioch. And the Patriarch too, perhaps in enough time to complete some vital assignment. But it was too late now. He glanced at Adele while putting an olive in his mouth, and he knew in his heart he would have changed nothing, that he could never live with himself if he had left her to the fancies of the Turks. And now, after five years together, he felt he could never live without her.

He opened the envelope and unfolded the letter carefully. It was four years old and the paper yellowed. An object fell out onto the flagstones. He looked down. "What's that?"

Adele bent over and picked it up. "Looks like a small pouch."

Ramiro took it from her fingers and opened it. "By all the saints! This must be the relic my mother mentioned in her first letter."

"What is it?"

He tipped the pouch into his hand and a small piece dropped out. "I think it's a thorn."

"A thorn? Well, what does she say in the letter?"

Ramiro held it at arm's length. "Again she writes in Castilian. But her hand is weak." He faced Adele and read softly.

> To my dear son, Ramiro, son of Sancho, greetings and God's blessing from your loving mother, Isabella.
>
> Alas, my beloved, if you read this then it is too late. I prayed to see you before my last days on earth but my prayers were not answered. Soon, I will pass over to Christ. I beseech you, pray for my soul.

His voice broke as he read and he took a moment to compose himself. Adele pressed against him to give him strength. His eyes watered and he fluttered his eyelids in an attempt to see. He took a deep breath and read on.

> It has been six years since I sent to you my first letter. Since that time, my son, there have been many rumors within the confines of the Church. It is said the Christians of Rome and those of the West Countries plot with the Greeks to free Jerusalem from the

*grip of heathen. If this is so, my son, you must position yourself
for the great Christian kingdom to come.*

*Take the Thorn of Christ I give to you, and become a Soldier
for Christ. Restore the Holy Land to God-knowing people. This
is my dying wish. May God be with you always.*

August 19, in the year of Our Lord, 1094.

Adele's eyes opened wide. "Is it really from Christ's crown of thorns?" She reached out to touch it.

He lifted one cheek in a skeptical grin. "Honestly, I don't know what to believe. My mother, God bless her soul, she believed it. But have you looked in the Christian markets? There are enough thorns for sale to make a hundred crowns!"

"Maybe so, Ramiro, but keep it with you, just in case – for your own protection." She tapped on the letter impatiently. "And what does she mean by 'position yourself'?"

"It seems she wants me to take up the sword and seek high office in this new kingdom." He shook his head slowly as he looked down on the letter. "I believe mothers are much the same in this regard. They all want what they think is best for their children."

She picked the thorn from his hand and studied it on her palm. "Is this what you'll do?" she asked with some distraction.

"Heavens no! I have no desire to take part in war and politics, nor to govern Jerusalem. This is not my path. I'm afraid my mother, may God bless her soul, was a little more zealous than I anticipated."

Adele picked up an olive from the paper napkin on her lap. "Then are we going back to Jaffa to find the Patriarch?" she asked before putting one in her mouth. "Are we going to Cyprus?"

"No, no. What's the sense in that?" he said, chewing. "I have nothing to give to the Patriarch. The cross is lost. And how do I know if any of this is still important?"

"So what do you plan to do?"

"I must speak to this Bishop Aliphas." He squeezed his hands together as he talked. "And I must try to find the cross. How can I face Abbot Hugh if I do not at least try?"

"That was nine years ago," she said. "I'm wondering if this cross is cursed."

"Nothing is cursed," he said with some annoyance. "People curse, that is all."

She took his hand. "Must you put your life at risk again, Ramiro? What if Khuda still has it?"

He shook his head. "He would have sold it by now. Or melted it down. It's not likely a Muslim would want to be seen carrying a Christian cross. I know it's not in Abu Ghosh... I checked everywhere. So he must have brought it to Jerusalem. This would be his best market for it."

"Where will we stay?"

"Abbot Hugh ordered me to the Benedictine monastery, the Monastery of Santa Maria."

"And where's that?"

Ramiro looked around and chuckled. "It's right there, across the street."

She looked up. "That's a mosque," she said.

"That building is, yes. That's the Mosque of Umar. But on either side and behind it is the Monastery. I saw the plaques earlier. It's more of a hospice really. Mainly to attend to sick and weary pilgrims."

Adele stared blankly across the street. She did not seem to hear. "What will you do, Ramiro?" she asked, squeezing his hand. Her smooth, freckled brow furrowed in concern.

"What do you mean?"

"Will you return to the Order of Benedict?"

"I'm not sure if I can. Although married men are allowed to be monks, as long as they take a vow of chastity afterward." He could feel her grip tighten. "But usually their wives enter a monastery too."

She looked down for a moment before raising her head again. "Is this what you want me to do? Become a nun?"

He put a finger to her chin and lifted her face. Her eyes watered and he bit his tongue to stop his own tears. The noisy plaza seemed to grow quiet. Pigeons waddled past them, pecking among the stones. Gently, he put his hand on top of hers. "No," he said. "That is not what I want."

BROTHER GERARD

A long, stone wall wrapped around the expansive grounds of the Monastery of Santa Maria Latina. Outside the wall, rows of end-to-end shops cluttered the streets, nearly obscuring the entrance. "Here it is," Ramiro said, opening a small iron gate. "Come on."

No one guarded the gate and the unkempt gardens and crumbling courtyard appeared abandoned, the only sound was the loud, hard whistle of a spectacled bulbul flitting between a few withering almond bushes. They followed a wide pathway separating two large buildings before stopping at one.

A heavyset nun came out to greet them. "I am Sister Agnes. What can I do for you?"

"We are pilgrims looking for accommodation," said Ramiro.

"We can give you a bed," she said plainly, waving her arm to one side. "This building is the hospice for women." She waved in the other direction. "And this one for the men."

"May I speak to the Abbot, Sister?"

"The abbot is not here. He was expelled by the Egyptians. You must see the superior, Brother Gerard."

Adele poked Ramiro in the back. "I'm not staying here by myself," she whispered.

He ignored her. "Thank you, Sister. And where will I find Brother Gerard?"

She pointed. "Go through that door - but no women," she said as Adele began to follow him. "You can wait with me, my dear. Come inside."

Ramiro climbed the low, stone steps and opened a black, wooden door. The hallway was empty and quiet. "Hello. Anyone here?"

A monk came out of a nearby doorway. He wore a black habit and his hair was cut in a tonsure, but days of rubble grew around it. "Please, come in," he said, rolling an arm. "What brings you to the hospice?"

The sight of a Benedictine monk sent Ramiro's thoughts racing back to Cluny and, in an odd way, filled him with a renewed determination to complete his mission. But he also felt some embarrassment, dressed as he was with a full head of hair and a beard. And he could not help feeling some shame that he had a wife. So he hesitated.

"Sayyid?" asked the monk after a long silence. "What troubles you?"

Ramiro emerged from his thoughts. "My apologies. I am Ramiro of Cluny. I was told to see Brother Gerard."

"He is busy in the infirmary. Is it important?"

"It is very important, Brother. I have come a long way and have a message for him."

"Very well," said the monk. "Go down to the end of the hall and turn left."

"How will I recognize him?"

"He's the bald one."

Ramiro heard the groans of pain long before he found the infirmary. Beds lined either side of the open room, interspersed with tall columns reaching to a high ceiling. Stained glass windows on one side added bright colors to the otherwise drab and dismal scene. Three monks tended to the patients, who were men of all ages. He soon saw the bald monk. He was not completely bald, a thin semicircle of hair stretched between his ears at the back. He had a prominent brow, a clean-shaven face and a distinct chin.

Ramiro approached him. "Brother Gerard?"

"Yes, I am he," he said, looking at him with a stern expression. "And who are you... and what are you doing in my infirmary?"

"I am Ramiro of Cluny, Brother. I apologize for disturbing your work, may God bless you for your devotion. But I come on an important errand."

"Do you?" he said, cleaning the stump of a severed leg. "Did you say you're from Cluny? Cluny in Burgundy?"

"Yes, Brother."

Gerard wrapped the wound in clean cotton before glancing again at Ramiro. "You don't look like a monk."

"But I am, Brother. The Abbot of Cluny ordered me here. I am out of habit only because of a difficult journey."

Gerard nodded as he left the bed and went to the next one. "Have you come to join us in God's work?"

Ramiro followed him. "I would be glad to help wherever I can, Brother."

"That is good," Gerard said in a matter-of-fact tone. "God knows we could use any help. Is that why you have come?"

"Well, no. I came to ask you if Abbot Hugh mentioned my name or if he said anything of my mission?"

Gerard looked up at him and smiled, almost laughed. "Your mission? No, I've never heard a word from Cluny - nor from the Pope for that matter. We've been asking for money and supplies for years, but it seems we have been abandoned." He stopped at the bed of a severely bruised young man who wore a cast of wooden slats about one leg. "Here," he gestured to Ramiro. "Help me lift him to the next bed."

"What happened to him?" Ramiro asked as he lifted the boy in his arms. The young lad groaned.

"He fell from his father's roof. Put him here. So tell me, Brother Ramiro, what is this mission of yours?"

"Abbot Hugh asked me to deliver a message to Patriarch Symeon."

"Well you are too late for that, he was exiled some time ago."

"So I have heard."

He motioned to a table. "Hand me those bandages. Do I dare ask what this message may be?"

Ramiro passed him a wad of cotton. "I'm really not sure. I was asked to deliver a cross to him."

Gerard frowned with a smile. "A cross? What is that all about?"

"The Abbot said it had something to do with uniting the Churches. I was hoping you would know more." He pulled out the ink drawing he had made in Abu Ghosh. "Unfortunately, it was stolen from me before I arrived. It looks like this. Have you seen it?"

Gerard lifted his head from his work and looked briefly at the drawing before turning back to his work. "No, it doesn't look familiar. As I said, no one spoke to me of it. How long ago was this?"

Ramiro felt his ears redden. "Nine years now."

"Nine years!" Gerard laughed. "You *are* late!" he laughed again. "I've only been here for five."

A loud moan came from one of the beds and Gerard moved to an old man with spiked gray hair who stared out from the covers, his eyes clouded by cataracts. "So where have you been all this time?"

"It has been a difficult journey," Ramiro said, not wanting to say much. "I was captured by the Turks and held at Antioch."

Gerard gave him a serious look. "Well, we can thank the soldiers of God for liberating the city and cleaning away the heathen. And the sooner these brave men take Jerusalem from these contemptible heathen, the better it will be for all of us. They treat us like slaves and hinder our good efforts."

"What of the massacre at Antioch?" Ramiro asked. "Does this not concern you?"

"Why should it? We are Christian."

"Yes, but I hear they killed Christians too."

Gerard nodded indifferently. "The Greeks, yes. But the French are of the same Church as us. It will indeed be a glorious day when they take Jerusalem."

Ramiro stared at the man, his simplistic view was deeply troubling. "Are not the Benedictines men of peace?"

"Yes, that's true, but what of Augustine's notion of a just war? Surely, this is what the Pope speaks of."

Ramiro was about to argue that Augustine's 'just war' was justified only in the defense of innocents and should be used only to restore the peace. But he thought it unwise to pursue the subject further, especially since the Pope himself had summoned this war.

"Perhaps you should see the Greek bishop," said Gerard, "... what's his name?"

"I believe you refer to Bishop Aliphas. I have an appointment with him on the morrow."

BISHOP ALIPHAS

Ramiro bowed low in the opulent reception room in the Palace of the Patriarch. "Bless, Your Grace."

"May the Lord bless you," Bishop Aliphas responded dryly as he raised his hand towards him.

Ramiro stooped to kiss his sacral ring.

Aliphas seemed impatient and distracted. "What did you say your name is?" he asked in a gruff voice.

"Ramiro of Cluny, Your Grace." He was a little surprised to see that Aliphas was an Arab. He had a thick shag of black hair and a black beard and looked ill at ease wrapped in his stiff, embroidered red cape, over which hung a rectangular scarf decorated with crosses.

"Please sit, Ramiro of Cluny."

"Thank you, Your Grace."

"Cluny?" he asked. "In the land of the Franj?"

"Why, yes, Your Grace."

"Are you Benedictine?"

"Yes, I am, but I do not wear my habit because I have been traveling through Muslim lands."

Aliphas nodded in understanding. "So you have come to work at the Latin monastery? In the hospital?"

"I may, but that was not the reason I was sent here."

"Then why have you sought an audience with me. I must ask you to be brief, I am a busy man."

Ramiro told the Bishop of his mission, how Abbot Hugh ordered him to Jerusalem with instructions to deliver to the Patriarch a certain cross which, he believed, contained some message for him, a message the Abbot deemed essential to the survival of Christendom. Alas, he said, the cross had been stolen by a Turk but he suspected it was somewhere in the city.

Aliphas looked at him with some skepticism. "That sounds a little preposterous," he said. "Are you sure it wasn't for some other reason you were sent here?"

"I swear in the name of God, Your Grace. If there is another reason, I do not know it." He had a sudden thought, remembering the letter he had given to the mufti, Ibrahim. "I sent a letter to the Patriarch in which I told him I am the legate of Abbot Hugh and that I was on my way with the cross. Did he mention this?"

"Not that I remember. Who delivered it?"

"A Muslim by the name of Ibrahim."

"Ibrahim? The Qadi?"

"Yes, that's right. He did mention he was appointed to the position of Qadi."

"How long ago was this?"

"A year to the month, Your Grace."

"Well, there are two things you should know. First of all, the Turks exiled the Patriarch and he fled to Cyprus at about that time, so the two may never have met. And secondly, the Qadi has gone missing. He either fled with the Turks or he's locked up - or he's dead."

"But why would they harm a Muslim scholar?"

"Do not forget, he is first a Sunni... and an important one. The Fatimids have already taken over all the mosques. Most of the Sunni clergy have fled."

"Is there any way to discover what happened to him?"

"You could ask the authorities... at your own risk. But why are you concerned about a Muslim?"

"Well... he was an acquaintance, that is all."

"So, do you still report to your Abbot?" asked Aliphas.

"Yes, Your Grace, whenever I can. But for long periods I could not. I was either held prisoner or had no way of sending a letter out. I resumed my reports after escaping Antioch but have yet to receive any reply. I am hoping Abbot Hugh will contact me here in Jerusalem."

The Bishop looked at him with a little pity. "Do you know why Patriarch Symeon was exiled by the Turks?"

"I have heard rumor, Your Grace."

"He was accused of treason... they say he plotted to facilitate the invading armies from Byzantium and the West. I dare say your Pope and perhaps even your Abbot were complicit in this affair. Now the Muslims fear the Christians in Jerusalem will revolt. Our activities are tightly controlled and we are watched by the askari, first by the Turks and now by the Egyptians."

Ramiro was not sure he understood. "You say the Abbot... the Abbot of Cluny was involved in this? How so?"

"Well, I am not entirely sure," said Aliphas. "But Pope Urban and the French armies seem to be well informed about the lay of the land and the military capabilities of the Turks and the Arabs. Rumor has it that much of this information came directly from the Abbey of Cluny. How? We do not know."

Military capabilities? Ramiro flushed. The Abbey? His mind raced. Can this be so?

"What's wrong, Monk Ramiro?"

Ramiro waved a hand. "Oh, nothing, nothing, Your Grace. I'm a little tired that is all."

Aliphas continued. "So I do not know what to make of this cross of yours. If indeed, it contains a message, I would be glad to receive it on behalf of the Patriarch."

"Yes, Your Grace, of course. I will do my best to retrieve it."

"A word of warning, Ramiro. Tread lightly - and beware the Arabs."

IFTIKHAR

Governor Iftikhar, the new Egyptian governor of Jerusalem, leaned over a table in the Castle Al-Jalud, a fortress built in the north-west corner of the city, just north of the Jaffa Gate. It served as his headquarters and housed a large garrison of mamluks. He was studying plans to repair the city walls damaged in the battle with the Turks when one of his lieutenants, a burly Sudanese, came through the door and handed him several sheets of paper.

"What's this?" he asked in a loud voice.

"It is an order of execution, my Lord," said the lieutenant as he bowed.

Iftikhar sat cross-legged on a large green cushion. An expensive red turban topped his big head, a matching red tunic covered his gleaming mail vest and a long, green cloak draped across his broad shoulders. He was a handsome man with olive skin, a thin beard, high cheekbones and a small nose. But his beauty did not conceal the determined ferocity of his oval eyes. Iftikhar was an ambitious military man and always kept his sword hilt jutting from his cloak. "And who are these people?"

The lieutenant pointed to the list. "These are Turk soldiers, my Lord. The ones that eluded us after we took the city." He pointed to one name in particular. He's a bad one, Sahib. We caught him at the gates. Dressed as a merchant he was. But one of our wounded men identified him. He deserves to die, my Lord. He curses Fatimids in an unholy and foul manner. I cannot repeat what he says."

"And the others?" Iftikhar asked.

"Turk brigands and spies. They were caught hiding in the city."

Iftikhar read the names and their titles. "You have Sunni mullahs on your list. Do you think this wise?"

"Yes, Sahib, they plot against us. And we have returned all mosques to the True Faith as you instructed."

Iftikhar nodded. "That is good, but you will not harm the mullahs. They may be Sunni, but they are Muslim. And, as you know, this is the end of Ramadan and first day of Shawwal, a time to show forgiveness and mercy. We will take their names off the list and send them packing to Damascus instead."

"But, Sahib," said the lieutenant pointing to another name. "This one is a spy and an agitator. He was the Qadi."

"Which one? This Ibrahim?"

"Yes, my Lord. He plots with the Christians against us."

"How do you know that?"

"We have confessions from the others, my Lord. They saw him with the Christian priest, the patriarch. Even his own kind view him with suspicion."

Iftikhar pressed his lips tight. "You may be right, Lieutenant. I will think on this. But leave him in the dungeon for now."

"Your wish is my command, Sahib." He bowed. "And what of the Christians, can we trust them?"

Iftikhar paused for a moment before he replied. "No, we cannot."

"We should drive them from the city."

Iftikhar frowned, thinking about the great loss of revenues this would entail. The Christian merchants were rich and paid steep taxes, and the poll tax brought in more. "No," he said. "We will let them stay for now."

"But Sahib, we hear the Christians in the north rebelled and allied themselves with the barbarians who took Antioch."

"I know, Lieutenant, but only a few Christians here present any real threat," he said as he recalled a letter sent to him by his master, the Vizier Al-Afdal. "The western barbarians are the ones to worry about. Christian fanatics, I hear. Call themselves Franj." He waved a finger at the lieutenant. "They are the ones we must fear the most. Our Great Vizier offered them half of Syria if they would cede control of Palestine to us. But they scorned his offer."

"They are deluded, Sahib. They cannot defeat our Vizier, may Allah keep him. His great army will destroy them all. We will stop them."

"There may be no need for us to stop them," said Iftikhar. "Allah has cursed them. Praise be to the Most High God, the heathen are stalled in Antioch and have fallen to disease."

"Yes, my Lord, they are weak."

"That is good. By the will of Allah, they will all die there." He reached for a pen, crossed out the names of the Sunni mullahs and signed death warrants for the rest.

• • • • •

"So what does all this mean?" Adele asked before she picked up her glass of orange juice. "Does Bishop Aliphas know anything about the cross?"

"Apparently not," said Ramiro. "I admit, I am confused." He took a sip of red wine and looked around the restaurant patio, there were few customers today. "Although I must say I am beginning to doubt there is any meaning to the cross. I hate to think I have been unwittingly used as a spy for the Abbot. I find that even more difficult to believe."

"Why is that?" she challenged. "It seems the Pope himself organizes armies."

He groaned and shook his head with incredulity. "Perhaps you are right, my love. Can I be so naïve? Now I hesitate to send another report to Abbot Hugh. But he should at least know that I'm in Jerusalem. At least here I will be in a position to receive correspondence from him. I'll ask him what I should do." He took a bite of his meal. "And I will send another letter to Brother Aldebert. I promised I would write as soon as I arrived. He must be back at Cluny by now... but just in case he gets any foolish notion about coming to Jerusalem, I will let him know it is not safe."

"Brother Aldebert," she said. "I barely remember him."

"I'm sure he will be very happy to hear I've finally arrived in Jerusalem. I hope he is in good health."

"Do you think he'll come?"

"No, no, he would need permission from Abbot Hugh, and that is unlikely." He wondered if he would ever see him again. And what would he say to him? What would Aldebert think to see him dressed like this, his head unshaved? Perhaps I should take up the habit once again. And what will he say when he learns I'm married? I will be disgraced, I vowed to forsake the world. He glanced at Adele.

"So, what are you going to do about the mufti, Ibrahim?" she asked.

"I'm not sure yet. I must be tactful." He thought fondly of Ibrahim, who had spent so much time petitioning Yaghi Siyan on his behalf. He wanted to help.

The noise in the markets got louder and louder. An excited crowd began to pass by the restaurant doors, all clucking like hens to the henhouse.

"What's all the commotion about?" he asked.

"Looks like something's happening near the Temple Mount. Let's have a look."

"But I haven't finished my wine."

"You've had enough wine, and the tavern holds more. Come on."

He emptied his cup and rose from the table, wiping his face with his kerchief. They joined the flow of the crowd as it moved east to a square near the Al-Marwani Mosque.

"What's happening?" Ramiro asked a stranger.

"It's an execution," the man said. "Enemies of Iftikhar are about to lose their heads."

Ramiro hesitated. He pulled on Adele's arm and put his mouth to her ear. "This is grotesque. I don't want to see an execution."

Adele pulled back. "Come on, I just want a quick look," she said with a hint of macabre fascination.

They jostled for position, eventually making their way to the edge of the square where a regiment of Iftikhar's askari stood watch over six battered and bloodied men who knelt on the flagstones, their hands tied behind their backs and tied again to their ankles, their hair sheared short to allow the executioner a clean cut with his heavy blade. They all bowed their heads in resignation.

All but one, who held his head up, bleeding and bruised. Red slashes from the jailer's whip crisscrossed his weathered face and blood oozed from his scarred nose. He cursed aloud in a deep, gravel voice. "Damn you all to hell! Cursed Shia! I curse your mothers and your sons! Sons of whores!"

Ramiro stared in shock. Gone were the long braids... but the voice... the voice was unmistakable. "It's Khuda!" he shouted before slapping a hand to his mouth.

Khuda had made the fatal mistake of joining forces with the Turks of Jerusalem. He surrendered with many others and may have been released. But he had the misfortune of being recognized by a former Egyptian soldier with only one leg, the same man he had viciously attacked on the road to Jerusalem.

Khuda writhed from the searing pain in his shattered knee - but he heard his name. And the voice... it was a voice he knew. He stopped cursing and, in a long, slow motion, scanned the gathering crowd with a black-hearted scowl. He saw them. It was them! The stinking, thieving kuffar!

Ramiro shivered as he caught Khuda's cold, piercing glare. The Turk's face reddened, clenched in a terrifying snarl. Never before had Ramiro seen such a look of raw hatred.

"It's you!" Khuda shouted in an explosion of rage. He tried to get to his feet. "You! It's you... you son of shit! The Devil foks your mother!"

The crowd gasped at his profanity. Two soldiers rushed in, clubbing him to his knees before holding his arms out. And before Khuda could utter another vile blasphemy, the big executioner swung his heavy broadsword down hard, severing his head with a single blow.

Blood spurted from the stump of his neck and his body slumped to the flagstones. His head flew forward, leaving a bloodied trail in its wake. And, in what seemed like a last defiant act, it tumbled slowly across the flagstones, rolling toward the crowd, where it rocked and shuddered to a stop – right at Adele's feet. Khuda's narrow, empty eyes glared up at her, his scowl frozen in death.

She screamed. The crowd laughed.

• • • • •

Much to Adele's relief, Ramiro abandoned any thought of staying at the monastery and instead, they rented a small room from the church. It was pleasant enough and had a view of David Street, which stretched from Jaffa Gate to the Dome of the Rock.

"He was a bastard!" she crowed over dinner.

"Good gracious, Adele," he sighed. "There's no need to speak like that. He was a thief, I'll admit. But remember that we took his bag of money and he believed we were thieves too."

"I don't care," she said curtly. "He killed my child. I'm glad he's dead. It was like living in a nightmare."

Ramiro nodded gently. He said no more of it.

She tossed her hair over her shoulders. "At least we can be fairly certain of one thing," she said.

"What's that?" he asked as he scooped a spoonful of fruit.

She put both elbows on the table and laced her hands together. "That your precious cross is somewhere in Jerusalem."

Ramiro lifted his head and stared long into her eyes. "Precious cross? What do you mean by that, Adele? Do you mock me?"

Adele noticed an odd flash in his dark eyes and felt a chill. She flinched. "Forgive me," she said, reaching for his hand.

AN OLD FRIEND

"Have you seen a cross that looks like this?" Ramiro held up the ink drawing of his golden cross.

The jeweler shook his head as he took Ramiro by the arm. "No, no, but look at these," he said. "Are they not beautiful?" he picked up an embellished cross. "I will make you a very good deal on this one. It is the will of God. You look like a good Christian to me."

Ramiro shook his head and forced himself away. "No, thank you, I am looking for this particular cross."

The jeweler clicked his tongue and waved a hand in dismissal.

Ramiro's reception was much the same at the other jewelers, and there were many of them. Then he tried every other shop, even the barbers. And there were many of these. But no one had seen his cross. So he returned home, taking a route that led him past the Church of the Holy Sepulcher. On the other side of the street, was the Mosque of Umar, built in commemoration of the Caliph who had captured Jerusalem many years ago.

The mosque looked small compared to the monastery, but it was always busy. Outside the door, a skinny old man stooped, sweeping the steps with a short-handled broom. The scene reminded him of Ibrahim. He walked over.

• • • • •

"Poor Ibrahim," Ramiro said. "The old man at the mosque said they keep him in the dungeon of Castle Al-Jalud. I'd like very much to hear his tale."

Adele wagged her finger at him. "Now don't get into more trouble. God knows we've had our share. Next thing, *you'll* be the one in that dungeon. Forget it! Let's just find the cross!"

He lifted his chest before letting out a long, slow sigh. "I've tried all the jewelers, even those of the Hebrews and Muslims, who thought I was completely mad, of course. Perhaps I am mad."

"Did you try the other churches?"

"Well... no. How would they get the cross?"

"I don't know, but what else can you do?"

"I suppose."

• • • • •

With little warning, the overcast skies burst in an autumn downpour, pelting Ramiro in a shower of heavy beads. He rushed into the foyer of the Church of Saint John the Baptist, shaking the rainwater from his cloak. A priest came out from an anteroom.

"Have you come for Matins?" he asked.

"Uh, no Father. I seek your help. I am looking for a particular cross."

"A cross?"

"Yes," said Ramiro as he reached into his pouch and brought out his drawing. "Have you seen this cross?" he asked.

The man looked at the drawing, turning it in his hands. Then he smiled.

"You have seen it!" Ramiro almost shouted.

The man frowned at him. "I have not. But it is unlikely you will find it in this part of the city."

"Why? What do you mean?"

"Your cross has an Armenian design. Try looking in the Armenian quarter."

• • • • •

The downpour stopped as quickly as it started and the sun began to peep through thinning clouds. Rainwater steamed on the warm pavement as Ramiro twisted his way south along Armenian Street, heading toward the southern walls and the Zion Gate. He stopped when he came to the Monastery of Saint James.

The monastery's gray walls reached almost to the street. A brass knocker in the shape of a cross hung from one of its iron doors. He took hold of it and banged twice. The resounding clang was louder than he expected and the door seemed to reverberate. A slat clacked open and he could see two eyes glaring back at him, two blue eyes.

"What can I do for you?" asked a smooth voice.

"I come in search of a cross," Ramiro answered.

"A cross?"

"Yes. Of a special design. If you let me come in, I will show you my drawing."

There was no reply. The eyes continued to stare at him.

"If you could help me please," Ramiro pleaded. "I just want to know if you have seen it."

The voice behind the door stuttered and choked. "Ma... Master? Master Ramiro? Is it you?"

Ramiro drew back at the man's words. He looked closely into those blue eyes. "Yes, I am Ramiro of Cluny. Who are you?"

The latch of the door slammed back with a loud clank and the door swung open, squealing on its dry hinges. A young man dressed in a full-length, black tunic stood in the foyer. Dark brown hair hung to his shoulders, draping beside blue eyes and a small nose. His attractive face was clean-shaven. Ramiro stared at him. "Jameel? Jameel is that you?"

"Yes, yes, Master Ramiro. Praise be to God Almighty! I thought I would never see you again." He rushed forward to embrace him.

"Blessed saints!" Ramiro shouted with a smile, returning his embrace awkwardly. "How you have grown since I last saw you. You are a man now."

"Come in, Master, come in. You must tell me what happened at Antioch. Did Yaghi Siyan capture you? How did you get here?"

Ramiro sat down and outlined his story as the young man busied himself serving sage tea and pastries in the anteroom. "And what did you do when you left Antioch? Did you travel with Tatran?"

"No, Master. Tatran rode right past me on that fateful day, chased by a regiment of askari. I have never seen him since. I waited for a year in Latakia, hoping you would come. Then I decided to go to Jerusalem. You always talked of Jerusalem and I thought perhaps you had made it safely by some other route. I have been here ever since."

"What do you do here?" Ramiro asked as he looked around. "Isn't this an Armenian monastery?"

"And Maronite. It's shared. Some are monks, others priests. I'm not a monk. They pay me to take care of the place and to keep unwanted visitors at bay. We are not well liked by the Muslims. They say the Maronites give them too much trouble in Lebanon - and now they blame Armenians for the fall of Antioch." He sat down. "And what of that red-haired woman, Master? What happened to her?"

"She's here too, Jameel. Her name's Adele. I married her."

Jameel let out a long, low whistle. "You married her? It must be God's will, Master, after all the trouble you went through to rescue her."

"Well," Ramiro replied demurely, "… I hardly rescued her. It was only by the fickleness of fate that we escaped."

"It was God's will, Master. Praise the Lord."

"And what of you, Jameel? Have you found a wife?"

A broad smile crossed his face. "Yes, and I have a son," he said proudly. "And maybe another on the way."

Ramiro felt an unexpected twinge of envy but leaned over and gave him a slap on the shoulder. "Congratulations! You will make a good father."

"You must come to visit, Master Ramiro. You and your wife. Come tonight. My wife, Layla, is an excellent cook."

Ramiro smiled. "We would like that very much Jameel, thank you."

"So what happened to your cross, Master?"

"Ah, yes." He pulled out his drawing. "It is a long story and I will tell you all about it when we meet tonight. In short, it was stolen by a Turk. I'm sure he sold it here in Jerusalem." He unfolded the drawing. "I know it's been some time since you've seen it. Hopefully, this will refresh your memory. A man at the Church of Saint John said the design was Armenian and sent me this way."

"Oh yes, I remember it," Jameel said as he glanced at the drawing. "It is very beautiful. And yes, I remember the design. Do you have any idea where it is?"

"Not yet."

Jameel rubbed his chin. "Hmm. Perhaps you should visit the jewelers. They have many crosses like this."

"I'm sure I've been to every jeweler in Jerusalem. I had no idea there were so many."

"Try the Armenian jewelers again," said Jameel. "One of them must have it."

MADTEOS

Madteos looked up at the customer in front of him. He glanced into Ramiro's dark eyes and felt himself shudder. "What can I do for you?"

Ramiro showed him the drawing. "Greetings, God bless you. I am looking for this cross. It is made of gold and silver. Have you seen it?"

"I remember you," said Madteos. "I've already told you I haven't seen it."

"Please, Sayyid, look again."

Madteos looked at the drawing. At first, he held it at arm's length, then he drew it closer and closer to his long nose. He pursed his lips and shook his head before glancing at Ramiro suspiciously. "Who are you?"

"Ramiro of Cluny, a land far to the west."

Madteos shook his head again. "Never heard of it. What do you want with this cross?"

"A cross like this was stolen from me some weeks ago. Stolen by a Turk."

Madteos leaned forward and pretended to study the drawing again.

Ramiro saw the nervousness in his eyes. "Are you sure you haven't seen it?"

"No, no," he said with annoyance. "I've told you – I've never seen it." He handed the drawing back to Ramiro.

"I see you have many crosses. May I look?"

"You can look all you want. It's not here."

Ramiro scanned the collection slowly. He kept one eye on the jeweler and pointed to a cross with a similar design. "It looks like this one," he said, jogging his finger. "But it has a center of wood, olivewood, actually."

Madteos pretended to ignore him. "Doesn't sound familiar," he muttered.

"I would be willing to pay handsomely for its return."

Madteos lifted his head from his work and turned to face him. "Maybe I can find a cross like that," he said with feigned disinterest. "But if it is made of gold and silver, it could be very expensive."

"How expensive?" Ramiro asked with a look of scorn.

Madteos opened his stained, dry hands and tilted his head. "Perhaps ten dinar," he said.

"Ten dinar?"

Madteos nodded.

"You jest with me. The cross I speak of does not contain that much gold. Much less, in fact. I will give you five dinar. That is more than it is worth." He paused and wondered how he could possibly obtain five dinar.

Madteos spat on the ground and waved an arm in dismissal. "Others will pay more," he said with a sneer.

Ramiro leaned over his desk, looking straight into his eyes. "The cross is mine, and I want it back. You know it's stolen." He raised his voice. "Perhaps I should report you to the authorities!"

Ramiro's loud retort caught the attention of two young men sitting at the back of the shop. They were cousins of Madteos, hired to protect him after Khuda had thrown him into the wall. The men rose from their cushions and approached in a threatening manner.

Madteos became emboldened by their presence and jumped from his chair. "I told you I haven't seen it! Why do you continue to waste my time?" His cousins moved forward aggressively.

Ramiro backed away. "My apologies, Sayyid. God's peace be upon you."

• • • • •

The markets closed and Madteos collected his wares in two large cases before he locked up. He walked home at a brisk pace while his two cousins followed. When he reached his house, he brought out an iron key to unlock a thick wooden door. He picked up his cases, entered quickly, and slammed it shut. His cousins went home.

"Madteos? Is that you?" asked a plump woman carrying a lamp.

"Of course it's me, stupid woman! Who else could open the door?"

She forced a smile. "Would you like some tea, my husband?"

"Not now, not now." He moved the cases to an inside door. The keys jingled in his hand. "Give me the lamp." He snatched it from her and held its dim light to the keys, picking one from the ring before turning back to the inside door. His hands shook as he turned it in the lock. Once open, he pulled the cases in and relocked it before working his way to a dark corner of the room. He knelt to the floor and pulled at a strap. A large, square tile at the base of the wall swung open to reveal a hole no wider than a man's forearm. He lifted the lamp to the opening. There, inside, was his long, rectangular strongbox, made of iron and sealed tight with two locks. He dragged it out and opened it.

Right on top of his hoard of gold and silver was a small bundle wrapped in oilcloth. He untied the string and unfolded it slowly. The cross glowed in the lamp light. He picked it up as if it were a frail flower. It is so beautiful, he thought, ...even if it is a little scraped. The workmanship, the engravings - a masterpiece! But his delight soon turned to a nagging anxiety when he recalled his encounter with Ramiro. What am I going to do about that damned foreigner! May God curse him!

• • • • •

"What about the cross?" Adele asked as she swept the floor. "Any luck?"

"As a matter of fact, yes." He told her about his encounter with Madteos. "I know he has it, he looked as guilty as a sinner at confession." He offered her a bowl of raisins but she rushed off to the kitchen. "And he was very defensive," he said loudly as he gazed out the small window. "But I looked around and I didn't see it there."

"How will we get it back?" she cried out. "We don't have ten dinar. Do you think Bishop Aliphas will give you the money?"

"I asked him already but he said it was too much. I believe the Church is short of cash with all this trouble brewing. And Aliphas doubts the importance of the cross."

"Blood in hell!" she cursed. "So how are we going to get it?"

Ramiro frowned. "I'm not sure. But it was good to see Jameel alive and well. You must remember him from Antioch. He was the boy who dressed as a eunuch at the palace - to give you my message. " He stroked his short beard. "About four years ago, I guess."

"I remember the incident, Ramiro," she said. "And how could I forget that dreadful place? But I doubt I would recognize him."

"Well, you'll have your chance tonight. We've been invited for supper."

She rushed out of the kitchen, wiping her hands on her apron. "Tonight?"

"Yes. What's wrong?"

"Oh dear, Ramiro. I'm a mess," she fretted, pulling back her long hair with both hands. "I'll have to wash and dress."

"Not to worry, you have time."

When she came back into the room, she had on her favorite yellow tunic and still fiddled with her hair. "Ramiro...," she said, "you know I love you." She walked over and took his hand. "But time is passing so fast. Let's go home. Let's forget all this and go back to France. Don't you miss it?"

He looked down, clenching his jaw.

She squeezed his hand. "I'm twenty-seven, Ramiro. Soon I'll be an old woman. God willing, we can still have another child."

He felt his temper flare but soon subdued it, his shoulders finally sagging in resignation. "Perhaps you're right," he said with some melancholy. "I see no way of fulfilling my mission now. In fact, I really don't know what my mission is anymore." He fell silent for a long moment before squeezing her hand gently. "Nonetheless," he said "... you must give me a little more time."

• • • • •

Jameel's wife, Layla, was a slight woman of Arab descent who covered her long, black hair with a patterned shawl. Like her husband, she had fine facial features and beautiful eyes. She was clearly pregnant beneath her loose tunic and her swaddling son squirmed in her arms. "Do you mind holding him while I make the hummus?" she asked Adele.

Adele reached out gingerly. "No, not at all, Layla." She took the child in her arms and cradled it on her knees, looking at him adoringly, caressing his small fingers and stroking his thin hair. But her faint smile soon faded to a look of sorrow. She clenched her teeth hard and tried to fight back a well of tears, but a single drop managed to trickle down her cheek. She brushed it away as quickly as she could.

Ramiro watched her, knowing how she felt. He felt the same empty pain and it was all he could do not to weep with her. He turned to Jameel. "You... you are a fortunate man, Jameel. I thank God you have done well. Do you plan to stay in Jerusalem?"

"We would like to stay, Master. But we are worried about the barbarian army. They say it's heading this way."

"Well, if they do get here, Jameel, you and Layla would be wise to flee. If but for a while."

"Will you stay, Master?"

"I will stay long enough to fulfill my promises, God willing. Hopefully, I can eventually retrieve the cross from Madteos and give it to Bishop Aliphas."

"What will you do in the meantime?"

"That's a good question. I suppose I can volunteer some time at the hospice, and I thought about establishing myself as a scribe."

"A good idea, Master. Jerusalem needs knowledgeable scribes like you."

A MIRACLE

"Where are we going," Adele asked, rushing to keep up.

"To the Jewish quarter," said Ramiro. "To the paper merchant. They say he has the finest paper - made in Baghdad." He walked in long strides. "I will need good paper if I'm to set up business."

Adele caught up to him. "We have little money left," she reminded him. "So just get what you need to start."

"I know, I know," he said with irritation. "But there are certain things I must have if we are to make any money at all."

"I suppose," she said, not wanting to push the matter.

The Dome of the Rock grew large as they made their way to the Western Wall. He pointed. "The place should be down this street. Come on, it's getting late."

"Don't you think it odd, Ramiro, that the streets are so quiet today?"

He looked around at the empty storefronts. "You're right, everything's closed. There's hardly a soul out."

"Except one," she said, pointing to an old beggar huddled in a corner of a gray building.

Ramiro walked over to him. "Peace be upon you, Sayyid."

The grizzled beggar returned a toothless smile and waved the stub of a malformed arm. "And to you," he said in a raspy voice. "Have you got a coin for an old man?"

Ramiro dug into his purse and handed him a few fals. "Tell me, why are the shops closed today?"

The man took the coins and looked askance at him, his small eyes clouded with cataracts. "You don't know what day it is?"

"Excuse me," Ramiro said as patiently as he could, "but I am new here."

"It's Yom Kippur," said the beggar. "All the men have gone to the synagogue."

Ramiro nodded in understanding. He thanked the man and turned away.

"What's Yom Kippur?" Adele asked when they walked away.

"It's a day of atonement for the Hebrews. It's a day when they seek forgiveness for wrongs against God and man." He began to walk away. "I should have known better but I've been too busy with other things."

"Ramiro wait! Let's walk around a little before we go home."

"Now? It's almost dark."

"But look at the moon. It's full and will soon be bright. And I want to see the Western Wall while we're here. It won't take long." She pulled at his sleeve.

The Western Wall, also known as the Wailing Wall, was the only section of the Second Temple not destroyed by the Romans many centuries before. The plaza in front of the wall was eerily vacant. Adele looked up and down, studying the stark section of gray wall constructed of enormous blocks of limestone that rose up the height of ten men. In the background, the roof of the Dome of the Rock glowed softly in the last rays of the setting sun.

The silence broke with the sounds of men yelling in the distance. Adele turned her head. "What's that?"

He turned in the same direction. "Sounds like it's coming from the synagogue."

"Let's have a look," she said, walking away.

"Careful, Adele," he warned, "women are not allowed anywhere on the synagogue precinct, especially gentile women." But she did not reply and continued on her way. Ramiro hurried to her side.

No sooner had the synagogue come into view when a great hubbub erupted on its steps. Bearded men crowded around one spot, many dressed in fine, white coats. Ramiro hurried forward while Adele held back.

"He's dead!" a man wailed. "He's dead!" Groans and cries of grief followed.

Ramiro stood beside the low steps, peering through the small crowd of men. He glimpsed a man lying flat on his back. His hair and beard were almost white and he was dressed in the robe of a rabbi. The huddle of men soon dispersed, leaving the body in full view. "What happened?" he asked one of them.

The man scowled at him. "It is no business of a gentile," he said with an air of intimidation. "He collapsed coming out of the synagogue."

"Is he dead?"

"Of course he's dead. Would we say he is dead if he were not?"

"Excuse me, Sayyid, I mean no offense, but I am a physician. Perhaps I can help."

"You are a gentile and unclean," the man said with contempt. "We cannot permit it. We have our own physicians."

Ramiro inched closer to the dead rabbi and stared at his face. It was hard and chiseled, and hairy eyebrows grew wildly over a strong brow. It was a face of strength and sorrow, but he looked at peace. Ramiro was about to turn away when he thought he saw the flicker of an eyelid. Or was it the torchlight?

"Move away!" one of the men shouted at him.

Ramiro did not hear. He watched the rabbi's face intently. There it was again. The flicker of an eyelid.

"He's alive!" Ramiro shouted. "He needs to breathe!"

"Move away you idiot!" the man shouted again.

But he paid no heed to the man's words. Instead, he jumped forward and spread his knees across the rabbi's torso. He put his arms under his midriff and lifted. He could hear a slight draft of breath pass through the rabbi's mouth. Then he let him down and lifted again, and again.

The Jewish men did nothing at first, completely flabbergasted at Ramiro's effrontery and sacrilege. But soon, in an indignant rage, they took hold of him and forcibly dragged him off the rabbi. They beat him with their fists and threw him from the steps. He tumbled onto the road.

It was just then that the old rabbi took a long gasping breath.

"He lives!" one shouted. "He lives!"

· · · · ·

"What are you doing?" Adele asked as she watched Ramiro tie a long rope around a small pillar in the bedroom.

"I'm making an escape route. If necessary, I'll throw the rope out the window and scale down to the street below."

She frowned. "Is it safe?"

"I think so. We're only on the second story."

She moved to the window and looked down. "And is it really necessary?"

He waved his hands in frustration. "Of course it is! I can't get out the door without being thronged by a crowd. They all want to touch me. They rend my garments. They impede my path. They bring their sick to me for healing. What nonsense! Brother Gerard says hundreds more await me at the hospice, people of all faiths."

"You have become very popular," she tried to restrain a smile but could not. "They believe you can raise the dead."

"Humph! But Rabbi Moshe wasn't dead - although he was close to it."

"What do you think was wrong with him?"

"He's old. He probably just fainted from lack of food and drink. Yom Kippur is a fasting period."

Adele tossed her hair over one shoulder. "Well, the word has spread to the Christians and Muslims. You've become a holy man of Jerusalem."

Ramiro groaned. "I don't want all of this attention. I would simply like to retrieve my cross. Then we can go back to France."

A broad smile stretched across Adele's face, her eyes beamed. "Really? Do you mean it? Back to France!"

Ramiro nodded with a grin.

"Then we really *must* find the cross," she said with renewed enthusiasm. She reached across the table and held up a small stack of letters. "But what of all these invitations! What are we to do?"

· · · · ·

Rabbi Moshe had not fully recovered and was still confined to a chair, but he welcomed Ramiro with open arms and made him the guest of honor. The other men milling about him were much more kindly than they had been a few weeks before on the synagogue steps. They talked in length of the weather, the crops, and the markets before finally asking Ramiro more pointed questions.

"So what of these Greek mercenaries?" asked the Rabbi in a hoarse voice. "They seem to be trouble for everyone. You know these people do you not?"

"I know of them, Rabbi, but I am not one of them. They are intent to capture Jerusalem, although it has been many years now since they came."

"We are very worried about these armies. We have heard of the massacres of Hebrews in the Western countries, and now at Antioch - the massacre of a whole city."

"It is a terrible, terrible thing Rabbi," said Ramiro in condolence. "If they do approach Jerusalem, I would suggest taking shelter elsewhere."

"Do you think that possible?" One of the men asked. "I hear they suffer from the plague and starvation. And their numbers shrink by the year."

"I really do not know," Ramiro conceded. "It is in the hands of God."

• • • • •

Adele threw herself on a row of cushions. "I'm already worn out with these festivities. But what a nice group of people! Look at all these gifts! I don't even know what some of them are."

Ramiro smiled. "I thought you would enjoy it."

"What are we doing tomorrow night?" she asked, becoming somewhat exasperated by the attention.

Ramiro watched her as she lay down. How he loved this woman, a love he could never explain with words, even to himself. Sometimes, she was as obstinate as an old mule and impossible to reason... and what a temper! Other times, she was a complete angel and he could literally feel her love radiate over him like a warm sun. But either way, he adored her. Every move she made was a dance to his eyes. He smiled again. "All this socializing has been good for you, Adele. And your Arabic is improving nicely." He picked up another letter from his desk. "Well, it seems Bishop Aliphas has invited us to a celebration of the birth of Mary. The actual name of the event is 'The Nativity of Our Most Holy Lady, Mother of God and Ever Virgin Mary' - quite a mouthful."

"I've never heard of it," she said.

"That's because you're from the West. The ideas embodied in the celebration do not agree with Catholic thinking."

"Why not?"

"Well, on one point, they do not agree that Mary transmitted original sin but rather that she was free of sin by the Grace of God."

Adele was quiet for a moment. "I like that idea," she said. "Maybe that's why the Greeks treat their women better. What do you think?"

"I'm not sure anymore. The older I get, the less sure I am about anything... except God's presence." He stood up and stretched. "Nonetheless, it is presumed to be a happy occasion and we should take part."

Adele sat up suddenly. "Ramiro," she said with some frustration, "... we simply must find the cross."

Ramiro slumped into his chair. "I agree. But we also need to make some money. I get paid nothing at the hospice, despite all my labors. Fortunately, Jameel was kind enough to find us a shop to rent near that jeweler, Madteos, so we can keep an eye on him. And Rabbi Moshe has promised to help with any supplies we may need."

ANTIOCH

NOVEMBER 1098

Drugo the Red was richer. Count Robert's men were among the first to storm the walls of Antioch and the first to kill and plunder. The mansion Drugo occupied in Antioch belonged to a prominent Muslim family, one he had personally slaughtered. The building was once beautifully decorated inside and out. But now it was ravaged. Magnificent sprawling gardens lay in ruins after frenzied searches for buried treasure. Inside, smashed furniture and everyday garbage littered the hallways, anything of value stripped away.

Drugo occupied a single room in which he stashed his hoard. He sat on one of the few remaining chairs, hunching his cold hands over a burning brazier. "Find some more wood or some charcoal," he said to Otto. "This will go out soon."

Otto of Bremen and Arles of Ghent, along with one hundred and fifty-six others, were all that was left of Drugo's original company of five hundred. Over one hundred were dead by the time they defeated the Patzinaks with King Alexios at Roussa. And, after joining Robert of Flanders in the Holy Crusade, Fulk succumbed to the heat of the Salt Desert, as did a score of others. More died at the Battle of Dorylaeum and some died of starvation during the long siege of Antioch. Now, after the final conquest, typhus ravaged the remainder.

"There's not much left, Sir Drugo. And there's no one to collect more." Otto looked frail and ill. The onset of typhus had drained him. But he lived.

"Blood of Christ!" Drugo shouted, slamming a fist onto the table. "Is there nothing to eat? There must be something left. Check the cellars."

"I've looked, Sir. There's nothing left. There's no food left in the city. There's nothing for miles around."

Antioch was nearly deserted. Its citizens were dead and the bustling life of the city, along with its commerce, died with them.

"God help us!" Drugo shouted again. "I thought the Greeks were going to send supplies."

"Apparently, the Greek King is angry because we haven't handed the city to him as promised."

"Nor should we! God damn him! We are the ones who died in its taking!" He rubbed his hands over the glowing embers. "Thank the good Lord that Count Robert rides to Maarat tomorrow. He plans to lay siege and we'll have a chance to gain more booty and get some food."

An obscene grin crossed Otto's face. "And a chance to kill more of those Godless pagans. God curse their filthy hides!"

MAARAT

Once again, the Crusaders gathered en masse outside the walls of Maarat An-Numan, led by Bohemond and Raymond. Their previous defeat here some four months ago was still fresh in their minds and they were determined to set things right. Now emboldened by their success at Antioch, they set out to seize more of Syria – and to seek their revenge.

The Turks and Arabs of Maarat greeted them with loud curses, screaming obscenities and taunts from the battlements. The Christians ignored them, setting up their tents just out of arrow range. But then the Turks did something that really caught their attention. In plain view, they hung makeshift crosses from the top of the walls – and these they began to abuse by smashing some with hammers and setting fire to others. Then, in a bit of animated theatre, one of them climbed up on a castellation and began to piss, directing his stream over one of the crosses.

The Christians went wild, screaming their own curses, the most vile they could imagine. The shrill voice of the mystic, Peter Bartholomew, rose above them all. "You will burn in hell! Foking pagans!" he screamed while jabbing the Holy Lance in the air. "I will kill you with my bare hands!"

• • • • •

Inside Maarat, the people worked furiously to resist the siege. Salim the physician and other hospital staff set up emergency beds, preparing to tend the wounded. Even Dawud the Silk Merchant helped to carry bundles of arrows from the armory to the battlements or to collect stones and bricks, anything they could throw down on the attackers. The Qadi watched from the citadel, barking orders to his lieutenants, who rushed back and forth coordinating efforts. This foreign army was much larger than the last one, too large for him to attack head-on as he did before. In worry, he sent a fast messenger to Aleppo to plead for Ridwan's assistance, but Ridwan had lost courage after his last defeat. They were alone.

• • • • •

The Crusaders worked at a mad pace, cutting trees from the closest woods to make longer, sturdier ladders as well as a formidable siege tower. Sappers rushed out to undermine the walls by chipping away the mortar of lower stones. The men of Maarat fought back furiously by hurling everything they had at them; stones, arrows, fire, lime and even beehives.

It took ten days to finish the tower. They built it higher than the walls of the city, moving it on four wheels of solid wood. Inside the tower, a hundred fighting men waited. Drugo, Arles and fifteen other men held on to the top story as it bumped and swayed along the rough ground. An arsenal of stones and spears lay beside them. As they advanced, one of the men blew a horn in loud, sharp blasts. Peter Bartholomew and the priests trailed behind, beseeching God in loud voices to defend his chosen people.

The Turks kept throwing all they had at the tower as it began to loom over the wall. Drugo took the advantage of height, grabbing stones with the others and hurling them down on the defenders, breaking their ranks. Then they threw out large grappling hooks to secure the battlements and dragged the tower tight to the wall. The tower door opened, slamming down.

Drugo was among the first to jump out. Arles was right behind him. Arrows peppered their ranks and men collapsed around them. They rushed at the Turks with their lances and the enemy fell back. But the Turks and every other Muslim in Maarat, driven by the fear of certain death, rushed at them again with desperate ferocity. Drugo and his men fell back in a frenzy of swordfight, some of them jumping from the walls in terror. But just as the Muslims began to gain the upper hand, the sappers below scored a success. A section of wall collapsed.

At the same time, the French overran an opposing wall amid heavy fighting and hand-to-hand combat. When the Muslims saw the Christians coming from two directions, and now pouring through the breach in the wall, they fell back in terror, retreating to the safety of fortified buildings. The Christians stormed over the walls, hooting and yelling – and the slaughter began.

• • • • •

Next morning, Bohemond left the smoking ruins and rotting corpses of Maarat to lead his men back to Antioch, fearing that King Alexios would take advantage of his departure by sending out a fleet of warships. Robert followed him, as did Godfrey, both abandoning the obsessive Raymond, whose arrogance they began to despise.

With bitter resignation, Raymond began to realize he would never wrest Antioch from Bohemond. So he turned his attentions once again to Jerusalem and gathered his men to march south alone. He was determined to be the glorious leader who would command the Holy Crusade to liberate Jerusalem from the shackles of unholy pagans.

He rode with an air of nobility, but deep inside he was worried. He was about to march into the unknown territory of an unknown enemy. And since his quarrelsome allies had abandoned him, his forces were perilously few. At most, he commanded a few hundred trained knights and about four thousand able men.

But his concerns were without warrant. When the Muslims heard that the invincible, barbarian cannibals were marching down on them, they abandoned whole countrysides in abject terror. The Emir of Shayzar, worried about his head, sent an embassy to the Franj, offering to send provisions and to sell them horses from the Shayzar market. Meanwhile, the Emir of Homs, also in a rush to save himself from the Christian scourge, sent Raymond horses and gold.

Raymond took advantage of the fear and moved on to the coast, where he besieged the fortress of Arqah in an effort to squeeze tribute from the Emir of Tripoli. He succeeded, and the Emir sent him fifteen thousand gold coins, horses, mules, and silk garments.

It did not take long for the news of Raymond's financial success to reach Antioch, where Bohemond and Godfrey heard about the amazing riches falling into his hands. And it did not take long for their greed and envy to overcome any animosity they harbored towards him. They set out to join his forces, now scattered around the Tripoli countryside. But when Bohemond reached Latakia, he heard that King Alexios had recaptured the Aegean coast and was approaching Cilicia with a fleet of war galleys. He soon abandoned the Holy Crusade and turned his knights back to Antioch.

Part Nine

YEAR 1099

~~~~~~~~~~~~~~~~~~~~~~~~~~~~~~~~~~~

JERUSALEM

JANUARY

Ramiro curled over his small desk, huddling in a shop he rented from the Monastery of Saint James on Armenian Street. A heavy cloak covered his shoulders and draped down to his wool leggings and fur-lined boots, keeping him warm in the cold, wet winter of Jerusalem. His shop was close to Madteos' and allowed him to keep an eye on the sly jeweler while offering his services as a scribe and translator.

Adele crouched at the back of the shop. She too, bundled herself in thick robes and kept busy with leatherwork, making quivers and bags as well as sheaths for sword and dagger, which she fronted to vendors in the market.

Their business flourished in a busy market. For the Christians, it was the last day of the Nativity Holidays and, for the Muslims, the week before the Prophet's birthday. Customers lined up for long waits in front of their door. But many had little use for Ramiro's services, they simply wanted to meet the miracle healer who had saved the life of Rabbi Moshe.

His desk straddled the front, where cushions and a chair awaited his clients. He was busy writing Arabic in a fast, clear script for a thin old man squatting on one of the cushions across from him. Ramiro listened carefully to all the man said and wrote it down verbatim. When the man finished talking, Ramiro dated the letter according to the Hijra calendar. It was the tenth day of Safar in the year 492. He took a burning candle and dropped a blob of wax at the end of the document before turning it around to face his frail customer, signaling for the man to step forward. He pointed to the end of the letter.

The old man stood uneasily, forming a fist with his right hand and pressing his ring into the warm wax. When all was finished, he took hold of Ramiro's hands in a firm grip and held fast for some time, as if his touch alone would bring him good fortune and good health.

Ramiro did not resist. He looked kindly into the old man's eyes and smiled. "Peace be upon you," he said gently.

Tears welled in the man's glassy eyes as he paid Ramiro for his services, all the time muttering Allah's blessings.

With a heavy sigh, Ramiro looked to the doorway for the next customer. He longed to lay down for a nap. He heard the muezzin's call to afternoon prayers sound from the minarets. The markets will close soon, he thought with relief.

Another customer began to enter his doorway when yells of outrage rang from the waiting line of patrons. The customer had hardly entered the store when another man, a soldier, barged in and forced him back with a rough arm, pushing him outside. The bulk of the man filled the doorway. He was Sudanese, a warrior of rank with weathered black skin and thick lips. A thin moustache and a thinner beard spread across his chiseled face, too thin to hide the pale scars that trailed across his cheeks like narrow lines of war paint. He stomped up to Ramiro's desk wearing a domed steel helmet and the coat of an Egyptian askari.

Ramiro almost blurted out something about bad manners but, with considerable effort, he stifled his words with a hard clench of his jaw and stood to greet the intruder politely. "Peace be with you. Please sit down. Would you like some water... juice?"

The man did not return a greeting. He looked down and hesitated a little before sitting awkwardly in the rough wooden chair. His chain link armor rustled and his sword clacked. He waved a thick hand in a curt manner. "No, I want nothing," he said in a deep, resonating voice.

Ramiro squirmed behind his desk, on which were neat piles of papers and envelopes held down by stone weights. Near at hand were inks of various colors and pens of varied shape. He put a piece of paper in front of him and looked up. The askari just stared at him.

"So, what can I do for you, Sayyid?" Ramiro asked.

"You are Christian?" asked the soldier, his wide nostrils flaring as he spoke.

Ramiro thought that was obvious, his iron cross hung about his neck in clear view. "Yes," he said with some apprehension. "So what can I do for you, Sayyid?"

The askari stared at him with narrowed eyes. "I hear you look for a Christian talisman... a golden cross," he spat the words.

Ramiro's trepidation vanished in hopeful elation. "Yes, Sayyid," he gleamed. "Do you know its whereabouts?"

The big man snorted in derision. "I know nothing of your diabolical cross – nor do I care." He leaned forward and glared at him. "There is something else that is of more interest to me."

Ramiro said nothing, his worries returned.

The askari smirked as if reading his fear. "I hear you speak the language of the barbarians from the West? The language of these heathen kuffar. Perhaps you are one of them?"

Ramiro could feel his heart beat furiously. "I... I know the language, Sayyid. But I am not one of them," he said, glossing the truth.

The askari reached into his cloak and pulled out a sheet of yellowed paper. He stood up and tossed it on the desk. "Tell me what this says!"

Obnoxious man! Ramiro thought as he picked it up. The first thing he noticed about the letter were the blood stains smeared across it. Carefully, he unfolded the page and looked over to the askari, forcing a thin smile before putting his head down to read. He expected to see Greek or Latin but this was different, the characters were Latin but the words were not. Then it became clear. Why! It's the script of Provençal. The language of Burgundy! He was stunned and glanced quickly up at the askari, who now towered over him, moving his hand from his belt to his sword hilt. "What does it say?" he asked even louder.

Ramiro studied the letter again and did not reply right away.

"What does it say, kafir! We know you understand this tongue. We know you are one of them! We have heard it from others. Translate it!"

Adele stopped what she was doing and looked up.

Ramiro felt a flash of dread. What does he mean by 'we'? He continued to hold the letter and stared at the guard in indignation. "Of course I know this script!" he said, taking a defensive tone. "And yes, I do come from the same land. But that was many years ago. I know nothing of these new armies and I have no communication with them."

The askari looked at him warily before speaking with irritation. "If you can read this letter... then tell me what it says."

Ramiro cleared his throat and began to translate.

> *Sir Guicher to Eleanor, his dearest and most amiable wife, to his beloved children and to all his vassals of all ranks, his greetings and blessings.*
>
> *By God's grace, our time of suffering in Antioch is at an end. The sickness has lifted and we have come to a quick recovery. Soon we will march...*

"Enough!" the askari yelled with some alarm. "Give it to me!" He held out his hand.

"It's just a letter to his wife," Ramiro said as he handed it back.

The askari barged behind the desk and took his arm. "You will come with me!"

"What do you mean? ... Now?" he sputtered. "What about my customers? Where do you take me? On whose authority?"

"On the orders of Governor Iftikhar. Come peaceably or face the consequences."

Adele put her work down and rushed to Ramiro's side.

He patted her hand. "Close the shop," he said to her. "Can you carry all this home?"

"Don't worry about that," she said. "I'll ask Jameel to help. But how will I know where you are?"

He shook his head as the big Sudanese dragged him away. "I don't know. In the Emir's castle I should think... or his dungeon."

• • • • •

A band of sunlight cut across the smooth skin of Iftikhar's olive-brown face as he peered through an arrow-slit built into a wall of Castle Al-Jalud. His thin beard and his small nose gave him a boyish look, a characteristic that belied his ruthless ambition. He fingered a string of prayer beads made of pearl and did not speak for some time. When he finally turned from the portal to face Ramiro, he sounded annoyed. "I hear you have become a popular man in Jerusalem, that you raise rabbis from the dead."

"It was nothing miraculous, my Lord," said Ramiro. "I merely noticed he was still alive and attempted to give him breath."

Iftikhar studied him intently. "So you make no profession to be a divine healer?"

"I do not, my Emir."

"That is good," he said with narrowed eyes. "I do not like so-called holy men leading the people astray and disturbing the peace. Only Allah, by His will, can perform miracles. Do I make myself clear?"

"Quite clear, Sahib."

Iftikhar continued to stare at him as he nodded lightly. "Very well. Now on to other business. My askari tells me you know the tongue of these Christian barbarians who invade our land. Is that so?"

Ramiro glanced at the huge Sudanese askari who straddled the doorway. "Yes, my Lord. But I have no association with these men."

Iftikhar handed him the French letter. "Read it to me."

Ramiro read the letter aloud.

"And can I take you at your word that your interpretation is correct?" Iftikhar asked, his voice echoing from the bare stone walls.

"I swear it, my Lord, just as I read it to you. It is a letter to his wife and all he states is that they are on their way from Antioch to destinations south. I believe he refers to Tripoli."

Iftikhar waved a hand in frustration. He looked down to his desk stacked with letters and reports. A lock of black hair fell out from his blue turban. "This is old news now," he sighed. "It tells me nothing." He motioned to a cushion. "Please sit. You must tell me all you know of these mercenaries, these Franj who fight for the Romans."

Ramiro shrugged his shoulders before he took his seat. "I hear what others hear, my Lord. About the battles at Nikea and Antioch... and recently Edessa."

"And now Maarat," Iftikhar said.

"Maarat An-Numan?"

"Yes, yes," he said quietly, his gaze becoming somewhat vacant.

"What happened, my Lord?"

Iftikhar swallowed and turned his head to the side. When he turned again to face Ramiro, he had a grim look. "I have no love for Turks," he said. "The more these barbarians kill, the better. But I cannot condone the wanton murder of good Muslims – it was a massacre!" He bent over and slapped an open hand on the table. "Stinking beasts! They are worse than animals!"

"But I was there last summer, my Lord. The Franj were turned back."

"Not this time," he said, sticking out his chin. "They came back with a larger force and took the walls." Once again, he fell quiet for a time.

Ramiro said nothing.

"Have you not heard?" Iftikhar said, raising his brow. "They slaughtered the whole city... over ten thousand people!" He drew a deep breath. "Muslim, Christian, Hebrew, it doesn't seem to matter to them. Roman, Arab or Turk – they kill them all!" He glared at Ramiro with ferocious eyes, as if he shared the guilt. "And then, by the will of Allah, the devil sons of shit starve because they have destroyed everything - they have nothing to eat."

Ramiro thought of Salim and Dawud and all the people he had come to know in Maarat, all the people he had toiled with at the hospital. He waved his head in disbelief, a hollow ache filled his chest.

Iftikhar started to say something else but choked on his words. He turned away quickly and feigned to look through the arrow-slit. A cold gust tossed his hair back. When he turned back to Ramiro, his hands trembled and his voice gnawed with revulsion. "Our spies watched these barbarians eat human flesh! They saw them dig up the bodies of the slain martyrs of Islam to strip their flesh with carving knives." His face screwed in angst. "They eat Muslims as if they were cattle! Godless cannibals! May Allah curse them and their bastard sons!" He bit his lip as tears welled in his eyes.

Ramiro reddened and looked down. He did not doubt Iftikhar's words and felt a wave of hot shame for his countrymen. He recalled the atrocities at Antioch and lifted his head to look into Iftikhar's glare of hatred. "May Allah's peace be upon them," he said sincerely. "I lived in Maarat, my Lord, for almost a year. The people were my friends. I am as deeply grieved as you are."

"Can I believe you, Scribe? Can I trust you?" he asked, tipping his head. "How do I know you are not a spy?"

"I assure you, Sahib, I am a man of God." He put his hands to his heart. "In no way do I condone any murder, Muslim or Christian or Hebrew. It is true, I come from the west as do the Franj, but I have lived and worked among the people of Syria for the last nine years."

Iftikhar inched his prayer beads through his fingers. "You will tell me all you know." His oval eyes sharpened. "And you will tell me what you have been doing here for nine years."

● ● ● ● ●

Iftikhar smirked after Ramiro finished his story. "And so this is why you ask around about a golden cross," he said. "That is quite a tale, Ramirah of Cluny." He leaned back on a cushion and stretched his arms out. Then he scowled a little. "But I find it sad and worrisome that you have no children. A man without sons is truly cursed."

Ramiro felt a sharp pang of anguish at the Emir's words. He bowed his head a little. "Yes, Sahib, in a way. But I must put all my trust in the good works of God and go where He guides me."

"Of course," said Iftikhar with some condescension.

Ramiro leaned forward on the cushion, trying to ease the pain in his back. "May I be so bold, my Lord, to ask your assistance in retrieving my cross?"

Iftikhar waved a hand in disregard. "I do not engage myself in the disputes of Christians. However, if you can find one Muslim to verify your story, I will reconsider my stance."

Ramiro nodded. "Thank you, Sahib, thank you." Mufti Ibrahim came to mind - but that won't do, he thought, he's Sunni.

"So you say you have been deep inside Turk lands," said Iftikhar. "This is also of interest to me. Tell me all you know about the Turks."

"Now, my Lord?" Ramiro asked in exhaustion. The evening call to prayer sounded from the minarets, as if to emphasize the time.

"Yes, now." His lips curled on one corner. "Would you like some tea?"

• • • • •

Adele sat at the window of their room near the Jaffa Gate. She looked down on the empty streets below and a single tear rolled down her cheek. Ramiro had been gone all night. She raised her head and looked across Jerusalem into the night sky. The golden Dome on the Temple Mount seemed to glow in the soft light of a half-moon. She fingered her prayer beads silently.

> *Hail Mary,*
> *Full of Grace,*
> *The Lord is with thee.*
> *Blessed art thou among women,...*

But no amount of prayer seemed to relieve her anxiety. Was he alright? What should I do? I can't open the shop by myself. I can't wander the streets without a man at my side. She put her head in her hands. Who can help? She thought of Bishop Aliphas and Jameel.

She slept in fits, waking at every sound, jumping to the window or the door. Is it him? No. She returned to her empty bed and lay down again.

The sun was only a hand off the horizon when a heavy knock came to the door. She jolted from bed, her heart pounding. "Who is it?" she squawked.

"It's me!" Ramiro shouted.

PAKRAD

"They killed Christians?" Madteos asked as he lifted his eyes from a golden cross he was cleaning.

"Even Armenians and Syrians, elder brother" said Pakrad. "No one was spared."

Madteos put down his work and wiped his hands on a rag. His brother was a priest, and priests always seemed to get the news first. Pakrad stood in a brown robe that draped loosely down to his sandals. He was short like himself and he had the same curly brown hair but, younger by ten years, his was not yet grayed. Madteos always had trouble taking Pakrad seriously. The man was educated and collected but he looked like a bumbling fool. His big ears jutted out from his long head, his nose was short, almost upturned, and his big eyes seemed to bulge from his head like those of a monkey.

"What are you going to do?" Madteos asked.

"Nothing for now. I can always move quickly. Not like you, brother, with all your gold."

Madteos looked at him with a little scorn. "And don't forget whose gold it is that provides for your family."

Pakrad blushed. "What will you do if the invaders reach Jerusalem?"

Madteos stared straight ahead. "I haven't given it much thought, Pakrad. But now... now it is worrisome."

"You should be worried. They'll come for your gold first."

Madteos picked up the golden cross and started to clean it again. "When the Emir is worried, I will go. Until then, I carry on business as usual."

Pakrad stared at the cross in Madteos' hand. "That's beautiful," he said, walking behind him for a better view. "It looks familiar. I think I've seen it before."

Madteos pretended he was finished and quickly began to wrap the cross in an oiled cloth.

"Yes, I remember!" said Pakrad. "That looks like the cross that Christian foreigner wants. You know - that man with an Andalusian accent who saved the Rabbi."

"How do you know what it looks like?" Madteos asked as he tied the wrapping.

"I saw his drawing. One of the attendants at the monastery passed it around."

Madteos got up from his stool. "You will keep your mouth shut! He has no right to it. I paid for it. It's mine!"

Pakrad stepped back. He seldom saw his brother flare into a rage. "Of course, elder brother. As you wish."

• • • • •

"There he is again," said Ramiro, looking out from his storefront. "The Armenian priest. That's the third time I've seen him in Madteos' shop."

"Perhaps he comes to perform some prayer service for Madteos," said Adele.

"That seems unlikely. But it is possible he sold my cross to the priest," he said as he stepped outside and watched him walk away. He looked up at the sky before rushing back inside. "It's almost noon. Close the shop. I'm going to follow him."

He trailed Pakrad through the crowded street. The priest headed south toward the Zion Gate, but he did not go far. In an instant, he turned and disappeared. Ramiro ran up to the spot. Praise God, he thought, looking up at the iron doors and the huge cross above the door. The Monastery... it's the Monastery of Saint James. What fortune! I'll ask Jameel who he is.

FEBRUARY

Iftikhar ate quietly in a lavish room of the Emir's Palace while servants rushed about with more plates of food and drink. He lifted his head lazily. "You say they got past Homs and Shayzar?"

"Yes, my Lord," said the Sudanese askari standing at a distance. "The barbarian army now besieges Arqah outside Tripoli."

"Let them come," Iftikhar said stanchly, trying to conceal his distress. "Our Vizier, may Allah protect him, has advised us to wait until they reach Palestine and head inland. Then they will be isolated, without food or water. That will be our chance to surround them and destroy them all, by the will of Allah."

"Praise Allah," replied the askari.

"But I am still concerned, Lieutenant. Another plague racks the cities of Egypt. Thousands more have perished, including many of our good soldiers. If it continues unabated, we will be severely weakened."

"We all pray to Allah for forgiveness, Sahib. We pray He will remove this curse from our cities."

Iftikhar did not respond.

"And what of the Christians, Sahib? Do you still wish to leave them be?"

"No. I want all of their prominent men detained. The Hebrews too. But we must wait until they finish their Easter celebrations. There will be too many pilgrims and any hostile actions now may just create more trouble."

"We should ban all Christian celebrations, my Lord."

"We will wait. We will wait for Jumada Al-Awwal. When that month begins, we will impose our restrictions and deportations."

"Yes, Emir. And what do you want to do with that Christian priest from the West, my Lord? You cannot trust him."

"I know Lieutenant," Iftikhar said quietly. "And I have no need of Christian heroes at a time like this. I want him watched at all times. I want to know everything he does, everyone he meets, every letter he writes."

"Yes, my Lord, as you command. And what of the golden cross he desires? If he obtains it, he may gain power over the Christian people."

"I thought the same. We will leave things as they are but, if by some chance he does get it back, you must tell me right away. In the meantime, I may think of some use for the man."

TRIPOLI

The Crusaders flocked to a mansion near Tripoli. Once occupied by a wealthy Muslim baron, the estate now served as Count Raymond's headquarters. The building stood three stories tall, surrounded with a low rock wall. Sunlight glared from its mosaic façade and beat upon its red tile roof. All around, apple and pear trees blossomed in thick sprays of white and pink. And further out, lush vineyards and fields of sugarcane spread out for miles.

MARK BLACKHAM

Within its cool, brick interior, a council of men, all dressed for war, milled about in an expansive reception room, still intact with Chinese vases, pearl-embedded oak furniture and the finest of Persian carpets. The air reverberated with loud and raucous boasts of daring feats, laments at the loss of friends, and vivid descriptions of the strange things they had seen.

The commanders sat at table, each accompanied by their lieutenants and clergymen, who stood watching the proceedings. Drugo stood among them.

Count Raymond banged his mace on the wide, oak table, shouting through his thick, gray beard. "Order! Come to order!" The room fell silent and he stood to speak. "As most of you know," he bellowed, "we recently received another emissary from King Alexios of the Greeks. I have his letter here." He waved it over his head for all to see while he scanned the crowd with his one eye. "He repeats his offer to join us in June with a sizeable army. I say we should accept. With his help, nothing will stand in our way."

Duke Godfrey stood up suddenly, standing a head taller than most. His long, blonde hair swayed across his broad shoulders. "With his help?" he asked incredulously, his imposing voice thundering in the hall. "Where in hell was he when we needed him?" Murmurs of agreement followed his words. "What about his whimpering men who abandoned us in our time of trial before the walls of Antioch? Abandoned us like mangy dogs running back to their master."

Raymond banged his mace again. His gray brow scowled, wrinkling his eye patch. "Let me tell you what happened, Duke Godfrey!" He spat his words. "Bohemond was the one who sent the Greeks packing because he wanted Antioch for himself!" His words trailed off as he fell to coughing.

"Better that," said Godfrey, "than letting it fall into Greek hands. We're the ones who died for it."

"By God's mercy!" said Raymond. "The king is a Christian!"

"He's a heretic! He's a damned Greek! He's not one of us. Half his men are heathen Muslims. How can we trust him?" He raised his voice to appeal to the council. "After all our sacrifices in the name of God, are we going to allow this conniving King of the Greeks to lay claim to our conquests?" Many men shook their heads and several 'nays' could be heard.

"If we need help," he went on, "we should look to our brethren in Genoa or Venice. They have no need of conquest as long as they profit from trade. Even now, they moor their ships at Latakia. I say we send them a purse of the Emir's gold. Tell them what we need. Tell them we march for Jerusalem and ask for their help."

"And where will they put to port?" Raymond asked. "The Egyptians have the southern coast and Jaffa. The King's ships can only help us to secure these ports."

"Will we rule the Holy Land?" Godfrey appealed to the men. "Or will we just hand it over to these heretics?" He paused for effect before glaring at Raymond. "And we are wasting our time with the siege of Arqah!" he shouted. "And we are wasting good men! We can't afford this. We must leave now to conquer Jerusalem!"

Raymond stood to face him. "I will decide when we leave, Commander!" he shouted in a hoarse voice. "And if we leave Arqah undefeated, the Muslims will think us weak." He looked around the room for support. He knew his argument was frail and he tried to look sure of himself, but felt he was losing his grip. If he could not take Arqah, could he take Jerusalem? Even his own men had started to grumble. He ground his teeth, wagging his gray beard.

"And if we stay to fight your fruitless battle, we soon *will* be weak!" said Godfrey. "It's spring. We are ready. Only a fool would be blind to this. Now is the time to march!"

Drugo and others nodded their heads in agreement. But not everyone agreed with Godfrey. A loud "No!" roared out from the crowd of men.

It came from the mystic, Peter Bartholomew, who stomped forward, slapping his boots on the marble floor. His thin face blushed red as he shouted at Godfrey. "How dare you speak to our Lord in such a fashion!" he said, trembling with his hands on his hips. "He carries the Holy Lance." He waved a hand in the air. "God has ordained the Count to lead us to victory over the heathen!"

"That's enough, Peter!" Raymond shouted, only to be cut short by a deep, racking cough.

But Peter continued in righteous indignation. "We are the ones who marched south!" he ranted. "We are the ones who cleared the path to Jerusalem while you idled your time in Antioch." He leaned forward. "In debauchery, no doubt."

Godfrey kicked his chair across the room and drew his sword so fast that few saw it come out of its sheath. Before Peter could utter another word, the tip was at his throat.

"Why you foking pile of horse shit!" Godfrey shouted. Spittle flew from his thin lips and stuck in his blonde beard. His hair dangled in front of his menacing eyes. "I'll take your ugly head right here and feed it to the pigs!" He feinted with a push of his sword and Peter's eyes went wide. "Even your precious Holy Lance won't save you from my blade!"

Raymond slammed his mace onto the table - he slammed it again. "Enough!" he shouted in a strained voice, and again he fell to coughing.

"And you, old man," Godfrey said as he turned on Raymond again. "You're too weak to lead us any further. You spend half your days in bed!"

Raymond could hardly speak and no one else stepped forward to defend him. Most of the men were at a loss. They respected the imposing and muscular Godfrey, who showed no fear and fought like the devil himself. But Raymond was of noble birth and Peter was his spiritual leader. Peter was the one who discovered the Holy Lance at Antioch but he was not well liked and, as the days wore on, many began to doubt this would-be prophet's story of the lance. And many more disagreed with Count Raymond's siege of Arqah.

In the tension of the moment, another man ventured forward, stepping before the council. He was short and thin, and the pallid skin of his face stood in harsh contrast to his greasy, black hair and darkened eye sockets. His long nose wrinkled in a perpetual sneer as he spoke. "Please men! I beg of you," he said through wet, red lips. "We must remain civil!" It was Arnulf Malecorne, chaplain to the Normans, highly respected by some because of his erudition but derided by others because of his drinking and womanizing.

With Peter humiliated, Arnulf saw an opportunity. "There is little to be gained by this bickering," he said, trying not to sound too condescending "We must all ask God for Divine Guidance." He held his hands in prayer. "We must all bear the Cross of Christ to Jerusalem." The men nodded, eager to have this feud settled and pleased that Arnulf had the courage to do it.

Godfrey withdrew his sword and sheathed it but, after a moment of hesitation, turned back to smash a fist into Peter's chest, heaving the frail man to the hard floor. Gasps and rumbles came from the councilmen. "One more insult," Godfrey shouted down as he gripped the hilt of his sword, "... and I'll gut you where you stand!"

● ● ● ● ●

Count Robert of Flanders met with Godfrey in a nearby house he had commandeered for himself. Robert had once allied with Raymond but now, since abandoning him after the siege of Maarat, he had warmed to Godfrey.

"What is it?" Godfrey asked, finding it hard to take his eyes from Robert's hawk-like nose.

"I just heard," said Robert. "Peter claims to have had another vision of Christ."

"Not another! Who the hell does he think he is? The pope himself?"

Robert smiled, lifting his high cheeks. "And wait 'till you hear this one. He says the Lord in person told him there were many sinners among us and that he, himself, was to be the one to root them out."

Godfrey guffawed. "What impudence!"

"But more disturbing," Robert continued without smiling, "is that he claims God has instructed him to execute those found wanting."

Godfrey shook his big head in disbelief. Then he laughed aloud. "Ha, ha, ha. That stupid shit! Does he think he can get rid of me so easily? I should have rammed my sword through his guts!"

"The men are outraged," said Robert. "And terrified. Even Raymond's own men."

Robert always seemed to wear a look of satisfaction and, perhaps, of mild humor, even when he discussed the most dire of issues. Some say his down-turned eyes and elegant eyebrows give this effect, and that he always has the same demeanor, even when he raises his sword against the heathen.

"It's a good thing they're outraged," said Godfrey. "It's about time someone put that vile peasant in his proper place. How could anyone believe his story anyway? That he so conveniently found this so-called holy lance. Horse shit!"

Robert returned a half smile. "And listen to this," he said. "Arnulf Malecorne has challenged him and his story."

"Arnulf... the one who looks like a raccoon," Godfrey chuckled spitefully.

"Yes," said Robert in his steady voice, "and the one who likes young girls and copious amounts of wine, I hear."

Godfrey laughed again. "This may turn to our advantage, Count Robert," he said with a wry smile. "If Arnulf has publicly challenged Peter's story... and the veracity of this Holy Lance, then he will be forced to prove himself by Saxon law."

"Yes," said Robert, not really understanding Godfrey's mirth. "But if he fails, Count Raymond could be discredited along with him."

Godfrey said nothing. He sat with an elbow on a knee and rested his head on a huge fist, biting his tongue to hide his glee.

GOOD FRIDAY

It was the morning of Good Friday and Peter Bartholomew stared at the tall stacks of blazing olive branches. This was his ordeal. By Saxon law, he would prove himself true. He watched the flames rise high above the crackling stacks, which were two feet apart, stood the height of a man, and ran a length of five to six paces. Their intense heat already burned at his face.

Thousands of men circled around him, all pressing for a better view. Only the flames and Raymond's Provencals held them back. But no one said a word.

I'll show them all, Peter thought as he readied himself for the flames. God is with me. Oh please God, be with me now. Please God, show these unbelievers that I am your Word, my Lord! He strode forward, his eyes nearly closed, and rushed into the flames. "God help us!" he screamed as the fire swallowed him.

The flames roared up, dry branches cracked and popped. Wide sheets of a red inferno shot skyward, driving waves of sparkling ash into a blue sky. Everyone watched, nobody breathed.

"Where is he?" someone yelled.

"There he is!" another shouted and pointed. "There he is!"

Peter jumped from the flames, his hair burnt, his skin red, his tunic charred. "God help us!" he screamed again.

A delirious roar deafened the air. Hundreds of hysterical men rushed forward to touch him, all crying "God help us!" They tore at his tunic for a piece of it and grabbed at his singed hairs. They pressed in harder and harder, and Peter collapsed in the mad melee.

• • • • •

Peter lived for two weeks after his ordeal. Some say he died of his burns, others blame the mob that broke his bones and tore his charred skin in the ensuing rush to touch him. Whatever the cause, those who once idolized Peter soon came to believe he had lost favor with God. And the once venerated Holy Lance became an object of ridicule.

Raymond was humiliated. For years, he had used the lance as a relic of sacred power. But now, it was defamed and his power to command waned in mockery.

SMYRNA

Emperor Alexios leaned back in his chair, allowing his servant to fit his knee-high red boots. Outside, he could hear the rolling waves of the Aegean crash against the rocky promontory below the tall citadel of Smyrna. Since he had taken control of Nikea, and now Smyrna after the death of the pirate Chaka, he was pleased with his on-going campaign to wrest control of the west coast of Asia Minor. But he knew he could never be entirely successful in this regard without possession of Antioch and, as time went by, he began to realize he may never have the opportunity. The Kelts had betrayed him, as he feared they would.

When he made an offer to join them in Tripoli, it was not so much to march to Jerusalem as it was a ploy for Antioch. He realized that any venture for the Holy City would spread his forces far too thin and he would have to contend with the might of the Egyptian empire, which he could ill afford to do. He hoped rather, that he could establish himself at Tripoli in order to create a base. Perhaps then he would have a better chance to squeeze Antioch from the south and the north.

But the Kelts in Tripoli again refused his offer of help and made veiled threats should he try. At this point, Alexios realized he had lost any control over their movements and began to think they had outlived their usefulness. Indeed, these Kelts had become a threat. Since they had taken Antioch and Maarat and now seized the territory around Tripoli, they had come to believe God ordained their victory and they no longer needed the help of the Byzantines, nor that of the Egyptian infidels.

He motioned to a waiting scribe. "Send a letter to the Egyptian vizier. Tell him we no longer have any control over these Kelts. I wipe my hands of the whole matter. They act alone."

BARI

When Aldebert received Ramiro's letter from Maarat last October, he vowed to join the Holy Crusade. But Abbot Martinus would not let him go. The Crusaders were still in Antioch at the time, and Jerusalem remained in the hands of infidels. Martinus did not want him to travel alone and he could spare no one to travel with him. Aldebert argued that many pilgrims go to Jerusalem at all times of the year, but the Abbot would not bend to his pleas.

Two things changed the Abbot's mind. One was a very important bit of information Aldebert gleaned at the docks - and the other was a letter.

Ramiro's next letter came from Jerusalem, taking seven months to get to Aldebert in Bari. Once again, it had taken the circuitous route of going to the Abbey of Cluny before being forwarded to him by Abbot Hugh.

But it was not the only letter delivered from Cluny. Another was addressed to Ramiro, from the Abbot himself. Ramiro's last letter to Hugh explained the situation in Jerusalem, that the Egyptians ruled and that the Patriarch was exiled. He had pleaded for instructions - and this letter was Hugh's response.

Aldebert put it aside and picked up the letter Ramiro had sent to him. In it, Ramiro warned him to stay away from Jerusalem because of all the trouble there. But Aldebert bristled at his warning. He had met many pilgrims in Bari who thought little of heading to the Holy City for Easter celebrations, even while the Crusaders continued to march south. Already, the Soldiers of God had reached Tripoli and readied for the final assault to reclaim the Holy City for the True Faith. It was a glorious time indeed. And now, more fighting men were willing to make the dangerous journey across the Mediterranean, hoping to join the Holy Crusade they had heard so much about. He yearned to go too.

Abbot Martinus was visibly annoyed. "Yes, yes, I am painfully aware that you want to go to Jerusalem, Brother Aldebert, but the Army of God is still in Tripoli."

"Forgive me, Reverend Father, but those two letters you gave to me yesterday – the one from Father Ramiro says he's safe in Jerusalem. He's at a Benedictine monastery." He paused and watched the Abbot, who continued to glare at him. "And did you know the other letter is addressed to Ramiro, from Abbot Hugh himself?"

"Yes, yes, I saw that. I thought you could take it to the port – find a ship going to Jaffa and send it on."

"I could take it myself, Reverend Father. Let me tell you what I heard at the docks yesterday..."

● ● ● ● ●

Aldebert huddled in his cold, stony cell within the Allsaints Abbey and leaned over to dip his quill before resuming another letter to Abbot Hugh.

> *To his Reverend Father Hugh, by God's grace, the Abbot of Cluny, Aldebert, his monk and humble servant, greetings.*
>
> *It is with great joy and many praises to Our Lord that I inform you, my Reverend Father, that on this day, I encountered on the docks of Bari, six vessels destined to the Holy Land in order to lend aid to the Soldiers of God who fight for the Holy Cause. Four of these are Genoese and the other two hail from distant Anglia. These galleys are laden with foodstuffs, tools, and supplies of every kind and, while at port, are taking on even more. With them are tradesmen skilled in the machines of war, and more men join them from Italy, including many good fighting men.*
>
> *Unfortunately, there are no clergy among these good men, no one to carry before them the mantle of the True Faith. So I was asked to join them, to carry the Holy Word. They know not where they will make port but will follow the Holy Crusaders south until such time, by the Will of God, they will be given an opportunity to unload their precious cargo. Seeing their need, I have asked Abbot Martinus for permission to sail with them and, by his grace, he has allowed me leave. In the name of the Holy Mother Church, I will continue to inform you of events.*
>
> *May 4, in the year of Our Lord, 1099.*

JERUSALEM

EASTER

On a cold Easter night, Ramiro and Adele moved through a noisy throng of pilgrims gathered at the Church of the Holy Sepulcher. People came from far and wide to attend the Vesperal Liturgy of the Easter Mass. From Byzantium, pilgrims sailed from Constantinople, stopping in Cyprus before sailing to Latakia and continuing south on the Via Mari. From Europe, they travelled to Italy and headed for the port of Bari, just as Ramiro did years before. From here, they embarked on ships to Jaffa before journeying inland to Jerusalem. And joining these venturesome pilgrims, were hundreds of Christians traveling from all parts of Syria and Palestine, many of them Maronites, Jacobites, and Nestorians.

The jubilance and devotion of the pilgrims gave no hint to the political turmoil of the time. Few seemed to care whether Egyptians or Turks ruled Jerusalem, even though most were aware that a hostile Christian army marched through Syria and was on its way to the Holy Land.

Some of the pilgrims, on hearing rumors of the Crusader's success at Antioch, and now at Tripoli, armed themselves to fight for the cause of liberating Jerusalem. But Egyptian forces at Jaffa quickly disarmed these misguided adventurers and confiscated their horses. Like the Syrians and Turks, the Egyptians forbade Christians to bear arms or to ride a horse. The more zealous pilgrims, angered by these restrictions, concealed their knives and clubs under their cloaks and headed north to join the Crusader army in Tripoli.

Inside the church, torch lamps flickered in every corner, casting dim shadows among the thousands of pilgrims gathered inside and out. "There he is!" Ramiro whispered to Jameel as the presiding priest read aloud from the Book of Isaiah.

"Who?"

"The priest I mentioned. That's him!"

"You mean the one reading?" asked Jameel, who sat beside them with his wife and son.

"No, no. The one standing at the far right. I watched him go to your Church."

"Oh, I know him. That's Pakrad, an Armenian priest. He's a pious man. Very kind. Why are you interested in him?"

"I have seen him often at Madteos' shop. Perhaps he knows something of my cross."

"I think he's a relative – a cousin or brother, I'm not sure. Why do you think he has your cross?"

"If he's a kinsman, maybe Madteos gave it to him. It does have an Armenian design."

"But the golden cross, Master. It is too precious for a monk to own."

The Liturgy ended and all torches were extinguished except for the dim perpetual flame on the altar. The whole church was cast into utter darkness, the blackness so thick that most were unable to see their hands in front of their faces. And here the crowd waited until the stroke of midnight when the high priest lit his candle from the altar. From this one candle, thousands of others were lit and the whole congregation, candles in hand, moved outside to join the ritual procession around the church.

Ramiro and Adele were no sooner out the door when the big Sudanese lieutenant stepped in front of them.

"You will come with me!" said the dark, burly man, taking him by the arm. "The Emir demands it!"

AN EMBASSY

"I'm glad you could come, Sayyid Ramirah," said Iftikhar.

"Apparently, Sahib, I had little choice in the matter," Ramiro replied sullenly, thinking with apprehension about the many hours Iftikhar had detained him last time. "... although it is always good to see you again, my Lord. And... uh, if it pleases my Lord, what matter does my esteemed Emir find pressing at this late hour?"

Iftikhar did not invite him to sit. "I will get straight to the point, Ramirah. It seems your invading countrymen in Tripoli have sent emissaries to meet with me. These barbarians have already met with our Great Vizier in Egypt and they have failed to reach any agreement with him. Now they approach me without the Vizier's consent. I believe their purpose is to discuss the fate of Jerusalem and I want you to join me when we meet."

"Me? But why, Sahib?"

"Because you are one of their countrymen, are you not?"

Ramiro shrugged. "Not really. At least no more than Egyptians would consider Syrians their countrymen."

Iftikhar gave him a suspicious glance. "Nonetheless, you are one of them, you are Christian."

Ramiro sighed. "I cannot deny I am Christian, Sahib. So what is it you would have me do?"

Iftikhar moved a little closer to him and spoke softly. "These men have their own translators, but none of my people know their tongue. I want you to write down everything they say, even if it's a simple aside to a compatriot."

Ramiro nodded. "I can do that."

"But," said Iftikhar, "... you will not be introduced - and you will not speak to them. You will sit behind me. When I motion to you, you will give me all that you have written. Is that clear?"

Ramiro bowed his head. "Your wish is my glad duty, Emir. Will I be detained for long? My wife is waiting."

"That is of no concern to you. My men will watch over your wife."

Ramiro stiffened, looking hard into Iftikhar's eyes. "I'm sure she will be safe in your gentle care, Sahib."

• • • • •

Iftikhar looked down on the three men of Provence, who sat awkwardly on cushions set in front of the dais. They looked uncomfortable and one of them kept stretching his legs out under the table. They were unarmed but well-attired in expensive vests and pantaloons, clearly adopted from local fashion. The man in the middle was about thirty, blonde, his round face reddened by the sun. He spoke Greek and did all of the talking. An Arab interpreter knelt beside him.

Two of Iftikhar's advisors positioned themselves to either side of the French ambassadors. Ramiro sat inconspicuously behind Iftikhar while two burly askari straddled the door, one of them the big Sudanese.

Iftikhar thought about the letter he had just received from his master, Al-Afdal, who warned him that the Greek King no longer controlled these bloodthirsty barbarians. They acted alone and he would have to deal with them as he saw fit. And Al-Afdal said their once mighty army was greatly diminished in size and their resources were thin. Armed with this knowledge, Iftikhar took a firm stance.

After long pleasantries and introductions, the Franj ambassadors began to discuss the purpose of their visit and presented their proposals at length.

"What did you say?" Iftikhar asked after a time. "You want me to surrender Jerusalem to you?" He sounded amused

The fretful interpreter kept his head down. "Yes, Sahib, that is what they ask."

Iftikhar chuckled. He put his hands to his belt and jutted his elbows out of his billowing blue tunic. "That is a preposterous request! The Vizier, may Allah bless his name, has already presented to you a magnanimous offer. Let me repeat this for you. If you stop where you are now, in Tripoli, we are willing to cede all Syrian territory to you without contest. In fact, we offer you an alliance against the Turks. We will aid and abet your efforts to conquer their cities." He leaned forward as if to accentuate his next words. "But we will continue to hold Palestine, including Jerusalem and all land west of the Jordan."

The translator spoke to the emissaries in a similar meek tone. When they heard Iftikhar's reply, one of them leaned over to the blonde man, speaking in the tongue of Provençal. "Tell this God-damned pagan their blood will drench the streets," he said in a venomous voice. "This is unacceptable. Do they not understand Jerusalem is ours? God wills it."

The blonde man put up his hand to dissuade him. "Don't be a fool. You will anger him and he will slit our throats where we sit. Be civil." He turned to Iftikhar and spoke in Greek. "I hear your offer, Governor, but you must understand that Jerusalem is the most holy city to a Christian. How can we come this far without free access to its most holy shrines?"

Inwardly, Iftikhar seethed at the effrontery of these arrogant barbarians. They had no manners and smelled like goats. But outwardly, he remained calm. "That is not a problem," he replied. "Every year, thousands of Christian pilgrims come to Jerusalem unhindered. You too are free to come and worship at any time. All we ask is that your visits are limited in number so we can more easily accommodate your needs."

Once again, the French conversed in their own tongue. "I don't trust him," one said. "It is a ruse of the devil to deflect God's holy plan."

"It is our duty," said the other, "to seize the Holy Sepulcher in the name of Our Lord."

The blonde man pursed his lips and shook his head apologetically as he spoke to Iftikhar. "We cannot accept your offer. Jerusalem is our holy right."

Iftikhar rose up in a rage. He could no longer tolerate these men. "So be it! I believe these negotiations have ended! Be warned - the armies of Egypt will stand against you if you march further south. We control the coast. We will strangle your supply lines."

The French got to their feet, mumbling and cursing amongst themselves.

"My men will escort you back to your quarters," said Iftikhar. "Prepare to leave Jerusalem before noon." Then he turned to Ramiro and spoke quietly. "Give me what you have." Ramiro handed him his paper of notes. Iftikhar took them and motioned towards the Provencals. "Go with the escort. Tell me all they say."

"You mean... go with them now, Sahib?" asked Ramiro.

"Yes, yes, that is what I mean," he said. He motioned again. "Go, go."

• • • • •

Iftikhar read Ramiro's notes after the French emissaries left the city. "Look what they say!" he said with a touch of alarm. "They know about our troubles in Cairo - about the plague and the rebellions. This is not good. The Vizier must send an army soon. We are dealing with fanatics!" he said angrily, handing the paper to his lieutenant.

"I agree, my Lord," said the lieutenant as he read them over. "We must destroy them now."

Iftikhar turned on him. "And what would you have me do, Lieutenant? Send our cavalry to Tripoli? We can barely hold Palestine."

"But, my Lord, this kafir... what's his name?"

"Ramirah."

"Yes, he says here he overheard talk of them seizing Jaffa and even Ascalon. If they do this, we cannot win."

"They cannot take Jaffa, half our navy is there. And the Roman ships will no longer assist these barbarians. The King has washed his hands of the whole affair and has nothing more to do with them." But despite his bold words, Iftikhar felt an inner dread. Fanatics were dangerous people, and he knew he should never underestimate an enemy willing to die for his cause - like the Hashashin.

"With respect, my Lord," said the lieutenant, "I would not trust the Roman king. He is a sly fox. And what about the Genoese fleets the kafir speaks of? And these Eng... Engleezi. What of their ships from the west?"

"We will ask our Vizier what we should do," said Iftikhar. He motioned to his secretary. "Compose a letter to Al-Afdal, may Allah keep him."

The secretary nodded. "As you command, my Lord."

"And we should expel the devil Christians," said the lieutenant. "Before it's too late."

"Not yet," said Iftikhar as his prayer beads rushed through his fingers. "Not yet... but make preparations." He was about to dismiss the man, but hesitated for one last question. "What about this Ramirah? Did you find the cross he looks for?"

"No, my Lord. But we think an Armenian jeweler has it."

"Why is that?"

"Our man says he watches the jeweler and all who come and go from his shop."

"Good. Then we will watch too."

• • • • •

"So now you're a spy for the heathen Muslims?" Adele asked with obvious scorn. "I don't understand you, Ramiro. Why are you so against your own people?"

"For the sake of Christ, Adele! Iftikhar threatened both of us. What would you have me do?" he asked as she glared at him. "And I'm not against *my* people, I'm against holy war. I'm against people who kill, steal and rape in the name of God."

"So you don't believe Christians should rule the Holy City of Jerusalem? The very place where Our Lord is buried. Instead, you'd rather have these infidels and heretics by your side?"

"Why do they need to rule it?" he argued. "Christians are free to worship in Jerusalem. You know that. As are Hebrews and any other creed. Can you say the same is true in France or Germany?"

Adele stomped a foot on the tile floor. Her red hair dangled in front of her eyes. "It's not right! The priests say the Messiah will return when Zion is complete. What about that?"

"Adele, my love, how can I make you understand? The Messiah has already come to teach us brotherhood, love and mercy - but still we reject his words. Can you really believe that the Son of God, whose message is of spiritual peace, will return in heavenly glory to vindicate these bloodthirsty men, and to stand victoriously over heaps of slaughtered Muslims? It is an abomination of the mind!"

"Oh, so now your own countrymen are bloodthirsty. Next you'll be calling them barbarians like the rest."

"They are barbarians, Adele. Only barbarians slaughter for the sake of slaughter. Only barbarians dare to eat the flesh of the vanquished like a pack of ravenous dogs!"

"God's blood!" she shouted, spinning away from him.

Madteos' Offer

Madteos wrung his hands in worry. "Are you sure, Pakrad?"

"Yes, Madteos, the barbarians are at Tripoli and will come this way. It's not worth the risk. They kill everyone. They steal everything." Pakrad's big eyes looked about in an excited manner, as if expecting trouble at any moment.

"Do you really believe Jerusalem will fall?" Madteos asked, staring at him with old eyes. "What of Al-Afdal and the Egyptians? Surely, they can defeat these barbarians."

"The barbarians took Antioch, brother. Why not Jerusalem?"

Madteos reflected for a moment. "So what do you think we should do?"

"Rumor has it that Governor Iftikhar will evict the Christians anyway. You're not safe. You should go to Bethlehem. Go to your son's house. You can always return when it is safe."

Madteos shook his head. "But I've got too much to carry. I'd have to hire guards, it would attract too much attention."

"Then sell what you have," he said. "Sell it here and take the money."

• • • • •

"Peace be upon you, Sayyid," came a small voice.

Ramiro looked up from his writing. A thin, old man with a wrinkled face and a wide gray moustache stood in front of his desk. It was Madteos the Jeweler. "And peace to you, Madteos," he said with a hint of surprise. "What brings you to my shop?"

Madteos opened his hands as he spoke. His bushy, gray eyebrows danced under his brown turban. "And to you peace, Sayyid. I uh... I think I have found the cross you are looking for. Are you still interested?"

"Yes, yes, of course," Ramiro answered, happily astonished that Madteos was willing to approach him openly. "But I cannot afford your price."

"Well, Sayyid, you must understand that my first price was only an estimate. An estimate based on your flowery description of a beautiful masterpiece."

"Of course," Ramiro replied with wry amusement. "So what will it cost now that you realize its true value?"

A forced smile cracked across Madteos' bristled face. "Oh, it is quite reasonable. I believe that only five gold dinar will secure it for you."

"Five dinar? Really?"

Madteos nodded in high expectation. "Yes, yes."

Ramiro fell silent for a long moment. He watched Madteos squirm and wondered why the old man was willing to take much less than he originally asked.

Madteos wrung his hands as he waited for Ramiro's response. "So what do you say, Sayyid Ramiro? Do we have a deal?"

Ramiro squinted at him. "Why this sudden change of heart, Madteos? What has happened?"

"Oh... oh nothing of any import, Sayyid. Except that now I see you for the holy man that you truly are. I hope that, by this small gesture of mine, I will gain your blessing."

He's a poor liar, Ramiro thought as he looked directly into his cloudy eyes. "I will give you three dinar," he offered.

"Please, Sayyid. I make no profit on this. But because you are a man of God, I will give it to you for only four dinar. Do we have a deal?"

Ramiro nodded. "We have a deal."

Madteos seemed happy enough. His smile looked genuine. "I will get it for you right away," he said as he began to rush off.

"Wait!" Ramiro called after him. "I don't have the money here. I will collect it tonight and see you in the morning."

"Yes, yes, of course, Sayyid, of course. I am a foolish old man. I will meet you here in the morning, God willing."

• • • • •

Bishop Aliphas looked annoyed. "With respect, Ramiro of Cluny, I'm not sure that I share the same sense of value towards your cross."

"You must trust me, Your Excellency," Ramiro replied in earnest. "Abbot Hugh thought it was essential that I deliver the cross to Patriarch Symeon. I admit I do not know the true reason. But what I tell you is the truth."

"And do you expect me to send it on to Cyprus? The Patriarch is old and frail and has fallen ill. I'm not convinced he could do much in your favor."

"Then you must open it, Your Excellency. It may have an important message locked inside."

"And you still believe this message is vital?" Aliphas asked with a thin smile. "Like you say, it has been ten years since you were first given this cross."

Ramiro felt himself redden in shame. It had taken too long, he knew that. But what could he do? He put his hands together, fingers interlocked. "Your Excellency, if you can find no importance attached to it, rest assured that the cross is well worth four dinar in gold and silver alone."

Bishop Aliphas curled one cheek and wagged his head slightly. "Very well, Ramiro of Cluny. I will give you the four dinar and trust on your honor as a Christian and a Cluny monk that you will deliver this cross to me. My secretary will draw up an agreement for you to sign."

TRIPOLI

For months, Count Raymond kept up his siege of Arqah. But the fortress, high on a steep hill, proved impregnable. His men died by the day in hails of arrows and cavalcades of stones. And now the siege appeared the worst of folly, a waste of time and men and, God forbid, that bastard Godfrey was vindicated. Even his own men joined the chorus to march to war.

And now, after his ambassadors returned from Jerusalem and their meeting with Governor Iftikhar, he could wait no longer. They advised him to march soon because the Egyptians refused to hand over the city and, praise the Almighty, they were weakened by disease and civil strife and were unprepared for battle. On hearing this, Raymond finally relented and quit Arqah.

Meanwhile, Duke Godfrey's prestige grew. He had proven to be a capable leader and a terrifying warrior. And now his admonitions to march were readily embraced. The men flocked to his side. Even Tancred, forever the opportunist, was no longer swayed by Raymond's gold.

And Arnulf Malecorne's scheme had worked. He quickly stepped into the mystical void left by Peter and worked feverishly to maintain the peace and to entrench his position. He declared a period of fasting, prayer and alms-giving to let tempers cool. And slowly, he nudged himself closer to Godfrey's side.

Before they set out for Jerusalem, the Christians of Tripoli, using the Emir's gold, fashioned a golden crucifix for Arnulf, on which they fixed a drooping figure of a suffering Christ. Having successfully discredited Raymond's Holy Lance, Arnulf felt the need to create a new icon around which to rally the faithful, *his* icon. He lobbied feverishly to forge a new following around it and convinced Godfrey to become its patron and protector. But not all were entirely convinced of its sanctity.

JERUSALEM

JUNE

The messenger's breath came in gasps. He raised a dusty sleeve to wipe the sweat from his brow. "The barbarians have left Tripoli, Sahib." He drew another breath. "They... they march to Ramla." Sweat continued to trickle down his face in the stuffy heat of the meeting room. The air outside the Citadel stood silent and still, offering no reprieve from the scorching heat.

"Straight to Ramla?" Iftikhar asked.

"Yes, my Lord. And they make great haste."

"Did they make no attempt on Beirut or Acre?"

"No, my Lord. And no one dares to come out in challenge."

"Surely, they will need to make an attempt on Jaffa. How else would they get any help by sea? Did any of our reinforcements arrive from Ascalon?"

"No, Sahib." The messenger looked down as if suddenly afraid to speak. "And Ramla... Ramla, my Lord, it is abandoned."

"What?"

"Yes, my Lord. The garrison has fled, everyone has fled. They left behind all they could not carry. The whole city is deserted, only ghosts remain."

Iftikhar flushed. "Cowards!" he belted. "May Allah damn them!" For a long while, he stood in seething silence with his face down and a hand to his chin. The men in the room kept completely still, the silence fractured only when the *adhan* sounded from the minaret of the Al-Aqsa Mosque. They all kneeled to pray.

"We have become too complacent," he said after prayers ended and everyone sat down. "The barbarians tarried so long in Antioch and then

Tripoli, we came to believe we had ample time. Now it appears not. They make great speed south."

"It is a foolish move, Sahib," said the Sudanese lieutenant. "If they move inland without securing the coast, they will soon run out of supplies."

"I agree," said Iftikhar, dabbing the sweat from his face with a napkin. "It's difficult to believe they can be so brazen and careless."

"We should attack, Sahib. Cut them down at once!"

"That would be even more foolish, Lieutenant. Do you suggest we leave Jerusalem unguarded?"

"No, my Lord," he said, bowing his scarred head.

"Our Vizier promised to arrive with an army next month. He has been delayed by the plague and has more trouble with rebellions. We must do all we can to hold them off until he arrives. Then, by the will of Allah, we will destroy them all!"

"Then we must prepare for siege, Commander."

"Yes, at once. Gather all crops, all livestock – kill or conceal any we cannot use ourselves. Leave only dirt for them to eat!"

"Poison every well and every pool, Sahib," said the Sudanese. "All of them within a farsakh of the city. We'll see how long they can last before they choke on their own tongues!"

"But what of the Pool of Siloam?" asked another. "Fresh water gushes from the spring every three days."

"How far away is it?"

"About two hundred paces from the south wall, Sahib. But low in the Valley of Qidron."

"Put two of our best archers on the wall," one said.

"And just to make sure, fill the pool with dead animals."

"What about materials, Sahib?" asked another. "We should collect anything they can use against us."

"I agree. Collect and burn all timber we cannot put inside the walls. All of it! I don't want a scrap left. Not enough for a single arrow! Nails, rope, axes... anything that could aid these accursed Christians!"

"What of the Christians in the city, my Lord?"

"Get them out, especially their priests. Close the churches and throw out anyone else with money or influence."

"As you command, my Lord."

Iftikhar lowered his eyes in thought. A burning slit of sunshine pierced through a portal and began to creep across his face. He raised his elbow for shade. "And bring that damned Christian scribe to me," he said. "The one called Ramirah."

• • • • •

Bang! Bang! Bang! The door rattled on its hinges. Ramiro and Adele jumped from bed, exchanging nervous glances. "Who is it?" Ramiro shouted.

"Askari of the Emir!" a man shouted back. "Open the door!"

"Again? God help us!" said Ramiro with hushed breath.

He rushed to put on a tunic. "Hold on!" he shouted again, "I'm getting dressed!" He turned to Adele in breathless apprehension. "Get dressed fast! Take the money! Go to Madteos and get the cross! Hurry!"

"How do I get out Ramiro? What if they take me too?"

He rushed to the window. "The rope!" he cried. "Use the rope! The one I tied to the pillar for an easy escape." He rushed over to the coil of rope, checked the knot at the pillar and threw it out the window.

Adele looked down and shook her head. "I can't do that!"

Ramiro nudged her to the rope. "You must do it, Adele. All depends on you."

Bang! Bang! "Open the door!" came another angry shout. "Or forfeit your life!"

"One moment, please!" Ramiro shouted. "I'll be right there!"

Ramiro held Adele by the arms as she stuck her legs out the window. "Grab the rope!" he whispered.

"Blood in Hell!" she gushed. "I've got the damn thing!" She started to lower herself but stopped. "My mace, Ramiro, hand me my mace!"

"Yes, yes," he reached for it near the bed. "Here it is. Go! Go!"

Adele stuffed the mace into her belt and began her descent. She stopped. "My shawl. I need my shawl."

"For the love of God, woman," he said looking around the room. "Ah! Here it is! Go!"

She started down again but her tunic got caught in the rope. "By the Cross!" she cursed.

Ramiro scowled as he reached down to get her free. "You shouldn't curse. It's most unbecoming."

She looked up at him and scowled. "Lunatic! Don't forget to untie the rope!" she said before sliding down to the alley.

Ramiro smiled down on her, he loved her spirit. He watched her reach the ground. She's down! Get the rope!

Crash! The door flew open and three askari barged into the room, swords drawn. Ramiro rushed out to greet them, closing the bedroom blind behind him. "What are you doing?" he shouted with indignation. "I told you I was coming! There's no need for this!" They moved towards him. "I am a man of God!"

They ignored him, sheathing their swords and grabbing his arms, squeezing hard. "You will come with us!" They looked around. "Where's your wife?"

"She's not here," said Ramiro. "She went to market."

One of the askari ripped the blind from the bedroom. He pulled at cushions and threw them about the room. Then he went to the window and looked down.

Ramiro held his breath.

• • • • •

"Did you bring the dhimmi scribe to me?" Iftikhar asked.

"Yes, Sahib."

"And his wife too?"

"No, Sahib, she was not there."

"Where is she?"

"The dhimmi said she went to the market."

"At this hour? You idiot! Send men out to find her – now!"

The lieutenant bowed. "Yes, my Lord, at once." He signaled to an askari who nodded and left.

"Did you manage to get his cross?"

"No, Sahib," replied the increasingly nervous lieutenant. "It was not in his room so we went to the jeweler's home this morning but found no one. He has left the city. We tore the house apart and found nothing."

Iftikhar glared at him. "May Allah curse your sons! Moron! Get out! Get out before I have your head removed!"

The lieutenant lowered his eyes and backed to the door in cautious steps.

• • • • •

Adele pulled her headscarf close about her fair face and kept her head down. She worked her way across the street, remaining inconspicuous, and headed for Madteos' shop. But the shop was closed and empty. She looked about in frustration before hurrying to another jeweler nearby. "Peace be upon you," she said as demurely as she could.

"And to you, Sayyidah" the man replied. "What would you like?"

"The jeweler – Madteos – where is he today, Sayyid?"

"I don't know. He didn't show up. Very strange,"

"Please Sayyid, where does he live?"

"To the south, near the Zion Gate. Ask the rug merchant at the end of the street. He will show you."

When she reached Madteos' house, it seemed eerily quiet. The narrow street was devoid of traffic except for a lone boy leading a gray donkey. She brushed her tunic and adjusted her shawl before approaching the door. She knocked. The door was ajar and it opened a little. She looked around again before pushing it further, just enough to slide into the dim interior. "Ya Madteos!" she said loudly. "Are you here? Madteos! I have money for the cross!" Silence. She ventured another step. Broken glass and pottery crunched under her feet. Even in the waning light, she could see the place was a mess. Something was wrong.

The door slammed shut behind her. Her heart beat into her throat and she swung around, straining into the darkness. "Who is it?" she cried. "Who's there?" She heard the grinding of another step, not hers. With shaking hands, she fumbled for her mace.

SIEGE, JUNE 7

Iftikhar stared out from the rooftop of the Tower of David. His long blue tunic billowed and slapped in gusts of warm wind.

"There they are!" cried the watchman. On the hill! Beside the Mosque of Prophet Samuel!"

He saw them. Rays of morning sun flashed from their steel as clouds of dust mushroomed from their midst and rose into the clear blue sky, only to be swept aside in an instant by an erratic wind. There they are, he thought. Ten thousand strong. An army of Christian fanatics! How is this possible? Will Al-Afdal come in time?

He heard the slap of steps and turned around. The Sudanese approached and stood nearby. "What is it, Lieutenant?"

"My Lord, they have already taken Bethlehem!"

● ● ● ● ●

The Crusaders pushed and shoved for their first sight of the Holy City, the very place where Heaven and Earth unite, the Centre of the Earth. After surviving three years of long marches, arid deserts, starvation, disease and the perils of war, they had reached their goal, the holiest site on earth, the Tomb of Christ. They fell to their knees and wept, as Ramiro did months before, giving thanks to God in loud voices.

Arnulf Malecorne held his new standard high above his head. On it, was his golden crucifix. He jabbed it into the air repeatedly, as if it were a sword. "Praise be to God!" he shouted as loud as he could.

By late afternoon, thousands of French, Germans and Normans gathered to the north, between Herod's Gate and the Castle Al-Jalud. These men followed Godfrey and Robert. By the time they reached the walls of Jerusalem, Godfrey had established himself as the chief warlord of the Christian army, and Arnulf Malecorne was his servant of God.

Meanwhile, Raymond, because of the rift between leaders and his rapidly declining popularity among the men, took up position in the south, outside the Zion Gate. Even some of his long-time allies abandoned him to join Godfrey at the north wall.

ANOTHER DUNGEON

Three gloomy men sat in the dungeon of Castle Al-Jalud and Mufti Ibrahim was the only one Ramiro recognized as the guards threw him to the floor. There was only one window in the large cell, and that was a small opening near the ceiling. It cast a gloomy, pale light over the stark interior. A carpet of straw covered the floor, crawling alive with camel spiders and weevils. Several benches served as beds, allowing the prisoners to rise above this creeping haven. A simple latrine, in plain sight, occupied one corner and a heavy stench permeated the stifling hot air.

The cell door slammed shut and Ramiro rose to his feet, brushing straw from his cloak. "Mufti Ibrahim," he said with surprise. "I am glad to see you well... even in these sad circumstances." The mufti's white tunic and turban were soiled. He looked thin and disheveled and his face showed bruises and cuts. His brown eyes, usually so stern and proud, had a look of defeat.

Ibrahim stared at him, not sure who he was.

"I am Ramiro of Cluny. Do you remember me from Antioch?"

Ibrahim began to nod ever so slightly. "The Christian," he said quietly as his memory returned. "The one looking for his woman."

"That's right," said Ramiro. Ibrahim's response made him think of Adele and he felt a shiver of fear. Did she get the cross? Is she safe?

"You must tell me how you escaped Antioch," said Ibrahim. "And how did you end up here?"

Ramiro sat down and told him his story, although he left out many details he had no wish to share. One of the prisoners, a Christian, sat at the far end by himself, scowling in their direction. The other man, a Muslim, sat closer to Ibrahim. He remained silent and morose.

"Tell me, Mufti," Ramiro asked, "did you ever have the opportunity to deliver my letter?"

Ibrahim nodded sadly. "Yes, I did, and it caused me some grief as I feared. Especially when the siege of Antioch began. The Turks became nervous. That's when they exiled the Patriarch and many others. Some feared I collaborated with Christians." He shook his head. "What nonsense."

"But it was the Egyptians who threw you in here," said Ramiro, feeling some guilt and regret.

"That's right – for the greatest crime of all."

"What's that?"

"Being a Sunni and an enemy of the Fatimids."

Ramiro nodded in understanding. "You must tell me, Mufti, did Patriarch Symeon recognize my name or say anything at all?"

"He seemed to have no idea who you were, although he did know the Abbot you mentioned."

"Abbot Hugh," said Ramiro with a distant look. What is going on? Perhaps the Patriarch just forgot over time. But does it really matter anymore? He put a hand to his iron cross.

A moment of silence gripped the cell. But in the distance, they could hear people shouting. The voices grew louder and louder. Ramiro could feel the tension in the air, the sounds of rushing feet, people yelling. "By all saints! What is going on?" He strained to hear. Only when someone yelled, "May Allah curse your mothers, Christian dogs!" did it dawn on him.

"The Crusaders have arrived!" he cried. "Blessed Mary! O Jesus! They're here!" He thought of the slaughter at Antioch, the massacre at Maarat, and he thought of Adele. Father in Heaven! Please God, keep her safe!

A rattle of keys came from the door and it opened slowly. A big man, armed with a dagger, came in with trays of food and some toiletries.

Ramiro rushed over to him. "Please, Sayyid, let me speak to the Governor. There is no need to keep me here. I will leave the city." The man made no reply, not even a simple yes or no. "I beg of you!" He grabbed the guard's arm. The big man turned, shoving him to the floor.

CRUSADER CAMP

The Christian camp spread out along the north wall of Jerusalem. They kept back, beyond arrow range and beyond the long curtain wall that dipped and rose thirty paces outside the main north wall. Governor Iftikhar moved from the Tower of David to Castle Al-Jalud to watch their movements. He stood near an arrow port to study the nearest camp.

"You see the big one?" he said to the Sudanese. "The one with long, yellow hair? He's their leader. See the way he commands his men?"

"I see him, Sahib."

Iftikhar was amused when he heard that a group of infidels covered themselves with their shields and rushed madly at the walls, smashing at stones with simple hammers, as if expecting them to collapse with a single blow. But he found they were easily dissuaded with boiling oil and boulders.

He was relieved they had no siege machines and, apparently, no means to construct any. Praise Allah. Let them hammer all they like. We will cut them down one by one.

Reports from the Zion Gate were similar. An old man with one eye was said to lead the Christians gathered there and he was busy guarding the Church of Saint Mary on Mount Zion.

Iftikhar knew the stinking kuffar had discovered the poisoned wells because his sentries saw them coming from miles in the distance carrying fresh animal skins full of water. He heard that a desperate and parched crusader crawled over the decaying filth of dead animals clogging the Pool of Siloam and found fresh water at its source. Hundreds followed after him, pushing and shoving and brawling for a single drink as his archers peppered them with arrows shot on high from the nearest tower.

"It's unfortunate," said Iftikhar, "but the barbarians seem to have enough to eat."

"Yes, Sahib. They stripped Ramla of its grain and other food, and now Bethlehem supplies them with more."

"Have we sent out our spies?"

"Yes, my Lord, three men dressed as peasants."

The air was dry and the heat, the dust, and the wind made it even drier. The stench of death filled the air. All around the walls lay the carcasses of horses, mules, cattle and sheep. If not killed on the orders of Iftikhar, they died of thirst and rotted where they dropped.

Iftikhar turned from the window with a pleasing sense of accomplishment. The Christians were unprepared for a siege. They would soon die of thirst and wither away. He rubbed his chin, barely able to conceal a grin. "Bring that dhimmi scribe to me."

● ● ● ● ●

Ramiro had no sooner entered Iftikhar's chamber when he blurted out, "Where's my wife? What have you done with her?"

Right away, the big Sudanese struck him across the side of the head with a heavy hand, sending him staggering. "Mind your manners, kafir!"

Ramiro caught his balance and rubbed his ear. "Excuse me, peace be upon you, Sahib."

Iftikhar clenched his jaw. He had little tolerance for disrespect, especially from a filthy Christian. "You would do well to guard your head, Ramirah of Cluny. You may still lose it."

Ramiro was about to correct Iftikhar on the pronunciation of his name but he bit his lip.

"Come with me," Iftikhar ordered. He walked through a small archway that took him onto the battlement. The lieutenant shoved Ramiro along until they came out into the open air.

That is when Ramiro first saw them - thousands and thousands of Crusaders milling about in the distance. He reached out to steady himself against a castellation. The height of the wall, the open sky, the stink in the air, it all made his knees weak.

"You see?" said Iftikhar. "These are your countrymen." He waved his arm in a broad arc. "They have come all this way from a distant land. And for what? To touch the shrine of Jesus?" He smirked, as if he had some hidden knowledge. "Peaceful pilgrimage to holy places, that I can understand. But these men come armed for war, ready to die. In some ways, I admire their resolve, but then again I pity their foolishness. Look at them now. Now they die of thirst and attack our walls with little hammers."

Ramiro looked out on the hordes of men. Strangely, they did not appear familiar. Their helmets, their armor, their dress, even their horses, they all seemed to have a distinctive Muslim character. Were it not for the few crosses sewn onto shoulders, and perhaps some red and blonde hair, they would be difficult to discern from any other army in the region.

"Do you recognize these men?" Iftikhar asked.

"Not at all, my Lord."

"You see no one you know?"

"No, my Lord, but my eyes are not as good as they used to be."

"What about an old man with one eye, does he sound familiar?"

"No, I'm sorry, Sahib. As I said before, I have been gone many years and have never seen these men before."

Iftikhar stood looking north, resting a hand on his sword hilt. His black hair rippled under a blue turban. "Well, scribe, you are of little use to me at the moment. Go." He waved a hand.

"Please excuse me, my Lord, but I am concerned about my wife. Do you know if she is safe?"

Iftikhar turned and looked at him with a deadpan face. "She is well cared for," he lied. "... as long as you cooperate."

JUNE 13

The first attack looked foolish and desperate. But the Crusaders were so convinced that God would deliver Jerusalem into their hands, they charged forward with one ladder, climbed over the curtain wall and attacked. They managed to steady it against the main wall near the Damascus Gate and men rushed to the top. The first man to reach the battlement lost his arm to a mamluk sword and fell to earth. A fierce onslaught ensued. Some managed to mount the inner wall to engage in hand-to-hand combat but they were soon repelled by reinforcements and a few survivors fled back to camp.

Demoralized and staggering from thirst, the men called a council to decide on a course of action. No more would they waste good fighting men with these futile assaults. They needed siege engines. But the nearest forests were thirty miles away and they had not a single axe or nail, and not a soul left among them knew how to build a decent catapult.

• • • • •

Ramiro could hear the din of battle in the distance. Then he heard another rattle of keys. The cell door opened and the jailer shoved four men into the cell. All of them wore the robes of a rabbi. One of them was an old man assisted by two others, it was Rabbi Moshe.

Ramiro rose to his feet. "Rabbi? Why are you here?"

Two men led Moshe to a bench and tried to make him comfortable. "It seems we are a threat to Iftikhar," he said in a raspy voice. He still looked pale and sick and his chiseled, gray face sagged in despair. "They are afraid we will aid the Christians. A preposterous claim! Why would we help them? They kill Hebrews."

"Iftikhar is probably afraid of any dissent at this time," said Ramiro, who was really not sure what to say. Moshe was right, of course, and he tried to comfort him in a clumsy way. The other rabbis remained sullen and were clearly worried.

Some hours later, the cell door opened again and guards pushed in six more men. One was Bishop Aliphas and another was Brother Gerard from the monastery. The rest were clearly Christian clergymen, some of whom he had met briefly. They were all badly beaten and Gerard looked terrible. Crude, blood-soaked bandages wrapped his hands and feet. He could hardly walk and had to be helped in.

"Brother Gerard!" Ramiro shouted. "What have they done to you?"

Red welts ran across Gerard's bald head, cut by the lash of whips. He spoke with difficulty through swollen cheeks and lips. "I've been charged as a traitor."

Bishop Aliphas broke in to speak for him. "We were all sent to the battlements, Ramiro. Iftikhar ordered us to throw stones on the Christians. Most of us refused so they beat us. And they caught Brother Gerard throwing them bread so they burned his hands and feet and beat him too, as you can see. Then they raided the monastery, where they took anything of value."

"Ramiro!" said Gerard gritting his teeth with the effort. "What are you doing here?"

"It seems that Iftikhar fears I will aid the Christians as you did. And those ridiculous rumors about me creating miracles did not help." He waved his arm to a bench. "Come, Brother. You must lay down here. Let me have a look at these wounds."

• • • • •

The days passed and the men in the dungeon soon found little to talk about. They waited for any word of events, but nothing came. Bishop Aliphas hardly spoke at all. In fact, he had said nothing for days. Most of the time, he knelt in prayer, letting the camel spiders scurry across his legs. It was difficult to know where he stood on any issue, while Brother Gerard left no such ambiguity.

Ramiro paced back and forth. Often, he went to the cell door and pushed on it, hoping that, by the will of God, it would open for him. It was still locked. He went back to the bench, sitting down hard. Adele, he thought, I hope she's alright. I hope she got the cross. She can't go home, not now. He got to his feet and paced again. What if they caught her? Where would she be? I must talk to Iftikhar. What in God's name is going on? He sat down again, gnawing on the knuckle of one hand. God forgive me. I should never have brought her here. You idiot!

"You look worried, Brother Ramiro," said Gerard. The swelling had gone from his face, though long, thin scabs remained. Rough bandages still wrapped his hands and feet.

Ramiro pulled his knuckle from his mouth. "How long will we be detained here, Brother Gerard?"

"For as long as Iftikhar wishes," he said, rubbing at the searing itch of his burns.

Ramiro nodded, still thinking of Adele. "You said all Christians were driven out. Are you sure?"

"I'm sure most were. Why do you ask?"

Ramiro was still uncomfortable speaking of his wife with a fellow monk. "I... I have many friends in the city," he said, veiling his thoughts. "I pray they are safe."

"So do I, Brother. And I pray these good men will conquer soon and bring the Holy City to Christian care."

There was no privacy in the cell and all men overheard his remark. "Unfortunately," said Rabbi Moshe in a raspy voice, "not all of us share your view. Surely you have heard of the massacre at Antioch?"

Gerard said nothing. He turned his head away from them and whispered to Ramiro. "Cursed Hebrews."

Ramiro reddened and stood up quickly, as if to disassociate himself from the man.

"And what of Maarat?" asked an indignant Ibrahim, breaking his silence. "There is nothing left! They killed everyone. Is this what you want?"

Gerard avoided looking at him too. Instead he stared straight ahead. "God's will be done," he said righteously.

Ibrahim rose to his feet. Defiantly, he addressed everyone, as if he were giving a sermon in the mosque. "When the great Caliph Umar conquered Jerusalem, he persecuted no one. He assured the Christians that their holy places would go unmolested. And this still holds true today." He turned his sad eyes to the Rabbi. "And was it not the Caliph who allowed Hebrews to return to Jerusalem after centuries of Roman exile? So tell me now, is it better the Muslim way or the barbarian way?" He sat down. "I will say no more."

GENOESE

Unbeknown to the Crusaders, the Egyptians had abandoned the port of Jaffa. Although Al-Afdal knew the barbarians gathered around the walls of Jerusalem, he believed that Jaffa was safe enough left alone and so he gathered his troops in Ascalon instead. So when the Genoese approached Jaffa warily, on the lookout for Egyptian ships, they were surprised to discover their good fortune.

The Crusader's plea for help, sent from Tripoli with bags of gold, had been safely delivered and the Genoese answered their call with six merchant galleys, four of their own and two English, bringing supplies of all kinds; tools, ropes, hammers, nails, axes, mattocks and hatchets, as well as food and shelter. Also sailing on these ships, were many craftsmen skilled in the building of war machines. And there was a monk, a single Benedictine.

Aldebert clung to the rail of a Genoese galley. Sea air lashed his face and rippled his black robe as tears welled in his eyes and rolled down his cheeks. The Holy Land! he thought with mounting exhilaration. Praise be to God, I'm here, I'm finally here! He felt for the Abbot's letter, the one meant for Ramiro. Please, Saint Benedict, I pray he is safe.

"Look, Father Aldebert," said Louis the Carpenter. "The docks are deserted. The cranes sit idle. No one is here. And no damned heathen. God paves our way."

When Aldebert boarded ship in Bari, he was shocked to find Louis, who he had heard was killed in Nicomedia after it was overrun by Abul Kasim. Louis told him his story, how he and Mathilda had watched in helpless terror as a band of raiders snatched up Adele and tied her to a horse, how the same cruel men came after them with their swords, how he watched in horror as they slaughtered poor Mathilda, and how her dying screams still haunted his dreams. He too, was pierced through and left for dead in a pool of his own blood, but shortly after the assault, a Greek farmer rescued him and nursed him back to health.

Louis was no longer the light-hearted man he used to be. He seldom smiled anymore and, every once in a while, Aldebert saw his round, rough-shaven face clench in a grimace, as if his old wounds had opened up again.

"You're right, Louis," said Aldebert. "I see no one, not even an animal."

"The bastards have fled in fear," said Louis with bitterness as he watched a skiff depart for shore. "But the Captain says he won't venture to port until an armed escort arrives from Jerusalem. Look," he said, pointing down to the skiff. "There go the messengers now."

• • • • •

No sooner had Iftikhar left the Al-Aqsa Mosque when his lieutenant rushed up the stairs of the Temple Mount to greet him.

"Commander!" he heaved. "Christian ships have arrived at Jaffa!"

Iftikhar stopped. Behind him, stood a servant who carried his prayer mat. He waved the man away. "How many?" he asked as he continued to walk away from the mosque.

"Six, my Lord," said the Sudanese, rushing after him. "And the Christian army already knows. We failed to stop their messengers."

"And where is our fleet?"

"The fleet awaits in Ascalon, Sahib, along with six hundred cavalry."

Iftikhar continued down the steps where a groom waited with his horse. "Send them out!" he yelled as he mounted. "Immediately!"

JAFFA, JUNE 17

The Crusaders roared with delight when the Genoese messengers arrived to tell them the good news. Godfrey immediately dispatched a hundred knights and fifty infantry for the one day journey to Jaffa, not realizing that six hundred crack Arab troops waited for them.

A vanguard of knights first sighted the Arabs east of Ramla and, despite being vastly outnumbered, they charged forward, confident that God would lead them to victory. But they were almost wiped out before the other knights, riding at a distance, received news of the battle and came galloping to their aid.

The Arabs had heard the grisly tales about these invincible, bloodthirsty barbarians who ate human flesh, and they were nervous. At first, thinking there were only thirty of them charging recklessly, they were confident in victory and fought with valor. But when they sighted a cloud of dust on the horizon, they were certain it was an ambush and that thousands more of the murderous infidels were on their way. In terror, they turned and fled. Godfrey's knights chased them down, and in the disarray, two hundred Arabs fell to the Crusader sword while the rest fled back to the walls of Ascalon, leaving all their possessions behind. The knights took much plunder, including gold and horses, and spent some time dividing the spoils before moving on.

When they arrived at Jaffa, there was a great celebration. They spent the night in festive drinking and feasting, telling wild tales of their victories to the excited Genoese. But in the hazy mist of dawn, when they awoke with pounding heads, they found themselves surrounded by the Egyptian fleet from Ascalon.

In near panic, they unloaded their cargo onto the docks and abandoned their ships. And before the Arabs could amass a land force, they commandeered every pack animal they could find and rushed to Jerusalem with their precious cargo.

War Machines

With supplies at hand, the Crusaders felt renewed vigor and confidence. Local Christians told them where to find wood in the forests of Samaria, thirty miles away and, with the help of fifty Muslim slaves, they soon brought back a train of timber-laden camels.

Iftikhar watched in dismay as the barbarians furiously constructed the finest war machines of the time, two huge towers, a massive battering ram with an iron-clad head, catapults, large crossbows, scaling ladders and portable screens. To the west, he watched Godfrey's tower rise up slowly between the Jaffa Gate and Castle Al-Jalud while, to the south, Raymond's rose higher than the Zion Gate.

"Are the catapults ready?"

"Yes, my Lord. We have aimed five at the north tower and nine to the south."

Iftikhar worried more about the Zion Gate than the north wall. There was no curtain wall to the south and he felt it was more vulnerable. "And the walls are prepared?"

"Yes, Commander. We have hung ropes and bags of straw to soften the blow of their missiles."

Iftikhar clenched his jaw in worry. In the name of Allah and the Prophet, when will Al-Afdal come?

• • • • •

Aldebert scurried through the crowds of fighting men outside the walls of Jerusalem. He recognized Robert of Flanders, who he had met in Bari, and was pleasantly shocked to find Drugo the Red still in his service. Drugo was now thirty-five. He was still one of Robert's best warriors, although he was not as fast as he used to be. His hair was cut short, finding it more convenient for battle, and his ruddy face boasted many more scars, wrinkles and broken teeth.

"Have you seen Father Ramiro," Aldebert asked.

"No," said Drugo bluntly. "I haven't seen him since Gallipoli. Do you really think he's still alive?"

With a shudder, Aldebert remembered that fateful day when the Turks captured Ramiro. "I believe he is, Sir Drugo. I received two letters from him. He must still be in the city."

"I doubt that," said Drugo. "All the Christians were driven out."

Aldebert could feel his expectations heighten. "And where did these Christians go?"

"Some have joined the fight. Some went to Bethlehem."

"Bethlehem! Maybe he's there at the birthplace of Our Lord," said Aldebert, feeling a thrill. "Uh... which way is that?"

A NOBLEMAN

Godfrey and his men yelled and hooted from a safe distance outside the Jaffa Gate. They paraded a stumbling captive back and forth, a corpulent man dressed in the finest Dabiqi cloth hemmed in gold thread. They had captured him on a foraging expedition near Bethlehem and thought he might prove useful.

Iftikhar recognized the man, it was the sheikh of Bayt Jala, who had come to him some months ago to pledge his allegiance. What were these barbarians shouting?

"Bring the foreign scribe to me," he told his lieutenant. "Quickly!"

Within minutes, his men shoved Ramiro in front of Iftikhar, who pointed out from the battlement of the Citadel. "Tell me what they say! What are they doing?"

The men laughed aloud as the fat sheikh stumbled and panted, his face bruised and swollen from a recent beating. Ramiro noticed two belligerent men screaming vile curses. One had red hair. The other was huge. Blessed Mary, Mother of God! It's Drugo! And there's Arles the Executioner!

A thin man with long black hair shrilled at the hostage. "Renounce your pagan faith before the walls of the Holy City! Accept the True Faith and live!" It was Arnulf Malecorne.

The sheikh shook his battered head. "I will not," he huffed. "May Allah and the Prophet be praised!"

"Then you will die!" Arnulf screeched. The squires who dragged him back and forth forced the man to his knees. Arnulf looked up at the Egyptians watching from the Citadel. "Look! You pagan bastards!" he yelled. "Look and learn the fate of all who refuse to accept Jesus Christ as their savior!"

A tall squire raised his sword and with a single blow of his thick broadsword, hacked off the sheikh's head. The men roared their approval and shouted more jaunts and curses.

Ramiro watched in dismay, interpreting all that he heard.

Iftikhar exploded. "Get the Christian priests! We will show them the fate of those who refuse Islam!"

Gerard and his fellow monks, six in all, were dragged limping to the battlement. Ramiro was shoved among them and they were made to stand in front of the castellations, facing the invaders. Iftikhar's executioner stood behind them, holding his sword with both hands.

But few Crusaders noticed. They had finished their amusement and were dispersing, going back to their work on their war machines. Drugo looked up to the Citadel just as Iftikhar's swordsman sliced off the head of a monk and tossed it over the wall. "What in hell's blazes are they doing?" he asked Arles. "Are those monks?" He could see the dark robes but these men had full heads of hair.

"Could be," said Arles. "But who gives a shit? Probably those Greek heretics!"

"Good riddance! It'll save us the trouble." Drugo said with a smirk and they turned away laughing.

Ramiro looked down. The slain monk's blood drained onto the smooth stones of the battlement where it pooled around his feet. He thought of Adele and worried how she would survive here alone. He heard the executioner step up behind him and he lifted his eyes to heaven, asking God to forgive his sins and to prepare his soul for life everlasting. The swordsman raised his blade to strike.

"Look Sahib!" Ramiro cried out. "They walk away! It means nothing to them!"

Iftikhar raised his hand to stay the executioner's sword. "Do they care nothing for their fellow Christians?"

"Not for the Roman Christians, Sahib!"

"What do you mean?"

"They think we are Romans, my Lord. Just as you hate the Sunni, these men hate the Orthodox."

Iftikhar nodded slowly, he understood the parallel. "Take them away!" he yelled at his guards. "And clean up this mess!"

A PROCESSION, JULY 8

Aldebert returned from Bethlehem in disappointment. For many days, he visited the churches and dallied about the markets, hoping someone would have seen Ramiro. But no one remembered a dark-haired, heavyset Benedictine monk.

So he returned to Jerusalem feeling downcast, but was soon swept up in the emotion of the moment. A holy man had a vision of the dead Bishop Adhemar, in which the bishop had told them to purge themselves of uncleanliness and to turn from their evil ways, to march around Jerusalem barefoot and, through the patronage of the saints, invoke the mercy of the Lord. And then, on the ninth day, he said, God would come to the aid of His servants and deliver them victory.

Aldebert believed it and eagerly joined the priests, monks and bishops who walked barefoot around the walls of Jerusalem. Arnulf walked up front, raising his crucifix high above his head. The rest carried with them many crosses and relics of the saints and prayed to Almighty God in high voices that He should not desert His Chosen people in time of need. Behind them, a long line of Christian warriors also trudged barefoot, carrying their standards high, piercing the air with trumpet blasts.

But the Arabs did not share their sentiments and shadowed the Crusaders as they made their circuit from the Damascus Gate to Mount Zion, standing on the battlements blaring their own horns, screaming curses and mocking them in every way. And, as at Maarat, they fixed makeshift crosses atop the walls in mockery and abuse. They beat them with sticks and smashed them against the stone walls, some they spat on, others they pissed on while hurling the most vile insults. And when the Christians arrived at Mount Zion, which brought them closer to the wall, they peppered them with arrows, killing some and wounding others.

Aldebert seethed in fury. God-damned pagans! They will burn in Hellfire for this! May God give us victory. But as they climbed Mount Zion, his thoughts turned again to Father Ramiro. Where is he? Do the godless savages have him? He shuddered at the thought.

The long procession eventually gathered near the Church of the Blessed Mary and Arnulf Malecorne, seeking to reassure his flock, raised his voice in sermon, reminding them that God would be merciful to all who followed Him, even to his grave.

• • • • •

In the dungeon, Ramiro heard the trumpet blasts, the shouting and loud commotion, as did the other prisoners. "Does the battle begin?" he asked, scowling in worry.

No one made reply, although some shrugged their shoulders before returning to their nervous prayers. Ibrahim prayed for a Muslim victory, even if it was to be Shia. Rabbi Moshe, who feared a slaughter, also prayed for the Arabs. Only Aliphas, Gerard and all their clergy implored God for a Christian triumph.

JULY 14

The Egyptian army was on its way, hurrying across the Sinai Desert. Word reached the Crusaders and they knew they had to attack soon.

For weeks, Iftikhar had watched Godfrey's men assemble their huge, wooden tower outside the western wall, near the Castle Al-Jalud. Now its black silhouette loomed higher than the wall itself. But he was prepared. He had the walls strengthened and buffeted, his catapults and ammunition placed ready at hand, tar heated, firebrands dipped.

To the south, Raymond's Tower was ready to advance toward the Zion Gate. Here too, Iftikhar's men watched and waited with a massive store of stones, arrows and firebrands. And when they saw the Christians filling in the dry moat, they knew they were going to attack soon.

• • • • •

"Sahib! Sahib! Wake up!" shouted the Sudanese lieutenant.

Iftikhar jumped from his bed and rushed to the door.

"Sahib, they have moved a tower!"

"What do you mean?" Iftikhar asked in confusion. "They moved it to the wall?"

"No, Sahib. They have moved it to Herod's Gate!"

"Herod's Gate? Impossible! That's almost a mile!"

The lieutenant bowed. "The impossible is done, my Lord. What shall we do?"

Iftikhar rushed to don his armor, jumped on his mount, and galloped to the north wall. He had underestimated Godfrey's intelligence and resolve. Unbeknown to him, the Christian lord built his tower in sections, so that it could be easily taken down and reassembled. Its construction outside Castle

Al-Jalud was a ruse. In the dark of night, the barbarians had carried it, piece by piece, using hundreds of men and slaves, to a site near Herod's Gate, on flatter ground that sloped down towards the wall and favored the tower's movement. Waiting beside the tower, was their huge battering ram and three giant catapults, standing ready to provide cover fire.

"Move the catapults!" Iftikhar shouted nervously. "Move it all! Let's go! Let's go!" He cursed himself for his stupidity. The north section of wall was one of the weakest and had no towers nearby to defend it. The battlements were narrow and his catapults would be restricted in movement.

Raymond's tower at the Zion Gate did not share these advantages. Even after filling in the dry moat so his tower could approach the wall, he still had rough ground to traverse, and it was all slightly uphill. He had no element of surprise and the Arabs had a vast arsenal waiting for him.

But Godfrey knew he had the advantage and the attack began. His huge catapults began an incessant barrage of stones and fireballs against the wall and fortifications. Under this cover, hundreds of men strained to move the massive battering ram, pushing it up to the curtain wall. Arrows rained down as they repeatedly pulled the heavy beam back before releasing it against the stones. And by late afternoon, a section collapsed, creating an enormous breach. As the ram smashed through, its own momentum drove it forward until it crashed against the city wall itself.

The Arabs began to drench the ram in burning oil until it roared in flames and, in a desperate bid to save it, the French began to throw their precious water at it and tried to pull it out. But Godfrey stopped them.

The ram had created a breach but now it blocked that same breach and was jammed between the curtain wall and the city wall. Hence, it blocked the path of the tower, which was the whole purpose of the advance. Godfrey realized their best hope was to let the ram burn to ash in order to clear the way. So he ordered his men to save their water and add more fire to it instead.

It did not take Iftikhar long to see their plan and, in a laughable reversal of tactics, he ordered his men to put the fire out and they started to throw buckets of water over it. But the flames were so intense by this time that the water had little effect.

Meanwhile at the Zion Gate, Raymond's men were under a deadly barrage of stones hurled from Iftikhar's catapults. And as they attempted to move the tower to the wall, thousands of arrows and firebrands fell upon them like a hail from hell, pounding the tower relentlessly. The men scurried around it putting out fire after fire, but they faltered under the weight of the Arab assault and, before dusk, pulled the damaged tower back to safety. As the sky dimmed, the battle stopped and both camps settled into a night of fear.

JULY 15

In the hazy light of dawn, both towers began another advance against the walls. The Arabs unleashed another deadly hail of arrows, firebrands and stones against Raymond's tower. Men shouted in defiance and screamed in death as stones pounded against them in a savage, incessant barrage. Balls of fire exploded in their midst and the air choked with burning tar and pitch. Raymond's tower began to burn and fracture in the hellish din of battle, and then it collapsed.

On the north wall, Godfrey kept up the bombardment with his catapults while his men sweated and heaved against the three-story tower, inching it forward. Arrows riddled them and balls of fire burned them alive, their dying screams piercing the summer dawn. A thick, putrid smoke hung about them in a black fog, stifling their breath. Inside the tower, hundreds of men waited, including Drugo, Otto and Arles. Godfrey himself was on the top floor as the cumbersome structure swayed and rocked towards the city wall. Arnulf's golden crucifix glittered from the tower roof as the Arab catapults pounded the wattle-and-hide covers. A stone crashed straight through the wattle, smashing the skull of a man standing right next to Godfrey.

As the tower edged to the wall, Iftikhar's catapults began to lose their effect. The tight confinement of the battlements made it impossible to adjust their range for close encounters. The huge structure approached and soon loomed high above. Now Godfrey and his men used the advantage of height to pelt the defenders with their own firebrands and missiles.

The Arabs fought back with a vengeance, throwing everything they had at the tower, now only a few paces from the wall. But the French firebrands had ignited the wooden infrastructure of the lower wall as well as nearby buildings and, in minutes, the choking smoke and searing flames drove the Arabs back. Godfrey's tower hit the wall, the side came down and his men stormed out. Drugo, Otto and Arles came out screaming war cries as a flurry of arrows peppered their ranks. Arles staggered back - an arrow stuck in his throat. He pulled at it madly, choking on his blood. But another struck him right between the eyes and the huge man tumbled off the battlements. Few noticed in the melee and the shouting men continued to pour out of the tower by the hundreds. The Muslims faltered, pulling back in hopeless terror. The Christians charged into them, hacking and chopping with fanatic fury, clearing the battlements of all resistance. Now heady with the scent of victory, they stormed through the city like a pack of wild dogs, thrusting and stabbing their way through the screaming streets.

To the south, Raymond kept up his attack with catapults and arrows but he had lost the advantage. Then, suddenly, the Arab defense stopped. There was no one on the walls. A heaving messenger ran up to him. "We have breached the wall!" he shouted. "Attack!"

With shouts of joy, Raymond's men rushed forward with their ladders and scrambled over Zion Gate.

• • • • •

Iftikhar saw all was lost. He jumped on his horse and raced through the city to the Tower of David, followed closely by his officers and guards. They locked themselves inside the Citadel and waited for the worst. Meanwhile his valiant men rallied around the Dome of the Rock, putting up fierce resistance, but the Crusaders soon cut them down by the sheer weight of their onslaught.

French, Germans, Normans and Flemings raged down every street, killing everyone in their path. They smashed down the doors of every building, slaughtering women and children, chopping and stabbing with knife and sword, seizing infants by their feet, splattering their skulls against stone walls. They spared no one. The blood of their victims drenched the narrow cobblestone streets and poured into the gutters.

The Jews ran for the safety of the synagogue and locked themselves inside, cowering in terror. They yelled out of the windows, begging for mercy. But the Crusaders scoffed at their pleas and set fire to the building, laughing aloud at the hellish screams of those burning alive.

Hours later, when the long trail of terrified shrieks and screams finally subsided, the Soldiers of God began to pillage, grabbing all they could. Men ran to and fro over the heaps of corpses, slitting open the bellies and groping into the guts for swallowed gold and coins.

• • • • •

No one in the dungeon spoke, but Ramiro still had to shout over the blood-curdling wails and screams of the victims. "It's a massacre!" he said, wringing his hands. He thought of Adele, sick with worry.

"The Protectors of the Faith have arrived and conquer," said Gerard with satisfaction.

"Protectors?" yelled one of the rabbis. "They are nothing but butchers! And for what? To gaze upon the sepulcher of your crucified bastard!"

Gerard lunged at the rabbi but the other rabbis stood as one and beat him off. "Scourge of Christ!" screamed Gerard as his monks held him back. "You will burn in Hellfire!"

"Hell is all yours, you Gentile shit!"

"God bless the Pope of Rome!" Gerard taunted. "And his almighty victory over the pagans and the unclean!"

"God damn the Satan of Rome and his wicked ways!" the rabbis shouted back.

"Enough!" yelled Ramiro as he stepped between them. "Enough! Are we going to start killing each other too?" The men settled back, still seething. And as the clamor in the cell died down, so did the din of battle outside. He went to the cell door and shouted. "Guards! Guards!" But there was no answer. He returned to his seat to wait in a frightening silence.

• • • • •

While Tancred took Castle Al-Jalud and Godfrey laid claim to the Temple Mount and the Emir's Palace, Raymond circled the Tower of David. He wanted to rule Jerusalem and was well aware of the strategic importance of the Citadel. He sent a messenger to Iftikhar, who was still holed up inside with his guards, and asked him to relinquish the tower, promising him safe conduct out of the city.

"Can we trust the old man, Sahib?" asked the lieutenant.

Iftikhar smiled in pity. "Trust? No, there is no trust. But what choice do we have? We will surely die if we stay here, but we may live if we accept." So he agreed to Raymond's terms and surrendered the tower. Much to his surprise, the old, one-eyed man lived up to his bargain and gave them safe passage to Ascalon.

• • • • •

Ramiro jumped to his feet when a group of bloody knights rushed into the jailhouse. The stark-eyed warriors, panting from their slaughter and still brandishing their swords, milled about the iron bars silently and stared into the cell. They were drenched in the fresh blood of their victims, which dripped in heavy beads from their hair and beards. "What goes here?" one asked. "Give us your gold!"

"Praise the Lord!" Gerard shouted at them. "Soldiers of God! Free us from these pagan bars! I am Brother Gerard of the Church of Saint Mary and these are my blessed monks," he said pointing to his men, who were dressed in black robes.

One of the soldiers went to the nearby guardroom and grabbed a set of keys. Eventually, he unlatched the door and opened it. "Give us your money!"

Gerard rushed towards him. "But we are prisoners, we have nothing." The soldier pushed him away and he stumbled backwards.

The man stalked into the cell with four others, eyeing the prisoners with a loathing sneer. "Look what we have here," he said in taunt. "A pack of foking Hebrews!" But only Gerard and Ramiro understood his words.

Rabbi Moshe understood their gestures and opened his hands. "We have nothing," he said in Arabic. The soldier did not understand him and did not care. With no further provocation, he brought his sword down on the old rabbi's head, splitting his skull. Moshe slumped dead to the floor and the other soldiers moved forward for the kill. The remaining rabbis, now splattered in Moshe's blood, began to weep, bowing their heads in prayer.

"Stop!" yelled Ramiro as he rushed forward in shock. By habit, he had spoken in Arabic and the blood-drenched knight, thinking he was an Arab, swung his arm out hard and smashed him across the head. Ramiro flew back against the wall, bashing his head again on the rough-hewn stones. He collapsed unconscious, bleeding at the temple. The soldier raised his sword to run him through.

"Stop!" Gerard cried. "Don't you see his cross? He's a Christian!"

HOLY SEPULCHER

Before the sun had set over the Judean Hills, the Soldiers of God gathered en masse at the Holy Sepulcher, the very place for which they had given so many lives and so many years. They surrounded the aedicule with their hair and beards matted with half-dried blood and their clothes crusted hard with it. In both hands, they carried hefty bags of loot, which they gripped greedily, even as they fell to their knees rejoicing and weeping and giving thanks to God, victorious and triumphant.

Arnulf Malecorne and the priests raised their voices in a ringing song of exaltation and the soldiers joined in, rasping their praise as hot tears streaked through the blood and ash blackening their faces. Arnulf made loud offerings and supplications to the Lord. "This is the day which the Lord has made," he cried, "let us rejoice and be glad in it! This is a new day, a new joy, the Holy Sepulcher has been liberated!" The soldiers howled in ecstasy.

Brother Aldebert fell to his knees as the reverence of the moment overwhelmed him. When he had first rushed into Jerusalem after the slaughter, he was ecstatic about their glorious victory. But even his wildest joy did not prepare him for what he saw. He was not a soldier. In fact, he was still haunted by the death of Wiker the Blade some years ago. So when he had to step over the grisly mass of dead, the sight overcame his zealous sensibility and he found himself fleeing back through the gate, heaving up his breakfast on the way.

But he soon heard from others that all were gathering at the Church of the Holy Sepulcher and he quickly summoned his courage to make his way through the gruesome, desolate city. Now, as great tears streamed down his thin face, he could hardly believe he was actually in the presence of the Tomb of Christ, the holiest place on earth. God had delivered them a great victory, as was His will. He lifted his tonsured head to the high ceiling of the rotunda and thanked all the saints, Mother Mary, the Most Highs, Jesus, and all the hosts of heaven.

AFTERMATH

Ramiro opened his eyes and stared up at the dim ceiling. The cell was quiet. He put a hand to his throbbing head and felt dry blood on his temple. He sat up and strained to his feet, steadying himself against the wall while rubbing his face with both hands as he tried to compose his thoughts.

When he pulled his hands away and his eyes cleared, he began to discern the macabre scene sprawled out before him in the murky light. Moshe and the other rabbis were all dead, strewn across the floor, drenched red with their own blood. Two were beheaded and another had his arms chopped off. Ibrahim was dead too. They had sliced his belly open and there was barely a part of him that was recognizable. But Bishop Aliphas, Gerard and the other clergymen were gone.

He turned his head away in a heave of revulsion. His stomach hurled but there was nothing to come out. He stumbled to the open cell door and, steadying himself with a hand against the wall, made his way down the narrow, dingy hall to the stairs leading into the lower chamber of Castle Al-Jalud. There was only one thing on his mind, and that was Adele. Iftikhar said she was safe. What did he mean? Did he confine her here - in the castle?

He made his way up a thin flight of stone steps. It was strangely quiet except for a distant scream, quickly silenced. He reached the top of the stairway and entered the lower hall. Mutilated bodies spread across the wide, blood-soaked floor; soldiers, clerks, servants, men and women. "By the blood of Christ!" he blurted in disgust and turned his head away again. But his eyes crept back reluctantly to the horrific scene. He had to know. Was she among them? He stepped between the corpses, looking at each one. Then he rushed through the castle, searching every room. Bodies lay everywhere but, with a twisted sense of relief, she was not there.

He saw no sign of the invaders and wondered where they had gone. Did they lay in wait for victims? He snatched a short sword from among the bodies and, from another, he took a thick vest of leather armor. His thoughts turned to his rooms on David Street. Maybe she was there. He ran out into the street.

But he was no sooner out the door when he tripped on a thick stack of corpses and fell face first into the slimy, gory remains. He jumped up in horror but slipped again on blood and guts and fell back. Slowly, he pulled himself up. The sight before him boggled his mind. Maimed and disfigured bodies lay knee-deep across the street. Mounds of torsos, heads, limbs, hands, feet and guts clogged his every move. The air reeked of burnt flesh and a thick, acrid smoke choked his lungs. His head reeled and he staggered from the shock. I've got to get home!

Covered in blood from his fall among the corpses, he worked his way down the street brandishing the sword. He passed the Church of the Holy Sepulcher, where he heard men singing inside. A few Crusaders milled about outside but paid him no heed. He made his way to the building on David Street and rushed up the stairs.

The rooms were a mess. His books and papers were scattered everywhere, the furniture smashed. "Adele!" he shouted in desperation, dashing into the bedroom. The mattress was slit open, and their clothes thrown about. She was not here.

In a daze, he sat on the battered remains of his desk and lowered his head. He looked down on his letters and books and stooped to the floor where, in trance-like movements, he began to pick them up, as if somehow they could help him piece his life back together. Cold tears rolled down his cheeks, streaking through the blood on his face.

"What are you doing here?" a voice shouted. "This is mine. I seized it! Get out!"

Ramiro looked up, not bothering to wipe away his tears. A bloodied soldier stood in the doorway carrying a heavy sack of booty that clanged and tinkled with his every move.

"Where's my wife?" Ramiro asked.

"Your wife?" asked the man. "Are you mad? We brought no women." Then he chuckled. "And already you've got yourself a wench. A sweet young whore, no doubt."

"The woman who lived here," said Ramiro. "Where is she?"

"There was no one here. Now get out!"

"You've killed her, like all the rest! You've murdered a Christian!"

"I tell you there was no one here. Who the hell are you anyway?" he sneered. "I'll wager you're one of Raymond's men. Get out!"

Ramiro waved the sword in his hand. "Where is she?"

The soldier drew his blood-stained sword and held his ground. "You idiot! I've told you. You know the rules. I seized the place and it's mine!"

Ramiro hesitated, feeling he was no match for this hardened warrior. He stared at the man, he looked familiar. Then he recognized his beady, green eyes. "I know you," he said accusingly.

"Do you now," said the man, still holding his sword. "Well then you would be wise to lower your weapon."

"You're Otto, Otto of Bremen."

"Yeh, so what?"

"You ride with Drugo the Red!"

"Yeh. So what? Everyone knows that." He stared at Ramiro, the eyes, the dark eyes. "Who the hell are you, anyway?"

"I am Ramiro of Cluny."

"Cluny? Then you are one of Raymond's men."

"No, I'm from the monastery. Do you not remember me?"

Otto stared at him. "I haven't seen you before."

"Yes you have, many years ago."

Otto's eyes went wide. "You're that damned monk!"

Ramiro nodded.

"We heard you were dead. But your dress, your hair. You don't look like a monk."

"I would have died a long time ago if I did."

"What in God's name are you doing here?"

"Surely you remember, Otto. I was heading for Jerusalem."

"Oh yeh, that's right. To see the bishop or something."

"The patriarch."

"Whatever the heretics call him," said Otto with annoyance.

"And these are my rooms you have destroyed."

"All's fair in war, Ramiro. This place is mine now, but I'll let you stay. You can pay me the rent."

Ramiro gave him a despairing look. "The rents are of no concern to me, Otto of Bremen. Besides, who is left to rent? You have slaughtered the entire population."

Otto's thin lips pulled back in a grotesque smile. "We have done marvelous works," he said with some pride. "The Holy City is now cleansed of filth and corrupt pagans."

"The Christians," said Ramiro. "Where are the Christians? Or did you kill them too?"

"Some of the heretics may have got in the way. But the pagan king threw most of 'em out."

"Where did they go?"

"I don't know and I don't care. Now, are you going to pay me the rent?"

• • • • •

Ramiro left Otto behind and rushed to the house of Jameel and his wife Layla. On his way, he saw every door smashed through, all the houses ransacked, the churches too. He found the house and climbed the littered stairs to their rooms. The door was open and he entered cautiously. But it was not long before he spotted their mutilated bodies on the floor, the baby too. He clenched his jaw and backed out the door. "Oh dear Lord my God," he said aloud in a strained voice. "A Christian family! How could this happen? Is this Your will my God?"

• • • • •

Muslim slaves heaved the corpses and body parts onto a huge mound of flesh and bone that grew steadily outside the city walls. Then, with bowed heads, they returned to the blood-caked streets to refill their carts with more of their wretched cargo.

Ramiro watched them work. He checked every corpse, looking for Adele. Once, he sighted a shock of red hair hanging from a cart and yelled out for them to stop. Now inured to grisly visions of the dead, he pulled on the hair and drew out a severed head, wiping the dead face with a rag. To his relief, it was not her.

He ran back and forth between the gates to inspect the many pyramids of dead, but it was too much. There were too many. For a full week, he kept up his gruesome task, returning to his barren and demolished room only for sleep.

One day, as he was standing near the Jaffa Gate, he noticed a number of Christians returning to the city. Many were clergymen who held their scarves tight about their faces to shield themselves from the putrid smoke of burning flesh drifting across their path. Ramiro stopped one of them before he entered the gate.

"From where do you come?" he asked the priest.

"I stayed in Abu Ghosh," said the man.

"Is that where all the Christians went?"

"Not all. They spread out to surrounding villages, staying wherever they could. I believe most went to Bethlehem."

"Have you seen a red-haired woman? Pale complexion, some freckles. Speaks poor Arabic."

The priest shook his head. "I'm sorry. I've seen no one like that. But I haven't had much time to notice people."

"How far is Bethlehem?"

"About four miles south of the Zion Gate."

"Is it safe there?"

The man sighed sadly. "As safe as anywhere if you're a Christian. The Franj seized it. A man by the name of Tancred rules the place."

THE ADVOCATE

Days after the slaughter, the Crusader nobility and the clergymen met in the Al-Aqsa Mosque on the Temple Mount, which they hastily remade into a palace for Godfrey. It was a chaotic scene, nearly everyone was talking and a few shouted to be heard.

The Bishop of Albara, an ally of Raymond, raised his voice above them all. "Count Raymond deserves to rule Jerusalem! He outranks you all. And he's the one who led us south to begin this Holy Crusade!"

Arnulf Malecorne jumped to his feet. "It was Godfrey who breached the walls of Jerusalem! It should be his right to rule!"

Another bishop spoke up, red-faced. "The holiest city on earth should have no secular king. It must be ruled by the Mother Church!" Most of the clergy agreed in loud voices.

Aldebert nodded his head but had no courage to speak.

"But we need someone to command the military," said Robert of Flanders. "We should choose one of us and I say Duke Godfrey deserves the position." Many knights nodded their approval.

Count Raymond stood up and held a hand high. His long, gray hair hung loosely to his shoulders. He glared around the room with one eye and the crowd fell silent. His gaze settled on Godfrey and he raised his voice in indignation. "Have you all forgotten that it is I who first met with the Pope himself to organize and lead this Crusade? And that I was chosen as commander-in-chief?"

The men fell silent for a moment and began to murmur amongst themselves. They knew Pope Urban had never proclaimed Raymond publicly, as was custom. Furthermore, the Count had lost credibility since he failed at Arqah. And here at Jerusalem, it was *his* tower that failed at Zion Gate.

But Raymond persisted. "I remind you all again that we will need the support of the Greek King if we are ever to persist in this endeavor. And I am the one who has established détente with the King while others seek nothing but to satisfy their selfish ambitions!" His look fell again to Godfrey.

Godfrey stood up in a rage, kicking his chair out. "You are one to talk of selfish ambition! Ever since this crusade began, you have done nothing but attempt to covet territory for yourself! And what has the King done for us? Our supplies were delivered by the Genoese and the English!"

"Yes!" Raymond shouted. "But you know they came from the Greeks!"

"Enough!" shouted Arnulf with new courage. "Let the men vote. They will decide."

"But no one will be king," said the Bishop of Albara. "Whoever we elect will serve only as a Protector of the Holy City."

And so it was, much to the seething anger of Raymond, that Godfrey was elected to the newly-created position of Advocate of the Holy Sepulcher, and he wasted little time consolidating his power.

BETHLEHEM

Ramiro washed away the blood and grime in a basin of water. He found some clean clothes among the rubble and donned his leather armor once more. Then he hung his sword from a belt strapped around his shoulder and headed off to Bethlehem on foot.

The road was eerily vacant, only a few Christians made the march to Jerusalem, and once he passed a long line of miserable Muslims, all bound together with ropes and herded by jeering knights who whipped them along.

Tancred's banner fluttered above the huge Church of Nativity in Bethlehem. He made his headquarters here, knowing he would never rule Jerusalem, and worked to lay claim to the surrounding region.

Ramiro milled between the rows of marble pillars lining the cavernous apse of the church, questioning all he met. Most were Christians exiled from Jerusalem before the assault. Learning of the slaughter, many were still leery to return.

"Have you seen a red-haired woman?" Ramiro asked a new arrival. "She's French. About this tall."

"There's an old hag who lives near the well," said the man. "She has red hair."

Ramiro found the house and lingered near the door to draw courage. He knocked and an old woman answered. "What do you want?" she asked. Her hair was red with gray streaks. It was not Adele.

"Sorry to disturb you, Sayyidah, but I am looking for a French woman with red hair."

"Franj you say?"

"Yes, have you seen her?"

"There's a new one who stays at the house of Abel."

"A man?"

The old woman cackled. "Of course he's a man, you fool."

"Is she his... his mistress?"

"I don't know, why don't you ask him?" She slammed the door shut.

• • • • •

Ramiro approached the door of Abel's house. His palms sweated and he felt short of breath. The closer he got to the door, the more his heart pounded. By the time he was ready to knock, he felt faint. The blood drained from his head and he reached out to steady himself against the door jam. He knocked.

A young man in a surprisingly white tunic opened the door a crack. "Peace be upon you, Sayyid. What do you want?" he asked cautiously.

"Peace to you. I am Ramiro of Cluny and I'm looking for a red-haired woman. She's French, pale face. Goes by the name of Adele. Have you seen her?"

"You are Ramiro?" asked the man.

"Yes, yes! You have seen her?"

The man motioned to him. "I am Abel. Please, come in."

Ramiro stepped into the tidy room, colorfully decorated with silk cushions and rich carpets. "Where is she?" he asked impatiently.

"I think she returned to Jerusalem."

"Praise the Lord!" said Ramiro loudly, barely containing his relief. "But how did she get here?"

"She came with my uncle, Pakrad."

"Pakrad? The Armenian priest?"

"Yes. Do you know him?"

"Yes, yes. When did she return to Jerusalem?"

"Just yesterday. She left by herself. I warned her of the dangers but she would not listen."

JERUSALEM

Ramiro ran most of the way back to Jerusalem, stopping only when he was out of breath. He hurried through the gates, ran down David Street, rushed up the stairs to his rooms - but she was not there. "Pakrad! The Monastery of Saint James!" he shouted and flew down the stairs, heading for Armenian Street.

The almost empty streets had been stripped of corpses, leaving thick, dried pools of blood over the flagstones. The hot air stank of it. He arrived at the monastery heaving from his run, only to find the door locked. He banged on it madly with his fist. There was no answer. He banged again.

The door slat opened but he saw no face. "What do you want?" asked a voice.

"Is Adele here?" he choked, fighting back tears.

"You are Ramiro?"

"Yes, is she here?"

He could hear the latch fall. The door opened. "Come in. Quickly!"

He stepped into the cool interior. It was the same place where he had met Jameel many months ago and he felt a sharp pang of sorrow for the bright young man so senselessly slaughtered. The place was dark. "Are you Pakrad?"

"Yes," he said as he shut the door and latched it. His big ears poked out from a shag of brown hair and his eyes bulged in a disarming manner. "Come with me."

Ramiro followed him through the rubble of pillage still cluttering the long hall. They went down a short flight of stairs before coming to the monk's cells, where he knocked on one of the doors.

"Who is it?" asked a familiar voice.

Ramiro tried to reply but a lump in his throat choked his words.

"It's Pakrad. There is someone to see you."

The door opened a little. Adele held her bronze mace in one hand and nodded to Pakrad before looking at Ramiro. At first, she was taken back, dressed as he was in a bloodied leather vest and carrying a sword at his side. But when she met his tearful eyes, she dropped the mace, slapped her hands to her face, and burst into a sob. Ramiro sprang forward, clutching her in his arms.

● ● ● ● ●

"Tell me what happened," said Ramiro when they were alone.

Adele kissed him again as he held her close. "When I went to Madteos shop," she said, "he was gone. So I went to his house and it was deserted. Everything was upturned, it looked like it was looted. Madteos was gone. But Pakrad was there."

"What was he doing there?"

"I don't know. I think he was looking for something. Maybe the cross. He scared the wits out of me. He said that Iftikhar's askari had ransacked the place. He thought they were rogue soldiers looking for gold before the battle." She rested her head against his shoulder. "I told him who I was, that I had come for the cross. But he said he knew nothing about the bargain you made with Madteos. That's when we heard the soldiers coming back. He told me to run but I couldn't return to our rooms, so he took me to Bethlehem, to the safety of his nephew's house."

"Did you meet Madteos there?"

"Yes, briefly. He said he didn't have the cross. He said he barely had time to flee with the clothes on his back. But he told Pakrad where it was and said we could have it. He said it was evil, that it brought a curse on his house." She stroked the back of Ramiro's head. "Is it cursed, Ramiro?"

"No, my love, it is not cursed. It is merely a thing among accursed men. Did he say where it is?"

"He said it was safely hidden. Will you go with Pakrad to get it?"

"Should I bother?" he said with a slight shake of his head. "It doesn't matter. The whole affair has been a failure. And what meaning will the cross have now? The patriarch is dead, they say. It's too late."

Adele drew back. "But we're so near. And if it's made of gold, perhaps we could exchange it for a house and new life in France."

"It's not mine, Adele."

"Then whose is it?"

"Well, it belongs to the patriarch."

"You mean the one that's dead?"

"Then it belongs to the church."

"The church?" Adele scoffed. "You've seen what happens to gold in the church. It fills the bags of these thieves."

Quest for a Monk

Aldebert kept asking every Crusader he met, but no one had seen a Benedictine monk named Ramiro. He renewed his efforts only after the exiled Christians returned, beginning to frequent the many churches and monasteries. Someone told him the Monastery of Santa Maria was Benedictine and he happily made his way through the gate.

"May I see the Abbot?" Aldebert asked in the dim foyer after he had introduced himself.

"Not at this time, Brother Aldebert," said the monk. "He has just returned from exile and is not feeling well. Can I be of any assistance?"

"I am looking for a Cluny monk by the name of Ramiro. Have you heard of him?"

"Ramiro? Oh yes, everyone has heard of him."

Aldebert lit up. "Really? Do you know where he is?"

"I have no idea, Brother, but he was well known for his healing skills. He came to work here often. Alas, I have not seen him since we were expelled."

"Is there anyone else I could ask?"

The monk scratched the back of his head. "You could ask Brother Gerard, he was the superior at the hospice."

"Is he here?"

"Oh, I am afraid he is no longer with us. He had a falling out with the Abbot."

"You mean he renounced the order?"

The monk leaned closer, eager to share his gossip. "Yes. A scandalous affair, I fear. Brother Gerard tended to many of the sick and wounded after the battle. He became very popular with the French and they offered him many gifts and rewards. But when the Abbot asked him to give it all to the monastery, he refused and left in a huff. Needless to say, the Abbot was very upset."

"Where is Gerard now?"

"The French gave him a building next to the Church of Saint John. He started his own hospice with the money he received. He now calls himself a disciple of Saint Augustine."

"Thank you, Brother," said Aldebert as he backed to the door. "Thank you." He rushed out.

● ● ● ● ●

Arnulf Malecorne set up home in the Palace of the Patriarch and relished in his new-found power. Just two weeks after the conquest, a council of bribed bishops appointed him the new Patriarch of Jerusalem. His friendship with Godfrey had paid off and he was vaulted over the heads of more senior clergy, who were infuriated because of his low birth and his seedy reputation as a womanizer. But others, especially the Provencals under Raymond, saw his nomination as a Norman plot, in which Godfrey made sure his own men held the reins of power. Meanwhile, the Greek Orthodox were outraged that their own candidates were not even considered for the position, which they felt was their traditional right.

And so, by the time Arnulf was making himself comfortable in the Palace, he had few friends indeed. And, not one to forget a slight easily, he seethed with resentment at the many rebuffs, secretly vowing his revenge. In short time, he put his own acquaintances into positions of power and, thinking enthusiastically of the tremendous income from church tithes, plotted to usurp the long-held authority of the Orthodox Church. Even among his own flock, he began to tighten the screws of office. Soon, the lewd stories about his nightly capers, which had grown so much currency on their long march, were quickly silenced.

Nonetheless, Arnulf realized in his scheming mind that he needed the support of his countrymen. But his golden crucifix, forged in Tripoli, had failed to rally the faithful and he began to fear it would be discredited just like Raymond's holy lance. He needed something else, something to bring him closer to the glory of God, something of great spiritual authority. He needed a powerful, holy relic.

"What have you found?" Arnulf asked in the privacy of his den.

"One of the men says he has a vial of the blood of Saint John," said Lothar, a cringing man with balding blonde hair and a wrinkled face. "And another claims he got a vial of the milk of Mother Mary from one of the churches."

Arnulf shook his head in displeasure. "But can we verify these finds?" he asked painfully. "It's got to be something genuine. Something to which everyone will give credence."

"Some say the bones of Saint James are here, Your Eminence."

Arnulf's sallow eyes narrowed in thought. He tucked his greasy black hair behind one ear. "No, that won't do. Our men believe the bones of Saint James are kept at Santiago de Compostela. I need something no one will contest. What of this rumor about a cross?"

Lothar rubbed his rough, stubbled face. "I asked the Greeks but they won't say much. All I've heard is that a piece of the True Cross was hidden away when the pagans took the city years ago."

Arnulf's wily eyes sparkled. "Praise God!" he said. "That's what I need! We must find this cross!"

"But no one seems to know its whereabouts," said Lothar.

"They know," he said ominously. "The heretics know where it is and we will find it. We will make them talk."

"It seems that someone else was looking for it too, Your Eminence. A holy man, a Christian."

"What do you mean?"

"That monk at the hospice - what's his name?"

"You mean the physician, Gerard? He was looking for it?"

"No, no, but I asked him if he knew of any relics. He doesn't seem to know any more than we do, except that he mentioned a holy man, a monk actually, who was in the city before the battle."

"So?"

"Well, he said the man was looking for a cross... a particular cross," said Lothar, shifting his eyes. "Said he had a drawing of it."

Arnulf sprung to his feet. "Where is this man?"

"I don't know, Your Eminence."

"Find him! And send Gerard to me first thing in the morning."

"Yes, Your Eminence."

Arnulf lowered his voice a little. "But before you go, bring one of those pagan girls to me... so that I may convert the wench to the True Faith."

Lothar bowed. "Yes, Your Eminence."

• • • • •

Aldebert dashed over to Louis the Carpenter, who was busy overseeing repairs to Zion Gate in the southern wall. He found him near an oxcart full of fresh beams of wood. The workers scurried back and forth, hammering, sawing, mixing mortar.

"Louis! Louis!" Aldebert shouted as he ran towards him.

Louis held up his arm to stop him in his tracks and yelled to the men. "Put your backs into it, men! The bloody pagans will return and we don't want them getting in the same way we did!" Then he turned to Aldebert, who seemed flustered, but he was often flustered. "What is it, Father Aldebert?"

"Father Ramiro is here!" he shouted.

Louis' stern face broke into a broad smile. "Praise the Lord! You have seen him?"

"Well... no. But I went to see Brother Gerard at the hospice and he said Ramiro was in the dungeon with him before the attack began. Said he left him unconscious but alive!"

"Is he alright? Where is he now?"

"No one has seen him since. But he must be alive and well because Gerard said he sent someone back to get him but he was gone!" He squealed and danced like a giddy child.

"By the grace of God," said Louis.

"Yes, yes!" said Aldebert bubbling with anticipation. "And I have more good news, Louis. Very good news!"

Louis furrowed his brow over his big nose and formed a half smile. "And, pray tell, what is that, Father?"

"Gerard said Ramiro was with a woman." He nodded as he spoke and licked his lips at the end of every sentence.

"Is this a good thing?" Louis asked.

Aldebert nodded with his whole body. "And her name is Adele!"

Louis stared at him, his face turning ashen white. "Do not jest with me, Aldebert," he said, glaring with such intensity that Aldebert took a step back.

Aldebert's smile faded. "I do not jest, Louis. That is what he said."

"Dear Jesus!" Louis tried to steady himself with a hand against the wagon but fell to his knees in the dirt. "My daughter is alive! Blessed Mary, Mother of God!" He made the sign of the cross on his forehead and clasped his hands together. Tears welled in his eyes as he looked heavenward. "Thank you, Lord Jesus!" he shouted and, as suddenly as he had dropped to his knees, he sprang to his feet again. "We've got to find them!"

"We will, Louis, we will. Brother Gerard gave me his address. Come with me!"

"Wait," said Louis. "I can't leave these men alone. But we'll be finished soon, it's almost dusk. Help me to pick up my tools and we'll pack the carts."

● ● ● ● ●

"You have met this holy man?" asked Arnulf Malecorne. "The one asking about a cross?"

"Yes, Your Eminence," said Brother Gerard, nodding his bald head. "Many times. He said he was a Benedictine monk from Cluny."

"From Cluny?"

"Yes, Your Eminence, but he dresses like a scribe."

"How can you be so sure he is a monk?"

"He seemed quite knowledgeable of Cluny and was a good medicina. And just yesterday a Benedictine monk from Bari came asking about him."

Arnulf began to feel anxious. "And you say he showed you a drawing of this cross?"

"Yes, but that was some time ago."

"Can you describe it?"

"I remember that he said it was made of olivewood but was framed in gold."

Arnulf leaned forward, trying to control his anxiety. "Is it a piece of the True Cross?"

"I do not know, Your Eminence, he did not say."

"Did the man ever find this cross?"

"I don't think so. At least not when I saw him last."

"I hear he was called a holy man. Why is this?"

Gerard told him about the incident with Rabbi Moshe and how he became popular with all faiths in the city.

Arnulf leaned back in his elaborate chair. He put a hand to his chin and looked down in thought. "You saw him consort with these pagans?"

Gerard nodded. "He went to a number of their festivities during his time here."

"What's his name?"

"Ramiro, Your Eminence."

"Where does he live?"

● ● ● ● ●

"Why is a Cluny monk looking for a particular cross in Jerusalem?" Arnulf asked Lothar when they were alone.

"It does seem odd, Your Eminence," said Lothar as his beady eyes darted about.

Arnulf paced back and forth. "He knows something. But we must be careful. Abbot Hugh is a powerful man... and a cunning one. He likes to get his greedy fingers into every pie. I'm sure he would like nothing more than to have the True Cross for his monastery. We must find it first!"

"I sent two men to search for this Ramiro... and to scour his rooms for the drawing. But they have yet to return. If he doesn't have it as you say, Your Eminence, perhaps we should ask the Greek priests again."

"Yes, Lothar, but this time we will not be so polite. Bring that Greek bishop to me. The one they call Aliphas. We will squeeze him until he squeals like a pig."

• • • • •

Bishop Aliphas tried to be courageous but the knights had a lot of practice with torture and terror and they soon had him wailing like a child. "I know nothing of the True Cross!" he cried, sputtering blood. "I swear! There is nothing hidden!"

Lothar brought his knife up under Aliphas' nose. "I'm going to slice your nose off for lying, heretic!"

Aliphas' wide eyes watched the blade. "It's all rumor! I swear!"

"And what of this man called Ramiro?" asked Arnulf. "He came to you about this cross? And he showed you his drawing?"

"Yes, as I said, Your Excellency. When I last saw him he said he had found it and I gave him money to retrieve it. But... but then the battle began."

"Did he say who had it?"

"He said the man was an Armenian, that's all."

"Armenian? And where would I find a filthy Armenian in Jerusalem?"

"Most fled. But some returned to their positions at the Church of the Holy Sepulcher, Excellency. And others may be at the Monastery of Saint James."

Bishop Aliphas, badly beaten and bruised, was then ordered out of the Church of the Holy Sepulcher, as were all other Christians of the Greek, Armenian, Nestorian or Jacobite followings. Arnulf not only loathed people of all other denominations but he also feared them. And he was convinced the True Cross was hidden among the stones of the Church and he wanted to make sure none of them retrieved it. So he interned them all and called them, one by one, for a brutal interrogation.

DAVID STREET

The building on David Street was strangely quiet when Ramiro and Adele climbed the stairs to their apartment. Gone were the sounds of children playing, of people laughing. Gone were the aromas of home cooking and potted flowers. Only bare rooms remained, despoiled, empty of life and stinking of rotten flesh and blood. Ramiro was about to open the door but it was already ajar. "What in heaven's name?"

"What's wrong?" asked Adele.

"Somebody has been here since I cleaned up. That damned Otto, I suspect." He swung the door open. "Blessed Mary! Not again!" The place had been ransacked and, once again, his books and papers were strewn across the floor, every drawer and every corner disturbed, loose bricks pried out.

"Whoever they were, they were looking for something. What the devil could it be?"

Adele went into the bedroom. "What a mess!" she cried. "Look at my clothes! They're filthy. Oh no, my blue dress, it's ruined."

"I saved what I could," he said.

"Do you think they were looking for the cross?" she asked, folding her clothes into piles. "But how would they know?"

"I'm not sure," he replied after a long pause. "But if that is the case, they must think me a fool to leave it behind. They must have wanted something else."

Ramiro wandered over to his broken desk and began to pick up his books and papers. He said nothing for a long while and appeared distracted.

"What is it?" she asked.

"Look at this," he said. "Every book has been opened and my letters and notes have been flung about. They were looking for something in particular."

"Perhaps a book is missing?"

He stacked the books one by one. "No, they are all here." He leafed through his papers and spread them across the desk. "But my unfinished report to Abbot Hugh is missing. And where are all my travel papers?"

"Who in Jerusalem would be interested in your report?"

"That's a very good question," he said as he continued to look about for any scraps. Gathering it all, he examined every one. "And my drawing is gone, the one of the cross."

They looked at each other. "Somebody knows," she said. "One of the returning Christians, perhaps. Maybe Gerard."

"That was my first thought, but why would he want my correspondence with Cluny?" He picked up a blanket and spread it over the floor. "Help me pack this up, it's no longer safe here. We'll take all we can, then we'll go back to the monastery."

"When is Pakrad going to get the cross?" she asked with growing apprehension.

"He said he would go tonight." He knelt to the floor to retrieve a paper. "He had to be sure no soldiers were wandering about."

• • • • •

They were only a block away from the Monastery of Saint James when they heard yelling and sighted the soldiers milling about the doorway.

Ramiro squeezed Adele's arm. "Come on, get off the street!" he said, pulling her into an alleyway.

"What's going on now?"

He peeked around the corner. "I'm not sure. Those are Godfrey's men. Wait. People are coming out. They have the priests and the monks. They're bound like slaves. Oh dear God, they've got Pakrad."

They waited where they were and slipped into the monastery after the soldiers left. Only a few boys and some patients remained.

"They were taken on the orders of the Patriarch," said one of the boys.

"The Patriarch?" asked Ramiro. "You mean Bishop Aliphas?"

"No, Sayyid, the new Patriarch, one called Arnulf. One of Godfrey's men."

"Where can I find this Patriarch?"

The boy shivered. "At his palace, Sayyid."

Adele pushed her way between them. "Did Father Pakrad take anything with him?"

"No, Sayyidah."

"He has something that belongs to us. May we look in his room?"

The boy shrugged. "The soldiers ransacked the rooms," he said. "But there was nothing to take."

• • • • •

"He doesn't have it," said Adele as they made their way outside. "We have to go to Madteos' house to look for it."

Ramiro shook his head. "Not now. What of Pakrad? Why have they taken these men? Perhaps we should go to the Patriarch and plead on his behalf. God knows what they will do to him. It's the least we can do."

"We can't go now," she said, pulling him south on Armenian Street. "It's too late. We'll go tomorrow first thing. Come on. Madteos house is near the Zion Gate. This could be our last chance, Ramiro, come on."

"But it's almost dark."

"All the better."

"Do you know where it is?"

"Not really. But it's got to be somewhere in the house."

"Very well," he sighed. "But we must be careful."

• • • • •

Some signs of life began to return to the barren streets as the exiled Christians returned. But they were a sullen lot. Most had returned only to find their homes plundered and vandalized. Many were penniless, but Godfrey's men demanded rent. So they found themselves forced into work gangs for their new overlords.

One of these gangs sauntered up the narrow street as Ramiro and Adele neared Madteos' house. They were led by a laden oxcart and beside the cart walked a black-robed monk.

"Out of the way, man!" yelled the monk as the cart rumbled over the cobblestones.

Ramiro was about to step to the side, but something stopped him. It was the monk's voice, he knew that voice. "Wait here," he said to Adele.

He stepped up to the monk and looked hard into his face. It *is* him, older now. But the features are unmistakable. "By the grace of God. Brother Aldebert?"

The monk turned to him with a look of annoyance. "You will address me as Father Aldebert!"

Ramiro smiled wide. "Aldebert! It's me."

Aldebert stared at the bothersome man blocking his way. He had shoulder-length black hair and a beard. He looked like one of the heathen except that he wore cheap armor and was armed with a sword. "And who are you?" he asked indifferently.

Ramiro laughed aloud. "I am Ramiro of Cluny!" He laughed again.

The blood drained from Aldebert's face and his bearing sagged in shock. "Father Ramiro? Is it really you?" The workmen kept walking to their homes but the man at the oxcart stopped and waited.

Ramiro nodded. "Yes, Father Aldebert. Praise all the saints you are well."

Aldebert continued to gawk. "By the providence of God. But... but your hair," he stuttered. "Your beard, your... your dress."

"It is a long story. I will tell you all about it later when we have time."

Aldebert gestured wildly to the man at the cart. "Louis! Come! It's Father Ramiro!"

Louis rushed up and stared. "Father Ramiro? Look at you! Aren't you a strange sight!"

Ramiro stared back, equally dumbfounded. "Louis the Carpenter? God bless you, man. We heard you were killed at Nicomedia."

Louis smiled. "It seems God has spared me for another purpose."

"Papa?" Adele asked in a strained voice as she stepped up behind them.

Louis looked at her for a long time. His eyes watered and years of suppressed grief swelled in his chest. "Adele?" he choked. "My darling, Adele. Look at you. You're a grown woman." Tears gushed down his round cheeks.

Adele sobbed too, flinging herself into his arms. "Papa... Papa... I thought you were... I saw..."

"Never mind, my love," he said patting her back. "I am here."

"And Mama?"

Louis shook his head. "I'm sorry, my sweet."

She burst into tears again and they stood in a quiet embrace as dusk faded into nightfall.

"We should move on," said Ramiro.

"You must come to my house," said Louis, wiping his face. "Come. It seems we have much to talk about."

Adele looked at Ramiro, her cheeks wet with tears, and they both thought of the golden cross. He nodded to her knowingly. "Of course. Thank you, Louis," he said. "We would be delighted."

• • • • •

Louis' house sat across the street from the Church of Saint John the Baptist, not far from David Street. It was claimed by one of Godfrey's men, who had ransacked the place. Louis paid him a small sum for rent and moved in shortly after the assault. It took him two days to clean out the debris and scrub the bloodstains from the floor. The night wore on with a few bottles of cheap wine and much banter.

"Where is our groom, Pepin?" Ramiro asked. "I hear he became a soldier for the Greek King."

Aldebert's face dropped in a sad look. "I told him to stay with God's work but he would have none of it." He shook his head. "Now he has paid the price."

"What happened?"

"I'm not sure. But I received a brief note from Commander Manuel. Do you remember him? The Byzantine?"

Ramiro nodded.

Aldebert lowered his voice. "He said only that Pepin had fallen in battle."

"A very sad business, indeed," said Ramiro as he thought fondly of the energetic young lad.

After a moment of silence, Louis spoke with some anticipation. "Now you must tell us your story, Father Ramiro."

Louis and Aldebert listened in amazement as Ramiro recounted his journey, falling deep into events of the last ten years. And when he told them how he had found Adele at the slave markets of Aleppo, they were astounded.

"That's incredible!" said Louis. "Surely God guided your feet, Father Ramiro."

And when Ramiro told them about his failed rescue attempt and how he was forced to marry Adele by the Emir of Antioch, they whistled in disbelief.

"Not to worry, Father Ramiro," said Aldebert. "If you were married in the Greek Church, we can have it annulled." He felt pleased that he was able to offer Ramiro some good advice.

Ramiro and Adele glanced at each other. He hesitated for a while before reaching out to take her hand. "No," he said, as if he had made his final decision in the face of God. "She is my wife and I love her dearly."

Aldebert leaned back, somewhat shocked. "But what of your vows? You know we cannot take wives or concubines."

Ramiro nodded. "I am well aware of the consequences. I will speak to the Abbot when I return."

"The Abbot!" Aldebert cried. "I almost forgot!"

"What?"

"I have a letter for you – from the Abbot himself!"

"Really? Well, that should prove interesting. He has finally replied. Where is it?"

"It's in my room at the church. I'll bring it tomorrow."

Louis beamed with pleasure. His daughter was finally married. And to a respectable man. He got to his feet, stumbling from the wine. "A toast!" he cried. "A toast to my new son-in-law!" He raised his cup and they all followed suit, although Aldebert still appeared a little dazed.

In his telling, Ramiro never mentioned the cross, and Adele, sensing his discretion, also remained silent on the subject. Aldebert never knew that Ramiro's mission was to deliver the cross. He was always led to believe that Ramiro went to see the Patriarch on some church business, that he wanted only to see his mother and worship at the Tomb of Christ, and perhaps to take up an honored position at the monastery or even at the Church of the Holy Sepulcher.

"Did you ever meet with the Greek Patriarch, what's his name?" asked Aldebert as he recovered.

"Symeon. No, he was exiled before I arrived."

"Then you must see Patriarch Arnulf. I've been assigned to the Holy Church and I'm sure he would be glad to give you a position. Perhaps... perhaps as a scribe or something."

Ramiro thought only of Pakrad. He intended to plead on his behalf. "Yes," he said. "I plan to see the Patriarch soon."

"I'll go with you," said Aldebert, who was becoming worried about Ramiro's appearance and state of mind.

"Very well, but not tomorrow. Adele and I need to look for accommodations." He squeezed her hand, knowing it was a lie. "But perhaps you can tell me why he arrested the monks at Saint James?"

Aldebert shook his head. "I'm not sure. But I know he doesn't trust the blasphemous heretics."

• • • • •

The next day, Aldebert and Louis returned to their work with heads throbbing from green Jerusalem wine. Meanwhile, Ramiro and Adele rushed again to Madteos' house. The place was nearly destroyed. Complete walls had been demolished, broken floor tiles were scattered everywhere and small piles of dirt lay beside hastily dug pits in the floor. They searched in every corner and Adele, remembering how Khuda had hidden the cross beneath his floor, pried at every loose tile. But they found nothing.

"Does it look the same?" Ramiro asked as rubble and detritus crushed under their feet. "Does anything look different?"

"I don't know," she said. "It was dark when I arrived and I never got a chance to look around. But it seems worse than I remember."

"That's what I fear." He took her hand. "It is over," he said with resignation. "We will leave Jerusalem and forget this whole business."

A HOLY RELIC

Ramiro and Aldebert arrived early at the Palace of the Patriarch and waited for hours in the elaborate foyer.

"Have you got the Abbot's letter?" Ramiro asked.

Aldebert knocked his head with one hand. "No, I forgot, I'll go now."

"Not now," he said. "We could be summoned at any moment."

While they waited in the foyer, Lothar and a servant waited upstairs outside the door of Arnulf's bedchamber. Finally, the door opened and a young girl rushed out, pulling the hood of her thin, cotton cloak tight about her face. But the hood did not hide her tears, nor her look of terror. The servant pulled her aside and led her away.

Lothar continued to wait. Eventually, Arnulf came out, dressed in the long, black cloak and tall hat of the Patriarch. In one hand, he held the golden-tipped staff of office and, hanging at his midriff was the large medallion of the Patriarch on a golden chain.

"Good morning, Lothar," he said with unusual cheer. "Is the procession prepared?"

"Yes, Your Eminence, it is all arranged. And all of the Latin clergy have been ordered to attend."

"And my Sacred Scepter?" He asked as they descended the wide, curved staircase.

"Yes, it is finished and ready for you, Your Eminence. We plan to depart from the palace at noon and lead the procession around the Church before finishing up at the Tomb of Our Lord."

"Excellent," said Arnulf with ebullience. He breathed deep, sensing his growing religious power with heady delight.

"Until that time, my Lord, there is someone here requesting an audience.

"Not now, Lothar, I'm much too busy."

"Yes, Your Eminence, but he says his name is Ramiro of León."

Arnulf stopped suddenly. "Of León? I thought Gerard said he called himself Ramiro of Cluny?"

"He did, my Lord, but not many go by the name of Ramiro, especially in Jerusalem."

"Give me an hour," said Arnulf as his dark eyes narrowed in a cunning look. "Then send him to me in the meeting hall."

"Yes, Your Eminence."

"And bring my Sacred Scepter to me."

• • • • •

Arnulf sat stiffly upright on the throne of the Patriarch. He held his staff in one hand and tried to appear regal. Behind him, stood the cowering Lothar and a number of hand-picked priests. One of them held a rolled document while Lothar held the Sacred Scepter in readiness. Arnulf put his hand forward and Ramiro stepped up to kiss his sacral ring.

"You say you are Ramiro of León, once of Cluny?" Arnulf asked.

"That is correct, Your Eminence," he said as he stood and stepped back.

"Does this mean you have renounced your vows to the Mother Church?"

Aldebert, who stood behind Ramiro, lowered his head in heartfelt shame.

"Only one," Ramiro said calmly. "I can no longer remain obedient to the Benedictine Rule."

"So you prefer the ways of the Greek monks?"

"No, that is not..."

"And you are the so-called holy man of Jerusalem?"

"That is a name used by others."

"And you are still Christian?"

Ramiro scowled at him. "I have dedicated my life to the teachings of Jesus, Your Eminence."

"So why have you come to me, Ramiro of wherever."

Already, Ramiro was beginning to dislike this man. Clearly, by his manner and speech, he was low-born and, worse yet, he was condescending. He glared right into the Patriarch's eyes. "I come to beg your leniency, Your Eminence."

Arnulf met his black stare with a shudder of cold fear. The eyes of the devil! he thought, but he soon composed himself. "Leniency? For who?"

"For the monks of Saint James Monastery, Your Eminence. I would like to say that I know them personally and would vouch for their integrity."

"You are a friend of these heretics?"

"I am a friend of all, particularly Christians."

Arnulf sneered. "And a friend of the pagan Muslims, we hear. Is it true you speak the language of the infidels?"

"Yes, Your Eminence, but please understand, I have been here ten years."

"And one who consorts with vile Hebrews?"

"I have met several Hebrews but I would not say..."

"You know what I think, Ramiro of wherever?" Arnulf said loudly. "I think you are a spy!" He raised a hand and a priest came forward with a document. Arnulf held it up for Ramiro to see. "This is the proof. I have your report and it clearly notes all of our defenses and the number of our men. You are a traitor!"

"That is not so, Your Eminence," said Ramiro, realizing that Arnulf held the report taken from his room. "I wrote this report before the assault. If you read it carefully, you will see those are the numbers of Egyptian troops, not the French. These documents are for the Abbot of Cluny, who ordered me here. The Pope himself, may God bless his name, was a monk of Cluny. How can you believe I am a traitor?"

Aldebert stepped forward. "He tells the truth, Your Eminence."

"Shut up!" Arnulf yelled. "You will speak when asked!"

Aldebert bowed silently and backed away.

"Is this the only reason you came to Jerusalem?" he asked in a calmer but suspicious voice.

"Father Aldebert and I were sent here to see Patriarch Symeon and to await his instructions."

"Is that so?" Arnulf smirked. "Now you tell me that the great Abbey of Cluny takes its orders from heretics?"

Ramiro glared at him, making no reply.

Arnulf banged his staff to the floor in anger and spoke in a shrill voice. "Well since you have come to follow the patriarch," he said, "it is only logical that you now serve me." He raised his hand again and Lothar came forward with his scepter. "Come forward Ramiro of wherever to kiss my Sacred Scepter and to vow your allegiance to the Church of the Holy Sepulcher." He held out his hand and Lothar stepped forward with the scepter. Arnulf braced it to the floor and motioned for Ramiro to step forward.

Ramiro looked at Arnulf with barely concealed loathing before his eyes travelled to the scepter, a long staff of gilded gold crowned with a golden cross. He clenched his jaw as he stared at it. It was a cross of wood framed in gold. "That's my cross!" he blurted.

Arnulf smiled in perverse delight as he gazed on Ramiro's awestruck face. "Are you saying that the True Cross is *your* cross?"

"It's from the Abbey of Cluny. I was told to deliver it to Patriarch Symeon."

"So you claim that you brought this cross with you to Jerusalem?" Arnulf asked, feeling a moment of panic. If this were true, it could be discredited.

"That is correct."

"Father Aldebert," said Arnulf. "Step forward." Aldebert shuffled to the front. "Can you verify this story? Have you seen this cross before?"

Aldebert looked hard at the cross. He glanced back at Ramiro sheepishly before turning again to Arnulf. "Well... well no, Your Eminence. I do not remember this cross and I know nothing of it going to the patriarch."

Arnulf felt a flood of relief.

"I can explain," said Ramiro. "It is my olivewood cross you see at the center, Father Aldebert. Unfortunately, Turk slavers at Gallipoli pried out the bloodstone. And the Sultan of Persia added the gold frame. I can tell you the story, Your Eminence."

Arnulf chuckled. "Turk slavers? The Sultan of Persia?" he said mockingly. The priests behind him chuckled too. "If indeed, what you say is true, then why were you searching for a cross you already had?"

"It was stolen by a Turk, Your Eminence, when I was captured in Antioch. I managed to retrieve it and hold it for a while but the same man chased me down just before I arrived at Jerusalem. He sold it to an Armenian jeweler."

As outlandish as Ramiro's story sounded to the others, Arnulf began to realize there could be some truth to it. His men found the cross at the house of an Armenian jeweler. But he could not afford the truth. "A ridiculous fable!" he shouted. "I should have your tongue cut out for your lies! You wanted the gold!"

"No, Your Eminence. As I said, my original wood cross is at the center. I believe it may contain some important message, a message for the Patriarch. If you open it, it will probably verify my story."

Arnulf laughed loudly. "Now you want me to destroy the True Cross just to satisfy your ludicrous tale? I begin to believe you are mad."

"If you would ask Bishop Aliphas, he will verify my story."

Arnulf smirked. "Rest assured, we have had a long talk with Aliphas."

Ramiro did not like his tone. "What have you done with him?"

"You seem quite concerned about these heretics. Let me suffice to say that we know he paid you to retrieve this cross. Is this not true?"

"Yes, but that money was to pay the jeweler."

"So even if we are to believe your hare-brained tale, you would have to admit the cross rightly belongs to the Patriarch of Jerusalem. Unless you wish to admit it was all a lie to steal money from the Church. In which case, you would leave me no choice but to hang you from the gallows."

Ramiro bowed his head. For the love of God, he thought, why do I bother? He raised his head. "Yes, Your Eminence, of course. I lay no claim to this cross."

Arnulf rose to his feet, glowing with satisfaction. "You are dismissed. Both of you will join my sacred procession around the Church so all can gaze upon the True Cross and see that it has been returned to the victorious, to the people chosen by God."

After they left, Arnulf sat back with a conniving look. The man knows too much. What if he discredits my holy relic?

• • • • •

"The man is an idiot!" said Ramiro, when they were outside. "I will go to see Duke Godfrey. Perhaps he will intervene for the Armenians."

"Oh no," said Aldebert.

"What?"

"Patriarch Arnulf has the favor of Godfrey. He won't help."

"Well, who should I see?"

"Uh, maybe Count Raymond," said Aldebert scratching his long nose. "He doesn't like Godfrey or Arnulf."

"So where does Raymond stay?"

"You can't go to see him now, Father Ramiro. The procession begins. The Patriarch ordered us to attend."

"You go. I have no more time for this business."

• • • • •

Count Raymond still held on to the Tower of David, refusing to hand it over to Godfrey. He brought in expensive furniture and tried to make it a comfortable home. But he had little company because most of the men, even some of his own, just wanted peace and resented his stubborn intransigence.

So Ramiro had little trouble getting an audience with him and both men sat out under the archways next to the open courtyard, sipping cool lemonade while the sun set over the Judean Hills, casting its orange rays across hot stone walls. Servants scuttled around, putting out bowls of fruit brought in from Syria.

"From the monastery at Cluny, you say?" Raymond asked as he dabbed at the sweat dripping from his brow, careful not to dislodge his eye patch. Already over sixty, the last few years seemed to age him even more. His wrinkles ran deeper, and his weatherworn face, burnt by the sun day after day, was pocked by old blisters.

"Yes, my Lord," said Ramiro, glad to finally meet one of the foremost leaders.

"I know your Abbot well," said Raymond. "He has been of considerable help to us in our Holy Crusade against the infidels. I admire his vast knowledge of events."

His words knifed through Ramiro's heart and a feeling of profound regret swept his mind. "Yes, my Lord," he said, trying not to think of the slaughter. "So what of the Armenian priests? Can you help them?"

Raymond shook his head slowly, furrowing his gray brow. "No, I cannot help you, sir," he said sadly. "It is out of my control. I have neither the ambition nor the men to help the Armenians." His eyes grew distant as he stared into the courtyard. "Cursed Normans!" he spat. "First that bastard Bohemond took Antioch and now Godfrey claims Jerusalem! And to make matters worse, he managed to get that greasy, wine-soaked womanizer appointed Patriarch – and he's a bloody Norman too! The bastards have betrayed the Church and the Pope!"

Ramiro did not reply, watching him.

"I'm sorry," said Raymond, smiling a little. "But let us not worry about these things. You must tell me more of your story."

AUGUST

Tancred came galloping up from Bethlehem with alarming news. The Egyptians had arrived. The vizier, Al-Afdal, led an army of twenty thousand and they were now at Ascalon, less than fifty miles away.

"Twenty thousand?" asked Godfrey with a grim look of concern. "We cannot remain here to be besieged!" he shouted. "The walls are not yet repaired. We should ride against them before they organize themselves."

"Against an army of twenty thousand?" asked Raymond, glaring at him. "I think not. We would be fortunate to get ten thousand men together. I say we would do better within the walls."

"Like at Antioch?" asked Godfrey with bitterness. "We'll be starved out in a month! The will of God is with us - I say attack."

"I'll go," said Tancred.

"And I," said Robert.

"I will reconsider," said Raymond, "when you can verify this tale."

• • • • •

Ramiro told Adele and Louis of his encounter with Arnulf Malecorne. "Wretched man," he said. "Claimed I was a traitor. After all I've done for the Church."

"And Raymond was no help?" asked Louis.

"I believe he would help us if he could," said Ramiro. "He feels the Mother Church has been betrayed."

"How much longer will we stay?" Adele asked.

"We must leave as soon as possible." He took a sip of thin, leek soup.

"But which way will you go?" asked Louis. "The Egyptians hold the coast. Jaffa is not safe."

"Then we will have to ride to Latakia."

Adele tore off a chunk of barley bread and handed it to him. "We will never find a horse," she said. "We'll be lucky to find a donkey."

"But I hear many of the men want to return to Europe soon," said Louis. "Perhaps that will provide an opportunity."

"What of Aldebert?" asked Adele. "Will he stay?"

"I have no idea," said Ramiro. "I suspect he's beginning to think I've lost my mind."

They began to hear chanting in the distance. The sound got louder and louder. Ramiro got to his feet and looked down on the road that ran south from the Church of the Holy Sepulcher to David Street. Louis and Adele rushed up behind him.

A long, trudging procession made its way down the street. Leading them, was Patriarch Arnulf walking barefoot. He clutched his new scepter of the True Cross with both hands while shouting loud glories to the Lord. Behind him were several clergymen and, behind them, were hundreds of knights and thousands of foot-soldiers, all of them barefoot, carrying their boots in their hands.

"What's going on?" asked Adele.

"I don't know," said Ramiro. "But we will soon find out." He stared down at the men who led the soldiers. "Tell me Louis, which one is Godfrey?"

"He's the big one with the long, blonde hair," said Louis. "The one on his left – the one with the big nose, that's Robert of Flanders. The younger one with brown hair is Tancred."

"Which one is Raymond of Toulouse?" asked Adele.

"You can't mistake him, dear. He's the old man with an eye patch, but I don't see him. Him and Godfrey don't get along."

"There's Father Aldebert," said Ramiro, pointing down.

"Where?"

"He's marching behind the Patriarch."

• • • • •

Duke Godfrey felt invincible. But even his unwavering faith could not disguise the fact that he was greatly outnumbered. His scouts spotted Al-Afdal's huge army after they arrived at Ramla so he sent a fast messenger back to Raymond, telling him it was all true, the Egyptians had indeed arrived. Raymond finally relented under pressure from his own men and reluctantly he left the city unguarded.

Still, due to the attrition of war, the Crusaders could amass no more than nine thousand infantry and a thousand knights. They were outnumbered two to one and, to make things worse, the Egyptian army comprised thousands of skilled cavalry. So Godfrey was forced to make a daring decision when his scouts spotted the enemy camp outside Ascalon. He decided on an age-old tactic - that of surprise.

Al-Afdal felt confident the barbarian rabble would remain huddled behind the walls of Jerusalem. He knew they had no allies within hundreds of miles. Tomorrow, they would besiege the city and wait them out. So when the blood-thirsty knights came charging down on their camp in the first light of dawn, they were stunned out of their beds. The sheer ferocity of the Crusader assault, fuelled as it was by a sense of fanatical righteousness, quickly overwhelmed one of Egypt's finest armies and the doomed battle soon turned into an all-out rout. The French hunted the Egyptians down one by one and hacked them to pieces, even as they groveled on their knees for mercy. Only Al-Afdal and Iftikhar and a few others managed to escape to Ascalon with nothing more than their horses and the clothes on their backs. And they soon left Ascalon for the safety of Cairo.

And so it was that the Crusaders returned victorious to the walls of Jerusalem, and Godfrey was again their hero, blessed with God's Grace. They brought back a vast plunder of gold, jewels, arms and horses captured from

Al-Afdal's camp, a treasure so great that the returning men could not carry it all. And then, in another grand procession, Patriarch Arnulf led the bloodied troops through the streets of Jerusalem, holding his True Cross high above his head and jutting it into the air as if it were a sacred spear. The people fell to their knees in awe of its power.

The resolute Crusaders had conquered the Holy Land against all imaginable odds and there was not a single army left to oppose them. The Byzantines still wrestled for control of the Aegean and Asia Minor and were more interested in regaining Antioch from Bohemond. The Turks were still embroiled in bitter civil wars since the death of Malik Shah and were no longer interested in the affairs of Palestine. And the Egyptians were decimated by war, disease, and internal strife. The ancient triangle of Middle East power had collapsed and in its midst was a new barbarian kingdom.

A TRAITOR

The soldiers arrived at Louis' house before dawn and banged on the door. Louis rubbed the sleep from his eyes and groveled for the door in the darkness. He opened it cautiously. "What can I do for you?" he asked.

"On the orders of the Patriarch," said Lothar gruffly, "we have come for Ramiro of León."

"On what charge?"

"That is not your business. Where is he?"

"I am here," said Ramiro as he came up behind Louis. "What does the blessed Patriarch want with me?"

Lothar unfurled a roll and strained to read by the flickering light of a torch. "By the order of His Eminence, the Patriarch of Jerusalem, it has been judged that Ramiro of León, formerly of Cluny, is a traitor to the Mother Church of God and to the Protectorate of Jerusalem."

"That's preposterous!" said Ramiro.

"You will come with us," said Lothar. Two soldiers grabbed him by the arms and dragged him away.

"Ramiro!" Adele screamed.

• • • • •

Lothar punched Ramiro in the back of the head before he shoved him to his knees. Arnulf held out his hand so Ramiro could kiss his ring. But Ramiro did not approach.

Lothar kicked him in the back. "Show respect to your superiors!"

Ramiro winced from the blow but remained still.

Arnulf turned away seething. He sat down hard on his throne. "You have come to me with lies!" he shrilled. "You are a spy for the heathen!"

"That's ridiculous!" said Ramiro.

Lothar belted him across the head. "You will speak when asked!"

Arnulf clapped his hands and motioned to a waiting servant. The man rushed forward with several documents.

Arnulf waved them in front of Ramiro. "We have proof!" He held up one paper and rattled it in his hand. "This one is written in the heathen tongue. We had it translated. It seems you are a servant of the King of Persia. How do you answer?"

Ramiro stared into his deceitful eyes. "As I alluded to previously, Your Eminence, I was in Persia, held as a slave. Those papers are merely a form of identification."

Arnulf glared at him. "So you say." He picked out another paper. "And I have another. Also from the pagans. It seems you work for the Egyptians as well."

"No, Your Eminence. That document is merely a tax receipt. It is mandatory for a Christian in Muslim lands."

"So you say, Ramiro of wherever, but the evidence is against you."

"All I have said is true, Your Eminence. I met with Pope Urban himself. He will verify my story."

"Pope Urban is dead," said Arnulf, almost with satisfaction.

Ramiro stared at him, not sure if it was the truth.

"Yes," said Arnulf, sensing his doubt. "We hear he passed into heavenly care just before we stormed the walls of Jerusalem - doing God's work as he bid us," he sneered. "While traitors to the Holy Cause plotted against us!"

Ramiro paused, thinking of the Pope. He had liked the man. "I speak the truth. Abbot Hugh of Cluny will attest to that."

"I don't believe you," said Arnulf who yet again, rattled another sheet of paper at him. "You say you are a monk, but we found this. You know what it is?"

Ramiro strained to look. "Ah... yes, well I can explain that too, Your Eminence. It is a marriage certificate issued by the Greek Church."

"A marriage certificate," he said derisively. "Since when do Benedictine monks take wives?"

"I was forced to marry, Your Eminence, under threat of death by the Emir of Antioch."

Arnulf looked at him with disgust. "The Emir of Antioch!" He tossed his head back and cackled a laugh. Then his white face sneered in malice. "Enough of your lies! You are a traitor and a thief."

"I am neither, Your Eminence."

Lothar slapped him again.

"Well what of this?" asked Arnulf accusingly. He held a small pouch in front of him. "Do you recognize it?"

"Yes, Your Eminence. It contains a thorn. It was given to me by my mother."

"Your mother?"

"Yes, my Lord. She was a nun here at the blessed Church. She claimed it to be a holy relic and left it to me on her deathbed."

Arnulf cackled again. "An outrageous story!"

"It is true, my Lord. If you will check the Church records."

"There are no records, traitor. We know you stole it from the Mother Church of God."

"That is not..."

Arnulf jumped to his feet. "Take him out of my sight!"

• • • • •

"What did you discover," Adele asked.

Aldebert pursed his lips, holding back tears. His face writhed in anguish and he bowed his head.

"Come on man!" she shouted at him. "Out with it!" She had little patience for Aldebert's stupidity.

He lifted his head. Tears ran from his red eyes. "The Patriarch has denounced him as a traitor and a thief. They..." he started to blubber. "They... oh dear God! They are going to execute him!"

Adele clenched her teeth hard and spun away from him to hide her shock. Louis stepped up and took her hand, but she pulled away from him and confronted Aldebert again. "Can't you do something? Why don't you tell the Patriarch who he is?"

Aldebert squirmed, his face went pale. "What can I do? He won't listen to me."

She slapped him hard across the face. "You spineless bastard! Coward!"

Aldebert, eyes bulging, rubbed his cheek in shock. Louis stepped in and spread them apart. The room went quiet.

"How?" she asked softly.

"Hung... hung from the gallows."

"Mother of God! When?"

Aldebert squatted to the floor and put his head in his hands. "Tomorrow!" he wailed.

"We should all go to the Patriarch to plead on his behalf," said Louis anxiously.

"What good will that do!" she screamed. "He will pay us no heed! A tradesman and his daughter!" She gestured to Aldebert. "And a whimpering, idiot monk!"

As if to prove her right, Aldebert moaned again. "And I never did give him the letter," he sobbed.

"What did you say?" She stood over him with her hands on her hips.

He looked up, his big cow-ears seemed to droop from his head. "The letter," he said again.

"What letter?"

"From Abbot Hugh. I brought it from Bari."

"Give it to me!"

He cringed. "It's for Ramiro – from the Abbot himself."

"Give it to me!" she screamed, putting a hand to her mace. "Or by God's blood, I'll beat you to death!"

Louis hovered over him, lending weight to her threat.

Aldebert backed away on the floor. He groveled in his pockets and brought out an envelope with a trembling hand. "You can't open it! It's God's business!" he belted out as a last defense.

"I'll give you God's business!" she said, snatching it from his hand. "Just like your bloody knights do! Don't you realize how important this is? It proves Ramiro is a man of Cluny!"

"I... I never thought..."

"That's right," she said. "You don't think."

"Calm down, Adele," said Louis cautiously. He was taken aback by the determined strength of his daughter, a side of her he had never seen. "We must think of something. We must know someone who can help."

"Drugo the Red is here," Aldebert said quietly. "I saw him."

"He's a common soldier!" Adele snapped. "And a savage brute! Have you forgotten what he tried to do to Papa? To cut off his hand for a crime he did not commit? And he never liked Ramiro anyway."

She paced the room in a frenzy, rubbing the back of her neck with her head down. "There is only one man who can stop this wretched Patriarch," she said. "And that's Lord Godfrey." She left the room for an instant and came back pulling her cloak over her shoulders. "Come on!" she ordered them. "We're going to see Godfrey."

"Me too?" Aldebert asked plaintively.

"Yes, you too!" she shouted. "Or I'll hang you myself!"

• • • • •

The rubbish and litter of war still cluttered the nearly-deserted streets. Adele rushed past broken doorways and shattered shutters. Louis and Aldebert struggled to keep up. The smell of death hung in the air, mixed as it was with the acrid smell of still-smoldering buildings. They passed the burned-out synagogue and came to the plaza near the Wailing Wall, now empty of life. Up the stone steps they went, through the narrow path leading to the Temple Mount where they came to the gate the Arabs call Bab Al-Silsilah, the Gate of the Chain. Two armed guards blocked the way.

"What do you want?" one asked in a challenge.

"We have come to see Lord Godfrey," said Adele.

The guard looked at her and smiled, then he turned to Aldebert. "Does this woman speak for you?"

Aldebert blushed.

"I speak for myself, soldier," she said defiantly. "I demand to see Lord Godfrey. It is a matter of life and death."

The guards were greasy-haired, filthy men who still reeked of stale blood. They smiled at her spunk. "You're a pretty one," said the other.

"She's my daughter, sir," said Louis, stepping forward. "Will you give heed to her request?"

"Is she now?" one said. "Well never you mind, Duke Godfrey is not seeing anyone today. Go about your business."

"This is my business, soldier," said Adele as she barged past them. But one reached out and grabbed her arm. She spun around and pushed him. "Let me go!" she screamed.

The other guard held a sword to Louis. Aldebert stepped back, terrified.

Drugo the Red emerged from the archway and limped to the gate. "What's the trouble?" he shouted. His once smooth, freckled face was now creased and hardened by war and adversity. Several of his teeth were missing, his hair and beard bleached by the sun. Heavy bandages wrapped one leg, a wound suffered in the attack on Ascalon.

"She demands to see Duke Godfrey, Captain. I tried to send her away."

"What's your business?" Drugo asked Louis.

"We have come to save a life, Sir Drugo," said Louis. "I'm Louis the Carpenter and this is my daughter Adele. Do you remember us, Sir?"

Drugo looked them over. "I remember the monk. And you," he said, pointing to Louis, "you're the man who makes catapults." If he remembered the time he almost cut off Louis' hand, he said nothing about it.

"That's right," said Adele. "And he served you well. Now we demand to see Godfrey."

Drugo glared at her with some hostility. He was not used to a woman giving him orders. "That's *Lord* Godfrey to you," he said. "What do you want?"

"It's Father Ramiro," said Louis interrupting. "He has been sentenced to death by the Patriarch. He's a good Christian, Sir Drugo. We are hoping Lord Godfrey will put a stop to it."

"Father Ramiro?" Drugo chortled. "So that damn monk is still alive, is he? Yeh, well I remember that trouble-maker. The Patriarch probably has his reasons. Good riddance, I say."

Adele rushed up to him and slapped his face. "You worthless mound of shit! You're not half the man he is!"

Startled, Drugo hesitated for a moment. Then, in a rage, he slapped her with the back of his hand, sending her reeling. "Bloody bitch!" he cried rubbing his cheek. She tried to run past him but he grabbed her by the hair.

Louis leapt to her rescue but the guards pushed him back with the tips of their swords. Meanwhile, Aldebert staggered in fear, spun around, and fled back through the gate.

Drugo pulled hard on Adele's hair and pushed her towards the gate.

"Let me go! You foking bastard! Rot in hell!" She kicked and beat at him. One of her kicks hit him squarely on his wounded leg.

He cried out in pain and released his grip. Then, in a mad fury, he drew his sword.

"What's going on here!" a voice yelled. It was Robert, the Count of Flanders. Unlike the other men, Robert kept himself clean and neatly trimmed, as if he had never fought a battle. His face remained handsome, smooth and unscarred.

"Cursed trouble-makers, m'lord," said Drugo, who limped even more.

"We are good Christians, m'lord," said Adele, straightening her hair. "We ask only to see Lord Godfrey on an important matter."

Robert smiled at her and bowed a little. "Enchanté, my lady. You must forgive these rough men. They are good soldiers, but unfortunately they are uncultured and have no manners. Come and sit. Tell me your story." He gestured to a number of chairs put out under the archway.

Drugo scowled as they walked away. He sheathed his sword and returned to the guardroom to tend to his leg.

• • • • •

In only a few weeks after the conquest, the Christians stripped the Temple Mount and converted the Dome of the Rock into a church, which they called the Templum Domini, The Temple of the Lords. At the same time, the nearby Al-Aqsa Mosque had been completely converted into a luxurious palace for Godfrey.

"She pleads for the life of her husband," said Robert as he took a seat across from Godfrey. "It seems Patriarch Arnulf will have him executed tomorrow."

Godfrey looked up from his plate of meat and bread. "You should try this, Count Robert. It's mule meat. Not that bad." His voice echoed in the vast nave of the former mosque, where two great colonnades of white, Italian marble topped with Corinthian capitals, supported whitewashed archways rising to a ceiling the height of eight men. Over one hundred stained glass windows reflected rainbows of light from the elaborate designs in mosaic walls.

But its beauty was marred. The place had been gutted of anything Muslim. The sacred *mihrab* was destroyed, as was the *minbar*, their remains burned, along with every book, in a huge pyre set on the plaza of the Temple Mount.

"No thanks," said Robert, watching the blood drip from Godfrey's blonde beard. "I'm not hungry. So what should we do? It seems this man was a Benedictine monk. The woman claims she has correspondence from the Abbey of Cluny that would verify this. Perhaps the Patriarch has overstepped his bounds." He secretly despised Arnulf, a greasy, common man who was merely Godfrey's puppet.

"You say he *was* a monk?" asked Godfrey before he took a draught of green beer.

"Yes. Apparently, he left the abbey about ten years ago on some mission and has since renounced the Order. Attires himself as a scribe."

"What are the accusations?"

"The Patriarch says he is a traitor. That he works for the pagans."

"Perhaps it is true," said Godfrey as he put his knife down and leaned back in his chair. His long hair swept over his shoulders.

Robert scowled, lifting the nostrils of his long nose. "Are you going to allow Arnulf to start executing Christians?"

Godfrey leaned forward again, putting his elbows on the table. He picked up his knife and pointed it at Robert as he spoke. "You must understand, Count Robert, that we have only recently established ourselves. And now Arnulf claims he has found the True Cross. It is a powerful relic and rallies the men. If I allow him to be discredited at this time, what will it say to the others? The foking Greeks would like nothing more. Besides, what is one more man in this great scheme?"

Robert remained quiet for a time, staring at Godfrey. Finally, he opened his hands and spoke. "You should at least look at the evidence, Lord Godfrey."

"Evidence? I'll give you shit for the evidence. It's the power that's important. We need to let the people know we are ruthless and will not be stopped. Let the matter drop, it costs us nothing."

Robert stood up angrily. "I cannot condone such practices."

"Think as you please," said Godfrey with a tone of finality. "But I will not interfere with Arnulf's designs at this time."

• • • • •

"What?" Adele yelled after Robert told her the bad news. "But this is madness! He's one of our own!"

"I am truly sorry," said Robert. "You must believe me, I do not in any way agree with Lord Godfrey's assessment. But I am powerless to stop it."

"Unbelievable!" she shouted. "You're a pack of bloody barbarians! Just like Ramiro said."

"I am sorry, my lady, but you will have to leave."

• • • • •

Adele broke down into sobs as soon as they entered the house. Louis did his best to comfort her, but to no avail. "I'll kill that bastard patriarch myself," she said in a croaking voice.

"That is unlikely," said Louis. "And it will accomplish nothing."

She wiped her face with her sleeve and reached into her pocket. "I'm going to open the Abbot's letter." She pulled it out. "What harm can that do now?" She ripped the envelope, taking care to keep the writing intact, and drew out the letter. For a while, she stared at the page, stumbling over the words. "What does it say, Papa?" Ramiro was still teaching her Latin.

"We need someone to read it," he confessed. "We could look for Father Aldebert." He reached out to hold her hand.

"No, Papa, he is useless. I don't trust him."

Louis brightened. "Then we'll take it to that Armenian priest that Ramiro mentioned. I hear he's back at the Monastery of Saint James. Arnulf released him after he found his precious cross."

THE ABBOT'S LETTER

Pakrad's face was still swollen and bruised from the beating he suffered at the hands of Lothar and his men. He felt guilty and ashamed. It was he who had broken down under torture, and it was he who had told them where to find the cross in Madteos' hidden cache. "I am sorry for all the trouble, Sayyidah. I never thought it would come to this."

"Never mind, Pakrad," said Adele. "No man could have done any better. Just read this letter for me."

He opened the letter, cleared his throat, and read aloud.

> *To my humble servant, Ramiro of Cluny, from Abbot Hugh of Cluny. Greetings in the name of Our Lord Jesus Christ.*
>
> *Be it known, good monk, that I have received several of your reports and letters and am happy to say that the Mother Church stands deeply in your debt for the great service you have rendered on behalf of Almighty God.*
>
> *As I write, the Soldiers of God now triumph in Tripoli and will soon head south to liberate the Holy City from the filth of pagans. You are instructed to brace yourself for much trouble and I command you, for your own safety, to remove yourself from the city for fear of retaliation by the heathen. You will travel north to join your brethren in Tripoli where you will serve as my personal legate to the brave men who fight for the Holy Cause. Here, you will join with Raymond, the Count of Toulouse who, even now, leads these men to a great victory.*
>
> *I pray for your safe return, as do all your fellow monks at the Abbey.*
>
> *March 2, In the year Our Lord 1099.*

Pakrad put the letter down. "How is this going to help you?"

"Raymond of Toulouse?" asked Adele. "Where is he now?"

"I hear he left the city in a rage. Went to Jericho after they drove him out of the Tower. They say he hates Godfrey and his new patriarch."

"So I have heard," said Adele.

"Which way is Jericho?" asked Louis.

Pakrad pointed with a thin finger. "About fifteen miles to the east."

Adele stood up and took the letter from his hands. "Thank you, Pakrad. I'm going to Jericho."

"But Adele, how will you get there?" asked Louis. "Nobody's going to lend you a horse and even if we had the money, you're unlikely to find one for sale."

"I'll find one," she said, pulling her cloak tight and fastening her mace before storming out.

Louis rushed after her. "Adele, be reasonable. You have no time for this."

"I'm sorry, Papa, there is nothing more we can do here. I refuse to stand by while Ramiro hangs from the gallows."

"Where are you going?"

"To Saint Stephen's Gate," she said, taking long strides. "I'm looking for a horse."

"But we have no money."

She felt for her mace. "I don't need money."

"Adele, my sweet, you're starting to worry your poor father."

They passed the Church of the Holy Sepulcher before coming to the Emir's Palace near the northern gate. A few horses were tethered nearby but she kept walking. She walked right through the gate where Godfrey's men checked everybody coming in. A long line of travelers waited to get through. With no hesitation she walked over to a man holding the reins of a thin-looking filly. She pretended to stroll past him, pulled her mace, then turned and struck the unsuspecting man on the back of the head. He had no sooner collapsed when she jumped into the saddle. "May God forgive me, Papa." She straddled the horse like a man and pulled it out of line before anyone knew what was happening.

"I'll come with you!" Louis yelled.

"Sorry, Papa, too much weight. Do what you can for Ramiro!" She dug in her heels and the filly galloped away.

• • • • •

The sun had just begun to rise over the Mount of Olives when a wagon creaked and groaned its way towards the plaza beside the Pool of the Patriarch, a city reservoir not far from Jaffa Gate. It was pulled along by a single mule led by one of Lothar's men. Ramiro sat on a box as it rattled along, his face blackened with bruises, his ribs broken, his hands tied behind his back.

The gallows was new, built of fresh timbers. But already, the bodies of two men hung from the beam, where they rotted in the sun. Arnulf stood nearby with Lothar and a few of his cronies. With them, was Aldebert, who sobbed uncontrollably. He had no desire to be there but Arnulf had coerced him, telling him he was a necessary witness. Louis stood by too. He came of his own accord, hoping he could do something to help. But Lothar's men were well-armed and he had nothing. He felt useless and despondent and, when he saw Ramiro's sad state, he was grievously shocked.

The wagon made its way under the gallows and came to a stop below a single rope. Lothar jumped on to fit the noose around Ramiro's neck. "Consider yourself lucky, traitor," he whispered with venom." If I had my way, I'd slit you open like a pig and strangle you with your own guts." He pulled the noose tight.

Lothar read the long roll of charges against Ramiro before passing a sentence of death. Then Arnulf led his clergymen in a long ramble of prayers asking God to have mercy on this poor sinner's soul. Ramiro waited for them to pull the wagon away. He listened to Arnulf's last prayer.

*In the name of the Father and of the Son and of
the Holy Spirit
Amen
May the grace and peace of Christ be with you...*

But before Arnulf could finish the last rites, a tremendous ruckus broke out at the nearby Jaffa Gate. There was much yelling and a clash of steel. Arnulf stopped reciting and his men ran to David Street to have a look. They no sooner arrived when they came running back again. "It's Count Raymond!" one shouted. "And all his men!" A roar of hooves beat upon the flagstones as the knights charged through the gate. Raymond galloped up Patriarch Street, whipping his horse, his gray hair fluttering beneath his helmet.

Arnulf saw them coming. He panicked and ran up to the wagon. "Ayyah!" he shouted at the mule, slapping its rear. The beast whinnied and heaved. The wagon moved out from under the gallows and, slowly, the rope went taut, pulling Ramiro off by the neck. And when his feet left the wagon, he swung just off the ground, strangled by the rope.

Aldebert's eyes rolled in his head and he fainted to the ground.

Raymond spotted the gallows, in plain view of the road. He saw a man swinging from the rope and charged onto the plaza, driving away Arnulf's men. He raised his sword, slashing the rope, and Ramiro collapsed in a heap.

Lothar and his men ran towards him, swords drawn. Raymond spun around to face them and, just as Lothar was about to strike, he brought his sword down hard, splitting the man's skull in two. The others backed away as the rest of Raymond's men charged up.

Louis was already at Ramiro's side when Adele jumped off her horse and ran over to him. Ramiro lay motionless, his face puffed out, red and black. Blood dribbled from the side of his mouth. Louis tried desperately to loosen the noose. Finally, he got it free and threw it off.

"Ramiro! Ramiro!" Adele wailed and wept. "Don't die on me now, dear God, not now." She put her ear to his mouth but could detect no breath. She beat on his chest. "Don't die!" she screamed, putting her eyes to heaven. "Mother Mary help me now!"

Meanwhile, Arnulf began to rant at Raymond. "Defiler of the sacred! God's curses on your head!"

Raymond glared at him. He jumped off his horse with the agility of a younger man and stomped over, grabbing Arnulf by the throat and putting his bloodied sword to his neck. "You low-bred dog!" he cursed as he tightened his grip. Arnulf struggled and paled, unable to speak. "Get on your knees, you slimy bastard! And address me for my station. Or I'll cut you down where you stand!"

Arnulf groveled to his knees. Raymond loosened his grip and stuck the point of his sword at his throat, ready to ram it through.

Arnulf cowered in terror, his face writhed in plea. "Please, honorable Count Raymond. In the name of God's mercy!"

"My Lord!" one of Raymond's men shouted a warning. "Godfrey comes!"

Arnulf's fear turned to elation and he looked up to Raymond with a devilish grin.

Raymond pulled his sword away. He pointed the tip skyward and pounded the hilt into Arnulf's head. The man slumped to the pavement. "Let's go! Everybody!"

One of the men held Ramiro's limp body in front of him in the saddle. Adele and Louis jumped on another horse and grabbed the reins. And before any of Godfrey's men could reach them, they all charged back through the Jaffa Gate and rode fast for Jericho.

LATAKIA

SEPTEMBER

The victory was complete and the exodus began. The Crusaders went home, all heading back with their bags of loot, returning to their homes and families in Europe. They left by the thousands, leaving Godfrey with only three hundred knights and a thousand foot-soldiers to guard his new kingdom. But they could not sail from Jaffa, the nearest port. Even though the Egyptian army was defeated, their fleet still ruled the coast and no Christian vessel would dare approach. So the Crusaders rode north to Latakia, which was safely guarded by the Byzantines, Pisans and Genoese.

Raymond's entire entourage of Provencals rode peaceably along the Via Maris. No one dared threaten them. And when they passed through Tripoli, they discovered the entire coast had fallen into the hands of Maronite Christians, who helped them along. But by the time they arrived in Latakia, they found Bohemond besieging the place, attempting to wrestle control from the Greeks. Raymond, fed up with the likes of him and Godfrey, rallied his forces and drove him off.

Over one hundred Pisan vessels waited for them in Latakia. But Raymond refused to leave. He had vowed to die in the Holy Land and eventually set sail for Constantinople to see King Alexios, where he hoped to find further opportunities. The rest of them boarded ships sailing to Bari and Pisa. Over the days, Robert of Flanders arrived, along with Drugo the Red, Otto of Bremen and, trailing behind in a dismal mood, was Brother Aldebert.

● ● ● ● ●

The large, square sails of the merchant galley unfurled into a stiff, warm wind and the oarsmen heaved at the beat of the drum. The heavy-laden ship pressed into the rolling waves.

"Over here, Papa!" shouted Adele. "This is our berth."

"How can we afford this?" Louis asked.

"Count Raymond paid for it," she said dryly. "And gave us more." She rattled the coins in her purse.

"Well, God bless the man! This is a long journey to stand on deck."

"He felt it was the least he could do," she said. "He was very grateful to discover all that Ramiro had done for them." She motioned to a bench. "Put him down there."

Louis struggled to the bench and put Ramiro down carefully, flat on his back.

Ramiro groaned when Adele knelt beside him. The swelling was gone from his face and the gash around his neck looked better, although many bones and cuts had yet to heal. He winced from the pain in his ribs and could not speak.

"God watches over him, lass," said Louis. "The fall was not enough to break his neck."

She put a hand to Ramiro's head, combing her fingers through his hair. "It's alright my love," she said softly and bent to kiss his cheek "We're going home."

CLUNY

APRIL 1100

Abbot Hugh would soon be seventy-six but he still ruled Cluny with an iron hand. And since Pope Urban had passed on, he now worked diligently with the new pope, Paschal the Second.

The news of a Crusader victory raced like a whirlwind across Europe, causing much celebration and a new-found sense of power. Paschal was so enthused by its success, he preached a new crusade and many young, eager men rushed to his call.

"I am very sorry to hear you are leaving us," said Hugh. "Pope Paschal needs men like you. You could be of great help to our Holy Cause."

"Thank you, Abbot, but I have had enough," said Ramiro. "I doubt I could survive another journey. How is Brother Aldebert?"

"He appears in good health," said Hugh. He shook his head sadly. "But suffers in mind, I fear."

"We will all pray for him, Abbot."

"I was deeply saddened to hear that Pepin died," said Hugh looking down. "But he gave his life for God and I think we can rest assured that his soul has found a place in heaven."

Ramiro sighed heavily but made no reply.

Hugh looked up with a meek smile, showing a few remaining teeth. "While I regret you are leaving the Order, I understand your situation and am sure God will forgive you. Needless to say, we are very grateful for all you have done for the Mother Church. I hear you have purchased a plot of land not too far away."

"Yes, Abbot, thanks to the generosity of Count Raymond. And, if I have your permission, my Lord, I am still willing to work in the library."

"Of course, I don't believe there is anyone here who could match your skill with languages."

"May God bless you, Abbot." He stood still, not sure how to ask his next question.

"Is that all?" asked Hugh.

"Uh, yes, just one more thing, my Lord."

"Well, out with it."

Ramiro looked at him hopefully. "What was in the cross?"

Hugh frowned and shook his head. "What do you mean?"

"Did it contain a message for the Patriarch?"

"There was no message, I thought I told you that."

"Then what was its purpose?"

"It was only a means to identify you to the Patriarch. Through our correspondence, we agreed that my legate would be identified by a wooden cross with a bloodstone at its center."

Ramiro clenched his jaw as he stared at Hugh. "I don't understand," he said irritably. "Why not just use a letter for that purpose, Abbot?"

"Only because we believed the cross would be more durable and have a much better chance of surviving the arduous journey than would a frail piece of parchment. We presumed it would never leave your side. What happened to it?"

Ramiro looked down to hide his rising ire. "It was lost in the fall of Jerusalem," he said curtly, unwilling to say any more.

"Ah, well, not to worry. We accomplished our aim with God's help - and we achieved a mighty victory."

"And what was I supposed to do in Jerusalem, dear Abbot?"

"Only what you did all along," said Hugh. "To send me reports and to coordinate our efforts with the Greeks. To aide in the Holy War."

Ramiro looked down, feeling another rush of indignation, but he bit his lip to still his angry thoughts. When he raised his eyes, he could think of only one phrase. "God has called us to live in peace," he said quietly.

Abbot Hugh's thin smile faded in bewilderment.

• • • • •

The small hamlet, which lay amid the fields of Burgundy not far from the monastery, consisted of eighteen thatch-roofed cottages. One of these nestled in the middle of a wild garden full of herbs and vibrant flowers.

"And did you tell him what happened to his cross?" Adele asked as she sat comfortably in a soft chair.

"No," said Ramiro, staring at the flames flickering in the small fireplace. "I sincerely doubt he would have believed my story. And what does it matter, it won't change anything."

She giggled.

"What's funny?"

"Look at her, Ramiro, she's reaching for you and smiling."

Ramiro smiled too. He rose from his seat and knelt beside her. "She's got your hair," he said as he stroked the baby's head lightly with his thick fingers.

"Your daughter still needs a name, my husband."

He pondered quietly. "Would you like to name her Mathilda after your mother? Or Isabella after mine?"

"No," she said, cuddling the babe to her breast. "I want to think of nothing but peace when I look upon her face."

He touched Adele's hand. "Then we should call her Irene."

She nodded. "I like that."

He gazed at the child, stroking its soft cheek with the back of a finger. "Blessed are the peacemakers," he said quietly, "for they will be called the children of God."

Adele smiled at the babe adoringly, rocking her gently on her breast. She raised her chin and, in a soft voice, she began to sing.

Epilogue

In every battle thereafter, the Latin patriarchs of the Kingdom of Jerusalem marched into battle carrying the 'True Cross' before them. But eighty-seven years later, in 1187, it was captured at the Battle of Hattin by the Sultan of Egypt, a man by the name of Salah Ad-Din, who defeated the Christians and recaptured Jerusalem later that year. The cross was never seen again.

ABOUT THE AUTHOR

Mark Blackham has a keen interest in the affairs of the Middle East, whether it be the Neolithic Period, the Medieval Age, or the state of current politics. He has conducted research in Syria, Jordan and Israel. In 1999, he earned a graduate degree in archaeology and anthropology from the University of Toronto and continues to delve deeply into the past, fascinated by the parallels that exist between contemporary events and the stories of ancient history.

NOTES

My apologies beforehand to the medieval purists, who may find some errors or omissions in my story. To the best of my knowledge, the major events described are of historical account. The one exception would be Abul Kasim's assault on Nicomedia, placed in the spring of 1090. Nonetheless, the evidence suggests that the Turks did take the city around this time.

And while Arnulf Malecorne did find the 'True Cross' in Jerusalem (its appearance roughly as described), its true origin remains a mystery.

LIST OF CHARACTERS
FICTIONAL

Adele	Daughter of Louis the Carpenter.	Flanders
Aldebert	Ramiro's assistant monk.	Cluny
Aliphas	Greek bishop at Church of Holy Sepulcher.	Jerusalem
Arles	Arles of Ghent. The Executioner - one of Drugo's men.	Flanders
Boris	Ramiro's Hungarian servant.	Antioch
David	Rabbi held in compound with Ramiro.	Antioch
Dawud	Silk merchant who paid for cross.	Maarat
Dmitri	Russian slave of Harun.	Aleppo
Drugo the Red	Captain of the Flemish knights.	Flanders
Fawwaz	Surgeon who tended to Aldebert.	Adrianople
Frederick	Captain of the Papal Guard, Rome.	Italy
Fulk	One of Drugo's lieutenants.	Flanders
Harun	Slave trader.	Aleppo
Huda	Harun's wife.	Aleppo
Ibrahim	Mufti in Antioch. Later the Qadi of Jerusalem.	Aleppo
Jameel	Christian slave left to care for Ramiro in Edessa.	Edessa
Khuda	Mamluk in Aleppo, later with Yaghi Siyan in Antioch.	Aleppo
Lothar	Aide to Arnulf Malecorne in Jerusalem.	Crusader
Louis	Carpenter travelling with Drugo's knights.	Flanders
Madteos	Armenian jeweler of Jerusalem.	Jerusalem
Mathilda	Wife of Louis the Carpenter.	Flanders
Moshe	Rabbi in Jerusalem saved by Ramiro.	Jerusalem
Otto	Otto of Bremen. One of Drugo's lieutenants.	Flanders
Ozan	Turk scribe who travelled to Isfahan with Ramiro. Later with Kilich at Nikea.	Nikea
Pakrad	Armenian priest, brother of Madteos.	Jerusalem
Pepin	Boy (groom) sent off with Ramiro.	Cluny
Qubad	Secretary to Nizam in Isfahan.	Iran
Ramiro	Benedictine monk of Cluny.	Cluny
Raul	Carpenter and brooch thief at Monferrato, Italy.	Flanders
Rolf	Assassin sent with Wiker.	Italy
Salim	A physician in Maarat.	Maarat
Sebuk	Brother of Hasan of Cappadocia.	Nikea
Toros	Armenian slave of Harun. Later with Khuda.	Aleppo
Wiker	Assassin sent after Ramiro by Giberto in Rome.	Italy
Yaqut	Highwayman who stole cross in Jisr Ash-Shughur.	Maarat

HISTORICAL

Abul Kasim	Emir of Nikea after death of Sulayman.	Nikea
Adhemar	Bishop and Papal Legate of Crusade.	Crusader
Al-Afdal	Vizier (ruler) of Egypt.	Egypt
Alexios	Emperor of Byzantium.	Byzantium
Al-Khanes	Atabek (advisor) and general of Kilich at Nikea.	Nikea
Anna	Mother of Alexios. Royal dowager.	Byzantium
Arnulf	Chaplain to the Normans. Latin patriarch of Jerusalem.	Crusader
Bohemond	A leader of first Crusade. Son of Robert Guiscard.	Crusader
Bolkas	Half-brother of Abul Kasim.	Nikea
Borsa	Ruler of Apulia, Italy. Son of Robert Guiscard.	
Buzan	Emir of Edessa and Turk general.	Turk Empire
Chaka	Turk pirate at Smyrna.	Byzantium
Danishmends	Turkoman dynasty in northern Asia Minor.	Asia Minor
Dukak	Son of Tutush. Ruler of Damascus after Tutush dies.	Damascus
Gerard	Monk in Jerusalem and founder of Knights Hospitaler.	Jerusalem
Ghazi	Leader of the Danishmends	Asia Minor
Godfrey	Of Bouillon. Norman leader of first Crusade.	Crusader
Giberto	Archbishop installed as anti-pope by King Henry of Germany. Pope Clement.	Italy
Gregory	Pope before Urban. A reformer.	Italy
Hasan	Son of Bolkas. Took Ramiro to Isfahan.	Nikea
Hashashin	Assassins of the Ismaili.	Turk Empire
Hugh	The abbot at Cluny monastery.	Cluny
Humberto	Norman nephew of Robert Guiscard. Byzantine mercenary, Adrianople, Nikea.	Byzantium
Iftikhar	Egyptian emir of Jerusalem.	Jerusalem
Isaak	Brother of Alexios.	Byzantium
John Doukas	Governor of Dyrrachium. Alexios' brother-in-law.	Byzantium
John the Oxite	Greek patriarch of Antioch.	Antioch
Kerboga	Ruler of Mosul. Led final Turk assault on Antioch.	Turk Empire
Kilich Arslan	Son of Sulayman. Jailed in Isfahan. Returns to Nikea.	Turk Empire
Malik Shah	Sultan of Seljuk Turk Empire.	Turk Empire
Manuel Butumites	Byzantine commander and envoy to Melfi, Italy.	Byzantium
Nizam Al-Mulk	Vizier to the sultan, Malik Shah.	Turk Empire
Peter Bartholomew	Young mystic who found Holy Lance at Antioch.	Crusader
Peter the Hermit	A leader of Peasant's Crusade.	Crusader
Raymond	Leader of first Crusade. Older man with one eye.	Crusader

HISTORICAL

Ridwan	Son of Tutush. Ruler of Aleppo after Tutush dies.	Aleppo
Robert	A leader of Crusade. Count of Flanders.	Crusader
Robert Guiscard	Leader of Normans in Apulia, Italy. Invaded Byzantium in 1085. Died 1085.	Italy
Sulayman	Ruled Roman lands in Asia Minor before Abul Kasim.	Nikea
Symeon	Patriarch of Jerusalem.	Jerusalem
Tancred	Leader of Crusade, nephew of Bohemond.	Crusader
Taticius	Byzantine general who commanded the Kelts.	Byzantium
Tatran	Byzantine lieutenant. A Turk. Ramiro's tutor.	Byzantium
Tutush	Prince of Syria. Half-brother of Malik Shah.	Turk Empire
Urban	Pope. Formerly, Odo of Lagery.	Italy
Walter the Penniless	A leader of Peasant's Crusade.	Crusader
Yaghi Siyan	Turk emir of Antioch.	Antioch

PLACE NAMES

Name Used	Current Name	Location
Acre	'Akko or 'Akka	Israel
Adrianople	Edirne	Turkey
Aleppo	Halab	Syria
Anatolia	Turkey	
Ankara	Ankara	Turkey
Antep	Gaziantep	Turkey
Antioch	Antakya	Turkey
Antioch Lake	Lake Amik	Turkey
Apulia region	Puglia	Italy
Ascalon	Ashkelon, Asqalan	Israel
Ash-Shughur	Jisr Ash-Shughur	Syria
Asia Minor	Turkey	
Askanius Lake	Lake Izmit	Turkey
Astacus Gulf	Gulf of Izmit	Turkey
Axios River	Vardar	Macedonia
Beirut	Bayrūt	Lebanon
Bethlehem	Bayt Lahm	Palestine
Bosporus	Istanbul Boghazi	Turkey
Byblos	Jubayl	Lebanon
Cairo	al-Qāhira	Egypt
Cilicia	Mersin province	Turkey
Civetot	Hersek	Turkey
Constantinople	Istanbul	Turkey
Danube River	Ister	
Daskerah	Arak	Iran
Dog River	Nahr al-Kalb	Lebanon
Dorylaeum	Eskişehir	Turkey
Dyrrachium	Durres	Albania
Edessa	Sanliurfa	Turkey
Filastin	District of Hashefela	Israel
Gallipoli	Gelibolu	Turkey
Haifa	Hefa, Hayfa	Israel
Hebron	Al Khalīl or Hebron	Palestine
Hellespont	Çanakkale Boğazı	Turkey

PLACE NAMES

Name Used	Current Name	Location
Heraclea	Eregli	Turkey
Hierapolis	Manbij	Syria
Homs	Hims	Syria
Iconium	Konya	Turkey
Isfahan	Esfahan	Iran
Jaffa	Tel Aviv	Israel
Jerusalem	Al Quds Ash Sharif or Yerushalayim	
Kayseri	Caesarea	Turkey
Kios	Gemlik	Turkey
Latakia	Al Ladhiqiyah	Syria
Ludd	Lod, Lydda	Israel
Maarat	Ma'arrat An Nu'man	Syria
Malatya	Melitene	Turkey
Mosul	al-Mawṣil	Syria
Nicomedia	Izmit	Turkey
Nikea	Iznik	Turkey
Orontes	'Asi River	Syria
Propontis	Sea of Marmara	Turkey
Ramla	Ramlah	Israel
Rus	Russia	
Smyrna	Izmir	Turkey
St. Simeon	Süveydiye	Turkey
Sung	China	
Tarsus	Tarsus	Turkey
Thessalonica	Thessaloniki	Greece
Tripoli	Tarābulus	Lebanon
Thrace	Rumelia	Turkey
Tyre	Sūr	Lebanon
Xerigordon	Unidentified but near Nikea	Turkey

GLOSSARY

Adhan	the Islamic call to prayer
Askari	royal or elite guard
Atabek	military and political advisor
Beyfendi	supreme lord or master (Turkish)
Dhimmi	a non-Muslim citizen
Dinar	a gold coin about the size of a silver dollar
Diwan	fiefdom with per cent of revenue
Efendi	sir, mister, or lord (Turkish)
Emir	military commander
Farsakh	parsang or farsang = 6.2 km or 4.8 miles
Hadiths	oral traditions of Islam
Hashashin	assassins, hash-eaters
Hour, ninth	about 3 pm
Hour, third	about 9 am
Kafir	unbeliever, infidel (derogatory)
Kafiya	traditional headscarf for men
Kuffar	plural of kafir
Mamluk	a slave-warrior, often of Turkoman descent
Mufti	a lawyer
Nativity Feast	Christmas
Qadi	a judge, often the ruler of a city
Roman mile	1.1 English miles
Sadah	plural of sayyid
Sayyid	like 'sir' or 'mister' (Arabic)
Sayyidah	feminine form of sayyid
Sharia	laws of Islam
Souk	marketplace
Synod	a meeting of bishops to decide issues
Talent	unit of weight, about 26 kg or 57 lb
Vizier	the top bureaucrat, ruler's right-hand man

Manufactured by Amazon.ca
Bolton, ON